# BEAUTY AND THE BILLIONAIRE

## LAUREN LANDISH

# ALSO BY LAUREN LANDISH

VOLUME 1

# BEAUTY AND THE BILLIONAIRE

# PROLOGUE

## Mia

THE DARKNESS IS COMPLETE, WRAPPING AROUND ME LIKE AN EBONY velvet blanket, cool and textural on my naked skin. I can feel it on my goosebumps, the air adding to my trembling.

My body, exhausted from the last ordeal, still quivers as I try to find the strength to move. It's so difficult, the waters of sleep still tugging at me even as instinct tells me there's something in the darkness.

A soft shuffle of feet on the carpet, and I can sense him. He's here, watching me, invisible, but his aura reaches out, awakening my body like a warm featherlight touch on the pleasure centers of my brain.

Arousal ripples up my thighs, fresh heat shimmering with the memories of last time. I've never felt anything like him before, my body used and taken, battered and driven insane . . . and completely, thoroughly pleasured in a way that I didn't think possible.

It was so much that I don't even remember coming down, just an explosion of ecstasy that drove me into unconsciousness . . . but now my senses have returned and I know he's still there, measuring me, hunting me, *desiring* me.

How can he have strength left? How, when every muscle from my neck to my toes has already been taken past the limit?

How can he still want more?

My nostrils flare, and I can smell him. Rich, masculine . . . feral. A man's man who could tear me apart without a second's effort. His breath, soft but shuddering, sipping at the air, savoring the conquest to come.

Another whisper in the darkness, and the fear melts away, replaced by a heightened sense of things.

The moonlight, dim now in the post-midnight morning, when the night's as deep as it will ever be.

The sweat on my skin and the fresh moisture gathering at the juncture between my thighs.

He steps forward, still cloaked in shadow, a shape from the depths of night, ready for a new kind of embrace.

He reaches for my calf, and at his touch, I start to tremble. I should resist, I should say I can't take any more. He's already had his fill. What more can he want?

He inhales, his nose taking in my scent, and the knowledge comes to me, a revelation that I've chosen to ignore.

He wants me to be his. Not just his bedmate, not simply a conquest to have and to discard. He wants to possess me fully, to own me, body and soul.

But can I?

Can I give myself to such a man, a being whose very presence inspires fear and dread?

Can I risk the fury that I've seen directed at others turned back upon me?

His tongue flicks out, touching that spot he's discovered behind my right knee that I wasn't even aware of before him, my left leg falling aside on its own as my hunger betrays me.

My mind is troubled, my heart races . . . but my body knows what it wants.

He chuckles, a rumble that tickles my soft inner thighs as he pauses, his breath warm over my pussy. He scoops his hands under my buttocks, and I feel him adjust himself on the mattress, preparing for his feast.

"Delicious," he growls, and then his tongue touches me . . . and I'm gone.

# CHAPTER 1

## Mia

THE ELECTRONIC DRUMBEATS THUD THROUGH THE AIR SO HARD that I can actually feel my chest vibrate as I look at my screen, my head bobbing as I let the pattern come to me.

I've had a lot of people ask me how I can work the way I do, but this is when the magic happens. I've got three computer screens, each of them split into halves with data flowing in each one. I'm finishing up my evaluations, I've done the grind, and now I'm bringing it all together.

For that, though, I need tunes, and nothing gets my brain working on the right frequency as well as good techno does.

I can hear the door to my office vibrate in its frame, and I'm glad I've got my own little paradise down here in the basement of the Goldstone Building.

Sure, my methods are weird, and I'm sort of isolated considering that I'm in a corner office with two file rooms on either side of me, but that's because I need this to make the magic happen.

Frankly, I wasn't too sure if I'd be able to keep this job, considering the number of complaints I got my first six months working here.

Part of it, of course, is my occasional outbursts—to myself, mind you, and more often than not in gutter Russian so no one can understand me.

That, with the random singing along with my tunes, meant I was labeled as 'distracting' and 'difficult to work next to.'

But the powers that be saw the value that I bring with my data analysis.

So, as an experimental last gasp, I was sent down here, where the walls are thick, the neighbors are paper, and nobody minds that my singing voice is terrible.

It works for them, but more importantly, it works for me.

And here I've remained for almost six years, working metadata analysis and market trends, making people with money even more money.

Not that the company's treated me poorly. I've gotten a bonus for seven quarters straight, and I've always managed my own investments.

For a girl who still has a few years until she hits thirty, I'm doing well on the ol' nest egg.

But I'm pigeonholed. Other than dropping off files from time to time, I almost never see anyone in my day to day work, which I guess is okay with me. I've never been someone who likes the social scene of an office.

On the other hand, I can wear my pink and blue streaks in my hair and not have to see people's judging glares. And I don't have to explain what my lyrics mean when I decide to sing along.

"Another one for the Motherland!" I exclaim as I see what I've been looking for. This isn't a hard assignment, merely an optimization analysis for some of Goldstone's transport subsidiaries. But I prefer to celebrate each victory, no matter how small or large, with glee.

I swipe all the data to my side monitors and bring up a document in the center and start typing. I've already included most of the boilerplate that the executives and VPs want to see, the 'check the box' sort of things that my father would understand with his background.

After all, he is Russian. He knows about bureaucracy.

Finally, just as the Elf Clock above my door dings noon, I save my file and fire it off to my supervisor.

"In Russia . . . report finishes *you.*"

Okay, so it's not my best one-liner, but it's another quirk of mine. While I'm as American as apple pie, I pay homage to my roots, especially at work, for some reason. It seems to help, so I'm sticking to it.

Heading to the elevator, I go upstairs before punching out for lunch and jumping into my little Chevy to drive to my 'spot', a diner called The Gravy Train. An honest to goodness old-fashioned diner, it's got some of the best food in town, including a fried chicken sandwich that's to kill for.

As I drive, I look around my hometown, still surprised at how big it seems these days. The main reason, of course, is tied to the dark tower on the north side of town, Blackwell Industries.

Thirty years ago, Mr. Blackwell located his headquarters here in the sleepy town of Roseboro and proclaimed it to be the bridge between Portland and Seattle. A lot of people scoffed, but he was right, and Roseboro's been the beneficiary of his foresight.

I've been lucky, watching a city literally grow with me. Roseboro is big enough now that some people even call this a Tri-Cities area, lumping us in with Portland and Seattle.

I get to The Gravy Train just in time to see the other reason that I come to this place so frequently for lunch wave from the window. Isabella "Izzy" Turner has been my best friend since first grade, and I love her like she's my own flesh and blood.

As I enter, I see her untie the apron on her uniform and slump down into one of the booths. Her normally rich brown hair looks limp and stringy today, and the bags under her eyes are so big she could be carrying her after work clothes in them.

"Hey, babe, you look exhausted," I say in greeting, giving her a hug from the side as I slide in next to her. "Please don't tell me you're still working double shifts?"

"Have to," Izzy says as she leans into me and hugs back. "Gotta keep the bills paid, and doing double shifts gives me a chance to maybe get a little ahead. I'll need it once classes start up again."

"You know you don't have to," I tell her for the millionth time. "You can take out student loans like the rest of us."

"I'd rather not if I don't have to. I owe enough to other people as it is."

She's got a point. She's had a tough life and has seen tragedy that left more and more debt on her tab, and student loans are tough enough without all the other stuff in her life.

And even though she always turns me down, I have to offer once again, just on the off-chance she'll say yes this time. "Still, if you need anything . . . I mean, I've said it before, but you can always come live with me. I've got room at my place."

Izzy snorts, finally cracking a smile. "You mean you want someone to stay up with you until two in the morning on weekends playing video games."

Before I can elbow her in the side, the bell above the door rings and in walks the third member of our little party patrol, Charlotte Dunn. A stunning girl who turns heads everywhere she goes with her long, naturally bright and beautiful red hair, she slides into the booth opposite Izzy and me, looking exhausted herself.

She settles in, sighing heavily, and Izzy looks over at her. "Tough morning for you too?"

"I think walking in the back and sticking my head in a vat of hot oil might just be preferable to working reception on the ground floor of Satan's Skyscraper," she jokes. "It's not like anything bad happened either."

"So what's the deal?" I ask, and Charlotte shakes her head. "What?"

"I guess it's just that everyone there walks like they've got a hundred-pound albatross on their back as they come in. No smiles, no greetings, even though I try. It's just depressing," she replies. "You got lucky, landing in the shining palace."

"Girl, please. I work all by my lonesome in the deep, dark dungeon of a basement," I point out.

Charlotte snorts. "But that's how you like it!"

She's not wrong, so I don't bother arguing, instead teasingly gloating, "And I get to wear whatever and work however the hell I please."

Our waitress, one of Izzy's co-workers, comes over with her order pad. "So, what can I get you ladies?"

"Something with no onions or spice," Izzy replies, groaning. "Maybe Henry can whip up a grilled cheese for me?"

"Deal. And for you ladies?"

We place our orders, and the three of us lean back, relaxing. Charlotte looks me over enviously again, shaking her head. "Seriously, Mia, can't get over the outfit today. You trying to show off the curves?"

"What curves?" I ask, looking down at today's band T-shirt. It's just a BTS logo, twin columns rising on a black shirt.

"Hey, you're rockin' it." Charlotte laughs. "It fits the girls just right."

I roll my eyes. Charlotte always seems to see something in me that I don't. Men don't seem to find me interesting. Or at least, the men *I* find interesting don't find *me* interesting.

Deflecting back to her, I ask, "How're things looking for you? That guy in Accounting ever come back downstairs to get your number?"

Charlotte snorts. "Nope. I saw him the other day, but it's okay. It's his loss."

She does a little hair flip and I can't help but smile. She hasn't always had the best luck with guys, but she never gives up and always keeps a positive attitude about the whole dating game. Her motto is 'No Mr. Wrongs, only Mr. Rights and Mr. Right-Nows.' Maybe not the classiest, but a girl's got needs, and sometimes it's nice to have an orgasm from a guy not named B.O.B.

We eat our lunches, chatting and gossiping and bullshitting as always. It's never a big to-do since we share lunch together at least once a week, if not more, but it's still nice to catch up. Izzy and I have been friends for so long, and Charlotte and I met in college. They're important to me.

"So, when do classes start up again, Izz?" Charlotte asks. "So you can, I don't know, get some sleep and not have fallen arches?"

Izzy snorts. "Too soon, I think. But if I can string together another two semesters—"

"Wait, two?" I ask in shock. "Honey, you're like the super-duper-ooper senior at this point. Seriously, some of the professors are probably younger than you by now."

"Hey, we're the same age!" Izzy protests, but shrugs. "You know, I had a freshman ask me if I was a TA the other day?"

"Ouch, that had to hurt," Charlotte says. "What did you say?"

"I pointed him in the direction of the student union and turned him down when he asked for my number. Seriously, I'm not sure if he even needed to shave yet. I don't have time to teach eighteen-year-old man-boys what and where a clit is!"

Charlotte and I laugh, and I punch her in the shoulder. "You'll get there in your own time, girl. But still, why the wait?"

"Mostly the internship," Izzy admits. "I can juggle classes and work, or internship and work, but I can't do classes, internship, and work. There's just not enough hours in the day."

I nod, understanding that Izzy has plans and dreams. But unlike most, she's willing to sacrifice and work hard to reach hers.

We shift topics, like we always do, until we've covered all the usual topics and my tummy feels pleasantly happy without risk of an afternoon food coma.

Wiping our mouths with our napkins, I glance at my phone, checking the time. "So, Char . . . rock, paper, scissors?"

"Nope, this one's mine!" Charlotte says, giggling as I lean into Izzy, preventing her from moving as Charlotte grabs the check and runs up to the counter.

"Hey! Hey, dammit!" Izzy protests. "I—"

"Should be quiet and let your friends pay for lunch for once," I whisper. "Or else I'll use my secret Russian pressure point skills on you!"

"Oh, fine, since you put it that way!"

Charlotte comes back, and she smiles at Izzy. "Chill, Izz. You bust your ass, and you've snuck us an extra pickle more than once. You're allowed to let me buy you lunch every now and then."

"We could all use some more *pickle*." Izzy chuckles. "Seriously, at this point, I'd settle for a one-nighter. No commitment, no issues, just a good old-fashioned hookup. As long he's well into his twenties, at least," she says with an eye roll.

"Mr. Right Now?" Charlotte asks, and Izzy nods. "Hmph. You find him, send him my way. I keep finding good guys . . . two months after they've met the girl of their dreams. Only single men I find are dogs."

"You've just gotta make sure you give them a fake number and a flea dip, and enjoy the weekend," I tease, though she knows I would never do anything of the sort.

"I'm lonely, but I've got rechargeable batteries."

We all laugh, and my phone rings. I pull it out, checking the screen. "Shit, girls, it's my boss. Says he's got a rush job for me to complete."

"How's he working out, anyway?" Charlotte asks as I finish my drink quickly. "And have you started working for The Golden Child yet?"

"Nope, I've never seen him except for the publicity stuff," I reply honestly. "He's the penthouse. I'm the basement. Twenty-four floors in between us. Anyway, I gotta jet, so I'll talk to you girls soon, okay?"

"Yup . . . I'm going to relax for this next ten minutes before I need to clock back in myself," Izzy says, stretching out. "Gimme a call later?"

I nod, blowing them a kiss, and head back to work.

# CHAPTER 2

## Thomas

L OOKING OUT OVER ROSEBORO, I FEEL LIKE I'M LOOKING OVER MY empire.

Of course, I'm joking . . . but maybe not so much.

Twenty-five years ago, this town was just a suburb of a suburb of Portland. Though it was already up and coming, I'd like to think that over the past six years I've added my fair share to this place.

I'd finished my MBA at Stanford and set up shop in the growing town, watching the landscape change and cultivating the business interests that serve me best. Because I haven't just watched. I've worked my ass off to get Goldstone where it is today.

Still, I made sure to keep the competition in sight, literally.

My office faces the Blackwell Building, a one-mile gap separating the two tallest buildings in the city. It helps me keep things in perspective. I came to town because I saw potential, even if Blackwell had already created something big here.

But this place is too fertile for him to fully take advantage of. A rose that, if tended right, can provide more blossoms than any one man could utilize.

I watch the morning sun hit the black tower. I'll give Blackwell grudging respect. His design might be morbid, but it's also cutting-edge. All that black is absorbing the solar energy and using it for electricity and heating. The man was environmental before environmental was actually cool.

*Too bad you'll never be that. You're just a wannabe, another young upstart who'll never stand the test of time.*

I growl, pushing away the voice from inside me, even though I know it'll be back. It never really goes away, not for long. No matter how much I achieve, that voice of insecurity still resides in my center, ready to cast doubt and shadows on each success.

The soft ding from my computer reminds me that my ten minutes of morning meditation are over, and I turn back around, looking at my desk and office. It's nothing lavish. I designed this space for maximum efficiency and productivity.

So my Herman Miller chair is not in my office for lapped luxury, or for its black and chrome styling, but for the fact that it's rated the best chair for productivity. Same with my desk, my computer, everything.

Everything is tuned toward efficient use of my time and my efforts.

I launch into it, going through my morning assignments, answering the emails that my secretary, Kerry, cannot answer for me, and making a flurry of decisions on projects that Goldstone is working on.

Finally, just as the clock on my third screen beeps one o'clock, I send off my final message and stand up. Locking my computer, I transfer everything to my server upstairs in case I need it.

I see Kerry sitting at her desk as I leave my office. She's well-dressed as usual, her sunkissed skin and black hair gleaming mellowly under the office lighting, the perfect epitome of a professional executive assistant. While she works for me, she has this older sibling protective instinct. It's not often that I need it, but I appreciate her looking out for me.

"Need something, Mr. Goldstone?" she asks.

"Just headed upstairs," I tell her.

"Of course," she replies, her eyes cutting to her computer screen. "Just a reminder, sir, the governor will be hosting his charity event tonight at seven. I've already had your tuxedo dry-cleaned, and your car detailer called. Your car will be ready and downstairs by three this afternoon."

I give her a nod. Three's plenty of time. "I just sent you a list of other projects to work on, by the way."

"Of course, Mr. Goldstone. I was looking that over, and I got an email from Hank also, the team leader you assigned the Taiwan shipping contract to. He said that he's going to have to take a day off Friday, sir. His daughter's going to college this year, and he promised her that he'd drive her up so she can get settled into the dorm."

I stop, pursing my lips. "What is her name?"

Kerry taps her desk for a moment, searching her memory. "Erica, sir."

"Tell Hank that I understand and wish Erica the best, but if he isn't at work on Friday, don't bother coming in on Monday."

My tone has grown serious, and Kerry's eyes tighten, but she knows Hank is crossing a line. He should've given notice, especially when he's working a contract this important.

He's usually a good employee. But he knew his daughter was starting classes. No excuse for that.

*No excuse for you, you mean. Failure just drips down from the boss's office down to Hank, that's all.*

Leaving the twenty-fifth floor of the Goldstone building, I take the stairs up a level to stretch my legs. Not many people even know about this floor other than the executives. To everyone else, the Goldstone Building has twenty-five floors.

The twenty-sixth is mine. It's my penthouse, and while it isn't quite as large as the other floors, it's still six thousand square feet of space that's just for me.

I strip off my dress shirt, tie, and slacks, depositing everything in the laundry chute before pulling on my workout clothes.

Today's upper body day, and as I go into my home gym, I swing my arms to loosen up my shoulders. They're going to be punished today. Starting with bench presses, I assault my body, pushing myself to press the bar one more time, to get the fucking dumbbells up despite the pain, despite gravity kicking my ass.

*Just like everything kicks your ass.*

The finisher for today is brutal, even for me. The 300 . . . 100 burpees, 100 dips, and 100 pullups, in sets of ten, nonstop. By the time I'm finished, sweat pools on the rubberized gym flooring beneath me.

I have to force myself to my feet because I refuse to be broken by anything, even something as meaningless as a workout that's supposed to do exactly that.

Instead, I jump in for a quick shower and meditate for twenty minutes after. I need to focus because running Goldstone is a mental exercise.

Closing my eyes, I force myself to push all the responsibilities away, to let it all fade into the background.

I push away the flashbacks, the voice in my head, the memories that threaten from time to time, and imagine my perfect world . . . my empire. My perfect Roseboro, deep red petals soft as velvet and eternally blooming, ready to be passed from my generation to the next for tending and care.

I know I can do it.

I *must* do it.

Changing into my tuxedo, I head downstairs to the freshly cleaned limo waiting to take me to this event. The Roseboro Civic Library is one of the newest public buildings in town, a beautiful hundred-thousand-square-foot building in three wings over two floors. The central wing is named for Horatio Roseboro, who founded the city in memory of his daughter, who died on the Oregon Trail, while the other two wings are named for the main benefactors . . . Goldstone and Blackwell. My only request was that the Goldstone wing contain the children's section, and they were more than willing to do that.

Tonight, though, it's the scene for a fundraiser for the governor's favorite charity. Governor Gary Langlee tends to ignore Roseboro most of the time—we're not his voter base—but when it comes time to get money, he'll go just about anywhere he can if someone will cross his palm with a little bit of green.

I arrive at just the right time, ten minutes before seven, in order to get the best of the press. I tolerate the leeches more than like them, but I do understand that the fourth estate has a purpose and a job to do.

And there are legit journalists who I respect. It's just the paparazzi and empty talking heads that I despise.

So I smile for the cameras, giving a little wave and shaking hands with our local state representative before heading into the foyer, where the party has already started.

"Ah, Thomas!" the mayor says, greeting me in that hearty way that really endears him to the locals. "I'm so glad you could make it."

"You know me, never pass up a chance to press the flesh," I reply, making him laugh. He knows I'm lying but thinks that I'm only here because of the press and good PR that Goldstone will get for tonight.

The reality is far different. While Governor Langlee and I might not see eye to eye on most public policies, I actually agree with the goals of tonight's event.

"I'm sure you'll enjoy yourself," the mayor says after a moment when I don't follow up.

Clearing his throat, he looks around. "If you don't mind telling me, Thomas, there's a rumor around town that Goldstone is looking into building a sea transportation hub in Roseboro. I'm not saying I wouldn't appreciate it, but if you are, I happen to know a man who's got about seven hundred and fifty acres just outside of town. It's county land, but I'm sure we could work something out."

That's the mayor . . . a good ol' boy to the voters, a sneaky dealmaker to those with money. The man would sell his grandmother's grave if it'd make him a buck.

*Oh, like you've been such a good son.*

"If we do move on such a project, I'll be sure to keep City Hall informed," I tell him with a smile that turns just a little predatory at the end. "But of course, I would do my due diligence on the property. No use wasting my money when it could be spent on a proper seaport instead of along the Columbia?"

The mayor blanches just a little, which is what I want. A tiny reminder that while he may hold office, I hold the funds that make this city thrive or fail. Or at least a large share of the finances that do so.

Leaving him, I do my best to 'mingle'. I know the faces. I've seen it all before.

A pat on the back here for a friend.

A backhanded compliment for the enemy whom you can't quite man up and call out in public. The icy stare from across the room at those whose families have somehow found the time to engage in feuds despite not having the time to make a difference in the world.

It's all old hat, and while some might find it interesting, I just tolerate it to get my goal here tonight done.

Finally, at nine o'clock, I can't do it any longer. I retreat to the children's section, which is relatively quiet in comparison, and I look over the newest books on the display.

"You know, I'm not too sure if *Long Way Down* really belongs in the children's section," a throaty voice says behind me, and I turn to see Meghan Langlee, Governor Langlee's daughter.

She's wearing a Chanel cocktail dress that fits her like a glove, highlighting a very fit body and a camera grabbing face. A former beauty queen like her mother, Meghan's parlayed her looks into a budding career as a political pundit.

"Actually, I personally insisted on it," I reply, turning away from her and looking at the books again. "While the subject matter might be a little dark and violent, the days of young people growing up needing little more than *The Andy Griffith Show* and reading Judy Blume are pretty much over."

"Hmm, well, I'll say my father would disapprove, but I understand what you mean," she says, stepping closer. "You know, Mr. Goldstone . . . mind if I call you Tom?"

"If you wish," I reply, sizing her up immediately. She must be up to something, she's coming on too hard, too boldly.

It wouldn't surprise me if she's been sent here on a mission. Her father's a weasel and would see no issue with using his only daughter this way.

She takes my arm, as if she expects me to suddenly escort her and be happy to do so, giving me a false coquettish giggle. "Ooh. I've heard your reputation Tom, that you're pretty *rigid* in your fitness routines, but wow, this tux is hiding a *beast* underneath all this worsted wool."

"Clean eating and good habits," I reply, already tiring of her and her lazily flirtatious innuendos. She tries to lead me back to the main wing, and I follow along simply to avoid any issues, but when she sees one of the press and starts trying to angle us in that direction, I pull my arm free. "Excuse me, Miss Langlee."

She looks surprised, anger hiding in her eyes. I doubt she's used to being denied. She reaches out and grabs my arm again, pulling herself close.

"Come on now, Tom. I'm sure we can find a little bit of fun."

I can't tolerate this any longer, and I pull away, my voice tight. "Sorry. I haven't had my rabies booster this year."

I walk away, cursing myself at that last crack. Turning her down cold? That's one thing.

But essentially calling her a disease-infested slut was probably too much.

"One of these days, you're going to piss off someone important," she says threateningly to my back. When I don't reply, she stomps her foot like a petulant toddler, loud enough to cut through the hubbub of the party as she calls out, "Bastard!"

Everything stops, and I nod, glancing back over my shoulder at her with a charming smile. "That's one of the things they call me."

I keep going, and as I pass by the governor, he gives me a dirty look. Reaching out, he puts a hand on my arm.

"You know, my daughter—" he starts, already conciliatory, which makes me think he knew exactly what Meghan's game was tonight.

I don't let him finish. I just shrug him off, ignoring the snapping cameras. I only pause at the door to reach into my jacket and pull out an envelope that I slide into the donation box.

It's unmarked . . . but that's just what I want.

# CHAPTER 3

## Blackwell

T HE SHADOWS OF THE UNUSED WING CONCEAL ME, JUST AS I planned. There are no lights up here, just the glow from down below, which is just how I like it.

Why should I waste my time mingling among the players on stage when I can be the director, up here in the shadows until the right moment for my cameo?

The velvet rope across the stairs to the upper floor sends a tasteful but pointed point to the people down below, giving me the privacy I want.

I sip my glass of Seleccion Suprema, enjoying the subtle tones of the fine tequila while watching Thomas Goldstone storm out of the library, the governor outraged and his little tramp of a daughter staring dark murder at him. It's exactly what I wanted.

"Scurry home, Golden Boy," I whisper, sipping my drink again. "Storm out of here, showing the whole world your weakness."

I've studied my adversary from afar for years, ever since The Golden Boy turned his attention from minor league playing the market and posting dramatic percentage gains to actually slinging weight in Roseboro.

I'll admit, I underestimated him at first. I laughed when Goldstone established his first 'headquarters' and even rented him the first building. The old three-story building had sat empty for awhile, caught in that gap between small business and big business and too difficult to divide up. I figured it could come to some use at least that way, but I'd thought Goldstone would crash and burn after a few years.

Little did I expect to have to look out of my office window to see Goldstone's own building, nearly as tall as my own, every morning.

I shake my head, wondering where I'd gone wrong. It should have taken him another decade or more to get to where he is now. It makes no logical sense for the Golden Boy, at just over half my age, to have already closed the gap on me so quickly.

I'd run the numbers and taken the time to double-check the figures personally . . . and knew the day after Goldstone cut the ribbon on that shining monstrosity a mile from my own tower that if I didn't do something to destroy Thomas Goldstone, he'd steal my throne as the richest man in Roseboro.

Goldstone is poised to relegate me to the list of also-rans, the men who were big but not the biggest.

History remembers Secretariat, not the horses who finished second behind him.

I have no intention of ending my life as anything other than the undisputed master of my domain. Some may call me a dictator . . . but at least they'll remember me.

And so I plot, and tonight, I confirmed a suspicion I've had for a long time. Thomas Goldstone's infamous temper is very real and rather raw when it comes to beautiful women.

He didn't show it outwardly, and I'll give him that much. There was no yelling, no screaming like I've heard rumors about. But to just impetuously pull his arm away from Governor Langlee like that? Ill-advised, to say the least.

I chuckle and watch the governor console his stupid, status-seeking daughter while trying to get the focus back on tonight's charity cause.

Men's dress shoes click on the tile flooring of the landing. I refuse to let my wing of the library be sullied with anything as plebeian as fuzzy carpet like Goldstone has in the children's wing. There's a reason they're called rugrats, after all.

Still, the shadows are so thick that even up close, I know the man can't see my face clearly, although the obsidian cufflinks on my tuxedo clearly reveal my identity.

Not too many people can pull off obsidian and platinum cufflinks while not mingling with the crowd.

"Sir, I assume you saw that?"

My operative is dressed like most of the men downstairs, in a suit that is appropriate for the evening but not a tuxedo. No, only the crème de la crème are wearing tuxedos, and I need my man to stay anonymous.

Which, in many respects, is very hard to do in a gossipy upper-crust crowd who eyes any newcomer with scrutiny and obvious analysis of their financial bearing. And unfortunately, my operative is as status-hungry as the governor's daughter, in his own way.

Not quite a peacock . . . but definitely not a chameleon. He's not quite seeking recognition though, which is useful to me. I need a snake, not a chameleon.

"Of course," I reply after a moment of savoring my tequila. Forget the flavoring, the mixings. Just let me savor the oaky vanilla tones of the extra anejo tequila while the agave essence sort of plays in my nose. "It went well."

"I apologize that he didn't leave with the girl. When I pointed her in his direction, I assumed he'd—"

"Never assume anything," I say, looking over at the man. Intelligent, and with striking eyes that most people assume is a product of his upbringing. I know different, and know the fire inside them burns with hatred for Thomas Goldstone. Yes, he's definitely not a chameleon.

But he's not half the hunter he thinks he is, either.

He expects that by playing Judas to Goldstone, he will garner himself favor with me. I can't blame him for the blossoming hope, since I planted the seed myself and have watered it with unspoken promises over these past few months.

The man has a future, as long as he keeps his eyes open. The very same knife he's helping me to slip into Thomas Goldstone can quickly be turned on him as well if he decides to think beyond what he's told.

"It doesn't matter. The Golden Boy has shown his weakness. All that glitters isn't gold."

"Excuse me, sir?"

I sigh and finish off my tequila. Perhaps my operative isn't quite as smart as he pretends to be. But at the same time, it reassures me. The man isn't smart enough to realize he's being played.

For a man who is betraying his employer, he still has an ironic blind spot. He's not very good at planning, just executing the plans of others.

"Piece of advice. There is a time when you set up, and plan, and project, and scheme. But there comes a time to just push that first domino and see what happens. Knowing when to do each . . . that's power."

My man says nothing, watching as the governor clears his throat and the party starts back up, tension starting to melt away . . . but I can see that many people won't forget the scene Goldstone created.

Least of all, the governor.

"Sir . . . what shall we do about him?" my man asks. "Any man confident enough to just walk away from Governor Langlee like that . . ."

I can't help but grin as I think through my plans. Goldstone is on his way to becoming a large enough problem that drastic measures will need to be used. It's not that I'm averse to that methodology, and in fact, I've nurtured a healthy relationship with operatives beyond the law.

But I prefer to stick with the quieter approach I've plotted, so as not to draw more attention to the famous Golden Boy.

I want the man crushed . . . not a martyr.

And there are so many, many ways to cut your enemy's legs out from under him. Quiet or loud, mercilessly or kindly, with confrontation or from the shadows.

"I have an idea . . . but for now, enjoy the party. After all, you have connections to make yourself, yes?"

# CHAPTER 4

## Mia

I GATHER MYSELF AS I KNOCK ON MY SUPERVISOR'S DOOR. BILL Radcliffe's been my boss for the past two years, and though I might feel nervous coming up here for any other boss, Bill's been a great one.

Best I've worked for, going all the way back to my part-time college gigs. And this week's update meeting should be a slam-dunk considering I'd completed his rush job with time to spare.

But I'm still awkward and uncomfortable up here in the land of the automaton office zombies, feeling like people are glaring at me.

"Hi, Bill," I greet him, adjusting my jeans. It's Friday, which means denim is more than fine, and I like being as casual as I can. Although I might be pushing it with the Ahsoka Tano T-shirt today. "Uhm, you said you had something you wanted to talk with me about?"

"Yeah, come on in and close the door," Bill says, leaning back.

I sit down, a little nervous. This seems odd. Usually, Bill's to the point, but I can see him gathering his thoughts.

"Uhm, is this about my BTS T-shirt last week? Or that mix I played earlier this week? I promise you, I didn't realize the lyrics at the time until I was halfway into it."

"The wha . . . never mind, no, there's no problem at all," Bill says, chuckling. "If I had a problem with your music, Mia, I'd have said something two years ago when I first walked into your office and you were screaming Nine Inch Nails at me."

I blush, nodding. It had been a 'rough time', as Izzy likes to say, and so my music had been a little rougher too. Still, your new boss walking into your office while you scream *I want to fuck you like an animal* is not the impression you want to make.

"Yeah . . . so, what's up?"

Bill takes a big breath and turns his laptop around. "You've been called upstairs. It seems that someone has recognized what I've seen for the past two years, and those Sherlock skills of yours are going to be put to the test."

I read the document he has up, a standard company email, and gulp. "I'll be reporting to Mr. Goldstone? Starting Monday?"

"Not quite," Bill says. "You're still with my group, but this assignment is for a short-term project team, something The Ruthless Bastard likes to do a lot. Ad hoc teams."

The Ruthless Bastard. I've heard more than one person call Thomas Goldstone that, though no one ever says why. Mr. Goldstone must actually like being called that because I can't imagine Bill saying it to me otherwise.

"So, what can I expect?"

"The team will be some of the best talent in Goldstone," Bill says, "and the rewards for a good performance can be substantial. You might even earn a ticket out of the basement, if you want, although I think you might actually enjoy being on your own."

"I could use a window," I joke. "I get pretty pale come summertime. But yes, I do enjoy it."

Bill rubs at his cheek. "Listen, Mia, if it were anyone else on the team, I'd send them up there without much more than a 'watch your ass' comment, but you . . . well, I happen to like you. You do damn good work, and despite your quirks, you make my life a lot easier. With you on the team, I don't feel so bad about taking the demotion I asked for years ago. Those bonus checks you help us get come in handy."

"Why did you ask for a demotion, Bill?" I ask, curious and glad for the opening to pry. I'd heard rumors but had never had the chance to ask him before.

"Six years ago, I was one of those folks who was burning up the corporate ladder. I'd come to Goldstone from Silicon Valley because I wanted in on the ground floor of an upstart again and saw potential almost as soon as Thomas Goldstone launched the company."

"You're an OG?" I ask, surprised. "I didn't know."

Bill chuckles. "Yeah, well . . . in my first three years here, I'd worked myself up. Literally, because when this building opened, I had a nice office on the twentieth floor. But I learned the same thing a lot of people have. This company's great to work for. The pay is good, the bennies are great . . . but the closer you get to Thomas Goldstone, the more you need them to tip the scale in your favor. Goldstone truly demands perfection, and the expectations and stress levels go up exponentially with every floor."

"'High achievement always takes place in the framework of high expectations.' Charles Kettering," I quote, but Bill shakes his head.

"Mia, before I joined the corporate world, I did four years in the Army, including a tour in Afghanistan. I did Ranger school, even if I don't look it now. A year being shot at in the mountains of Kandahar, a year of Ranger school . . . and Thomas Goldstone broke my ass in one project team. Nope, I'm happy here on three."

I nod, thinking. I never knew that about Bill, but I'm not really surprised. He strikes me as that sort of easygoing leader who still gets his people to perform and sort of makes do with what he has available.

"Okay . . . and what if I were to turn down the assignment?"

"It'll be reassigned to someone else but noted upstairs that you turned down the opportunity, which isn't a great look for you," Bill says. "This company has plenty of data analysts. You're just the best . . . in my opinion."

His compliment means a lot to me, and I sit back, thinking. "I'll do it. I mean, a window in my basement cave would be sweet." I wink because we both know that'll never happen. "And, well . . . I want to prove what you said. That I'm the best. Challenge accepted."

Bill nods. "My wife's going to kill me for this. My daughter needs braces and those are expensive as hell, and with your reassignment, my quarterly bonus just poofed into thin air, but you're right . . . everyone's entitled to their shot. More than one, if they want to take it. So let me give you some pointers. One, be prepared to work harder than you ever have in your life. I mean, you need to be on point every minute of every day. That means when you're in a meeting, you need to listen and be able to comment on anything. One of Goldstone's things is he'll ask people their feedback on something that doesn't seem to be in their lane. It's both a test and a way for him to get fresh insight from different perspectives. Second . . . I hate to say it, but Goldstone's a bit old-school, and at least for meetings and stuff, you're going to need to be more . . . traditional."

He gestures at my attire and my dyed hair. I get the point, but he didn't need to say that. I wouldn't show up wearing my usual casual wear.

"Right," I murmur, nodding. I tug at my hair, which today is totally awesome with a blood-red fringe on the lower two inches, wishing it a silent goodbye. Hello, boring old blonde Mia. "Got it."

I stand up, but before I can leave, Bill holds up a hand and grins. "Oh, one other thing . . . got any ideas on the news?"

"Which part?" I ask.

"The White Knight," Bill says. "He struck again." His gleeful curiosity is apparent, as is his joy at being the one to spread the gossip to me.

Ah, the White Knight. He's almost a local myth, and any anonymous act of charity in the Portland/Roseboro area is attributed to him. They say he's even done stuff up in Seattle as well.

"How much was it this time?"

"Half a million," Bill says with a smile. "That's going to help a lot of homeless vets."

Vets this time.

Last time, it was an animal shelter, and before that an orphanage and a drug treatment facility, originally starting off with an at-risk children's center.

Each time, a white envelope with a cashier's check or a white paper-wrapped package of cash was delivered totally anonymously.

Rumor has it the local news is stumped because the checks are connected to some shell corporation out of the Bahamas. It's just . . . urban legendary.

"Honestly?" I reply, shrugging my shoulders. "I think whoever it is wants their privacy, so I figure we should respect that. Whoever it is, they're doing good. Why mess with that?"

Bill nods. "Yeah, guess so. Still, if you told me I could work for the White Knight instead of The Ruthless Bastard, I'd take that offer in a second."

"My sweet little girl, you look beautiful," my father greets me, grabbing me and kissing me noisily on both cheeks. Some things he'll never give up. "How is my little Anastasia?"

"Papa, how many times must I beg you to stop with that?" I ask. "I'm no princess, and she ended up dead."

"Bah, that's just what the Party wanted everyone to believe," Papa says, waving his hand. "She still lives on in the hearts of all true Russians. Even now, her daughter is somewhere, waiting for her country to need her."

I shake my head. Papa will always love the Motherland in his heart. Even if we're meeting in a Thai restaurant for dinner. "Whatever you say. Come, let's enjoy dinner. I have good news."

He sits rapt as I tell him about my day, his smile growing as I tell him about the project group. "See? I have always told you, Mia, you have the brains of a genius and the beauty to match. Now you have your opportunity to show the rest of the company the same thing."

"Papa, they're looking for my brains, not how I look."

Papa scoffs, sipping his beer. "Nonsense, sweetheart. You are as beautiful as any of those girls in magazines and on the television. All peasants compared to my Mia!" His voice rises like he's singing my praises not just to me, but the whole room.

I'm blushing, staring at my appetizers as Papa finishes his declaration, wishing he'd be a little less supportive. "Papa, I'm just brains. God made me smart, not . . . that!"

Papa lowers his voice a little, almost to a whisper. "Oh, but you are a beauty. And one day, you'll pull your nose out of your numbers, look into a mirror, and finally realize what I've known all along."

I smile. Papa has always spoiled me with compliments, even when money was tight. I'm sometimes amazed I haven't ended up weirder than I am.

"Anyway, back to the job. I've heard that the stress is pretty high on these projects. There's a real risk of failure, flopping on my butt in front of the boss and the whole team."

Papa shakes his head, his smile dimming. "That's not going to happen. You are smart, and you are capable of being anything you want to be. And now you have the opportunity to show your bosses, of grabbing your future with your own two hands."

He grabs at the air, fisting his hand to emphasize his point. "And in that, I will always be proud of you."

"Don't ask for it," I whisper, and Papa quirks his eyebrow. I shake my head, smiling. "Nothing, Papa. Just something you said reminded me of

Eureka Seven, one of my animes. A character says, 'Don't ask for it. Go out and win it on your own.' You just made me think of that."

"Those Japanese cartoons of yours," Papa says, tsking. "I suppose it would be too much to ask that you'd just want to enjoy normal television that I know? Watch *The Bachelor* like an American girl, or the news so we could discuss politics."

I laugh. Papa has never understood my fascination with nerd culture . . . but he lets me be me. And for that, I love him more than I could ever explain.

"Yeah, well . . . right now, what I want to be is well-fed," I reply, seeing the waiter approaching. "What'll it be, Papa? My treat."

Papa sighs and quickly looks at his menu. "What on here won't give me heartburn?"

# CHAPTER 5

## Mia

THE CONFERENCE ROOM ON THE TWENTY-FOURTH FLOOR SEEMS huge, but maybe it's just the people involved. I mean, there are only six people here, and the table's no bigger than the team meetings I would have on Bill's team.

But the power in this room means a lot, and the view out the windows . . . I know I'm being silly, but I swear that at any moment, a cloud's going to come drifting by and a bird's going to roost on the little antenna sticking out below the window. I think that's a cellphone point, but my tech knowledge is in using the system, not designing it.

"Can I have everyone's attention?" the man at the front, a handsome, broad-shouldered guy with slightly wavy black hair and a chin that would make a cowboy proud, says.

He's got startling blue eyes and teeth so white I wonder who makes his bleaching product. Still, the thousand-dollar suit he's wearing, and the fact that he's put his tablet at the head of the table, tells me he's somebody.

"Let's go ahead and get started, shall we? For those of you who don't know me, my name's Randall Towlee, Vice President of M&A here at Goldstone. Since some of you might be new to this sort of format, let's go around and do introductions. Just your name, your department, and your specialty."

The other five are all from different departments in Goldstone. One's an accountant, another is in real estate, while there's a lawyer and finally, a contracts specialist. They all seem okay. Nobody's breathing fire, at least.

Last of all, it's my turn, and I do my best to not fidget as I fight the urge to scratch my neck and shift my thighs in the unfamiliar 'professional' pencil skirt I've got on.

"Hi, everyone. I'm Mia Karakova. Uhm, I've spent the past few years working with Bill Radcliffe's team down on the third floor, though I house in the basement."

*Shit.* Why did I say that? They probably know about the weirdo girl in the dungeon. *Shake it off.*

"I'm a data analyst. Most of the time, I do metadata trendspotting, but Bill likes to call me Sherlock." I smile like it's a funny joke, but no one laughs.

Short, but not too short. Nothing too embarrassing. Okay, first hurdle passed.

"Nice to have you with us," Randall says, flashing me a smile. "Everyone, I was the one who asked Mia to join the team. I've had the chance to read her reports and analyses for the past few quarters, and she really is a trend detective. And we've been handed a corker of a problem."

Janice, the accountant who's been looking at Randall like she wants to eat him alive, cock first, gives me an appraising look. There's some frost, and maybe a touch of aggression.

Okay, well . . . she can have him. I don't want drama, and Randall doesn't do anything for me.

"What is the problem, Randall?" Janice asks. "It must be some sort of M&A issue if you're leading the charge, although nobody matches wits quite like you, so it could be anything."

Oh. My. God. She's laying it on thick.

Randall beams at her praise. "Actually, Mr. Goldstone is looking at expanding into the healthcare field and you've each been selected to help us address any issues with this new direction before he proceeds."

"If you don't mind," Danny, the lawyer, asks, "where *is* Mr. Goldstone?"

"Busy, but he told me this morning that he'll stop in," Randall says, his picture-perfect smile not dimming in the least. He launches into the details as he hands out a short document with the bare bones on the deal.

It's stupid and petty, but just another thing I don't like. He's got a tablet, this room has a giant freakin' display screen, and we've all got email. Did he really have to kill the trees to hand out a document he could have shown us digitally? It's the twenty-first century, for fuck's sake.

"So, bottom line," Randall says, reaching the end of his ten-minute speech, "Mr. Goldstone wants to buy a hospital. I'm sending you each an email now."

He clicks around on his tablet, and I hold back my smirk that he could've just done that in the first place. Redundancy, meet Randall.

"I've included the list of hospitals in the area that could be targets. We're not looking at launching a whole project from scratch. That's just not happening here. All the hospitals are in the PNW area, and it's going to be your job to research them. Figure out how we could get control of each of them, what the financial outlays are, projections on growth, things like that. Feed all your results through Mia. She's going to be meta on this, but Mia, I want you sharing your analysis back out. We double-check everything around here, got it?"

I nod. That's something I expected. "Got it."

"Good," Randall says, clearly aiming his attention back at me. "Okay, everyone, let's scatter, and you know the deal. Noses, grindstones, and all that."

The five of us get up, heading for the door, when I hear Randall say, "Mia, if you'll hang behind a moment?"

Janice gives me a look, but I can't tell her out loud that I'm not trying to run clitorference on whatever game she's got with Randall. And she doesn't seem to get the message I'm sending with my eyes.

Randall is shuffling his papers, and I stand by the window, admiring the view for a moment and hoping that Randall isn't about to kick me off the team already.

It isn't until I'm turned around that I remember that this skirt's a little tight through my hips and I'm definitely giving him a show. I turn back around, crossing my arms over my chest and looking down.

"What can I help you with, Mr. Towlee?"

"Two things. First, I know what it's like to be on your first action team here at Goldstone," Randall says, mostly sounding like a nice guy, but I didn't miss the way his eyes shot upward when I turned around. "You're going to be nervous, and I know you're probably not used to other people checking your work."

I shrug. "I do work alone, but I'm sure someone does check whatever I send up. Bill usually, but others too. I'm just probably not the best at verbally explaining it because most people hear 'data analysis' and instantly get bored."

"Okay. You do your data magic, and I'll handle the talking," Randall reassures me, standing up. "I'm pretty good at speaking tech, and I promise that you'll get your name on the report."

I nod, not really saying anything. I expected my name to be known if I am on the team and doing the work, so it's not like he's offering something I wasn't already entitled to.

"Also," Randall says, lowering his voice and stepping a little closer, "if you'd like—"

"Towlee!"

The name booms through the air so loud I swear that whoever said it is actually in the room, but it's not until two seconds later that the door opens and my breath catches.

It's the first time I've seen Thomas Goldstone in the flesh. And the PR photos don't do him justice.

Rich brown hair, sharp cheekbones, and eyes that blaze with green fire, lit from within with an intelligence and intensity that take my breath away. And that's just from the neck up. His shirt looks custom-tailored over an upper body that I'm pretty sure is carved from granite, almost to the point of looking like a superhero in disguise, Bruce Wayne in the boardroom.

Even his suit looks absolutely perfectly tailored to fit his body, or maybe he just has the perfect body for suits. I can't tell, and I know something about suits.

But Thomas himself . . . he's just that powerful. He's magnetic, a man with his own pull and charisma that might be able to overpower the force of gravity if he so desires. Though he's only one man entering the room, it suddenly feels infinitely smaller with his aura pressing in against mine.

"Thomas," Randall says, clearing his throat and stepping back like he just got his hand caught in the cookie jar. "How can I help you?"

"What is this garbage you sent me about the Yakima project? I told you to give me a detailed analysis of their advertising budget usage over the last decade."

For the next three minutes, I stand to the side, trying to stay small while I watch in fear and fascination as Thomas Goldstone performs an absolute verbal castration on Randall Towlee. It's an exercise in utter mastery of the English language.

He never curses.

He never gets personal.

Other than his initial name callout, his voice never even rises.

He just carves the document apart with a tongue like a scalpel, pointing out half a dozen places where the report didn't meet his standards.

It's totally professional . . . and totally emasculating. By the end, Randall, who was John Wayne in the group meeting, looks like a little kid wearing cowboy boots with his diaper as Thomas flips the report dismissively onto the table.

"Get me a *proper* analysis," Thomas finishes up. His eyes for the first time glance over at me. He looks me up and down but doesn't say a word, and then he walks out.

In the silence, I look at Randall, who's trying to gather together the last tattered remnants of his manhood that are left after Thomas just finished slicing, dicing, and feeding them to him by the handful.

"So that's what we call being put on blast," Randall says with a weak, watery laugh.

"And everyone has to handle things like . . . like that?" I ask, wondering how I'd react if Mr. Goldstone really put me on blast. Would I wilt like a flower in the face of an August windstorm, or would I find the strength to stand my ground?

Randall somehow laughs again, already recovering from Mr. Goldstone's onslaught. "That? That wasn't even that bad. You'll learn soon enough. You've got a lot of work to do and a short timeline to do it in. Welcome to the team."

"Thank you," I reply as Randall walks out, leaving me alone in the conference room.

In the suddenly empty space, I can't help but think about what I just saw, think about Thomas Goldstone. My knees shake a bit as I catch the slightest whiff of his cologne. It smells powerful and impressive, just like the man. And I feel fear . . . and arousal? Yes, that uncomfortable clenching in my gut isn't my belly, but decidedly *lower*.

Fear . . . and arousal.

# CHAPTER 6

## Thomas

T HE WARNING ALARM ON MY COMPUTER DINGS, AS IT ALWAYS DOES at 4:45, reminding me it's time to push away from my desk and to review the 'regular day'.

It's one of my *things*. I've tried to push the habit down on the rest of the company, but most don't take to it. Work hard, work fast, and do it by taking two fifteen-minute spots to intentionally do nothing except think.

By taking the first fifteen minutes of my day, I lay out exactly what I have to do. I review my long-term goals and then break them down into what I'm going to do that day. Then I get to it.

Of course, the day isn't always going to go to plan. In fact, a lot of days, things get torpedoed before I even get to lunch. But that's what this time is for. To reflect, to adjust, and to update my priorities.

There's nothing fancy to it. I don't have a meditation rug or trippy ambient music to put me in the proper mood. They're not needed. I turn away from my desk and close my eyes, letting what happened today wash over me.

It was a good day. The reports I got, the results generated, the plans that I sent out . . . they came back to me in good time and the quality was acceptable.

Still, everything didn't go to plan. I had to lay into Randall Towlee for his report on the Yakima project. It may not have been as bad as I made it seem, but I expect more from him, so he at least partially deserved some feedback.

Thinking of that early morning confrontation, I feel my heart quicken in my chest and my blood start to flow a little faster. It's not the memory of Randall Towlee's report causing it, either.

Randall, for all of his qualifications, is someone who only does what needs to be done. It's gotten him a long way, but that's not what I'm about.

I want perfection.

I want to exceed expectations.

But what my mind keeps going back to is the girl. With a few clicks, I review the email list to figure out her name. Mia Karakova. Amazingly, she's worked for me for years without my seeing her. Apparently, she's been trapped in the basement with Bill Radcliffe's team.

But in a glance, I can't wait to see her again. Her blonde hair hung in cornsilk waves down her back, with a few strands curling over her shoulders, framing a face that shouldn't have been as pleasing as it is.

Her eyes, while beautiful, are too wide-set, almost doll-like behind funky plastic frames, and her nose was a bit too upturned, naturally pixie-like, and her lips just a bit uneven, as though she'd been biting her puffy bottom one. But all together, somehow, it is sweet perfection.

Everything about her is impossible. Her body's no lines, all curves, all of them going in different directions but somehow coming harmoniously together in a multifaceted ballet that's interjected itself into my thoughts.

Her demure, almost shy sexiness inflames me, and I can barely focus for the rest of the fifteen minutes of my meditation. In fact, when five o'clock comes, I realize that I've spent the entirety of my meditation time researching her.

But in her very beauty, she scares me. I don't have a great history with beautiful women, and that history goes all the way back to my childhood.

*"You know, Tommy, you're a very lucky little boy," Mrs. Franklin tells me as my friend Ben and I enjoy some midafternoon cookies. "What with the mommy you have."*

*I don't really know what she's talking about. Mommy's . . . Mommy. I mean, they all have their good points. Mrs. Franklin, for instance, makes the best chocolate chip cookies in the world.*

*They're even better than Keebler's.*

*"Why?" I ask, trying to use words to explain all my thoughts. It's really hard, I think because there are ideas running around in my head that I don't even have the words for yet.*

*They say I'll learn more when I go to big kids' school next year.*

"Honey, Grace Goldstone is a classic beauty," Mrs. Franklin says, her voice sounding both happy and maybe a little angry. "Every time we go shopping, I'm reminded just how much so. Most women would kill to have looks like hers."

I think about Mommy and shrug. The long cloth thing hanging by the fireplace that says Miss Teen California and the pictures of her with that sparkly thing in her hair say it too. But Mommy's job until she had me was to be pretty. That's what she said, at least.

"Honey, before I had you, people paid me thousands of dollars to take my picture," she'd say. I didn't quite understand why people would do that, but if Mommy said so, then it was true.

Ben and I finish our cookies, and then it's time for Ben's bath, so Mrs. Franklin walks me to the corner. I'm a big boy now. It's okay for me to walk the other half block to my house by myself. I know to stick to the sidewalk, and when I get to my house, I turn and wave at Mrs. Franklin just like I'm supposed to.

She waves back, and I walk up to my front door. But I stop with my hand on the screen handle as I hear arguing inside.

"How could you, Grace?" Daddy screams. He's very angry. "In our own bed?"

"It wasn't like I planned it, Dennis!" Mommy yells back. "It's not like you've been here anyway!"

"What does that matter? I put in long hours—"

"Hey!" I call out, opening the door. "I'm home!"

The memory hits me hard, and I shake my head, trying to blink it away, but it's already rolling like a movie screen in my mind.

The bus drops me off, and I hurry inside. I open the door, and everything's quiet. That's pretty normal. Mommy's been taking afternoon naps a lot recently, and she sometimes forgets to set her alarm. Checking the bedroom, I see her lying under the blankets, and I let her be.

Adults are weird sometimes.

At school, they make us take naps, and I hate it. Why nap when there's fun to be had?

But adults, who can stay up late and watch the cool movies, take naps by choice.

Whatever.

I go back to the living room, where I watch cartoons for I'm not sure how long. I just know it's time to turn it off when the stupid 'Power Princess' cartoon comes on.

Finally, I get really hungry, and I put my toys away. Mommy's still not up, *but I can't really wait anymore, so I walk into the bedroom where she's still lying on the bed. The lights are off and the shades are pulled down. "Mommy?"*

*She doesn't move, her eyes closed and her hair all loose over her face like she does when she's asleep. I pat her shoulder through the blanket, but all she does is wiggle a little.*

*"Guess you're on your own, buddy," I tell myself, using the nickname Mommy sometimes uses for me.*

*That's okay, I'm a big boy now, so I go into the kitchen. Using the step stool, I get the box of chicken nuggets out of the freezer before looking at the microwave.*

*I'm not supposed to use this, but I've seen it used a lot of times and it's not that hard. A few minutes later, I'm eating from my plate of hot nuggets when the door to the garage opens and Daddy comes in, his suit coat still on and his tie pulled halfway down.*

*"Hey, buddy."*

*I smile, hoping he doesn't ask how I got these nuggets.*

*"Where's Mommy?" he asks, putting his briefcase on the table.*

*"Uhm . . . she's taking a nap," I admit, looking down. "I got hungry so I made these myself," I say, nodding to the plate. "I'm sorry, Daddy."*

*Daddy looks worried, and I'm afraid I got him angry, but he says nothing as he goes to the bedroom. I stuff my last nugget in my mouth and get up to take my plate to the sink. I'm halfway there when Daddy's scream scares me, and I drop my plate.*

*For some reason, the sight of the Batman shattering on the floor of the kitchen is what I'm going to remember most.*

I sit up, gasping for air as I'm jerked back to the present.

Sleep . . . she wasn't sleeping. Six years old, and she'd left me.

The most beautiful woman I've ever known had cheated on her husband and killed herself afterward.

# CHAPTER 7

## Mia

"WELL, WELL, IF IT ISN'T THE BEAUTIFUL STRANGER," CHARLOTTE teases me as I slide into the booth at The Gravy Train. The diner's busy, but this is a Friday lunch on payday, so it's not too unexpected. "I swear you've been a ghost the past week. No texts, no phone calls . . . if you hadn't shown up, I would have had to come down to your office just to get proof of life."

"Sorry, girls," I reply, sighing gratefully as I stretch out, "but I've been busting my ass with this project."

"Yeah?" Izzy says, trying to sound encouraging. "What's it about?"

"Well, I'm not supposed to spill any details. It's all corporate hush-hush, but I've been pulling long hours all week. There were team meetings four days this week, and after that, I had to really put the pedal down and bust my butt to even get home before ten o'clock."

I chuckle, though it sounds more like exhaustion escaping than mirth. "I haven't seen the sunset in a week."

"Damn, girl," Charlotte remarks as our lunches come. "Is it worth it?"

I shrug, trying to wrap my head around Thomas Goldstone's presence. He's been at every meeting, at least stopping in for a quick check-in.

And each time, I walk out of the room feeling like I just stuck my fingertip into a light socket.

"I don't know. But I do get seen by Mr. Goldstone . . . the boss."

"Yeah, well, he sounds too demanding for me," Izzy says, jumping in. "He'd better be worth all your attention."

Oh, my God, if she only knew. That man is sex on a stick. He could demand anything from me and I'd give it willingly, even if he does come off as an ass.

But I don't tell them that.

"I've heard people say he can be a jerk," I reply, stirring my soup and taking a sip, "and I get it. He maintains a lot of pressure on us to perform, but . . . we've got the heavy lifting done now, I think, so I guess his tactics work."

"So, no more pressure? No more crazy hours?" Charlotte asks, and I nod.

"I sent my report to Randall, our team leader, right after this morning's meeting. So while the project isn't done yet, I think most of what I'll have left is convincing the others why I think my analysis is correct."

Defending my ideas . . . that's definitely my weakness. While so far, corporate politics and turf fighting haven't come into play, the idea of standing in front of Thomas Goldman and trying to say anything coherent makes my head pound and my gut churn.

The man's just too handsome, whether it's in slacks and a dress shirt or jeans and a T-shirt. Oh, yes, I did manage to catch him in casual wear one evening when I was working late and went upstairs. I would've thought he'd look odd, so much power in such a rough wrapper, but the soft wear on the jeans had given me all sorts of dirty thoughts about teasing my hands along his thighs.

And now I don't know which fantasy image I prefer—rough and casual, or slick and formal.

His burning gaze, the powerful clench of his jaw as he chews over what other people are saying, the flex of his muscles straining against his shirt even as the fabric panics to release its hold on his perfect flesh . . . I might be getting home after ten, but I've been up until midnight just trying to get my mind calmed down.

Not that a man like that would notice a girl like me. I've barely spoken up in the meetings, spending most of my time burying my head in my tablet or pretending to be obsessed with the PowerPoints everyone else is putting up like experts.

Yeah, I've answered questions when someone's directed something my way, but for the most part, I've put all of my effort into my meta analysis, and that's not something that can get broken down into daily PowerPoint presentations.

"Earth to Mia, anyone there, cosmonaut?" Charlotte teases, waving a hand. "You spaced out for a minute there."

"Sorry. Guess I'm just mentally drained. What'd you say?"

"I said, is he as hot as he is on paper, or is it just airbrushing?" Charlotte asks. "Gah, he looks like Prince Charming to me."

"Prince Charming?" I ask, snorting. "Sure, he's good-looking." I make sure to play it down. Good-looking doesn't even begin to describe Thomas Goldstone.

"But he's not charming in any way, Char. He's less prince and more god-like." Before they get too excited, I continue, "Really pretty packaging on an arrogant, controlling center. Watch me control the winds, the lightning . . ."

I stab my fingers in the air like I'm directing weather forces and throw my head back in a villainous laugh.

Both girls grin at my antics. "Yeah, yeah, yeah. Babe, I'm not asking if he's *actually* charming," Charlotte laughs. "You know what I meant, and I think I got my answer. 'Really pretty packaging.'" She mimics my words with a waggle of her brows and a smirk.

"Okay, yeah, I guess I did answer. Fine. He's *really* nice on the eyes," I admit. "Still, that's all he is."

"Ooh . . . a hot but arrogant control freak?" Izzy sums up. "I don't know, I could work with that. For one night, at least."

I nod, matching her smile, but inside I'm not so sure. It's strange, because yes, Mr. Goldstone's been hard and domineering, just bordering on going over the asshole line most of the time he has been around, but there's something in the way he delivers each rebuke, each time he tells the team to work hard. To do more.

It seems to come from a place that . . . I don't know.

Maybe I'm just better at understanding numbers than people.

After lunch, I head back to my office, where there's an email from Kerry. *Please report to Mr. Goldstone's office at four thirty this afternoon.* My stomach drops and my heart races. Why would he want to see me? We just gave preliminary reports this morning.

I quickly grab my laptop and go upstairs to Bill's office. "Hey, Bill," I say, thankful for his open-door policy as I knock on the doorframe of his office, "you didn't get cc'd on this. What's up?"

Bill looks over the short email, his lips narrowing as he hums. "I'm not sure, but be careful. I don't want to scare you, but that's always been Goldstone's 'killing time'. He brings people up at four thirty to pink slip them personally. Guess it saves them the humiliation of walking out in the middle of the day, but at the same time, it feels like a long ride down to get your shit together. I know how I felt when he and I had our face to face about my transfer down here."

"But I've been busting my ass on this project," I protest, and Bill nods, giving me a supportive smile.

"Good. Then make sure he knows if he doesn't already. That's one thing about him. He does respect strength, Mia. Don't forget that."

I go back to my office, and for the next two and a half hours, I do everything I can to review what I've done this week. I play out the meetings in my mind and go over the numbers on the spreadsheets once more.

I can't find a flaw in my analysis. I looked at each of the properties and ranked the top four from best investment on down, highlighting the methods needed to gain influence, the hurdles in the way, the outlays, the sunk costs, the potential returns on investment . . . everything.

Four properties, fifty-eight pages of work including charts. I even did an extra five-page summary so that someone could gain a quick grasp on the subject if they needed.

Finally, at four fifteen, I grab my laptop and head upstairs to the twenty-*fifth* floor. Goldstone's floor. I've never been up here before, and I'm surprised at just how . . . efficient everything looks.

The hallway layout is simple at best, with only four doors excluding the shared bathroom . . . at least, I guess it's a shared bathroom. There's only one sign sticking out.

It only takes me two minutes to find Mr. Goldstone's office, or more specifically, his secretary's. We've swapped emails, but this is the first time we've met face to face. She's a well put-together woman, probably in her mid-thirties but could be a young forty, her black hair pinned up stylishly and her makeup flawless.

"Hello, Kerry? I'm Mia Karakova."

Kerry turns around, nodding as she looks me over. "Of course. You're right on time. He's expecting you."

Nervously, I cross the space toward Mr. Goldstone's door, my heart in my throat as I reach up and knock softly. It feels like I'm being asked to enter my own execution chamber.

"Mr. Goldstone?"

"Come in," he growls from the other side of the door, and I quiver and glance over my shoulder to Kerry before remembering what Bill told me. Strength.

He respects strength.

Tugging on the hem of my T-shirt with one hand in my best Picard Maneuver, I wish I'd dressed better today. We'd had a meeting today, but past the first introductory one when I'd dressed up, I've reverted to my usual more semi-casual wear. Thank God I at least have on a denim skirt and flats with my T-shirt, considering it's Friday.

I open the door and step inside. If I thought that the outer office was designed for efficiency, then Thomas Goldstone's inner office is like the epitome of Spartan efficiency.

"Mr. Goldstone, you asked to see me?"

He looks up from his desk, where he's set aside his keyboard to look at a bound folder instead.

"Sit down, Mia."

He indicates the chair in front of his desk, an uncomfortable looking black metal and nylon chair that at least has a little padding under my butt, which barely touches the cushion before his eyes start blazing.

"What have you been doing all week?"

"Sir, I'm not sure what you—"

"When Randall said to give you a chance to join the action team, I was initially hesitant. You've put up some good results but have a bit of a reputation as an oddball. I wondered how you'd work with a diverse team, especially when I expect so much. And now a week in, and *this* is what you turn out?"

He tosses the binder aside like it's nothing more than Charmin in a portfolio.

"I—"

Nope, not going to get a word in edgewise. Instead, for five whole minutes, I feel what it's like to be 'put on blast' by Thomas Goldstone. Every word is like a battering ram to my confidence, every word a cut to my pride.

Just like with Randall, he never loses his temper, but he chews up my report line by line and spits it out.

"Like this," he says, his voice dripping with bitter disdain for my work.

"Fifteen million in debt servicing and issuance of new stock for the Columbia River Community Hospital. What led you to—"

"Stop."

I don't know where the strength in my voice comes from, but it cuts through Mr. Goldstone's monologue, and he slams his palms down on his desk, his computer monitors shaking but nothing tipping over.

"What did you say?" he asks, seemingly shocked and for the first time bordering on true anger.

"I said stop," I repeat, whipping open my laptop and pulling up my files. "You've been downing my report from the moment I walked in the door. But what you just said . . . it's wrong."

"Wrong?" It's said with a silky edge of darkness.

I need to keep up my momentum. "Give me a minute to explain, sir."

He looks at me, and I wonder if he's going to grab me in those massive hands of his and hurl me through the window.

Stupidly, my brain tries to calculate just how long it would take for me to fall twenty-five floors before I impact on the street below. But instead, he sits down, his brows knit together as he crosses his arms over his chest.

He nods. "Proceed." It's more challenge than permission, but I jump in.

"Mr. Goldstone, for a whole week I've worked my ass off doing analysis for this project. I took figures and work from the other team members, re-did half of them myself, and then gave you a spot-on analysis. Here's what I've been doing this past week."

I stand up, boldly moving around to his side of the desk to set my laptop down in front of him. Standing at his side, I pull up my files.

"Now, CRCH . . . first off, I didn't even put that in my top four list for the exact reason you stated. They're absolutely drowning in debt. And it's in an area that already has three hospitals, two of which are part of state university systems, which doesn't help CRCH's case. There's no edge to it. It's not a Goldstone brand move. How that even made it into the possible acquisitions you're reading, I'll never know."

He grunts, and I know I'm gaining some wiggle room. I've turned the corner on this meeting, and a manic energy fills me, telling me to seize as much advantage as I can.

I use my energy and take the next twenty minutes going over what I produced. I show him everything, the analysis, the data . . . I even show him the muck on the wall Excel spreadsheet that I created to allow me to group and extrapolate the trends that I used.

His eyes follow my every word, from number to number, line to line, and I realize that not many people understand me when I deep-dive into the figures this way. But he is catching it all. Not just the data, but the extrapolations and analysis. He understands what all this dry information actually *means* the same way I do.

When I finish, a sheen of sweat coats my forehead, and I'm afraid a drop or two may have run down my neck to disappear into my T-shirt. I'm breathless, flushed . . . and my nerves have changed into pride at what I've done.

"I know my numbers are solid, Mr. Goldstone. And I am confident in my decision when I say you should invest in Pacific Cascade Children's. It makes financial sense, and while it's not my area of expertise, the less tangible image rewards of investing in a children's hospital make it the best bet on every front. So if you're going to fire me, do it. Go with whatever other choice you think is better. Just remember what I said when I'm proven right."

I turn around, leaving my laptop on his desk because I'm sure that I just got myself fired with my big mouth. I can't imagine that anyone says much other than *Yes, sir* to Thomas Goldstone.

In fact, I bet when I open this door, building security will be waiting for me, ready to drag me down the stairs and out the door if I don't go quietly.

But I'm not going to give them the satisfaction. I cross the room with my head held high, reaching for the door handle when Mr. Goldstone's voice rumbles across the room again.

"Stop."

My hand freezes an inch from the handle and I turn around.

Mr. Goldstone taps his fingers together, his eyes still sparking with anger . . . but I swear behind that, I can see something else.

"You think you've got it all figured out, don't you? You handed me your little perfect analysis, drop the mic, and strut out the door like this discussion is over. I do believe it's my turn for rebuttal now."

"I . . ." I reply, hating the quaver in my voice as I do. "I didn't plan on the mic drop. I figured I just got myself fired."

Goldstone frowns. "Why would you think that? Have you not done your research on me? That surprises me."

"I . . . I've done some analysis on you," I admit, a blush creeping up my neck as I realize how that can sound. Guilty as charged though. A lot of my analysis has been of him physically, though I did Google the hell out of him after that first meeting.

"I'd like you to share that analysis, and perhaps we can discuss my take on your hospital recommendations. Tonight, eight o'clock?" he says, the question not so much a request but an order couched in just enough politeness as to not make it totally sound that way. "I'll pick you up at your place."

I can't decide if this sounds like a date or a continued business meeting, but my racing heart in my throat knows which I want it to be.

"But how—"

He ignores me. "Dismissed," Mr. Goldstone says, this time a clear order. "Remember, eight o'clock. A dress. Formal. Have Kerry help you if that's a problem."

He looks me up and down, and I fight the urge to twist my toe into the carpet, wondering what he sees when he looks at me.

Nerdy? Cute but careless with my appearance? Those are definitely true, but the light in his eyes says he might see just a little something more too.

"And Mia?"

"Yes, Mr. Goldstone?"

"Call me Thomas . . . never Tom."

# CHAPTER 8

## Thomas

A DJUSTING THE KNOT ON MY TIE, I CHECK MYSELF OUT IN THE
mirror. It's only seven fifteen, but I told Mia I'd pick her up at eight
and I don't want her to wait.

For a week, I've wanted her. From that first glance, images of Mia
Karakova have burned themselves into my mind. I can't get enough of her,
but I've had to push myself away from the meetings, from drinking her in
and obsessing over her. She's got a thousand and one little ways that she's
teased me and she doesn't even know it.

The way she bites the end of her pen, her lips nibbling at the plastic
making me want her mouth and teeth on my skin.

The way her eyelashes flutter behind her lenses as she absorbs someone else's prattle. I want to make her eyelids flutter like that as my tongue
sends shivers up her spine.

Lust isn't the word to describe the driven thirst coursing through my
veins for her. I've never felt this way about any woman before, but by some
miracle, I've been able to stay professional.

Until this afternoon.

The first time I had her alone, I caved.

I'd needed to prove a point, to myself and to her, that I'm in charge. So
I'd burst in with both barrels blazing, taking control of the conversation.
And at first, it'd worked as she shrank beneath my criticism.

But then . . .

The way her eyes sparkled behind her eyeglasses, the intensity in her voice, the way her breath quickened and her body seemed to grow before my eyes. I couldn't resist, and watching her storm out, her ass flexing in her denim skirt, made me thankful I'd instituted denim Fridays at the office.

But nothing was as much fun as the few moments where I'd teased her. She tried to stay strong, and she could be, especially after the way she said she's analyzed me. I'd been glad I was behind my desk because my cock sprang to full attention at that comment, with the way her cheeks blushed and she unconsciously bit her lip.

It doesn't take me long to drive to Mia's apartment, a decent place in a decent part of Roseboro. Still, I know she can afford more than this. She must have either some outstanding debts, or more likely, knowing what I do about her, she's socking it away, because while it is a nice enough place, she could afford more.

I walk up to her second-floor apartment, knocking on her door just as my watch says seven fifty-eight.

"Just a moment!"

One minute later, the door opens . . . and I'm floored.

She's a goddess, wrapped in a black, deep V-necked cocktail dress with floral accents along the top of the thigh-high slit that makes every inch of her flawless alabaster skin look succulent.

I'm almost tempted to push her back inside her place and take her right here, taste her to see if her skin's as creamy sweet as it looks.

She's even changed her glasses, going with some black frames that give her perfection a subtle quirky, geeky twist that only highlights just how unique she is.

"Mister . . . Thomas," Mia says, biting her lip but still smiling. "Uhm, I hope this is okay? I don't often dress formally."

"It's perfect," I reassure her, checking her out all the way down to her open-toed heels that show off toes so precious I want to suck them until she giggles or orgasms, whichever comes first. "You look beautiful."

It's so true that my stomach clenches tightly, threatening to send this date careening off the rails before we even get to the restaurant.

I grew up with Grace Goldstone as the epitome of female beauty in my mind. She was my mother, but as I grew up, I could still admit how gorgeous she was.

And she'd abandoned me.

*But Mia isn't Grace Goldstone*, I keep telling myself, and it helps me calm down a little. *She's too . . . unorthodox.*

I'm more surprised than ever when we get out to the parking lot and she pulls away to run her hand over the fender of my car.

"Whoa . . . Acura NSX with a hybrid twin turbo. Super-rare here in the States."

"You like cars," I comment, and she turns, blushing a little. "No?"

"Not exactly. I'm just a geek," Mia explains shyly. "One of my favorite animes has a character who drives an NSX."

I nod as though I typically discuss cartoons with my dates, but I tuck the information away, escorting her around to the passenger side and opening the door for her.

She gets in, revealing a long stretch of subtly toned thigh that has my cock jumping in my pants again, and I have to take a moment to adjust myself as I go around back and get in the driver's seat. I look over at her, where she's wide-eyed, checking out the interior.

"Never saw the inside of one."

"I've customized it some," I admit. "It's a better driving experience for me this way."

It's about this time that I expect Mia to try to play off the fact that my bank account dwarfs hers with either an unfunny joke or an obvious money grab. In my experience, that's what women tend to do when faced with an in-your-face show of my wealth. Instead, she smiles, relaxing a little as the leather seats of my car support her body.

It's not a long drive. Roseboro's not large enough for anyone to have to worry about a long drive anywhere, but what the city lacks in size, it more than makes up for in quality. Quality I help cultivate with selective loans, support, and donations.

Case in point . . . Moreau-Laurent's. A husband and wife partnership, they may not have the huge name that comes with having a restaurant in a bigger city, but they do have a James Beard award, and more importantly, they have passion for their cuisine. And they've done so well in Roseboro that they paid off their loan with me in record time.

"I've driven by this place but never been here," Mia admits as we sit down, the white damask tablecloth just draping to our laps. "What do you recommend?"

I grin, seeing how she's not trusting in the waiter but in my opinion. "I tend to always get the smoked salmon, but . . ." I let my voice drop deeper and quieter as if I'm sharing a secret. "I know what I like."

I'm looking directly at her, and judging by the way she squirms in her seat, I think she recognizes I'm not talking about the food.

"Oh?" Mia asks, lifting an eyebrow. "I thought we were here to discuss the hospital figures?"

It's a challenge wrapped in flirtation as she traces a finger along the rim of her water glass and looks at me through her lashes.

She's testing the waters, wanting me to make my intentions crystal clear before she steps off the corporate straight and narrow, which doesn't surprise me about a number cruncher like her, even if she's definitely not a rule follower.

But I left that path a week ago when I first saw her, and I'm the bastard who's going to pull her into the deep end with me, regardless of whether she can swim with the sharks or not. I'll hold her, protect her, buoy her, if need be.

"Mia, though there's absolutely no pressure either way, I think we're both well aware that this dinner has nothing to do with the project." I pin her with my eyes, daring her to disagree.

"Aren't we—and by 'we', I mean you—getting a little ahead of ourselves?" she backpedals, but I can see the fire in her eyes.

The longing is so clear, and I realize that for all her sexiness, perhaps she's shy or inexperienced. The former is surprisingly adorable, a word I don't think I've ever actually used, not even in my mind. The latter can be delightfully corrected.

"Maybe . . . but when I want something, I go for it. Question is, Miss Mia Karakova, do you?"

She pushes her hair behind her ear, meeting my eyes as she lifts her chin defiantly. And it's game on.

Dinner is delicious, but more sumptuous is Mia. She keeps the conversation light, even touching on Roseboro and Goldstone Inc. But I don't mind, because intermixed with the first-date conversation, it seems we're tossing innuendo back and forth like this is a tennis match.

By the time the check comes, the sexual tension is like a tractor beam pulling us together, and it feels natural to let my hand fall to her waist as we walk out.

"So, what did you think?"

"I think I haven't tasted a damn thing since the chicken was taken away," she admits. "The company was too magnetic."

"Too bad. You missed a great dessert."

Mia's lips twitch, and I laugh. "Yes?"

"Oh, I was just waiting for the come-on line about how you've got another dessert waiting for me," Mia says, and I can't hold back my smirk.

"You said it, not me."

I drive back to the Goldstone building one-handed, my right hand resting on Mia's thigh, squeezing and stroking the muscle higher and higher over top of her dress. She's biting her lip again, but I can see her nipples hardening through the top of her dress, and I grin. If she's wearing a bra that thin . . . she's been thinking the same way I have.

"Why are we back here?" she asks, a little confused as I pull into the parking garage in the sub-basement.

"Just trust me. You'll love this," I reply as I lead her over to my elevator. There's one floor that's not accessible on the touch panel, only available when I insert my key card, and the motor starts.

As we start to ascend, I crowd Mia against the side of the elevator, pulling her glasses off and tucking them in my breast pocket. "Thomas—"

I kiss her hard, claiming her mouth, and she freezes in shock for half a moment before giving in to me, her hands coming up to my neck and pulling me in deeper.

Her kisses are soft caresses against my lips combined with the strong, powerful twist of her tongue as she greedily tries to taste me, our mouths opening up to each other.

I breathe her in, her unique scent searing its way inside me before I give the air back to her and she moans in ecstasy.

My hand runs up her thigh, lifting the hem of her dress as I trace the delicious contour of her leg, realizing that she didn't wear any stockings. The soft sexiness I've been watching all night was just her natural skin. My cock throbs in my pants, pressing against her hip.

"Is that . . . for me?" she asks, moaning as I grind against her.

I grin, promising her with my eyes. The elevator dings, and I take her by the hand, pulling her out into my entryway.

"Welcome to my home."

I don't give her time to respond as I pull her to me, crushing her in my arms as I consume her with another powerful kiss. I'm barely able to watch where I'm going as I drag her to my bedroom, ready to conquer her.

Somewhere along the way, her dress gets unzipped and my jacket and tie get pulled off, a button popping and bouncing away noisily before we're in my bedroom. My shirt is half undone, exposing my chest while I look at Mia on my bed, her breasts cupped in a lacy midnight-blue bra with matching see-through panties.

"Gorgeous, naughty girl."

Mia lets out a seductive smile and reaches for my belt. I step back, shrugging my shirt the rest of the way off and undoing my pants, stripping naked for her while she watches. Her fingertips stroke her nipples and drift between her legs, and she gasps as I come into view, fully hard and ready for her.

I lie down on the bed next to her, pulling her to me and kissing her again, licking over to her neck to nuzzle against her ear.

She moans, and I growl in triumph, cupping her ass and squeezing hard as I explore her body. Every inch of her skin pressed against me is an erotic revelation, a symphony of sensation crackling up and down my nerves until my cock is twitching, oozing clear drops of precum even before I have her panties off.

I push her onto her back, my need taking over. Mia barely has a chance to take a breath before I tug her panties to the side and thrust two fingers deep into her pussy, making her cry out.

"Oh . . . fuuuuuu—"

I love the way she draws it out, her eyes rolling back as I nip and suck on her throat, sucking hard enough to mark her and give her a hickey. My thumb brushes against her clit, and electricity leaps through her body, making her cry out as her hips lift up to meet me.

She's tight, so tight my fingers are squeezed almost numb as I pump them in and out of her, and dimly, in the part of my mind not taken over by my animal passions, I'm glad that I'm doing this to prepare her instead of taking her hard with my cock first.

I don't want to hurt her.

But another side of me wants to be rough. It wants to hear her cry out as I pound her, and that side eventually takes over, though I hope she's ready for me. I pull my fingers out, licking them half clean before shoving them in Mia's mouth, startling her into sucking her own juices off my fingers.

"Like that, don't you? You taste so fucking good."

Mia's eyes close, and she moans around my fingers, but I pull back. "That's enough. I'm just getting started."

She whimpers but spreads her legs wider for me. I look down at her pussy for the first time, my inner beast tamed just slightly by the beauty that I see. Her pale lips are puffy with need, slick with her desire, and her core is deeper pink, beckoning me to come closer.

As I guide my cock inside her, I take it slow so I can watch her pussy suck me inside, each inch stretching and disappearing inside her. Mia moans, her eyes rapturous as she watches too until I'm all the way in, my hips pressed against hers.

"More," she whispers, and in her quiet plea I hear damnation and salvation. I grab her wrists, pinning her to the bed as I pull back, pausing for just a moment before thrusting hard into her again.

Her pussy is the tightest, most amazing embrace I've ever felt. With each thrust she pulls me in tighter, wanting more of my cock, and each time I pull back, her body clings to me, not willing to let go until she's wrung every bit of pleasure she can out of me.

I let go of her wrists to clutch her tightly, greedy to feel her skin against mine, her lips against mine, her tongue wrapped around mine.

She *must* be mine.

My bedroom fills with the deep animal sounds of our fucking, my hips slapping against hers as she tilts her hips up, begging me to give it to her deep and hard. I'm growling, pounding her with everything I have as my inner beast is unleashed.

I grind against her, feeling her body tighten and squeeze around me, her orgasm rushing through her like a thunderbolt.

"Thomas!" she screams, her nails digging into my back, but I don't let up. If anything, I thrust harder, faster, filling her clenching, spasming pussy with my thick shaft until I feel my balls tighten. She's moaning deeply too, her eyes open and staring into mine as she feels me swell. "Please . . . I'm so close again . . ."

It's ten seconds of eternity, holding back my climax until Mia comes again, this time deep and savage as she grunts out a curse.

I cry out, my balls exploding as I fill her with my cum, my body spasming and shaking as I press her body tighter against the bed. My back and neck arch to the point I can feel crackles going up and down my spine even as the last droplets leave me, but I stay inside her for a moment, enjoying the depth of the connection.

I collapse on top of Mia, and she holds me close, sighing happily.

# CHAPTER 9

## Mia

"Oof," I grunt to myself as I settle into my chair on Monday morning.

Never have twenty hours done so much to my body. Wanting more in the morning turned into a double-dose of aggressive, intense sex with Thomas that left me so weak and unable to move that morning quickly became four o'clock Saturday afternoon before I could drag myself away, part of me still wanting to stay behind.

Twenty hours . . . and I've never been more grateful for having a Saturday night alone. I'm not too sure if my body could have taken another night of Thomas Goldstone.

Even today, my body aches in all the right ways. My nipples are chafing pleasantly in my bra from where Thomas almost gnawed them half off, my pussy still pulses with my heartbeat, and as I settle into my chair and pull up eight hours of chill-hop to let me just glide through the day, only one thought goes through my head.

*When's our next date?*

I'm just getting through a weekend's worth of bullshit emails when there's a knock on my door and it opens to reveal Randall Towlee, looking bright-eyed and bushy-tailed. He's freshly shaven, with a recent hair trim, and his suit looks like it just came from the dry cleaner's yesterday.

"Hey, Mia, how was your weekend?"

"Not bad," I reply carefully.

*Oh, God, does he know?* "How was yours?"

"Eh, same old, same old," Randall says. "Listen, I know this might be a little weird, but last week during the meetings, I kept feeling a vibe in the air. You did too, right?"

Huh? Is Randall asking about me and Thomas? "I'm not sure—"

"I'm asking because I was figuring, since the group's pretty much over with now, just a few once-a-week meetings . . . how about we go out and celebrate? Six thirty tonight? I know a good little bar that has your name on it."

It's hard not to thump my head on the desk. Seriously, I feel like I've just walked into the *Twilight Zone.*

Has something been dumped in the water of every man in Roseboro over the past few days? I've gone six months without a guy so much as looking at me, and now I've met two men, both of them handsome, intelligent, and more than well-employed, and they've asked *me* out.

Me.

The girl who spends most of her time buried in numbers to create meta-analyses that most folks couldn't understand even if I could explain it to them.

The girl whose idea of 'making an effort' is to pull her hair back into a ponytail and who treats her hair like one of those tablet dress-up apps. Pink and green? Cool!

The girl who wears glasses, watches anime, and scream-sings trance metal music . . . in Russian.

But when I'm suddenly smacked in the face with the fact that both Randall Towlee and Thomas Goldstone seem interested in me, the choice is pretty easy.

"I'm sorry, Randall. I'm flattered, but I don't mix . . ." I start before realizing that whether I'm trying to say 'no' nicely or not, I'm not going to be a hypocrite about it. Mix business and pleasure? Uhm, I mixed it three times between Friday night and Saturday afternoon, and I came seven times in the course of doing so.

I may not think Randall's sexy at all compared to the human video game god that is Thomas Goldstone, but I'm not going to lie to him.

"It's just not a good idea. Sorry."

His face gets cloudy and his eyes pinch in, like it never occurred to him that I might say no. "Are you sure about that?"

"I'm sure," I reply, surprised at the strength in my voice. "But I think we've done some good work on the hospital project. I'm looking forward to this week's meeting update." It's an obvious redirect back to professional ground, but Randall doesn't exactly take the hint.

"What are you working on now?" he says, leaning against the edge of my desk and eyeing me up and down, though he can only see to my waist since I'm sitting.

I feel like he's trying to get under my skin. "Well, considering it's nine in the morning on a Monday, I'm just going through my emails, getting a start on my week." I hope he'll hear that I'm busy, because while I'd kind of love to tell him to go back upstairs where he belongs, I can't really kick a VP out of my office.

"You are always a morning person. One of the reasons I chose you for my team over some other analyst. You don't start slow. You hit the ground running."

Under normal circumstances, that'd be a compliment. But the way Randall says it makes it come off flirty. A few days ago, I probably would've been excited to have a cute guy flirt with me a little, but it's different now, though I can't explain to Randall why that is.

Awkwardly, I stand and go around the other side of my desk, heading for the door to put some space between us. My voice is bright and falsely high as I say, "Yep, as Mr. Goldstone said, gotta get out there and sell those cookies!"

I'd actually laughed at that one the first time I'd heard Thomas say it. Comparing our work to the Girl Scouts probably isn't politically correct, but it'd struck me as funny.

Randall walks toward me and pauses in the doorway. "You're sure?"

I nod. "I'm sure. Thank you for the invitation, but I'll have to politely decline." It's as gentle of a letdown as I can give because I want to be crystal clear.

"Let's not let this become unprofessional."

"Don't worry," I reply sweetly, so saccharine that a Tic Tac wouldn't melt on my tongue right now. "I won't."

He leaves, and I sit back down, wondering what fueled all that. I mean, first off, asking me out? I just don't get it.

I'm not some uber-hottie. If this were *Scooby-Doo*, I'd be Velma, not Daphne.

So why are two guys who are certifiable studs making moves on me?

*So, how was your day?*

I glance at the text message, grinning. Of all the silly things to be doing, I'm at home, it's eight o'clock at night, and I'm swapping texts with Thomas.

*OK. U know how much I luv my little cave. New music mix today had me jamming.*

*Oh? Who?*

I laugh, shaking my head. *U don't wanna know. Total geekdom.*

*I happen to like the fact that you're an unabashed geek.*

*Really? Y?*

*Because you're smart. Smart is sexy.*

I feel a tingle between my legs, and I smile, letting my free hand drift down my shirt. Yup, I've got high beams going too.

*Even if I dye my hair?*

*What do you mean?*

*I like to put streaks in my hair. I change it almost every week. I cut two inches of Bright Blood-Orange-Red out for the project meetings to look professional. I might be a little salty about it still. ;)*

*Hair doesn't make you professional. And I'd take you salty or sweet.*

He adds a tongue emoji and I can't decide for a moment if that's cute or cheesy. I decide it's a bit of both and that I like it because it reminds me of his tongue licking me all over.

*I know. So . . . U don't mind?*

*Not at all.*

Whoa. I grin, a bit surprised because I'd expected him to be a bit more traditional and prudish about my wild hair, but maybe I should've given him more credit because he has been inordinately accepting of my vast musical taste and anime chatter. I type again, looking for ideas. *So . . . what's your favorite color?*

*Depends. What does the old jelly bracelet code say?*

*Oh, the flashbacks that brings up . . . and if you choose the color, you get what that means?*

*No,* Thomas sends back. *I'll get what I want either way.*

I should be turned off . . . but I'm not. If anything, his swagger and confidence have me even more turned on.

*Somehow, that doesn't surprise me.*

*Speaking of what I want,* he says, shifting back to the full spelling he uses from time to time, like he's back to being 'professional', *tomorrow morning, come to my office.*

*Uhm, that doesn't sound like the smartest plan?*

That's putting it mildly. I can't just waltz into his office like nothing has changed. Hell, Kerry will be able to read it all over my face as soon as I step off the elevator, and the last thing he probably wants is gossip about the basement girl coming and maybe *coming* in his office.

*That was an order, Miss Karakova.*

*Why?*

*Our next date. It's a political fundraiser down in Portland, and I need you fitted for the event.*

Wait, next date? He didn't even ask, he just . . . *Is my cocktail dress not good enough?*

*Not for this. You need a full-length gown, and I have a stylist coming in. They'll do the fitting tomorrow, and Friday night's the fundraiser. We'll discuss details tomorrow after your fitting.*

I have a chance to say no. I mean, he didn't ask, he's just demanding. But I could still tell him no, especially about something big and public like this. He's assuming that I want to go with him, and that I . . . *OK. What time?*

*9:15.*

*OK. Then let me get my beauty sleep tonight. See you in the morning?*

*You're already beautiful, but sleep tight. Goodnight, Mia.*

*Goodnight . . . Tommy.*

He doesn't reply, which I take as a sign of approval. I didn't mean to call him Tommy when he made me come that next morning, but once I did, it just fit. Like it was something just between us.

# CHAPTER 10

## Mia

THE EXECUTIVE MEETING ROOM ON THE TWENTY-FIFTH FLOOR IS perhaps the most luxurious room I've seen in the Goldstone Building. In a place that's designed around efficiency at every turn. This room's dripping in luxury, from the carpeting so thick it looks like it could cushion a tap-dancing elephant to leather chairs that creak only to mellowly remind you of how buttery rich their upholstery is. And the *piece de resistance* is the crisp display paneling the far wall, so large it's almost over the top.

All in all, the room's amazing.

You could throw the Super Bowl party of all Super Bowl parties here.

But right now, corporate meetings are the last thing this room's set up for. Instead, there's a trio of mirrors, a huge rack of gowns, and a bunch of other stuff that I honestly don't quite grasp the use of.

But the biggest thing in the room is truly . . . huge. As in, a bald man who looks like he's nearly seven feet tall, with a barrel-shaped upper body that's clad in . . . lilac velvet?

"Hi, uhm I'm—" I start before the giant of a man turns, a huge smile spreading across his face.

"My next canvas to show the world how fabulous life can be," he says melodramatically, his voice sounding nothing like I would expect, given what he's wearing. It's as deep as James Earl Jones's voice. "Come in, come in.

I'm Damien Rayie, the artist who will transform you into the princess you should be."

It's a hell of an introduction, and I feel weird as I step inside, closing the door behind me. "Hi, I'm Mia Karakova."

"Lovely to meet you, Mia. Come now, let's start with that hair. What did you do with it?"

"Uh . . . black and green streaks?"

Damien shakes his head. "Not that, I mean the style, the style! Oh, we have our hands full today!"

He sits me down as an assistant pops out from behind the rack of dresses, and for the next hour, my head's the center of attention while Damien talks constantly.

"So this event, it's a political fundraiser, which means I'll have to restrain myself. It's a shame, because I have rarely seen such a perfect set of raw materials for me to work with. Such is life, but maybe we can have another opportunity." He winks conspiratorially.

"Wait," I ask, sipping at the tea that another assistant gave me. "What do you mean, perfect raw materials?"

"What do I mean?" Damien asks, looking like I've taken leave of my senses. "What do I mean? Do you really not know, or are you mocking Damien and his vision?" He eyes me sharply, and I get the sense that he's seeing into my soul.

"I'm not mock—ow!" I answer as the person on my hair tugs a knot free. "Come on, I condition my hair three times a week. It can't be that bad!"

"Hush now, darling. Stella knows what she is doing. I do think those streaks are very you, and yes, when I say raw material, I mean *raw material.*" He lifts my chin with one finger, looking deeply into my eyes. "I don't think you realize how beautiful you are, but don't worry. If you didn't before, you will when we're done."

After the hair, Stella moves around to focus on my makeup.

"Why are we doing all this now? The fundraiser's not until Friday."

Damien hums. "Trial run. And to choose the proper dress, one must be conscious of the total vision. I can't have you trying on gowns with a messy bun and a bare face." He shivers like the mere thought is off-putting, which makes me laugh.

Stella huffs her annoyance, and I straighten, sitting up tall and still for her to work. I close my eyes, letting the brush strokes along my face soothe my nerves.

This is crazy, like some sort of fairy godmother shit, and though I don't want to get my hopes up, there's a piece of me that hopes Damien can do something with me to make it so that I feel right when I walk into the fundraiser on Thomas's arm. Otherwise, I'm afraid I'm going to stick out like a sore thumb and be an embarrassment, not to Thomas but to myself.

Stella intones, "Open." I open my eyes to see her scanning my face critically. "It'll do."

*And that's exactly what I wanted to hear,* I think, holding back the eye roll but saying, "Great. Mother Russia is not amused."

Damien doesn't even get caught by my weird little jokes to myself. "Now, the lingerie! What are you wearing now?"

I've never felt so deconstructed but at the same time supportively rebuilt. Damien forgets nothing, scheduling a mani-pedi and full-body waxing for Thursday evening, then picking out a set of lingerie for me that feels . . .

"My God, where did you find this?" I ask as I look at myself in the mirror. It's not slutty, but sexy and supportive at the same time. I feel like my breasts have been lifted by magic, and they look damn good, from what I can tell.

Damien's being nice, letting me try everything on in a little ad-hoc changing room behind a curtain, but I almost want to show him how good this looks. "It's amazing!"

"Damien has his suppliers, darling," Damien replies behind the curtain, chuckling. "As I said, a true artist does not depend on labels but on the materials. This comes from a little boutique in Seattle. Now for the dress!"

We go through a dozen dresses, each one more fabulous than the previous. Damien doesn't let me look at the results though, just him and his assistants as they study me. "No," he says at the first. "With hair like hers, that tone just isn't right."

Next.

"Washes out her skin, and I don't want to risk that silk with a bronzer."

Next.

The fifth, he laughs at, shaking his head. "Only if we want someone to call you Elsa . . . no, try the yellow-gold one. It's dramatic, but maybe that's what we need."

Finally, he hits on *the dress*, and Damien's face blooms into a wide smile. "Yes! That's the one!"

"Can I see?" I ask, and Damien nods. He points to his assistant, who uncovers the mirrors, and I turn.

The sight of me takes my breath away. The skirt is full and elegant, clinging to my waist before puffing out just a little in golden yellow waves that are a shade darker than my hair, while the top shines with encrusted crystals, framing my stomach and breasts in contours that highlight my figure.

I blink, and my fingers shake as I adjust my glasses, which somehow compliment the whole ensemble even though these are just my work glasses.

"I . . . I'm beautiful," I murmur, but it's more than that.

For the first time in my life, I see myself as not just brains, not just 'meh' looking, but beyond beautiful. I'm fucking *gorgeous*. With my hair piled on top of my head the way it is, my neck arches gracefully like a swan's, and the ringlets that have been allowed to escape the updo frame my face and make me feel . . . "Damien, thank you!"

"It is nothing, darling," Damien says, grunting as I turn and hug him tightly. "Mia, my dear, is this your first time understanding?"

Tears threaten to spill from my eyes, and I nod, looking up at him. "Papa calls me his princess, jokes I'm Anastasia, but . . . but . . ."

"But he is your Papa, and that makes it easy to dismiss," Damien says, patting my shoulder gently with his massive hand. "Trust me, I understand. Now, we are not finished. A few accessories, not too many. As you said, you are beautiful as you are. Just enough to accentuate, not distract. First . . . a necklace to match your glasses. Or do you wear contacts?"

"Never," I admit. "They irritate me."

"Come, I have a dark crystal set that'll go perfectly with that and the hair colors."

I just get the necklace, obsidian and pearl with a smoky dark gray diamond in the middle, clasped around my neck when there's a knock on the door, and Thomas comes in.

"I came to see—"

His voice stops as he sees me, and I gulp, doing my best little curtsy for him as I smile widely. "What do you think?"

Damien looks eager to hear praise as well, but Thomas's eyes never leave mine as he studies me.

Silently, he crosses the room, taking in my hair, my skin, and my curves and looking at me with a fire burning in his eyes that both scares me and turns me on. Either he's about to explode . . . or he's about to *explode*.

"Everyone out," he says, his eyes fixing on mine. "Now."

Damien opens his mouth, snapping it shut after a moment and waving his assistants out. He tosses me a wink and a big grin before calling out, "Lovely to meet you, Miss Karakova."

Thomas walks them to the door, closing it and throwing the lock while I stand next to the conference table, trying to figure out whether he's angry or turned on.

"Thomas?" I ask, and he crosses the room, grabbing my waist and pulling me to him before crushing my lips in an intense kiss.

Question answered.

# CHAPTER 11

## Thomas

I'D WAITED AS LONG AS I COULD, FOR HOURS AS DAMIEN LAID CLAIM to the executive conference room. I knew that he was going to take his time, and when he was done, Mia would see and feel what I see in her. But he's an artist, and artists are . . . inefficient in their genius. So I tried to be patient, imagining what they were doing in there.

But I'm still shocked at the vision before me as she stands in her heels, her body wrapped in golden silk that makes her glow in the midday sunlight coming through the windows.

"Thomas?" she asks, but my animalistic instincts have kicked in, and I'm barely able to keep myself together long enough to lock the door before I'm on her, pulling her to me and claiming her as mine.

My hands tug at the gown, lifting the hem as I push her against the table, her lips and tongue finding mine. I move down her jaw and neck, my mouth fastening on her skin again, inhaling and tasting her unique scent.

She's not wearing perfume. It's just her natural essence driving me wild and making my cock harden instantly inside my pants.

I've never done this, not here, not like this. But in this moment, I don't care about appropriateness and rules. I want her and I'm going to have her.

This isn't like me. Though most would say I'm a risk-taker, every gamble I make is after solid research and thoughtful consideration, and only then do I throw everything in the kitty. But with Mia, I'm going about it differently, no brakes, no brains, no bluff. Just all in from the get-go, mentally obsessed and physically addicted from just one taste.

I didn't even want to let her leave on Saturday afternoon, and just texting back and forth last night was murder on my patience, something I'm definitely not known for. I had to resist the urge to jump in my car and drive to her place to take from her what I needed. The only thing that held me back was fear that in doing so, I might scare her with my possessive need to be with her, around her, inside her.

Now having her like this, her silky thighs pressed against me as I slip my hand under her dress to grab a handful of her taut bubble ass, is more than my senses can take. I grip the firm flesh, almost pinching as if to make sure she's real and not some figment of my imagination. She responds by pressing her tits against my chest with a throaty moan I can feel as I trace the pulse in her neck with my lips.

"You're so fucking sexy," I growl, reaching for my belt and undoing it, freeing my cock from the painful restraints of my slacks and underwear. Mia's eyes drop down, her jaw dropping open hungrily when she sees my thick hardness. I stroke myself with a tight fist, teasing us both, and she whimpers in need. "I want to see you, all dressed up like a fucking queen, sexy and sullied with my cum. Get on your knees."

I shove her down, but she hurries to obey, swallowing my cock even as I thread my fingers through her hair and thrust forward. Her mouth is amazing, and my cock lights up with pleasure as I pump in and out quickly, groaning with pleasure.

"Look up at me," I rasp as my hips pump all of my thick inches in and out of her eager lips. "That's it . . . you want my cock, don't you?"

"Mmpfh!"

The vibrations of her reply make my knees quake, but I can tell she's agreeing with me. "You're mine, Mia. I'm going to fuck you, take you, and never let anyone touch you. You're totally mine."

I know I'm promising things too quickly, but I can't help it. The words pour out unfiltered and dangerously full of truth. And though she doesn't say anything back, her mouth too full of cock to speak, I can see the hope shining in her eyes as she looks up at me.

Suddenly on the edge, I pull my cock out and jerk her to her feet before turning her around and pushing her chest-first into the table.

I'm going to claim every inch of her, but right now, with the promises hanging around us like fog, I need to be balls-deep inside her to come the way I want.

Lifting her skirt is like revealing the world's sexiest Christmas gift. She's spread her legs automatically, giving me access to the beautiful, perfect half-globes of her pale ass, just barely parted by her thong. She's writhing, grinding in search of relief, and I steady her with a hand on her cheek, then trace down her leg to the stockings she's wearing.

I can smell her arousal. Whether it's from me or from her finally recognizing just how sexy she is, I don't know and don't care.

Instead, I smack her right ass cheek, planting a bright red handprint on it and making her yelp.

"Ah!"

"You're wearing foundation over my mark. I left it on your neck intentionally," I murmur ominously into her ear as I lay over her, pinning her to the table with my weight, but with the threat, I tug her thong to the side and rub the head of my cock over her pussy lips, coating it with her honey. "You're not allowed to," I decree, as if my word is law. But for her, for Roseboro, it is.

"But people will see."

"Let them," I roar, slamming my cock balls-deep inside her. She's so hot and tight, and both of us cry out as I ram home inside her perfect body. The heels she's wearing have brought her pussy and ass up to just the right height. I don't have to adjust at all as I pull back and thrust again, grinding deep inside her. "Show them all that you're mine."

I grab her hair, lifting her tits up off the table as my hips thrust hard and deep inside her. I pull the dress's bodice down, cupping her left breast and tugging on her nipple.

In response, a fresh gush of Mia's wetness coats my cock, so I repeat the motion, twisting the nub until she squeals in equal parts pain and pleasure. I watch in Damien's mirrors, overwhelmed as the view of her from every angle amplifies the sweet agony of her velvet walls gripping me.

My cock hammers in and out of her, my mind washed with wave upon wave of intense pleasure. I know this is dangerous, but in this moment, I am more animal than man, more primal than civilized, and I rut into her like a savage. Miraculously, she meets me stroke for stroke, not shying away from my roughness, and in her ability to handle me, small cracks shatter in my façade.

I am not Thomas Goldstone, billionaire entrepreneur. My most important title is . . . hers.

And she is not Mia Karakova. She is simply . . . mine.

My chest heaves, my heart pounds, and with each slap of my hips against Mia's upturned ass, I feel myself bound tighter to her.

I want to etch myself on her skin. I want to claim her as mine forever, my captive to keep and do as I wish. I want her to be my angel, my fucktoy, my . . . my everything.

It's insane, but right now as my cock throbs deep inside her and I hear the symphony of her gasps of pleasure, I'm allowed insane thoughts.

Letting go of her nipple, I grab her around the waist, spreading my legs a little for strength before I start hammering her as hard as I can. I look down, my mouth watering as I watch the obscenely sexy vision of my thick, glistening cock blurring in and out of her tight pussy, her lips clinging to me even as I go harder and faster, thrusting with everything I have.

"Oh, fuck . . . Tommy . . . Tommy . . ."

"Say it again!" I roar, not caring if anyone hears me. Or her.

"*Tommy*!" she cries out as she comes, her pussy clamping around me, and I roar in triumph as I feel my balls contract, my seed spilling and marking her inside and out as I cry out senselessly. I give myself over to the breakdown of everything as our shared climaxes wash over me and I surround myself in her warmth, her comfort, her beauty.

We stay there, connected as one until our hearts slow, and I pull out by inches, regretfully rearranging my clothes and pulling my underwear and slacks back up. A Neanderthal impulse inside me revels that I'm coated in her cum, and with a glance at her abused pussy, a cocky smirk takes my face that she is just as messy with mine. Mia rearranges her thong, attempting to put herself back together, but she's still so weak from what just happened that I have to reach out and help her with the dress.

"So . . ." she says after a moment, her upper body still heaving as she catches her breath, "I guess that means you like the dress?"

"I fucking love it," I reply, adjusting my tie. "Though we might need to have it dry-cleaned before Friday's fundraiser."

She smiles at the lewd joke, brushing her hands across the skirt and smoothing out the wrinkles where I'd bunched it in my hands.

Mia looks up, her eyes flashing with happiness and questions behind her frames. "I can't tell if you're bullshitting me or not."

I know she's not just talking about whether I like the dress but if *this* is something more. She'd let me walk away, I know she would.

She'd write off the possessive things I said while we fucked as dirty talk, and we could go back to some semblance of professional stasis. It's too fucking bad that that's not at all what I want. I meant every word, both the ones I said and the ones I thought but bit back.

"I never bullshit," I say evenly. "I might skirt the truth from time to time in business . . . but I never bullshit."

The tension builds between us, and though we don't say it aloud, we both know something powerful is changing between us in this very moment. An acknowledgement from us both, an acquiescence on her part, an acquisition on my part.

Finally, she turns away, going behind what looks like a changing screen, and I hear her unzipping her dress and then shuffling as she changes.

"I'm not ashamed of what we just did," Mia says, coming out from behind the partition still wearing the high heels she had on but dressed more like she normally does for work. She looks just as stunning, but I can see that she's armored herself against me with the T-shirt and slacks she must've worn this morning. "I mean, we probably took the corporate conduct rulebook and lit it on fire . . . but I'm not ashamed."

"That's good, because—"

"Wait," she says, holding up one finger to make me pause. "I'm not ashamed, Thomas, but I have to say one thing. I'm not going to be your 'office girl'. This isn't *Mad Men*, and I'm not going to trade on whatever attraction you have for me. God made me smart, and apparently, Russia made me beautiful . . . or at least that's what Papa tells me. But I make my own future, with my brain and no other body parts."

I nod, relieved that this is her only concern. For a moment, I'd been able to see the weight on her shoulders and had thought she was going to write me off.

*Like you deserve. Waste of oxygen, thinking you're worthy of a goddess like her. She'll realize soon enough.*

"You're much more than an office girl, Mia. I think we can both feel that." I pull her to me, kissing her softly and swallowing the soft sigh that passes through her lips as I pray that she doesn't find me lacking and leave me so soon.

Keeping my arms wrapped around her, I tap her temple. "Actually, Miss Smarty Pants, you were right, and I don't say that often or lightly. I looked over your computer when you mic dropped out, and the file you showed me and the report that hit my desk were two different things. I need to look into what happened in between to update the numbers and see if it'll change our direction, but in the meantime, I'm not going to go easy on you just because of this."

Mia smiles but then snarls comically as she adopts a thick accent. "Good. Because in Mother Russia, hardworking analysts fuck you."

I growl, dropping a hand to squeeze her ass and grind against her a bit. "Yes, you did." Her laughter is infectious, making me smile broadly. "Hey, what's with the heels?"

"Damien says I need practice," she says simply, looking down. "Although I'm really going to have to figure out how to coordinate these with my normal wardrobe. Maybe my friend Izzy will have something I can borrow. She's sort of a discount fashion queen."

From outside the door, the bustle of the office working away gets louder and reality starts to creep back in.

"I should probably get to work. My boss is a real asshole if I slack off." She winks as she teases me. "Anyway . . . see you later?"

"You definitely will," I reply. She opens the door, and I call out, "And Mia?"

She turns, her smile warm but melting into a more professional version. "Yes, Mr. Goldstone?"

"I expect great things from you."

# CHAPTER 12

## Blackwell

THE PARK IS SMALL, BUT THE POND IN THE MIDDLE OF IT IS PERFECTLY picturesque and the shadows around the south shore deep as I sit on the bench, watching the basketball game.

Footsteps approach on the gravel path, and I look over, my man appearing precisely on time. He sits down, trying to look casual and failing.

Me? I don't care if someone sees me. I control this game. I am above most of the rules.

"Sir."

His tone holds excitement, news he's eager to share. And because of that, I make him wait, drawing out the moment of anticipation, both for my own delight and the man's frustration.

"Look at them," I start in conversationally, keeping my voice low.

I indicate the game across the pond, where the sweaty group of young men continue to pound the asphalt with their rubber ball, wasting their time with their stupid game.

"And they wonder why they'll never get close to touching power or influence. Some of those boys have been out there for over an hour."

"It's a fun sport," my man says, looking across the pond. "When I was in high school, I played on my school's team. Small forward. I even got All-Conference my senior year."

"Hmph," I reply, unimpressed. I'm finished with the rare attempt at small talk I used to delay the man's delivery. If he won't learn from the crumbs dropped from my table, he'll learn the hard way eventually. "You said you have an update?"

"Yes, sir. It seems that our mutual . . . acquaintance is dipping his pen in a company inkwell."

"Is that so?" I ask, amused. The Golden Boy, Mr. Perfect, finally doing something that could be turned to my advantage? The timing couldn't be better. "And how do you know this?"

"Everyone in the vicinity of the twenty-fifth floor on Tuesday around lunch knows," he says with a degree of disgust. "It was . . . obnoxious to hear his name screamed so loudly. Oh, and she called him 'Tommy.'" The man's eye roll is worthy of a teenage brat.

"Hmm, I would've thought the Goldstone Building had better soundproofing."

My man laughs bitterly, nodding. "It does. She's just that loud."

Something about the way he sneers is almost more telling about his thoughts than the actual words. He dislikes this woman. Or maybe likes her, and feels affronted anew by her actions with the Golden Boy.

Curious.

I file the information away in my mental rolodex of data in case it ever becomes useful. Frankly, it's those little tidbits of information that people hand away all the time that make my life possible.

"And Goldstone, he's enamored with this woman?" I ask, and his man nods. "Interesting."

"He's taken her out once, they're attending the fundraiser on Friday, and he fucked her in the meeting room," my informant says. "I'm not sure how serious it is, but it's certainly a vulnerability, even if it's only because she's an employee."

"Then we simply need to apply pressure at the right times, in the right ways," I muse, feeling the first nebulous tendrils of a plan start to swirl in my mind.

"I want you to bring me every bit of information you have on this woman. We'll push him, even if there are risks. But we need to move relatively quickly. This deal is worth more than millions. It's worth a legacy. *My* legacy."

"I understand."

My man gets up and leaves, and I lean back, watching the young men across the pond continue to waste their time playing their stupid game.

I have never been one for such a dirty game. Power is more than your ability to toss a rubber ball through a metal hoop like a trained monkey. Even growing up, I shunned the common games of my classmates for pursuits more befitting someone of my class. Chess, polo . . . even a bit of squash to maintain the heart.

Still, I have to admit, the strength that sports like this form in the young men is admirable. They don't know it, but it's building the muscle and dumbing down the mind so that later on, they can become good little minions in the games of the truly powerful.

Like me.

And that, I muse, gives the basketball players a sort of noble futility, poetic in their usefulness. So let them play their games.

"After all," I whisper, getting up while still remaining totally in the shadows of the warm summer evening, "we all have games we enjoy playing."

# CHAPTER 13

## Thomas

T HE FRIDAY MORNING SUNSHINE IS WARM, AND KERRY DOESN'T SAY
anything when I tell her I'm leaving on a personal errand. She knows
that I don't shirk my work that often and probably figures I need to
get ready for the fundraiser tonight.

Besides, she's probably glad that I'm getting out for a little bit. While I
doubt she's already got the tequila flowing and is dancing on her desk, she is
probably happy to take her foot off the gas for a few hours.

At least I won't be able to dump any more work in her lap.

But starting yesterday for no apparent reason, I just couldn't get the
voice out of my head.

Hammering me.

*Weak.*

*Stupid.*

*A failure.*

So I knew I had to get out or else explode.

Going up to my penthouse, I go into my closet, where I quickly change
into my disguise for the day, a baggy old-school Clyde Drexler Trailblazers
jersey, shorts, custom-fit blond wig, and a snapback hat. Armed with a small
duffel bag and using my keycard, I lock everyone out of the elevator all the
way down to the sub-basement parking garage, where I get in my ten-year-old
F150 that I use when I don't want to be noticed.

I wish I could go talk to Mia. It might help. But I can't. For two days, the prospect of having to do this event tonight has ratcheted up the pressure cooker that is my temper and my soul, and I can't let her see me like this. I need to have my head on straight when we waltz into that room tonight because I won't let her down when a public appearance like this is a big deal, and we both know it.

I need to let some of the anger and rage and pain out. And this ... this helps. In fact, until this past Friday, it was just about the only thing that did help for more than a few hours.

Roseboro is beautiful as I pull away, a picture perfect warm blue sky with a few clouds that scream for kids to be running beneath them, pretending they're one of their sports heroes.

As I drive, I wish for the millionth time that I could learn to enjoy days like this like normal people, maybe go for a walk or have a picnic and appreciate the gift of the sunshine, but I'm anything but normal. I can't be normal ... was never brought up to be anything of the sort. I was raised to be hard, suspicious, a hard shell wrapped around a dark pain that I could never discuss.

The eastern half of Roseboro is my destination for the day. This part of town is decidedly not the best, a far cry from the downtown bustle and the quaint suburbs. While Roseboro doesn't have any real inner-city ghettos, it does have its bad areas.

And it's from those dirt-lot parks full of single-wide hellholes that the kids I get to see today come from, orphans who were either abandoned by their families or just taken when their parents decided that alcohol or meth were more important than taking care of their progeny.

I get out of my truck at the Roseboro Boys' Home, looking around at the old but well-maintained building. It's been a personal project of mine, no publicity, no naming of any buildings ... just my place to have a release. Slipping on my sunglasses, I get out and stretch, eager for what's about to happen.

"Hey, Tom!"

I normally hate that name, but when I hear it from the excited mouth of an eager nine-year-old boy whose face is split with a huge smile as I approach the fence to the orphanage, it's more than worth the instinctual flinch I hide inside.

"Hey, Frankie," I greet my young friend and mentee, one of a dozen that I work with here. Going around to the back of the truck, I grab a big plastic cooler, wheeling it behind me. "How're you looking for school next week?"

"You know how it is," Frankie says. "I mean, I do okay, but what's the point?" He shrugs dismissively, his eyes more haunted than any child's should be.

"You know what the point is," I reply, unzipping my bag and pulling out a football. "How're you going to ever play for the Seahawks if you can't get into college?"

Frankie grins, the old fantasy still having enough tread between us to at least let him hope for a moment. He's barely a shade over four feet tall, and if he weighs fifty pounds, it's because he's soaking wet and someone's put bricks in his pockets. But he's a good kid, and he solidly catches the ball when I toss it to him.

After checking in with the orphanage staff using my fake ID, I follow Frankie out to the best part of the facility, a large grassy play area. It's not big enough for all forty kids to play at once, but for the dozen who wander out to play some pickup football with me, it's more than enough.

"Okay, guys, now who's going to play QB?" I ask, waving my hands when everyone points at me. "Oh, no, I told you guys last time you'd have to work on your spirals. I want to catch once in a while too, you know."

In the end, I actually end up not playing at all, which is what I want. Instead, I act as a ref, coach, and cheerleader as the kids strike up a spirited, sometimes rough, but still clean game of touch football.

Laughter, some smack talk, and joy fill the air as the ball flies back and forth. Frankie even catches a touchdown, which he celebrates with a half-respectable spike before all is said and done.

After the last pass, I open up my cooler, passing out Gatorades to everyone as they gather around.

"Okay, guys, good game today," I tell them, closing the cooler and sitting down on the lid. "So listen, I heard what everyone was jaw jacking about during the game . . . seems you're *excited* about Monday?" I'm trying to rename their emotions in a positive light, even though their chatter was full of nervousness and anxiety.

The groans around me are universal. Frankie's not the only kid who's not looking forward to school on Monday.

"Yo, Tom," one of the guys says, "why should we be excited? Same bullshit, different year. Kids are gonna rag on us about our clothes, rag on us about being losers, all that shit."

"Maybe they will," I admit, and the guys nod. It's probably what gives me a chance to connect with these kids better than a lot of the so-called volunteers who come down here. I give it to them straight, but at the same time, I encourage them.

So I'm going to be bluntly honest because that's what they respect.

"I know most of you are going to say that I'm full of shit, but let me give it to you. A lot of kids, you know what happens to them? They sort themselves into some slot in their heads right about the same age you guys are, and they cruise in those slots. You see it now, the kids who just sort of know in their heads that they're going to go to college, those who're going to be blue collar, and then . . . well, you guys."

"You mean the losers?" one of the boys says, copying his cohort's word choice, and though they all laugh, I'm betting they've heard that and worse.

But I don't laugh. "A lot of people probably already see you that way. Teachers who won't give you that extra chance to fix mistakes that they're giving Timmy Bank Account who comes from a 'good family'. Other kids who have no idea what it's like to wonder where your next meal is going to come from are going to bag on your PB&J lunch. You get a bit older, and you're going to be pushed into a few categories. Those of you who have skills, folks will sometimes encourage you, especially if you're good with a ball."

There are cheers for Jeremy, who is a pretty sick point guard, and he flashes a thumbs-up. "Good . . . go for it, man. The rest of you, it's not too late, and sports aren't the only way out."

A few of the boys look down, and I clear my throat. "Don't let *them* write your future for you," I tell them. "I come down here because I look around and I see possibilities. I see a ball player, a lawyer, a writer, a business owner."

"Man, I ain't ownin' no business," someone says, and I shake my head, growling.

"The only thing stopping you is you. It isn't going to be easy, and it won't be fair. You guys, more than anyone, know that life isn't fair. But that's okay. Because having to fight that much harder means you're going to be that much stronger. So when I look at you guys, I see someone who's going to be a man someday, maybe with a wife, a couple of kids, and a good home. And he's going to look back at this place and see what he's accomplished."

I look at the building behind us, bland and institutional. "Turn around and look. That building right there—that's *where* you are, not *who* you are. Where you're at right now is beyond your control, but who you are? That's your choice, today and everyday. Make the right choices and ultimately, you'll get to be where you want to be too." I let that sink in before adding, "Anyway, I'll stop by sometime next week to see how school goes. I expect to see your heads held high. Deal?"

Of course it's a deal. A lot of these boys are desperate for affection in any form, and more than one of them sticks by me as we gather my stuff up and get ready to leave. For a lot of these boys, it's the only time adults give them the time of day, and it pains me to think that I'm somehow acting in a big brother or father figure role for a lot of them.

They deserve better than me.

The office door finally cuts me off from them, and Reba, the staffer on duty right now, signs me out. "How were they today?"

"Good boys," I reply before starting to cough. "Sorry, Reba, you mind grabbing me a cup of water or something? Little dusty out there."

While Reba's back is turned, I slip my envelope into the incoming mail, wait until she comes back, and sip the water. "Thanks."

"No problem. The boys here really are glad you come by."

"I told them I'd be back sometime next week. I'll give you guys a call, see what we can work out," I reply. I figure she wants me to continue to come by but didn't want to ask directly. She doesn't need to. I enjoy this.

In some ways, I need this as much as the boys do.

"Thanks again, Reba."

"Have a good one, Tom," Reba says as 'Tom Nicholson' walks out of the Roseboro Boys' Home. I get back in my truck, and I'm able to make it out of the parking lot and all the way to the nearest supermarket parking lot before I have to pull over, the memories too strong to deny anymore.

*The Cadillac waiting outside of school is expected but unwanted as I come out of Briarwood Elementary, my bag over my shoulder and my new jeans still stiff and uncomfortable.*

*I didn't get to 'break them in' like they call it. Nobody wanted to play with me . . . again. Since Kenny Tyson came to school talking about Mom and what his dad, who's a cop, told him, everyone seems to not want to play with me.*

*But that doesn't mean I'm looking forward to the ride in the big black Cadillac.*

*Still, I don't want Dad honking like he does if I go too slow, so I hurry across the parking lot and get in, buckling my seatbelt.*

*"Hi, Dad."*

*"Tom," Dad says coldly. It's the only thing he says for the whole ride to his*

*office, where my 'after school corner' is set up in the firm's coffee room. I know to go right to work and sit down, looking at the math worksheet Mrs. Higgins sent home with me.*

*But homework doesn't take me long, and by five o'clock, I'm done. I even read my library book for the third time, but the story about the frog and the pig is just boring by now.*

*Getting up, I go out to the hallway, walking carefully down to Dad's office. The other lawyers in the office seem nice, but I don't want to make them angry. Dad says I'm not to bother them or else.*

*But Dad's secretary, a pretty girl named Christina, is nice. "Hi, Thomas!" she says, smiling as I walk in. "What can I do for you?"*

*"Uhm . . . I'm done with my homework," I say, but before I can say more, Dad's office opens and he walks out, stopping when he sees me.*

*"Go back to your work," Dad says, barely even looking at me. "You're not—"*

*"Sorry, Mr. Goldstone. I asked Thomas to help me with some stapling," Christina says quickly, smiling at me. "He's already done with his work, and I figured, well—"*

*"Whatever," Dad says, leaving the office and walking out. I let out a sigh, wishing Dad would be like he was before Mom died.*

*"Come on, Thomas," Christina says in that voice adults make when they're not happy but don't want us to know, patting the chair next to her. "You can help me do . . . something."*

*Actually, something turns out to be fun as Christina puts me behind her computer, pulling up a game website. Protecting my castle from the monster blobs is fun, and I'm starting to smile when a little bubble pops up that says* Email: RE: Autopsy, Grace Goldstone.

*I don't know what an 'au-top-si' is, I think, sounding out the unfamiliar word like Mrs. Higgins taught me, but Mom's name makes me click on the bubble, and a new window opens. It's a picture of some kind of paperwork, and a lot of it I can't understand, but I recognize Mom's name, our old address, and a few other things.*

*The first thing I see is* Cause of Death. *A lot of the words make no sense, but I learned what it meant later . . . suicide.*

*Something else highlighted makes my eyes fill with tears.* Time of Death . . . three thirty PM.

*I know three thirty . . . that's when Animaniacs comes on.*

*"No . . ." I whisper, and suddenly, Christina's next to me, curious as to why I'm crying so hard. I want to be a big boy, I'm not supposed to cry, but I can't stop.*

*"Thomas, what . . . oh, Jesus," Christina says, seeing the screen. She hugs me, stroking my hair. "Honey, you weren't supposed to see that."*

*"Is it true?" I ask. "Was . . . was Mommy alive when I got home?"*

*Christina pulls away, looking into my eyes. "Thomas . . . Tom, never, ever blame yourself for that. What your mother did is her fault, not yours."*

*"But if I'd not watched cartoons, if I'd checked on Mommy earlier—"*

*"No!" Christina says, hugging me again. "Never, ever blame yourself, Tom."*

But I already did. I wipe my eyes, blinking back the pain. Starting up my truck, I drive back to the Goldstone building, parking and going up to my penthouse. I smell, I'm sweaty, and I need to shower before I get ready for the evening.

As the water runs over my shoulders and I'm letting the conditioner soak into my hair, I think about things. Twenty years from that day, and Christina's words still ring hollow.

Because I do blame myself.

If I had focused, if I hadn't been weak . . . if I had been a good son, I could have gotten the ambulance there in time.

I could have had my mother . . . and I could have really had my father instead of the cold, distant man who's never shown me love since that day.

*You deserve it. You failed her.*

Maybe that's why I go to the orphanage to help out from time to time. I especially go before events like this dog and pony show tonight.

Those kids, from Frankie to Jeremy to even shy little Shawn, who've got issues even deeper than mine, understand. Like understands like, and they see that, regardless of whether my father's still alive or not, I'm just as much an orphan as they are.

# CHAPTER 14

## Mia

THE SENTINEL HOTEL IS ONE OF THOSE PLACES I'VE DRIVEN BY A multitude of times, mostly on my way to the famous Powell's Bookstore that's nearby, but I never thought that I'd actually be walking through the lobby of the restored classic hotel.

"There's a red carpet," I murmur as Thomas and I arrive in the limo he's arranged for tonight. "You didn't mention a red carpet."

"Well, there will be VIPs from all over the Tri-City area," Thomas informs me. "We make enough of an impact on the state that the governor wants to keep us in the loop."

He doesn't say it, but I can hear in his tone that he doesn't really like these events. I adjust my glasses and take his hand.

"If you can do it, I can do it." I get out and glance down. "Still, I didn't think the carpet would actually be red."

The cameras are almost blinding, and I'm shocked that so many people would be interested in taking photos of Thomas. Not that he isn't the hottest guy in like, the entire universe, but he's no sports star or actor or anything. He's a businessman, and a relatively private one at that.

"Why so many photogs?"

"The governor's looking at angling for a national presence next election," Thomas whispers as I take his arm and he stops us to pose for a few seconds before leading us on. "It's why he wanted this on a Friday. It'll be too late for the local coverage, but he figures he can get on the weekend news cycle, get invited onto *Meet The Press* or *News Sunday* or something."

I nod, still sort of awestruck as I recognize some of the celebrities in attendance. Sports players, some movie stars, but Thomas doesn't seem all that out of his element. When one of the sports players gives Thomas 'the nod', I'm surprised.

"You know that guy?"

Thomas smiles a little, giving the guy 'the nod' back. "Yes. He runs a charity for kids in Portland. I helped out some last summer. Decent guy . . . terrible cook though. He served up more bricks at his barbecue than he did all last season on court."

I don't really know what to say, just chalking it up to the growing wonderful mystery that is Thomas Goldstone.

Holding onto his arm tightly, though, I walk with him upstairs to the fourth floor, where I'm stunned by the opulent room we walk into.

Thomas notices my gawking.

"The Governor's Ballroom," he says as he also takes in the scenery. It's beautiful. White-fluted marble columns flank each of the huge windows along the walls while inlaid decorations and a rich mostly blue carpet make the whole space look like a European palace. There's even a quintet of classical musicians, a string quartet with a French horn adding their tones to the whole surreal experience.

"It's beautiful," I whisper, ignoring whether anyone's looking as my head goes on a swivel, trying to take in everywhere at once. There are people, music, and even waiters with drinks and appetizers mixing through the room. I snag a flute of champagne, and Thomas follows. "I knew Damien was like a fairy godmother, but now I truly feel like I just walked into a fairy tale."

"Too many people for a fairy tale," Thomas whispers, giving me a smile that makes me blush as he toasts me. "And though Damien may have worked some magic, the beauty has been in you all along. He simply let you see yourself the way I do."

I blush, dipping my chin and unconsciously shaking my head. I know I look good tonight, had even stared at myself in the mirror in disbelief for more than a few minutes after Damien and his team had left my apartment, but Thomas's bold words lay my insecurities bare.

"You're the most beautiful woman I see at this party. Take a moment and look around again . . . you'll see that I'm right."

I do look around, but as I do, I feel even more like a fish out of water. The women all look stunning, but it's more so that they have an air of confidence and comfort in this environment, something I lack even if I'm decked out like one of them tonight.

But Thomas never even glances at them except when they greet him, and in every conversation, he makes sure to include me.

"Mia, this is Willa," he says, introducing me to a famous local TV anchor. "We met years ago when she interviewed me for a piece about Goldstone. Willa, Mia's the best data analyst I've ever met. She'd put three-quarters of your stock market people out of work if she wanted to. However, she has one significant flaw." He pauses dramatically, giving me a sly smile. "She has terrible taste in men, which is how I've found myself lucky enough to accompany her tonight."

"I see." She raises an eyebrow, giving me a smile that's warm, but at the same time, I can see her mind working because it's a look I wear myself quite often. "I love the hair and glasses. Just the right touch of uniqueness at a cattle call like this. Please tell me they're not non-scrip?"

"Nope, I can't see a thing without them," I reply, relaxing a little that she's not putting my odd choices down. "If I didn't have them on, I couldn't tell you from Beyoncé."

She laughs. "Well, rest assured I won't be busting out in song and dance moves, so if you see Beyoncé, let me know and I'll squeal with you." She smiles, and despite the perfect face, the telegenic smile, and the look that's been practiced so long it's probably second-nature to her, Willa seems to be not that bad. She points in the general vicinity of my head. "The streaks are a great look on you. So how long have you known Thomas? I met him for a profile piece I was doing for the station."

"I, uh . . . I work in the company, but we just met recently," I reply, not sure how much Thomas wants everyone to know about our situation. But when I glance at him, he's smiling easily.

A man comes by and pats Thomas on the arm, whispering in his ear for a moment, and Thomas nods. "Of course . . . Mia, if you'll excuse me, the governor would like to have a word with me. Back in five minutes, ten at most."

"Okay," I reply, and Thomas disappears into the party. As he goes, Willa smirks, and I turn to her, lifting an eyebrow. "What?"

"He's into you," she says, grinning. "*Really* into you."

"Why do you think that?" I ask, trying not to shy away. Thomas wouldn't want me to, and after all the work I've done this week to prepare for this thing, I plan on keeping the empowered feelings that started Tuesday rolling. "He needed a date for the event, that's all."

"Uh-huh. He's been showing up stag for these snore fests for a while now. I don't see why this one would be any different," she replies, nodding as though she's putting the pieces together. She must see the look of panic on my face, though her words delight something deep inside me. "It's okay. I'm not working tonight, so it's all good. But the main reason I can tell is the way he talks to you. He's actually . . . nice. It's like you tamed the monster. You're the Beast Whisperer!"

I blink, trying to think about the way Thomas and I talk to each other. I guess I've seen it with him grilling the team, and he started out that way when he called me to his office that first time, but since then, he's always been . . . Thomas.

Willa notices I'm not quite following and rolls her eyes.

"Oh, please," she says, snorting. "The reason he left you with me is because he's going to have to deal with the governor, and Thomas is . . . mercurial around people like that. When I went with him to one of these things three years ago, purely professional as part of that profile, he had no problem showing me that he's three-quarters asshole, one-quarter genius."

"No, I know what you're saying, and I've seen that side of him," I counter. "I mean, he basically put me on blast in our first real meeting."

"And yet you're still here tonight? Gutsy." Someone calls her name from across the room, and Willa turns, raising a glass. "Excuse me. It was a pleasure, Mia. Good luck."

She leaves, and I'm left confused. Good luck? Good luck with what? Thomas? I would chalk it up to cattiness, but she sounded totally honest and heartfelt in her words.

"Maybe it's just the TV side of her," I wonder aloud, sipping my own champagne and wiggling my nose at the bubbliness. "Or maybe she meant something else."

Slightly disturbed, I try to set aside my worries and just enjoy the party, not gawking too much at the luxury and splendor around me. I've always prided myself at being levelheaded and not so shallow as to get wrapped up in all the fine clothing, expensive jewelry, and fancy décor, but I can't help it when it's on display like this.

"Papa would be so surprised to see me right now," I murmur as I start playing a mental game of ranking the hierarchy of attendees. It's perhaps a bit tasteless, but it's the way my mind works, finding patterns in the randomness. Actually, it's interesting, seeing the generational trends of couples grouped by age, race, and even flashiness of jewelry.

"Mia!"

I turn, surprised when I see Randall Towlee approaching. Like many of the men, he's wearing a tuxedo. And while Randall looks good, he's still a pretender compared to Thomas.

"Randall, this is a surprise."

"Stepfather's a state assemblyman," Randall says, nodding toward a rather rotund man in the group near the governor and Thomas. "So I get a mandatory invite to all of these sorts of events. I think he wants me to follow in his footsteps."

I nod, unsure what to say next. Since his failed attempt at asking me out, he's sort of avoided me, except for one meeting on the hospital team, and that was strictly professional. And I'd love to think he's let the whole thing go, but there's just something in the way he looks at me that tells me that he's not giving up after being rejected.

"You look lovely tonight."

"Thank you." That feels safe enough, platonic and common for this environment, even if I'd squash him for commenting on my appearance at the office.

"So, what are you doing here?" he asks boldly, lifting an eyebrow. "I mean, I've heard rumors, but . . ." He lets the syllable linger, like he wants me to ask him exactly what he's heard.

"Thomas asked me to be his date," I answer him, trying to sound confident but casual. "I didn't want to make a deal about it at work."

"Oh, I can understand that," Randall replies, and though there's not malice in the words, it feels like a bad dream coming true. Like I can see the moment where he loses respect for me and I have to remind myself that his perception is his problem. I haven't changed and neither has the quality or content of my work.

At that moment, Thomas returns, his face cloudy but clearing when he sees me and I smile back.

"Hello, Thomas."

Never mind, the clouds are back. "Randall, didn't think your father would invite you to something so . . . dry."

"Oh, this is exactly the type of thing he loves for me to attend," Randall says, grabbing a champagne. "He says that it's events like this where I'll learn how politics really work. I keep telling him I'm not interested but . . . well, you know how family can be."

Thomas's eyes tighten, but he gestures with his head. "Of course. If you'll excuse us, Mia, I have someone I'd like to introduce you to."

We walk away, Randall giving us a little salute with his champagne as we go.

"Thomas, I'm sorry. I didn't expect him here, and when he asked—" I rush to explain.

"You said you're my date," Thomas finishes for me. "Good." His soft smile reassures me that I did the right thing. It's funny. When it's just the two of us, everything feels right and easy, but in the stress of this room, these unfamiliar expectations are getting to me.

There actually is someone for me to meet, the president of a small computer manufacturing company in the area. We get into an interesting discussion about computer systems, nerding out over processors, RAM chips, video cards, and more. By the end, I somehow feel like I've just placed an order, and as Thomas leads me away, I look at him out of the side of my eye.

"What was that?"

"That was you meeting someone I felt you'd have something in common with," he says with a smirk. "You're definitely not his typical customer, but I'm sure your enthusiasm made his evening."

"Who is his typical customer?"

"The alphabet soups," Thomas says, chuckling again when I look at him in confusion. "DEA, CIA, FBI, IRS, FDA, all those government agencies that take big names and shove them down into three little letters. He makes high-speed, high-security computers for them. And if he starts recruiting you to steal you away from me, I'll have to make sure the alphabet types step in to help."

It's a bit outrageous and possessive, but it makes me laugh.

The governor gets on stage to make his speech, and while it's short, I immediately see what Thomas means about how he's angling for national attention.

About halfway through the speech, out of the corner of my eye, I see Randall, who's watching me intently while drinking another champagne, totally ignoring the speech.

"What's the deal with Randall? I didn't know his stepdad's a politician."

"It's part of the reason I hired him," Thomas says mysteriously, clapping at a line in the governor's speech that I've totally missed. "He wants to make his own way, and his ambition is . . . useful. I just have to remind him from time to time that I don't care who his family is, whether he was president of his frat in college, or who his father knows. I just need him to give me his best effort."

The governor finishes his speech, and things sort of morph into that cocktail party that everyone's seen in a dozen movies but up until this moment, I've never actually thought I'd get to attend.

"This feels a lot like my high school prom," I tell Thomas at one point. "Although the band's a lot better."

He chuckles and takes my hand. "Then how about a dance?"

He leads me into the center of the room, where a sort of nebulous dance floor has emerged. The lights are dimmer here, and as I take his hand and put my other one on his shoulder, I'm glad I've spent the past week working with these high heels. There's no way I'd be able to do this comfortably otherwise.

"Uhm, Thomas? I can't dance for shit," I whisper. "I can't even macarena."

He laughs lightly at my candidness, a deep rumble in his chest that reverberates in the space between us.

"Just follow my lead and relax."

His touch on my hip is strong but gentle, and as we weave in and out of the half-dozen other couples out here dancing to something jazzy and classical, I let him take control of me.

Moving our bodies together just feels right, and my heart starts to race, my body flushing as I look up at him. His eyes burn with an inner desire, a fire that tells me that if it weren't for the few hundred people in this ballroom right now, he'd have no problem claiming me right here in the middle of the dance floor. I almost want it to happen.

"You're having naughty thoughts," he says, pulling me closer. "Want to share?"

"Not if you want to stay for the rest of the party," I tease. "Let's just enjoy this and see what happens after that?"

As soon as our dance ends, someone approaches us, requesting Thomas's presence again.

He looks to me questioningly, and I tell him to go. I'm a big girl and can mingle at a party.

I decide to go over to the refreshment table, thinking that I'll either get some stimulating conversation with the small group working their way around the table or at least some delicious food. My stomach is rumbling, and I've barely had a cocktail shrimp all night. I grab an *hors d'oeuvres* I don't recognize but that looks pretty, and I almost have it in my mouth when Randall approaches again.

"You looked beautiful out there on the dance floor. I'd be remiss if I didn't ask for my own turn."

"Sorry, Randall," I reply. "But no, thank you. I'm here with Thomas."

"And that's twice now he's left you to do what? Schmooze?" he asks, stepping just inside my personal space zone. "You deserve better than a rich bastard who'll use you and desert you."

I'm surprised at his nerve, both presumptive and erroneous. But mostly just ballsy as fuck, considering Thomas is his boss. And like Willa said, he's quite known for being an asshole.

"Randall, let me be clear. I enjoy our professional work relationship, but that is all I'm interested in," I reply, turning away to scan for a familiar face . . . ideally Thomas, but I'd take Willa or Gene, the computer guru. I'm walking that line, the one between where I tell Randall off in a blaze of glory that'll definitely draw some unwanted attention at a soiree like this and the one where I can control my urge to slap the shit out of him.

And then I feel his hand on my shoulder, and I turn to him in anger, my palm itching.

"She said to leave her alone," Thomas says out of nowhere before I can give him a piece of my mind, his voice rumbling just below a roar.

Randall turns, his own eyes flashing as he goes nose to nose with Thomas. They're nearly the same height, both athletically built, but the rage flashing in Thomas's eyes is like a force of nature, even as Randall stares back, his own ego making him stand up.

I think they're about to come to blows when finally, blessedly, Randall remembers himself and yields.

"Just entertaining Mia. You know how awkward these events can be when you don't know anyone and your date disappears on you."

The barb is supposed to be sharp, but Thomas doesn't flinch. His voice is a quiet version of his reputed 'blast'.

"Randall, she said no politely. At this point, I'm both concerned about your personal ability to accept a decline and your professional responsibility to recognize harassment. Where she has been nice, let me be clear. Mia is *mine*."

The threatening tone in Thomas's voice is clear, and Randall recoils as if he's been slapped. But then his eyes narrow shrewdly, and when he speaks, it feels false and sycophant-esque. "My apologies, sir. I didn't realize it was quite that serious."

Something in the way he says it makes me think that all of this was just to get that admission from Thomas, and I wonder what Randall plans on doing with the information.

I'm suddenly foreseeing a whole host of judging eyes glaring at me on Monday after Randall spreads the news of how I spread my legs for the boss. It's not like that, or at least it doesn't seem that way to me, but I have no doubt that Randall will make it sound as seedy as possible.

Randall steps back, turning to leave, and Thomas watches him before he looks at me. "Let's get out of here."

The ride back to Roseboro is confusing. It's not even an hour, but neither of us says anything as I look out the window, the lights flashing by as my mind tries to make sense of it all.

What had Randall hoped to gain by still hitting on me? I turned him down clearly at the office, and he should have seen in our first talk tonight that I'm not interested.

But then Thomas saying I'm *his*. He didn't say it like I'm his date but like I'm his. Like I belong to him, a possession. It should turn me off, but instead, as I look across the bench seat of the limo at him, I'm tempted to climb into his lap and see if we can do a few more movie fantasy scenes in the time we have left.

I shake my head, trying to figure out what I'm feeling beyond lust, when we get off the Interstate and we're back in Roseboro. Thomas looks over at me, his eyes calmer but still that fire burning in them as he looks at me.

"We'll be back at your apartment soon."

I clear my throat and suddenly make a decision. Though tonight was odd, with more going on below the surface than I was prepared for, I desperately want Thomas right now. There will be time enough for analysis and evaluation, but right now, I'm going with the time-honored tradition of following your gut. "You want to come up?" I ask, reaching over and taking his hand.

He doesn't even think about it and without answering reaches forward, hitting a switch on the control panel. The partition to the driver drops down, and Thomas rumbles. "Change of plans. You'll be dropping both of us off at the first location."

# CHAPTER 15

## Mia

THOMAS REACHES FOR ME AS SOON AS THE DOOR TO MY APARTMENT'S closed, but I step back, putting a hand on his chest. "Would you like a drink?" I ask, playing hostess. It's a slight stall, and though I can feel my heartbeat in my pussy, I do feel like we should talk about what happened tonight.

Thomas nods and shrugs off his tuxedo jacket, looking around for somewhere to hang it up.

I take it from him, hanging it up before leading him into my living room.

Blushing a little, I tell him, "Make yourself comfortable. Let me get changed." I slip off my heels and carry them down the hall to my bedroom.

I quickly slip into something more *me*. My dress is gorgeous, but stepping back out into the living room wearing cotton shorts and a *Sailor Moon* T-shirt, I feel more comfortable, more in control of myself and the situation.

This is perhaps the first time I feel like he's in my world versus me being in his. I pause for a moment to relish it as I study him.

He's sitting on my sofa, his back to me as he looks at the arrangement of game controllers and remotes on my coffee table. He picks up my newest acquisition, an aluminum-bodied, unbreakable wireless PS-style controller, turning it over in his hands and pursing his lips.

It's adorable to see his mild confusion by something so routine to me, and yeah, my heart melts a little as he quietly whispers, "pew, pew" at my television. How can I not get all gushy over that?

"I've always been a bit of a tech nut," I say, interrupting his study. Thomas sets my controller down, turning his head and looking me over appreciatively as I come around and sit down next to him. It's a little strange, me in what you could call pajamas while he's in three-quarters of a tuxedo, and it only highlights the differences between us.

But at least he's undone his tie and slipped his shoes off, almost like a sign that I'm getting him to relax incrementally. It feels like a win to see the precise, tight grip he holds himself under loosen.

"Mostly around the house, it's gaming, although the PC here is hooked to my TV too. You ever play?" I'm pretty sure I know the answer before I ask the question, but it seems the obvious next inquiry. What I don't expect is the shadow that crosses his face.

"No, not since I was a child. I last played some game with blobs attacking my castle. After that, I never . . ." He pauses, and I can see that he's somewhere else in his mind. It's on the tip of my tongue to ask him what's going on in that brilliant mind of his, but he shakes it off and says, "I like your setup. It's . . . efficient."

I can hear in his words that he means it. And considering being *efficient* is one of the most important things to him, I take it as a compliment. I do wonder what it is that drives a man who seemingly has it all to be so unrelenting in his drive for more. But that seems rather like a truth that is revealed slowly, not a question to be answered, so I let my curiosity sink and stay with the topic at hand.

"Thanks. It probably seems a bit too nerdy to you. But it's . . . me. Papa would try to get me to get out and do things when I was younger." I mimic his voice, "How about ballet, *dochenka*? Softball? Let's go for a walk!" Returning to my own voice, I finish with, "But he realized quickly that wasn't for me."

"Papa? Doche . . . ?" He stumbles over the endearment.

"*Dochenka*. It's Russian for daughter," I explain.

"Oh, yeah, I remember from your file. Your dad is Russian?" Thomas asks, and I nod, chuckling.

"As Russian as vodka. He was still a young man, barely nineteen when he first came to New York, and the issues with the crackup of the Soviet Union caused him to leave. He struggled for a while."

Thomas hums, nodding. "I could see that. It must've been quite the shock to his system. What did he do?"

"He put himself to work. He had enough savings to pay up his apartment for a few months, and it was above a tailor's shop. He started off as a shop assistant, running errands and stuff, and worked his way up. Eventually, he worked his way up to doing his own work. He used to laugh, too, because my grandmother insisted that he learn how to sew when he was in the Soviet Union. He hated that, said it was so unmanly . . . yet it was what put a roof over his head."

"So your Papa becomes a seamstress . . . but it was a while before you were born," he points out. "What happened?"

"Don't let him hear you call him that," I say, laughing. "He says he repairs and adjusts clothing the Old Country way, and therefore, he's a tailor." I smile, having heard the phrase a number of times over my life. Continuing on with the story, I say, "The fact is that Papa's very talented. He mostly does men's clothing, suits and things, but he likes to dabble from time to time, and he made dresses for me and my friends that were better than anything in the stores. Anyway, Papa met Jennifer Appleman. She was Upper East Side, and he was . . . the opposite.

"He thought it was forever love, and I guess at first, they were happy. Papa was beneath her, he says, a tailor to her family money. I suspect she was playing at slumming it with the immigrant bad boy."

Thomas lifts an eyebrow in silent question, and I clear my throat.

"Anyway, she left him. I think if I hadn't come along, they would have split even earlier, but when Jennifer got pregnant, she faced a lot of pressure to get married. She may have been New York money, but there are those who flaunt it and live it up, and there are families whose asses are wound up tighter than a banker's on tax refund day. Jennifer's family was the latter."

Thomas snickers, lifting an eyebrow at my terminology, but he keeps his composure mostly, sobering as my face tightens.

"So, she just left?"

"Two weeks after my second birthday," I say quietly. "I don't even remember them living together. All I remember is that they lived in separate places. I'd go from house to house, and when I was with Jennifer, it was . . . I felt like an annoyance and a game piece. Everyone made sure I was quiet and out of the way, but then Jennifer would buy me things to try and turn me against

Papa. I spent more time with a babysitter than Jennifer or her parents, even though it was their house."

Thomas growls lightly, reaching out and stroking my shoulder. "What was it like with Papa?"

"We had almost nothing some weeks. He worked hard, but New York is expensive and sometimes, he had to make difficult choices on which bills to pay. I remember one time we spent the whole week 'camping' around the stairwell in the living room. We did that so we could catch more of the heat drifting up from the shop downstairs, because Papa didn't want his boss to know how tight things were. Honestly, it was one of my favorite weeks because he made it seem fun and like an adventure. Ironically, it was that week that led to his getting full custody of me."

"How so?"

I lean back, sighing a little. "I was still cold, and Papa took off his jacket, laying it over me. He only had a short-sleeve T-shirt, but he wanted me to be warm. I noticed that Papa had a Band-Aid on the inside of his elbow. I asked him what it was, and he took it off, showing me a fresh hole on the inside of his arm. He'd started going to a couple of plasma centers, lying about how often he was donating to get enough money to support us. The day before he'd picked me up, he donated twice. He showed me the hole in his other elbow, and I told him it was like the holes in Jennifer's arm. She had a whole line of them going up the inside of her left arm. I was too young and naïve to know what that meant."

"Drugs?" Thomas asks, and I nod. "So he told his lawyer?"

"And his lawyer had a cop on Manhattan Vice who owed him a favor. One tail of Jennifer Appleman while I was with Papa, one trip to the right nightclub, and boom . . . the family courts don't look kindly when you're picked up in the biggest drug bust of the year. I don't know all the details on what happened to her. I just know Papa got temporary full custody that ended up permanent. We moved to Roseboro soon afterward so Papa could open his own shop, and I haven't seen her since then. I even reached out to her and her parents. Papa helped me write the letters. The last two were unopened, just marked *Return To Sender*. That's all I needed to know. It's been me and Papa ever since."

Thomas nods, giving me a sympathetic smile. "I was wondering why you didn't call her Mama. I . . . I lost my mother when I was very young too. She died when I was six years old."

He looks lost in his thoughts, and I wonder how many people know this about him. I certainly didn't before now, and I've checked out his corporate profile and online presence like a tenth-degree clinger. There's a lot about Thomas's education, his rocketing up the business world, and the accomplishments he's had as the head of his own corporation, but nothing about his family life. It's as if he sprang forth as a fully-grown man in college, having never existed before age eighteen.

"What happened?"

"She . . ." he starts but then swallows thickly. "I can't talk about that," he admits, and while it's not the same information dump I just shared, his confession feels like he's giving me a vulnerability, trusting me with a weak spot and hoping I won't pick at the scab. He clasps his hands together between his knees, head dropped low, and I want to reach out to him.

He clears his throat, blinking rapidly. "Suffice it to say that while both of our mothers might have left us with our fathers and the resulting baggage of that loss, my subsequent relationship with my dad was not full of fun adventures." I can feel the pain it costs him to say those words, and I doubt he's ever let them pass his lips before.

He sighs and plops back on the couch, shoulders hunched, back rounded, and I think it's the most real I've ever seen him, like he's too exhausted to maintain appearances. I like that he's willing to do that with me, like he's letting me in bit by bit, sometimes with big leaps and sometimes with small steps, but closer to the core of who he is all the same.

"Sorry. I think we've brought up enough bad memories for the night."

I kiss his lips softly, rewarding the gift he's given me tonight. Not the fancy outing with limo and expensive clothes, but his truth. "It's okay. So . . . you want to play a video game?" I ask lightly, wanting to give him a chance to reset and re-center. "Nothing hard, just a little beat 'em up?"

Thomas busts out a small laugh, and we slowly walk away from the abyss of his childhood. We swap little tidbits back and forth as we play, mostly me telling him about myself as I beat him at every turn. But when my clock beeps and I see that we've come up on midnight, I've seen more of Thomas than I think anyone else ever has.

"So, tell me," I ask, setting the controller down and taking his hand, "you made some rather serious claims tonight. Are you sure you're ready to handle a woman who's kinda nerdy, likes to play video games while listening to death metal and techno, makes weird leaps of logic that you might find hard to follow, and has a father who's taught her how to curse fluently in Russian?"

"I suppose," he says with a smirk. "As long as you're willing to deal with a man who has a deep streak of asshole in him for reasons he sometimes isn't really sure about himself."

He seems less sure that I'm going to accept him as he is.

I chuckle, rubbing his shoulders. "Will it come with the good side of you too?"

"Like what?" he asks. "Oh . . . I forgot. You like my car."

I laugh, leaning over and kissing his cheek before climbing in his lap. "I can think of about two dozen things I like about you more than your car. It's a sweet ride, but that's not your good side."

"What is?" Thomas asks, his hands naturally coming around my waist to rest on my hips as he looks up at me, his body reacting even as his eyes search me, like he's trying to figure out what the answer is himself.

"You've got something to you, Thomas Goldstone. It's hard to see sometimes because you keep it under layers of barbed wire and jagged glass to keep anyone from getting too close." I trace a finger along his smooth jawline and then outline his lower lip.

He swallows. "I know. I want to be . . . a better man."

"You're already a good man. I'm just the lucky girl who gets to see it."

He shudders, and I think something in my words might've healed a small crack inside him, but then his eyes light up with devilry. "I've got something else you can see too. If you want."

I smirk back. "Let me see it all."

# CHAPTER 16

## Thomas

I CARRY MIA DOWN THE SHORT HALLWAY TO HER BEDROOM, LETTING her give me directions as we go.

I inhale her scent with every step, marveling at how some words can change things so much. It's the same woman, the same silky skin, the same soft hair tickling my nose . . . but it feels so different. Because now she is mine. And we both know it.

Her bedroom's just like Mia, a quirky mix of nerdy and sexy, and I take a moment to notice everything as I set her down on the mattress and stand up, stripping off my tuxedo shirt. I want to memorize everything she is, never forget anything, because she's just so . . . her.

Her bed's just big enough for the two of us, with colorful sheets and a little pink blanket sitting at the foot. She's also got one of those furry Russian hats on top of her dresser, along with a snow globe, of all things.

But all the baubles and trinkets in the world can't distract me for long with this beautiful vision in front of me. As my pants fall to the floor, Mia finishes pushing her shorts off, leaving her in sexy lingerie that matches the dress she wore tonight. That she left it on when she changed tells me she's wearing it just for me.

The pale gold lace is a few shades darker than her creamy skin, drawing my attention even more to her lush curves. Her nipples, pink jewels on top of snowy peaks, peek through the golden veil, and between my legs, my cock rises to full, almost painful hardness.

"Hmm, and I've barely touched you," Mia jokes, brushing a pink-tipped toe up my thigh to trace my cock through my underwear. "Should I wear this more often?"

"If you let me, I'll buy you a whole wardrobe of stuff like this," I promise her, capturing her foot in my hand. I resist the urge to attack her this instant, my desire for our emotional bond overwhelming my primal need to fuck her senseless. "But it's not the wrapping. It's the package itself. It's you who does this to me, Mia. Just you."

I climb onto the bed on my knees and kiss the arch of her foot, making my way up her leg. She moans louder when I lick the back of her knee, and inside my mind, I'm memorizing every reaction, learning how to bring her the most pleasure with a single touch.

As I reach her core, I see how wet she is through the soaked lace and groan, not sure if I can take this slow any longer. She has a way to bring the beast inside me out.

I lean forward and lick her from bottom to top with a wide, flat tongue, savoring the bouquet of her taste and scent while Mia moans.

"Oh, God . . . how are you so good at that?"

It's simple, really.

I love her taste.

I want to consume her, to have her ground into every pore of my skin, to carry her with me everywhere I go, every moment of the day. So I suck and lick, feasting on her from behind the lace until neither of us can hold back.

She lifts her hips, rolling her panties down until I pull my mouth away just long enough for us the get them out of the way before I'm on her once again, pushing her knees up and back, making her watch as my tongue dips deep inside her.

Mia bites her lip, gasping as I tease her inner folds, tracing and snaking my tongue along her pussy. "Hold your legs open for me, Mia."

She does as I instruct, hooking her legs with her hands but spreading them wide, knees near her shoulders.

Freed, my hands come up to cup her breasts, my thumbs rubbing over her lace-covered nipples while I flick her clit slowly with my tongue, making her squirm while pinned underneath me.

"Feel good?" I tease as I pull back, lowering her body back to the mattress as she trembles, keeping her on the edge.

"More," she pleads.

I kiss up her body, taking my time tasting wherever I fancy until I reach her lips. I hold myself above her, our skin just brushing as our mouths and tongues wrap around each other, sliding and lighting our bodies on fire.

It's a game for me, a challenge to hold myself back while bringing Mia to the quivering edge again and again. Through denying us both, prolonging the torturous agony, I'll bring us both to new heights, making the wait worth the reward.

I use my fingers, my lips, even the press of my body against her as I explore her, dipping my fingers into her tightness before swirling them over her clit, stroking until she's breathless, her head thrashing back and forth before I finally give her the final stroke she needs to shatter into a million pieces. It's a gorgeous display of release, my Mia at my hand.

"Enough?" I ask, and she nods, tears of ecstasy rolling down her flushed cheeks.

"Yes! Goddammit, Tommy, please fuck me!" she begs, reaching over and pulling me on top of her. My body's more than ready, and I sheathe myself in her pussy in one savage thrust, her legs locking around my hips as she cries out. She instantly comes on my cock, the convulsions almost continuously washing through her since she's barely recovered from her first orgasm.

Her arms lock around my neck while I watch her rapturous face and feel her velvet walls spasming around me, tempting me to let go with every pulsing squeeze.

I don't let her come all the way down before I pull back and thrust again, my inner animal fighting at my mental leash. I've been restraining myself all this time, torturing myself even as I've given her ultimate pleasure, and now my control's nearly frayed.

No woman has ever gotten this far past my defenses, made me reveal so much about myself. I was weak in front of her, and my ugly self-hatred wants to turn that back on Mia, punishing her for making me think about things best left buried. But rationally, I know it's only punishing myself to delay the inevitable.

So I don't hold back.

Punishing her, punishing me. Pleasuring her, pleasuring me.

With every stroke, I pump harder, deeper, relentlessly grinding against her even as her pussy swells around my cock. I kiss her hard, pulling the very air from her lungs as I fuck her brutally.

Inside me is the nice guy who wants to keep giving her the sweet dream she likely wants. The nice guy wants to keep things gentle, not test the limits of what her body can take and not dole out the depth of what I can dish out.

I want to worship her, to show her that I think she's an angel and that I'm enraptured with her, that I want to give myself fully to her just as she shared her pain with me. She's so strong, and I want to prove to her that I can be that strong as well.

But that side of me is not in control.

Instead, the beast inside me is, and it's going to punish this blonde goddess for daring to see through my façade. My hips slap against hers, her tits bouncing out of her bra from the hard thrusts.

She shouldn't be able to take all this. And she'll likely see me for the monster I am after this is over. But I'm being driven by lust and . . . fear, sweat dripping down our bodies from the effort and stinging my eyes.

But I don't let up, my cock growing with each plunge, my soul enraged as she cries out not in pain but in pleasure, grabbing my forearms and holding on as she comes again, her voice an angelic scream of release that obliterates my blackness. And I cry out, coming deep inside her. Not with fury and pain, for she's somehow cleansed that away for a freeing moment, but with utter happiness.

My back arches, and I purge myself, giving her everything as she accepts me, miraculously. I gather her in my arms as I collapse, holding her tenderly as tears mix with my sweat . . . but somehow, Mia doesn't mind. Instead, she holds me until the darkness swells over me and I let myself fall into sleep.

*You don't belong here.*

Go away.

Twenty years I've been hearing this voice, the familiar deep disdain and hatred. Every day, every task, every night, it's there.

Can't it at least give me some peace at a time like this?

*How can you even think of ruining this girl with your pathetic weakness? You think you're going to do better this time?*

I wasn't responsible for that. She was thirty-one. I was six!

*And? You failed her . . . your own mother. You let her die.*

I didn't! I didn't feed her those pills!

*You failed . . . and you'll fail Mia too.*

I sit up, my chest heaving and night terror sweat rolling down my face. The sun's just creeping up over the horizon, and next to me, Mia sleeps, a soft smile on her lips as she murmurs in whatever dream is in her head.

I don't want to wake her up from that.

Shakily, I get up and find her bathroom, where I take a morning piss before washing my hands and face, looking at the haunted eyes staring back at me from the mirror.

What am I doing here?

I'm being greedy, that's what I'm doing.

Mia's beautiful, inside and out. Instead of letting her personal tragedy strike her down, she's come out stronger, smarter, and simply more than a man like me ever deserves.

I shake my head and know that I need to get out of here.

Going back into the bedroom, I find my clothes, pulling my pants on before sitting down next to her, brushing a lock of hair out of her face. Mia hums, her lips twitching.

"Tommy . . ."

"Shh, Beautiful," I murmur, kissing her forehead. "Go back to sleep. I'll . . . I'll call you later."

*Fucking coward. Too weak to even walk away like you should. Can you do anything right? You know you're just going to disappoint her. Like you do everyone else.*

"Tommy?" Mia whispers, her eyes fluttering open. "What do you mean? Stay."

I shake my head and kiss her lips softly. "I want nothing more than to stay. But I need to go." It's the truth. I wish I could curl up in bed with her and use her body and cries of ecstasy to drown out the twisted voice in my head. But that would be wrong. I don't want to abuse her that way. "There are some things I need to take care of, and I don't want to ruin your morning by obsessing over them instead of you."

It's not a lie, but it's not the full truth, and it tastes bitter on my tongue.

"Then don't," she says. "It's Saturday. Can't you take the day off? You're the boss, you know?" Her smile is sleepy as she sits up on her elbow.

I smile back, shaking my head, so damn tempted to lie back down with her, to watch the sunlight brighten on the walls of her room, and to share coffee or something, maybe even go out to breakfast in last night's tuxedo while she wears . . . well, whatever she wants. I imagine her in a cartoon, no, an *anime* shirt. That's what she called the shows she watches last night.

But the hated voice inside me won't be denied much longer, and I know if I stay, I'm going to destroy what my good side wants so desperately. It's a sharp-edged balance, one I don't truly have experience walking. But I won't risk her, risk this, by pushing too far. The ugly whispers are already getting louder.

"I'm sorry, Beautiful, but this one won't wait. I'll call you this afternoon. Maybe we can get together this evening?" It's a weak promise but one I hope that I can keep.

"Maybe," Mia says, humming as she drifts back off. Her voice strengthens with wakefulness, "Oh, wait . . . I promised my friend Izzy that I'd stop by The Gravy Train. She's working a double and can really use the tips."

"Sounds like a date to me," I reply, smiling hopefully. "Seven?"

Mia smiles and lies back, her breasts so enticing as the sheet falls from them. "You don't have to. It's just a diner."

"I want to," I return, standing up. "I'll call you this afternoon, okay?"

I grab a cab back to my penthouse, where the elevator can't take me upstairs fast enough. Running to my bedroom, I change clothes and go to my gym, where the spin bike awaits me. With four switches, everything is prepared, and as screaming guitars, angry bass, and lyrics fill my ears, I get on the bike.

Two minutes on, thirty seconds off. It's rough, a brutal level of high-intensity intervals, but it's what I need. I'm not interested in the training effect. I'm interested in . . . absolution.

In pain.

In brutalizing my body to the point of exhaustion so that the voice shuts up and gives me a few hours of peace.

So as the lactic acid builds up in my quads and my lungs burn, I scream along with the music, the veins in my forearms bulging as I race away from my inner demons. Electric fire pulses through my nerves, making my muscles cramp before my veins carry the pain back to my heart and lungs, only to be recycled into my brain.

But still the past lashes at me, each memory a whip that drives me another round, and another round, and another. I shouldn't be able to do this.

The flywheel on the bike is so warmed through that I can feel it like a baking hellish coal between my legs while my demons cackle in the background.

Finally, the machine can take no more. In a loud *twang,* the overloaded tension belt snaps and the machine rolls totally free just as my vision clouds over and I collapse against the handlebars, my stomach heaving as sweat pours off my body to puddle on the floor.

Weakly, as the stereo continues to scream at me, I stagger off the bike, pausing with my hand on the mirror before flipping the switches, cutting off the music just as the bass riff starts to wind down and the anger ramps up.

Leaning against the wall, I wait for my vision to clear before going to the bathroom. I shower with scalding hot water, scrubbing the salty sweat off my body and wishing it were as easy to wash away my painful past. Even though it's Saturday, I still shave before putting on a T-shirt and jeans. My stomach's so queasy still that I skip breakfast before opening my laptop.

I didn't quite lie to Mia. I do have work I should catch up on. Emails, correspondence, and reports piled up yesterday as I played with the kids at the orphanage and then got ready for last night's event.

While Kerry handled as much as she could, I still have a pretty significant string of unopened messages, decisions to make, and things to reply to.

The chance to immerse myself in work instead of my inner doubts and hatred allows me to escape even more than my workout did, and I'm so immersed in the numbing regularity of work that I don't even hear the beep from the elevator or the sound of shoes on the tile in the entryway.

It isn't until I hear a familiar, hated double-knock on the kitchen island granite that I stop and turn around in my home office chair to see my father standing in there, for some reason still in a suit even though it's a Saturday.

"Dennis."

It's been years since I've called him 'Dad,' and we're maybe beyond the point of even caring any longer. Then again, I did give him a card access to the executive suite and the penthouse, so maybe . . . I don't know.

"Tom," he says, the same way he has for over twenty years. Bastard, motherfucker, cocksucker, cunt . . . none of those can hold a candle to the way my father can make my name sound, and none of them can cut me as deeply. "You didn't answer your phone yesterday."

"I was busy," I reply, standing up and purposefully walking past him to the kitchen. I give him my back, something I wouldn't have done in my younger years, but things are different now. But still, I've found it's safer to have something physical between us, although the reason's changed over the years. He hasn't laid a hand on me since I turned fifteen and he realized his 'boy' was no longer going to take his shit.

But he doesn't need the physical threat anymore. He has other weapons that he can use.

"I assumed that," my father says, standing on the other side of the island while I grab some eggs from the fridge along with butter and leftover vermicelli. "I see you still like Rita's recipes."

"Yeah. For a housekeeper, she was a good cook."

She was also the only person in the house who cared for me back then.

"Too bad you chased her away, but then again, you do that with most people in your life," he says, turning the same screw he always does. I squeeze the egg in my hand so hard the shell shatters, but luckily, I'm over the skillet, and most of the shell fragments stick together. He chuckles. "I see you're still a clutz in the kitchen."

He's trying to get a rise out of me, but I'm not going to let him. "What brings you here on a Saturday?"

"Where were you last night?" he asks, hands in his pockets. "I came by your office to discuss the quarterly dividend, and your secretary said you'd left early. She wouldn't tell me where."

"I was preparing for the governor's fundraiser," I reply, staring at my skillet while I add the already cooked vermicelli and start scrambling it all together like fried rice.

"So you were slacking off," he retorts, sighing. "How you're able to turn a profit with this clusterfuck of a company you run is beyond me. Guess it proves PT Barnum right. There's a sucker born every minute."

"This company is beyond reproach and has been profitable every year of operation," I remind him for what has to be the thousandth time. Sighing, I set aside the bowl of food and turn to my father, not ready to eat yet. "Everything you need to know about the dividend was in the quarterly report." It's a tactic I learned long ago. Don't ask him questions and don't give him a lead-in, because by giving an inch, he'll take a mile.

"I want to know why you declared a quarterly dividend of only fifty cents a share when the finances clearly show you could have declared fifty-five!" he yells. "Your ineptitude cost me thousands of dollars!"

"As the report showed, and you're well aware, I did it to reinvest it in the company," I reply, trying to keep control of my emotions. "That five cents a share means a lot of capital for the company to expand and acquire—"

"Who gives a shit? It isn't like you don't have enough leverage to get more! For fuck's sake, you don't just call the bank, you *own* the goddamn bank! Take the capital out yourself, not out of my money."

The argument goes back and forth, although like most of our discussions, it's a one-sided affair. No matter what I do, no matter how I explain it to my father, there's always a flaw in my thoughts, in my planning, in my reasoning. It's always been this way, and I wish I could go back in time to warn my younger self not to take his paltry investment in my upstart. At the time, it'd seemed like a turning point for us and I'd wanted to believe that he finally saw something worthwhile in me. The small percentage of shares in a company I hadn't even begun hadn't seemed like a risk. Now, I can see it was just another way to keep me tied down, to control me even as I finally made something of myself in spite of his influence.

"You know what, Tom? Monday, you will declare another dividend and make this right!" my father explodes after fifteen solid minutes of ranting. It's an order, a command. "If you can't run your company right the first time, you can at least make up for it." He rolls his eyes and murmurs, making sure I can hear him, "Such a stupid boy, useless waste—"

I slam my hands on the counter, my patience lost. "Shut up, Dennis! I've made you a lot of money. I've repaid you a thousand times over for the small investment you made. If you think you can do better, cash out your shares and invest in yourself. Or approach the board and see what your voting rights get you."

My father snorts derisively. "You can be outvoted, you know. I could take your own company right out from underneath you. You own fifty percent, but every move you make needs a majority. I could take you out at the knees."

I lift an eyebrow at the threat. Once upon a time, he did literally take my legs from underneath me with a hard push. I'd been young enough that I'd repeated his description of a 'fall' to the ER doctor when he'd asked how I banged my head on the ground hard enough to get a concussion. But this threat about my business, it's something he's never dared to voice.

"I trusted my own hard work and backed myself. Then and now. You could try getting every other shareholder on your side. But you'd fail."

My father's lips lift in a snarl, and he's pissed. Good. "You little . . . you should have been the one taking those pills, not—"

"Get the fuck out!" I yell, finally pushed too far. As I get closer, I warn him, "Get out of my house, and don't ever come back!"

He shrinks for a split second, like he knows if I take this physical, the way he used to, he's already lost. But though I'm a monster, I'm not him.

When he sees I'm not going to strike him, he looks like he's about to argue, but then he takes the smallest step back and smiles wanly, adjusting his tie. "I will be filing a formal grievance, as per Goldstone corporate rules."

He leaves, and I clench my fists, holding back the explosion until he's gone before picking up my bowl and hurling it in the direction he just went, the whole thing exploding in a giant mess on the wall. The fact that I now have to clean it up as well as not have any breakfast yet infuriates me more.

Never. I can't . . . I can't see him again.

A crazy thought drifts through my head, and it helps me calm enough to get the broom and start cleaning up.

The Gravy Train.

She said the food there is good.

# CHAPTER 17

## Mia

"Y OU'VE GOT A BOYFRIEND," IZZY SING-SONGS LIKE WE'RE TEN.
I laugh, nodding as Izzy sits down across from me for our stand-ing Friday lunch. It's just the two of us today. Charlotte's got some sort of thing going at her job that has her working extra time, so she texted her regrets with a picture of a sad brown bag lunch.

It's not the same without her, but Izzy and I have been buddies since we were sharing Oreos on the playground, so we're used to the Two-Girl Power Trip.

"I guess so. Though calling that man a boy-anything is a little strange to hear," I answer, chuckling as I think about Thomas. No, even with the little I know about his childhood, I can't imagine him as a little boy running around in dirty sneakers and a tank top.

Izzy smiles, and I press her. "So, what'd you think?" She's one of my best friends and I trust her opinion. I want her to like Thomas just as much as I do.

She sits back, humming. "I mean, on one hand, the man left me a $150 tip on a twenty-dollar order. For that alone, I'm giving him a chance. But Mia, I just . . ."

Izzy's voice trails off, and we're distracted for a moment as we give our orders. While I wait for my drink to arrive, I sip at some water, eyeing her.

"Come on, Izzy, spill it. We've been friends long enough that nothing you say is going to hurt our friendship."

She sighs and runs a hand through her hair. "It's just that ... okay, maybe it's me. I mean, I'm the first to admit that I've got a pretty dark view on men."

"Ohh ... you don't say?" I ask sarcastically. But then my smile drops. "So you didn't like him?" I replay our dinner over in my head. He'd picked me up last Saturday just before seven, had seemed perfectly comfortable in the ragtag diner, and had been his usual charming self. What's not to like? Okay, maybe not quite his usual charm. There'd been a bit more of the "professional" Thomas in his mannerisms, not rude or Ruthless Bastard style, but a little colder than he usually is with me. I'd chalked it up to nerves at meeting my friend, the way I'd been a bit awkwardly star struck at the fundraiser.

She shakes her head, putting a hand on mine, "It's not that I didn't like him. The whole thing just seems ..." She pauses, searching for the word she wants and then settles on, "Fast. I don't want your hormones to run away with your brain. Like, you've been on a couple of dates, but I could tell that man thinks you are *his*, in the possessive sense of the word. That's just a bit brake-worthy to me."

I don't tell her about him claiming me that way at the fundraiser and how it had made me eschew the brakes and go full-throttle, pedal to the metal. Instead, her words remind me, the story falling out unbidden, "Do you know what he did on Monday?" I don't wait for her answer, continuing, "He tried to get me to move up to his floor. It was an 'invite' but I don't think he thought I'd have a problem with it. Mother Russia was not amused."

Izzy cringes. "What'd you say? What happened?"

"I reminded him that I don't want any favors at work, so unless he was moving the whole data analyst team up there, I was staying where I am. Plus, I reminded him that while he thinks my quirks are cute and eccentric, most people, myself included, prefer me to work in the quiet basement where I can rock out and geek out in private. And then he saw the error of his ways and apologized ... on his knees."

Izzy gasps, eyes wide with shock. "In the office?"

I nod, grinning. "In his office, overlooking all of Roseboro."

Izzy plops back against the booth and fans her face. "Dayum, where do I sign up for that benefit package?" Her face sobers, and she purses her lips. "Look, babe, everyone's got a good side, though Thomas Goldstone is more known for his asshole side."

I interrupt her, holding up a finger. "As crazy as it sounds, I think he's actually uncomfortable showing his nice side. Kinda the opposite of most guys where they put on the nice front to cover the asshole lurking underneath. Tommy wears a mask of a jerk to hide his good side."

She presses her lips together, thinking about that. "If he's good to you, good for you, enjoy the ride. Have fun, go do some one-percenter stuff that we never thought we'd get a chance to do, and get yourself royally laid. But be prepared for the crash."

"The crash?" I ask, thinking of the darker side of Thomas. Already, his nickname of The Ruthless Bastard has been yammered in my ear constantly, and while Bill Radcliffe's been cool about things, especially considering the influx of looky-loos who want to see the data analyst crazy enough to date twenty-five floors above her station, he's not the only person who's thrown in the towel when it comes to trying to put up with Thomas's hard-charging nature and angry outbursts. More than a few warning stories people have shared about him call him a user, and while not an abuser . . . I've raised a few eyebrows among both the men and women around the Goldstone building.

"The crash," Izzy confirms. "Come on, don't make me spell it out for you. You're in the fairy tale phase of the relationship, and that's cool. Everything's refreshing, sparkling, you've got more pep in your step than I've felt in . . . shit, I can't even think of the last time I felt as happy as you look right now. But there are too many instances where that fairy tale turns into a bad dream, babe. I'm just saying . . . fairy tales don't always come true. You know that from your own history, or did your dad being Soviet Cinderfella not teach you that lesson?"

I sigh, nodding. Reaching into my pocket, I pull out today's gift and set it on the table between us. "I know, Izzy. But then there's this."

Izzy picks up the card, looking it over. It's black, unmarked except for the chip embedded in the surface. "He gave you a credit card?"

"No . . . something more important," I tell her. "It's a keycard to his penthouse. He gave it to me this morning, saying that he understands why I don't want the office upstairs . . . but that if I ever need to, I have access to his penthouse and his office. To him, anytime and always. He said that after this weekend, I'm one of three people with those cards. The other is his secretary, and he has one. Everyone else has to be buzzed in. He's quite literally letting me inside."

"Wow," Izzy says, pursing her lips before sighing. "Okay. Like I said, any guy who's willing to give me a hundred and fifty bucks on the sly is worth a shot. But be careful, and if things go to shit, I'll be here for you."

"I know," I say as our lunches arrive and I put the keycard away. "I've got you and Char for sure, and if anything, Papa said he could give a call to some people he knows."

"Your dad knows Russian Mafia?" Izzy asks, surprised, and I laugh, shaking my head.

"No, the closest he knows to Russian Mafia is Father Vasiliev at the Orthodox Church. If you've ever heard him give a sermon asking for more donations . . . now *that* man's a gangster."

Up until now, I've been a pretty big PC and video game nerd, but that was before I really started getting in deep with work and Goldstone. I guess 'adulting' has its consequences.

Gone are the games that need daily logins or lots of grinding. So bye-bye to *Eve Online*. Bye-bye even to *WoW*, or *Final Fantasy Online*.

I refuse to get beaten down to *Fortnite* level yet, so instead I've started up *TERA*. It's action-packed, lots of fun, and not so complex that I can't leave my character for two weeks without major problems.

And tonight's the night to get my game back on. I'm just about to fire up my PC and log on when my phone rings. I see it's Thomas, so I pick up my phone, leaning back on my sofa.

"Hey, Tommy, what's up? Please don't tell me you're still in the office. I know it's hump day, but you don't actually have to be at the top of your mountain of paperwork to slide into Friday."

"Nope. I stick to my policy of leaving the office by no later than six," he says. "Though sometimes, I take work upstairs with me, but that doesn't count." He laughs at his own joke and I grin. "Actually, there's something I wanted to talk to you about, but I wanted to wait until after work because I didn't want you to think I was trying to hit on you in the office."

My smile falls as I sit up, clicking into a more serious headspace. "I appreciate that. What's up?"

"I've been presented with an opportunity for Goldstone. And I need to put together another project team. This is a big one, so I'll be taking the lead on it and selecting the team myself. I'd like you to be on it, but I understand if you think that's muddying the waters too much. You're the best choice, but I won't be offended if you'd rather not." His voice is serious, showing how much he has listened to my rants about people gossiping about us and how it's not right that everyone looks at me as playing up, not him playing down. Not that either of us is playing at this point.

"I can keep it professional. I mean, we wouldn't be together all the time, right? We're twenty-five floors apart. How hard can it be?"

"That's the thing," Thomas says. "The deal isn't one that can be done in the office. Do you have a passport?"

"Uhh, yeah. I got one for a trip to Vancouver last year. Why?"

"The job is in Japan. I'm putting together a team for a week-long trip overseas to tour a resort location and their company headquarters to see if it's a good fit for a capital investment. We leave a week from Friday. Until then, we'll be buried to our eyeballs doing prep work. What do you think?"

I grin so hard my jaw aches. "You realize you just asked me if I want to go on a business trip to the home of anime, video games, and all sorts of nerdy paradise that gets my geeky heart going pitter-patter, right?"

Thomas's laughter is silent, but I can still hear the way he's breathing. He's gotta be almost heaving on his end of the line. "Is that a yes?"

"Of course!" I half scream, trying not to boogie on the couch.

"But honestly, it's just because you'll be working with me, right?" he teases, knowing that he's basically offered me a dream gig. Japan, a work opportunity, and him.

Thinking of him, I say, "Now, you've got two options. Either you let me get off here so I can play the game I was about to start, or you get your ass over here and help me work off this energy another way."

There's a two-second pause on the other end of the line, and then Thomas growls. "Pack a bag for work tomorrow. I'll be by in ten minutes to pick you up."

# CHAPTER 18

## Thomas

W HEN I INCORPORATED GOLDSTONE, I DIDN'T SET THINGS UP
the way a lot of corporations do. Quite frankly, the idea of an
elected board with politics and horse trading being the primary
reasons certain decisions are made disgusts me. It's as much an issue of
covering your ass as it is 'good corporate governance', so I avoided it.

Pretty easy when I'm the largest single shareholder.

But still, as an olive branch to my initial angel shareholders who gave
me the boost I needed—including, regretfully, my father—I do have meetings with them, usually including my senior executive vice presidents on a
semi-regular basis to give a recap on their respective areas. Mostly, they're in-
formal things that go according to plan. As long as my dad doesn't make one of
his rare appearances to decree Goldstone a failure and demand more profits.

But before projects like this, we have a more formal sit-down to address
any concerns before proceeding.

I've given the basics of the project and the potential growth we could
achieve if this investment plays out, and thankfully, everyone seems to be on
board. "Okay, so we'll be flying into Tokyo Narita, and from there we'll—" I
say, going over the travel plan as a bit of a wrap-up.

One of my executive VPs, Stanford Truscott, clears his throat. "Yes,
Stan?"

"Thomas, I have no concerns about this project, but something connected to it," he says, tapping the table in the way he does when he's got something uncomfortable on his mind. He's a great lawyer, head of my legal department, in fact . . . but the man's got enough tells that I'm shocked he's ever been able to win a court case. Maybe that's why he does his hardest negotiations around a conference table instead of in a courtroom. "It's about Mia Karakova."

Her name on his lips freezes me and I narrow my eyes. "What about Mia Karakova? She did great work on the last project."

Stan glances across the table at some of the other VPs, who give him a supportive nod. It seems I've walked into something of an ambush. But Stan's the one who has apparently been elected to face the executioner. The fact that he agreed to challenge me almost makes me respect him a bit more and lessens my impression of the remaining men and women sitting around the table like lemmings.

"I don't think anyone disagrees with that. And it's not that we don't want you to have a social life, but she works in the company."

"Your point?"

*Stop getting your dick sucked by your analysts?*

Not that damn voice. I don't need it here.

"By all reports, she's a bit of an odd wunderkind with numbers. In a month, she's gone from being given a chance with a team here in Roseboro to being seen with you at a major public event, and now you've given her a jump up the ladder to an off-site team. To say there are whispers of . . . influenced decision making is an understatement. And as your lawyer, it makes me concerned."

I look around the room, noting the faces looking at me. There's a lot of experience in here, 'advisors' and executive VPs who have been with Goldstone since the beginning. Still, I know their thinking, and I know their number-one concern is quarterly reports and stock prices. Not a one of them cares about me beyond what I can do to fatten their portfolios.

"I'm only going to address this subject once," I reply, pushing back from the table and glaring at the entire assembled group. "My relationship with Mia Karakova has nothing to do with her being part of either research team. It has everything to do with the fact that her professional results speak for themselves. She was given a shot on the hospital team because of her work for Bill Radcliffe. And her analysis was spot on. In fact, you all voted for Goldstone to proceed with her recommended course of action, the one that forecasts record returns on your investments in less than two years' time. She did that."

I can see that some of them are nodding now, on my side, and the fact that they are so easily swayed by dollars and cents only proves my point that money is all they care about. They just wanted to hear me say it.

"Still, Thomas, I've reviewed Miss Karakova's employment history," Stan says, trying to stay on point. "There's a rumor you tried to have her office moved up to your floor?"

"That's not a rumor. That's a fact." I've had enough of this, and my patience is wearing thin. I lean forward, planting my palms on the conference table where I fucked Mia just weeks ago. Fuck, has it only been such a short time. It feels like I can't remember a time before her, like I've blocked it out in favor of the happiness she brings me, even if only for a short time.

"Let me be transparent here. Mia Karakova is a factor in my life, and that's *not* going to change. But she is not affecting my business decisions any more than I take her analysis into account the same way I do each of you. You have all made millions of dollars from trusting my decisions. This one should be no different. But at the end of the day, it's my name on the building out there, and I'll stand by my actions. If you can't, feel free to let Stan know and we'll begin dissolution paperwork of your relationship with Goldstone Inc. Any questions?"

I cross my arms, fixing every person in the room with a stare. No one says a word, most of them unable to meet my eyes. I know I have a reputation for putting people 'on blast', but I certainly hadn't thought this was how today's meeting was going to go.

With a sigh of disappointment, both in my board and in myself, I tell them, "Meeting adjourned."

Everyone files out, leaving me to fume. Who are they to question me on bringing Mia into this project? If it weren't for my decisions, we wouldn't be a billion-dollar company right now in less than ten years.

*It's pure luck, no skill on your part, stupid boy.*

It's not her fault, but I'm brooding and I barely give Kerry a glance as I head into my office, closing the door behind me and sitting down. I close my eyes and will myself to relax. I'm not going to let them hold me back, and I'm not going to let them force me to doubt myself.

If I'm going to be worth anything, I have to be the best, and I can't be that by being pissed off that someone questioned my decisions. I am better than this. I have to be.

*You'll never be worth anything anyway. No matter what you do.*

There's a quiet knock on my door, and I open my eyes, shutting the voice down with a growl. "Yes?"

Kerry opens the door, sticking just her head in. She probably saw my face, heard my tone, and wants to make sure I'm not about to rip heads from shoulders.

"Excuse me, sir. Mr. Truscott's here. He was hoping to have a private word?"

I take a deep breath before nodding, sitting back as Stan comes in. Kerry asks if he'd like a coffee, hurrying off to get a cup for him while Stan sits down in my guest chair and stares me down.

I asked him to be my legal VP for a couple of reasons, not the least of which is that he can deal with my fiery temper when it comes to work and isn't afraid to ask the tough questions.

So I remind myself why he's here in the first place. I hired him exactly for this.

"Something else, Stan?"

"Thomas, believe it or not, I came in here to see how you're doing," he replies, unbuttoning his jacket and getting comfortable. I raise a challenging brow, and he says, "And maybe to share a little advice. That is, if you'll listen."

"I have a few minutes," I say, sitting back and refusing to give him a banal response of 'fine' about how I am because we both know that's not true.

Stan didn't need to come to Goldstone. He'd already made a good life and career for himself as a named partner in his own firm. He earned my respect before ever stepping foot in the building as an employee, and he has done even more to impress since coming onboard, even if I do think he's too conservative on his business ideas most of the time.

"Did you know," he says, pausing as Kerry comes back with his coffee and he thanks her with a polite nod, "before I agreed to join the company, I did my research on you?"

"I'd have expected nothing less. What did you find?"

"I found a man who's smarter than the average bear, that's for sure," Stan replies, "but who's no genius. Now don't take that the wrong way, because there are too many geniuses in this world who are cashing welfare checks for me to draw any relationship between brains and success."

"So, what's brought me to the top in your estimation?" I ask, curious what he sees.

"You're successful for the same reason Jerry Rice, Michael Jordan, and every other overachiever is, at least if you look at what people thought of them when they got started. You want to prove people wrong. You compete with yourself, with what others expect of you. That desire to be the best is second to none, and you're willing to work hard to be number one. I also know what fuels it."

His analysis is not incorrect, which makes me wonder what he thinks my driving force might be. "What's that?"

Stan shakes his head, sipping his coffee. "You know, you could create the world's largest company. You could become president. You could craft world peace . . . and it won't matter. Not to *him*."

The fact that he throws that out there so casually infuriates me, but I school my features into a poker face, refusing the tell that would give me away.

"Your father," Stan says, acknowledging the elephant if I won't. "My research and discretion are more thorough than most. That's what you pay me for, after all. And after meeting Dennis at my first board meeting, I felt some inquiry was prudent. Not to be condescending, but you deserved a childhood far different from what you had. You may have had things when it came to money, but money isn't everything, as you're well aware. The way he treats you"—he leans forward, meeting my stare—"and treated you after your mother's death, is criminal. And that's coming from a lawyer."

He's pretty spot-on, but this is a little too deep for Stan and me, so I just want to move this along. "You said you had some advice for me?"

"Yes," Stan says. "Mia Karakova is the first person I've seen in my five years here who seems more important to you than your drive to be the best."

"It seems like that would be a good thing. A more well-balanced leadership?"

Stan smiles sadly. "You'd think that'd be the case, but you're a jet engine on stage-five afterburners, just about two steps short of blowing up if you keep going the way you have been these past few years. And all it takes is for you to be put in just the right situation, the right circumstances, and those two steps will hit you like a ton of bricks. In a situation like that . . . you could hurt yourself, you could hurt her, and you could hurt the business. I'd prefer if you didn't reach that point."

"So, what are you recommending? That I stop seeing her?"

"No," Stan says with a laugh. "I wouldn't dream of asking that of you. What I recommend, what I advise, both professionally and personally, is caution and consciousness. Be aware and be wary, of her, of yourself. And even of others' perceptions, not because they are true but because they can affect your placement as the best on whatever scoreboard you're keeping. Dennis isn't going away, but you can be happy. Not in spite of him, but simply because he no longer has any hold on you. That is what I would like for you."

It's probably the most caring, dare I say *fatherly*, speech anyone's ever given me. That Stan sees beyond the face I present, whether because he's looking for my tells from knowing my history or because he actually cares, is oddly reassuring. His willingness to broach this conversation, both in the meeting and again in private, speaks to his character, and I respect that, and therefore, his advice.

"I would like that as well," I offer.

He stands, offering a handshake that I return. But before he goes, he says, "Investing in a woman isn't like investing in a company. You can't just cut your losses, follow the contract guidelines, and walk away when it's all over."

He's right . . . and wrong.

I know what I'm doing. Mia isn't just an 'investment'. She's someone special. And I have no intention of walking away from her.

And all the old bastards in the company can doubt me. They can doubt my decisions and my skills . . . but I won't let them stop me.

Even Stan doubts that I can have the perfect ending, worries that I can't have my company and Mia.

We'll see.

# CHAPTER 19

## Mia

WATCHING TOKYO UNFURL UNDERNEATH ME IS LIKE A DREAM come true. Sure, at several thousand feet in the air, it pretty much looks like every other city I've flown over in my life, but at the same time . . . it's different.

"You look like you're ready to geek out," Thomas whispers from the business-class seat next to me.

"I am . . . but it's all good."

I was surprised that he's back here with the rest of the team, but when he sat down next to me, giving me the window seat in the front row of business class while he took the aisle, I was so excited that I've barely slept the entire eleven hours.

Instead, I've binged on movies, talked with Thomas, and tried to keep my voice down as he's made me laugh even as the people around us have slept.

That was hard, as somewhere over the Pacific where I could just see the aurora borealis out my window, he insisted on whispering things he wanted to do in Japan into my ear . . . very few of which we could repeat out loud. The ideas that go through his mind fill me with heat, and more than once, I had to stifle a moan as he teased me with naughty thoughts about what we're going to get up to.

And that was without even touching me as he reminded me of my demand for professionalism. I'd been *this close* to saying fuck it and skipping down the aisle to the tiny bathroom to join the Mile-High Club, and he'd known it. He'd delighted in it, in fact.

All work and no play? Thomas likes to pretend that's how he is, but it's the exact opposite. His hard, efficient work means he plays just as hard, and for hours over the Pacific, he told me exactly how he wants to play.

My excitement fades a little as we circle into Narita Airport and go through the exhausting rigmarole that is customs. Even Thomas's money and influence don't swing any weight with these guys, and by the time we step out into the underground train station that links the airport to the rest of Tokyo, I'm already exhausted.

"Please tell me this takes us directly to a hotel."

"Sorry," Thomas says, shouldering his bag while wheeling his other behind him like any other traveler, "but our limo's waiting for us at Tokyo Station. And at least the train's fast."

Fast is one thing, but more importantly, the Narita Express is *quiet*, and Thomas doesn't seem to mind that I use his shoulder as a pillow while I close my eyes. It's comforting, watching him act so normal but so protective. It lets me sort of half-doze, and I have good dreams as I feel his warmth against my cheek the whole trip.

"Come on, we're here," he says, gently nudging me.

Our team isn't that large, only five people, but the other three don't seem to give a second thought to Thomas's possessive closeness with me. In fact, in the last couple of weeks, nobody's said anything to me at all about Thomas and me going 'public' with our relationship, probably for three reasons.

One, almost nobody comes down to my office anyway since the gossip-mongers all got their fill.

Two, I'm still busting my butt for Bill and he's pretty much the coolest supervisor I could ask for in this situation.

Three, I'm pretty sure Thomas's simmering anger and reputation have made anyone who considers saying anything keep their traps shut out of fear of 'the blast.'

I don't care. I'll prove the naysayers wrong the same way that I've won Thomas's respect . . . with my results. I'm strong, I'm powerful, I'm one sexy bitch . . . but most importantly, I'm smart.

Emerging onto the streets of Tokyo is like a dream come true. The crowd, the sounds, the music, the signage . . . I feel like I've just walked into one of my animes.

"It's beautiful."

"Too bad we won't be able to see what it looks like at night," Thomas reminds me, looking around before turning to Kenny, who's serving double-duty as translator and Japanese legal expert. He directs us to our ride, and we make our way over.

The limo's not quite a limo but more of a large, luxurious minivan that takes us where we need to go. I want to watch Tokyo city life blossom around me, watch the hustle and bustle, the children walking to school in groups with their uniforms, hats, and backpacks, the young people looking much more colorfully arrayed, and the housewives on their bicycles. I want to watch the herds of 'salarymen' on their way to work . . . but it all passes too quickly, even if we are dealing with city traffic.

It turns into a hazy slide show, and before I know it, we're at Odaiba Bay, where we get off in front of something I can't believe. "A seaplane?" I ask.

"I figured it'd be more fun than the ferry, and I want to look at incorporating this service," Thomas replies as we climb aboard the sleek, modern-looking plane.

The flight's about ninety minutes, and while nowhere near as quiet as the business-class airliner we took to get to Tokyo, the view's worth it, and I'm reminded of old reruns of *Fantasy Island* as we come in for a landing.

The island's beautiful, a tropical paradise, one of a small grouping, volcanic hills hunching out of the deep blue Pacific and covered in deep green forests. Along one side there's a small town, beaches, and a dock.

It's about as far from the *normal* image of Japan that I've seen, and while the view up here is amazing, I'm excited to get on the ground and see it.

"My God, it's beautiful," I whisper as we land in a huge spray of water that's amazingly smooth, considering what we're doing.

Thomas nods. "When we get off the plane, take mental notes," Thomas says to everyone, all business as we approach the dock. "I want your impressions, market ideas, everything. We know our preliminary research, but I need confirmation."

Colors. Every day, I'm reminded of just how Technicolor this resort is. Five days of waking up in a tropical paradise to the sound of waves, tropical birds, and a gentle wind stirring the curtain outside my window should be enough for anyone to unwind and relax. I sit up in the morning and look out into a riotous collage of blues, greens, whites, and natural browns, of birds dipped in reds and yellows, of fish that dance like golden sparkles and starlets in clear blue bays.

I should be putty in bed, lounging around. I mean, I don't even need to wear pants. Everyone around here wears shorts most of the time.

I should be relaxed . . . but I'm anything but. Part of it, of course, has been that I haven't been able to spend much time with Thomas. While he might be the most efficient worker I've ever met, the locals are on their own idea of what good work means.

Unfortunately, that means a lot of 'work longer, not better,' and he's had huge chunks of his time taken up with meetings, teas, and the like where there's a lot of nodding, a lot of professional smiling, and not much else. I think poor Kenny is getting a sore throat from all the translating back and forth.

By the time Thomas gets back every night, he barely has time to catch up with the rest of the team, to share a small bit of time with me, and to shower before he has to crash and be ready for the next day.

As for me . . . I've got my own challenges.

After a breakfast of rice and *furikake*, a seaweed, salt, herb, and fish flake mixture that's used as a seasoning on top of a lot of stuff all around Japan, I try to go back to work.

Which brings me to my main problem, the working situation.

While the proposal Thomas has been presented with is to buy the resort, with its twenty-eight guest rooms and two meeting spaces, and turn it into a high-end escape for Fortune 500 types who want to mix their business with pleasure, the professional capabilities are severely lacking.

Our team's work room isn't much bigger than my office back in Roseboro, and while there are only three of us in here, we're having to share four outlets for three tablets and six laptops. There's no way we can even fit everyone in here at once unless we want to share bad breath.

To top it off, the Internet is ridiculously slow. As in, I could send a carrier pigeon back to Roseboro faster than this.

"And . . . I'm going to go do my hair," Randy Ewing says, shaking her curls, which are much frizzier than when we arrived, and pushing back from her space. She's responsible for looking at renovation ideas and has been working harder than anyone. "All this heat and humidity is terrible. I'm already planning a salon trip when we get back, but for now, I just need this mop braided and out of my face. I figure by the time I get it done, my email might actually be finished downloading." She taps the laptop she's working on like her harsh words might make it connect faster. "What about you, Mia?"

I mutter a few tasty curse words in Russian and glare at one of my two laptops. Looking up at her, I shrug. "At least you've got something. Did you know the current owner keeps all his business records on paper? Not even an Excel spreadsheet . . . handwritten entries in a bound book like it's 1985. Seriously, how am I supposed to see any trends with that?"

"Best of luck," she says, shaking her head. "By the third time I had to bicycle all the way into town to even check my texts, I'd made up my mind. We'd have to sink too much into this place to make it anything close to what Thomas is thinking. God knows what it'd take to get a proper renovation team up here, and that's before the actual materials cost even kicks in."

Randy leaves, and I chug away at my information as best I can. Finally, just before noon, I see Thomas come in, his eyes red from last night's activities.

"Ugh . . . I don't know what they put in the local version of *sake*, but it smelled like kerosene and kicks like a mule."

"Good morning to you too, sunshine. Or good afternoon," I grumble, slamming my laptop closed. "Please tell me that you're making progress on your side of things?"

"I think I am," Thomas confides. "I feel stupid that I haven't learned Japanese and have to rely on Kenny to translate for me, but I've gotten the flow of how they do things around here. Somewhere in between *Dancing Queen* and *Gimme Shelter* at the karaoke bar, there was a nod, a little grunt passed in between two men who were pretending to be drunk but were nowhere near as wasted as their singing excused, and I've gotten the approval of the village head honchos. If we want to make the deal on the resort, we can. I hope it's worth the headache, and I hope Kenny forgives me for my bad rendition of Elvis. Apparently, the karaoke bar in town doesn't have the most up to date database."

"Databases . . . ugh. God, what I'd give for a fucking database right now. I'd run algorithms, maybe even make a chart. Databases," I say longingly. I lean back, growling at the word while I tug at my hair. I've reached my limit. I never thought I'd be tired of being in Japan . . . but the Japan I want to see is nowhere near here.

"What's the problem?" he asks, rubbing at his temples. "Internet is on the list of needed upgrades. Along with a revamped power system."

"It's not just that. You need data analysis, but I can't get my hands on the data. You want me to spot trends, but without having the ability to see the complete picture, I simply can't. I've got twenty-year-old technology, fifty-year-old data collection systems, and a power grid that can't even keep up with what we're asking of it. I'm working one-armed and in the dark. And I don't want to let you down."

"Mia, figure it out. That's what we're here to do," he says dismissively, sitting down in the empty chair. "You're smart. Think outside the box."

"Excuse me?" I ask, my frustrations boiling over. "Thomas, I've been stuck in here because the tools I need to use—"

"Use your brain, not the technology!" Thomas snaps. I stop, shocked at how he's pushing me. It's not that I think I'm immune from his 'blasts', and in fact, have demanded that he treat me the same as everyone else, but this is the first time he's actually done so, and the charge in the air between us is staticky and buzzy.

He pauses for a moment, taking a breath before continuing in a calmer voice. "Computers are tools, yes. But that's just it, they're tools. They're never going to replace what's inside your head because that brain's better than any computer can ever be. I do need your skills to dissect the clusterfuck this resort is, judging by everyone's complaints. But that can be done at home if the technology isn't here. There's more here to evaluate than just dry figures."

Somehow, it feels like he doesn't even know me. I live for dry figures, columns of numbers that magically add up correctly every time, and the things I can learn from rows of data. But he says there's more?

"What do you mean, 'more'? *This* is why you brought me," I say, gesturing to the laptop in front of me.

Thomas, amazingly, chuckles. "We're not making a decision and cutting a check today. If we do want to move on this deal, it's going to be a fiscal year at least while all the right people put all the right signatures on all the right pieces of paperwork. I honestly think this island's held in place in the ocean by paperwork. But while we're here, I need the team's insight—no, I need *your* insight—into this deal."

I pause, surprised by the meaning in his words. I venture, "Do you realize that we've been on this island paradise for four days and I've barely had time with you as my boyfriend and not my boss? I know we're here on business, but maybe we can take a small break?"

He presses his lips together, and I can already hear him telling me that he can't budge from his schedule. "How about if you spend today compiling every bit of information you can get your hands on and getting your numbers pulled together to take home, and tomorrow, we take twenty-four hours just for us? I'll give the whole team the day and let them pull their own impressions too so we have a solid look at everything this proposal has to offer."

I grin, giving him a little sass. "That was the most unsexy request for a date I think I've ever received."

His smirk is full of arrogance, and he raises an eyebrow. "Not a date, Miss Karakova. We're keeping things professional, remember?"

I bite down on the end of my pen pointedly, remembering how he told me he thought I'd been intentionally driving him crazy in our first meetings. His eyes zero in on my mouth the way I'd hoped they would, and I tease him further. "Anything you say, Mr. Goldstone." My voice is pure sex and suggestion.

"Starting tomorrow when you wake up, you'll be totally unplugged. And totally mine, Mia."

# CHAPTER 20

## Mia

"GOOD MORNING."

Two simple words, but the way Thomas looks at me tells me so much more as his eyes explore me. I'm not naked. I've pulled a tank top on over my bikini top, and I swear I've slathered so much sunscreen on my arms and face that I must look like a ghost, but Thomas's eyes tell me that he doesn't mind in the least.

"Good morning," I reply, putting my backpack over my shoulder. "How'd you sleep?"

"I'll be honest, upgrading beds is on my agenda here," Thomas says with a stretch. "Seriously, futons are not my thing. Come on, let's get some breakfast. You look lovely, by the way."

"My Russian roots are going to do a number on me tomorrow. I'm gonna be sunburned neon pink tonight," I say with a laugh as we leave the resort. "What is for breakfast, by the way?"

"Just down the road, you'll see," Thomas reassures me. "And what other roots do you have, if you don't mind me asking?"

"Not at all. According to what I was told in the little bits I remember, the Appleman side of me is mostly English. So you've got pale and paler. How about you?"

"American mutt, from what I know," Thomas says casually. "Honestly, I sort of treat heritage like zodiac signs. It's an interesting factoid, but it doesn't define us as people. You can toss it out as a conversation gambit, but it doesn't define you. Even if you're from the Motherland."

"Hey, I'm mostly joking—" I start but stop when Thomas takes my hand, entwining our fingers.

"That's culture, not DNA. You can be proud of that and what your father taught you. You've taken the good and hopefully dropped the rest. At least, I'm hoping you aren't planning on wearing a babushka or stuffing me full of borscht?"

"Gotta admit, I hate borscht and my headwear is more headband than babushka."

Thomas grins, giving my hand a little squeeze. "Good. Here's breakfast."

It's a fruit stand, and the selection's stunning. I don't know what the vendor offers me, but as I bite into the softball-sized golden fruit, sweet and sour and utter deliciousness roll over my tongue and I find myself gorging myself on whatever it is as Thomas hands me another piece.

"Mmm . . . this is like the food of the gods."

"Isn't it?" he asks, biting into a green thing that has a deep chromatic red flesh inside. He hums happily, his eyes twinkling before he offers me a bite, and I eat from his hand, licking the juices from his thumb with a flirty look.

He brushes the fruit over my lips, and I suck it for a sultry moment before biting into it with a chomp. "Delicious," I say, grinning at the quick change of his expression from arousal to fear. "Don't worry, I won't bite into you that way, at least not anywhere important."

We laugh and start off walking, exploring the island. There's a lot to find, starting with the small town with its tropical slice of Japanese life, complete with a seeming unending plethora of convenience stores, vending machines, posters adorned with cartoon characters, and other little things that just sort of pop out of nowhere.

"I know I sound like a total tourist right now, but that's just strange," Thomas says as we pass a construction site. Instead of regular signs to warn people, the plastic temporary fence posts themselves are shaped like a man in a construction helmet, his hand up warningly, a bubble coming out of his head to say something in Japanese. I can only guess it means *Caution*, or *Warning*, or maybe *Stay the Fuck Out*.

"It does get the message across though," I point out as we swerve around the metal poles. "What made you look here to invest, anyway?

It's a bit beyond your usual scope, though I know you've invested beyond Roseboro, obviously."

"Because of the unrealized potential," Thomas admits. "Well, someone realized it, hence the resort we're looking at purchasing, but they weren't able to make it a reality. I've heard that the owner is a motivated seller."

"What's his weak point? Financial? Health?"

"Not quite. His daughter and grandchildren live in London, and he's ready to retire and be closer to them," Thomas replies.

I nod, setting aside business as we keep walking. We don't push the pace. We just wander, and after a light lunch at a noodle shop in town, we head back toward the resort, exploring the fifty acres of land there. As we do, the afternoon heat starts to soak in and I strip off my tank top once we reach the shaded privacy of the walking paths that ring the property.

Thomas grins and pulls off his own T-shirt, exposing his chiseled muscular torso and leaving him in just some board shorts. "Need some more sunscreen?"

"Nicely played, though not exactly subtle," I tease, taking the bottle and rubbing a fresh layer onto my thighs, calves, chest, and belly.

"And you think you're being sly stripping down to a bikini top that shows me damn near everything? You started it." The way he looks at me leaves me feeling a lot more than the tropical heat, and as I hand him the bottle, I know my nipples are starting to tighten inside my top.

"Think you can behave?" I challenge.

His hands on my back are thrilling, rubbing lotion into my flesh while at the same time kneading my shoulders, lighting up my body, and leaving me glancing around to see if we're alone.

His hands drift lower, to the curve of my spine, and I almost want him to drop below the waistband of my tiny denim shorts to grab ahold of my ass.

"I can behave . . . when I want to," Thomas purrs in my ear, a thumb rubbing up my side and sending a delicious tickle straight to my heart. "But do you *want* me to behave?"

"For . . . for now," I admit, turning around and putting my hands on his chest. "You know this is hard, right?"

"Getting there," he jokes. But when he sees I'm not being salacious, he asks, "How so?"

I hum as I run my fingers through the light hair on his chest. "Because

I want this, but there's a part of me that is still worried. Nobody is saying anything, at least not anymore, but I can see it in their eyes. And I don't want the reputation as the girl who slept her way to the top. I want to earn my spot because I deserved it. Because I do."

"I agree," Thomas says, placing his hands over mine. "Mia, of course work's going to play a role in all this because that's part of who we are—a brilliant analyst and a dashing CEO." He smiles and touches his forehead to mine. "But I do want us to be . . . *us* as well."

It's a good answer, and one that I can respect. "I want us to be us too."

It feels like we both just made a major confession, or perhaps a promise. Our version of one, a vow to not change each other and to accept each other as we are in all our geeky, scary, bossy, analytical ways.

I look up at Thomas through my lashes, taking a deep breath. "So, what do we call this? Izzy said you were my boyfriend, but that just seems so . . . not enough." I'm still analyzing, labeling, and he smiles.

"The name doesn't matter. The feelings do," he declares, wrapping his arms around me. In the shaded privacy of the heavy forest, I lean against his warm body, feeling Thomas's aura envelop me, making me hum in happiness.

"How do you always know just what to say?" I murmur, rubbing my hand over his forearm and biting my lip as I feel his muscles tremble.

"I tell myself that everything in the universe is in balance. For every dark, there's a light. For every luxury, there is a sacrifice. And for every beast . . . there is a princess. And I just say what I think my princess would like to hear."

His words strike me to my very heart, and I look back at him, somehow loving that he called me his princess even though on some level, it pisses me off that I like it because I'm not that girl. But I'm going to take a lesson from Papa's rulebook and let it go and just enjoy the endearment without judging myself. I'm about to press back into his shorts when we hear voices, and we step apart, keeping our hands locked as we keep going. I don't know what trails we're following. I don't care. I just trust in Thomas.

Suddenly, we're headed downhill, and the jungle opens up, revealing another unexpected scene from paradise that seems to dot this island like gems to be discovered, one after another.

I gasp as I look down on the sheltered lagoon below us. We're on the eastern side of island, and the hills below us slope down to a narrow pristine beach.

By some miracle of erosion, the entrance to the lagoon is covered by a natural stone archway, leading to a pool that's not much larger than a small, deep pond . . . but what it lacks in size, it makes up for in utter beauty.

Thomas leads me down the path, his grin audible in his eager breathing. There's a bounce to his step, a joy and lightness to him that I've never seen before. It's another view into the man Thomas could be . . . and the man he is . . . and the man I realize I'm falling for.

Falling? Fallen? It's an analysis I'll have to do later because for now, I'm living in this moment, enjoying this beautiful day with him.

Getting closer to the crystal-clear water, we both freeze, watching fish swim in front of us. The schools of tropical creatures are so colorful, I almost feel like I'm in a pet store or in one of those BBC nature documentaries.

Slowly, we sit down on the sand, just watching until Thomas looks over at me and grins. "Thank you. For giving me a chance."

I lean in, cupping his face as I sense the meaning of so much behind his words that I can't imagine he said lightly. He doesn't have to question, and maybe that's the funny thing. He's spent so much time being this hard-driving neo-Alpha perfectionist that not many want to get close, if he'd even let them.

"Tommy—" I start before a rumble booms overhead, and both of us look up to see storm clouds coming in quickly over the mountains. I curse the sky as the first drops fall. "The Motherland is *not* amused!"

He chuckles, and we get to our feet and I cast a final look at the lagoon, reminding myself that this forest and this beach bore witness to the leap Thomas and I both made today. It feels special, like a secret only we share, and someday, I want to come back here.

We get back on the path and hurry back, the trip up much harder than the one down. The rain hits hard just as we're cresting the hill. The trees help some, but in less than five minutes, both of us are soaked to the skin.

"Well, this is why I said swimsuit!" Thomas says while we take temporary shelter underneath a tree. "How are you doing?"

"I can't see shit!" I complain, pulling my glasses off. "Here, nearsighted is better than blind as a bat. Can you put this in my backpack?" I hand him my frames and turn so he can unzip the bag to slip them inside.

"Here, hand it to me," he says, taking the bag. "The straps are already rubbing you pretty raw."

I look down, seeing the faint red marks, and help him adjust the straps to fit over his broad back. It's actually funny and cute, seeing Thomas's muscular frame carrying a miniature pink backpack.

"I'm so taking a picture when we get back," I tease him, wiping my eyes before pulling my hair back over my shoulder. "You look cute in pink."

"And you look hot in white," Thomas says, his voice full of heat as he looks at my bikini top which might as well be translucent by this point. He pulls me in close and kisses me, but before we can do more, lightning splits the sky and thunderbolts pierce the clouds and crack almost directly over our heads. It's so close that both of us jump, and I can feel the hair on the back of my neck trying to stand up despite the deluge.

"Should we make a run for it?" I ask.

"I think we're safer under cover," Thomas says, and we watch as the path turns to mud before our eyes. We go deeper under the heavily fronded palm tree, letting the leaves create a semi-shelter against the torrent.

And suddenly, we're kissing, ravenous for each other. I don't care that we're outside. I don't care about the rain or my soaked feet. I don't care that the drips coming through the imperfect foliage roof are sending chills down my spine, because Thomas's hands are equally hot, cold and heat blending inside me and sending my heart racing.

Thomas reaches up, rubbing a thumb over my nipple through my soaked bikini top, and I moan, reaching down to cup the huge thick heat of his cock, tugging at the drawstring of his shorts.

"Fuck me," I moan in his ear. "Right here, right now."

"I can't wait to be inside you," he whispers, pinching my nipple before sliding his hands around to cup my ass through my shorts, kneading my cheeks and making me moan louder. "You're mine."

"I'm yours," I whisper, tugging the Velcro fly of his shorts open and wrapping my fingers around the warm girth of his cock. He's huge, masculine, and thick, with the flared mushroom of his head pressing into my fist as I stroke back, making him gasp. "All of me. And right now, you're mine."

I emphasize my point with a swipe of my thumb over his head, collecting the pre-cum there and spreading it down his shaft.

"Always," he groans. "Not now, always."

He pulls me to him, my hand and his cock pressed between us, and he grabs my ass with a punishing grip as I buck my hips into him. His fingers drift toward my rear cleft, and I nod, whimpering when I feel a single digit stroke down my ass and over my hole, thrilling and naughty.

"There?"

"Even there," I promise, pumping his cock with my hand. "Do you want it now?"

Thomas's finger probes, but he withdraws, shaking his head. "Not yet. Turn around."

I nod, letting go of his cock and pressing my shoulder against the tree. I feel his hands on the waistband of my shorts, but out of nowhere, a horn blares.

Thomas pulls back, quickly tucking his cock back in his shorts. "What the fuck?"

"We were worried! Went looking for you!" the voice calls, and out of the rain, a man appears. It's the same resort worker who picked us up from the dock. I think he's probably the only guy besides the owner of the resort who speaks any English, and he's grinning widely while I hurriedly try to hide behind Thomas and unzip my backpack to grab my tank top. Everything's a matted mess, and the first thing I get out is Thomas's shirt, but I don't care. I yank it over my head while Thomas shelters me.

"How'd you find us?" Thomas asks, and the man smiles widely.

"Saw the pink bag in the distance!" he says, and I'm struck with the insane coincidence that I was just about to have sex, outdoors, in the middle of a rainstorm, and it was interrupted because somehow, the guy driving around looking for us saw my bright pink nylon bag hanging from Thomas's back right before he was about to get my shorts down.

Of all the fucking luck.

Thomas gives me a wry smile as we follow the man, and both of us are surprised when we realize how close we were to the main road. At least the heater in the truck is blasting, chasing the chill from my body a little bit.

"We still have the rest of the afternoon," Thomas whispers in my ear. "My room's more private than yours."

And I feel a warmth rush through me that has nothing to do with the truck's heater.

Unfortunately for us, as soon as we step out of the vehicle, Randy's there along with Kenny, who're looking thankful that we're back.

"It's getting nasty out there, Thomas. I'm glad you're safe," Randy says, a hand on her chest. "Uhm, I hate to bring even more bad news, but Randall Towlee's been calling non-stop."

"What the hell does he want?" Thomas asks, confusion marring his face.

"Something about the hospital project, he says it's important that you talk to him immediately."

Thomas turns to me, a regretful twist on his lips. "Looks like work calls."

# CHAPTER 21

## Blackwell

"Your report?"

I don't like talking on the phone. I feel like it's a needless risk, but at times it is needed. I just have to be careful what I say.

I grew up in an era where tapping someone's phone was a simple matter. Anyone could tap a landline with two alligator clips and a headset. Meanwhile, cellphones have gone from bricks the size of my thigh to things barely larger than an old-fashioned cigarette case, and because of that, I distrust the electronic gadgets in an inherent, primal way that cannot be explained away. And with technology comes more and more ways to exploit it for eavesdropping.

But my contact uses them casually, carelessly. I'm not sure if it's a condemnation of the man or the times we live in. Probably both.

"My friend says that he's distracted for sure," my contact says gleefully. "Reports from Japan show that he spent time with *her* every day, sometimes just minutes, other times much longer." The man's disdain for Goldstone's action is obvious. "He's due to come back in two days."

"Here's what I want you to do," I command, leaning back in my black leather club chair and letting my operative know what I need. It's nothing too complicated, mostly taking guts, timing, and a little bit of work . . . nothing he will be unfamiliar with

Of course, what my operative will do with the results . . . ah, now that is the crux of the matter. The simple, beautiful blow to Goldstone's reign over Roseboro.

If discovered, it's at least a firing offense, if not a felony.

And my operative is not exactly someone trained in the methods of the CIA. So the risk is real, but calculated.

But the operative hates the Golden Boy nearly as much as I do . . . and hate makes a man ignore the risks easily. Still, a more prudent man would wonder if I was using him. A truly cautious operative would consider every angle of the possible repercussions, but this man is blind, malleable.

Just the right kind of operative.

"Sir, no offense, but this could be dangerous. There's no way I'll be able to hide my presence on the security cameras if someone suspects and checks."

Not stupid . . . just malleable. "But you are capable of forging the time and date stamps on your work, correct?"

"Of course, sir. If anyone even checks."

I can feel his hesitation, even through the buzzing line.

"Remember, the prize is often left unclaimed because victory favors those willing to take the risks to grasp it." I pause, letting the words sink in until they're pregnant, roiling in this man's brain, festering until they're a pimple ready to burst. Only then do I squeeze. "So, what kind of man are you?"

The release is immediate, poisonous, and just what I desire. "I'll call you when the job is done."

# CHAPTER 22

## Mia

"**G**OOD JOB, EVERYONE," THOMAS SAYS AS THE TEAM GETS OUT OF the van in Tokyo, and I notice it in the way they're acting. They're not sure what to make of a smiling Thomas. And because of that, they don't trust it and are waiting for the other shoe to drop.

On the island, we all sort of relaxed. Now, they're more professional, but Thomas is probably more jovial than they've ever seen before.

Kenny glances at me while Randy gives me an appraising look. She grins, and so fast I think I might've been seeing things, she flashes me a thumbs-up and grins before schooling her face back to neutral.

"Enjoy your flight," Thomas offers. "Considering you're getting empty seats next to you, you should be very relaxed for our meeting on Tuesday."

Kenny pales a little, and his and Randy's eyes meet. Thomas might be relaxing, but he isn't *that* relaxed. "Of course, Mr. Goldstone."

When they're all loaded up, I look at Thomas, half in shock and half in amazement. He turns, giving me a raised eyebrow.

"What?"

"What?" I reply, smirking. "Tommy, you have to notice that you're acting . . . *strange.*"

To say I'd been shocked when he'd suggested that we stay back for an extra two days of pure vacation time on our own would be an understatement. Actually, I'd laughingly asked if he'd ever been on vacation and he'd thoughtfully said no. That he wanted to do this with me was somehow . . . everything. And more than I could've dreamed.

Thomas shrugs, reaching out for my hand. "Maybe I've learned a thing or two from you. Or maybe you just make me happy. And guess what? From now until we get on the plane back to SeaTac the day after tomorrow, I'm yours. You'll have to show me how to 'vay-cay-shun' because I'm not sure I know how."

I laugh at his childlike sounding out of the word. "You may come to regret that," I joke as we head toward the train station. I already told Thomas that if I'm going to do Tokyo, I'm going to do it the right way. Forget taking taxis around everywhere. I want to experience the real thing—the subways, the trains, everything.

The hard part is that there's so much I want to do, but my inner geek knows there's one place I want to go first.

"So . . . what do you know about Japanese pop culture?" I ask as we buy our tickets at the little electronic machine. "Ever watched anime or listened to the music?"

"I've looked up some of the bands you've mentioned," Thomas says, warming me with his first answer. "I actually found one to add into my workout mix. Don't ask me what it was, but I liked it."

I clasp my hands to my chin, batting my lashes melodramatically behind my lenses, cooing. "You know just what to say to make my heart go pitter-pat. I'll make a nerd out of you yet."

His face lights up, and for the entire forty-five minutes it takes us to make our way to our destination, I do my best to make him smile again and again. I do it because this is the Thomas that I think nobody else in the world gets to see. Just for me. Mine.

It's not his professional smile, roguishly charming or great-white threatening, depending on the need. It's not his ironic smirk or his amused half-smile. This is the full-on, blindingly beautiful teeth and secret dimple that I adore smile.

That's the smile I want, the smile I keep getting from him, and with every flash of it, I find myself falling deeper and deeper for him.

Yep . . . *falling.*

But somewhere in the middle of that rainstorm on the island, as we slogged through impenetrable curtains of rain and I was miserably wet, I knew I wouldn't trade it for anything else in the world. I wanted to be with him, and I knew I'd fallen.

But I just keep falling, more and more, deeper and deeper.

I'm not just going to date him. I'm not just going to explore what it's like being 'his' or letting him fuck me three ways from Sunday and seeing if I can crawl out of bed the next day or if all my bones are still jelly.

There are still a lot of things we don't know about each other, and those unknown things could sink us like the Titanic meeting an iceberg, minus Celine Dion. But I'm climbing on this ship willingly and excitedly, ready to take the trip with him wherever it may go, even if we sink to the bottom of the Atlantic Ocean. As long as it's with him.

"What's on your mind?" Thomas asks as I smile secretly to myself. "You look like the cat who just got the cream."

I chuckle and kiss him on the cheek. "I feel like the girl who just got the fairy tale. Girls like me, it takes a lot to get underneath all the layers to our emotions."

"But what I've found underneath is worth the searching," Thomas replies, pushing a lock of hair behind my ear and cupping my face.

My heart leaps with joy, and as we make our way off the train, I announce, "Welcome to the Mecca of All Things Geeky," I tell him. "Akihabara!"

"Wait . . . Akihabara . . . you mean that group you were teasing me about?" Thomas asks, and I nod. "You're serious."

"AKB 48 . . . Akihabara 48," I explain to him as we walk. There's music, lights, noise, and neon everywhere, even here in the middle of the day. "This area's known as Electric Town, and it's the pulsing, nerdy, slightly pervy heart of all things anime, manga, and video games in Japan. If you've seen a Japanese game, if you've listened to a Japanese song, if you've seen an Internet meme about weird shit in Japan . . . nine out of ten chance it came from here."

We see it all. Thomas shocks me as right out of the gate, he asks to stop at the first store he sees. Thankfully, it's on my checklist too, and we go into the famous Don Quijote discount store. We fight our way through the crowd, laughing at the crazy wildness as a whole gaggle of teens sing and dance to the video playing on the huge screen.

"What are you doing?" I ask, laughing as he holds up his phone and snaps a photo of me in front of some plush figures from *Naruto*. "I'm a mess."

"You're the most beautiful woman I've ever seen," he reminds me, snapping another pic. And then he flips it around and takes a shot of the two of us together.

We both admit that the crowds are a bit much after a few more minutes, and the incessant jingle playing through the speakers is more than our American ears are ready for.

Everywhere we turn, it's another advertisement, another crush of people, another speaker screaming for attention or lights flashing or . . . "I swear, shopping in this place is like going through Vegas!"

Thomas laughs. "Vegas on New Year's Eve!"

We move on, out into the slightly quieter streets, and Thomas is great. He listens as I explain my love of anime and manga in the stacks of a used bookstore, watching me hunt down treasure after treasure.

He insists on buying them, but I refuse, explaining to him that it's not the books that are important to me but the stories themselves.

"So why not keep them as collector's items?"

"Mr. Efficiency is telling me to pick up collector's items?" I ask as I pluck the *Eureka Seven* DVD out of his hands and put it back on the shelf. "Tommy, first, I have this entire series downloaded onto a flash drive back home in full HD. Second, I don't speak Japanese, and these don't come subtitled. While the purists will say that there's nothing like listening to it in the original Japanese and going with subs if you need them, that doesn't mean I need them like this. I just want to see them, hold them for a minute." I pause to see if he understands my weird logic, and when he shrugs, I tell him, "Besides . . . you're buying lunch."

"Lunch? Where?"

I grin, knowing exactly the type of place I want to take him to . . . if I can find it. "Come on, you're gonna flip over this one."

Twenty minutes later, we're seated in a cafe while a girl in a French maid's uniform takes our order, her obscenely short skirt barely covering her ass as she giggles and gives us both looks while flirting shyly with Thomas the whole time. As soon as she walks away, though, he rolls his eyes.

"I've said it a dozen times today . . . this place is nuts."

I look around the cafe, which does its best to mimic an old-fashioned French chalet while still keeping to modern architecture, and nod. "Yeah . . . but it's a bucket list thing. Don't you have a few items on your bucket list?"

"Sure," Thomas acknowledges as he sips his water. "I'd like to learn how to fly a helicopter, I'd like to go hiking in the Rockies sometime, and I'd like . . . never mind." I swear he's blushing a bit as he dismisses whatever dream crossed his mind.

I reach across the small table, taking his hand. "It's okay. You can tell me, you know."

"I'd like to start a school . . . or a scholarship," he says quietly. "For kids . . . give something back to them."

His words shock me at first. It seems so unlike the staunch businessman who chases profits and annual reports. But as they sink in, I realize that this dream is more *him* than anything inside the big gold building back in Roseboro. And I love that he shared it with me, letting me in deeper, closer to the root of his soul. "Then do it," I tell him, smiling. "If you want, we can even do it together. Well, not the scholarship thing. I'm pretty sure any scholarship I can fund wouldn't even be able to pay for textbooks. But I can help in other ways, research and stuff."

"You'd do that?" he asks, surprise widening his eyes.

"Hell, yeah. I'd also hike those Rockies with you and climb in the helicopter with you. I'm afraid to say, you might be a little stuck with me, Tommy."

Thomas swallows and smiles bravely. "Even if I crash and burn?"

I feel like he's not talking about a rough landing in the helicopter he doesn't know how to fly, but something more abstract. But I keep the metaphor going.

"I've never, in my entire life, known someone who has a smaller chance of crashing and burning than you do. I think . . . I think if the blades came off the rotor and it was falling to the ground, you'd keep that helicopter up by the sheer force of your will, if necessary. I trust you that much."

Thomas flushes and nods even as his face pinches a little. I wonder what inner demons are whispering in his ear but don't push. He's letting me in bit by bit, even as he's gushing to support me. And I want to give him time, to trust me and to want to share his story with me. It's his past to reveal whenever he's ready, and I'll accept that as long as he's making his present and future with me.

After lunch is over, we continue exploring, working the back streets just as much as the main drag of 'Electric Town.'

We visit a small shrine, elegant wood and water nestled in between two large shops that somehow seem to be in their own quiet little sub-universe.

We poke around in 'recycle shops' that are filled to overflowing with used computer parts, haggling with shopkeepers over prices on stuff I don't really want or need.

But mainly, we do a lot of people watching.

We see people in Super Mario costumes whizzing down the streets in go karts while anime ninjas patrol the sidewalks, magicians do tricks, and guitarists are somehow trying to make themselves heard over everything in between.

"Oh . . . my . . . GOD!" I scream at one point, totally fangirling out as I see a poster hung on a wall. "They made a new movie?"

"A new movie of what?" Thomas asks as I grab his hand and drag him over. It's even better than I could have imagined. "Mia—"

"*Sailor Moon*!" I yell over the throngs of people gathered around an outdoor screen. "It's the new movie!"

Thomas obviously doesn't get it, but he's smart, and as I join in with the dancing crowd, yelling excitedly, he joins in. I wish I had it on video because the image of a man built like Thomas in the midst of all this and jumping around with me has to be a sight.

Afterward, the noise quiets a little and he pulls me aside.

"Sailor what?" he asks.

"*Sailor Moon*," I repeat. "It was . . . I guess it still is my favorite anime. When I was a teenager, I was really struggling with some body image issues, some other stuff. For the first time, I sort of missed my mother. Well, not *my* mother, but having *a* mother, know what I mean? Puberty had hit, and Papa, for all his love, wasn't quite sure how to handle his little girl becoming a young woman."

"So, how does that relate to the show?" Thomas asks, leading me toward a cafe. This one's a cosplay cafe, and ironically, our server is dressed as none other than Sailor Moon herself. As we sip our cream sodas, I give him the down and dirty about the show, and he listens intently the whole time.

"So in the end," he says, stroking his chin, "the girls transform from normal girls into these . . . Sailors, go kick ass, take names, and look good while doing it?"

"There's more than that. There's a lot of interpersonal stuff, relationships, all of that," I admit. "I mean, it was like, ninety episodes or something that I've chunked down to five minutes here. But it was *so* cool and made me feel like I could handle things too."

Thomas smiles, chuckling. "I get that by how you talk about it. So what's this about cosplay?"

"Getting dressed up like the characters," I say, pulling out my phone and showing him some pictures. "I know it sounds stupid, but we could . . ."

"We?" Thomas asks, lifting an eyebrow. "I hope you mean the guy in the tuxedo."

"Of course, although I'm sure we can find a costume your size in this part of town," I joke. "You'd make a *great* Sailor Pluto."

"Ha-ha." Thomas looks at the picture, then at me, his eyes gleaming and his voice low. "This isn't something you can wear in the office."

"No," I purr, leaning in, "but maybe in our hotel room? You did make a reservation tonight, right?"

"You'll see. Fine . . . but you're going to owe me for this," he says, pointing at a picture of a rather slutty version of a Sailor Moon costume.

We go to a few shops, but eventually, I find what I want, even if it does cost more than I'd ever spent on a costume. But Thomas sees my eyes light up as I try it on.

"Thomas, this—"

"Looks great on you," he says, his voice husky with desire. "And at least you don't need the wig."

It feels strange, walking around for the next two hours while the shop makes the adjustments to my costume with the promise that it'll be delivered to our hotel. Thomas doesn't even reveal what hotel that is to me, merely humming, a twinkle in his eye that leaves me wondering just how in charge I am of our little jaunt through Tokyo, even if it is more my bucket list than his.

I don't care. I'm having fun and enjoying time with Thomas as we watch the sun go down and the lights of Electric Town really light up.

"This place," Thomas says, watching the hustle and bustle that never stops, "it's special. It's weird, it's unique . . . but I like it."

"It's been fun," I admit, holding his arm, "and thank you. This was near the top of my bucket list and has been the best day I could have imagined."

"It's not over yet," Thomas promises me. We flag a taxi to get to our hotel, and as we pull up in front of the Ritz-Carlton, he holds my hand. "My lady."

*My lady.* I do *feel* like his lady, and as we check in, I look forward to being his even more.

Our suite is luxurious, looking out over the city lights, and as soon as the bellhop leaves, I turn to Thomas, my eyes brimming with tears. "Tommy, all of this, I—"

He takes me in his arms, holding me close as he brushes my hair back and shakes his head softly. "I'm doing this because I want to," he murmurs, touching his forehead to mine. "I'm not a good man, Mia. So I'm doing this for selfish reasons. Because seeing you happy makes me happy. Because I savor your happiness."

"Then . . . how can I make you happy?" I whisper, hugging him. "Because I want to see your happiness too. I think I have here lately, but I don't want it to end when we leave."

Thomas crushes me in his grip, and I wrap my arms around him. There's no passion, that'll be for later, but instead the comfort and closeness of our burgeoning relationship.

Forget titles. Forget boyfriend, girlfriend, Mia, Tommy . . . forget all of it.

Instead, I give myself to him in this hug, in the closeness of our bodies, and he gives it back to me just as much, two separate souls slowly growing together.

When we step back, I can see it in his eyes too . . . or maybe it's always been there and we're just seeing it for the first time. I think he's about to say those three little words, but he swallows and says, "I'll call room service if you want to get settled in."

I'm not disappointed he didn't say it. I can feel it, and I know we'll get there and are in fact making progress. The thought warms me. "I'm going to rinse off. After you order, why don't you put on that mask you bought when you thought I wasn't looking?"

Thomas grins at being caught and nods. I sashay away, going into the huge bathroom where I strip and give myself a quick wash. I don't want to get my hair wet, so I just spray off the city smell I've soaked up.

I want to transform for him.

My costume's hanging on the back of the bathroom door, and as I take it out, I feel my body responding. I can't believe I'm doing this, but I am.

I skip the bloomers to put on the short blue skirt, the shiny satin whispering against my thighs and ass and making me hum in desire.

Looking into the mirror, I can see my nipples tightening, and if Thomas came in right now, I'd let him have his way . . . but instead, with shaking hands, I get my hair pulled up into the iconic twin curled ponytails with tiara. It's not quite long enough to match the character, but I don't care. I love it, and I do a quick touch-up to my makeup before pulling on the top.

The tailors made it so I don't have to wear anything underneath, and the silk lining tingles against my naked skin, my pussy clenching lightly as I tuck the zipper tab underneath the red bow on my chest.

Last are the boots, knee-high red heels that cling to my calves, followed by the white elbow-length gloves with their red cuffs. Looking in the mirror, the only thing different from my anime fantasy are my glasses, and I slip them off, marveling at myself.

It's hard to hold myself back from going out there, but I force myself to wait until I hear Thomas sign for the room service and for the server to leave. Thomas gives me another few minutes, then clears his throat.

"Mia?"

"Are you ready?" I ask quietly, my heart in my throat. I feel sexy, I feel powerful, but I'm also so vulnerable right now. This character, what she helped me with when I was an awkward teen . . . this isn't play to me.

Thomas hears me, though, and I hear him moving around on the other side of the door, and a switch flips. "I'm ready."

Swallowing my worries, I open the door, my breath immediately taken away as I see what he's done. The room's filled with candles, at least two dozen golden lights around the room turning the suite into a romantic chamber.

Even more impressive is Thomas. His tuxedo isn't quite perfect. It's a modern style instead of the cape and tails from the anime, but considering he's pulled this off somehow on the sly while I was getting fitted and adjusted, it's amazing. And his mask is textbook perfect, the red carnation on his lapel iconic. He's even got a top hat in his hands. He looks me over, bowing when he sees me.

"Fucking beautiful."

I thought I was turned on before, but watching him as he adjusts his mask and holds out a hand fans the flames inside me. I cross the room to him, putting my arms around his neck and kissing him, chuckling as for the first time, I'm the one who has to adjust to the other person wearing something on their face.

"This means so much to me," I whisper.

"You mean so much to me," Thomas replies, gasping as I reach down and grasp the clasp on his tuxedo pants. "What about dinner?"

"Later," I promise, slowly lowering myself to my knees and opening his pants.

Like me, he's not wearing any underwear, and his cock emerges from the black zipper already hardening as I wrap my lips around his shaft and start to suck.

I'm no blowjob queen . . . in fact, I'd refer to myself as a relative newbie. But the feeling of Thomas's cock sliding over my tongue and lips as I look up into his eyes is pure molten heat. He tastes like a man, feral and powerful, satiny skin over a steel core that pulses when I pull back.

I swallow him again and again, moaning when his cock gives me a delicious bead of precum that I suck down greedily. I hum around the head of his cock, making him growl, and I realize that *I'm* in charge.

I bob up and down on his cock, and my pussy quivers, arousal dripping down my inner thigh. I want to touch myself, but I'm in total control here, and Thomas is what I'm devoting myself to.

"Oh, fuck," Thomas moans, gripping one of my ponytails but letting me control the speed. "That feels so good. Suck that fucking dick."

I look up at him, swallowing him as I seal my lips around his shaft, my hand and my mouth working together as I speed up. He moans, his hips taking over some and thrusting in and out of my eager mouth, both of us giving to each other as I worship his masculinity while he abandons himself to me.

I'm guided by his sighs, the deep throaty rumbles in his chest as he's pushed higher and higher. I can tell he's trying to hold out and enjoy the experience even as I push him to give me all he has. I feel him swell, his breath catching in his throat before he groans deeply and the first splash of his salty, tangy cum hits my tongue.

I love it.

It's just like Thomas, unique and manly, thick and creamy that pulses out of him to fill my mouth until I'm straining to hold it all in.

I don't let a drop out, though, instead pulling back to show him the naughty, sexy sight of my cum-filled mouth before I swallow, licking my lips and moaning as my pussy clenches beneath my skirt.

"Fuck," Thomas says, pulling me to my feet and carrying me in his arms to the bed. He sets me down, and I get onto my hands and knees, bending over to let him see my gleaming sex while he strips out of his pants and shoes, leaving him in just his open tuxedo shirt, jacket . . . and mask. He climbs on the bed behind me, his voice dripping with fresh desire. "So damn gorgeous, Mia. Look at this pretty pussy dripping wet from sucking my cock. Delicious."

I can't see him. My skirt is hanging down, blocking my full vision, but I can feel his breath on my pussy and his hands on my ass, rubbing softly and making my hips squirm in time to some silent music going on in his head.

"I'm only going to say this once," Thomas says, "and maybe I'm a coward for not being able to say it to your face. But when we started this, I didn't know what came over me. I just wanted to fuck you, I'll admit. But that's changed. My life's never going to be the same. It's all changed since I met you."

I don't have a chance to reply before his tongue invades me, knowingly finding every spot that has me burying my face in the bedspread and my hands balling up, moaning.

"Tommy . . . oh, Tommy, yes . . ."

He doesn't stop, his hands massaging my ass while his mouth voraciously consumes my pussy from behind, sucking and slobbering and licking until I wantonly shove my ass in his face, desperate for release. He reaches his tongue out further and strokes my clit, just once, and I explode, coming hard while his mouth sucks my juices out, kissing my lower lips in a deep, naughty open-mouthed Frenching that has me shaking, crying out.

I collapse into the bedspread, but a jolt galvanizes my spine when I feel his tongue trace up, leaving my pussy to tickle the space in between before he pulls back, his thumbs spreading my cheeks as he blows warm breath over my ass.

"You said this is mine," he says, his voice low and the breath warm on my tight hole. "Is it?"

"Yes," I rasp, breathless after just coming. "It's . . . only yours."

"On the right night, I'll claim it," he promises me, and a wave of such utter devotion floods me as I realize he's heard what I meant to say but didn't.

I've never imagined someone licking my asshole, but when Thomas does, my eyes roll up into my skull. It's amazing, it's wonderful . . . it's the whole fucking thesaurus squeezed into a single sensation and sent from my most private of places to explode in my brain.

I'm giving him my most tender, private place, and he's feasting on me, taking it and telling me with every wide lick, every probing press of a stiffened tip against my ring of muscle, every soft suck, that he's going to do his best to take care of me. It's what makes me open up to him, and I let out a cry of joy, release, devotion, and desire.

It builds me, it stokes my need, and as he darts deeper into me, it's almost like the sensations hit my pussy before exploding in my chest . . . in my heart.

"Tommy . . . I need you," I beg, and he pulls back, his cock ready and stiff again. For a moment, I think he's going to take my ass despite his words, but instead, he plunges deep into my pussy, filling me and making my joy complete.

Complete.

I'm complete when I'm with him like this, woman and man joined together, bodies locked in an embrace of passion and desire. His hands are on my hips, my skirt fisted, as he pumps in and out of me deep and hard, and I push back into him, meeting him as we build to a new peak, higher than we've ever gone before.

Lovemaking . . . not fucking. No, there's a time to fuck, but what we do is different. It's hard and soft, sweat and breath and blood and soul mixing together, delivered by way of cock stretching pussy and pussy gripping cock, electricity crackling through us.

It's pure.

It's honest.

It's beautiful.

My climax starts from somewhere inside me that I didn't even know existed, cascading over itself and sweeping away all other thoughts.

I know Thomas comes too. I can hear him cry out, and this time it's different than ever before. Before, when I've come, everything fades away except the pleasure.

This is different. In an instant, I feel like I truly am superpowered. I see everything, I hear everything, I smell and touch . . . everything. More than that, I can feel Thomas's thoughts, I can feel his heart and his soul, I can feel his pleasure as he gives to me.

It's a moment that I will cherish forever.

# CHAPTER 23

## Thomas

"YOU REALLY WANT TO DO THIS?" I ask MIA AS WE CLIMB OUT OF the shuttle bus. We've sent everything to the airport except for our passports, phones, and wallets. Our flight's the last one out of Tokyo and we won't need anything else.

"Absolutely sure," Mia says, seemingly totally refreshed after yesterday's long shopping trip and the passionate costumed encounter that led to us eating room service in bed.

My mask was ruined after I ate Mia out and she gushed on my face . . . but I can't imagine a better souvenir than the slightly stained fabric that I tucked into my suitcase this morning.

We approach the ticket gate, and I reach into my pocket and pull out my wallet. Inside is a simple black card, and if you don't look closely, you wouldn't notice the Mickey Mouse ears embossed faintly in the plastic.

"May I help you?" the park attendant asks, her eyes widening as she sees my card. "Yes, sir!"

I let Mia stammer in surprise as we're whisked through the normal gates, a simple signature on my part getting her free access to everything, and suddenly, we're inside the park, although in a part not many people are familiar with. Finally, she can't take it any longer.

"What was that? Are you CIA or something?"

"Close . . . Club 33," I reply, showing her my membership card. "It's sort of Disney's VIP club."

"I didn't know you liked Disney that much."

There are so many questions in her eyes, and I'm on the verge of telling her why I have this card, but now's not the time.

I clear my throat, thinking back with a smile. "I . . . it's a long story. So, where do we start?"

We end up starting with Splash Mountain, skipping the already eighty-minute line to climb right into the front of a log after only five minutes of walking, and as we go over the falls, it sets the tone for the day.

Again, we do a lot of people watching, and as we do, I notice the differences between Anaheim Disneyland and Tokyo Disneyland.

"Is that ten or eleven Snow Whites?" I ask Mia as we walk past It's A Small World while munching on some strawberry flavored popcorn.

"I stopped counting anything after fifteen Elsas," Mia says, giggling as a trio of princesses goes running by. "And I thought we enjoyed dressing up last night."

"I doubt we could do that here," I remind her with a chuckle. "Wrong genre, remember?"

We hit everything. The Mountain Trio, Splash, Space, and Big Thunder. Star Tours. Pooh's Hunny Hunt. In each ride, we get to skip lines, going all the way to the front, even passing up the Fast Pass people to just walk onto a ride. All it takes is flashing the small rubberized wrist bands that we're wearing, and we're able to take the entire park at our own pace.

Even better are some of the 'extras' involved. "This is so cool," Mia says as we walk through the VIP entrance to the Haunted Mansion. "It's like a whole new ride!"

I agree. In the VIP section, the pictures move, the paintings are a little creepier in a fun way, and even the music's different. It doesn't take away from the ride but adds to it, like we're getting the full attraction.

"Each park's a little different in the VIP areas," I whisper to her as we leave the Haunted Mansion. "I remember . . ." I start and then stop myself before exposing too much.

Mia hears it in my voice, and her smile dims. "Remember what?" She says it casually, not prying but just inviting me to share with her.

I shake my head, forcing a smile even as I see another group of happy children and teenagers go by, a knife suddenly jabbing in my heart as a father and son walk by holding hands and laughing. A pang of hurt washes through me, the little boy in my heart wishing for a moment that it had been my life. But wishes don't always come true. Even at the happiest place on Earth.

"Nothing. It's a long story and for another time."

It's not exactly a lie. It is a long story, and I redirect while I can. "Come on . . . I'm hungry. Let's get something to eat."

The Blue Bayou cafe, just across the water from the start of Pirates of the Caribbean, is quiet and refreshingly cool after the muggy Tokyo afternoon. Sitting down, Mia waits until after the waiter's come and taken our orders before reaching across and taking my hand.

"Hey," she prompts, and I know what's coming. She's not letting me off the hook that easily, but she doesn't force the issue, just asks, "You okay?"

"Sorry," I whisper, my eyes drifting to another happy family in the middle of the restaurant. "I shouldn't have come here."

"Why not?" she asks, giving my fingers a squeeze. "I mean, yeah, it was kinda strange to listen to Davy Jones in Japanese, but it didn't really take away from the ride."

I can tell Mia has a feeling there's something more going on and is trying to lighten the mood and give me time to corral my thoughts.

"Not that," I admit, taking a deep breath. Yesterday, I could see the nervousness in her eyes when she shared her childlike things with me, but she did it anyway. Now, I'm almost trembling like a leaf, frightened shitless. "I guess this might be the happiest place on Earth, but I never got to go even though it was something I always wanted as a kid."

"Dad?"

*The house is pretty quiet, but I've gotten used to that. Since Mom died, Dad never really turns on the TV much . . . when he comes home at all.*

"I'm in here."

*I enter the dining room, or at least that's what it used to be. Dad had the furniture all taken out. Now it's his home office. With Mom gone, he can't travel for his work as much as he used to. He's still a member of his 'firm' where he's a lawyer, but his career's supposedly stalled. At least that's what he says when he talks at me.*

*Not to me.*

*At me.*

"Dad, I got my report card."

*He turns around in his chair, his face pinched and his eyes already flinty as he holds out a hand silently for the card. I'd like to lie to him, but he knows the school calendar pretty well . . . and I have to bring it back by Friday with his signature.*

*I fidget from side to side, my shoes squeaking on the hardwood flooring, wishing I could evaporate as he reads off the grades. "Math . . . A minus. English . . . A. Social Studies . . . A. Physical Education . . . A plus. Science . . . B plus."*

*I can see it in his eyes, and I try not to panic as he folds the report card and puts it back in its cardboard envelope. "I—"*

*"Pathetic," he says, staring at me. "I provide for you, and the best you can fucking do is a B-plus in Science and an A-minus in Math."*

*"I screwed up one test, that's all. I'd just—"*

*"So stupid, that's what you are," he sneers, getting out of his chair. The quiet label hurts more than what comes next as he gets louder and louder. "I should beat your spoiled rotten ass raw! Maybe you'd learn your lesson then! Such a disappointment!"*

*His hand raises, but before he can strike, I retreat to my bedroom like usual and go to my special hiding place, feeling at least a little secure. But I heard his words as I scurried out, and they echo in my head, even as I put my hands over my ears trying to drown them out. "Run away, just like you did while she died."*

I sigh, coming out of the past to see Mia's stunned face. A part of me wants to clamp my mouth shut, keep it bottled up the way I always have, but it's like I've been uncorked and I keep going.

*"And Thomas Goldstone for the touchdown!"*

*My chest's heaving, but after having run ninety-five yards in the fourth quarter of what's been a high-scoring game, I think I'm allowed to be a little gassed. My teammates are all excited. With this touchdown, we've put the game out of reach for Westwood, and those cocksuckers are our biggest rivals. They knocked us out of the playoffs last year, and this year we're going to be the ones dancing on the fifty-yard line while they go home to listen to the state championship on the radio.*

*Still, as I jog back toward the sidelines, I scan the bleachers for what's probably the hundredth time tonight, and the thousandth time this year, even though I know it's pointless. Because in all of the eight thousand screaming, cheering faces, I know the one person I want to be here most isn't.*

"He never went to a single game?" Mia asks, and I shake my head. "Why?"

"He never thought I was good enough. I'd absorbed it and had gotten used to it by then. Honestly, if he'd come, he probably would've just told me what I'd done wrong and made it worse. But there was that little boy inside who still dreamed I'd look up and see him in the stands, smiling and proud, you know? I still feel it even today. That desire to finally impress him, but the practical side that never wants to see him again. Does that make me awful?"

"Of course not! Why?" Mia asks, horrified. "Why did he do that to you? That's so horrible, Thomas. I'm so sorry." Her words tumble out, but before I can answer, she pulls me in for a hug, her arms wrapping around me and taking the edge off the atrocities I've told her.

Pulling back, she looks me in the eye, cupping my jaw. "And why do you still put yourself through it? He's not worth it."

"Because of my mother," I reply before I can stop myself, telling Mia my deepest, darkest shame. She listens intently as I tell her the memory, our food forgotten. In the end, I have to choke out the last few words. "So that's what happened. I watched cartoons while my mother died from a drug overdose. I let her die, and he blames me for it." I've never actually said those words aloud.

I wait for her judgement, her criticism, her horror at what I did. I wait for her to pull away from me once she sees the truth of what a monster I am. And I try to prepare for it, but there's no way to be ready for your heart to be ripped from your body. And that's what she will do if she scorns me now. She holds my heart, my soul, my future in her hands as I hold my breath.

"And you internalized that and are always trying to make up for it," Mia says like she just figured something out about me, and I nod. She looks at me, and there isn't disgust in her eyes, nor pity. Instead, there's just . . . something I'm not ready to name yet.

"I try to break the cycle, but I always get sucked back in. Eventually, I decided if I couldn't be perfect enough to get his love, I could damn sure be perfect enough to make sure he couldn't ignore me anymore," I admit, thinking back to those days as well.

"The day I left for Stanford, he never even said goodbye. I didn't care, or at least that's what I told myself. I went to college, got my degree while using my extra scholarship money to invest, multiplied it, and when I graduated early, I went to him with the plan for my company."

"Why'd you go to him?" Mia asks. "I mean, did you think he'd be happy for you?"

I shake my head, sighing. "No, I knew I was giving him a noose to hang me with, but I was still too young for a bank to back me and I was desperate. So I worked a deal with him. He gave me a loan, and I gave him shares of the company and signed away my inheritance. I took that money and what I'd saved up myself from my successful investments . . . and in three years, I turned it into twelve million. From there . . . well, now you work in my building."

"Which I happen to enjoy, by the way."

I nod, watching as a boat full of a laughing family goes by, making me sad at what I didn't have. "Somewhere along the way, I realized that he was never going to forgive me."

She tries to interrupt me, but I shake my head. "I know, there's nothing to be forgiven for. I was just a kid. But the narrative's been written in my head over and over. So when I realized he was never going to forgive me, was always going to try to keep me down, I decided to stop making my success about him. I work my ass off, push myself harder than even he would to be my best, and I do a damn good job running my company. Not because of him, but in spite of him. And that eats the shit out of him."

I grin, and I know it's tinged with spite, but I can't help it. There's too much history, too much ugliness for it to be anything but a vindictive victory.

Mia reaches over and squeezes my hand. "You're a good man, Thomas. Regardless of what your father thinks, you were not responsible for your mother. And even with a lifetime of his beating you down, you rose. Because deep down in your core where it matters, you're a good man. And I see that."

Her words heal something inside me I thought was a never-ending gaping wound. I memorize the words, wanting them to battle back against the voice in my head when it inevitably returns with snide insults. With her acceptance, her acknowledgement of the side of me only she sees, I feel stronger, better than I have in . . . *ever*. It's comfortable and uncomfortable at the same time, to be so exposed, so seen.

"I think you're the only person who thinks I'm a good man. Most folks would describe me as a monster, an asshole. Oh, a Ruthless Bastard," I say, quipping with the name I know is muttered around the office to describe me. I let it slide, and besides, the reputation helps with making sure people do their best work.

Mia smiles brightly and winks. "Well, that's because you like to put on that mask. But I happen to think you're best without it."

I let the lighter mood wash through me, reveling in the fact that she's not running and screaming from my baggage like I expected. In fact, as she snuggles into my arms, she seems almost relieved that I finally spilled. Shockingly, I am too. Though I hate that she had to hear all that about me, the weight on my shoulders is lessened from the sharing.

I lean down, whispering hotly in her ear, "You didn't mind the mask last night."

She giggles, and I let the sound brighten my soul. And then she looks up at me. "I'm truly sorry you went through all that. Can I ask you a question?"

Without hesitation, I say, "Yes, anything." And I almost mean it.

She bites her lip. "With a shitty childhood like that, how'd you end up knowing so much about Disneyland? Why'd you get that fancy VIP card? Isn't coming here like poking at the bruise from your childhood?"

She's a smart one, I'll give her that.

"That's a story for another day. But suffice it to say that I've been to Anaheim Disney more than a few times, and once to Orlando. Club 33 is just one of the perks of being me." It's almost the truth. After all, Tom Nicholson doesn't have a card, though he's the one who takes kids on a dream daytrip, but Thomas Goldstone is the one with the black card in his wallet. Funny thing is, they're feeling more like one and the same with every healing moment with Mia.

She nods, letting me keep that story, and we're quiet for a moment. It feels like I just ran the most important touchdown of my life, celebrated on the field with the guys, and now I'm blessedly alone in the locker room, replaying and letting the joy wash through me. Except this isn't a game, and I'm not alone. This thing with Mia is real, and it's everything.

Her voice is muffled by my chest, but I hear her anyway. "Do you worry about being perfect, about proving something to your dad, about your past when you're with me?"

I sigh, not taking the question lightly because I can hear that she didn't ask it carelessly. "With you? No, when I'm with you, I just . . . am. I feel . . . free."

I can feel her cheek move against my chest, the smile against my heart warming me. "Good, because I want you to spend your time with me smiling, relaxing, and having fun. I want the real you, the one you hide, the one you don't let anyone else see. Just me. Mine."

I tip her chin up with my fingers, looking into those gorgeous blue eyes. "And you're mine." Our gazes lock, and though we've said so much, there is more left unspoken in the blue seas of her eyes. I kiss her softly and then whisper, "If I'm yours, what are you going to do with me?"

I expect her to say something flirty back. Most women would take full advantage of an opening like that. Mia, of course, is not most women. And somehow, I'm surprised, but not really, when she pops up and grabs my hand.

Her eyes light up with childlike joy. "We're gonna make Disney our bitch! Let's ride, Tommy!"

And though a part of me would like nothing better than for her to ride me, she knows on some cellular level that this is what I need. A day in the park, innocent wonder at every turn, an experience I should've had many years ago but one that she can give me today.

# CHAPTER 24

## Mia

I GLANCE UP FROM COMPUTER, MY MOUTH FREEZING WIDE-OPEN AS I sing Rammstein's big hit *Du Hast*. It's German, not Russian, but the repetitive nature of the chorus means just about anyone can sing it. Though judging by the barely suppressed laugh on Thomas's face, he's not going to join me in the next round.

I curse in Russian, mixing up all my languages when I tell him, "Shit! You scared me!"

He laughs. "I thought it was just a crazy rumor, you know, like fables they tell the new hires. *Beware the psycho in the basement!*" His voice has a mumbo-jumbo, woo-woo waver to it. "But it's actually true, and it really is you."

I roll my eyes, laughing. "Well, yeah. Have to keep up my street cred so everyone leaves me alone to crunch my numbers."

It's still a bit weird to have the big boss coming all the way down to my basement office, but I like seeing him here, in my space. I suspect he likes the escape just as much as I do. He looks around at the spartan space, taken up mostly by my desk and multiple monitors. But there are several pops of color in the framed posters on the wall.

With a grin, I lift my chin toward my latest acquisition. "Like it?"

Thomas touches the frame gently with one fingertip, a soft smile spreading his face. "Sailor Moon? Any particular reason?" His words are laced with memories.

"Got to see the latest movie in Japan. Did a little cosplay. The poster reminds me of good times," I say, the flashes just as fresh in my mind.

He looks at me. "I came down to ask you to lunch. But now I'm thinking of something a little sooner." He glances at the hall outside my door. "Does your office lock?"

I blush, so turned on by his words I can barely think. "Of course, it does. But I've gotta crunch these numbers. Boss is a real stickler on deadlines. And this is a big job."

It's not a flirt, though the words could be construed that way. I really am mid-analysis on the resort figures, and Thomas was right that doing the work at home had been the right way to go. With the data being in multiple locations, compiling it was my first step, and I'm only just beginning to actually make comparisons and projections. "And I don't know that a mid-morning quickie in the office is really the message we want to send."

He sighs, the sound an admission that he knows I'm right, but the look in his eyes says he wants me anyway. "Fine. Lunch it is. You're a tough negotiator, Miss Karakova."

I smirk. "You have no idea, Mr. Goldstone."

He comes closer, tipping my chin up and leaning forward as he locks me in place with his eyes. Our lips are only a breath's space away and I'm ready for his kiss, lips parted and wet and wanting. And that's when he says, "I can be rather persuasive myself."

I feel the heat of his words, knowing that he wouldn't have to persuade me to do a damn thing. I'm putty in his hands, and I slump as he walks to the door, leaving me cold without his closeness.

He adjusts himself, intentionally letting me know that he's just as affected as I am, a small gesture on his part. But then he stands straight and stiff, his professional persona clicking into place like armor.

"Yes, I'll need those figures as soon as possible. Get to work, Mia."

If anyone was in the hallway to hear, it'd sound like he was dangerously close to putting me on blast, but I see the spark in his eyes, so I play along. Though I do it in my own way.

Knowing he's the only one who can see me, I flash him double middle fingers and stick my tongue out like a child. I can see the clench of his jaw where he's fighting back the laugh.

"I'll hold you to that promise. Lunch today, noon."

He leaves, and I'm a swirl of giddy heat. That a man like Thomas is play-ful with me, while at the same time actually fucking brilliant and powerful, is a combination that hits me right in my heart. And lower.

I get to work, cranking through as much of the analysis as I can, know-ing that it'll be a process that takes weeks to truly get a thorough look at the resort's financials. And before I know it, the morning has flown by.

I hurry upstairs, walking into Thomas's twenty-fifth floor office to see Kerry rather obviously listening to a meeting behind the closed door.

"What's going on?" I whisper.

She jumps a foot in the air, eyes going wide. But then she glares at me for scaring her and I shake to keep the laughter quiet.

We're not exactly best buddies, but things are friendlier after our lunch trip to The Gravy Train yesterday. I'd invited her, wanting to get to know her.

*"So, I have ulterior motives for lunch today," I'd told her boldly.*

*"I expected as much. Look, I'm strictly Thomas's assistant. There's never been anything between us, never so much as a wayward glance. On his part or on mine. And it's going to stay that way." She nods her head with certainty.*

*With a grin, I reassure her. "Honestly, that hadn't even entered my mind, but thank you for that. What I was thinking is that we're all part of the same team, both for Goldstone and for Thomas. I just want to know the woman who controls Thomas's work life and admittedly, get you on our side so that any gossip-hounds won't use you as a source."*

*I'm never one to beat around the bush, but this is as blatant as I can be.*

*I can see the leeriness on her face as she carefully says, "Uh, I like my job. Like how it lets me pay for my kid's braces without taking out a second mortgage. So I'm not inclined to do much of anything that'd put my paycheck on the line. And that includes gossip, about you or to you."*

*"Oh, no, this isn't a twisted way of pumping you for info! I'm going about this all wrong, I guess. I just want us to be friends, or friendly. I just . . . Thomas is important to me." I slouch, feeling in over my head and like my good intentions didn't pan out as planned.*

*She pats my hand, letting me off the hook. "I understand. Can I tell you some-thing? Not gossip, but just an observation?" At my nod, she says, "I've worked for Thomas for years, since he had a tiny office in a building of suites. Well before he was Mr. Goldstone of Goldstone Inc. with the second-largest skyscraper in all of Roseboro. Point is, I've seen a lot. And this is the happiest I've seen him. That's because of you. He's never had someone, not his family, not friends, not women. But with you, there's something different."*

*Something in the way she listed out who he's never had gives me pause.* "What do you know about his family?"

*Kerry shakes her head.* "That's getting closer to gossip, and I won't do that, but I know his dad is on the short list for security to keep an eye on if he comes in without an appointment. And I know that you have free access to his office and the penthouse." *She smiles, the importance she places on those things apparent.*

Back in her office, she whispers so quietly I have to lean close. "Thomas has Nathan Billington in there on blast."

"Eek," I mouth soundlessly. "How bad?"

She presses her lips. "Grade-three on a scale of five."

I shrug, smirking. "Not so bad, right?" Her perfectly sculpted raised brow says otherwise.

Through the door, we both hear Thomas's raised voice. "Get the fuck out, Nathan!"

Ouch. I'd call that a four.

We scramble back to Kerry's desk, her plopping in the chair and me perching on the edge unnaturally. I'm sure we look just as guilty as we are, but Nathan stomps by red-faced without a glance our way.

Kerry looks at me with the most saccharine of smiles. "Mr. Goldstone will see you now."

Though we don't laugh, there's a shared giggle in our eyes. She just might be the Thelma to my Louise yet. At least at the office.

I knock lightly on the door, sticking my head in carefully. "Hey . . . bad time?"

Thomas is standing by the window, looking over Roseboro with his hands in his pockets. He doesn't look back as he invites me in, his voice calming down as he talks. "No, lunch is just what I need." But the words are heavy, as if they cost him to say.

I go to him, running my hand up his back, tracing the tension in the muscles there. "What happened? I mean, if you want to talk about it."

He turns, and I can see the storm clouds in his eyes as he growls, "Billington had a sexual harassment claim filed against him. Nothing hardcore. He told a classless and tasteless joke, but it was overheard by someone. He's a VP, for fuck's sake. He knows better."

Thomas' jaw works as he grits his teeth, and then he says in a measured tone, "And when I called him out on it, he had the audacity to say that at least he wasn't seeing someone from the office. He didn't use the words, but he might as well have said I was 'fucking the help' like it's 1954 or some shit."

I gasp, shock and discomfort washing through me that Nathan would've dared to throw our relationship in Thomas's face, especially in such a crass way. One, that doesn't seem like a smart thing to do. Two, our relationship is nothing like that. We're consensually dating and being intentionally careful to not do anything that would smack of favoritism.

"*Mudak.* That asshole. Look, we know it's not like that. If he threw that out there, it's because he was desperate and knew he'd fucked up. Don't let him push you to a place you don't want to go. Blasting people or not, it's not about them. It's about you. I just want better for you because I know how hard that is on you."

His shoulders drop, and he looks at me sideways as if he can't fully meet my eyes. "I hear it sometimes, you know? Hear the words coming out of my mouth and hear my father screaming at me. But I don't know how else to push—them or me."

I smile, shrugging it off. "You just choose differently. Not everyone is motivated the same way, so you have to vary your approach to the person you're reaming out. Sometimes soft, sometimes hard, sometimes direct, sometimes in a roundabout way."

"Is that what you do with me?" he asks seriously. "Decide if it's a 'Thomas might break' kind of day? Or if I can take the brutal truth?"

I shake my head, feeling more relaxed. "No, unfortunately, I'm a bit like you too, stuck in my ways and a bit 'take it or leave it', but maybe we can both work on being softer. Together?"

Before he can answer, there's another knock at the door and Kerry bustles in. "Lunch is served." She's carrying two brown bags from a café down the street.

"I thought we were going out to lunch?" I ask, looking at Thomas.

Kerry answers, setting the bags down. "Yep, that was the plan. But every floor from here to the front door is talking about Nathan's little snit, so I figured the two of you walking out hand-in-hand for a lunch date would send the wrong message. I took the liberty of ordering in for you."

Thomas laughs as Kerry winks at me and mouths, "I got you."

"Whose side are you on here, Kerry?"

She pats her hair, grinning. "My side. And that means keeping the boss happy. And that means keeping his woman happy." She points between the two of us. "I also took the liberty of ordering myself lunch. On your card."

As she shuts the door, she calls back, "Don't forget you have a conference call at one."

Her whirlwind has broken the tension, settled the dust from Thomas's anger and my shock, so we sit down to eat, making the most of the few minutes we have.

"Oh, I'm sending out a meeting request to the hospital group for tomorrow. I'm going to announce my decision. I'm going with your recommendation."

"Which one?" I ask, rolling my eyes. "The first or the second one?"

"The real one," Thomas replies, his smile reappearing but still weak. "I still haven't figured out how the file was changed. I had IT look into it because of the discrepancies, and the print order was done from Randall's computer. But they checked his files and the network, and both show the file was unchanged. The changes happened between your email and his inbox, which isn't possible, but it's the only thing that makes sense. And that worries me."

"It's probably just a blip. Just a random ID-ten-T error," I say, confused but mostly just glad we caught the error.

"I'm not an idiot, nor do I think this was a random error. In fact, I was wondering if you'd help me with a special assignment?"

I lick my lips, wiggling my eyebrows. "What'd you have in mind?"

"Well, that too," he says with a laugh. "But the fact that an error like that could happen once makes me curious whether it's happened before. I want you to go back through the last few years' projects, investments, and such. Focus on the ones where we didn't do as well as early projections had forecast. I want to see if there are any trends."

"Well, I can tell you one trend right off the bat," I tease.

"What's that?"

"One person made the final decision each time. PEBKAC." I say with all seriousness.

"PEBKAC?" Thomas asks, and I nod. "I'll bite. What's PEBKAC?"

"Problem Exists Between Keyboard And Chair," I answer. "In this case, it could just be that you've made some bad decisions, Thomas. No investment is risk-free."

Thomas nods, and I see his shiver as he considers my point. I'm saying it clearly that he's possibly made mistakes. He's not perfect . . . he could be wrong.

"Point taken," he finally acknowledges, "but if that's the case, I need to know that too. Focus on the resort analysis first, but after that's done, if you can start the big job, I'd like you to keep me up to date."

"Of course."

"Speaking of dates . . . you up for dinner at my place after work tomorrow night?" he asks, pointing upstairs. "I know it's a long way, but—"

"But you want to give me time to pack some spare work clothes," I remark, getting to my feet. "I think I can be convinced of that . . . if you let me have a little bit of space in your closet to hang things up. I demand at least two hangers."

"Tough negotiator, but I'm pretty sure I can do that," Thomas says.

# CHAPTER 25

## Thomas

THE 'SUPER WAREHOUSE' IS HUGE, 100,000 SQUARE FEET OF JUST about everything possible in bulk boxes, bulk bags, and bulk crates. There's enough food here to feed all of Roseboro, I think . . . but it doesn't matter.

*Of course it doesn't matter. You're just pissing onto a forest fire, thinking it'll make a difference. Like you could make a difference.*

Instead, I focus on what I'm here for. The big cart in front of me is already heavy as I load a second fifty-pound bag of rice onto it. Thankfully, this place doesn't do normal shopping carts but industrial-strength carriers that can easily hold hundreds of pounds.

Up next are vegetables. I get a variety, from corn to green beans to carrots. Sadly, there aren't tons of options. I'd love to buy fresh from the farmers, but that would mean leaving a trail, and I can't have that.

I tug my ball cap lower as I turn the corner, and it's sauces. Lots of pasta sauce, then on to pasta itself, spaghetti being the main one, of course, along with a case of that dried cheese that's total shit but kids love.

Sausages, chicken breasts, oatmeal, milk . . . all of that's going to get packed into thermal cases, and by the time I'm done, I'm straining to push the cart. It takes the cashier nearly fifteen minutes to ring everything up. Thankfully, one of the stock boys helps me load up the back of the truck, and he pats the tailgate appreciatively.

"Man, whatever you're planning, I wanna be there. You've got enough here to feed a crowd. Tell me you're buying beer next?"

"Not for this party," I reply, tipping him a ten and a handshake. "Thanks for the help."

The drive takes longer than usual, mainly because I'm going south all the way over the state line, off the main roads and ten minutes into what looks like woods. When I heard about this place, I couldn't do anything at the time, but as I try to coast silently around the back, I start to tear up.

The Cabin looks almost normal on the outside. A large traditional-style house, a little rundown but cared for in a piecemeal sort of way that tells the tale of money coming in in fits and starts. Its eight bedrooms house sixteen kids, all of them rescued from abusive homes.

There are specialized programs here for the kids, therapy and job training, a chance for them to get their lives together. A chance for them to have a fresh start away from the roughness of their early days.

When I approached this place as Tom Nicholson, I'd heard what some of these kids went through. I hadn't been able to sleep a wink that night, the pain from my own past brought to the surface by the shared shittiness of our childhoods. I'd had to put myself through hell in the gym to purge myself of the emotions, and they still nearly crippled me for two days. But I'd gotten over it and set out to help.

Because they're struggling.

While the building itself might have been donated by an Oregonian who had the property and the foresight to see that getting these kids out of the environment they'd been in would help them more than a large urban 'rehabilitation factory', they don't get as much as they need. Politicians see the budget and the number of kids helped, and the bean counters take over.

Which is why I'm out here at nearly eleven at night, doing my best to unload the truckload of supplies onto the covered back porch without making any noise.

Actually, the fact that I'm having any success tells me that the next trip out here needs to include a security camera and some floodlights. Harder for me to sneak in like Santa, but definitely safer for these kids who deserve to feel safe for the first time in their lives.

I know it's stupid, keeping my charity work secret. If the PR team at the company knew about this, they'd be going gaga over it and trying to get my name in every paper up and down the West Coast. They'd probably preemptively clear a space on the wall of the bottom floor somewhere for all the awards they'd expect I'd get.

But that's exactly why I haven't told anyone. It's not for the recognition. I almost don't want to be recognized, actually. It's why I've taken the steps I have, the shell company, the cashier's checks on that account, the disguises, all of it.

Though I've thought about telling Mia. Maybe she'd understand, but I'm not sure yet. Not because I'm not sure of her but because I'm not sure about me.

My whole life, when my father was smacking me around, not giving a shit about me . . . no one really cared. They took me at face value as a charming, good-looking guy, someone who easily got good grades without the teachers' special attention, and who could play ball and win for the team. There were definitely signs something was going on, but no one cared enough to find out. They took the easy way out and I paid the price.

And I don't want the kids thinking I'm doing this at their expense, riding the coattails of their pain for accolades and awards. It's not about that, and if anyone knew it was me, that's what it'd morph into. I won't use them that way. So here I am, sneaking around in the dark.

Stacking the boxes with the two basketballs and the football on top, I reach into my pocket and pull out the white envelope, tucking it under a five-pound can of tomato sauce.

Getting back in my truck, the door closing sounds loud and shocking in the quiet of the night. I wince and put the truck in neutral so it rolls a bit, looking behind me.

I see a slice of light as a door opens, a wide man and a smaller silhouette at his side dark against the bright backdrop. Through the open window, I hear his words carry on the night air.

"Good Lord, look at all this."

Already caught, I crank the engine and gun it for the main road. But even over the engine, the man's yell reaches me. "Thank you! Thank you so much!" His sob touches me, bringing a sharp burn to my eyes.

*It's still not enough. Just a drop in a bucket. You'll never be enough.*

# CHAPTER 26

## Mia

I DON'T COME TO THE GRAVY TRAIN FOR BREAKFAST OFTEN. IT'S REALLY out of the way from my apartment.

But . . . I didn't spend last night at my apartment. In fact, I haven't spent three out of the last five nights at my apartment, and I've gotten used to taking advantage of Thomas's amazing shower.

Seriously, two pulsating shower heads will do things to your body that you only dream about. Especially when you're not showering alone.

The shower's not all I've taken advantage of, but I promised the girls that this morning we'd get together, so I pried myself out of bed while Tommy gets an early start on his agenda for the day.

Izzy comes in, looking fresher than I've seen her in a long time. "Hey, Mia, babe, you're looking . . . freshly fucked."

"What? I just got out of the shower!" I joke, even though it's true. "You look a lot brighter and more bushy-tailed than I've seen you in a while yourself. What's up?"

"Just a moment," Izzy says as Charlotte comes in the door. "I figure I just wanna say it once."

"Ooh, someone else on the man train?" Charlotte teases, grinning. "I mean, I figured you'd be trying out for the nunnery after you finished your degree, but maybe you went all Von Trapp on us?"

Izzy rolls her eyes, shaking her head. "I'm not that bad, but I do have good news."

"What's up?" Char asks as she slides in next to me.

Izzy pauses, then smiles big, the excitement she's been holding back bubbling out. "I got the scholarship!"

We all squeal, a harmony of shrill happiness, and clap loudly for her.

"Way to go, Izzy!" I cheer her.

"It's only five thousand dollars, but hey, it's five thousand dollars," she says. "It's some wiggle room for tuition and cost of living."

"So does that mean you're going to stop pulling insane shifts here?" I ask, and Izzy shakes her head. "Babe, come on!"

"No, I can't," Izzy says. "Listen, it's wiggle room, but not *that* much. My laptop's going to shit, and before you say it, Mia, I won't take yours so you have an excuse to buy a new one."

"Too much hentai anime on that thing anyway," Charlotte teases. "I have a strict three-tentacle per hard drive limit."

"Hey, I haven't gone there . . . yet." I laugh, and they both laugh with me.

"Hey, by the way, how's domestic life? I still can't believe you're spending time with us instead of with Hunky McDollarSigns," Izzy says. I give her a sharp look, checking for any sign of jealousy. We all know Izzy has the most money trouble of the three of us, but she's proud and wants to stand on her own two feet. Even so, having a friend who suddenly hooks up with the likes of Thomas Goldstone must make her a little salty. But in her eyes, I only see happiness for me, not a hint of envy, cattiness, or shallow ugliness. And that's why she's one of my best friends. She's good, down to her core good.

"It's not the size of his bank account that has Mia worked up, I bet," Char teases. "Tell me, honey, seriously . . . how long before you kick us to the curb in favor of ladies who lunch and splurge on a cucumber in their water?"

"Oh, please, it's not like that at all. Hell, Thomas isn't even like that. Besides, what would I ever do without you guys?" I ask, and Charlotte laughs.

"You'd be busy, that's for sure," she says. "On your knees, bent over the desk, in bed, in the shower. I mean, I'm sure we can't compare to Thomas Goldstone."

"Well, that's true. *All* of that is so true," I say with a smug shimmy of my shoulders. "But he can't compare to you guys either," I counter. "I mean, seriously, who's going to listen to me complain when I come in all bloated and crampy with PMS?"

"I don't listen to you now," Charlotte jokes. "Do you, Izzy?"

"Nope, never," Izzy teases. "I mean, if we were friends, maybe I would then, but you're just this psycho who comes into my work so much I'm kinda forced to hang out with you."

"Yup," Charlotte says before busting out singing, "F-R-I-E-N-D-S, that's how you fu—"

"Shh!" Izzy says, slapping a hand over Charlotte's mouth. "First of all, I hate that damn song. Second, I do work here still. I don't need you cursing at the top of your lungs and cracking glass with those shrill notes." She rubs at her ear like Charlotte's howling at ear-splitting levels. She's not far from the truth.

Charlotte sticks out her tongue, wiggling it. "Fine, but you know I sing just fine. When I was a little girl, the pastor in church kept saying I was the best at making a joyful noise during the hymns."

"Emphasis on the noise," I tease. "Charlotte, you're not as bad as me, which isn't saying much, but I say this with the brutal honesty only a friend can give you . . . scratch your plans to try out for *American Idol*. You don't want to end up on the loser reel."

She feigns shock, hand to her chest for a moment before conceding. "I know, I know, but I'm still pretty fabulous, if overlooked." She straightens and sips her drink. "All jokes aside, seriously, how're things with Thomas?"

"Really awesome," I admit shyly. It's not that I'm unsure about what we're doing, but sharing just how much I feel about Thomas with them before sharing it with him seems out of order.

Because I am feeling things, a scary four-letter thing. And I've never felt this before, not like this. Not a fizzy, bright bubbliness on top of deep, earthy richness, not a fire so hot I don't know if I can withstand it but all I want to do is try.

But I do feel all that and more with Thomas. And that both thrills and terrifies me. What if I'm not enough? What if he can't get out of his head? What if this is all just physical and new and I'm making it into more than I should because I've fallen for him?

But I know in my heart that this isn't one-sided or casual. I can see it in his eyes every time he looks at me. He's just as new at this as I am, maybe even more so. But that's okay, we can take our time and get there together.

I realize that while my mind has been whirling, Charlotte and Izzy have been waiting expectantly for a fuller answer. "Japan was everything I thought it'd be, and then some," I say cryptically, spreading my hands wide like I can't possibly encompass all that I saw, felt, and did into a few words.

"Because of the company," Charlotte adds wisely, and Izzy nods.

I sip at my coffee, agreeing. "Yeah, because of Tommy. He's . . . not what I thought when I first met him. He's so much more. It's complicated. He's got this persona as a hardass, but when he's with me, he's gentle and nice. Japan was . . . enlightening."

Charlotte leans to Izzy, stage-whispering in her ear so I can hear, "Sounds like she's literally tamed the beast. Has him wrapped around her pretty little finger."

I smile cheekily and wave my pinky finger at her.

Then Izzy whispers back, "Or maybe he has her wrapped around his thick cock. Did you see her hair when she came in this morning? Definite morning BJ."

Instinctively, I reach for the back of my hair, smoothing it down as my jaw drops open. When they both burst into raucous laughter, I chastise them. "Guys! That's not funny!" But I finally laugh with them, asking through punctuated breaths, "Is my hair really okay? I have to go to work!"

But that just makes them laugh harder.

# CHAPTER 27

## Thomas

"TOMMY?"

I look up and realize I've missed something Mia's said because my inner voice was whispering in my ear again. The same never-ending mantra of how I'm unworthy, but it's enough to distract me.

Shit. I growl lightly, and Mia's forehead creases as she sees my face.

"Sorry, lost in thought about work," I lie, but it at least eases her worries. "What did you say?"

"I asked how your morning appointment went," Mia says, relaxing. "I was looking forward to talking with you about some of the projects you sent me, but you popped out pretty quickly, Kerry said. I know I went to grab a coffee and boom, gone from the Motherland you were."

"It went well," I answer, thinking about the quick run out to the boys' shelter. Most of them were in school, of course, but Frankie's laid up sick with the chicken pox, so I brought him some Reese's Peanut Butter Cup ice cream before helping him with his math homework. That kid's a fiend for peanut butter.

After that, I came back to my place and did a workout before checking in with Kerry, and now dinner with Mia in my apartment. It's been a full day.

I rub at my temples, willing the voice to stay at bay. Just give me an evening of peace, and it can harass me to sleep later.

"By the way," I ask, hoping to change the subject, "how's the research going on the idea I gave you about someone maybe kneecapping me?"

Mia hums, setting her fork down. "I'll be honest. You've got a lot of oars in a lot of waters. It's been a ton of data to slog through on top of my regular projects that actually make the company money."

"I'm sure you can do it though . . . right?" I ask, forcing myself to keep my voice soft even as the voice in my head yammers at me.

*Just do it! It shouldn't be that hard if you actually try, you lazy shit!*

I take a deep breath. The voice almost sounded like it was yelling at Mia, but I know it's just a repeat of something my dad said to me once when I had a hard time building a mousetrap car in junior high school science class. Not that he could've done it either, and I did eventually figure it out. *Got an A, fuck you very much,* I tell the voice.

Mia nods her head, giving me a smile. "I said it's a lot of data to slog through, but I've got it. I'm starting by identifying the outliers in terms of prediction versus outcome, and that's not as easy as it might seem."

Okay, that I can understand. There's a lot of factors that can screw with a prediction, and some of them are out of our control. "What do you think?"

"I think it's too early to tell, though signs are looking good that I'll find something," she says, but there's heat in her voice and with a glance her way, I know she's not talking about the research project at all. Or at least not *only* about it.

"Oh, you think you've found something good?" I prompt back, playing along.

She bites her lip. "Oh, definitely. You're not perfect, and I wouldn't want you to be. But I'm really happy, Tommy. I'm sure this project is going to yield some very enlightening results, maybe even increase our ultimate profit margin."

Her not wanting me to be perfect is a balm to my soul, more healing than she probably realizes. And her play with work talk and personal talk is turning me on. Maybe that's weird, but I'm a businessman at heart. And apparently, my cock likes a bit of market chatter too, judging by the growing bulge in my slacks.

"So what exactly are you doing to develop these figures?" I let my eyes roll over her figure, taking an extra-long glance at the hint of cleavage on display in her slashed-neck T-shirt. It's from a band I've never heard of, of course, but most of her clothing is like that. I enjoy the way her blush creeps up her neck, pinkening the skin before my eyes as her breasts heave a little faster.

"Well, I can't just look at profit and loss because some projects are short-term, others long." She lets the word drag out sexily. She's geeky, nerdy, and turning me on more with every word from her sexy brain.

I lean forward, refilling her wine glass. "Nothing wrong with a quickie investment. Get in, get the goods, and get out," I rumble.

Her smirk is pure evil, her eyes wide and innocent, and the mix drives me wild. "But other times, to really get the payoff, you have to take your time, be patient, and really work every avenue for maximum impact. Milk everything you can out of it before you're fully satisfied."

She takes a sip of the red wine, and I watch raptly as she licks a droplet from her plump lower lip. I take a sip of my own, wanting to taste her but wanting to continue our game a bit longer.

"Really, getting everything sorted has been a bit of backbreaker, really hard and intense. But I'm making sure I do a good job on this for you, for professional pride but also because I don't want to give you a reason to bust my ass."

She's still playing, teasing about me sexily spanking her, but the words . . .

*Get over here! I work hard to provide and all I ask is that you work hard too and stay out of my way. Maybe if I bust your ass, you'll finally amount to something. You asked for this. You knew I'd bust your ass.*

Memories of me literally getting my ass 'busted' suddenly course through my brain, and I clench my jaw, regretting my action immediately as Mia takes it as my admonishing her for her sexy words. "Tommy?"

The mood is broken, the heat in my body replaced by a coating of cold sweat on my back. And judging by the way she's eyeballing me, I must be pale because Mia looks worried.

I hang my head, not able to meet her eyes. "Sorry . . . just a bit of a flashback."

She puts her hand on my back, rubbing me gently. "It's okay. Happens to everyone, about good things and bad."

Her acceptance of my freakout when we were mid-flirtation should make me feel better. Instead, I've never felt smaller, less like a man. I revert to what I know, dry business talk to distance myself from the shit show in my head. "It's just that I've figured out there might be some level of corporate espionage and sabotage. Maybe something going on for a long time. And I'm furious and disappointed in myself for not realizing it sooner."

Mia shakes her head. "This is slick, if there's even anything there yet. Which I haven't decided there is."

"I know," I say with a heavy sigh. And then I admit, "It's . . . I'm learning how to trust, with you. Basically for the first time. And with this over my head, it's even harder now. I'm sorry if that seems cruel to you or if I'm being an asshole. But I guess that's what I'm known for."

In my head, I see me yelling at Nathan Billington. But then superimposed over my face, my father's face appears. Red, veins bulging, hate in his eyes. Am I really that bad? How did it get this bad?

*Like father, like son. He broke your mother so badly she killed herself rather than face life with him, with her own son. How long do you think Mia can withstand you? Like father, like son.*

Mia shakes her head, taking my hand. The soothing touch pushes my inner demon back for a little bit, and I feel my pulse slow a little as she strokes the back of my hand with her thumb.

"Tommy, I know this is going to be difficult. And honestly, part of me wishes you'd get some help on your issues, even more than what I can do. Your dad did a number on you, but you don't have to let him have space in your mind. Kick him out, for fuck's sake!"

She mutters something in Russian, even feigns spitting on my dining room rug, so I decide she's cursing my dad. As stupid as it is, it helps. It makes it feel like she's on my side.

"But I'm not going to push you on going to therapy. You'll go when and if you're ready. In the meantime, I'll just earn your trust as best I can, because . . . well, I want that. And more."

"I know." I swallow, almost afraid of everything she's asking for. "And this may sound insane, because it shouldn't be this way, but that 'more' is coming faster than the trust." It's the closest we've gotten to saying the words, and she offers me a small smile, letting me know she feels the importance too.

"That's okay. We'll make our own path," Mia reassures me. All I can give back is a nod as I blink the burn in my eyes away.

She leans back, giving me space before clapping her hands as if she can clear the air between us. "As we were saying, with this data mining, it'd help if you had a guess as to who I could start my search with. It's not always a great idea, but with the sheer volume of data I'm combing through, I could use a good yard marker . . . unless you plan on my taking the next two months just doing analysis on all this."

"I don't know." I grit through my teeth. "I've tried tracking back through some emails myself, though I'm no cyber-security expert, and I've searched my brain and the company directory for anyone I thought might either want to hurt me or might benefit from a Goldstone loss. And nothing. Your mic drop performance was the first time I'd really considered that something might be wrong. You helped me."

"How'd I help?" Mia asks. "I mean, I just told you that you were wrong. And it was not a mic drop," she argues again, the same as she had done that day. It seems so long ago, but at the same time, I feel like so much has happened. It helps, seeing that sass and fire. It reminds me that Mia's on my side, and she's smart, and beautiful . . . and mine.

So I don't mind giving her some of my own back, even if it's professional. "You had evidence to back up your claim. Most people just backup their data to the company server. But you hard saved your own copy of the data on your laptop. So I had a place to start the comparison, follow the trail, and compile a smaller group to work from."

"The hospital project group," Mia murmurs, and I nod. "But the only person I sent that file to was Randall."

For some reason, even hearing Mia say his name pisses me off. "I know, but Randall says he didn't make any changes, and like I said, his computer's clean. Also, I looked back through my own files about some of the projects I knew didn't go according to plan, and for some of them, he was nowhere close to the team. It's a start, but I don't think it's strong."

"But you don't like him," Mia points out, and I shake my head.

"I trust him to do his job, but no, I don't like him. It's in his face, in the way he acts sometimes. Like when I had to get in his face at the party. Every once in a while, it's like the mask slips, showing me someone underneath who's my enemy. And if anyone knows about masks, it's me."

Mia chuckles. "Yeah, that party . . . it's funny, Tommy. I know a lot of folks would say that caveman behavior was wrong. Even that I should've left you both standing there, measuring your dicks. But I felt safe with you. I could see that your anger wasn't directed at me."

"And you have no idea how much that means to me. I was surprised at my reaction that night too," I admit, thinking back. "I was angry at how Randall wasn't listening to your polite no, but deep down, I just wanted to beat the shit out of him for daring to look at what was so obviously mine."

"And I'll admit that scares me, but the point is, you didn't. You held yourself back," Mia says. "So you can do better, be better. But Tommy . . . it's also what makes me worry. You're hell-bent on building a world for yourself, and I can see a place for me in it. But it's a world that's being built on a shaky, flawed foundation because you've got all this inner anger, this rage. What happens the first time a really big earthquake comes along and shakes it up?"

I nod and get up, going around the table and pulling her to her feet. "I've had the same thoughts every day. But that's something else you help me with."

"What's that?" Mia asks, her breath catching when I pull her close.

"When I'm with you . . . I feel like for the first time in my life, I feel . . . peace. I feel like when that earthquake does come, maybe I can survive it."

Mia smiles and takes off her glasses, setting them on the table before wrapping her arms about my neck. "Maybe we can survive it together. Ride it out together."

Her words are back to having a double-meaning, this one about acceptance, about wanting me to grow but taking me as I am, fucked-up mind and all. But on top of that deeper meaning, the heat returns between us, flashing fire through my every nerve, burning away my thoughts about work, my family, my shortcomings, and leaving in its wake only . . . need.

I pick her up, carrying her over to set her on the couch, loving the image before me. She's still the quirky woman I first met, still has the streaks in her hair—purple and blue today—but she's been wearing skirts more often. I suspect it's both to drive me wild with the flashes of her sexy legs and to make after-work access that much faster.

Today, her skirt is black denim, jagged at the hem in a flirty, sexy way . . . and already halfway up her thighs. I kneel, pushing her knees apart even as she spreads for me, showing me what she's wearing today.

"You wore a thong under that skirt?" I marvel, tracing the outline of the lacy triangle over her smooth pussy. "Maybe you're lucky I stayed out of the office today."

"Mmm, but you would have so loved the mid-afternoon snack I had in mind," she teases. "I was hungry and thought to myself that I could easily fit under your desk."

Though we've been trying so hard to corral our actual fucking to outside work hours, the image of Mia on her knees under my desk, sucking me off while I try to maintain a semblance of normalcy, feels naughty and invigorating.

"Tomorrow, maybe. I'll send Kerry out on an errand of something or another," I joke before rising and kissing Mia. I want to feast on her, but after such a hard day, my cock needs attention more than my tongue, and I pull back. "Wait."

"What?" Mia asks, her flushed face looking so fuckable I can barely hold back. But I want more than just torn clothing, tossed aside shirts, and frantic pawing at each other.

I want to be in control . . . of myself. Of her.

"Stand up . . . and strip for me," I reply, getting up so she can stand. As soon as she does, I take her place on the couch, watching her.

She shimmies her way out of her skirt and then begins teasing at the hem of her T-shirt, pulling it up and shoving it down to give me quick flashing peeks. And then with a smile that says she knows exactly how wild she's driving me, she pulls the shirt over her head.

She's a vision in sheer lace, bright pink against her pale skin. Her tits are pushed up high, cupped in a way that makes me want to free them, want to see their heaviness bounce. The lace at her center is but a bare scrap, giving way to thin strings that go over her hips.

I palm myself distractedly, looking for relief from the wellspring she's drawing up inside me. But she notices and with a bite of her lip demands, "Let me see."

I growl, giving her what she wants only because it's what I want too. I pull my shirt open, buttons flying but I don't give a fuck. And as I reach for my belt, I rumble, "Get on your knees for a closer look."

Her eyes flash to mine, and for a moment I think I went too far, not in the words because I know Mia can handle that, but in the tone. Bossy, demanding, arrogantly forceful. Like I'm entitled to have her suck me off. But then I see her blue orbs darken, and she drops in one movement, sagging like someone simply knocked her down. Or like someone took control of her body.

And I realize that someone has. Me. And she's letting me.

I rip my fly open, shoving my pants and underwear down over my ass. My cock stands heavy between us, and she waits for permission, for an order. She waits for me. "Suck me off, Mia. Like you would under my desk. Wrap those lips around me and swallow every fucking inch."

She moves forward, taking me into the hot wetness of her mouth, not inch by painstaking inch but all at once to the hilt. I surge into her throat, grabbing at her head and finding purchase with fistfuls of her hair. She makes a *gluck* sound in her throat and it's my undoing.

I push into her mouth over and over, pleased beyond measure as she swallows me at every interval. Her hums of pleasure vibrate through my shaft, and all too soon, I'm on the edge.

I hold her back by her hair, and she pouts that I've taken her treat away, though I can see the mess I've already made of her, drool and pre-cum mixing and dripping off her chin to her chest.

I guide her up, and she climbs into my lap, our hands exploring each other. I lean in, kissing her chest before sucking on her stiff nipple through the lace, flicking my tongue over the peak as Mia rubs against my cock, the wispy thong preventing nothing but my filling her.

"Oh, God, Tommy . . . I want you every day," Mia moans, pushing my head away to kiss me tenderly. "I promise you, I'll do whatever I can to make you a happy man."

"I promise you . . . I'll never hurt you," I reply. "I'll protect you, even if it's from me." It's a promise I hope I can keep.

She shakes her head, her hair brushing along the backs of my hands where I hold her hips. Though her eyes are closed in pleasure as she grinds against me, her words are crystal-clear. "I don't need protection from you. *You* need protection from you. That demon inside your mind only wants to hurt you. But I won't let it. I won't let it have you. You're mine. My *good* man."

The demon scoffs in my head. *You're barely even a man, much less a good one.*

But when Mia slips her thong to the side and reaches down, rubbing the head of my cock between her wet lips, her words are the ones echoing in my mind, shutting the voice up.

I pause, not forcing her down on my iron-hard member but letting her control it, feeling the electric thrill as she rubs just the crown, her honey oozing over my tip and down my shaft until I'm gleaming, and Mia whimpers.

"Your good man," I reply, needing the power of the words in the air between us. I hiss as she lowers herself onto me. Her pussy grips me in a tight, slippery vise that draws me into her until I push down on her ass, seating my cock deep inside her. "And I've wanted you all day. Now I have you, and you have me."

Mia leans in, kissing me before she starts riding me, lifting her body

and bringing her nipples to my mouth. I suck deeply, her other side rubbing against my cheek as she bounces, planting her hands on the back of the
couch as she takes me.

I . . . I like this. Like our time in Tokyo, I let her have what she wants,
entranced as she rolls her hips, her thighs tightening while my cock plunges
deep inside her. Watching her through half-lidded eyes, I can feel my soul
yearn for her happiness and pleasure, exaltation sweeping me as she throws
her head back, crying out when the head of my cock rubs over her G-spot.

"So good. *Soo* good."

"Beautiful," I rasp, and she looks down, smiling. Reaching down, she
grabs my hair and pulls my head back into a soul-searing kiss that ignites the
feral side of me like gasoline on a fire.

Grabbing her ass, I squeeze tightly, my fingers digging in and holding
her still as I thrust deep into her, her pussy clenching around me as I hammer upward, my hips flexing hard with each savage stab deep inside her. I
clamp my lips around her right nipple, sucking hard until she cries out in
pain and pleasure.

"That's it," I growl, letting go of her nipple and flexing my arms, adding
all my strength into the deep stroking, fucking her with my whole body. Her
hips must be aching. She's clapping up and down on my thighs so hard that
the sound echoes even above our panting breaths and the roar of my heart
beating in my chest. "Take it."

*Why pretend? You're not good enough for her.*

The whispered voice that I thought had abated drives me into a fury,
and I pull Mia off me, pushing her over the arm of the sofa before plunging
back inside her, holding her by her hair.

She cries out, but it's not in fear or pain, and she pushes back into me. I
pound her, smacking her ass with my free hand while my cock pumps deep
into her.

Sweat rolls down my cheeks, and I can hear her groaning as if I'm being too rough, but I can't stop. I just need to give her everything that I feel
inside me. I need her to feel what I feel, all the fear and the desire and the
hope and the anger.

I give it all to her.

And she takes it, somehow pushing back against me. I feel her pussy
choking my cock before she starts to shake, and her climax crashes through
her as she clamps down on me.

My name is a guttural howl of devotion on her lips, and I roar, my cum splashing deep inside her as her cry unlocks my release. I feel my balls emptying, the white-hot pleasure and pain mixing and scourging me of my agony, telling me that somehow, I've found my one and only.

The words are right there on the tip of my tongue but I hold them back. Not because of Mia. She deserves my truth, and I'm learning that more and more. But because I need to be stronger, better before I give her that last bit of me. The words are a promise, and I want to be the man she thinks I can be before I make that vow. But heart and soul, she's marking me as much as I'm marking her.

It scares me, but at the same time, I want more of it.

More of her. More of me. More of *us*.

My hand relaxes, and I pull her back, cradling her body in my lap as she shudders, putting her arms around my neck and nuzzling against my neck.

"Thank you," she whispers. "For giving me everything. For not holding back."

"Thank you . . . for letting me be myself."

# CHAPTER 28

## Mia

I SHIFT IN MY SEAT, MY ASS AND NECK BOTH ACHING FROM LAST NIGHT'S hammering. There are times, especially during and right afterward, when Thomas's intensity feels amazing.

And I love the way he protectively snuggles me in his arms when we're done. He's the world's best blanket buddy.

And yeah, I sort of take pride in walking just a tad bit bowlegged when I meet up with Izzy or Char for lunch. Their looks of amused jealousy are more than worth it.

But when I'm sitting at my desk trying to get my work done, an ache in my neck while I constantly shift around trying to get comfortable isn't the best feeling.

Not that I'd trade the feeling that Thomas gives me for anything in the world. The feeling of waking up this morning in his arms, of the safety and security that comes with it, is beyond compare. I even felt just as safe and secure as he was fucking me so hard that my spine crackled last night as I did this morning when he gave me a soft kiss before we came downstairs to start work.

Speaking of, it's time to get to work. I've got a day full of clickity-clacking away on my computers in front of me, analysis and compilation.

But first, I need data. Thankfully, my new position and my new assignment from Thomas give me administrator viewing privileges to everything in the Goldstone database, only one step below Thomas's own access or that of the IT department's VP.

I even have ghost mode, which means nobody but someone who's actively checking the database at the time will know any files are even being looked at. Sneaky . . . but effective.

It doesn't cover everything. I can't see the passwords for bank and other financial transactions, for example, but it does enough.

"Okay," I tell myself as I turn on my favorite Spotify techno channel to get things rolling, "let's put all these multiple cores to work."

Thankfully, my computer can handle the load of running multiple separate database searches at the same time. I went full geek mode on it, and I'm pretty sure it could run The Matrix if needed. Actually, the slowest part will be the data stream to the Goldstone servers, but that's fine.

First, I shunt my resort numbers to my far screen, then I pull up my main search on the other two screens. On the right, I run the first of two algorithms I wrote. The first one scans for server access that falls outside job title parameters I've set, like an HR assistant opening an IT file, which could be sketchy. The second assigns everyone a home floor based on their department location and then scans the data access points of their card usage for anomalies.

That'll help me find out if Susan down on three heads upstairs to the executive level bathrooms at ten every morning, or it will catch if someone is sneaking out to the parking garage outside set factors of lunch and quitting time.

Both checks result in huge heaps of data, but I'm hoping that it'll be useful to catch someone where they shouldn't be, either physically or electronically, and correlate it back to the questionable project figures. It's a long shot, but it's either in-house or an outside threat, and statistically speaking, in-house sabotage is much more likely so I want to scan from every possible angle.

On the middle screen, I work through my project figures of the ones Thomas pointed out as concerns.

The music and the hours go in sync, with the beats and grooving flow of the music allowing me to pull up files on bad deals the company's made.

Not all of them lost money, which is what makes it hard. Whoever's done this has been really, really subtle. There were deals that broke even, or deals that made a profit, but just a small one. The only consistent thing is that they underperformed.

For example there's the real estate deal, a large tract in an expanding suburb of Seattle. Everything around it seemed great, the area was up and coming, and Goldstone had a contractor ready to turn the whole area into a housing development . . . until after the contracts were signed and the contractor went belly-up at the last minute.

While the housing development was done, the cost in the delays, the taxes, and more meant that what should have netted the company tens of millions of dollars barely broke even.

Or an aircraft parts company that was ready to sell to Goldstone until at the last minute pulling out and selling to a Chinese government-backed consortium. It made no sense because the company made military parts, and by selling to a foreign entity, they lost out on twenty years or more of contracts that would have netted the company billions.

The strangest part was, Goldstone had actually outbid the Chinese, but the supplier was privately held and sold to the Chinese anyway.

Those are just two of the anomalies. I keep finding them. I know that at least half of these are going to end up being dismissed during my search as just plain old bad luck. Even with Thomas's superhuman drive to be the best, it's business.

Even in an era where the stock market can gain or lose a thousand points in a week, there's always that thirty to forty percent of investments that go opposite of what the rest of the market does.

But I have to investigate each one, draw out the data and plug it into my matrix. From there . . . trends will emerge, and I'll try to find that one common thread in the whole fabric.

I feel a little bit like a detective searching for clues to a crime . . . and maybe I am. *Like a forensic analyst,* I think, picturing me surrounded by computers with a flap-eared hat and pipe like Sherlock Holmes. I have always been someone good at finding patterns and clues, but this feels different. More challenging. More important.

"Face it, Mia, you just need a dog and some Scooby Snacks and you'll have the entire schtick down," I murmur as I close a file on a chemical research deal that hasn't increased in value but hasn't decreased either. I move it into my list of *Investigate Later* and keep going. "Well, that and a kickass orange sweater. Ooh, knee socks! Actually, those might be kinda hot," I murmur, appreciative again that no one can hear my weird chatter.

By lunch, I take a break, rubbing my eyes and checking in with Thomas, who's plugging away at his computer. He's muttering to himself, but his face looks calm, and when I knock, his first reaction is a smile. I'll take the win.

"Hey, I thought the fat cats at the top of the corporate ladder were supposed to sit around in their offices listening to, I don't know, Huey Lewis and the News or something." I sing dramatically, "It's hip to be square!"

Thomas claps, a laugh teasing at the edges of his smile. "You geek out on the old stuff too?" Thomas asks, sitting back. "What's up?"

"I was going to grab a little bite down the street. You want to join?"

Thomas shakes his head sadly, his mouth narrowing. "I'd love to, but I can't. It seems *someone* is trying to throw a wrench into the hospital deal. I'm getting a request from them. Well, more like a very strong suggestion that I see a doctor."

"What? What's wrong?" I ask, surprised. "I know it's not a performance issue."

"No, not like that," he replies, sitting back and rubbing at his temples but not laughing at my joke, which worries me. "You should have heard what they said, total corporate word salad . . . *In the interest of maintaining our commitment to public health and to good corporate image, we'd encourage you to take advantage of the same perks that all of our corporate officers share and complete a full physical and mental checkup so you can feel comfortable with our offerings . . .* blah, blah, blah. They want me to know what I'm buying firsthand, I guess. Basically, if they're going to sell to me, I have to do this."

"I mean a little ahh while some doc looks at your tonsils isn't bad, but a mental checkup? That seems odd, right?" I say hesitantly. I'm not averse to Thomas getting a little professional help and have even said as much to encourage him to do so, but doing it as a requirement of sale seems beyond the pale.

"I wondered the same thing," Thomas says, glancing out the window. "Either it's legit and they just want to show off a bit, or someone encouraged them to require this as a condition."

"Ouch. So when's the first appointment?" I ask.

Thomas looks up, lifting an eyebrow. "Who said I'm going?"

I can't help but chuckle. Maybe I am starting to read him because though his face is dead-serious, I can see the twinkle deep in his eyes. "Thomas, I know you, remember? You'd crawl naked through fifteen miles of army ant-infested manure in order to get what you want, and you want that hospital."

"Army ant-infested manure?" Thomas asks. "Where did you hear that . . . another one of your Russia-isms?"

"Nope, that's a total Mia-ism. So?"

"This afternoon . . . in about two hours," Thomas says, and I can hear the dread in his voice. "Which is why I'm chugging away at this."

"How, uh, open and honest are you planning on being with them?" I ask.

"As little as I can get away with being. I don't need a shrink poking their fingers in my emotional wounds and asking how that makes me feel. This is a business transaction. Truth be told, if the return on investment wasn't so high, I'd tell them to shove it. But like you said, I can say ahh, let them listen to my heart, and tell a therapist that life is grand and be out the door with their promise to sign on the dotted line."

"Sounds like a plan. Though maybe skip the bloodwork too? Just suspicious, and I don't want them cloning you from your DNA," I joke, though my Velma senses are still tingling. "So, dinner later then?"

"Do you think we can do breakfast in the morning? I think after all this, I might need to work off a little frustration and I won't be very good company."

His answer disappoints me, but I understand. I've seen how much wear and tear he's put on his home gym. "Sure. You know, if you want, I can introduce you to some of my games. It's not as sweaty as your ways, but there's something to be said for the rush of slashing a troll in half with a giant sword and how it calms the nerves."

Thomas smiles a little, relieving me. He's not that bad off, and maybe he'll do okay today. "I can do that. Say, if things aren't too bad . . . ?"

"You might find that I wouldn't mind a visitor tonight," I promise him. "I'll keep a half-pint of ice cream ready for you, deal? It's another guaranteed stress reliever."

"Deal."

I head to the elevator, my mind still ticking over what's going on. Someone is trying to break Thomas, I'm sure of it. I've seen enough of the data to know that Thomas isn't paranoid in that regard.

And this, now? He's got a lot on his plate, but everyone's well aware the hospital deal means a lot to him. Financially and personally. With that on the line, the last thing he needs is the additional stress of having a shrink, therapist, whatever, poking the bear that is his emotional baggage.

Someone knows this, and they're applying the pressure to him. As the elevator doors close, I promise myself that I'm going to do whatever it takes to help him. Still, as I eat my chicken wrap, I force myself to think about everything but Thomas and his twin mysteries that are on my work plate.

It's part of my secret, just letting my mind work unfettered by conscious steering. Sometimes, it works faster that way.

Not that I plan on a revelation coming to me out of the blue while I'm eating lunch, but stranger things have happened.

When I get back from lunch, my scans are still chomping away, but at least one of the algorithms is done. The last thirty days of access card scans that hit outside my set parameters are compiled into a report. It's not much, just a bare-bones start, but I figured fresher figures would be my best bet to see if this approach will even yield useful information.

I can't help it, my eyes scan for Thomas first. Not to be snoopy or spy on him, but just because I'm curious. Okay, and maybe a little possessive. I like knowing what he does all day. It makes me feel close to him, even if he's twenty-six floors above me.

Nothing too unusual. Data points for him heading back and forth to his apartment mid-day, visits to other floors, but that makes sense for the CEO, and several exits to the parking garage. And I realize with a smile that the last line is his exiting to the garage just a few moments ago.

He is heading to the doctor appointment at the hospital. I'm proud in a weird way. Even if it's only because he wants the hospital deal so badly, the mere fact that he's going to sit down with a therapist bodes well.

I cross my fingers and say a little Russian prayer Papa taught me, hoping that Thomas is protected. From whomever is messing with him, and from himself.

And then I turn back to my computers with a groan and turn up the volume on my music. "I've got a lot more data to go through."

# CHAPTER 29

## Thomas

THE OFFICE IS A SERIES OF PASTEL BLOTCHES THAT I'VE READ ABOUT in interior design magazines. It's supposedly meant to reduce stress, support positive mental states, and be totally non-threatening.

To me it looks like someone tried to harness their Jackson Pollack, but with nothing but pastels and earth tones. It's Army camouflage meets Lululemon and throw in a good dose of Lena Dunham annoying, and you have the décor of the office.

"Hello, my name's Thomas Goldstone," I tell the receptionist. "I'm here to see Dr. Perry?"

There's no answer for a moment. Instead, the receptionist, who looks very professional in a 1985 sort of way with her puffy hair and tie at the neck of her blouse, just keeps typing away . . . but considering that she's only using the arrow keys on her keyboard, I suspect she's not exactly doing data entry.

"She'll be with you in a minute," she says without looking up from her computer. I swallow my frustration, making mental notes about everything I've seen here as I sit down in a plum-colored chair.

From the front door, everything had been pretty well-maintained. Clean and bright, maybe a little outdated. And the workers on the first floor had been smiling and helpful. Then, I'd met with an internist, Dr. Maeson, who'd basically spent the appointment time trying to sell me on Botox and Juvéderm injections and very little time actually giving me a real checkup. It's a good thing I have a primary care doctor of my own. And now here I am, at the pin-nacle of my downfall.

*So . . . finally, you've been reduced to this. And I thought you had some pride.*

I do have pride, but you were the one who kept telling me pride goes before a fall. I'm not going to fall.

*You keep saying that. But you're going to fall anyway. You think you'll be able to get through this interrogation without the doc realizing you're fifty shades of fucked up? Good luck with that!*

I squeeze the arm rests on the chair until my knuckles are white as the de-mon's laugh echoes hollowly in my head, drowning out everything around me.

Dimly, I become aware of someone calling my name, and I look up to see the receptionist. Judging by her sigh, she must've called my name repeat-edly before I heard her.

Getting to my feet, I follow her down the short hallway to what pretty much looks like your standard shrink's office, although instead of the couch, it seems Dr. Perry prefers the super-comfy club chair arrangement.

I take a seat, and the receptionist leaves, closing the door behind her and leaving me alone . . . except for the voice in my head.

*What are you going to tell her? Maybe you should start with how you let you mother die while you ate chicken nuggets?*

The door opens, and Dr. Perry walks in, and I'm cringing already.

She's younger than I expected, maybe mid-twenties, but dressed in a buttoned-up, almost prudish way that makes her seem even younger. I have a biting thought that maybe the receptionist is her mother. There's just some-thing about Dr. Perry that screams she has no life experience and would be offended by the most minor peek at my true history.

I'm not normally one to judge people on appearance. I know just how much a fancy business suit can hide, after all. But how am I supposed to 'con-nect' and share with someone who looks like her biggest concern is whether she should have a bran muffin or treat herself to Mini-Wheats for breakfast?

How am I supposed to share and gain insight from someone I already think has never dealt with the same things I've dealt with?

Not that I have any real intention of getting help from Dr. Perry or any-one else. This appointment is strictly so that I can proceed with the hospital purchase plan.

*Aw, you know you can't get rid of me anyway. And this hospital deal is going to be a failure, just like you.*

"Thomas, it's a pleasure to meet you," Dr. Perry says, something else that puts me on edge. While I encourage the use of first names within the Goldstone offices, outside I'm always professional. You don't use my first name without getting permission first. "How are you today?"

"I'm here," I reply, cautiously guarded. "You?"

"It's been a good day," Dr. Perry says, and I notice she doesn't offer her first name. Instead, she looks me over before sitting down and picking up a clipboard next to her. "So, let's talk ground rules."

"Ground rules?" I ask, lifting an eyebrow. *Remember the deal. Remember the deal . . .*

"Yes. First, I am going to need you to be open with me. That's the only way to delve into any areas that need clarity. Perhaps we should begin at the beginning. Tell me about your childhood."

The things I do to be the best.

The elevator can't open quickly enough as I get back home, my anger barely held back.

I'd spent the better part of an hour redirecting Dr. Perry away from every hot-button issue I have and trying to steer her toward information pertinent to the hospital sale. But she'd been relentless, almost to point of it becoming an interrogation as she calmly asked questions about my parents, my school years, my business, and my personal life, all the while making checkmarks on her clipboard like the whole thing was an automated process for her.

Check yes here, ask follow up question there. And when I'd gotten frustrated at her repeated inquiries, she'd had the nerve to tell me that I need to *accept* my anger, let it *teach* me, and *grow* a healthier future. It might as well have been an inspirational quote from her Pinterest board for all the insight she offered.

She'd basically turned me off therapy, and between Dr. Maeson and Dr. Perry, my biggest concern with the hospital purchase is the caliber of its employees. Well, and that someone had managed to wrangle that whole rigmarole in the first place.

I strip quickly out of my suit and look in my closet, finally choosing the clothes that match my inner anger and rage. The white undershirt's tattered, bloodstained, and patched in half a dozen places, looking more like

Frankenstein's T-shirt than something belonging in the closet of a man who has more money than he knows what to do with.

For two years, I wore it under my shoulder pads for every football game, every team lift, so that by now, it barely hangs together. But it's raw, it's torn and battered . . . and so am I, full of rage, venom practically dripping from my lips as I pull on my heavy compression shorts and go into my gym.

Grabbing my belt from its hook on the wall, I start up the music, Carl Orff's *O Fortuna* setting the right mood as I set up the squat rack.

Time to get ugly, to make the pain flow.

By the time *Venom* pounds through the speakers, sweat stains my shirt, my thighs are flooded with blood, and my chest is heaving as I stare at the 375 pounds on the bar.

*Do you think this will make you feel like you've accomplished something? It won't. You're just going to fail.*

"That's the fucking plan," I growl, slapping myself across the face. This isn't exactly safe. You're not supposed to push yourself to maximum effort under heavy weight without anyone here to spot.

But I built this gym with that in mind, and I've got the equipment to protect me. The nylon safety straps looped around the upper supports of my power rack are capable of catching the weight when I can't do any more.

I slap myself again, rage and anger and hatred for myself, for my life, for everything that I've been through coursing through me. Jamming myself under the bar, I revel in the punishment of the steel pressing into my back, the inch-thick bar digging into that space right below my deltoids and across my back before I drop into 'the hole'.

One.

*You're never going to make it. Your best is twelve . . . you're weak.*

College. Standing on stage. Nobody in the crowd for me. I was the twenty-one-year-old *wunderkind* who graduated with his MBA at the same age most people were figuring out which beer they liked best. Dennis Goldstone? Didn't attend, didn't send a gift, didn't send a congratulations.

"Bastard! Two!" I yell as the music screams with me.

High school. The state championships. Giving the valedictorian speech. Never once did he attend.

Three . . . and I can feel it in my back. I've spent so much time over the past month doing things besides putting in time under this bar, my back is tired already. Fighting it, I push my stomach out against my belt, bracing myself and dropping again.

Four . . . five . . . my thighs are flushed with blood, the muscles in there quivering with each breath, sweat pouring down my face and dripping onto the flooring beneath me, but I still go down.

*I bet you won't even be able to do ten.*

Six . . . God, the pain's blinding . . . seven . . .

*You really think you're the best because you can push some pussy weights around? The best perform to their capability every time, always pushing further, deeper, better. And that's just not you.*

Junior high. Scoring a perfect on my PSAT, then a 2250 on the then SAT scale in ninth grade. No acknowledgement from my father except to point out that over 400 students got perfect scores.

Nine . . . I take a deep breath, my vision narrowing to a pulsing red-black tunnel that barely allows me to see my depth as I go down again. I feel wetness on my upper lip and realize I've burst a blood vessel in my nose, but I don't stop, going down into the hole again.

*Stay down! You're fucking weak, stay down!*

My mind flashes, remembering the 'discussions' with my father, the time I told him if he'd come, I'd hit a home run in Little League . . .

I groan, pushing as the world spins around me until I'm standing up, pain pulsating through every fiber of my being. My back's on fire, my legs are numb, I can't feel my fingertips, and my heart's pounding so hard that I can't even hear the music anymore.

But I go down again.

My knees are almost in my chest, and everything's strained in ways that men are not supposed to strain themselves, and for this eleventh rep, the hole feels like the deepest pit on Earth, the weight of the entire building on my shoulders. I'm in hell, and the only way out is my rage and my own will.

My thighs quake, my calves threaten to cramp, and everything becomes a single explosion of pain as I push to get the weight back up.

I'm a quarter of the way there when the cramp paralyzes my left thigh and I pitch forward, unable to stop myself. The safety straps catch the weight just as planned, saving me as I fall face first to the ground, unable to even stop myself with my arms.

I lay there, blood pooling under my face, trying to will my thigh into relaxing. The pain's enormous, and even after my leg releases, I can barely move. I have to crawl like a baby out of my workout room, all the way to the bathroom. I'll clean up the mess later.

My tub is built into the floor, my only obstacle a six-inch lip that I lean on as the water fills and I peel my T-shirt off and use my toes to get my shoes off. I try twice to get my shorts off, but my back and legs won't let me move, so I leave them on, rolling over the lip of the tub and into the hot water.

Luckily, my arms are moving, and I push myself into a sitting position before calling out, "Alexa . . . play Enya." The screaming death metal from my workout room stops, replaced by soft music in the bathroom. It's cliché, perhaps, but everyone jokes about Enya music being relaxing for a reason . . . it is. And with a touch of a button, the jets in the tub turn on low.

I lean my head back, and shame fills me as the voice in my head gleefully taunts.

*Told you that you'd fail. You've gotten even weaker, if that's possible. She's done that to you.*

"No," I whisper, shaking my head. She's made me stronger, and I can't imagine not having Mia in my life anymore. I have to have her, and I have to keep her with me.

# CHAPTER 30

## Blackwell

"Y OU STEERED HIM TO WHOM?" I ASK.

"Only the worst therapist in the entire system for him. She's young, has a one-track mind, and not in the fun way, and is about as interesting as Cream of Wheat."

I chuckle, sipping at my snifter of brandy. The firelight flickers behind my chair, casting my body into dark relief as my man sits across from me in the study, his vengeful smile slightly off kilter and bloody in the burning light.

While I would not normally risk another face-to-face meeting so soon with such an underling, this one is amusing. He has a twisted sense of vengeance that most people wouldn't associate with him, underestimating him on appearances alone.

"Wouldn't Goldstone just walk all over her?"

My man grins maniacally, shaking his head. "Perry's too stupid to realize if he was. She goes from question one to two to three, no variance. Ever. So he could try to skirt around her questions, but she just wraps back around and around until she can check if off. Maddening woman. Met her at a Christmas party once. She's a good reason to indulge in too much eggnog."

"You have a stroke of deviousness to you."

It's high praise. I rarely meet people who are worthy of it.

"Thank you, sir. I learned from some of the best."

I hum, wondering if the man is giving me a backhanded compliment. I doubt it. He hasn't been under my tutelage for long. And he's experienced enough to know that mocking me is a potentially deadly choice.

"And does the hospital suspect you of planting such a poison pill in their potential deal?" I ask.

The man's smile is wide. "No, they thought my idea to really show Goldstone all the hospital had to offer was genius. I was able to make it as a casual suggestion through a buddy of mine. Made it easy for their board to take it as a good recommendation. But they have no idea about . . . this."

"So are you assured that you've been able to poison the deal?"

"It isn't perfect," my man admits. "You know he's driven, and more than once, through sheer force of will or stubbornness, he's made chicken salad out of chicken shit."

My mouth pinches, and I set my brandy aside. I understand my man's background has taught him such language is acceptable in the company of men, but I have other expectations.

"You should learn that a foul mouth is best saved for only the most exclusive of situations. Overuse of it in inappropriate times only makes you seem uneducated and crass. Although, Golden Boy does deserve stronger language than what you might normally use."

"That's true, sir. I can assure you that the Ruthless Bastard is going to fall. The only question I have is, will I let him know who's slipped the knife in his ribs when he goes down, or will I just enjoy the fruits of my labor?"

I shrug, unconcerned. Still, I know when I'm being asked for advice. "You know what cost Marcus Junius Brutus his life?"

"Killing Caesar?"

I pick up my snifter again, downing the rest of it in a single gulp. "No, his error was in letting it be known that he'd done so."

The truth, of course, is much more complicated. Entire books, entire careers, have been made on studying the political machinations of the transition period between the Roman Republic and the Roman Empire. It's actually a delightful bit of study that I've indulged in, and far more than what any television show or movie has been able to replicate. It makes *House of Cards* look like *Sesame Street*.

A more nuanced answer would be not that Brutus let it be known, but that he then didn't crush his adversaries when he had the power to do so.

Not that my underling would grasp the nuances of power. He sees power as a blunt tool.

"Of course, sir. May I ask, what will you do while this is . . . ripening?"

I chuckle, a chilling sound that makes even my man shiver. Ripening . . . it's a fine choice of words.

"What I always do. Consolidate power."

# CHAPTER 31

## Mia

TWO MORE DAYS, AND MY RESEARCH HAS SPLIT.

I've been forced into a rather uncomfortable pair of possibilities. And either one is dangerous for Thomas.

One, there's an outside puppet master involved in all of this, someone pulling strings inside Goldstone. If that's the case, I just don't have enough data. This puppet master could have multiple agents inside the company, and I would be chasing phantoms for years without knowing where to focus attention.

Goldstone has so many business rivals, so many enemies, that I'd have to do an active investigation, and I'm no private eye.

I'm just a data hound.

I don't care if I want to call myself Velma while I'm working at this and I don't care how sexy I think I look in glasses. I'm not an actual private eye.

The more dangerous possibility, though, is that there's a high-ranking traitor involved. I consider every angle of how the decisions are being made, from data pulls to meetings to PowerPoint presentations.

As hard as it is, I even consider Kerry as a suspect. I mean, in most mysteries, the butler does it. And while Kerry definitely isn't the butler, she's the one who filters all of Thomas's info to him. Thankfully, after a whole day of work, I can't find any data that supports that and I happily cross her off my mental suspect list.

Past that, I look at those with corporate powers. And considering the number of investments and the scattershot way I've seen them done, it would have to be a major shareholder or one of the Executive VPs. Only they have the ability to see all the projects that the company is undertaking, and only someone with such power would be able to apply pressure in the right way.

But why would a major shareholder or VP want to see the company hurt? Their fortunes rest on the company's continuing to do well. Why would a VP, who would want a good track record with the company even if they wanted to jump ship, undertake a complicated exercise in corporate sabotage?

And why would the shareholders, whose wealth is literally pegged to company performance? Thomas certainly wouldn't, and he's the largest shareholder in the company.

Looking over the list of major shareholders who would have access to enough information to slit the throat of all the projects I've found, there's only one name who'd have potential reason for wanting to hurt Goldstone . . . and it's a Goldstone after all.

Not Thomas. Dennis.

But would Dennis Goldstone really want to hurt his son that much?

Would he be so hateful and hellbent on ensuring Thomas's failure that he would sabotage him just to prove a point? Thomas told me about their argument, but even if Dennis is a greedy bastard, this seems unfathomable.

And then I remember the other unimaginable things Thomas has told me.

I might not be a private eye, but I can at least do some investigating.

I grab my phone, dialing Kerry and saying another prayer that I think she's legitimately a good thing for Thomas. "Hey, Kerry! I had potential lunch plans with Thomas today? Any word on his morning meeting?"

She scoffs, and I can imagine her shaking her head at her desk. "Definitely a no-go. His meeting is running long. He sent me a message a few minutes ago to give you apologies and order lunch in for the whole group downstairs. Bunch of bloodhounds are probably just yammering away in the hopes of getting a free lunch anyway. But he says sorry, and I've gotta run. Unless there's something else?"

I smile, relieved. "You're the best, you know that? But that's all I was checking on. Thanks!"

"Just make sure your man knows that and we're golden!" she replies, and then she hangs up without another word.

It seems like a sign, a perfect maelstrom of opportunity, information, and curiosity. And I'm going to Sherlock the hell out of it while I can.

I use my downloaded records to get Dennis Goldstone's address from the corporate database. Despite his supposed disdain for Thomas, he actually lives in Roseboro, having moved to town approximately one year after the Goldstone Building opened up. He even has a business address, a law office in a suburb just outside Roseboro.

I grab my keys. It's time for a road trip. Feeling good, I flip on the tunes as I drive, singing along in my terrible voice as I head out of town and into the pleasant suburb.

I'm a little surprised when I get there. I expected more, considering Dennis Goldstone's history of being a partner in a law firm. But Dennis's office is small, not much more than a pleasant-looking medium-sized house, and if it weren't for the plain wooden sign out front, I wouldn't be able to tell it apart from any of the dozen other small offices and houses that dot this tree-lined street.

I get out, noticing that there's only one car in the driveway, and go up to the front door, knocking three times and waiting. I wonder, does he work by himself?

Or maybe I'm just here when his staff has the day off?

Just as I'm about to ring the doorbell, the door opens and I get my first view of Dennis Goldstone.

I didn't realize until this moment that I'd expected a monster, not a mere man after the things Thomas told me. But before me is just a man. I can see the resemblance, faintly, if you took away about thirty pounds of muscle from Thomas and replaced it with maybe ten pounds of middle-aged pot gut.

Still, the eyes are the same, and while he's got the same jawline, it's obvious that Thomas got most of his good looks from his mother.

"Can I help you?" he asks.

"Mr. Goldstone? My name's Mia Karakova. If you don't mind, I'd like to talk with you about Thomas."

At the mention of his son's name, Dennis snorts, though nothing is funny in the least. But he steps back, waving me inside. "So you're *her*, huh? Come to see the Boogie Man, I suppose?" His tone is sarcastic, biting, and I can only imagine that it's what the voice in Thomas's memories are like.

I step inside Dennis's office, and I'm immediately struck by two things. One, that while Thomas's sense of style tends toward the efficient regardless of the aesthetics . . . Dennis is just cheap. The man made 1.8 million dollars in dividends on his Goldstone stock last year based off the declared dividends, but his office looks like it was furnished with page 62 of the IKEA catalog.

Still, his desk's nearly military neat, and the carpet looks freshly vacuumed this morning. Okay, he's gotta have staff working for him. They're just not here right now because nothing about this man says he does his own household chores.

The next thing I notice as I look around is the total lack of pictures on his wall. He's got his undergrad and law degrees framed and hanging behind his desk, and he's even got a couple of other certificates, thanks, and awards from various civic groups in Roseboro and other places.

But there are no pictures. Nothing of Thomas, nothing of his deceased wife . . . no family pictures at all. It seems strange, considering it is his office.

"So, what do you want to know?" Dennis asks, sitting down in his chair. I take the other, immediately wishing I had my office chair instead. The foam's shot, and I can feel the seat post actually pressing against my butt.

"What do you mean, sir?" I ask, doing my best to stay polite. Thomas may not like his father for good reason, but that doesn't mean I have to be hostile to him too. Especially when I'm trying to decide if he's the one trying to hurt Thomas. *More flies with honey,* I repeat to myself.

"I saw your picture in the paper with Tom, and there's no reason for someone from the company to come see me. The only people I talk to are my son and that bitch he has screening his phone calls. Unless . . . did he send you?"

*Kudos, Kerry. I owe you a cupcake or something.*

"No, Thomas didn't send me. He uh . . . he doesn't know I'm here, actually." And the impact of what I'm doing hits me full force. I truly am one of 'those meddlesome kids', thinking I have any right to Velma my way into not only Thomas's company business but his private affairs with his dad.

I squirm in my seat, the post prodding me and making me want to make a run for the door.

Dennis narrows his eyes in suspicion, his face pinching. "But you are dating my son? Are you looking for a payoff?"

I flinch, my jaw dropping in shock. "Yes . . . I mean no." I sigh, calming myself and speaking more confidently, "Yes, I am seeing Thomas. No, I don't want a payoff. That's absurd!"

"Uh-huh," Dennis says, leaning back. "So then you probably want to figure out why my son hates me so much. Like I said, you've come to see the Boogie Man."

"No, Mr. Goldstone, I wouldn't—"

"No, it's fine. He does see me that way, no sense in denying it. I already know it's true. So I repeat, what do you want to know?" His eyes are sharp, challenging me. No, *daring* me. This is a test, I know it in my gut.

This man has belittled Thomas, testing him and setting him up for failure since he was a little boy. And I no longer feel the need for polite niceties and falsely civilized conversation. Dennis Goldstone goes for his son's jugular at every opportunity, and it's high time someone went for his.

"I want to know why you blame Thomas for your wife's death? I want to know why you punished him, a six-year-old little boy, for something that wasn't his fault? And I want to know just how deep your well of hatred goes and what you'd do to hurt him now that a backhand won't do?"

It's harsh. I know it's harsh, but I also know from my time with Thomas that strength is important. And in this case, it's like son, like father. Dennis stares at me for a moment before grunting, leaning forward and planting his forearms on his desk.

I hold my breath, refusing to bow to the fury swirling in Dennis's eyes, so similar to the anger I see in Thomas's sometimes. I'm already expecting the blow, verbal or physical I don't know, but I'm ready either way.

But I'm not prepared for the way Dennis deflates before my very eyes.

"You're a ballsy bitch, aren't you?" He makes it sound like a compliment.

"I've been accused of it before."

"Fine, you want the whole sordid story? Then here you go." It sounds like he's about to tell a roomful of kids there's no Santa Claus, Easter Bunny, or Tooth Fairy, and dread fills my gut. I almost stop him, knowing this isn't my place, but I need to know too badly. I think it might be the only way I can truly help Thomas. So I don't stop him, instead letting Dennis dive into the past.

"I was a junior associate in one of those big firms when I met Grace. She was so beautiful. And we were happy, for a bit. Until she shattered my soul like it was nothing. Heartless bitch."

His words are deep, dripping with hurt, and I blink, wondering what they mean. "Shattered your soul? You mean the suicide?"

He bares his teeth at the word, like I just bade him to bite into aluminum foil. "No, she killed me long before that. See, what you need to know about Ms. Grace Lewis was that she was a beauty queen, always thought she'd marry up, live a life of luxury. Eat bonbons or some shit, I guess. But that's not what she got. She got me. And I was living in a dog eat dog world back then, working from sunup to midnight just to stand a chance at making partner one day. She got bored, told me she wanted to have a baby to play with. So we had Tom, and I thought she'd finally be happy and leave me alone to work. I was getting close by then, you see? Moving off the grunt work, living the American dream, it seemed like it was all going well."

He pauses, lost in the past, and I prompt him, "But?"

He slams his palm on the desk, his eyes flashing with decades of pain and fury. "But she was fucking everyone from the mailman to the Avon lady behind my back. Some dream!"

I'm shocked and the look on my face says everything. Thomas didn't say anything about his mom cheating, not that it excuses anything, but it's another puzzle piece clicking home.

"Yeah," Dennis growls. "Imagine, coming home early after busting your ass and you walk in to find your wife fucking someone in your own bed. The first time it happened, Tom was over at his friend's house. Grace even tried to defend herself, saying she'd always sent the boy over to play. Made me wonder just how many people were in on her little games. The whole time, I was being played for a fucking chump."

I shake my head. "But why blame Thomas?"

"Because he never said a word to me about going over to this kid's house! I would have known something was going on! While the cat's away, I guess the mice were having a fucking party." Bitter pain drips from the words like venom.

Horror fills me as I realize the depth of Dennis's anger. Somehow, he still blamed his son for all of this. Or at least blamed him for part of it. He hadn't known, had no concept of what she was doing, and maybe doesn't even remember that, but still. And in this moment, I'm just as angry at Grace Goldstone as I am at Dennis.

"I should have left her then, but I didn't."

His voice catches, and he swallows before continuing. "I gave her another chance. I didn't even hold it against her. I didn't need to cash in my chip and play tit for tat. I was trying to fix it if I could, even suggested counseling . . . and then she did it again. Walked in on her with my boss, said she was trying to help me at work, then pulled out that if he could get home by dinner time, then why couldn't I? She'd set it up on purpose, I think. I told her then that I was going to talk to a lawyer. Two days later, she killed herself while Tom sat munching on chicken nuggets and watching fucking *ThunderCats* or something."

And there it is.

"Dennis, he was six years old."

"So?" Dennis explodes, his eyes glaring in rage and anger. "He was a smart boy. He could have done something!"

I swallow back my own anger, not wanting to get into a screaming match with this man.

He blames Thomas? Where was *he*?

I'm not saying that Grace was right to cheat on her husband, but he was the one who abandoned her to chase his way up the legal ladder while assuming she was fine being a housewife.

I don't excuse Grace Goldstone for doing what she did.

But I don't blame her for what happened to Thomas, either.

Twenty-plus years of torturing his son mentally, abusing him emotionally and even physically . . . and it comes down to one afternoon.

"Did he tell you I got fired then? I was grieving my wife, trying to figure out what to do with a kid, and I was fired because they were afraid I was going to kill the last man who'd stuck his dick in my dead wife. And he was the one signing my paychecks."

Another nail in the coffin of the life Dennis Goldstone thought he had. And I can't imagine the pain that caused him, but this story doesn't end there. Not for Dennis, and not for Thomas.

"Dennis, I'm not going to tell you not to be pissed at Grace. She was selfish, and she betrayed her trust as both a wife and a mother. But your son has suffered for over twenty years, not because of what she did . . . but because of what *you've* done."

"And what did I do?" he asks quietly.

"You're not stupid. I think you know. I can see it in your eyes," I reply, having come to a realization.

Dennis is just as much a pained monster lashing out at the world as Thomas sometimes is, but where Thomas has me, Dennis has no one. His rage and misdirected anger at his wife are hurting Thomas, but I don't think he's the villain in the sabotage scheme.

He's definitely Thomas's Boogie Man, but he's not the spy. I'd bet on it, and I only gamble when I know the odds.

I stand up, done with this. "I came here because someone's trying to destroy your son's company. I thought maybe it was you, but from what you've told me, I'm sure it isn't. But Thomas has many enemies and not enough friends. He could use another ally. Even more, he could use a father. But make no mistake, if you hurt him in any way, physical or mental or emotional, I will make you wish for the release of death to ease your pain." I mumble a little Russian threat after I finish. I doubt he could understand, but I'm sure he gets the message either way.

Dennis sits pondering for a few moments before nodding, though not speaking any words.

After two decades, words must be hard to come by.

I give him my office number and email, writing them down on a piece of paper. Dennis takes a look and stands up, offering his hand. I'm so surprised that I shake it, just to see what he has to say.

"You're a strong woman. Smart, too, from what I've heard. Good luck."

We shake, and I leave, heading back toward the office.

I'd thought I might get a little insight on the man behind the monster, see if he was the one pulling the strings to hurt Goldstone, and I definitely got a lot more than I expected. I'm just not sure if that's a good thing or a very bad thing.

# CHAPTER 32

## Mia

THOMAS ARRIVES AT MY PLACE RIGHT ON TIME IN CASUAL sweatpants and a T-shirt. With his hair sort of disheveled like he's just gotten out of the shower and finger combed it, and a touch of five o'clock shadow . . . it's honestly the sexiest look he's ever had.

"Hey," I greet him, pulling him inside before kissing him softly. Tonight will end up with us in bed unless someone sets off a hand grenade . . . but that's still hours away, and I want him to see this side of me more. "How was your post-work workout?"

"Light," Thomas reassures me. After watching him limp for a day or two, it's nice to hear he does know how to throttle it back a notch. I didn't ask him what had triggered him to punish himself so much, but I've made a few assumptions and trusted him the rest of the way. "So, what's on the agenda?"

"TERA," I tell him, leading him over to the couch. "I've already got an account ready to go for you. You just need to pick your character name and we'll walk through the rest."

I turn on my TV and show him the basics of the world, what the deal is behind the game, and all the other stuff he needs to know. It'll be hours before he really gets it, but as he listens and flips through the various options, I can see him nodding in understanding.

"Uhh, what type of character do you use?" Thomas asks, and I grin as I open another window and show him my current favorite character. "You're one sexy elf," he says with a cheesy bite of his lip.

"Thank you. Just remember I can shoot the hairs off your ears at half a mile," I tease him. "You're going to need a lot of leveling up to get anywhere near my skills."

"Well then, since this is just for fun, how about . . . Castanic?"

I grin, the two of us deciding on a Castanic Brawler, his massive fists encased in the 'power gloves' of the game. It's a character and role that'll let him have fun while releasing some tension for sure.

I especially like how Thomas picks facial features that, while not ex-actly mirroring his own, certainly suggest the handsome man I've got seated next to me.

Thomas picks up the controller while I guide him through playing. Unfortunately, TERA isn't a game where we can both be onscreen at the same time, but that's okay. I enjoy coaching him through the basics.

We decide to swap the controller back and forth, Thomas watching as I hit a few button combinations and show him how to trigger the skills he's starting out with. Still, as he plays, I can see he's tense.

"What's on your mind? The game isn't the kind that you need to grit your teeth. I mean, you're beating up a mushroom right now. Not even Mario gets this tense."

"Sorry," Thomas says, rubbing his hands together. "Just trying to play well, but there's a helper in my head telling me that I'm going to crash and burn. Can you even do that in this game?"

I nod slowly. "Yeah, but you're safe here in this area. It's a learning and training ground. Just relax. This is supposed to be fun."

Thomas nods and takes the controller back when the pizza comes. I grab the large extra pepperoni pizza and bring it back, surprised when I see Thomas jamming buttons, his face flushed and his lips drawn back in a sneer.

"Tommy, what—" I ask just as another player turns him into a pile of goo. He'd attacked a high-level player outright?

Thomas growls and slams the controller into the cushion of my couch. Thankfully, I've nerd-raged a few times myself, and my wireless controller is strong enough to take it. I've learned that one from experience.

"Dammit!" Thomas growls while I come around, setting the pizza down on the table.

"You fought a guy twenty-six levels above you. There's no possible chance to win that."

"I should be able to." He pouts.

I climb into his lap, and he shuts up, his eyes still sparking with anger. "There's a method to the madness, steps and progress to take along the levels. You can't skip stuff. Just like in life, you've got to explore everything."

My sexy tone is melting his anger, turning it into molten lust before my very eyes. "Explore. Every. Thing?" he says darkly.

"Mmmhmm. Every emotion, every nook and cranny, every bit of it so that you're ready for the next level."

I see a flush wash over Tommy's face, and then he whispers hotly in my ear, "And are you ready for the next level, Mia?"

I could take his words as flirtation, because they most definitely are. But there's something underneath the sexy tone, a longing, a plea from this beast of a man, and I look into his eyes, wondering what would bring him to the point of begging. And I know.

He can't be the first to say it. He's simply not able to make that leap first and needs me to lead him there. But I can do that. That's what partners do, take turns leading each other sometimes, walk side by side sometimes, and even carry each other when one needs help.

So I press his palm to my chest over my heart. "Thomas Goldstone, you have let me into your heart and into your life, trusting me when every bit of life experience has told you not to. You may be a ruthless bastard to others, but to me, you're a brave man, beautiful on the inside, scars and all. I love you."

I can see the relief wash through him, the light filling him. I think I even see a glassy shine to his eyes, but I can't be sure because he pulls me down, kissing me hard and taking my breath away. I don't need it, but still my heart leaps when he breaks our kiss, whispering in my ear, "I love you too." And I feel the last wall crumbling between us, exposing even more of us to one another.

I grin like the cat that got the cream, so happy I could burst, and then I laugh out loud, the jiggles of my body rubbing me along Thomas's cock.

"What's so funny?" he demands, but I can see that he's not worried, just curious.

I try to sober but barely get the words out. "It's like Grand Theft . . . coronary. You stole my heart."

He blinks, and I think he doesn't get the reference to the popular video game, a crime against gaming everywhere, but then he busts out laughing too. "God, that's corny. It's a good thing you're cute."

I fake offense, swatting him with a throw pillow, and he smiles back. It feels good, like we said this really big thing, but we're still us.

And as *us*, the heat returns in an instant when Thomas kneads my ass, grinding himself against my pussy.

"I'm all yours, Tommy," I promise him as I swirl my hips, feeling him grow harder in his sweatpants. "Take it . . . *all* of it."

"You know what that means, right?" he asks, and I nod, grinning.

Thomas reaches under my legs, and standing up feels like a thrill ride in itself it's so smooth and powerful. He carries me down the short hallway to my bedroom, where he lays me down on my bed before stepping back, pulling his shirt off.

My heart hammers in my chest, watching his perfectly sculpted body flex with power and strength that's understated but fills the room. His muscles flow and bunch with organic grace as he unbuttons his jeans and slides them down his hips, pausing just before his cock pops out.

"This isn't all on me," he says, using his chin to gesture at my still-clothed body.

I grin, biting my lip naughtily as I sit up and pull my top off, my nipples tightening and my chest flushing as his eyes drink me in. "You're so beautiful, Mia. And so . . . mine. I love you."

The words come easily this time, but I return them anyway, wanting to reward him for the gift.

"I love you too."

I lift my hips and shimmy my pants down in time with him until he stands before me, a hulking, powerful god of love and sex, his cock standing thick and hard from his body.

"Spread your legs," he commands.

I do, stretching myself as wide as I can and letting him watch me, my legs as straight as possible before running my fingertips up the insides of my thighs, stroking my pussy softly for him to watch.

"So fucking hot," Thomas growls, reaching down and wrapping his fist around his cock as I keep rubbing until the warmth reaches its sexy tendrils down the insides of my thighs. I spread myself open for him, his fist slowly pumping his cock as we tease each other, our eyes glued on each other.

His cock is perfect. Even his massive fist can't make it look small as he squeezes it before he strokes back, pumping in and out of his hand. A clear drop of precum oozes out to hang on the tip of his cock like a jewel of morning dew before sliding down and off, a thread of delicious light gleaming in the bedside lamplight.

"I'm thirsty," Thomas says, dropping to his knees, his eyes fixed on my stroking fingers. "I'm going to suck your pussy dry until you come all over my face, but I want you to do something for me. Get your favorite toy for me?"

I nod and reach over with my free hand to open my bedside table. I take out my vibrator and the small bottle of lube just in case, setting them on the bed next to my hip. Thomas picks up the vibrator and inspects it, finding the switch and turning it on.

I blush, and he smirks knowingly as he picks up the bottle of lube. "This . . . this, we'll use later."

He lowers himself slowly, teasing and tantalizing me, his mouth just hovering over my pussy until I can't wait any longer, and I lift myself up, offering myself to him. The first touch of his tongue on my pussy is a dam breaking, and the sound he makes as he sucks on my tender lips is ravenous, starving, animalistic in its intensity.

He consumes me lovingly, his tongue stiffening to drive deep inside me before he scoops out my juices, sucking and drinking me like I'm a fountain for him.

"Mmm, that's it, Beautiful," he says as I toss my head side to side, somehow overwhelmed even though I knew what was coming—namely, me. "Give it all to me . . . and I'll give you more. Make this sweet pussy gush for me."

His tongue strokes my clit, and in the dim, sex-addled recesses of my mind, I hear the sound of my lube being opened. Thomas scoops under my ass to lift me before tucking a pillow under my lower back, and I look down blearily at him as he smiles between my legs, a conqueror ready to truly show me what he can do.

I gasp as his slick finger finds my ass, the breathless sound turning into a deep moan as he sucks on my clit, pleasure and trepidation teasing me as he massages the ring of muscle in time to his strokes.

I know we talked about it in Japan, and his tongue was wonderful, but can I really take him there? I open my mouth to say something when his finger pushes into me at the same time he licks my clit hard, and I cry out, instantly coming around his finger while his mouth sucks on my pussy, literally drinking and draining me of everything.

I don't know how long I writhe, but his free hand holds me still, trapped as his finger starts to probe deeper, slipping all the way into my ass before pulling back as he slowly finger fucks my backside.

"Mmm . . . I can read your eyes, Beautiful," Thomas growls, scooting up my body so that he's reaching between my legs to keep his finger moving against my clit, massaging it at the same time as he slowly slips in and out of my ass. "You think you can't take my big cock in that tight, heart-shaped ass of yours?"

I nod, whimpering as he lowers his mouth to my left nipple and sucks, my fingers twisting in his hair as he bites down lightly, keeping me trembling on the edge of pain and pleasure. My ass is starting to relax, and a deep feeling of accomplishment and wanton lust flood me as I feel him slip another finger inside me, stretching me more.

"Oh, fuck, you'll split me in half," I whimper as he speeds up. It feels so good now, my body taken in a new way while my clit slips and slides against his hand. "But I trust you."

"Then you'll love this," Thomas says, withdrawing his fingers from my ass. I squirm. The suddenly empty feeling has me trembling in need and he knows it.

He grabs my vibrator and holds it up, covering it with slick lube before teasing my asshole with it while at the same time kissing me deeply. I feel his smile and know it's a warning, one last chance to stop this, but I want it. I want it all. He swallows my cry as he pushes, the vibrator sliding into my ass and sending me over the edge.

I cry out, bucking against him as my clit throbs, the vibrator lodged deep inside me as I come around it and Thomas holds me close, his tongue invading me.

"Mmmhmm, one more . . . for now," Thomas says when I come down, limp and almost unable to move. "Trust me, Mia. I love you."

His repeated declaration of his love is what I need, and I nod, lifting my knees up as he gets between my legs. I think he's going to take the vibrator out to replace it with his cock, but instead, he reaches down, twisting it a little as he searches for the switch, but when he does . . .

"Oh, fuck . . . I can't, you'll drive me insane."

I've never tried this before . . . but each second, my body is pummeled with sensation as the vibrator turns my ass into a center of pleasure that I've never thought it could be. It's like he's pushing my limits, taking me, and cherishing me all at the same time, and as the tingles start to spread again, a new type of heat fills my body.

He grins, his cock long and proud as he grabs the lube again, rubbing it over himself . . . and I realize what he's going to do.

"You make me insane every time you look at me. Every time you kiss me, you drive me wild. I'm just giving you a taste of what I feel."

His cock gleams as he wraps his hands around my thighs and pulls me into him. I feel his thickness press against my pussy, but there's no way he'll fit. My body's already being taken over again from the vibrator and—

"Now!" Thomas grunts, driving his cock balls-deep into me in one savage, powerful stroke. I cry out, tears springing to my eyes even as my body comes again, my pussy clamping around his slick cock as he holds me paralyzed with pleasure and pain from the dual intrusions.

So full. I've never been this full.

My heart freezes, the air steel in my chest as Thomas doesn't stop, pulling back before stroking in slowly this time, drawing it out. My mind's exploding, my neck aching as I toss my head back and forth, but I don't know what I'm denying.

Is it that I can't take any more? That I want more? That I'm overwhelmed by what I'm feeling? That I can't believe what he's doing to me?

Yes. Yes and yes and all that and more. He presses into me, my pussy tightly clenching around his huge cock. Thomas presses me into the bed, letting go of my thighs to plant his arms on each side of my head, using all of his massive strength to drive his cock hard and deep into my exhausted, quivering body.

I've heard of this type of never-ending climax. I mean, what nerd hasn't? Wave upon wave of pleasure crashes through me, my body shaking and my muscles losing all sense of control. I'm helpless, pinned underneath him and barely able to feel anything except the constant barrage of white-hot explosions with each stroke of his cock. It's a fairy tale, it's a fantasy, but it's real and it's happening to me.

"That's it, honey . . . take my cock, cream deep all over me, and I'll fuck you over and over. I'll pound you, I'll hammer you . . . but I won't break you," Thomas rasps between thrusts. "I love you."

"I love you too!" I scream with the last conscious thought in my mind, and he howls, his cock swelling as he thrusts as deep as he can one last time. Liquid heat flows through me, pure release, but no sound escapes my lips. I can't even breathe anymore. Instead, I let the darkness take me because I know that in the darkness, there will be my Thomas . . . and I'll be safe in his arms.

# CHAPTER 33

## Thomas

Love.

Terror.

It's amazing how similar the two emotions feel as they dance around in my chest and my head, dueling with each other.

On one hand, I am in love. Mia's simple declaration sealed it, and the trust she put in me later melted any doubts I could have ever had from my heart.

I'll fight for her.

I'll conquer for her.

I'll win for her.

If she asks, I'll even die for her.

But can I be a better man for her?

I want to be, and I know I need to be, but am I capable?

And that desperate thought is what has me returning to this wellspring of hell.

I'm back here at Dr. Perry's office, sitting in her chair while she looks at me with eyes that judge me even before I've opened my mouth. Maybe it's fair game since I did the same to her when I saw her, but she's supposed to be the professional.

"So, Tom—"

"Excuse me, Dr. Perry, but if you don't mind, can you call me Thomas?

Tom is . . ." I start before searching for the right buzzword to use with her. It takes me a moment, but it comes to me from irony. "Triggering. Being called Tom triggers me."

Dr. Perry lifts an eyebrow and scribbles a note on her clipboard. "Why is that?"

"My father calls me Tom," I explain, clearing my throat and taking a sip of the herbal iced tea that's at my side. At least that's pretty good, I'll give her that. "And since my mother killed herself, it's been used more as a curse than as a name."

"I didn't know your mother committed suicide," Dr. Perry replies. "Tell me about that."

I'm not sure I can. Not sure it'll do any good other than give her a reason to add a checkmark to her list. But this is for Mia. And maybe for myself a bit too. Even if Dr. Perry can't help me, just saying this out loud is an accomplishment. And maybe she will have some insight. Or maybe she'll tell me to switch my breakfast cereal to something less stimulating like bran.

It's hard, and the words start slowly, in little fits and stops until momentum takes over. I hate reliving the memories, the voice in my head damning me the whole time, but I tell her about the day my mother died, trying to purge myself of the bad memories as she hums and says, "Tell me more," at regular intervals.

"After he screamed, I went into the bedroom and my father was trying CPR. I didn't know what it was at the time, and he kept yelling, 'Breathe, you bitch!' I didn't know what to do, and suddenly, he looked up, throwing his phone at me and yelling at me, 'Call 9-1-1!' And I did, but they couldn't save her. Since then . . . things have been bad."

*Because you fucked up.*

It takes me a long time to go over what my father did to me growing up, the mental and sometimes physical abuse. For the first time, Dr. Perry looks at me sympathetically before clearing her throat.

"Thomas, you have a lot of anger, but part of me feels like you're not being totally clear as to *whom* you're angry with."

"My father."

She looks at me blankly. No checkmark to her clipboard.

*Wrong answer, shithead.*

"You mean, am I pissed at my mother?" I ask, my hand clenching and my voice raising. "You're goddamn right, I am! I was just a boy and she left me.

And ever since, my world has turned upside down!" Shame blasts through me. "I shouldn't be mad at her. She couldn't have known how Dad would re-act, the things he'd do. She was just a depressed, lonely woman, or at least that's what I heard the ladies call her at the wake while they ate finger sand-wiches like it was any regular luncheon."

I'm out of the chair, pacing back and forth on the carpet, and Dr. Perry watches with a detached demeanor that infuriates me. As if I'm not enough already.

"You know it's not your fault," Dr. Perry says. "Rationally, you know that. Suicide is not about the survivors. Your mother likely couldn't contemplate what her choice would do to you because all she could think was what it would do to her. Suicide isn't about ending one's life. It's about ending one's pain."

It's a little mental health brochure-ish but startlingly insightful.

*But her life ended just the same. All while you watched cartoons and ate a snack.*

I'm getting nowhere, just circling the same drain I always dance around, and I'm done. At least for today, maybe with Dr. Perry, maybe forever. But I need to go.

"That's enough. I'm out of here," I growl, grabbing my jacket. I storm out, ignoring everything and everyone as I jump into my car and fire up the engine. The angry growl of the powerful motor echoes my inner turmoil, but it somehow focuses me enough that I don't crash as I drive back to the office and take the elevator upstairs.

It's just before the end of the work day, and I'm surprised Kerry's already gone, but I don't care right now. I should do my usual fifteen-minute medi-tation, but that seems like a dangerous proposition with where my head's at right now. Instead, what I want to do is check my email, and then head up-stairs and—

"Dennis?"

He's standing in my office, dressed as he always is in his suit, but with him is Mia, who looks up and smiles. They've been talking, obviously, and I blink, stunned. How could she . . . how could she let *that* man into my office?

"Thomas, I'm glad you're back. I'm sorry. I thought your schedule was clear, and—"

"He was probably wasting time," Dennis says in that voice he has. "I've been sitting on my ass for a half hour waiting on you, Tom."

"Don't call me . . ." I rasp, my anger flaring at the name I hate. "You know what, never mind. Just what in the hell are you doing here?" I go around to my chair, needing to put the desk between us. I'm not sure if it's for his protection or mine.

Dennis reads my tone of voice and sniffs, offended. "Well, if you're going to act like that . . . I came because Miss Karakova convinced me that I've been missing out on something by not having a friendly relationship with you. So I came bearing gifts to bury the hatchet." He tosses a box on the desk in front of me.

I glance at it and then back at him, unbelieving. "So that's supposed to be it? A present and that's supposed to wash away the years of abuse?"

He scoffs, rolling his eyes. "Oh, come on, 'abuse'? Don't be melodramatic. I kept a roof over your head, put you through school, even got this ivory tower you like to sit in started for you."

I stand, indignant fury coursing in my blood. "Melodramatic? Are you fucking serious? That roof over my head just gave you a place to slap me around. And the school you 'paid' for? You didn't pay one red cent. I earned that admission and that scholarship in spite of your telling me how stupid I was every fucking day. And the only reason you keep holding the startup money over my head is because you know I'm *better* than you. I did all this," I say, gesturing at my office, "and all you've amounted to is a wife who killed herself to get away from you and a son who wishes you were dead."

I've never been able to wipe that smug look off Dennis's face before, but those words sure did it. Maybe a little too evil, perhaps, but it does surprise him.

He stares at me, absolutely shocked before speaking up. "You should have died with her."

"Get out!" I bellow, crossing my office and grabbing him by the jacket before shoving him toward the door. Dennis stumbles out, and I have just enough time to close the door to my office before I turn to Mia, who looks aghast.

"Why? I told you those things in confidence. Why did you stick your nose in the one place I didn't want you to pry?" I beseech her. But then the fury reignites, aiming directly where I know it'll hurt her most. "I trusted you!"

"Tommy, I'm sorry," Mia whimpers, cowering away as I cross my office and pick up the package. It's a box wrapped in shiny plastic wrapping paper, the kind that looks like sparkling foil if you tilt it this way and that way in the light. "I went to see him about the sabotage stuff, and—"

"And what? You ended up having tea and fucking crumpets with the man who tried every day of my life to destroy me? And you thought, 'Hey, you know what'd be great? If I just blind-side Thomas with his asshole of a dad, and then ta-da, it'll be happily ever after.' How'd that work?" My words are caustic, sharp and jagged as I stab her with her every sarcastic syllable. But I hurt, so badly. And I can't stop the lashing out.

"You pried into my family relations!" I scream accusingly. "You brought that man into my office, knowing what he's done to me. You know better than anyone—*anyone*—why I can't be around him. But still, you thought you knew better."

"I . . . I know," she says, sobbing. Dimly, I realize I'm going too far, but the animal's loose, the rage overwhelming, and I can't stop it with so much emotion boiling over. "He told me about your mother, and then he called me and seemed to want to reconcile. I really thought—"

"No, you didn't think!" I yell, slamming the gift down on the desk.

I slam the gift down again and I hear something inside snap. Maybe it's in me, maybe it's the gift, I don't know. The sound triggers something primal and enraged deep within my soul, and I pick up the misshapen box, using the last of my self-control to turn away from Mia before hurling it against my office window. The thick security glass cracks from top to bottom, making a Y shape that echoes the question inside me.

Why? Why did she do this?

Why did he have to come here?

Why did she have to die?

Why do I hate everything about myself?

Mia gasps, and I hear a loud thump before the door opens, leaving me in my memories.

*Dad is yelling as I hold my hand over my bleeding forehead, praying I don't spill any blood on the carpet. "I just bought that bike!"*

*"Dad, I'm sorry, I didn't—" I try to explain. I don't care what they say about wearing helmets. Smacking your head into a tree branch when a snake pops out of nowhere, sending you tumbling down a dirt hillside, sucks the big hairy one.*

*But it's going to suck even more if I bleed on the carpet.*

*"You were careless and clumsy! Don't think you're getting another bike. You ruined that one so you can walk to school, for all I care!" Dad yells. He picks up the remote control to the TV and throws it, where it goes crashing into the fish tank, cracking the glass. Water spills out, and I can see Goldie and Mr. Colors, the two*

*fish my best friend Andy across the street gave me for my birthday, start panicking as their home drains onto the living room rug. "Goddammit!"*

*"No!" I scream, ignoring my head to run to the kitchen. I know where the big spaghetti pot is. Maybe if I fill it with water in time, I can save them.*

*I turn, running for the living room, but the water strikes again, or maybe it's that I'm still dizzy from my bike crash. I slip on the wet carpet, my head spinning as I crack my head on the edge of the fish tank, but somehow, I still get water into the pot. Scooping it in deep, I get Goldie and Mr. Colors out, sobbing as I watch them swim in their new home. It's gray, metallic . . . they're trapped. But they're safe.*

*"When you're done being a baby, clean that shit up," Dad says, his voice still raw and ragged from screaming at me.*

*He leaves, and I sob, watching Goldie circle around Mr. Colors, his mouth opening and closing. The water ripples, and I realize it's my tears.*

I gasp, jerked back to the present as I look at the crack on my window . . . just like the one on the fish tank.

My God. I've become just like him.

No. I've *become* him.

# CHAPTER 34

## Mia

WATCHING THE GIFT, I DON'T EVEN KNOW WHAT IT IS, PINWHEEL through the air and crack into the window, a Y-shaped lightning bolt splitting the thick safety glass, is one of the scariest things I've seen in my entire life.

Maybe that sounds silly, but seeing Thomas lose control absolutely terrifies me. In a blind panic, I turn and run for the door, but somehow, my hand slips and I literally run headfirst into the door before I get it open, the world spinning as I flee.

I must have hit my head harder than I thought, because the next thing I know, I'm outside of Papa's shop, tears running down my cheeks.

I open the door, and before I can even say a word, Papa sees me, his sewing machine stopping immediately.

Coming around the counter, he wraps me in his arms, murmuring the soft phrases he used to when I was a little girl, little Russian words that gave me comfort then and comfort now.

I'm transported back, back to the days when the world was big and scary, but my Papa was bigger and scarier and could protect me from anything. It's just that his lap has shrunk, and instead, he holds me as we stand up and I sob my eyes out.

"Mia . . . Mia, darling, what happened?" Papa asks after a few minutes of consoling me.

"He was so angry . . . I didn't mean to," I hiccup before fresh sobs rack my body. I feel miserable, like I've wrecked everything when all I was trying to do was help.

"Who's angry, Anastasia?" Papa says, helping me over to a chair and guiding me to sit down. He goes into the back, returning with a bottle of water that he hands to me. "Sip slowly and tell me what happened."

It's disjointed, my head's still not quite working right between my scare and the hit to my head, but I get it all out.

"I . . . Thomas asked me to look into who's been doing some corporate espionage, hamstringing the company," I start, holding the bottle against my head where I feel the biggest throb. "While doing that, I went to meet his father, Dennis. Things were weird, but when Dennis reached out to me, I figured it would be good to try and clear some of the air. Oh, Papa, there's so much between them, really bad stuff, and I . . . I was so scared."

"Shh, it's okay," Papa says softly, stroking my hair again. "Mia, whatever happened, you're safe now. I won't let anything happen."

I nod and struggle to get the rest of the story out. I explain my first meeting with Dennis Goldstone more, and how Thomas and I exchanged our love vows, and how I just wanted to ease the pressure on Thomas.

"Papa, he's under so much self-inflicted torture. I couldn't let him keep punishing himself, driving himself crazy with whatever Dennis has done to him."

"I understand, but Mia, how'd you get hurt?" Papa says, brushing my hair back. "You have a lump the size of a golf ball on your forehead. Did that man do that? I'll kill that son of a bitch if you say yes." The words are quiet but a promise of violence.

Oh, God, I didn't even realize.

"Papa, no!" I cry out, grabbing his wrists. I explain the disastrous meeting, that I bumped my head and it wasn't Thomas, but that the sight of him losing his temper terrified me.

Papa stops, and I can see he's trying not to scoff at me. "Mia . . . tell me the truth. I've heard that before—even on the TV, they say it. *I walked into a door. I fell down the stairs. I slipped on some ice.* You—"

"Papa, I'm serious. I ran into the door when I was running out. I came straight here."

He eyes me carefully, looking for the slightest sign that I might be lying to him. But finding none, he sighs, hugging me close once again.

"Okay, so let me see if I have this straight. You know your Thomas has bad blood with his father, and yet you set up a meeting without his knowledge, no preparation, no decision on his part on whether he wanted to mend fences, as the Americans say?"

Papa's words are eerily similar to Thomas's. Less angry and accusatory, of course, but the gist is the same and I break out in fresh tears.

"Shh, don't cry, Mia. Though it pains me to say it, I believe you have made a mistake. Perhaps this Dennis even used you to hurt your Thomas. Another pawn in their hurtful game."

Papa spits air at the ground beside us, and I wonder if he's cursing Dennis, Thomas, or me. I'm too afraid to ask, because he's right. I made a terrible mistake.

"Oh, God, I need to go back and apologize." I move to pull away, but Papa holds me tight.

"No. You may have made a mistake in judgement, but it was with good intentions and hope for a better outcome. Your Thomas reacted violently, like an out of control toddler. I can't let you go back there. Not now. He may come to see the error of his ways and come groveling back to my princess, but you both need time to settle. Let him calm, Mia. Let both of you calm." His voice is soothing, hypnotizing me into agreement.

I nod silently.

"Good, now you will stay with me tonight. I do not like the look of that bump on your head and want to keep an eye on you." He pokes at my forehead with gentle fingers and I wince. "I will wake you every two hours to make sure you can see properly and know who you are."

"Papa, I have work tomorrow. I have to go home," I argue even though staying buried under a pile of blankets on Papa's couch while he makes me soup sounds like just what I need right now.

"Then go home and get your things. But you should call in sick tomorrow. You have a perfect excuse." Though he looks at my head, most of my pain is coming from a point further south . . . my heart. "You should not work for a man who can't control himself."

I look into Papa's face, and I see a rocky stubbornness that is hard to crack. "Papa, I'm not just going to quit, but I'll call in sick and maybe take a vacation while I decide what to do, deal? And I don't mind staying with you for a few days. Let me go back to my place and I'll pack some things."

He goes to object, but the door to his shop opens and a customer comes in. Papa takes a deep breath and turns back to me, nodding.

"Fine. I promised Mr. Smith his suit by tomorrow and I have to get to work. But you go, and you come back here. Understood? How is your head?"

"It's fine," I assure him. "It hurts, but I'm fine."

"Oh, Mia . . . you have surely gotten yourself into something this time, but if it is right, it will be. Trust and truth are vital parts of love. But so is forgiveness. Let us hope that you both have enough in your heart to give."

We both close our eyes, exhaling and sending the prayer heavenward.

I get back in my car and see my phone flashing. There are two missed calls . . . both from Thomas.

I decide to take Papa's advice and give us both a little space. Instead, I start driving, trying not to think about what Papa said but failing miserably, as it seems I'm not really registering what's in front of me.

A horn blares, and I come to a stop just inches from the side of a UPS truck, the driver glaring at me. "Fuck, lady! Eyes ahead!"

I give him a little wave of apology, wishing it were that easy with Thomas. But I make it to my apartment without further incident, where I start packing my bag with the basics for staying with Papa for a few days.

I don't even know why I'm doing this, other than not wanting to deny Papa. It's not like I fear Thomas coming over or anything, but maybe Papa can help me get my head right. Figure out where I go from here.

A whisper in my head tells me that I just want to hide out, run away from the pain, the embarrassment, and the fear. And I wonder if this is what Thomas's inner demon is like, calling him on his bullshit and not letting him get away with anything. I suspect my inner voice is rather nice and polite compared to Thomas's though.

My phone rings again, and I'm about ready to ignore it when I see that it's not Thomas but Izzy instead. She's supposed to be on at The Gravy Train, and I pick up the call, worried something might be wrong with her.

"Izzy? What's up?"

"What's up?" Izzy asks, frantic with worry. "Mia, are you okay? Are you at the hospital?"

"What?" I ask, confused. "What do you mean, at the hospital? Why would I be there?"

"Babe, why aren't you at the hospital?" Izzy asks. "After what happened, I'd be getting checked out while calling the fucking police on his ass!"

"Izzy, you're making no sense. What are you talking about?"

Her voice is tight as she says, "Flip on Channel Eight. You're top fucking news."

I turn to my TV, finding my remote and turning it on, and a picture of Thomas flashes on the screen.

# CHAPTER 35

## Thomas

"WHILE THE OUTCRY FROM THE INTERNET HAS BEEN IMMEDIATE *and outraged, so far, there has been no official response from either Goldstone the company or Thomas Goldstone himself."*

I shake my head as the video plays again behind the voiceover. It's the fifth time I've watched it this morning, and each time, I wince.

It's a video, taken from the hallway outside my office.

At first, the visual isn't too damning, but you can hear the yelling, cursing, and hurled insults, all obviously my voice. You can clearly hear every word of my family's dirty laundry as I scream about my mother's suicide and wish my father dead.

And then the door opens, showing me physically shoving him out the door. I look mad, crazy-eyed and red-faced. In the background of the image, you can see Mia's pale face, horror written plainly in her expression. Then more closed-door yelling, and the crash as I throw the gift box against the window. But without knowing about the box, the shatter of glass sounds ominous, especially when a moment later, you hear a solid thunk against door. And then Mia runs through the video frame, holding her head with curled-in shoulders and runny mascara tears streaking down her cheeks.

"That's enough."

Irene Castellanos, my head of public relations, hits the pause button on the remote, and the video stops. "Someone's already pieced together a story about Mia, calling her your 'basement babe' and speculating on your relationship. I'll be honest, Thomas. The way they put this whole thing together, it looks like you were out of control and hit her."

"But I didn't!" I argue for the millionth time, rubbing at my eyes. I didn't sleep at all last night and I feel like sand's been poured behind my eyeballs.

Deep breaths . . . just deep breaths.

That's what I'd told myself when Mia ran out. Calm, breathe . . . over and over like a mantra. Dr. Perry would've been proud. Well, except for the raging tantrum I'd thrown. But I'd calmed, or more like collapsed like a deflated balloon, when I'd seen just how far I'd gone.

The news had broken by six, like the network had just been waiting for a chance to throw me under the bus. They aired it first with a lot of speculation and started asking leading questions later. And there have been a lot of them, because the phone calls demanding interviews have been coming in non-stop.

*And now they all know what a fuckup you are. Can't hide now!*

The voice in my head is gleeful as fuck, dancing around like it's won the lottery of fucking me over. At this point, I guess that's true. Everything's a mess . . . me and Mia, my company, my head.

Irene clears her throat, yanking me from my downward mental spiral.

"Sorry, Irene. You're right, but that isn't what happened. I was yelling at my father . . . for the most part. We have history."

"Yeah, I know. I heard. Everyone knows that now, if they didn't already. Too bad your father so far isn't willing to make a corroborating statement on that," Irene replies, tapping at the notepad in her lap. "I've reached out to him twice since I learned about this, and he's sticking with 'no comment' like I'm a member of the fucking press too."

That Irene cusses tells me just how bad this is. She's a consummate pro, experienced, and has pretty much seen it all. And she's losing her shit. That doesn't bode well for me.

A sudden thought goes through me, and I realize how exhausted I am that I didn't think of it earlier. "Have we found out who sent the video to the news? There's got to be a trail there."

Irene opens her mouth, then shakes her head. "I'm sorry, Thomas. I didn't think of that. I've been handling the PR side, trying to squash it, not track down where they got it since it's obviously real."

"Hold on that," I say, heaving myself to my feet and stepping out of my office. Kerry's frantic at her desk, talking with someone on the phone while typing furiously, and she's refused to even look at me all morning. I don't blame her. I haven't been able to look at myself all morning either.

But right now, I have something I need to find. "Kerry, I need you to call Smithson Security. Have their best investigator here today. If they can't come, see if they can recommend someone who can. And Kerry, be discreet, please."

If looks could kill, I'd be a dead man where I'm standing. "Yes, Mr. Goldstone."

I don't have time for this, but I stand directly in front of her, giving her a hard look. "Kerry, I'm only going to say this once, so listen closely." I can see her bracing herself, ready to be put on blast, or worse. "I didn't hurt Mia. Yes, I lost my temper, but I didn't lay a hand on her."

Her face softens a degree or two, but she's still not happy with me. "Shit, Thomas. What the hell is going on around here?"

Irene clears her throat, interrupting. "Actually, Kerry. You weren't here when all this was going down, correct?"

Kerry turns a frosty glare to Irene, and I intervene, holding up a hand. "Nobody's accusing you of anything. But you were gone when I came into the office. Did you know Dennis and Mia were here?"

She nods, looking pained. "I did. I asked Mia if she knew what she was doing, and she said she hoped so."

I swallow thickly. "Okay, so when you left, did you see anything suspicious? Maybe someone up here who shouldn't have been?"

Though I can see her racking her brain, she's already shaking her head. "I'm sorry, I didn't see anyone. I just headed out for my daughter's recital. I rode the elevator down with a bunch of folks, I don't know who, and then walked out the front door. I waved at Michael, the security guard, and then caught a cab. I didn't know about this until late last night because I had my phone on silent while Cami danced. I'm afraid I'm no help."

I pat her hand, and she grabs mine, holding on tightly. "I'm sorry, Thomas."

I grimace. I scared Kerry, angered her, hurt her trust in me, and I never should have. She's been the one person I could always trust before Mia . . . and I'll make it up to her.

"It's okay. Can you just call Smithson? I really need someone here, pronto."

"On it," she says, grabbing her phone and clicking around on her computer to get the number.

Irene gestures for me to come back into my office and shuts the door as I sit back down. "Okay, so what's the fallout here?"

"So far?" Irene asks, picking up her notepad she'd left on my desk before. "Well, Goldstone, both you and the company, have been condemned by every women's rights group from NOW to LOLA."

"What's LOLA?" I mutter.

"Ladies of Liberty Alliance . . . yeah, I had to look them up myself," Irene admits. "If you could see the sidewalk from up here, you'd find a group of marchers downstairs right now on the sidewalk protesting. I don't know what group they're from except that they're pretty much calling for you to finish breaking that window, preferably with your head, before you go falling to the street below."

The window. Turning around, I look at the Y-shaped crack, haunted by my rage. The gift had ended up being a photo cube, of all things, with pictures of my parents and me when things were happy embedded on each side. I didn't even know those pictures existed and certainly wouldn't have thought Dennis had saved them all these years. And last night when I'd finally opened the box, alone in my office in the ruined tatters of my life, the pictures had seemed more of a taunt than anything healing.

*See what you did? If only you'd helped her, this is the life you could've led. But look at you now . . . broken and alone.*

That's what the demon had said on repeat last night, and I shake my head, not wanting an encore performance of the vitriol.

"What else?"

"Well, your net worth is highly tied to Goldstone stock . . . and it's down ten points so far today. So you've lost a significant amount of money. Probably a millionaire instead of a billionaire today." It's a hollow attempt at a joke, both of us knowing I couldn't care less about money right now.

I shrug, not giving a shit. For once, business success isn't foremost in my mind. "Forget Wall Street. How's it affecting the company?"

Irene sighs. "So far, not too badly. There's an uptick in callouts. Some in protest, some because they don't want to cross the crowd below. Most of them just opted to work from home for the day, so it's not like anyone is hair-flipping out. I told HR not to say or do anything about it until you gave a directive. I'd suggest letting it slide . . . especially in Mia Karakova's case."

Mentioning Mia hurts, and I look out the window toward her apartment across the city. The simple fact is, I chased her away. She hasn't returned my calls and has ignored my texts, and I'd called down to her manager, Bill, this morning to see if she'd come in. He'd carefully said she called in 'sick' and I'd heard the questions in his voice. I'm not sure if I'm going to ever get her back.

"Agreed," I whisper. "Nobody gets punished for my fuckup, understood?"

My door opens, and Randall Towlee pokes his head in. Like I don't have enough problems to deal with. "Thomas, got a moment?"

I wave him in, sighing. More good news. "Sure, invite everyone in while you're at it. We can get to the execution faster that way. Sorry . . . what's on your mind?"

"Not to pile on, but I just forwarded you an email from the hospital project liaison. Basic idea is that they're cutting ties with Goldstone until this is resolved. There's some verbiage about negative public image, but they're basically running scared."

I sigh. *Of course.* "It's fine. I'll reach out to them."

"One other thing." Looking like he'd rather be anywhere than passing along the news he's got, he says, "The Board has called a meeting to discuss your behavior and the news coverage. Rumor is, they're concerned you've broken your own corporate bylaws."

I nod, exhaustion hitting me like a wave. "Tell them . . . tomorrow."

"They may not want to wait that long, Thomas," he says. "The damage to our corporate image—"

"Can wait at least twenty-four hours," I reply. "Tell them tomorrow, noon, conference room. Thank you."

He leaves, and I look at Irene. "I'm putting you in charge of that. Develop a plan to get ahead of the news cycle. I put us in a nosedive, but I'm going to need you to pull us out."

"That'll need you, Thomas," she says. "I can develop a plan, and I can be the corporate press presence, but to really change things around, the public's going to demand that you do it. Personally, and probably in public, to let them get their pound of flesh from you."

I nod, but I'm too tired. I'm shaken. For the first time in a long time, I actually do feel weak.

"I know," I whisper, heaving myself to my feet. "But not right this moment. You're in charge of that. I know you can pull magic out. If you need me, call Kerry."

I leave the office, point up, and Kerry nods. She'll screen things for me, but right now, I can't handle it. Instead I leave, each step feeling like I've aged fifty years in a single day.

As I enter my living room, something out of place catches my eye, pink and white, and I walk over to tug a T-shirt out from under the edge of my sofa.

I remember this. Mia wore it the last weekend she stayed over. I'd peeled it off her before we made love on the couch, and afterward, we'd soaked in the tub before making love in the bedroom. I guess in all the passion, we just sort of forgot where our clothes ended up.

My eyes burn, and I lift the shirt to my nose, inhaling that soft scent that's unmistakably Mia. She's not someone for perfumes, nothing eye-watering, just her natural scent that's honest, pure . . . and I've hurt her.

I feel wetness run down my cheeks and it isn't tears of rage or shame, it isn't sweat or chopping onions. I can't stop seeing the terrified look on Mia's face from the video.

I hurt the woman I love.

How am I supposed to recover from that? How am I supposed to move forward?

Out of everything I've lost today, she's the most important thing and what I cherish most.

For the first time in years, I don't know what to do, so I lay on the sofa, holding Mia's shirt to my chest while I cry myself to sleep.

# CHAPTER 36

## Mia

"*FREEDOM IS SOMETHING YOU HAVE TO FIGHT FOR, RATHER THAN something you're given. Being free means being prepared to carry that burden,*" the rather handsome hairy-chested man on the computer monitor says, flashing a thumbs-up to the young boy watching him. It's been years since I've watched *Eureka Seven*, but next to *Sailor Moon*, it's one of my favorite animes.

Lying in my sweats, my hair a mess and a bowl of Cocoa Puffs in my lap, I have to pause the video, setting it aside to wipe at my eyes. It's been three days, and I still can't stop crying at moments like this. It's part of the reason I still haven't gotten through the fifty-two episodes of the show . . . there are just so many feels.

I keep watching, rapt even though I know what's going to happen, and when the episode ends, I see that it's already getting close to eleven, and I get off the sofa to head for the shower.

Papa's place is a little bit bigger than mine, but most of it's been converted into his sort of home workshop-slash-storage area, so it seems smaller.

But still, it feels good to be back, surrounded by the dressing frames, the bolts of cloth, and three broken sewing machines that Papa picked up at an estate sale when I was in college. He vowed then to fix them, and it's become a running joke that he's never so much as turned a screw to start their repair. But somehow, their broken-down presence is just as much a part of 'home' as the whir of Papa's working machines.

I have just enough time to wash up and run a brush through my hair—to ensure I don't have a single obscenely matted blonde dreadlock hanging down my back—and pull on some jeans and a T-shirt before I head out. I stop down in the shop to give Papa a kiss on the cheek.

"Grabbing lunch with the girls."

"Are you sure it is safe out there for you?" he asks, peering out the windows. It'd taken fewer than twelve hours for the press to track me down, first at my apartment, then here at Papa's. Finally, I'd turned my phone off once the voicemail had gotten full. Izzy and Charlotte have been checking in with me via Papa's landline.

But today, the street is blessedly empty and I'm getting out for a little bit. I desperately need to so that I can get out of my head, even if only for a few minutes.

"Seems clear for now, at least, so I'm making a run for it. I'll call you before I come back to make sure no one has set up camp while I'm gone. See you later. Maybe I can help out down here some? I'm getting cabin fever upstairs."

"I would love for you to keep an old man company . . . and I do think I have some buttons that need work," Papa teases. "You know me. I'll make you work for your keep! Oh, and tell Isabella I have something for her to try! A skirt I made!"

I leave with a smile. Papa is always generous with Izzy. It's the first one to appear on my face in days, and I drive to The Gravy Train where Izzy's already waiting for me, twirling the straw in her Coke and looking nervous. "You're late. I was getting scared."

"Papa," I reassure her.

"*Eureka,*" she says with a smile.

I laugh softly, nodding. "Yeah, you know me too well."

She reaches up, hugging me before I sit down. Having been forced to sit through many an episode with me, she knows my routine. "Has it been that rough?"

I shrug, looking out the window. "I don't know. I know I'm not ready to go back there. If I face him, I'm going to have to make a decision, or maybe he's already made one, and I'm not ready for that yet. So I've just avoided the whole mess, hiding out at Papa's."

"You know, if you're that upset, you could always have your father talk to someone in the Russian Mafia," Izzy jokes, trying to lighten my dark mood incrementally. "I bet there are a couple of guys who could teach Thomas some manners."

"Papa doesn't know anyone in the Mafia," I protest, but Izzy snorts.

"Tinker, tailor, soldier, spy," Izzy chants. "When I saw the book in the library, I just thought of good ol' Papa Karakov. I've never even read it."

It's my turn to snort. My father's the last man who'd be a spy. "Izz, you've gotta get out more."

She smiles and takes a sip of soda. "Seriously, though, you could walk away. Cut ties with Thomas and with your skills. You could get a job anywhere, even with the notoriety you've got now. Maybe especially because of it. I bet you could even sue his ass for a nice ten-foot-high pile of cash if you wanted to."

"No!" I protest, though I know she's not being serious. But she's pushing me to think, to consider what I want now that I've come out of hiding. "No, I'm never going to do that. I just . . ."

Words fail me, and Izzy sets her Coke aside, which means she's really worried about me. The girl never sets aside calories. She needs them too much with as few as she gets.

"Talk to me, babe. What are you feeling?"

I close my menu, biting my lip as I try to form my thoughts into words. It's been swirling in my head for the past three days, and honestly, it's been easier to just sit back and let myself get lost in video games and anime. But the thoughts never stop.

"I love him," I say simply, and Izzy's shiny eyes mirror my own. "But I'm not sure if he's in the right state of mind to be in a relationship or if he'll ever get there. We were doing so well, and I . . . I really fucked up, Izz. I shouldn't have interfered."

I'm saved from her rebuke by the waitress coming up. I order a cheeseburger and fries and Izzy orders a grilled cheese with bacon.

By the time the waitress leaves, I jump back in, not letting Izzy patronize me with words that none of this is my fault. Because it is, and this isn't like Thomas internalizing something he had no control over. This is a mess of my own making. Not the media stuff, but the part between Thomas and me.

"Izzy, there's just something about Thomas," I tell her. "Yes, he's got issues. Yes, he's got a temper and a lot of emotional baggage. But I don't think he'd ever hurt me. I know the world doesn't believe me, but I did run into that door. And my mind keeps flashing back to the little things he's done. I don't even think he knows that I've noticed."

"Like what? The big tip he left me? Honey, I don't care about that. I want to see you happy," Izzy says. "I'd give the money back if it'd help you feel better. If I hadn't spent it already."

"It's not that," I say, thinking.

"It's other things. It's hard to even explain, but despite his reputation, there's a gentle side to him. The way he's made love with me is just part of it, and no, I'm not just talking with my hoo-hah. But taking me on a dream trip through Japan, remembering my favorite brand of juice and stocking it in his fridge, and sharing with me, even when I know how hard it was and how much it cost him to appear weak that way to me. Not that I think he's weak for what he went through as a child, but *he* thinks he was. He's got this need inside him to be strong, be the best, and he broke down in front of me, Izzy. He broke down *for* me, trusting that I would help him pick up the pieces. And I tried. I just solved the puzzle all wrong."

Izzy covers her mouth with her hands, and she sighs deeply. "Honey, I am so sorry. Tell me how I can help. Do you want to call him? It sounds like you both have apologies to make."

"I know, but——"

Izzy's phone buzzes, and I see that it's Charlotte. Izzy picks it up, putting it on speaker. "Hey, Char, what's up?"

"Hey, turn on Channel 7," Char says. "You're gonna want to see this."

"Hey, Elaine!" Izzy yells, her diminutive body exploding in the voice of someone's who's worked in a diner for a long time. The waitress on duty pokes her head up, and Izzy points. "Turn on Channel 7, pronto! And turn it up!"

"You got it, Izz," Elaine says. She flips the TV in the corner over to Channel 7 and cranks the volume up as loud as it'll go. "There you go!"

It's the noon news, and the little info bar at the bottom says the camera's set up outside the Goldstone Building. There's a crowd outside, a mix of media and a lot of pissed-off-looking women protesting.

On a quickly setup podium, Irene Castellanos, who I've met once in my time at Goldstone, gets on the microphones.

*"Thank you for coming today,"* she says simply, looking as professional as possible in her tailored suit and skirt combo, somber but not funereal. Dimly, in the part of my mind that isn't stunned by what I'm hearing, I note that she's

striking the right tone for a press conference. *"Mr. Thomas Goldstone would like to say a few words."*

The reaction by the crowd as Thomas steps up is loud and ugly. I'm almost surprised nobody throws a tomato at him, but the first thing I notice is that he looks like hell. He's shaved, sure, but the bags under his eyes are noticeable, and he looks haggard, exhausted as he smooths out the paper in his hand on the podium surface.

*"Ladies and gentlemen, thank you for being here today. My name is Thomas Goldstone, and I've come to address the recent incident and the video that has surfaced of me."*

*"Abuser!"* someone screams at him, and Thomas winces like he's been slapped. I wince with him, knowing that of all things, that label would be one that cuts deeper than most.

Thomas waits for the crowd to quiet, holding up a hand until he can be heard again. *"There are many things that people have called me over this. And many of them I deserve. There is no excuse for my behavior in the video, though the whole story is not reflected accurately in what you've seen. The truth is, I did lose my temper, and I behaved in a way that is inexcusable, raising my voice and throwing a box at the wall of my office. But, let me be clear. I did not lay a hand on the woman in the video, and she was never in any danger from me at any time."*

*"I'm aware of the nickname I'm known by, and the video showed me a man..."* he says, pausing before continuing, *"showed me a man I do not want to be. So first and foremost, I'd like to apologize to the employees of Goldstone. I've pushed, I've demanded ... I've been ruthlessly harsh."* His words speak to the ones running through everyone's mind ... Ruthless Bastard. *"For that, there is no excuse, and no amount of apology can compensate for the hurt feelings, the hurt souls, I've caused."*

*"More importantly, though, I owe an apology to the woman in the video. Some of you have found her name, so I feel comfortable saying this. Mia, I'm truly sorry. I'm sorry for scaring you. I have more to say, but you deserve to hear it from me directly."* His eyes look deeply into the camera, deeply into my eyes through the TV screen. It's like feeling him right here, in my very soul.

*"To the shareholders and the people of Roseboro and around the world who have come to know the Goldstone name, I swear to you that I will work tirelessly to restore your faith in this company. There are good people here, thousands of them. Don't let my mistake ruin all of their hard work. Therefore—"*

"The rest of it's mostly just stuff Irene made me put in there," a deep voice says from the entrance.

Izzy and I both look up in shock as Thomas stands at the edge of the booth, still wearing the same suit as in the video but looking even more haggard. I blink, unable to form words while Izzy just gawks.

Finally, I force out, "How—"

"It's on an hour tape delay," he says quietly, barely audible over the TV. Izzy waves to the waitress, and she turns off the press conference, and suddenly, it feels like everyone in the diner's looking at us.

They probably are.

"Listen—" Izzy says, but Thomas interrupts her before she can dismiss him.

"Wait," he says, his eyes shimmering with tears and exhaustion. "Mia, I know you're still angry at me, and maybe you're even scared of me. I've prayed for three days that you aren't, but I have to admit you could feel that way. I'm just asking for a few minutes."

I look up at him, and I can see everyone watching with bated breath to see what I'll say. Finally, Izzy interrupts the drawn-out silence.

"Mia? You need to do this, but you *don't* have to do this now if you're not ready." She eyes Thomas carefully.

"Give us a minute, Izz?" I ask, and she nods, sliding out of her seat before moving to the counter seat closest to our booth and sitting down.

"I'm gonna sit right here, and if I hear even a raised voice . . . buddy, I don't care how many muscles you've got. I'm gonna have your balls," Izzy says to Thomas with a falsely sweet tone. "And hurry. I'm hungry."

He slides into the seat gratefully and the waitress comes up. Thomas waves her off with a shake of his head and clears his throat. "Mia, I came here because I need to ask you for your forgiveness. I was wrong, I hurt you, and I've probably sent you running for the hills. I'm so sorry."

"You didn't *hurt* me," I remind him. "You did startle me a bit, but I ran into the door myself. We both know that video is bullshit."

"True, but my outburst caused it, so I still feel responsible," Thomas says. "Fuck, seeing myself in that video . . ."

"I get it, Thomas. I love you, but . . ."

"I know," he rasps, his voice thick with emotion. "And I know some people may tell you I'm not worth the trouble. For three days, I've realized that I've become the man I tried not to be."

"Like your father?" I ask, and Thomas nods again. "That is why I forgive you. Because you know that and want to be better. Yes, you lost control, but I was the one who pushed you off the edge, knowing your grip was precarious at best. I didn't realize . . . I mean, I knew what you'd said about how bad it was. But Dennis seemed like he wanted to reconcile, and I just thought I was going to give you this fairy tale ending." I bite my lip, swallowing the sob down. "I'm sorry, Thomas. I shouldn't have forced it. It wasn't my place."

He takes my hands in his across the table. "Don't you see? You did give me a fairy tale, but not with my dad. With you. That's what matters."

The impact of both of our apologies fills the air between us, washing through us, burning up the pain of the last few days and resetting us. Not back to where we were, but somewhere else on our journey, closer to a healthy place because we've both touched the fire and know the burn, know just how close we can get to it without getting singed.

Tears flow messily down my face, and a sniffle from my side tells me Izzy is sobbing too. "The heart wants what the heart wants, and I'm not about to give up on us so easily. I love you, Thomas Goldstone."

Thomas looks at me intently, and the hope in his eyes pierces my soul. Here's the Tommy I've been missing, the one he's hidden from everyone but me. "I love you too, but are you sure, Mia?"

"You've told me what he's put you through, and for so long . . . that's not something you can just brush off, but I know it's not who you are or who you want to be. We will get through it. And call me stupid, but I do hope that someday, you two can . . . I don't know, mend things? On your terms and no one else's. Your mother's death did more than end her life. It ended your childhood, and it ended something in him too."

I swallow the sadness down at how the loss of one woman has reverberated through decades, changing everything for Dennis and Thomas, and I wonder if she had any idea about the dominos she'd set in motion.

"But I need you to know, I didn't go to him for that purpose. I went to him to ask him a few questions relating to the sabotage situation."

"I remember," Thomas says. "I remember what you said."

"Right. It wasn't to set all that up. But as bad as Dennis was to you, I don't think he's the one sabotaging you. He's angry at you, but that's just it. He's too scattered, too emotional, too focused on hurting you to do something this calculated. He just can't. So I don't know who it is, and I've been thinking about it for three days to distract myself from us."

"You're probably right about that," Thomas says. "But the company's second. You're the most important thing."

I take a big breath. "Then let's try this again . . . but there's one thing."

Thomas's relieved smile dims. "What?"

"Well, you have your family issues. And I, uh, have mine."

From beside us, Izzy snorts. "Ooh, good luck with that one, boy. You've got one very pissed off Russian tailor who'll cut you into pieces and you'll never be seen or heard from again."

Thomas's eyes ping-pong between us. "Your dad?"

"If it were me, I'd just find a new girlfriend," Izzy interjects, raising an eyebrow when I cut my eyes to her to see her turned all the way around, watching us, amused. "What? I'm just being honest. Your Papa's more stubborn than I am."

"Should I tell him you said that? With that new project of his almost ready with your name on it?"

Izzy's eyes widen, and she shakes her head. "Hell, no! Papa's the nicest, sweetest teddy bear in the whole world!"

"How hard can it be?" Thomas asks, and I nod, giving his hands another squeeze.

"Words of wisdom, something I was reminded of recently and might be useful," I tell him. "Don't beg for it . . . earn it. Do that, and you'll be rewarded."

# CHAPTER 37

## Thomas

I REMEMBER THE TIME I WAS JUST SEVENTEEN AND STOOD OUTSIDE THE Dean's office at Stanford. There I was, a kid whose driver's license still practically smelled of freshly-minted plastic since my father wasn't willing to sign the parental authorization form until he realized if I could go to college, I'd be out of his hair.

I'd worn my best shirt and tie, feeling like a fool and wondering how I was going to tell a man three times my age that I deserved to get a full-ride scholarship when my father was economically well off. I was so nervous, I had to go into the men's room and splash cold water on my face before going in. But I'd done it, and I'd gotten the scholarship.

Then there was the time I had to go for my first major investor pitch. This was after I'd sunk everything I had made in four years of online investing into getting Goldstone Inc. off the ground and had even hit up Dennis for ten thousand in exchange for his shares, and I was ready for the majors. This was my first 'big' meeting, and again I was a nervous wreck. But I'd done that too and had gotten the money.

But standing on the sidewalk outside Vladimir Karakov's—in Russian, he's Karak*ov* and she's Karak*ova*—shop and apartment, I'm more nervous than I've ever been in my adult life. My palms are sweating, my throat feels tight, and despite not having drunk anything in hours, I swear I need to pee.

Because as much as that scholarship and investment changed my life, this meeting and Vladimir's blessing will make or break my future.

The sun's going down. Mia made me promise to let her go in first to smooth the introductions and to let me handle a little bit of corporate business.

Maybe that's why I'm here. I've spent the past three days thinking almost exclusively about Mia. Anything I said about corporate responsibility or public trust in the press conference? That was put in by Irene. My apology to the workers inside the Goldstone Building? Okay, I did want to do that, but the rest of my thoughts have been about Mia.

But she wants me to take care of myself, of the company.

On our way out of the diner, she'd even made me promise to go work hard, to try and clean up some more of the mess before coming over.

So I did, and now . . . here I am.

I turn, my stomach clenching, but maybe it's that I haven't eaten anything since that 'power smoothie' Kerry got me before the press conference.

I hear the door to the shop open behind me, and I turn around to see a stern-faced man, his cardigan vest and white shirt looking somehow old-fashioned for someone who Mia told me is a tailor.

"Mr. Karakov?"

With a grunt, he jerks his head inside, and I follow him in. I see Mia behind the door inside the shop, and she gives me a supportive thumbs-up.

"Papa, I'll keep things going down here. You said Mr. Smith was going to stop by to pick up his shirts?"

The man turns to his daughter, his icy demeanor immediately thawing as he gives Mia a kiss on the cheek.

"Thank you, darling."

He turns back to me, Siberian winter once again gripping his eyes. "Upstairs."

I follow him, and as we start up, I swear I hear Mia chuckling under her breath as we mount the narrow staircase in the back of the shop. The space is made even narrower with boxes of what look like sewing supplies stacked along the right side of the stairs, and I find my left shoulder rubbing against the wall the whole way up.

He heads into his apartment, and I follow, stopping in the entryway. He turns, eyeing me left to right, top to bottom. With a sound of annoyance and some muttered Russian, he approaches me, his hand reaching out to-ward my face.

To my shame, I flinch, and his eyes soften as he brushes some lint off my jacket. It must've brushed onto me as I touched the stairwell wall. Feeling more comfortable that he's not about to kill me where I stand, I let him do his thing.

He touches the seam at my shoulder. "Custom-made. Worsted wool, handmade buttonhole." He flips open the lapel, examining the inner lining with a hum. As if speaking to himself, he murmurs, "I can learn much about a man by his suit, what he values, what he fancies, where he will cut corners, and where he will indulge."

Feeling like a dog at the dog show, I stand straight and tall. "And what does my suit tell you about me?" I venture.

He grunts, stalking away from me on heavy feet. He heads into the kitchen, and I follow uncertainly, not sure if he's actually inviting me fur-ther inside. He takes two tumblers out of a glass-fronted cabinet and pours a healthy measure of a clear liquid in each one. The bottle is completely unlabeled.

*Could be water, could be vodka, could be poison, for all I know,* I think as Izzy's words run through my head. He hands me one.

"Drink."

It isn't a question, and as I lift the glass to my mouth, the smell hits me. Whatever it is, I'm pretty sure I could power a rocket to space on it. But there's no question about just sipping at it, and instead, I toss it back, praying that I've got enough 'power smoothie' left in my stomach and bloodstream so as to not make me piss-drunk in about two minutes. It burns hotly down my throat, but I force the gasp down.

Karakov smirks as he drinks his own vodka easily, then sets the bottle aside. "You hurt my Mia."

I nod, clearing my throat before I can speak. "I did, sir."

"My only daughter, who is more precious than the world to me," Karakov continues. "A young woman for whom I'd burn the world down."

"I did. And I'm sorry, sir," I reply honestly. "But I want to be clear that I never raised a hand to her, would never."

Karakov hums and stares at me from across the kitchen counter. "My daughter . . . she says the video was not the total truth?"

"No, sir. Though I did lose my temper, even in my rage, she was not in danger. But in her fear, she bumped into the door herself. I feel awful that happened, even if it was not my direct doing. It was still my fault for scaring her."

"I see. And she says you love her?"

I nod, blinking as the alcohol starts to hit. Jesus, what was that stuff, a hundred and fifty proof? "I do, sir. I know that I'm an asshole. But I'm working on being better for her. I'm not worthy of Mia's love yet. She is a pure and beautiful heart. And maybe that . . . maybe that's why I love her so much."

"Why?"

"Because if there's any hope for me," I reply, the words coming easier, probably due to the vodka, "any chance that I can be a good man and not the beast that I've become, it's her. When I'm with her, I see an end to the pain. I see a future. I see happiness."

"And if you're wrong? If you can't change?"

"I know I can. I won't fail. Because a single smile from her is all the strength I need to overcome anything."

Mr. Karakov nods, his eyes still icy cold. "When Mia's mother left us, I promised myself that I would give her the love of two parents. From what she has told me, when your mother left you, the exact opposite may have happened. You haven't been shown how to love properly."

"You might be right, sir. But with Mia, it feels natural. I don't think I need to be taught. And if I do, rest assured that the woman you've raised will set me straight."

He grins, pouring another two fingers of vodka into our glasses and raising his toward me. "It won't be easy. You'll make mistakes. Every man does, because a woman is a mystery that time, wisdom, and all the efforts of men to decipher have utterly failed at throughout history. But I believe you will still try, because that is what love is. And you will love my daughter with all your heart, or you will walk away now."

It's a threat wrapped up in an expectation. Something I'm familiar with, but something tells me Vladimir's follow-through would be different from my father's.

I agree, nodding gravely. "Yes, sir."

Karakov smiles. "Then you have my blessing. You're a lucky man, Thomas Goldstone. Mother Russia may be harsh, but Papas . . . we are harsher when it comes to our daughters. Now drink!"

I pick up my glass, sniffing before setting it down. "Forgive me, no disrespect, but I'm pretty sure this is rocket fuel, and I haven't eaten much the past three days. This is probably not the best idea and I'm trying to make smarter choices."

"Oh, but that's when the vodka is best," Karakova says with a soft laugh. "But I understand. Stay for dinner then?"

I nod, grateful as Karakov, I guess I need to start thinking about him as Vladimir, leads me over to the couch. "It'll be nice to have a dinner guest," he confides softly as I sit down and he comes over with a packet of Ritz crackers. It's simple, but right now, they taste delicious on my suddenly ravenous tongue.

Vladimir smiles. "For three days now, the only thing I've been able to get Mia to talk about are her animations and her two girlfriends. That and her data . . . always data with her. Though I understand none of it. But you sit, eat the crackers, and stay for dinner."

The moon's already passed its zenith when I leave via the back door of Vladimir's home, adjusting my tie as I do. Thankfully, he didn't insist on any more of that rocket fuel vodka of his, and the world is no longer spinning.

More importantly, though, Mia's with me, and inhaling her scent as I hug her next to my car is all the reassurance that eventually, things will be right between us.

"Thank you," Mia says, wrapping her arms around my waist. "For everything you're doing."

"And thank you for everything you're doing."

It's poignant, both of us having made mistakes, big, ugly ones, but able to still find our way out of the darkness by holding hands and taking it step by step. Together.

"I'd like very much to sweep you off your feet right now, carry you back to my place, and make love to you," I tell her, holding her tight, "but I feel like we need to work our way back to that. Like I need to earn you back."

Mia smiles and gives me a kiss on the cheek. "You already have my love. As for my body . . . you're right. We both need to work back to that, earn each other. And we'll both be rewarded. I'll see you at work tomorrow."

"It's a date," I say with a wink, feeling better than I have in days.

# CHAPTER 38

## Mia

I T FEELS COMFORTABLE BACK IN MY OFFICE AT WORK AFTER THE FEW days off. And I thankfully get to bury myself in numbers and figures and data. It's my dream come true, except all my reports have been crunching away without me, and now I have mountains of results to analyze.

Today is my first day back, and when I walk into Bill's office this morning, I expect him to chastise me for falling prey to Thomas's charms. But he simply looks up and smiles, welcoming me back with barely a mention of the mess even though I know it left him in the lurch.

"Hey! The gauntlet outside let you through? I got screamed at. I haven't been called so many nasty things since high school homecoming."

"Homecoming?"

"Short version? Rivalry game, star quarterback, smack talk," Bill says. "But seriously, you okay?"

"Once they realized who I am, it shocked the hell out of them. Some of them yelled at me for being weak, while others seem to have grabbed their ball and gone home," I reply, shrugging. "Whatever. Just leave me alone, you know?"

Bill chuckles and stands up, offering his hand. "Welcome back then. To be honest, it's been too damn boring around here without you. I even missed your loud music, though I'll deny it if HR gets another complaint about the volume. Only thing I'll say about this whole issue is that if anyone gives you any flak at all, you tell me. I'll be the one handing out ass kickings and name takings."

He lowers his voice, looking toward the door, "And that includes the boss man, Mia. I won't stand for any of my people to be mistreated. He's a lot to handle and fairly fucked in the head, judging by what I saw. You deserve better."

I shake my head. "No, it's not like that."

He lifts a brow, shrugging. "If you say so." I can tell he's not convinced. "Anyway, back to what we do best, data analysis. Go crunch those numbers. Your machine's been beeping like crazy."

He's right, and it takes me several days to get close to being caught up, and that's mostly on the resort figures because I missed a project team meeting in my absence. Finally, I'm starting to have time to split my attentions, getting pulled back to the saboteur puzzle again and again.

But the work has been a great focal point for my days and I feel like things are getting pretty much back to normal after almost two weeks back. I mean, I've yet to go with Thomas upstairs to his penthouse again, but I don't see it as our taking a step back. We've both acknowledged that our feelings for each other haven't changed.

Simply put, I still love him.

And he still loves me.

We hashed that part out the first weekend after I decided to come back on one of our dates. He and I sat at one of those Brazilian steakhouses for hours, mostly because they never give you shit about not leaving, especially when Thomas plunked an extra hundred-dollar bill under his red button the second time the guy with the skewer of beef came around and saw we were talking more than eating.

But with our conversation, I'm surprised I ate even a bite.

*"After my mother died . . . well, I told you how my father was,"* Thomas says, *looking about a thousand percent better than he did yesterday. It's shocking what a decent night's sleep will do for a man.* "But I didn't tell you about the voice."

*"The voice?" I ask, still at that point chewing a little bit of* picanha. *Maybe I'd been skipping some meals recently too.*

*"It first started in junior high school, but it really ramped when I left home to go to college,"* Thomas says, *nibbling at his own sirloin.* "It's Dennis's voice . . . *and he's just as vicious in my head as he is in real life. Maybe even more so. A bit ironic that when I finally got out on my own, that's when his grip got tightest and*

*he didn't even realize it. He'd just brainwashed me over the years to the point where I didn't even need the real deal anymore."*

*"That's a heavy weight to carry around in your head," I admit. "I mean, we all talk to ourselves in some way or another but . . . I'm guessing this wasn't rare?"*

*Thomas shakes his head. "It's like a constant presence on my shoulder, just instead of protecting me or encouraging me like an angel, it's the devil telling me that I'm going to fail, that I'm going to fuck it up. So many times, when people are thinking I'm pissed at them, it's not so much them but me getting angry at hearing my father's voice in my head, and they're just the unfortunate recipient of the cruelty."*

*I nod and take a sip of tea. "Is that why you actually tried with that, what was her name?"*

*"Dr. Perry," Thomas says, nodding. "Who, by the way, has already called me, trying to get me to go see her again."*

*"And are you going to see her?" I'm not going to push him. I've learned my lesson painfully, but I still think a bit of guided processing wouldn't hurt with the book of wrongs Thomas is hauling around.*

*"No, but I am going to see another therapist. One I can trust, and one who understands me. But I'll find someone who can help. Someone other than you."*

*"Fair enough. I'll take those times to go hang out with the girls or something," I tease. "Maybe I'll join a Zumba class or hot yoga, work off some of my own stress as well."*

*"You can always use my place," Thomas offers. "It'd be nice to see someone using that gym as a joy and not a burden."*

*He tells me about the night he nearly passed out under the squat bar, and that's it for dinner for me. "Tommy . . . the voice pushes you that hard?"*

*He nods, rubbing at his cheeks. "There was only one thing, before you, that made me feel better. It was . . ."*

*His voice trails off, and he sighs. I set my drink down and reach across the table, taking his admittedly slightly sticky barbecue sauce-stained fingers. "You can tell me. I'm not going to judge anything you say. I'm here for you, and I love you."*

*Thomas nods and swallows, and I wait for him to drop some awful huge bomb on me. Drugs, hookers, illegal underground fighting. Okay, that's a reach, but . . .*

*He shifts in his seat, only making me more nervous. We've conquered so much already. He'd shared such deep things. What could make him this twitchy?*

*"Okay. Well, I am . . . him."*

*"Him?" I ask, utterly confused, though he clearly thinks the words have meaning.*

*What does he mean? The man for me? Duh, I've kinda figured that out. But what's the coping mechanism he's hiding?*

He nods and looks up. "I was trying to find some way to quiet the voice. It kept saying all these awful things, and one night, sitting in the dark with just my thoughts, it started in like usual. But that night, I'd been to one of those corporate gala things, just a stupid reason for rich people to get dressed up and feel like they were doing something good while eating fancy food and drinking champagne. And I'd given a check like every other bastard in the room. So when the voice started in, I talked back, like the check had been this major thing. But it helped. Even though I knew the charity probably overpaid its director, and only a portion of the funds went to those who needed them, it helped me. So I did it again."

I nod, not quite getting it. "Okay, charitable giving is a good thing. Unless you're giving away everything you have? Are you telling me you've donated so much you're poor now? Because I'd love you even if you were penniless."

"No, that's not what I'm saying. I'm saying that I'm him. The White Knight. Maybe I'm partially doing it for selfish reasons, but I keep telling myself that at least it's doing some good, right?"

And everything started to make sense. *Of course he is . . . he was robbed of his childhood, of attention and affection, and so he gives of himself to those who have nothing.*

I hug him so hard, right there in the middle of the restaurant. "I knew you were a good man. I mean, I already knew, but this clinches it. My Ruthless Bastard. My White Knight. Why is this some huge secret though? I mean, this is a good thing."

He smiles, looking bashful. "I know, but that's why no one knows. I want the kids to think I'm doing it because I care about them, not some award. I have the people I help, the ones I support, but there are no PR photoshoots exploiting those in need. Just quiet, direct help."

I smile at the memory, warm bubbles rising in my belly, and if I was one of my anime characters, I'd probably have big pink heart eyes right now. My computer dings, breaking my happy buzz.

After a spin in my chair, legs kicking wildly, I focus on the finished report. It'd occurred to me yesterday that I needed to run a specified filter on the card access and see who'd been on the twenty-fifth floor the afternoon everything had gone to shit. Someone there had filmed that video and the suspect pool has to be rather small. Honestly, I was pretty pissed at myself for not thinking of this sooner, but I'd let myself off the hook since I'd been wallowing in the pits of despair, then buried in backlogged data, neither putting me at my best analytical skill level.

I scan through the report, line by line, moving a few folks to my *Look Into* list and dismissing others. After more than an hour, my suspicions are narrowing down.

Uncomfortably. These are people I work with, chat with over lunch, and see on a daily basis.

I turn to my secondary monitor, looking at the list of projects I'd been concerned about before my impromptu vacation, looking for cross-references and connections. And time and time again, my list gets shorter.

Nathan Billington had been on the twenty-fifth floor, a peculiarity for him since he offices on sixteen. But the project data doesn't pan out.

Kym Jenkins is an admin who frequently works on twenty-five, so her presence is logical, but she also served as an assistant on three of the five most suspect projects.

Randall Towlee wasn't on twenty-five at all, but he's been on all but one of the concerned project teams. Technically, I should mark him off the suspect list, and the rational side of my brain almost does it, but my gut roils. He doesn't fit the parameters, but something about him just makes my Scooby senses tingle, so I go ahead and put him on the short list with an asterisk to note that he's an outlier and an unlikely suspect.

I go through several others, and though I hate the answer, I'm pretty sure I know who is sabotaging Thomas. I double-check and then triple-check, even diving into the server files. I need to be sure because I'm about to accuse someone of some rather serious charges. Like felonious. And I don't want to make a mistake. I need to proceed with caution.

But everything I see, it all points in one direction. I save it to my personal hard drive, eschewing the network server, and put another copy on a flash drive, not wanting to take any chances. I feel a little like Sherlock, truth be told, but where he was this fictional brilliant badass, I'm just me. And the trip to the elevator and upstairs feels riskier than ever.

My heart is racing and my faced is flushed when I get out on the twenty-fifth floor. I even look up and down the hall, feeling like there are eyes on me. Truthfully, there probably have been since I haven't been back that long, and the gossip mill is still churning inhouse, even if the media has found bigger fish to fry.

But twenty-five is its normal deserted self, and I finally get to Thomas's office and Kerry looks up. "Mia, are you okay? You look as pale as a ghost."

I shake my head, keeping my voice low. "No, I need to see Thomas." I quickstep across the room, heading for his doors, but Kerry calls out.

"He's with someone right now."

Shit. Too late, I've already opened the door and interrupted. Thomas stands when he sees me, worry instantly etching his face. "Mia? What's wrong?"

# CHAPTER 39

## Thomas

**M**Y DOOR OPENS, INTERRUPTING MY MEETING, BUT WHEN I SEE Mia's face, I know it's for a good reason. Or a bad reason, judging by the complete lack of color in her cheeks. "Mia? What's wrong?" I ask the question, uncertain if I want to know the answer because I'm not sure I can handle anything else today. Normally, that'd make me feel like an absolute weakling to admit, even to myself. Hell, *mostly* to myself and my demon. But it's noticeably quiet, and I'm a bit emotionally spent. Understandable, I suppose, after my morning session with my new therapist had drained so much out of me.

Dr. Culvington has helped me make some rather quick strides in just a few appointments. He's a former military guy and suffers from PTSD, and the help he received led him to become a therapist himself. His approach today was pretty aggressive too, which suits me.

*"Okay, Thomas. Give me the basics of what you know is fucked up and we'll go from there."*

*"Uh, I don't usually . . ."* His eagle eye had glared at me, making me feel like *I was in boot camp and my choices were pushups or spilling my guts. While the pushups sounded easier, that was exactly the point, so I took a big breath and went the harder route. "Mom cheated and killed herself while I watched cartoons in the other room, Dad lost his shit, abused me my whole life, I worked my ass off in spite of him, not to spite him. Got my degree and started a successful company,*

*but his voice is in my ear, still beating me down at every opportunity. I need it to shut the fuck up. I want to be better. There's a woman. I love her."*

*I'd never summarized everything that succinctly before, and when Dr. Culvington had smiled, I felt like I'd already accomplished something.*

*And ever since, we've been making strides. He knows about voices, said he had a few of his own too after a rough tour, so he's taught me some helpful tricks for shutting them up. Mostly, to ignore them as much as possible to lessen their influence, challenge with positive messages, and while it makes me feel silly, to actively praise myself in my head. The awkward 'atta-boys' are weird as hell, but Culvington says I need to create a new methodology for my inner monologue, give it new messages to repeat.*

The memory helps me gird my mental loins, so to speak, so that when my inner voice pops up upon seeing Mia's face, I'm ready for it.

*I don't like him.*

For a moment, I'm almost intimidated again, but I can hear it now, the notes of petulance and fear in that voice . . . the voice of a father who blames me for his failures.

*Fuck off. I like Dr. Culvington,* I tell the voice.

*You can't handle whatever Mia is about to say. She's leaving your worthless ass and you're going to explode again, hurt her again.*

I force the breath into my lungs, filling them slowly and carefully as I refute that and let it go, secure that Mia and I have withstood trials and will handle whatever is wrong now.

She rushes to me, shocking me as she hugs me tightly. Not that I'm surprised she's doing it, but that she's doing so in front of an unknown guest in my office. We've been decidedly careful about who sees any of our PDA. But I know who he is, so I hug her back, rubbing the knotted muscles along her spine. My heart thumps as she whispers in my ear.

"I know who's doing it. Get him out of here. We need to talk. Now."

I look down in alarm, my heart thumping for a whole new reason. "You know?"

She nods, and I see the certainty in her eyes but also pain. "Mia Karakova, let me introduce you to John Smithson of Smithson Security. He was just about to share with me what he's found about the video, but perhaps you can share with us first?"

She shakes his hand but then looks at me sharply, silently questioning me if I want to air our company laundry this way. But I brought John in on this personally, and he's had his team examining the video's cyber-footprint as carefully as the FBI itself would.

She sees the answer in my eyes and goes over to my laptop, clicking some buttons as I sit down, giving her some space to work. "I need to remove any server access for this."

"It's all protected so that no one can get into my work. Shouldn't that suffice?"

She shakes her head, talking into the monitor as she focuses. "Better safe than sorry. Easier in the old days when I could just yank the fiber line. So here's what I found."

She's pulled up two files, splitting the screen into rows of data that make zero sense to me, but John leans forward, eyes scanning left to right, back and forth. He's got a background in cyber security and can probably see what Mia's saying faster than I can.

Mia paces as she speaks, like she needs the physical movement for her brain to function best. "I've been running data checks on unexpectedly low-performing projects like you told me to look into. I've identified several of interest," she says, pointing at the left side of the screen. "There are others, but these seemed the most obvious outliers, where the profit margins or the way the project played out made the least sense. Like the Chinese buying the aircraft parts company. So, I had these, but the overlap between players, project team members, departments involved, et cetera, was just too big. And then I had a thought."

"What?" I feel like this is her big build-up moment, but I'm eager to hear the results. "What'd you do to whittle it down?"

"Uhm, this isn't exactly legit, and you didn't ask me to go this far, be this intrusive, but I hope you'll think the result is worth it." I narrow my eyes at her, but John smirks as if he approves of whatever she's done even before she explains. "Okay, so I thought weeks ago that it might be helpful to track people's movements inside the company, both electronic and physical. I was hoping I might find some trend in someone being in the server files where they shouldn't be, on a floor they shouldn't be, or just weird comings and goings."

She looks at me, a slight blush to her cheeks. "I swear, I'm not some stage-five clinger, Tommy. I wasn't just tracking you. I was tracking . . . everyone."

I feign a mad look, then wink. "Stalker," I say. "Besides, maybe I'm one of those split-personality types."

John misses the wink and only heard my rough voice, so he comes to Mia's defense and corrects me. "Security."

He looks up, recognizing he's missed something, and realizes we're sharing a private joke. "Can we get back to what you've found?"

Reminded of why she's here, Mia resumes her pacing. "Yeah, of course. So, I've had that algorithm running for weeks, compiling loads of data. It's like freakin' terabytes worth. But then I realized, I didn't need to know about weird floor access six months ago. I only needed to know who—"

John interrupts, "Who was on the twenty-fifth floor to record the video that one day." Mia nods, and I can see that she's pleased John understands where she's going. "So, did you figure it out? Who was here?"

Mia gulps. "I did. But not only that. I got the list of who was on the floor that day, tracked if they'd exited and not returned, like Kerry. That gave me a shorter list of who was on the floor. But then I took that data and cross-referenced it with the project lists to see if anyone was on both lists. There were several, and I've been whittling them down, trying to figure it out."

She bites her lip, tears springing to her eyes. "It's Bill Radcliffe, my boss."

I search through everything I know about the man. Former military, has worked for me for years, took a move a few years ago, said he needed less stress and more nights at home with his family, but that's all I've got. He's just not a big blip on my radar.

Honestly, the move downstairs is the only thing I remember because it was unusual. Most people who can't cut it just move to another company. I normally even give them a letter of recommendation when they do.

"What? Why? Are you sure?" I ramble, not really questioning Mia's work, because I know it's above reproach, but just trying to make sense of it.

She nods, sighing. "I'm sure. I realized I was going about the project search wrong. It wasn't the team members themselves who were the biggest suspect pool. It was who had access to the data. Bill filters every bit of data through himself as a supervisory measure for those he manages. He didn't have to be on the project team. He could tweak the data itself to whatever he wanted. I found some server accesses that don't make sense, but I suspect he's running something sneakier to change the data. But that's beyond my cyber skills. I'm an analyst, not a security specialist."

I sag back in my chair, and Mia rushes over to sit in my lap. We hold each other for a moment. "I thought this was going to make me feel better, an answer to the puzzle, but this feels like shit," she says quietly, and I realize just how much Bill's actions have hurt her.

"I thought I was going to be mad as hell, rush out to kill someone or at least ream them, and I do want to do that, but mostly, I just feel confused," I admit.

John clears his throat, drawing our attention. "Not to hit pause on your pity party or anything, but I've got some info too." He looks to Mia, his eyes admiring. "First off, I'd like to say good work. The algorithms you thought to run, the data you slogged through, quite brilliant. And if you ever want to leave Goldstone, leave the corporate drudge and mill grinding behind, I'd have a place for you at Smithson."

I growl dangerously at him, holding tighter to Mia. "Over my dead body."

Mia pats my chest, chuckling. "Down, boy. Thank you, Mr. Smithson. But I'm good right where I am."

He shrugs like I'm not about to rip his head from his body. Okay, I'm probably not because then I'd have to set Mia down, and I rather like her in my lap, patting me. But I still give him a harsh glare. We've been professional acquaintances for years, but I can always find another security firm if need be.

"I suspected as much, but I had to extend the offer. Just business, you know?"

He looks at me, not apologetic but as if to say *you'd do the same thing*. "So, I took a different approach to your issue, focusing on the video itself because most people aren't tech savvy enough to erase all the markers. Actually, most people don't even realize there are data markers on every picture and video you take with your phone. First, I had to get the video. No small feat because the media was not interested in sharing their source, no surprise there, and copied versions off the Internet did me no good. Let's just say it took some work, but I got the original file and the email of where it was sent from."

I don't know what John had to do to get that access, and I suspect he wouldn't tell me even if I asked, but I trust he did it willingly and smartly. That's why he charges the exorbitant rates he does, because he's good at his job and goes all in for his clients.

"Once I had the info, I had my guys check it out. For your protection and mine, I won't share how we do that, but I tracked the phone back to one owned by Goldstone itself. It's in my report. I assume you can match that up with your records. The email was a blank account, basically the online equivalent of a burner phone, but from the metadata, I got the IP address as well. I think between what I have and what Ms. Karakova has found, it's pretty damning evidence. Prosecution might be a reach because explaining this to most juries is a crapshoot, but it's definitely enough for termination of employment and likely a civil suit."

John sets a plastic-coated folder on my desk, sliding it toward me. "Here's everything I have. Let me know if you need anything further, on this or anything else."

With a handshake, he's gone, and it's just Mia and me.

"What are we going to do?" Mia asks. "I'm in over my head here. I did the data work, but I don't usually have this much invested in the results and what you do with them. But this time, I do. I just don't understand why he'd do this."

I squeeze her tightly, using her body to ground me and keep me from charging downstairs like a raging bull.

"You know, part of me wanted it to be Randall Towlee," I growl lightly. "Since that thing in Portland-"

"I know," Mia whispers. "He's a jerk . . . but there's a difference between being a jerk and being a traitor."

Surprisingly, the urge to charge down at Bill, while definitely present, is something I can stave off. As long as Mia's with me, I have that inch of control I need. But distance is probably a good idea until I work out just what I'm going to do with all this information.

"Let's get out of here for a bit. Go to lunch or something."

"Upstairs?" Mia asks, her voice soft and silky.

I press my lips to her forehead sweetly and grind my cock against her ass roughly as I groan. "Fuck, Mia. I want nothing more than to take you upstairs and use you to make all this go away. Just lose myself in your pussy and pretend none of this exists. But I can't. I won't use you that way. Not for our first time taking it back to that level. When we go there, I want it to be just the two of us. No drama, no voices, just you and me."

She cups my jaw in her hand, looking up into my eyes. "You're a good man, Thomas Goldstone."

And another jagged piece of my soul sears over, the glass heating and reforming solid and whole. She is going to burn me to ash, but I want it because she's putting me back together bit by bit with her love.

She pops off my lap, pulling me to stand beside her. "Come on, I know just what you need. We're going to The Gravy Train and you're getting the biggest, greasiest burger they have, a whole plate of fries, and a milkshake. It's thinking food, and we're gonna think this whole shit show through and figure it out piece by piece, analyze the fuck out of it. Because Bill might have thought he was fucking with Goldstone, but he's fucking with my man. And Russian women, we don't put up with that shit."

She fake spits on the floor and mutters something, and in that moment, she is utterly beautiful. In all her weird streaky-haired, Russian-spouting, anime-loving, videogame-playing, metal-music-blaring, healing angel, avenging demon ways. I love this woman, and I will do whatever it takes to be worthy of the love she gives back to me so freely.

# CHAPTER 40

### Izzy

I SET A REFILL DOWN ON TABLE SIX, TAKING A DEEP BREATH AND schooling my face. How in the hell did I get myself involved in this? Oh, yeah, Mia. Of course. That girl could get me to do just about anything and definitely has over the years.

We've joked that we're each other's 'bury the body' friend. You know, the one you call when you accidentally-on purpose kill your cheating SOB of a boyfriend, and when you call them, they show up with a shovel and the gasoline? Yeah, *that* kind of friend, so this shouldn't be too bad.

In theory. At least that what Mia and Thomas had said.

*"You two okay? Looks like somebody pissed in your Post Toasties. And just to be clear, I would never do that to a customer's food,"* I say with a smile, hoping to get a returning one from Mia at least. I don't know what it'd take to make stone-faced Thomas smile, but Mia's easy game.

*"Not really, Izz. Just some work stuff that's hard and sad and infuriating and all the emotions rolled into one, basically."* She sighs and reaches for Thomas's hand, comforting him as he returns her sigh.

*Okay, tough crowd.*

*I pour their coffee. "Anything I can do to help? I mean, I'm no corporate genius, but the chocolate cake has solved some pretty serious problems before, especially with a scoop of vanilla ice cream on the side. Free of charge, of course. Benefits* of friendship." I frame my face with my free hand, highlighting the awesomeness Mia gets by being my friend.

"Actually, yes. Cake for lunch is just what we need. It won't solve a damn thing, but I could go for some feeling stuffing right about now," Mia says.

I plop a shareable slice on a dinner plate—no little side plates for my girl— and then add two scoops plus a drizzle of chocolate syrup. Feeling stuffing, coming right up. I've got you.

I set it down between them, interrupting.

"... understand why Bill would do something like this?" Mia says.

I can't help it, I hear everything that goes on in this place. It's like tying an apron on makes people forget you're human and they basically ignore you until they need something. Mia's not like that, but I can't help what I overheard.

"Bill? As in your boss, Bill? He comes in here often. Eats quick and leaves, not much for conversation. BLT with double bacon, onion rings, and Diet Coke, like that makes a damn bit of difference with that meal. Nice guy, though, tips me a fiver every time. What'd he do?"

Two sets of eyes turn to me, and Thomas says, "You know Bill Radcliffe from Goldstone?"

"I don't know him, know him. But I know lots of people from Goldstone. We're the best diner around, you know that," I reply with pride and not a bit of sarcasm. It's the absolute truth.

Thomas looks at Mia with an expression I can't read, not that I could begin to read him in the first place. But apparently, Mia can because they start some whole silent conversation with just their eyes and I excuse myself from their weirdness to go serve my other tables.

I return a few minutes later, and Mia asks me if I'll do her a 'small favor'.

This right here, this madness is no small favor. But I'd do anything for Mia, I remind myself. I give Elaine a wink, letting her know that I'm about to start my weirdness. I'd had to tell her I was doing something for Mia so that she wouldn't think I'd lost my marbles when this whole farce starts. The door opens, and Bill comes in, heading straight for his usual seat at table ten, right by the window.

I pinch my thigh hard so that tears spring to my eyes and think about those commercials with sad-eyed puppies in the rain, begging for your thirty cents a day. It works, and I get a good cry on before I approach Bill's table.

"Hey, Bill. How're you tonight? The usual?" I say, my voice flatter than Henry's pancakes. Actually, our cook and part-owner, Henry, makes great pancakes. So maybe that's not the best description. Flatter than my Grandma Sue's pancakes. That woman could make frisbees out of food.

"Yeah, that'd be great," he replies, and then he looks up at me. "Shit, you okay, Izzy?"

I swipe a tear from beneath my eye and glower at the window to the kitchen. "Yeah, I'm fine. Henry's just being an ass and it's making for a rough night. I'll get your order in. Maybe the King will deign himself to cook without bitching me out this time." The lie flows off my tongue as slick as turpentine. Henry's a great guy and a great boss, but that truth doesn't serve Mia's purpose.

I place Bill's order and return with his Diet Coke while the food's cooking. Like the heavens part and sing down praises on this ridiculous plan, Henry looks into the dining room and calls out.

"Izzy, fries up, girl. Show some hustle." He's not even in on the plan. His words are meant to be fun and just a part of our camaraderie, but they play right into Mia's evil hands and my twisted luck.

Grabbing the fries, I deliver them to table nine and scoot past Bill's table. A little more attention tonight, nothing too crazy as to raise his suspicions.

He tells me, "Chin up, Izzy. You're doing well."

I sniffle and offer a watery smile.

I grab Bill's food and deliver it to his table with an eyeroll that'd make a teenage girl proud. "Oh, my gosh, he's such a bear tonight. Of course, I might've had a little something to do with that," I say, holding up my finger and thumb an inch apart.

As I hoped, Bill raises his brows. "How's that?"

I glance over my shoulder at Henry and hunch down a little, whispering, "So just between us, Henry is like the biggest, absolute worst caffeine addict in the world. Buys this fancy ground coffee, blah, blah, blah special roast. So when he's giving me an extra-hard time, I offer to make him a pot. Out of the kindness of my heart, you know?"

I add a bit of devilment to my voice and then smirk. "And then he drinks that all night long. What he doesn't know? I don't make his fancy high-octane coffee. Nope, I use grocery store stuff, the cheapest swill I can find. And it's *decaf*." I say the word like it's poison.

And then I slap my hand over my mouth like I just told state's secrets to the mob, horror taking my expression. "Oh, my God, don't tell him about that.

Please, Bill. He'd fire me in a heartbeat. I don't know why I told you that." I look over my shoulder at Henry, who's oblivious to his usefulness in this plan.

Bill chuckles. "No big deal, Izzy. I won't tell. Though you'd better make sure my coffee is the good stuff."

My eyes widen. "Really? You won't say anything? You're a lifesaver. Thank you. I'd get tossed out of here in the middle of dinner service if he found out."

I don't want to lay it on too thickly, but it's my big play, the breath-holding moment in all this charade.

Bill is still laughing. "Really. We all do it to asshole bosses who deserve it. A little decaf here, a little fudged number there. It's no biggie."

I sigh in relief at the flippant share, but I want to really make sure the screw is tight. "That's right, you're a numbers guy. You'd really do that? I'm not a horrible person for getting a little revenge?" I hang my head ashamedly.

He shakes his head. "We all do it in some way. One little slip as I'm typing, and oops, that four becomes a five."

I look up in hope, like his casual comment makes me feel so much better. Then I shake my whole body like I'm letting go of the worry and smile sweetly.

"Thanks, Bill. I needed that. You know what you get today?" I point at the counter with my thumb. "One of our pieces of chocolate cake, on the house. Consider it 'hush cake', and hell, I guess I'd better go make a pot of coffee too. You want some? Caffeinated, I promise. And the good stuff."

"Sure, coffee and cake to go, please."

Minutes after Bill's left, a guy named John comes over and casually pops the bug off the bottom of the table. If I hadn't watched him put it there earlier, I would've been none the wiser. He gives me a subtle nod and is gone.

Operation Spy Izzy: success.

I think I'll get a slice of cake for myself too.

# CHAPTER 41

## Thomas

NOT EVERY FLOOR OF THE GOLDSTONE BUILDING IS STRICTLY meant for business. In fact, most of the ground floor is open to the public, including tonight's room, the large 'atrium' that can, and has been, rented out for large gatherings.

But tonight, it's strictly for Goldstone purposes, and it's a perfect setup, fun for almost everyone.

Except Bill Radcliffe.

"Thomas?"

I turn around, once again floored at the sight before me. Since we said we love each other again, Mia and I have not spent a night together, ironically. We've shared time during our days and have spent hours over long talks, but that's it. Step by step, bit by bit, better for her, better with her.

The physical piece of it will factor back in soon, and we can hopefully stop our torturous nights of phone calls where we invariably end up hanging up with fantasies roaring in my mind and my cock hard throughout the next two hours.

It's not enough, not nearly, but it's giving us time, and I've got a long and rather creative to-do list of ideas once she gives me the go-ahead. I'm hoping that's tonight, but if not, I'll wait as long as she wants to. Because she's already earned her way back into my good graces, my healing heart, and my soothed soul.

I'm not sure she ever really left, even when I was so hurt and angry, but either way, she owns me completely now. I just want to own her heart again too.

I walk over to her, taking her hand and twirling her around so I can get a better look. Her black gown is satin, hugging her curves sexily, and it's apparently a Vladimir Karakov original. Not bad for a man who says he's just a tailor who specializes in menswear.

But the piece de resistance is the under-layer of the skirt that flashes Barbie pink with her every step and matches the two inches of pink she's added to the bottom of her hair.

"You are stunning. I'm going to be the luckiest man in the room tonight."

She presses her free hand down her dress, smoothing invisible wrinkles, grinning. "Pshh, you're going to be the luckiest man in Roseboro tonight. Not because I can fill out a dress, though Damien and Papa really outdid themselves, but because this mess is finally going to all be over."

I don't want to talk about that right now. I'm a little nervous that everything won't play out as intended, especially with John still handling some last-minute details. I'd wanted to be there for that, but Stan said he'd handle it and John had agreed.

*You'd fuck it up. You always do.*

"It's going to be fine," I tell myself and Mia. "But let's not jinx it. Shall we?" I offer my arm, and we take the elevator down.

The party's in full swing already, our fashionably late entrance having just the right firework that I'd intended. People clap lightly, and I wave as Mia holds onto my arm for dear life, even though she's surrounded by friends and coworkers.

Or maybe that's why. It's easier to fake it when you just have strangers around you. It makes it different from the charity event in Portland, and besides, there's an air of something potent in the room tonight.

We work our way through the space, small talk here and even a few photos there. Apparently, some of the workers actually do like me . . . or more likely, they realize Mia's stunning.

Kerry signals me, and I make my way to the stage, taking the microphone the DJ hands me.

"Excuse me, if I could have everyone's attention, please?"

Conversation dies down as eyes turn my way. I meet Mia's eyes, gaining the strength I need to say the things I'm about to say.

She blows me a kiss and offers a thumbs-up with a big grin.

"First, I want to say thank you for coming tonight. I know it's been a rough couple of weeks for us, both Goldstone the company and Goldstone the man," I say, pointing over the crowd and then to myself. "But I appreciate your taking the time to come tonight."

There's a polite applause, more out of expectation than enthusiasm, which is understandable. Nobody likes an executive who gets up on the mic and makes it all about himself. Especially if it's a pity party.

"I've been the cause of a lot of concern and some media coverage, and you've paid the price for that along with me. And for that, I'm sorry. I said it in the press conference, but I'm saying it again. Profits don't mean much when they don't consider the people who produce them. And the simple fact is, I've spent too much time over the past six years thinking I had to put all of you on my back to drag this company up the hill. But the reality is, you are the hill, and I'm standing on the shoulders of giants. The giants who work on every floor, every day, busting your ass and not getting credit beyond a quarterly bonus from time to time."

I can see heads nodding and some surprise that I'm being so harsh about how I've run the company, but it's the truth. And I can see that now.

"But that's going to change. It's already changing, and I hope that you can feel that, in the building, in your departments, and in your dealings with me. We have some changes still to make, but it's going to be a new era at Goldstone, starting fresh tonight. I'm still going to ask each of you to give your best, but I'm also going to give you *my* best. And if I don't, I'm sure there's a smart Russian woman who will put me in my place."

I wink at Mia and the crowd laughs. "I watched a cartoon this week," I start.

Mia calls out loudly, "It's not a cartoon! It's anime!"

I grin and conspiratorially tell the audience, "I like to tease her, but I know the difference. God help me, I know the difference between a cartoon and an anime." Everyone laughs again as I look heavenward. "So I watched anime this week, and something resonated with me. It said, 'Don't ask for it, go out and earn it. Do that, and you'll be rewarded.' And that's what I want to do, and what I want you to do. Let's earn our way into making Goldstone the best it can be. We can reach that reward together. Thank you."

The applause starts quietly, and I'm surprised as it grows organically. Leaving the podium, I make my way through the crowd to Mia and take her in my arms.

"How'd I do?"

She smiles, kissing my cheek. "You did excellent."

More rounds of the room follow, and while everyone seems rather accepting of our relationship, especially considering the long weeks that have given time for the shock to wear off, there are still quite a few looky-loos. There are even some faces that let me know not everyone is pleased.

Before, I would've taken that challenge head-on, calling them out for daring to so much as have an opinion about who I keep company with. In fact, recalling one such board meeting, I cringe but then consider just how far I've come and decide the progress is worth celebrating.

Ironically, it's Stan who approaches me as I think back to that meeting and then the one afterward in my office. He'd been correct in his advice, and I think I've followed it in a round-about, messy way.

"Thomas, if you'll come with me. They want to run everything by you one last time."

I nod and start to follow, bringing Mia with me. I need her with me every step of the way on this because I know how hard this is for her. Bill has been a great boss while she's worked for him, and she's told me how hurt she is that he'd do something like this. She's a by-the-book, solve-the-puzzle type, and no matter which way you twist and turn this, Bill's actions just don't make sense. And that's eating at her, slowly but surely.

This needs to be over, for her as much as for me.

But she pulls back. I turn, questioning, "Mia?"

She swallows thickly, keeping her voice low. "I know this is happening, and I want it to happen. This needs to be made right. But while you do your last check, I think I'll go ask Bill to dance. One last time."

I cup her jaw, looking in her eyes. "Are you sure? If you say the word, I'll let it go. I have to fire him, but it doesn't have to be this way." I gesture to the full room around us.

She shakes her head and squares her shoulders. "No, this can't be hidden in the shadows like he's been doing. He needs to be called on the carpet, but not put on blast. And you need to show that you have the utmost control, of the company and yourself. This is where the fresh start begins, with you showing that you're better now."

I press my lips together and nod. "I'll be right back."

I walk out with Stan but glance back over my shoulder to see Mia smiling sadly as Bill sways her back and forth.

In the hallway, John is waiting for me with the city prosecutor and the police.

"Thomas, they feel like there's enough to proceed with a criminal case if you want to press charges."

I sigh, the moment suddenly real. I'm scared I'm going to lose it when I go back in there and see Bill's face as the accusations fly. Especially if he's confrontational.

*You're going to make an utter fool of yourself, just like always. You deserve his fucking with the company. You're going to run it into the ground anyway. Might as well let him get a head start.*

I shake my head, refusing to let my voice have the final say. *I run a successful company, with the help of a great team. One team member needs to be removed for wrongful actions of his own doing. This is how I keep the company healthy. I will keep my cool.*

The demon quiets, and I give John and Stan a look before nodding.

"Let's do this."

My entrance into the atrium ignites even more fireworks this time when uniformed officers are following me in. I head for Mia as every eye in the room watches. Her eyes meet mine, no doubt in them, and she steps to my side.

"Bill, these officers are here to arrest you." My voice is steady, calm, belying none of my anger, none of my sadness.

One of the officers moves forward, taking Bill by the arm. "What? What the hell's going on, Thomas?" he yells. "What are the charges?"

The silence from the crowd is shattered as whispers start. I can hear the soft murmurs of 'What's happening?' and 'The Ruthless Bastard strikes again.' But I don't let their words touch me, not now.

"We know you've been changing data, which in turn cost the company millions of dollars among the multiple projects you sabotaged," I reply, making sure my voice carries through the entire atrium. "And we know you were the one who filmed the video and sold the lies that I'd physically hurt Mia."

"I didn't. I wouldn't," he argues, trying to pull away from the officer who clamps down even harder.

"Don't resist or I'll have to cuff you, Mr. Radcliffe," he says quietly. "Don't make me take down a fellow vet."

Mia cries out, her emotions bursting through. "I know you did it! I'm the one who found the proof, Bill. I didn't want to believe it at first. All the files you accessed, you were so careful but not careful enough. And the reporter gave you up. Was the ten thousand worth everything? How could you do that to me?"

Bill's face is red, his breathing ragged. "I didn't do anything to you. This bastard did! He's the one who scared the shit out of you and hit you!"

"Don't do that. He didn't hit me and you know it," Mia argues loudly.

Bill rolls his eyes, huffing. "Fine, I sold the video, but you have nothing on the data manipulation."

His smug arrogance as he admits to selling the video sends a shockwave through the room. They know how much hell we all went through because of that—the protestors and media presence, the influx of phone calls, and lost stock margins. A lot of the people in this room own shares of Goldstone, and his actions have hurt everyone.

And with Mia and me both explaining repeatedly that, as crazy as it may sound, she really did run into a door, everyone believes the truth. That one of our own could do something so heinous and use Mia that way doesn't sit right with any of them any better than it did with me.

John holds up his phone and Kerry rushes the microphone over. She's good. I didn't even know he was going to need that, but she's on top of things, as always, anticipating everyone's needs better than should be humanly possible. John holds the mic to the speaker on his phone and Bill's voice fills the room.

*"Really. We all do it to asshole bosses who deserve it. A little decaf here, a little fudged number there. It's no biggie . . . we all do it in some way. One little slip as I'm typing, and oops, that four becomes a five."*

"How did you . . . that bitch!" Bill rages.

"Why?" Mia cries.

"Why not? I served this country for years! Saw shit that spoiled little brats like him would never understand! All I needed was a little fucking breathing room, a fucking break! Take your foot off my neck a bit, you know? Never once did he even give a shit whether I was okay."

He sneers at me. "Not that you care, but I was fine. And ready to move back upstairs. And when I asked to transition back, you know what you said? Absolutely nothing. I emailed you, I left you messages, and you couldn't even be bothered to respond. You trapped me and then left me there to die. Fuck you, Golden Boy!"

The officer hitches Bill up by his arm and starts forcibly leading him out of the room. At first, he's frantically looking for help from others. "Guys, this is wrong. He's the Ruthless Bastard, not me."

But when no one moves to help him, he gets more agitated, exploding at the door just before the police take him out. He turns, yelling, wild-eyed and crazy, "This isn't over!"

The threat hangs in the air, mixing with shock.

This is my moment to lead my people, to do better for them. I take the mic from John. "I'm really sorry you had to witness that tonight. And I will say that I probably have hurt many of you in the past six years. I can only say again that things will change. And I hope with a committed team of people who truly want Goldstone to succeed, we can move forward with the fresh start I spoke of earlier. Regardless of what I've done, Bill has been undermining our team for far too long, and I demand better. Not for me, but for you, the heart and backbone of Goldstone. Please enjoy the party tonight, celebrate the good things we've accomplished, and plan for the greater things we're growing toward. Good night, everyone."

I take Mia's hand and together, we walk into the hall. John and Stan give a quick wrap-up with the city prosecutor, and then they leave as well, promising an update as soon as they have one. In a moment, it's just the two of us.

"How're you holding up, Mr. Goldstone?" Mia asks softly, her hand on my chest.

"Better than expected, Miss Karakova. Though I suspect you have something to do with that." I hug her tightly, laying my cheek on the top of her head.

"Let's go upstairs," Mia whispers, and for a second, I think I imagined it, but when she pulls back and looks at me, I can see it in her eyes. Not just lust, but pride and love.

"Earned it?" I ask, cockiness creeping into my voice.

She laughs, tugging on my tie. "Fuck yeah, you earned it."

I kiss her lips lightly, but the passion is already igniting beneath the surface. "Good, because you earned me back a long time ago. You're a hard sell," I tease.

She adopts her thick accent, humming. "Mother Russia is not easily amused, but I could be courted to your point of view."

I sweep her into my arms and run for the elevator, not able to wait another moment to be inside her.

# CHAPTER 42

## Mia

BY THE TIME THE ELEVATOR OPENS TWENTY-SIX FLOORS UP, MY DRESS is already unzipped and puddling around my waist. I'm sandwiched between Thomas and the wall, our bodies on fire at every connection point. His tongue chases mine, twirling and teasing.

He backs me into his bedroom, and when my knees contact the edge of the bed, I fall back into the soft mattress. He pulls my dress the rest of the way off and then makes quick work of my black bra and panty set too, leaving me bare in my heels while he's fully dressed. It feels decadent and sinful, like he's going to use me, pleasure my body while taking none for himself.

But I want him to get pleasure too. This is us reconnecting, moving to a new level after some really tough challenges.

"Take off your clothes. Let me see you too."

Thomas unbuttons his shirt with deft fingers and flings it off carelessly, but when he slides his belt free from his slacks, he pauses and looks up at me.

I'm already expecting a flirty suggestion about him using the belt to tie me up, but what I'm not expecting are his next words. "Mia, I hurt you and I am so sorry. I feel like there's no way for me to prove to you that I won't lose control like that again. But I think ceding control to you might be a start." He offers me the belt. "It's not . . . who I am, but I can do it to prove to you that I have the strength to give you everything, to be the man you deserve."

I sit up on the bed, thinking and asking, "Is this something you want to do or something you think *I* want you to do?"

He shrugs, and I can see the sad boy inside him, the one who would do anything to make his dad happy. But I don't want that type of control over him. I don't want him to give in to me to the detriment of himself. I want to build him up, accept the flaws, and celebrate every change we both make, individually and together. I want a partnership.

"No," I say, and Thomas winces visibly.

He steps away from me, his eyes falling. "I understand. I'm sorry, so sorry."

"No, I won't tie you up because you think you need to prove something. I won't let you punish yourself, physically or mentally, for something we've already moved past. I don't want to change the way we make love unless it's exploring something we both want. I happen to like the rough way you fuck me, take me, and own me, every inch, every cell, every corner of my heart. So, if you want *that*, then take your damn clothes off."

He freezes for an instant, and I think he's actually thinking about it, like I might let him walk out of this room and leave me. He thinks he's possessive, but he's got nothing on a Russian woman, and I'll drag him back in here by his cock if he tries to go.

But then his face breaks out into the most beautiful smile, wide and happy and scrunching up his cheeks so much that little lines crinkle around his eyes. "Fuck, I love you," he says.

"Still not naked," I warn. But as he shoves his pants and underwear down his legs, I say earnestly, "I love you too."

In a flash, he's on me, or more to the point, he's on the bed. But he lies on his back, yanking me up to straddle his face. "Give me that pussy. Fuck my mouth."

Just the spread of my legs around his head feels naughty, but when I dip closer and his tongue licks along my slit, I'm lost, wanton with need that's been building for days. He lets me set the pace as I buck against him, but as my moans get louder and my movements erratic, he holds me still and feasts on me. His tongue delves into my pussy, stiff and fucking me like a precursor to what he's going to do with his cock. And when he slips up to circle my clit with wide strokes, electricity and love galvanize my body into a shuddering release.

I grab his head, holding him against me as I chase every spark of orgasm, and he drinks me down, gulping and slurping to get every drop.

As I relax, I sit back, making sure I didn't smother him to death, but he's still smiling happily. "That was fucking amazing."

All of a sudden, I'm flying through the air and Thomas has switched our positions, putting me on my back as he looms over me. "I think you also asked for me to fuck you rough."

I wiggle my eyebrow, challenging him. "Give me all you got."

He teases the crown of his cock against my slippery folds. "I already have. You have all of me. I love you."

I start to say the words back, but Thomas shoves into me with one powerful thrust, snatching my breath away. He's deep and nearly splitting me in two, and . . . "I love youuu!"

The howl begins before I can finish telling him, but I think he gets it, judging by the cocky smile on his face.

He pounds into me fiercely, our lovemaking raw and primal as our hips slap against one another in a sexy symphony. But through the animalistic fucking, our eyes never break contact.

This is us, our lovemaking. Sometimes rough, sometimes playful, but always a true expression of the deep love we feel for each other and the acceptance for who we are at our cores. There is something extra-special about this time, like it's the final puzzle piece of the rebirth of our relationship. We've been through work wildness, family feuds, and some hard self-awareness growth, but it's all brought us to this moment. Thomas thinks he doesn't deserve me, not yet, but he couldn't be more wrong. I love every part of him, the Ruthless Bastard he's moving away from, the secret White Knight he hides, my boss, my love. My Tommy.

And as he grunts, pistoning into my puffy pussy with his sweat marking my skin from his efforts, I realize he's one more thing. My beast.

# CHAPTER 43

## Blackwell

"*AND NOW IN HAPPIER NEWS, THOMAS GOLDSTONE, HEAD OF Goldstone Inc, seems to have found the magic touch again, this time not in business but in his personal life. He has just announced his engagement to Mia Karakova. The couple made headlines just weeks ago—*"

My thumb jabs at the remote control, turning off the TV, casting my office almost totally into shadow. Other than the bloody sunset coming in behind my desk, there's almost no light in the room. It helps me think.

How did my plan go awry? I'd set things up so carefully, years of work slowly ratcheting up the pressure on the Golden Boy, cultivating the connection with Bill Radcliffe, the vengeful Goldstone employee . . . and now my plans lay in ruins.

The hospital announced yesterday that they were accepting Thomas Goldstone's offer, and Goldstone Health is now a reality. Thomas Goldstone's star is even brighter than it was before, and I can already feel the sun setting on my empire like it's setting now outside his building.

My desk phone rings, and I pick it up, knowing select few have this number. "Yes?"

"Sir, please, you have to help me," Bill Radcliffe's pathetic voice hisses in my ear. Yes, he served his country, but obviously, men change. "I don't know what else to do. I've stayed loyal. I didn't mention your name. Yet. But they're saying they can pin the Chinese deal on me ... that's real prison time. They're talking years if I can't give them something."

I growl, knowing exploitation when I hear it. "Do not threaten me. An attorney, a good one, mind you, has already been provided for you. That is contingent upon two things. One, you will keep your mouth shut. You will never say my name to anyone. Not the police, not a lawyer, yours or otherwise, not even in your sleep. And two, you will never contact me again. You do these two things, and the attorney will do what he can for you. You choose any other option, and you will not be enjoying Federal custody for long."

I hang up before he can respond and sit back, tapping my desk. The grandfather clock against the wall starts to chime, and just as the sixth bong gets somehow swallowed by the cavernous air in my office, the outer door opens and my secretary walks in.

She approaches the desk slowly. "Sir, your evening appointment is here."

"Show him in," I command, watching her carefully.

"Of course, sir," she replies, scurrying out. She's dressed as provocatively as always, her curves on full display as she shows my appointment in, but I have to give the man credit, his eyes never acknowledge her as she leaves. It's a good sign, considering the job I'm hiring him for.

For the target is very eye-catching, and this man must be able to resist such ... primal urges.

"Mr. Blackwell," the tall man says, his charming face and boy next door smile doing nothing to hide the ice in his eyes from my perception. I've built an empire on both light and shadows, and this man definitely knows the shadows. "It's an honor. I've heard not too many people get invited to meet you here."

"Not many are deserving," I reply, standing up and going over to my wet bar, considering what to serve. "But for the man known as the Fallen Angel, well, exceptions can be made. Drink?"

"Absinthe, if you have it," the man replies. A fine choice ... unique, but certainly tasteful. "What is the nature of the job, Mr. Blackwell?"

"I recently had certain plans of mine backfire," I explain carefully. Before I reveal any extra information, I want to know if this man is on my payroll or not. "Unfortunately, the main parties involved are, if not beyond my reach, at least high enough in notoriety that I do not want to risk stirring too many pots right now. But there is one person I want eliminated. Their death will send the right message to the right people."

My guest nods, unperturbed by the macabre conversation. I have done my research thoroughly, how this seemingly charming man, as handsome as any television star, with a background that should make him a hero, has instead turned to such pursuits.

While he's not the best in the underworld and definitely does not have the highest body count, his background and demeanor are unique. It's given me leverage, for I just happen to know a few things that could help this man . . . if he does what I ask.

"I see. Hearts and minds?" he asks, lifting an eyebrow. "Show them not to mess with you?"

"Something like that," I admit. "This person's death would rattle my enemy, tell certain people to shut their mouths, and also, quite frankly, please me to no end. They were only an instrument, but even an instrument shares some blame for the damage they cause."

"Anything I should know? And before we proceed further, I assume they meet the aforementioned criteria I gave you?"

"That they do. And they aren't well-protected or even aware that they could be a target. It should be easy to make it look like a tragic accident. An easy payday for you."

The Fallen Angel nods and shifts as he takes the drink I hold out, swirling the glass for a moment before sipping. It's a good absinthe, and he savors the flavor before speaking again.

"Understood. But you realize if I take the contract, I do it on my timetable?"

"I know that is how you operate, but I would prefer a faster resolution to this issue. Wait too long, and the message loses impact," I tell him matter-of-factly.

"And the target?"

I cap the absinthe and pour myself a tequila before walking back over to my desk. Opening the lap drawer, I withdraw the photograph inside and slide it across the desk. It's a good picture, framed properly to give the Fallen Angel a good image to work from.

"Her name is Isabella Turner."

# EPILOGUE

## Thomas

"Hey, Frankie, this is my friend Mia. I thought she could hang out with us today. That cool?"

He shrugs. He's still too young to really care about girls. "Ms. Reba say it's okay? If so, it's good by me. She can be the cheerleader for the game," he says, laughing. But Mia's having none of that.

"Excuse me, mister man. But just because I'm a girl doesn't mean I'm automatically a cheerleader. I happen to be a brilliant data analyst, a video game virtuoso, and I know more about anime than anyone you know. So just because I'm female, you shouldn't assume I can't play football." She huffs, and I swear I almost see a neck swivel as she sets him straight. And she does curse, but at least it's in Russian so Frankie doesn't understand. She promised me no cursing in front of the kids.

"Oh, uh . . . sorry?" he says, apprehension in his eyes. "So, uh, want to be the QB?"

Mia smiles sweetly, tossing her hair back over her shoulder. "Just messing with you. I have no idea what a QB is. I don't play a lick of football, but you shouldn't assume that I can't."

She winks and laughs while Frankie looks at me and mouths, "Your girl is crazy."

"You have no idea," I mouth back.

And then we're all laughing.

Eventually, Mia does play ball with us, and all the guys are running around, doing their best to make up for her lack of skills. And while she can't catch, she can at least tag, and she runs decently enough to play defense on kids.

But what she lacks in experience, she makes up for with hard work and motivation. She's a natural cheerleader, encouraging the boys and helping them while we play, but I'd never call her that aloud.

Well, not now, at least, but maybe if she was wearing a costume.

Hmm. Might need to pick one of those up.

After the game, we pass out Gatorades and high-fives, along with promises to come back soon for a rematch. I tell Reba a quick goodbye, slipping a white envelope into the mail stack on her desk when she hugs Mia. And then we're back in my dusty old beater truck.

"Thank you for letting me come along today. I know this is kind of your thing," she says softly. "Don't know about the wig though. I like your real hair."

I shake my head, scratching where my scalp still tingles some. "Now it can be our thing, if you want. Look, I know you wished I'd make peace with my dad someday, but that's not going to happen, and I think that's for the best. He's off the board, out of my company, and out of my life. And I finally feel like I can breathe deeply for the first time in . . . ever. I might never be the son he wants, but I can be a role model for those boys at the home. And maybe one day, I'll be the dad I wished I'd had to a son of my own."

It's a big confession for me. Wanting kids seems scary as fuck since I don't know how to parent, and I'm reasonably certain a few hours here and there playing ball doesn't cut it as parental training.

I look over at Mia. She's wearing her favorite black distressed jeans, a rock band T-shirt from a group I've never heard of, and Converse. After a run of purple, her hair is a soft pink from roots to tips, and she has not a lick of makeup on. She's never looked more beautiful. Or happy.

"You'd be a great dad, Tommy."

I'm a bastard, a billionaire, and a beast. A man no one ever cared enough to get to know because of the monstrous mask I wore, but she saw beneath it so easily. Her Papa may think she's a Princess, but I know the truth. She's my savior, my angel.

*We're going to be one big happy family, just Mia and me and however many kids she wants to have.*

I wait for the demon to argue, but it's silent. Only my positive hopes for the future echo in my head like a promise.

# VOLUME 2

# NOT SO
# PRINCE
# CHARMING

# PROLOGUE

## Gabriel

THE PRE-DAWN SUNLIGHT PEEKS THROUGH THE WINDOW, AND faintly, I can hear the train rolling through town though the tracks are miles away.

I sit on the edge of the bed, my mind whirling and my back to the cause of my breakdown.

*Will you, or won't you?*

It's not that simple, though. When I'd accepted this job, I hadn't known the possibilities, couldn't have anticipated what was going to happen.

I hadn't planned on her beauty, her full lips puffed out as she softly snores, her head turned sideways on the pillow and her face so innocent.

I hadn't planned on the way her hair spreads out on the pillow, rich chocolate waves that, even in her sleep, flow around her like a messy halo. I curl my hand to stop myself from reaching out to stroke them, feel their silken threads against my rough palm.

Looking over my shoulder, I watch her, hating that I've been forced from the warm paradise of her embrace by nightmares of who I am, of what I've done. Of what I'm supposed to do.

I'm chased by the monster I've become.

*If you're a monster, then why not be a monster? Why not do what you were hired to do? You've done it so easily before, time after time.*

But I'm not sure if I can do it any longer.

I can't help myself as I slowly peel the sheet back so as not to disturb her. I need to see her, need to commit every curve and angle to memory. Because one way or another, I will lose her. I know that already.

She's an angel. A sleeping beauty whose glamour pulls me toward her, regardless of the dangers she represents.

*Then why are you continuing to stay here? Why not just walk away?*

Because I know if I walk away, then someone else will do the job, and I can't let that happen.

Unable to wait any longer, I reach out to see if she's real or just a hallucination caused by my own tortured conscience finally snapping.

She doesn't stir as I run my fingertips over her shoulders, brushing a stray lock of hair away from her cheek and allowing me to see the graceful swan-like curve of her neck.

My fingers keep going, tracing the light knobs of her spine as I descend, my own arousal growing with every inch of flawless skin I touch.

Somehow, despite all the years of hard work and struggle she's faced, her skin's still silky soft and flawless.

It's lightly tanned just enough to tease at the naughty side of my mind because I want to trace those tan lines with my tongue, revel in being the only one to see the natural creamy paleness of her breasts and ass.

I find the tiny dimples at the base of her spine and the tattoo she's got there. She calls it her *tramp stamp*, but she couldn't be anything further from that.

She has this daintiness and dignity that can only come from a well of great inner strength. A strength I admire, a well I wish I could tap into to find some fortitude of my own.

I leave the sheet over her hip, tracing back up her body as my cock rages in my boxers, but she doesn't move, doesn't stir as I feast on her curves with my touch, holding back on my desire to roughly take her.

That's the other side of me. The ugly side that wants to be purged, to violate her purity with my darkness.

*To do your damn job.*

But despite my nature, I want to treat her the way she deserves to be treated, like a queen.

Perhaps that alone shows that this ugliness is not my nature, but rather a depravity I've nurtured and let bloom inside my soul.

But this is no pretty flower, more like a weed that refuses to die and instead grows mightier each day, changing me, weighing me down, and strangling any attempts I might make to be better or do differently.

She hums, and a small smile forms on the pink bow of her lips. "Lower."

She doesn't open her eyes as my hand strokes lower, pulling away to slide under the sheet by her ankles and run up the outside of her legs. I find the swell of her hip, and she sighs softly, a breeze on the air that tells me that she's enjoying this.

I run my fingers inward and am rewarded by the warmth of her cleft, already wet and waiting for me. "Were you having a good dream?"

"Mmm-hmm," she whispers, gasping lightly as I slide a finger into her. Warm, slick velvet envelops me, and I slide deep inside her, pulling out just enough to find the nubby ridge of her inner spot and massage it.

She loves it, lifting herself and arching her back, all the while keeping her eyes closed as she playfully pretends to still just be waking up.

That stops, though, when my thumb finds her clit and her dark brown eyes fly open, already alight with arousal as she gasps.

"Oh, my God."

"Shh . . . just let me," I whisper, my fingers and thumb rubbing all the right places inside her.

But she can't seem to stay quiet now. "Yes . . . oh, fuck, yes. Right there, Gabe," she says.

She's moaning my name over and over, her hips pushing back to meet my plunging fingers as I fill her deeper and deeper.

"Do you want to come?" I ask, and she shakes her head.

She knows what she wants, and she lies flat on the bed, arching her back to lift her ass tantalizingly in the air, trusting me to give it to her.

But I don't deserve it, even if she does trust me. I shouldn't be this attached to her.

Somehow, in the weird alchemy of the universe, I've found the one I'm meant to protect and keep safe for the rest of her life.

But how am I supposed to protect her . . . when I'm the one who was hired to kill her?

The question floats away as I hover over her, holding my weight off her. Lining up my rock-hard cock with her slit, I push into her, slow and easy.

Letting her heat envelop me.

Letting her honey anoint me.

Letting her pussy absolve me.

But I can't be saved, not even by her. As she clenches around me, I wonder if the reverse is true. Can I save her, even from myself?

# CHAPTER 1

## Gabriel
*Weeks Earlier*

*Y*OU KNOW WHY YOU'RE DOING THIS.
    *It's not about the girl.*
    *There is no girl.*
*There is only a target.*

I repeat the mantra in my mind as I get out of the shower, my body freshly scrubbed and my skin tingling with the exfoliating scrub I always use in preparation for a situation like this.

It doesn't totally eliminate shedding skin cells, but I don't get paid to take chances, so I take all the precautions I can.

Looking in the mirror of the cheap motel room I'm currently renting, I get dressed on auto-pilot.

*Remember . . . in, out, and don't think. Just do.*

First is a cotton T-shirt, black, Hanes. You can get these at any discount store, and that's why I wear them. I don't need some hotshot CSI finding a scrap of cloth and somehow tracking me down based on my clothing purchasing habits.

On top of my undershirt is my long-sleeved blue hoodie pullover. It's fashionable enough that I won't stick out here in Roseboro, with its working-class population, while at the same time, it's dark enough that I will blend into the shadows.

*It's just like they taught you in the Boy Scouts. Be prepared.*

Black jeans, a basic pair of bootcut Wranglers, and underneath, a pair of common, run-of-the-mill black leather workboots.

Everything I'm wearing is commonly available at ten thousand stores around the country, and nothing is over fifty dollars. Considering I'm burning all of this after tonight, there's a good reason why.

On the bed are my main tools for tonight. First, a pocket knife. I've used this Leatherman for a very long time, the multiple tools and attachments being more useful than a lot of people would recognize.

Next, my lock picks. I'm prepared to break a window to get in if I have to, but I'd prefer not to.

The fewer details I leave behind, the greater the chance that I'll be sipping beer and watching the game before the Roseboro police even know something's wrong.

Finally, tonight's weapon of choice, a snub-nosed .38 Special revolver fitted with a silencer. Not the highest power of pistols, but accurate, and no shells will be left behind for forensics.

I finish up, tucking my ski mask into my pocket, knowing I might need it later, and put black leather gloves on before walking out to the plain-Jane Ford truck that I'm using for this job.

*Time to go to work.*

The house isn't exactly in the best part of town. It's maybe one of the oldest in Roseboro.

Once upon a time, it was probably considered rural, but as Roseboro expanded, the plot of land with a short row of near-matching houses is now on the edge of the industrial district. The cheap galvanized chain-link fence that surrounds the tiny two-bedroom 'mill' house is a product of a bygone era, back when the biggest employer in this city was Cascade Cider House.

But the national expansion of the big beer chains closed Cascade Cider by the seventies, and now the only things left are a few of these tiny breadbox-style places that used to be filled with people who smelled of fermenting apples nine months out of the year and fresh apples the other three.

It's a miracle any of these places still survive, but this house is one of the few, and while it's old, and nowhere near what anyone would call a dream home . . . it's been loved and cared for.

I see it in the way the trim is painted, not always in the same shade of blue, but carefully done anyway.

Or in the way the little brick flower garden underneath the tiny living room window is still bordered in tightly-fitted bricks, although the flowers are now replaced with hardy herbs that don't take nearly as much care as petunias.

I park across the street underneath an old, twisted scrub pine that's shed a thick blanket of needles all over the uncurbed grass that lines the backstreet. It's the sort of neighborhood where your parking space is the chunk of dying grass next to your mailbox.

I sit in the shadows of my truck, waiting and watching. The first step is to make sure my target's there, that she's alone, and that I'll be uninterrupted.

I know her schedule. She got out of her last class twenty minutes ago. She should be home soon to drop off her books before heading in for a late-night shift at The Gravy Train, where she'll work until the last of the late-night bar-flies get their greasy plates eaten.

Then she'll come home, crack the books until her head drops onto them, and do the whole thing again tomorrow morning.

Whether now or after her job, it ends tonight.

I see her pull up on her scooter, a little 50cc thing that a lot of people around here call a 'DUI bike' since you don't need to insure them.

She has a car, a beat-up twenty-year-old Honda that she inherited from her aunt when she passed away, but insurance and gas mean the scooter's her vehicle of choice more often than not.

I'm tempted to just take the shot here. It'll be easier and faster, although riskier and less controlled.

But I do have a few rules to my work, an honor code, even though what I do is less than honorable by anyone's standards, including my own.

First, be patient, hence my learning her routine and doing my research. I'm good, not because I'm the fastest, or the nastiest, or the strongest. I'm good because I take my time and do it right.

Second, absolutely no bystanders. I won't take a shot on anyone if there are innocent people who could get hurt if something goes wrong.

The last thing my conscience needs is me accidentally shooting some eight-year-old kid because I didn't see them or a bullet bounces off a lamp post.

Third, don't get too close. But I don't want to think about the third. Because I'm pretty sure I'm breaking the hell out of it with this job.

As I watch her shake out her long brown hair, nearly black in the deepening dusk, I grip my steering wheel a little tighter.

I know she doesn't try to be, but Isabella Turner is uniquely striking in her beauty.

Her hair falls simply, nearly halfway down her back, waving in the air like a dark curtain that frames her lean face.

Her eyes are large, almond-shaped and framed with thick lashes, like she's a princess hiding in this working-class setting, just waiting for her chance to be restored back to the throne that's waiting for her.

Of course, I'm being foolish, maybe a little whimsical. But I do this with every target.

Usually, I'm trying to make them go the other way. Paint them with a brush that pushes them fully into the 'evil' category.

So, the drug dealer isn't just a guy selling drugs but someone who's stealing kids off the streets, carelessly taking their potential future by hooking them on his poison smack to fund his criminal empire.

The stock broker isn't just a shady trader but someone who's laundering billions of dollars of crime money while robbing poor, innocent grandmothers of their retirement savings.

It helps me sleep at night, and quite honestly, isn't that hard to do. Not with the contracts I've accepted.

I've killed a lot of bad people. Hunted them down, snuffed out their miserable existence, and not felt much remorse about it.

Occasionally, I even feel like I'm doing something darkly noble, protecting those who can't do what I do from the evil in every corner of the world.

But no matter how hard I try or how much I look into her past, I can't make Isabella Turner 'bad' in my eyes.

But if I don't do this, I'll never get the answers I need. Blackwell hired me for this job, making it very clear that this is a tit-for-tat-only negotiation. I do this, and he gives me what I want . . . a chance for justice.

Considering carefully if this is the moment, I scan the street, looking for potential witnesses. As my hand reaches for the door handle, I freeze, seeing a man approaching the house from down the street.

His hair's long and greasy, the two-day-old growth of beard on his gaunt cheeks making him look even scuzzier than the ripped long-sleeved Nirvana T-shirt he's wearing.

"Hey, Izzy!" he yells, and I shrink deeper into the seat, willing myself to be invisible, my eyes narrowing as I rest my hand on my pistol. Something about this puts me on edge. "Izzy Turner!"

The look on her face tells me everything that Miss Turner feels about the man calling her name, and mentally, I quickly go through my research on this mission to place a name to a face . . . Russell Carraby. Thirty-five, single, currently listed as 'self-employed' according to his most recent tax records. And Izzy's landlord of sorts. He doesn't own her house, but Russell inherited the land Izzy's house sits on.

Seems the Carraby family got along quite nicely with the Cascade Cider people and that's how these houses came to be built out here. Back then, it was probably a sweet deal all the way around. But now, people who own their house, like Miss Turner, still have to pay a small fortune to sharks like Carraby because of where their home sits.

Meanwhile, Carraby gets paid doing jack squat.

But the financial data I'd run on Isabella Turner had seemed dry and unimportant, just a list of bills she paid off each month like clockwork. This moment with Carraby feels decidedly more threatening than a monthly invoice.

"What do you want, Russ?" Isabella asks, her shoulders slumping as Russell gets closer. "I already paid you for the month."

"No, you paid me catch-up money," Russell says, his ferret-like eyes clearly undressing Isabella even as he smacks the large wad of gum in his mouth. "Not all of it either. Late fees can be such a bitch." He shakes his head like he's sad, but even from across the street, I can see the joy he's taking in this moment. "Long story short, you're still behind."

Isabella isn't ready to back down, though. "You need to check your books. I paid you extra last time."

"Nope . . . you still owe," Russell says, smirking. "I got it all in my computer back at my place. If you'd like to come see?"

"There's no way in hell I'll ever go inside your house, Russell," Isabella growls, her anger flaring. "And trust me, I keep my own records too. Of every single red cent I give you. So you can stop looking at me like that. I'm not going to whore myself out over a damned land lease I've already paid."

"Just being neighborly. If you can't pay in cash, I'd be open to letting you pay another way," Russell threatens with a shrug and a smile, like he'd be doing her a favor. "Hell, it might even be fun. And I know you haven't had a man in a long time."

Even as that intel does dangerous things to my cock, my hand tightens on my pistol. I'm about ready to shoot Russell on principle when Isabella pokes a hard finger into the front of his dirty shirt, denting the doughy skin of his chest. She takes several steps forward, and like the coward he is, Carraby backs up under the weight of her fury.

"The next time you mention something like that is the time I call the cops on your ass," Isabella yells.

The threat, combined with her pushing against him, causes Russell to take another half-step back.

"I'm gonna give you one week, and if I don't have my fuckin' money by then, I'm going to take you to court," he says. "Don't fuck with me, Izzy. I know the sheriff. You might just have more problems than looking for another place to live."

But he's adding to the space between them, already walking away without giving her his back. Coward. Smart man, considering the balls on this girl, but still a gutless way to try to intimidate her.

"I bet you do know the sheriff . . ."

She pauses dramatically. "Since he's arrested you twice before," Isabella calls after him. "As for court, you bring your records and I'll bring mine."

She's taking aim at his every threat, but I can see it in the way her shoulders slump a half-inch that the fire's dimming. Still, she fakes it pretty well until Russell's disappeared around the corner, and she goes inside her fence.

This is the time I should be moving, taking advantage of her shaken state, but I can't do anything but watch as she fumbles, trying to get the keys to her house into the lock before giving up.

She drops her bag to the concrete stoop and collapses into the small, cheap plastic chair, discount lawn furniture at its finest, next to the door, burying her face in her hands.

She doesn't sob or cry loudly. Instead, she just sits there, her shoulders shaking quietly, her body looking like she's exhausted. She's carrying the weight of the world on her shoulders and she's tired out from doing it. I can almost see the scrabbling grip she has on the end of her rope, but still, she fights to hang on.

I watch, my soul touched. I want to go to her, to take her into my arms and tell her that the world isn't so hard and cruel, even if it's a lie. I want to . . .

*Do your fucking job!*

I clear my throat, blinking slowly as I pick up my ski mask, slipping the breathable Lycra over my head and then down my face, leaving just my eyes peeking out.

I pull up my hoodie, but I'm frozen, unable to move as she finishes her moment of weakness.

Then, in a show of resilience that makes my mouth dry, she stands up, wipes her face, and glances at her watch before opening up her front door enough to drop her book bag off and leaves immediately.

*You need to finish this.*

No.

I rip the mask off, stuffing it in the console. I need to find out more. I can't risk violating my most cardinal rule, that I don't kill the innocent. This is something that I could never come back from if I'm wrong.

Ever since I was given the contract to end Isabella Turner's life, I've broken myself trying to find something she's done wrong. She's not perfect, but she's done nothing deserving of death.

And Blackwell's reason for hiring me doesn't carry enough water with me. I know everyone is a pawn in someone else's game, but I refuse to the be the Grim Reaper for a soul that doesn't deserve it in some way.

My gut is telling me there's something more here, a puzzle piece I don't have yet. And I won't make a move until I have the full picture.

Isabella gets on her scooter, tucking her hair into her helmet again before taking off. I let her get a good block away before following. The streets in this neighborhood aren't busy and I already know where she's going.

The Gravy Train is that rarity to find anymore, an honest to goodness old-fashioned diner. The long silver bullet-shaped building resembles an old train car, and the inside decoration is a color I swear only comes when you take white paint and expose it to ten years' worth of fried onions, splattering greasy meat patties, burps, belches, and other bodily emissions.

I park in the lot, watching through the huge windows as Isabella goes inside and talks with another worker, who nods and clears away a spot at the counter for her. She brings her what looks like a grilled cheese while Isabella consumes it in four large bites before heading to the back, and I make my move.

So far, I've never gotten close enough to actually let her notice me, but something about her is calling to me, promising answers.

I push my hoodie down, not wanting to look suspicious, and my hair springs free, sticking up every which way, but I don't give a shit. I lock my pistol in the truck and head inside.

Taking an open booth, I pull out my cellphone, pretending to be obsessed with the screen while I surreptitiously watch for Isabella.

"Hey, honey, you orderin'?" a waitress asks, all sass and big hair and saucy attitude. She looks like she's about to tell me I need to order or move along, but one look at my face tempers that.

I'm used to women softening at my looks. I'm not arrogant, but I know that I'm easy on the eyes, and I've used it to my advantage more than once.

"Just a coffee for now," I order. "Decaf, if you have some ready."

"Honey, of course we've got decaf," the waitress says, turning around.

She gets me my cup before Isabella comes out, the two obviously swapping out as one goes off shift and the other comes on.

I nurse the coffee for a good half hour, watching Isabella at work. She's exhausted, almost sleepwalking through her shift, and while she keeps a smile on her face, it looks nearly painted on.

Still, as she keeps working, I find myself drawn to her more and more. It's not just physical attraction. I felt that the first moment I saw her picture in the office of the man who hired me to kill her. No, this is more than that.

How could he? How could he hire me to kill a pretty woman who mostly seems to be desperately struggling despite working her fingers to the bone?

She can't have any bearing on a man like that's life, they're literally worlds apart. There must be something I'm missing. There must be something he's not telling me. Surely, even he's not this cruel, this reckless.

"Hey, Izzy!" the cook in the back yells, banging on the little chrome bell next to the pickup window. "Come on, you got plates waitin'!"

"Yeah, sorry, Henry," Isabella says, grabbing them.

She hands them out to the three guys waiting at the old-fashioned sit-down counter before going over to the register, where another waitress, an older woman in her fifties who looks like she's done this her whole life, is tallying up a bill. I'm close enough that I can hear them.

"Hey, Elaine, I'm gonna grab another coffee. You mind?"

"I don't say nothin' about drinking the mud," Elaine says. "Don't let Henry get on ya, honey. Just his ulcer acting up again."

"No . . . no, I've been shit so far," Isabella says, yawning. "I can't keep going on three hours of sleep a night. But I don't know what else to do."

"You keep busting your ass, you're gonna end up like me, fallen arches and all," Elaine says encouragingly. "Seriously, what could have you scraping for every dime like you are?"

"Russ came by my place again," Isabella says quietly, recounting the confrontation at her house briefly. "I've got enough to pay the bastard but—"

"But then you won't have enough to live on. Don't say anything else," Elaine says. "Next week, you come in, you order what they allow us, and if it magically turns into a full chicken-fried steak and gravy dinner, well shit, I guess I just need to get my eyes looked at."

I see Elaine give a huge wink, like it's a brilliant conspiracy, and Isabella smiles. "If you do your studying here, you can have my shift meal too. That'd get you two per day at least. Make one of them the Country Plate Special and you can take the toast and little peanut butter packets and get a sandwich later too."

It's a kind gesture from the world-worn waitress, and with how quickly she throws that idea out there, I can tell she's been through some rough times too. Isabella nods quietly, touched, but I can tell her pride is stinging that she needs to take such charity. "You know if it was just any old house, I'd say fuck it, move into an apartment or something, but—"

"I know, honey," Elaine says. "I know."

Isabella clears her throat and finishes off her coffee. As she comes around the counter, I clear my throat and she looks over.

Our eyes meet . . . and inside me, I feel more conflicted than ever.

Because in the first meeting of our eyes, I feel what I've thought doesn't exist.

The Spark.

# CHAPTER 2

## Isabella

"Happy little clouds," I murmur to myself as I swirl my finger along the top of my touchpad, wishing for the millionth time that I could do this again with real paints and canvases.

But real art equipment costs money, and money is something I don't have. So instead, I use GIMP, which is free, and pray my laptop doesn't die again before I finish college.

Right now, I'm working on my own version of the *Mona Lisa* . . . if Gal Gadot were posing for the famous painting. Well, that and my color choices are a little surreal, but I sort of like the idea of putting light green clouds in a lilac sky behind the eternally smirking diva.

It's a lot more colorful than my real life, and I can go for a little bit of that before I have to slog my way through another day.

An insistent *meow* on my left gets my attention, and I look over to see Nirvash, my cat.

Technically, it's my best friend Mia's cat, but her former apartment lease didn't allow pets, so when she brought me the little ball of fur and begged for me to watch after it, I couldn't help myself.

Now, the miniature monster is mine, and I probably wouldn't give her back even if Mia begged. Not that she would. She knows what this cat has come to mean to me.

Sometimes, I wonder if Mia didn't plan the whole thing to trick me into getting a pet for my own good.

"Thanks, Vash. It's that time?"

Vash *meows* again, and I get up off the couch, stretching a little. Vash takes the opportunity to climb onto the keyboard, though she knows she's not allowed, and looks at the screen before turning her nose up and walking away.

"Humph . . . everyone's a damn critic. Well, I'm not done with it yet."

*Meow.*

"Yeah, yeah. I know, feed you before you get angry," I reply, heading into the kitchen and picking up the quarter-carton of nondairy creamer on the counter.

It, like a lot of the food I've got, is scraps from The Gravy Train's kitchen, since they can't keep opened containers overnight. I'm not sure that's a real rule, but Elaine had vehemently insisted it was true as she foisted the creamer and a large to-go bowl of soup on me.

She means well, and though it was a hit to my pride, I had taken it, knowing it'd help. The creamer is Vash's little treat and she loves it. "Is this what you want?"

*Meow.*

"Fine, fine . . . but you only get a little along with your real food," I reply, filling the shallow bowl Vash uses for food.

I check my clock and see I've got five minutes to be out the door before I'm late for my first class of the day. I toss the carton back in the fridge and hurry to the bathroom.

It's my own damn fault, really. When I'm painting, I'm able to escape, let my mind relax, and not worry about all the crap that's weighing down my life, even if only for a few minutes.

But that also means I let time get away from me, and as I quickly brush my teeth and pull a brush through my hair, I'm rushing.

"Okay, Vash baby, be good and keep the mice company!" I toss over my shoulder as I grab my bookbag and rush out to my little scooter.

The morning air's chilly, but until we get snow or rain, I need to be frugal, and using my scooter instead of my car saves me several dollars a day on gas.

As the wind blows in my face, numbing my lips, I curse myself for forgetting to use Chapstick before leaving. I've got some in my bag, but it'll have to wait until class. I just don't have time.

Like a lot of my life, I just don't have time for a lot of things. I barely have time for friends. I don't have time to take care of myself. I don't have time for anything except work and school.

I don't have any family left. The closest thing to family I have is Mia, my other bestie, Charlotte, and a cat that earns a good portion of her food through keeping the neighborhood rat population under control.

Other than that, my life's empty.

No time for self-pity though. I console myself with the idea that soon enough, I'll be able to take the next step after I finish my degree. Just one more year like this and then everything will be better.

The thought doesn't comfort me much when I hear an approaching truck motor and see Russell driving up in his Chevy. "You're up early," I mutter, tugging on my helmet and palming my keys. "Must really be running low on meth."

Russell comes to a stop next to me, putting his truck in park but leaving the motor running. "Izzy, where's my money?"

I growl, buckling my helmet. "You told me last night that I had a week, Rusty."

I've known Russell since I moved into this house, and I know for a fact that he hates that nickname.

Still, I'm just too tired and too hungry to think clearly about poking the bear, or honestly, to give a rat's ass about his bullshit this morning, especially since I've got class soon.

Russell's face reddens at the name, and he rubs at his cheek, where it looks like he's been doing the junkie shuffle all over his face. A shiftless kid who spent most of his teenage years trying to score beer and terrorizing the neighborhood middle-schoolers, he hasn't improved with age.

He scored his first drug conviction at twenty-two, but Russell's father got him out of those charges. Russell Senior had owned a lot of land on the outskirts of Roseboro, and as the town grew, he flipped a lot of the flat, empty pastures that weren't worth much to housing developers who needed easy plots for subdivisions. It'd made him bank, and money makes you powerful.

By the time Russell's parents died five years ago, a heart attack behind the wheel that resulted in a fiery crash that killed them both, Russell had inherited over a million dollars.

And he's burned through it all. Literally. A certified smoke hound, if you can put it in a pipe and smoke it, Russell Carraby's put it in his lungs. Quite a few rumors say he's moved on from smoking to straight up injecting poison into his body. All in all, it makes him unpredictable and desperate, which worries the shit out of me.

But money buys you lots of friends, and since Russell hasn't yet shit where he eats in terms of drug violence, the local cops don't do anything to stop him. I have a feeling the influence his money has bought is coming to a firework-worthy finale though.

He's down to his house and the deed to the land that my house and a few others sit on. He's like the slumlord of outer Roseboro, but with only the small pool of our row of old homes to dip into. And he's digging in with a damn shovel, trying to squeeze out every last drop he can get.

And that's what I owe him, a freaking land lease that I never had to pay to his parents. They had charged a small annual sum, more for show than anything, but when Russell inherited it, he used his connections to get a court order saying I have to make up for back payments. Stupid me never had a contract with Russell Senior, having just continued the deal they'd always had on the property and trusting that would always be the case, an honorable verbal agreement between all involved parties.

Russ isn't nearly the reasonable businessman his father was though. He's desperate for money, and I know it. He probably doesn't even remember telling me I had a week just last night, whatever memory he once had ruined by chemicals. The fact that he's back here so quickly tells me he's looking for a fix before the next payment is due.

Danger warnings ring in my head. Technically, I'm meeting the agreed-upon court ruling with my monthly payments to him, all documented carefully because I'm no fool. But the fact that I do owe him the money, at least legally, does cloud matters because if we go back to court, they could order me to pay it in one lump sum. And I'd be done for. So keeping him at bay is imperative, even if it means making smaller weekly payments rather than a monthly sum.

Because he still holds a lot of the cards in this little scam he's trying to run on me. And for all his drugginess, he's still smart. Sometimes.

Like now, he's technically not on my property, staying outside the fence, but the intimidation is just as effective and even more of a threat than taking me back to court.

"I said, where's my fuckin' money, bitch?" Russell says again, slapping the hood of his truck. "What, you want me to fuckin' go in your place and just take what I need to even us out?"

I see the blinds across the street twitch, and know the neighbors are watching this showdown. But they're just as scared of Russell as I am because he holds the land lease on their homes too. In a perfect world, we'd all band together and fight the evil slumlord. The reality is, they'll happily leave me to the wolves if it means the wolf isn't trying to blow down their house.

So I'm on my own. As always.

"You take one step through that gate and I swear I'll call the cops!" I yell back, reaching into my pocket and pulling out my phone. "I'm sure they'd love to offer you a field sobriety test, maybe search your truck?" I toss out the threat, hoping it's enough to scare him off because sure as the sun sets in the west, there are drugs in that beat-up ass truck of his.

He presses right up to the fence, hands on the top like he's considering vaulting over it. I measure the distance between me and the front door, deciding that my better bet would be to bean him with my helmet if he comes over the fence. "You owe me, and one way or another, I'll collect!" Spittle flies from the corners of his mouth as he yells, his eyes narrowed and mean.

"I'm calling, Rusty. Nine, one, one." I press at the black screen, feigning that I'm dialing because I know that even if I call, no good will come of it.

He throws his hands up, backing off. "Fine, but your bony little ass better get my money. Or else."

He drives away, and my hand shakes as I put my phone back in my pocket. As I do, I have a moment of hysteria that a junkie just called me skinny. Looks like Elaine's help isn't doing as much good as I'd thought. Vaguely, I wonder how Russell manages to stay so soft and round when all he does is smoke, putting every dollar to drugs and none to food.

My mind clears and I realize just how badly that whole interaction could've gone. Don't get me wrong, yelled threats and almost dialing 911 are serious. But Russell is escalating and I need to watch out for that. He knows I'm here alone, he's getting more desperate for money, and it's reaching the point where he has nothing to lose. The thought that he could get worse terrifies me. I'm so frightened that I nearly run my scooter into the fence, and it's only a last-second jamming of my brakes that prevents me from not going to class today at all.

My scooter stalls, and I push it a few steps back, looking around to make sure things are clear before I restart it. As I do, I do a double-take, swearing I see Russell's truck again, but despite them both being the same shade of silvery-gray, this one's a Ford, not a Chevy. I haven't seen it before and it's parked in front of Old Mrs. Petrie's house. She never has visitors other than her son, who lives a few towns away and drives a red Camry. I remember seeing the blinds twitch at her house and wonder if maybe she has someone over.

But the blinds are in place now. Still, I feel like I'm being watched, and as the hairs on the back of my neck stand up, I try to get a better view of the truck since it's the oddity in our same-shit-different-day neighborhood. The sun's at the wrong angle, though, and I'm forced to ride by it slowly to see inside. When I do, I see it's empty, and while that should relieve me, for some reason, it doesn't.

The Gravy Train beckons like the vampiric temple that it's been for the past three years for me. The long, train-car-like exterior glimmers in the late afternoon sunlight, and after four hours of classes this morning and some study time at the campus library, I'm not looking forward to slogging through another six hours of waitressing.

But if there's any chance that I'm going to keep Russell off my ass, I need to hustle and bust my butt for the tips. Dinner's the best time to get tips too.

Still, the next six hours will require me to keep my mind in a special place, clicking along as I work and provide smiling service even to surly customers—because trust me, the customer is definitely *not* always right—while simultaneously not focusing on the looming thundercloud of debt over my head. As I walk in the door, I'm not sure if I can keep it up.

The smell of the grill and the fryer, which probably makes most people's mouth water, smacks me in the face, making my stomach roil. In hunger or disgust, I'm not sure which. After three years, six days a week of that smell permeating every pore of my skin, it oddly feels like home, but some days, I swear I'd give anything for a salad. Unfortunately, fresh produce is a luxury I can't afford. Not if I'm going to keep Russell at bay and my school payments up to date.

And there I go already, letting the storm take over. I take a deep breath, letting the French fry-scented air fill my lungs as I shake my head, willing the dark thoughts away.

*Smile, Izzy. You can do this. You always do.*

"Hey, Elaine, order up!" a big voice hollers from the kitchen, and I sigh. Henry's the head cook at The Gravy Train, and while normally, he's an overgrown teddy bear, for the past month or so, he's been increasingly short-tempered. He says it's an ulcer, and I guess if I were a forty-year fry cook who had an ulcer, I'd be upset too.

"Hold yer horses, Henry, I'm comin'!" Elaine, the head waitress, tosses back as she throws me a wave. "How're you doin', Izzy?"

"Is that Izzy?" another voice calls from the back. "Tell her to come back here!"

Elaine rolls her eyes, since obviously, everyone in downtown Roseboro heard it. She tilts her head at me, adopting a faux fancy voice like she's a phone operator at one of the big skyscrapers downtown.

"Martha'd like you to stop by her office."

I grin at her over-the-top antics, appreciating the levity, and head back to the office, which is more like a storeroom closet with a desk, where I find Martha. Short and heavyset, she's the business manager while Henry's technically the owner . . . but we all know who really runs the show, both in their marriage and around here.

"What's up?"

"Hey, I just wanted to tell you I put you down for a double on Sunday," Martha says, typing away at her computer and not bothering to even look up at me. "Apparently, the new girl decided the Taylor Swift concert this weekend is more important than her job."

I sigh, nodding. I don't feel any pity for the new girl. She was here so short a time that I didn't even have a chance to learn her name. And I did tell Martha to let me know if she needed coverage for any extra shifts so I could make some more money.

Unfortunately for me, that's meant Martha penciling me in without really consulting me. It's fine, I need the shift, but the thought of another Sunday double, with cheap tippers after church and a basically dead dinner rush, doesn't sound like a worthwhile investment of my time.

"Is that a problem, Izzy?" Martha asks, sounding concerned. "I can always ask someone else, but you told me you wanted as many hours as you could get."

"No . . . no, I did say that, and I do need it," I reply, trying to keep my voice cheerful and utterly failing. "Thanks, Martha."

I get changed quickly. Thankfully, The Gravy Train did away with the ridiculous skirts for uniforms a long time ago, and black jeans, a diner T-shirt, and an apron are all I need. Coming out, I double-check that I've got my order pad and my two pens ready before sagging.

*I just can't take this anymore.*

No . . . no, I have to.

*Why? So Russell can take all your money and still take the house?*

"It's all I've got left," I whisper, wiping away a stray tear. I know I shouldn't be crying. It's just a broken-down old house that probably isn't even worth the wood it's made of anymore, but it's my 'inch.'

*"Izzy, don't tell Mommy we're watching this, okay?"*

*Daddy smiles and hands me the bottle of lemonade, and I grin as I take a sip. Of course, Mommy knows that Daddy sometimes lets me watch 'grown-up' movies, but she says it's okay because they're on cable.*

*I don't quite know what she means by that, but that's okay. It's just a reason for me to hang out with my Daddy.*

*And on the screen is one of his favorite movies. A tired-looking old man in a red shirt and black jacket is talking to a bunch of football players, and as he talks, the players get more excited.*

*"On this team, we fight for that inch," the man says, and the players cheer. He keeps going, and while I don't understand all of it, I still giggle as I hear where the bad words were changed for TV. There's a lot of them in this movie.*

*"I am still willing to fight, and die, for that inch. Because that's what living is! The six inches in front of your face!"*

In my head, I can see my daddy on the couch, eyes on the screen and mouth moving along with the famous speaker I later learned was Al Pacino. *Okay, Daddy, for you, I can keep going.*

Even if those six inches seem impossible.

"Izzy, you okay?"

I look over and see Elaine with her head through the swinging door, a concerned look on her face. She's a diner lifer, and I've appreciated her sassy, occasionally foul-mouthed mentorship.

"Yeah, I'll be okay, Elaine. Just got offered a double shift on Sunday."

Elaine whistles, but her face is still lined with concern. "You sure? You came in looking like you were ready to pack it all in already, honey. You need a break, at least a solid day to do absolutely nothing but laze around with cucumbers on your eyes and conditioner in your hair."

A sad smile twists my lips as I think about wasting a cucumber that way. If I had one, I'd probably just bite right into it, maybe with a little Tajin seasoning.

I follow Elaine back out into the main diner area, nodding. "Yeah. It's not only the work. Rusty's being a jerk again."

"What? Didn't you say that boy gave you a week just yesterday?" Elaine asks, her brows knitting together. "You know, his parents weren't exactly what I'd call the best apples on the tree, but ooh, he's just a rotten one."

"Yeah, well, Sunday'll help," I reply. "I'll figure it out. It'll be fine, always is." I'm trying to convince myself as much as her.

"Hmph. What you need to do is kneecap him with a Louisville Slugger the next time he comes around your way," Elaine says. She lowers her voice. "By the way, seems you've got a fan."

"Huh?" I ask, following Elaine's pointed gaze.

It's *him*. The guy from yesterday. He only ordered a plain meal, burger and fries, but in the few moments that we talked and our eyes met . . . I swear I'd felt human for the first time in ages, not like an automaton going from one job to the next.

No, not human. I'd felt like . . . a woman. Something I haven't had a moment to be in way too long. Elaine's chatter breaks into my daydream of what a man like that could do *with* and *to* a woman.

"Mmm, mmm, mmm . . . and I used to think the mud pie was the yummiest thing in these four walls," Elaine says teasingly. "But that man looks so good I wanna just sop him up with a biscuit."

My eyes are locked on the man, but I can hear Elaine making smacking sounds like she's devouring something delicious.

"Come on, he's just a customer," I murmur, but I sound fake as hell and I know it. The man's so handsome that my heart's already hammering in my chest, with piercing brown eyes, a boyish curl to his lips that seem to promise an eager smile even when he's looking serious, and just enough scruff on his cheeks that he looks . . .

Well, to steal one of Elaine's weird sayings, like I'd love to sop him up with a biscuit.

"Uh-huh," Elaine says. "The man came in a half hour ago, ordering just coffee . . . *again*. I bet if you go over there and bat those pretty brown eyes of yours at him, though, he'd order a meal. Or if you're lucky, make a meal of you. I'm just sayin'."

Just saying. Meanwhile, my brain and my primal urges are saying something else, that it's been a long, long damn time since I've looked at any man and felt more than a tired toleration of him.

But this guy, I don't even know his name, and I'm feeling fluttery inside.

I feel like a teeny bopper at a Justin Bieber concert just looking at him. I swear I have to hold my arm at my side so I don't hold it in the air, waving around as I yell, "Pick me, look at me!"

I'm not that girl, never have been, but suddenly, I think I could be if only for a moment. Which is a sure-fire sign that I need to slow my roll. Guys are the last thing I have time for. Even for a one and done.

"Elaine, I—"

"You're going to go over there and take his order," Elaine says with a laugh, pushing me lightly. "Go on now, git!"

My heart in my throat, I nod and approach the man with my pulse roaring in my ears. "Hi. Can I take your order?"

He looks up, and again our eyes meet. *My God . . . he's gorgeous.*

"Yes, *you* can."

It's only three words, but in those words I can hear a promise. Maybe Elaine was right, that he was waiting for me. But why? No matter. The way he's looking at me right now makes me feel something . . . something I haven't felt in far too long.

# CHAPTER 3

## Gabriel

S HE'S ABSOLUTELY STUNNING, EVEN ON THIS SECOND MINI-conversation, and as she holds her pen and pad in her hand, I feel myself almost split in two.

*Charm her . . . get her off guard, lure her in, and get the job done.*

But that's where the divide is. One part of me is screaming the 'job' is to touch her, mark her, fuck her, and claim her as my own. All the basal, primal urges she draws up in me with the barest of smiles.

The other part is reminding me of the job I was sent here to do and my blood runs cold.

"So, what would you like?" she asks, a pink flush overtaking her cheeks that makes me wonder what's going through her mind right this instant. I'd like to imagine it's something dirty, something involving the two of us and sweaty sex in the bed of my truck.

But probably not. She's a nice girl, I think, likely accustomed to taking a lover in her bed, gentle and sweet after dating for a while.

She smiles expectantly, and I realize I've been staring wordlessly for an awkwardly long time and not answering her question. The smile is a little brighter than what I saw yesterday when she talked with other customers. She's smiling for me.

"A burger again?"

*She remembers. Then again, I remember everything that happened between us yesterday as well. And how that bastard Russell harassed her this morning as I watched from across the street. Luckily, I hadn't had to intervene and then was able to duck down behind the wheel of my truck in time when she rode by on her scooter.*

"What's your favorite on the menu?" I reply, painfully aware of the way her uniform is hugging her body.

She's not voluptuous but rather lithe and lean, and the slim shirt and tight jeans show off her every slight curve and angle. Again, I'm struck by the image of her being a princess. She should be wearing a tiara and a ballgown, not worn-out and faded rags.

Even exhausted, her cheekbones are high and proud, making my palms itch to cup her face. The precious bow of her lips makes me want to trace it with my tongue.

As I watch, her lips twitch upward at the corners, like she's actually enjoying talking to me. Even though I know I can talk my way into anything, and could probably sell porn to the Pope, it doesn't seem like work with Isabella.

I just want to see her smile for me, to know that I gave her a moment of joy.

Dammit, how can I even consider killing such a beautiful creature? It'd be like double-tapping a unicorn.

"Well," Isabella says, biting her lip in a way that makes my cock twitch in my jeans, "I gotta be honest, I usually get the big plates if I can around here. If you're hungry, that means the Country Plate Special. It's an eight-ounce chicken-fried steak, hashbrowns, eggs any way you want 'em, two slices of toast, and two sausage patties."

"Phew, that sounds like a lot," I reply, chuckling. "And you can eat all that?" I let my eyes trace down her body quickly, judging her reaction.

"I usually have to doggie bag it," Isabella says with a laugh. "Actually, it's so big that when the Roseboro High football team's coach wants to fatten up some linemen for the season, he sends them down here before summer workouts. Now, I'm not bragging or anything, but that little high school's sent three kids to Division 1 schools in the past three years. So take it for what you will."

I laugh. She knows how to turn on the diner sass while still sounding authentic. "And if I don't want to be a linebacker?"

"The Reuben," she assures me automatically. "With or without the gravy dip. It's the best sandwich in town, hands down."

"Hands down?" I ask, smiling. "You sound like someone who's speaking from personal experience. Perk of the job?"

"Sometimes," she admits. "But more often than not, I stick with a grilled cheese with bacon. I'm too worried I'll get a mustard seed stuck between my teeth in the middle of a shift."

"Ah," I intone wisely. "The dreaded mustard seed. Nearly as deadly as that dastardly bastard spinach. Nowhere near as painful as its cousin, the popcorn shell, though."

Isabella laughs, tucking a stray lock of her beautiful hair behind her right ear. "True. It's a hard part of the job, but I deal with it. What about you? Any dangers lurking about in your daily life?"

Experience keeps me from freezing, even as my mind calculates whether she knows who I am and what I'm doing here. But the flirty smile lets me know she's just making conversation without any ulterior motives, so I answer accordingly.

"My job? Oh, there are all sorts of dangers and threats," I reply, grinning though I sound dire. "I mean, paper cuts can make even a tough guy cry."

She laughs again, and it's like listening to angels from above. Her laugh is musical, genuine, and pleased, and when she looks at me, I feel that same *spark* I felt yesterday pass between us.

But this time, it's not just a spark, it's damn near a flowing current, white-hot in the air between us as I look up at her from my bench seat.

"I don't mind it if a man cries . . . for the right reasons," she teases. "Paper cuts might make the list, under the right circumstances. Big paper?"

"Oh, the biggest," I tease back, a moment later realizing how naughty that sounds.

I see the flash in Isabella's eyes when she gets the unintentional innuendo too. She looks down at her order pad, twirling a toe against the floor nervously. "So, what'll it be?"

*Too far, man. Don't scare her off. Not yet.*

Returning to the innocuous conversation, I say, "Hmm, such a tough decision. How about this . . . you bring me one of each, and I'll brown bag whichever my stomach feels like not eating?"

"Deal. You know, if you're going to come in all the time, I'm going to have to start remembering your favorites and your name. Personalized customer service is kind of our thing around here."

It seems like a big step for her to ask my name, like she's not used to doing that. And I wonder if it's because guys follow her like the Pied Piper or if it's because she doesn't date at all. Either way, I'm glad she set us back on course, leaving the awkwardness of a second ago behind.

"Gabe . . . and when I find what I like, I'll make sure you're the first to know," I reply, smiling easily as she writes my order down and walks away. "Wait, what's your name?" I ask, remembering to cover my ass even though I already know the answer.

She stops, looking over her shoulder with a smile that nearly stops my heart. "Isabella, but everyone calls me Izzy."

While she's gone, I watch her interact with the other customers, the cold, ruthless part of me cataloging the ways I could do the job without leaving a trace. I already know so much about her . . . her routine, her vulnerabilities, and even a way to make it look like Carraby did it. Maybe a little posthumous justice for Isabella, and punishment for a bastard like Carraby is always warranted.

But I . . . I can't find that detachment.

I can't judge her as evil.

No matter what I do, what mental gymnastics I've twisted through my head over the past couple of weeks, I can't.

It's never been a problem before. Clean or messy, I get it done before disappearing like smoke in the breeze. I've never felt guilty about it.

Not since . . .

"Okay, I talked with Henry, our cook, and he says the sauerkraut isn't good today," Isabella says, interrupting my thoughts and actually surprising me a little. "So would you maybe like to change that into a grilled club?"

"No, I'll just tackle the Country Special," I reply, smiling. "As long as you don't mind me sitting here for a couple of hours afterward, letting it settle."

Isabella blushes a little, nodding. "Not at all."

"It'd be a lot nicer if I could have someone to share, say, a slice of that mud pie I see behind the counter with. Maybe?"

I can see it in her eyes, a flash of excitement, and I can see she's just about to say yes when there's a dinging sound from the kitchen window, jangling and cutting through our talk.

"Hey, Izzy! Order up!" Henry yells from the kitchen, and Isabella's eyes pinch down a little.

Jolted back into reality, she sighs, looking tired again, more docile. It pisses me off, because watching her eyes light up when I flirted a little with her . . . it was like discovering a treasure that nobody's ever discovered before, a diamond in the rough unearthed in front of my eyes.

Now it's hidden again, buried under minutiae and unimportant details.

By the time she comes back with my Country Special plate, the fire in her eyes is just a dim ember, barely flaring when I give her the patented heart-stopping, panty-dropping smile that I've had since long before I got into this line of work.

"Here you go," she says, setting the admittedly huge platter in front of me. "Anything else, Gabe?"

I like the sound of my name on her lips, would love to bend her over this table right here and make her scream it. "How about that mud pie?" I ask instead, raising an eyebrow. "Or better yet, your number? It's less embarrassing than coming in for lunch here tomorrow."

I have the number already—it was part of my background check—but I would absolutely do it, come in day after day just to see her. As I look at her expectantly, every little detail comes into sharp focus.

Not just her beauty but her exhaustion. It makes me feel like a shit for thinking obscene thoughts about her, and suddenly, I imagine myself caring for her, laying her in a hot bath, rubbing the knots out of her shoulders as she soaks away the stress weighing her down, and curling up around her and holding her as she sleeps.

She's mulling it over, and I can see her pen moving toward her order pad like she's going to write her number down when her face falls and with a frown, she looks down.

"Ah . . . I shouldn't. I'm sorry. I need to check on the other customers." The words are mumbled, disappointment woven through them.

She scurries off, and as I watch her go, I can't tear my eyes from her. She glances at me again before taking an order from a young couple obviously here on a cheap date, her flawless skin flushing before she turns back to her work.

I look at my Country Special, and I realize I've got a problem in front of me. There's no way in hell I can eat all of this. The plate's nearly as wide as my shoulders and covered in about a week's worth of food. No wonder the football coaches send their players here to get hefty for the season.

I also have a professional problem. Because no matter how much I twist it, no matter how hard I try, there is no way I can justify killing Isabella.

But the most powerful man in the Pacific Northwest hired me to do just that.

# CHAPTER 4

## Blackwell

*R*OSEBORO COMMUNITY HEALTH FAIR! *SPONSORED BY* GOLDSTONE *Health. With special thanks to Thomas Goldstone!*

I turn away, growling at my driver. "Get us out of here."

He responds immediately, no questions, no hesitation as he accelerates, turning right at the next intersection to remove that hated name from my sight.

A year ago, I had the world in the palm of my hand. Well, maybe not the world, but at least the city of Roseboro, and with it, the linchpin of the entire Pacific Northwest. If you wanted to make an impact anywhere between San Francisco and Vancouver, you came to me.

While I never greeted anyone with *buona sera*, and nobody called me it, I was *the* Godfather.

Until he came along. Thomas Goldstone . . . the usurper, the upstart . . . the *Golden Boy.*

At first, I was content to let him build. I found his forays into business amusing as he made choices I would never consider, stepping left when I would recommend right. He'd been like an experiment playing out before my very eyes.

As out of sorts as I found his style to be, he was successful, shockingly so, and at first, I'd been delighted, like he was my own personal dog and pony show. But he wasn't supposed to be *this* good, *this* fast.

I'd assumed he'd be the one to take over the mantle of Roseboro after I'm gone, not that that's on the horizon anytime soon.

But I thought I'd pass along my empire to capable hands, ones that would laud my brilliance and impact on Roseboro and beyond. He was supposed to be just a caretaker, maybe add a little few pebbles to the mountain that I'd built . . . and now he's eclipsing me.

I can't have that. I *won't* have that. My legacy will live on.

One weakness Thomas Goldstone has is that while he's smart, and he's nearly as ruthless as me, he won't go as afoul of the law as I will. I can't believe he's totally innocent. No man with as much money and power as he has is totally clean, but he's never cultivated the connections I have.

So I started hamstringing him. At first, it was subtle, using my backdoor connections to take profits away from him, hobbling him through several projects he'd planned.

Yet still, he rose.

I stomped his dreams into the dirt. I destroyed his attempts at expansion.

Yet still, like a phoenix from the ashes on a mighty wind, he rose.

Finally, I had to take direct action, and through a bitter, angry employee, I conspired to break him, to destroy not just his business, but his mind, his very soul.

I had him. I was so close . . .

And yet he rose.

Now, he's more successful than ever.

He's gone from one of the most well-known men in this part of the country to the darling of the entire *nation*. There are already whispers that when the next election rolls around, Thomas Goldstone would be a shoo-in if he chose to throw his name in the ring. Senator? Representative? Governor?

There've been whispers that the governor's mansion wouldn't be his last stop, either.

He's untouchable. I've spent millions trying to find more skeletons in his closet. Yet my best attempt, the most direct intervention I could try . . . and now he's actually *gained power* from it.

I could cry over the failure, beseech the gods to grant me this demand, or I can change direction and try again. I already know my course of action.

I'm going to teach Thomas Goldstone about the nature of power. Power isn't just money or fame. It's fear. It's pain. It's about being willing to go all-in and do the ugly deeds truly required to intimidate and inspire those around you.

And I'm going to give Thomas Goldstone a very educational lesson.

Reaching into my jacket pocket, I pull out my phone and dial. It's my normal phone—no reason *I* should be the one buying 'burner' phones.

*"Hello?"*

"You're taking too much time."

On the other end, the man hums. *"You knew when you hired me that I do things at my own pace. I don't rush."*

"There is such a thing as taking your time, and then there is wasting *my* time," I remind him. *"Do not* cross the line between the two. I want to see results. Soon."

*"As in?"*

"You have seven days. Or else . . . I will be upset."

The line goes dead, but I don't mind. My message was received.

Up ahead, a flash of white and silver catches my eye, and I wince as I see the building we're approaching. The Gravy Train Diner.

Where *she* works. Isabella Turner.

The woman who took my carefully-laid plan using Goldstone's employee, a man I'd manipulated for months, and demolished it in a single conversation.

She thought she'd been doing her friend a favor, but favors have consequences, and I have seen to that personally.

Within a week, she'll get her comeuppance. I have hired the best of the best to see to her punishment. And the happy byproduct is that it will devastate Goldstone and his woman, crumbling their very foundations and insuring that they understand just how vulnerable they truly are.

Though the thoughts race through my mind, I whisper them to the window, giving them power by declaring them aloud. "Soon, very soon, my little waitress, you will be doing *me* a favor of sorts."

My limo slides past The Gravy Train and we start to approach my building, my tower . . . my home. "You'll help me send The Golden Boy a very important message—don't interfere in my business. This is still *my town*, and your death will prove it."

It *almost* makes me smile.

# CHAPTER 5

## Isabella

THE MUSIC PLAYS ON THE TV, AND I FEEL A WAVE OF ENERGY FILL me. It's not the tune, a tired old piece of trumpet fanfare that's been used by this station since I was a kid. It's what the music represents . . . the hour it represents.

"Tonight on *News at Ten*—" the voice in the background says before Elaine turns it down.

"I don't need to listen to the organ grinder of doom three times a damn day," I say, putting the remote back down. "Anyone wants to find out what's going on, they can read the captions." I say it like I'm daring the handful of customers to argue about it, but no one so much as blinks at me.

I nod silently as I take a late-night order for pork chops from a delivery driver who just got off shift, but my brain's on cruise control.

It's him. *Gabe.*

I know it's stupid. I mean, I totally chickened out when he asked me for my phone number, reminding myself again that I don't have time to get involved with anyone.

But still, I'd gone home last night to an empty house and kicked myself in the butt for not at least considering. I mean, even if it didn't lead to much, a slice of pie with a hot guy or maybe *more* would be the highlight of my week.

All right, more like my year. But I'm focused, determined . . . and lonely.

Hot dreams had kept me tossing and turning all night, and in the light of day, he's been on my mind constantly. The way he smiles, the little twinkle in his eyes as we tossed a few double entendres back and forth . . . the dimples on his cheeks that highlight his perfect teeth.

I mean, how weird is that? I'm getting heated up thinking about a guy's *teeth*.

For the first time in I don't know how long, I've gotten through the day without feeling like hundred-pound weights are tied to each ankle.

I've felt lighter and brighter, like my lungs are full of helium and there's a glimmer of sunshine warming my back. It's been like this all day, through classes and the first four hours of my shift here at The Gravy Train.

Glancing over at the table where he sat last night, I remember the note he left on his bill, along with the tip, and I swear my belly floats up to the rafters.

*Bella . . . gotta be out of town tomorrow, but I'll see you Wednesday. Gabe*

Yeah, it's stupid, but I can't stop thinking about him. Even the fact that he called me Bella. I've been Izzy ever since I was five. Almost everyone calls me Izzy. But the way Gabe wrote it . . .

Well, to quote my besties, I left work moister than an oyster. I shiver at the word *moist*. There's always been something about it that makes me cringe.

But more than that, in the few minutes I've talked with him, I've been able to forget about the shit storm that is my life. I felt almost . . .

"Hey, you alive over there? Bueller? Bueller?"

I look up, realizing I've been spacing a little as I wipe down an already clean salt shaker. The delivery driver who wanted the pork chops is trying to get my attention, full-on snapping at me with his dirty fingers.

He seems to have missed the lesson on rule number one of diner life— don't ever snap at your waitress. Fixing my best coolly professional smile on my face, I walk over, clearing my throat.

"Did you need something?" I intentionally don't apologize because fuck his rudeness. I might've been off in la-la land for a moment, but he got his dinner in less than five minutes and looks to have been shoveling it in Hoover-style.

"You can start by answering the question," the driver challenges sarcastically, his mouth twisted in an ugly sneer. "You alive?"

"Sometimes, I'm not even sure myself," I answer honestly, blanking out my face.

I know this guy's type. He's been dealing with shit all day, probably been stressed out by half a dozen things that have forced him into having dinner here at ten at night. So of course, he's going to try to make me share the pain.

Misery loves company, they say, but I ain't visiting the Sad-Lands to-night. Not with Gabe on my mind, even if it's just a pretend fantasy where I'd given him my number and we'd gone out on a date.

"Can I get you something?" I ask with faux pleasantness.

"These pork chops . . . they're overcooked and dried out," he says, poking a fork into the small amount of meat left on his plate. "Unacceptable."

I can hear that it's a word he probably uses often. I do my best to limit my eye roll and pick up his plate.

"Can I get you something else instead?"

It's a pretty common scam for someone to eat half their plate, complain, and then want a replacement. Sometimes, I call them on it, but right now, I just want this guy to eat and not kill my happy buzz.

"Burger. Well done," he barks. But I see the tiny uptilt of his lips as he internally celebrates his successful schtick.

I head back to the kitchen. "Henry?"

"Yeah, I heard the asshole," he growls quiet enough the customers don't hear, a fresh burger patty already sizzling on the grill. "Son of a bitch should be glad I don't serve him a fried shit burger and make him choke on it. He sure as fuck ain't getting fries though."

"How's the ulcer?" I ask, and Henry grumbles again. "That bad, huh?"

"No, what sucks the most is that the doc's got me on the special diet," he says, sticking his tongue out to let me know exactly what he thinks of his modified menu.

"Prilosec and yogurt, but no milk or real cheese. Kimchee, sauerkraut, any sort of cabbage until I'm swimming in the shit, but no way can I have a sausage to go with it. All this weird frou-frou hippie dietary crap, no real food. And no booze. How the hell am I supposed to get the eight hours they say I'm supposed to get if a man can't have a post-work beer before bed?"

"Don't know," I answer honestly. "Hope you get back to normal soon. You're more fun that way."

"Yeah, well, tell Happy McAsshole out there five minutes and I'll have him another round of dinner," Henry says, giving me a pained smile as he rubs at his bothersome belly. "At least it ain't the big C, am I right?" He kisses his fingertips and holds them up, looking beyond the ceiling. Henry's not particularly religious, but I guess he figures a bit of prayer won't hurt.

I nod, going out to Delivery Driver and passing along the news. "Five minutes? I'd better be getting a discount."

"I'm sure we can. I just have to ask my manager," I reply sweetly before going back to the register to help someone with their bill. After ringing it up, Elaine comes over, smirking.

"You're so busy with the UPS guy that you didn't see Red come in," she says, pointing to the far corner table where one of my besties, Charlotte Dunn, is sitting. "Go take a break. I'll handle everything for a bit, and I'll have two slices of mud pie over there lickety-split."

"You're the best, Elaine," I murmur, handing her my order pad. "Thanks."

"I know it, and you're welcome," Elaine says, shooing me off when I warn her about the grumpy delivery guy.

I walk over to the booth and drop in, suddenly feeling the long day. "Hey, Char, what're you doing here this late?"

"They had me on late shift at work for a special project," Charlotte says, smiling that happy smile she always has.

Seriously, Char's like the chirpiest person I know as long as you're not talking about men. She's had an especially bad run lately, and even her usual mantra of 'there's no such thing as Mr. Wrong, only Mr. Right and Mr. Right Now' has been trashed. But you could dump her in the middle of the Sahara in August with nothing but a ski outfit and she'd be happy about how the goggles help keep the sun out of her eyes.

"Another girl called out sick and the copies had to be made and filed today."

"Ah . . . Blackuenza?" I ask, using my made-up term for when people who work in the Blackwell Building just say fuck it and quit with no notice. "I seriously don't know how you put up with it, babe."

"I don't work for the man directly, remember?" Charlotte says with a smile. "I honestly can't think of the last time I saw him even come inside the building. And the pay's okay for now."

"For now . . . how'd we end up in this fucked up cul de sac of life?" I ask, shaking my head. "I mean, Mia found her way out, but I feel like I'm circling the drain most days."

"Yeah . . . you were ready to castrate her man not that long ago, remember?" Charlotte asks, and I laugh. That's true. I was.

But Mia's guy, Thomas, came through in a big way for her, like grand gesture style, and I'd happily watched from the sidelines as she got her fairytale ending. And I am thrilled for her, truly and completely, but it is a reminder that while people around me are making leaps and bounds, I'm drudging along with baby steps.

Forward, but at a snail's pace that's basically killing me most days.

*Today was different*, a voice whispers in my head.

"Okay, okay . . . so what brought Roseboro's most vivacious ginger in tonight?"

"Redhead, not ginger. I got a soul!" Charlotte teases. "Mostly just wanted a little comfort food and to catch up with you. Been a few days."

Elaine comes over with two of the biggest slices of mud pie I've ever seen on each plate. Seriously, she had to have hand-sliced them.

"You should tell Red about your Prince Charming hottie."

She doesn't wait for me to say a word, turning straight to Charlotte and spilling, "He came in the past two nights in a row. Whoo-wee, that man is a good two hundred pounds of pure American beefcake if I've ever seen it."

She closes her eyes, grasping her hands at her chest and moaning, "Mmm-hmm."

"Oh, God, don't start," I groan, dropping my head as Elaine laughs. "Seriously?"

"Beefcake, huh?" Charlotte asks, eyes ping-ponging from Elaine to me. "You know how I feel about that." Her look of disdain says everything.

"Red, please. What you need is to go find yourself a good man too," Elaine says in that motherly way she has. "Your friend Pinkie Pie got herself wise. Now you two need to as well."

I grin at her calling Mia 'Pinkie Pie' because while Mia's hair goes through a rainbow of colors, she does tend to dye it pink more than anything else. With her calling Char 'Red', I wonder if she calls me 'Brownie' in her head to keep with the hair color theme, but it doesn't seem the time to ask as Charlotte's gearing up for her soapbox speech about not needing a man to complete her life.

"'Bye, Felicia," Charlotte finally says, wrapping up her latest story about the guy she kicked out for telling her to make him a sandwich.

I mean, he actually said that to her, unironically. Charlotte said he even scratched his balls as he said it, but I suspect she's embellishing there. But she's smiling a little as Elaine leaves. "That woman's a trip and a half."

"Don't I know it," I reply as I cut a big spoonful of chocolate yumminess and chew slowly. "Remember, I'm the one who works with her damn near every day of the week. But she gets a pass when she serves me big pieces of pie like this."

"Mmmhmm," Charlotte agrees before putting her spoon down. "Now, tell me about this man? Catch me up?"

"Just a cute guy who came in the past two nights," I demur, trying not to gush too much.

I give Char a rundown on Gabe because it's fun to think about him and gossip with my friend since I usually have zero to contribute to social life chats.

"Oh, and he's got that thing where when he smiles, only one side goes up and then the rest of his mouth catches up in slow motion. Like you can see the smile race across his lips. Makes me want to chase it. With my thumb or maybe my tongue." I can hear the wistfulness in my voice.

"True sign of a player," Charlotte says even as she gives the same sort of lopsided smirk. "What about life outside the diner? Classes okay?"

"I suppose," I reply, remembering that I have a test coming up. A test I know I'm not ready for.

"You sure?" Charlotte asks, piercing through my veil of toughness pretty quickly. When you've known each other as long as we have, that's not too hard, and I'm sure she can see the weariness I wear like a cape most days. "If it's not school, what is it?"

"Well, Russell's starting to harass me." I start telling her about his threats and visits to my house demanding payments.

I've always tried to minimize my financial difficulties with my friends, not hide them, exactly, but I don't go around whining about how tight my bottom line really is. But they can read the silent little signs like they're neon lights. I know they'd help me if I'd let them, but I don't want their charity. I want to handle things on my own.

But this thing with Russell is becoming something else altogether. Not just a bill, but a real danger, so I've tried to talk about him the least.

So when I'm finished, I'm shocked at how long I've been blabbing and how much I shared.

"Anyway, he's a huge pain in the ass. And if you get a call from the county jail, answer it and bring me some bail money because I've probably maced him for lurking around my fence and mouthing vulgar shit."

Charlotte's pissed. "That son of a . . . I should kick him in the balls so hard they come out his nose."

"I'm not sure that's possible, Char." But her vehemence makes me smile a little despite the ugly situation.

"I don't care!" Charlotte hisses. "I'm worried about you, babe. I mean, he threatened you!"

"He's woofin', that's all."

"Uh-huh. Still, if it were me in your position, I'd forget the mace and get a gun. You never know what's out there, and that guy is a piece of shit, Izz."

I freeze, the last bite of pie suspended on my spoon, shaking a little. "A gun?" I say in shock.

I mean, I've never even held a gun and would definitely be the dipshit who accidentally shoots themselves in the foot if I ever wrapped my hands around one.

"Babe, you live alone. In not the best part of town. And you've got a dope fiend hitting you up for cash. I'm not saying you need to be Rambitch and lug an Uzi around, but something small? Enough that if someone does force things, you can defend yourself. That's a good idea."

She makes good points, but there's one kink in her line of thinking. "Yeah . . . and how'd I buy one when I'm barely getting by?" The words slip out before I realize how they sound.

Char reaches for her purse, but I stick my hand out. I've got a hard policy, no pity pennies from my friends. "Char, no!"

"Fuck that. Listen, I've got a coworker, Brady. His brother runs a gun club just outside of town. Brady always said that if I gave his brother this card, he'd hook me up with a good deal. Lessons, a starter gun, everything. Just give him a call and see what it costs. Maybe it's not that bad?"

"Yeah, well, thanks, but I don't need a gun."

Char still holds out the card, and finally, I take it, tucking it in my pocket. "You know this is ridiculous. Guns are just . . . I don't know."

"Listen, honey, in most instances I'd be right there with you. I'd be more inclined to shoot some asshole's swinging dick off with it than use it to defend myself," Charlotte jokes.

At least I hope she's joking. "But really, your situation is different . . . oh, hell, no!" she says, smacking the table.

"What?" I ask, and Char rolls her eyes, sighing heavily like she's disappointed in me.

"I make one dick joke, and your eyes went all spacey on me. You were thinking of Beefy McSmiles again, weren't you?" she points a manicured finger at me accusingly.

Caught red-handed, I look down, a little embarrassed. "His name's Gabe, not Beefy McSmiles. Although that has a nice ring to it," I tease, and then quietly fake a porn-star breathiness. "Ohh, Beefy!"

"Gabe, Beefy, Tyler Durden, what does it matter?" Charlotte sputters, shaking her head. "Come on, we took the pledge together. Don't tell me you're backing out?"

She holds up three fingers, her thumb holding her ring finger down, and her face solemn like she's taking an oath.

"No, but really, Char, a pledge to become celibate married lesbians if perfect men don't sweep us off our feet by thirty?" I ask, remembering the promise we'd made each other in a drunken night of commiseration a few years ago. "Not saying you're not my main girl, but you really want to marry me and totally give up on men?"

"It's not like I'm into you that way," Charlotte reminds me. "But you're a good cook, you make me laugh, and best of all, we'd never fight over the toilet seat in the middle of the night. Actually, the best part is I can trust you, and that's worth sleeping in separate bedrooms the whole time."

"I'm also an utter slob," I argue, though that's not at all true. More seriously, I say, "You know I've got your back no matter what, Char, but isn't life more hopeful than that?"

"So says the girl who has zero social life, much less a sex life, lives in a shack, and needs to learn how to handle a gun."

I growl in frustration, arguing back the only thing in her list I can refute. "I do not live in a shack! It's not that bad!"

"Hey, I'm not hating. At least it's *your* shack," Char reminds me. "I rent my place so I don't have room to talk. But I'm serious. I don't want to hear about you on the news with your body parts scattered all over Roseboro because I am not adopting a mommy-less Vash. She's cute and all, but I'm a dog person."

"Hey, Izzy, last charge!" Elaine calls, and I raise a hand to acknowledge her.

"Listen, I need to help with the drunk rush before closing time and start cleanup. It's good to see you though. Thanks for coming in, Char." I do appreciate her stopping by because between all the other things on my plate, a girls' night out isn't likely to happen anytime soon.

She gets up and drops a five on the table, even though we both know Elaine's not going to charge for the pie.

"Seriously, babe, think about it. The gun, that is. And about Mr. Beefcake, check him out before you get too hung up. Remember, Mr. Hitachi will never *ever* let you down."

"We'd never work. I don't speak Japanese," I joke, and Charlotte laughs. We hug, and I squeeze her tightly. "I promise, I'll be okay, hon."

"Okay, I'll check in soon."

Elaine and I handle the last batch of customers that come in as we finish the prep work for the morning crew. After we lock the door and run the numbers at the end of the night, I look at my totals for the shift. Maybe it was easier back in the day when most tips were cash, but now with so many people paying by card, I have to wait until the end of the night to see my final tally . . . and it's pretty damn pathetic.

"Fuckin' Pork Chop Guy didn't even round up to the nearest dollar," Elaine complains as she looks at the printout on the register receipt. She sees my downcast face and pats my shoulder. "It'll be okay, hon. Payday's on Friday, at least."

I force a smile, rubbing the back of my neck. "Let's just get cleaned up."

Elaine nods, and I see her slip an extra twenty from her own tip pile into mine as we clean, but I'm too defeated to say anything. There go my damn morals.

"You know, hon, why not talk to your friend's fiancé?" Elaine asks as we get ready to leave. "Seriously, the man can buy half of Roseboro, and you'd pay him back, I know it. Hell, I'd hate to see you go, but maybe he could even set you up with something that pays better."

She looks through the dark windows to the night outside, and I wonder if she ever dreamed of getting out of here when she was younger. Her lips purse, and I amend my thought, wondering if perhaps she still dreams of it.

"I . . . I'd prefer not to, that's all," I admit. "Guess my pride's still pretty mixed up in all this. I want to stand on my own two feet."

"Yeah well, sometimes, we have to accept a little help, even when we don't want to, to get to where we're going. I'm sure that Goldstone boy would help. You could pay him back, and when you get to solid ground, you return the favor and help some other stubborn girl who could clearly benefit from a bit of a boost."

She looks at me hopefully, like she wants me to hear the genius of her idea.

I nod and mount my scooter. "Maybe," I say, but it's a lie.

# CHAPTER 6

## Gabriel

"*You have seven days. Or else I will be upset.*"

Blackwell's words replay in my mind, weighing upon my shoulders like a ton of bricks as I dissect them repeatedly. There's not much to the two sentences, a deadline and a threat. But it's the threat's ambiguous nature that turns over and over in my head.

What is he willing to do?

How far will he go?

I pause to take a breath and look up. In front of me is a nearly sheer rock wall.

While I've always been a good athlete, nothing quite gets my blood pumping and my endorphins going like nature. It's the one thing that helps me clear my thoughts and center myself.

Which is what brought me to this spot, about twenty minutes to the west of Roseboro, in the middle of a national forest.

"You know you don't have to do this," I tell myself as I wipe my hands on my shirt. It's the truth. I passed the sign for the hiking path to get to the climbing entry point I'm at now.

Yeah, I could take the easy way to the top . . . but this'll help.

I approach the wall, one last visual of the line I've chosen up the face of the cliff. And then I reverse my way down until my eyes land directly in front of me and take the first grip, lifting myself off the ground and adjusting my feet.

Free climbing is like no other form of climbing. There's no rope, so I can't take the same risks that someone who's tied in would. At the same time, I can't go too slow, because with each passing second, my ankles and forearms are being tested. One release, one slip, could be instant death.

But it's exhilarating, and as the fire starts up my calves, I can feel my head clear. It's like I split in two, half of me focusing on staying alive this very second by picking out the next handhold, the next place to put my foot, while the other half of me chews over my problem, unfettered and free to jump from idea to strategy to potential consequences without logic or rationality to get in the way.

Isabella Turner . . . my *assignment*.

Blackwell's paying me a shitload of money to make it happen, but the information he promised is far more valuable. That information is the whole reason I'm in the life I'm in.

Still, that doesn't change the fact that she's someone who doesn't deserve the fate chosen for her. If anything, she deserves to get a hand up in life.

An image of her proudly serving customers, head held high as she works herself to the bone, flashes through my head. Followed by one of studying hard in the library to better herself, and then standing her ground against an evil shit stain of a man who's obviously trying to take advantage of her.

If anyone deserves a lucky break, it's Isabella Turner.

But luck has nothing to do with this. And I'm definitely not a lucky charm, more like a tragic curse.

My left foot slips slightly, and I dig in with my right hand, pulling myself up a bit higher before my foot can find purchase again. I'm halfway up the rock face, but from here the going seems easier. There's a relatively large crack in the rock that looks wide enough for me to get both a hand and a foot inside, and it runs nearly all the way to the top of the cliff itself.

I pause, shaking out my hands and feet by alternating rest holds, and cruise the rest of the way up, reaching the top with a good amount of sweat built up but more excitement than anything else. It's been awhile since I've had the chance to really freeclimb, and I've missed it.

You learn about yourself on the rockface with nothing to catch you, no safety nets and no do-overs. You learn about who you really are when you have to look death in the eye and know that it's chasing you and the only things holding it back are your own will and skills.

It's a sad commentary on modern society that someone can go their

entire life without ever learning whether they're a coward or not. I forget
who said that, but it's true. And while I might not be a good man, at least I
know I'm not a coward.

Going to the edge of the outcropping, I look down, seeing that the
fifty-foot drop is definitely worse at this angle than from the bottom. There
are all sorts of jagged-looking rocks and outcroppings that would kill anyone
unfortunate enough to slip off this cliff face.

But I didn't fall. Not this time. I made it to the top, cheated Death once
more in the poker game I'm not sure he knows we're playing.

I shake my head and take a deep breath, banishing the idea and looking
around. The walking path continues off to my right, and I decide to follow
it, stunned a moment later when the trail curves around the mountain and
I'm treated to a view of the valley.

It's beautiful, rugged and untouched, pure forest that reminds me that
no matter my struggles, my pain, or my promises . . . the world doesn't really
care. It's not sad. It's almost liberating.

I can see, though, where I can make a difference. Because the forest thins
out, a power line here, a fire road there, a stream that diverts and slows, forming a lazy river, and slowly, Mother Nature gives way to man, and Roseboro
emerges to dominate the middle distance, a small idyllic city that looks
postcard-worthy from this vantage point.

Of course it's not idyllic. Even from up here, I can see some of the older
areas of town, and my eyes are drawn to where I think I can pick out Isabella's
neighborhood, close to the railroad tracks that run north and south through
town.

Every town's got that wrong side of the tracks. Even ones without
railroads.

Still, the scene stretched out below me is iconic, beautiful, and as I sit
down on a rock to watch, I marvel at the twin towers that dwarf the city.

Closer to me, there's the Blackwell Building, dark and foreboding, looking like a spear that's been shoved into the ground, piercing and penetrating
the city, plundering. Ironically, it's the older of the two buildings, and the
city actually grew from it.

The other, Goldstone Tower, rising up and reaching for the clouds
above, shorter than its older cousin but somehow more inspiring with its
golden-hued glass. It's the yearning of the city for a better future, unafraid to

shoot for the stars, secure in the knowledge that it's only through the risk of failure that great successes are built.

"You're getting sentimental again," I chastise myself, turning away and looking at the pool behind me. The water's not totally still, the waterfall and the outflowing stream guarantee that, but it's peaceful in its perpetual motion, tranquility in the churning bubbles.

I reach down and gather up a handful of pebbles, tossing them in one by one to watch the ripples flutter over the surface, and my past sneaks up on me, reminding me of another pool.

*"Jeremy!"*

*My little brother, Jeremy, stops and turns back to me, a grin splitting his face. We're close in age, so close that my uncle calls us 'Irish twins', which confused the hell out of me when I was younger. We're not Irish at all, from what I know of our family.*

*"Come on, Gabby. It's just the Union."*

*I sigh, tossing a rock across the small pond that we've been sitting next to for the past hour, watching it skip across the flat green water, the white stone so bright in contrast that it makes me stop, watching it bounce five times before dropping beneath the surface with a soupy plop.*

*Eleven months apart . . . we're actually somehow in the same grade in school, but I swear Jeremy's nothing like me. Like today. Mom and Dad told us to stay close to the house, and the pond technically qualifies since I can squint and still see the house from here.*

*But the Union? Where all the high school kids hang out and play basketball? Of all the places in town our parents don't want us to go, that's the one they've both named specifically.*

*And of course, Jeremy wants to go there. He's been working on his layup recently and wants to put himself to the test, even if we don't start junior high until August.*

*"Come on, Gabby!"*

*"Jeremy, stop calling me Gabby!"*

A breeze blows across the valley, and tears threaten as I think about my brother. He was always the adventurous one, the one willing to break the rules.

That first time we snuck off to the Union, he was six inches shorter than everyone else there, but he already had big brass ones. Even though he got elbowed right in the eye at one point, he still kept going for that damn layup and wore that purple bruise like a trophy for his gutsiness.

"Why'd you never slow down?" I whisper, shaking my head. "And you somehow kept getting me to go along with it, too."

Go along with it. Isn't that what I'm supposed to be doing now? Just go along with the plan, or pick from any of the half-dozen that I've formed in my head already, and kill her?

Yeah, it'll suck, and I'm going to feel like shit . . . but I felt like shit for three days after Jeremy got into a fight with Mickey Ulrich and his buddies and the two of us got stomped out royally.

I still never regretted jumping in to save Jeremy's ass, even if it was six on two.

I never regretted sticking with him.

Until the one time that I didn't.

*"Jeremy, come on!" I growl, looking up from my keyboard. "I get it, you wanna show off for Jenae, but newsflash . . . she's not feeling ya, brother. And I've gotta get this damn history report done by tomorrow!"*

*Jeremy scowls at the dig about the girl he's tailing after, his stringy cotton tank top already hanging off his toned shoulders, showing off a body that's changed a lot over the past year. I guess I got the jump on him there. I've got two inches on him and I'm already having to shave, but Jeremy . . . with his looks and personality, he's going to be getting girls long before I do.*

*"Blah, blah, blah, Pilgrims, maize, We the People, and sum it the fuck up!" Jeremy jokes. "You really want to tell me that you'd rather do a history report than play ball with the girls watching?"*

*"Yes, I do."*

*"Tiffany Robinson's going to be there."*

*My fingers falter for a moment, and I think of Tiffany. I swear she's looked at me from across the room in math class, and while I can't be sure she's interested, it's gotta be a good sign. I mean, we run in different social circles, but stranger things have happened, right?*

*He's got me, and judging by the slick grin on his face, he damn well knows it. "Not yet," I growl, looking down. "Just . . . gimme a half hour to finish up, and I'll go."*

*"Sorry, bro, but Jenae's got work later," Jeremy says. "Listen, I'll head down now, and you can join me when you can. I mean, even if Tiffany has already left by then, it'll still be fun, right?"*

*He's right. It'd be fine if it's just the guys playing, but he's even more right that it'd be better if Tiff were there.*

*Jeremy's words help fuel a furious bout of rapid-fire typing, and twenty minutes later, I feel like I can take a break. All that's left is the bibliography and figuring out what I'm going to say when I have to do the presentation on it in class later this week. But I can bullshit my way through that with the paper as a foundation.*

*I hurry and get changed, yanking on an old Angels T-shirt and some shorts before pulling a ballcap on. I think I'll see if Tiffany will hold it for me while I play, and if I'm lucky, she'll wear it herself. It'd be a good look, that girl in my hat.*

*I jog down to the Union, praying she's still there. I'm almost courtside when I hear something that I swear sounds like a typewriter, or firecrackers, and then the screams start.*

*"Jeremy?" I ask, my heart stopping in my chest as someone else screams his name. "Jeremy!"*

"I promised you I'd find out who did it," I whisper, watching the ripples in the pool but talking to my brother's ghost in the wind. I feel the responsibility of the vow I made to my brother's grave to get vengeance for his death.

It wasn't grief talking then. It was fury, it was righteous justice that no other family need go through this.

"And Blackwell says he can point me in the right direction. But it's complicated, Jer."

In my pocket, my phone buzzes, and I'm surprised I get a cell signal up here. Pulling it out, I see I've got a text from a blocked number. Still, I know who it is.

*I'm waiting for your word it's done. There's a difference between patience and stalling.*

I don't react, my emotions going cold as I put my phone away and stand up.

I knew this assignment wouldn't be easy, knew I'd have to get my hands dirty. But it'll be worth it to fulfill the promise I made.

At all costs, at any expense. Even if it's my own soul. Even if it's her life.

# CHAPTER 7

## Isabella

WEDNESDAY COMES AND GOES, AND AS I WIPE DOWN THE counter, I sigh. It's nearly nine o'clock now, and still no Beefcake. For days now, I've been daydreaming about him. While that's admittedly more than a little creepy, a ridiculous infatuation with a man I've shared a total of five minutes of conversation with, I can't stop looking up every time the bell over the diner door dings. And I can't help feeling a stab of disappointment each time it's not him.

Maybe Char's right. I don't need Gabe . . . I need Hitachi.

"Izzy, you have a minute?" Martha asks from the door to the back, waving me toward her. I glance around the diner and see we're pretty quiet. We're in between the dinner rush and the late-night surge. The other waitress on duty, Shelley, can handle things by herself for a few, but still, I glance at the door one more time before heading back.

"What's up, Martha?" I ask when we get to her office. "Everything okay?"

Martha always does paperwork on Wednesday nights, which usually means she's locked in her office for the bulk of the evening. Hopefully, whatever she needs won't keep me here long because I need to get back on the floor after having to scrape my bank account down to six dollars and thirty-two cents to get together enough cash to keep Russell off my ass, I need every extra quarter.

"Not quite," Martha says, picking a receipt up off the table with a perplexed look on her face. "You got a complaint over the weekend."

"What?" I ask, surprised. "Who?"

Martha hands me the receipt, and I glance at the time and date. Sunday night, near closing . . .

"Oh. That guy."

"What do you mean?" Martha asks as I look at the note he wrote on the back of the receipt. *Weitress is crap. Zombie the hole time. POS servus.*

It's not the bad spelling that hurts. It's the big fat double zeros in the tip space on the receipt, not even rounding up to the nearest dollar. Not even a line through the space . . . a big set of double zeroes.

"This guy came in last week too," I explain to Martha, handing the receipt back. "He bitched about the pork chops, sent them back, and scammed for a burger. When he came in this time, he sat down already bitchy. I did my best, but I don't think he'll be happy, no matter what."

"He's a regular?" Martha asks, and I shrug. "What's he look like? Somebody I'd know?"

"He's a delivery driver," I reply, sighing. "He comes in occasionally. I guess you could call him a regular. Anyway, if you want backup on his attitude, ask Elaine and Henry."

"No, your word's good with me. Next time, feel free to give him a little sass or have Elaine take care of him. We don't need troublemakers like that around, so if we can run him off nicely, all the better. Otherwise, I'll pull out the big guns," Martha says.

I appreciate that she has my back and that she'd be willing to kick the guy out for being an asshat, because she is definitely the big gun that takes no crap and tells you what's what with blunt efficiency and a solid lack of fucks about what you think.

"There is one other thing, though. I need you to cover another shift."

"Another?" I ask, torn. Right now, I've got twenty-one dollars to my name, including the few dollars I have in the bank. I do some fast figuring and think I can make it last, but a couple more bucks would make it easier.

But I'm also struggling to stay awake in class, and I know my grades are starting to suffer because of it.

*You're still passing classes though.*

"What do you need?"

It's the sound of the hamster wheel turning.

Martha looks at me carefully for a moment, then turns to the calendar on the wall. "Hiring a new server for the front's been tough. I wanted to see if you'd like to pull a double this Saturday, and next month, I might need you to do Wednesdays."

"Martha, that's potentially like an extra twenty-five hours next month, and a double on Saturday?" I ask, torn between joy and frustration. On one hand, it's money I desperately need. On the other hand, Vash is going to forget what I look like, and I'm going to have a feral cat by Christmas at this rate.

Martha blinks. "Shelley can't do it because of the kids, but I can ask Elaine if you want me to?"

*Way to guilt trip me*, I think. Elaine is fierce and feisty, but I know the years of being on her feet caught up to her long ago. An extra shift each week would kill her. "Okay, you know I'll try my best."

Martha starts scribbling my name on the color-coded calendar, and all the orange 'Izzy' entries make me a little dizzy.

"Thank you. Listen, I can't do much on the pay stub side of things, but I'll talk with Henry. Maybe we can at least help you on the tip side of things. Uncle Sam doesn't need to know about an extra twenty bucks cash you get as a shift incentive."

"Thanks," I reply, knowing that over the next four Wednesdays, I certainly won't be pulling in eighty bucks in cash tips. Still, Martha's trying and I appreciate that, especially considering how she's always had my back with my changing school schedule and lets me study at the counter when we're not busy. "I should go help Shelley."

I head back out, reminding myself that I was the one who came to her saying I needed extra hours recently. She's just giving me what I wanted. But the enormity of my schedule is killing me, slowly but surely.

As I hit the diner floor, I look around, hope that Gabe has arrived blooming in the desert of my heart. But the room's empty other than Shelley, who is marrying ketchup bottles in a booth by the window.

Stupid heart. Gabe's no Prince Charming, sweeping in to save me from the stress of my crazy life. Not even as a momentary distraction.

I grab a bottle of sanitizer and a rag, making my way to the table in the corner furthest away from the door. Ducking my head down, I get to work. Not once do I look at the door or even out to the parking lot for headlights. It feels like a hollow victory.

"I think Char's right," my other best friend, Mia Karakova, soon to be Mia Goldstone, says. We're not at The Gravy Train for once, but at a coffee shop near campus, mainly because she's buying and it's got free Wi-Fi.

"Are you nuts?" I reply before rolling my eyes. "This isn't a new bra she wants me to buy. It's a friggin' gun."

"Obviously, but that doesn't change the fact that Charlotte's right," Mia repeats, sipping her latte. "Russell's bad news, Izzy."

"I'm not disagreeing with that. He's an idiot, and as soon as he gets his next hit, he'll forget all about me," I repeat, even as I wish I hadn't told Charlotte about my problem with Russell at all.

I know she means well, but I don't need to hear about it from two sides at once, especially since that lets me know without a doubt that my besties have been talking about me. I know they worry, but their comparing notes on me brings back too many crappy childhood memories.

Plus, Charlotte's not even having coffee with us today so I can give her shit about selling me out. I stick to my usual party line, hoping it shuts down this attack as well as it usually does.

"Seriously, next week, I'll be fine."

"You've been pitching that same line for a long time now," Mia says, disappointed in me. "Next week, you'll be fine. Next paycheck, you'll be fine . . . same thing ever since your aunt passed away. You're more stubborn than even Papa, and he's worse than a damn mule."

"Then you know not to argue with me," I reply, hoping to sidetrack the conversation to safer ground. "How is he doing, anyway?"

"Gushy. He can't wait for the wedding," Mia admits. "It's sort of cute. But stop deflecting. You want to be stubborn, I'm going to be blunt."

Before I know it, Mia's reached into her pocket and pulled out a piece of paper. She plops it on the table in front of me. It unfolds on its own, and I feel a stab in my gut as I see the number of zeros on the check Mia's giving me.

"Mia, come on, this is bullshit! You know I can't accept this!"

"I'm not *giving* it to you," Mia says simply. "It's a loan. Izzy, we've been friends since we were munching on Lunchables together. I've subjected you to hundreds of hours of anime and video games, and meanwhile, you keep refusing help from the friends who love you, choosing to work yourself to the bone instead. Do you think Char and I don't know how tough things get for you?"

I startle, wondering exactly what they know because I thought I'd done a decent enough job hiding the rougher aspects of my life. Sure, they know I'm busy and strapped for cash, but definitely not that there are days I only eat my employee meal and that I've uselessly searched my couch for coins to keep the lights on.

But my pride still won't let me take the check. "I appreciate it, I do. But I can't." I try to shove the check back her way, but the paper sticks to my fingers. Well, okay, it doesn't stick so much as my thumb and pointer finger won't let go of it.

"Look, I know I've let you push off help, but that was when we were all struggling to some degree. Things are different now. I've got enough money to help you, and I promise my bank account won't feel it."

"Feelin' your privileges now?" It's a tacky and vicious thing to say, and I'm not jealous of Mia's fairy tale. She deserves it, worked for it with the beast she calls her man, but I can't help the shock of pain that goes through my gut at her ability to write a check like this and not give it a second's thought.

Mia stares at me with enough venom that I blush in embarrassment, looking down in shame. "Sorry, Mia. I know you didn't mean it like that. And I'm glad you're doing so well. You're my hashtag-goals, you know that. Degree, a job you love, and a guy you adore."

"It's okay," Mia says gently, thawing a little. "Listen, babe, I get it. I remember the way kids used to bully you. I remember those busted ass hand-me-downs you wore through high school. I know why you didn't go to prom, and I know why you still rode a bike to school after everyone else had their licenses. And as if that wasn't enough, fate bitchslapped you again when your aunt died. You've struggled for so long, I think it's just your normal. But this thing with Russell is different. And I've got the means to help."

"I feel more comfortable working for it, though," I reply with finality. "Mia, I love you. You're my number one girl—"

"Your future wife's gonna hate hearing that," Mia teases, knowing about the drunken pact Charlotte and I made. I smile a little at the joke.

"But I have to refuse this. It's too damn much! And I've heard too many stories about friendships getting ruined over dollar amounts a lot less than this. I won't risk *us* on *that*," I say, pointing at the check.

Before Mia can reply, I pick up her check and tear it in half, then in half again two more times before dropping the pieces in the glass of ice water that came with my Americano. Mia sadly watches the paper soak through and sink into the glass, then looks up at me.

"I was going to drink that," she deadpans.

"Didn't you just say you've got stupid money? I'm sure you can afford another glass of free ice water," I joke, grinning. "You mad?"

"I can't be mad at you for long," Mia says, leaning back. "But I want you to promise that if Russell amps up his stupidity, you'll reconsider. You can't pay anyone back if you're dead because some junkie got grabby hands for your cash or your other assets."

It's probably the reason she and I are best friends, because as I look her over, you wouldn't know she's getting married to one of the richest guys on the West Coast. She's still the same Mia she was a few months ago, with a green streak and red tips in her hair, a T-shirt for some Korean boy band, and ripped jeans.

If there's any difference in her lately, it's that she's got a little bit of a happy glow to her . . . probably from all the bedroom gymnastics she's getting up to, because I know she's not pregnant. Her Papa would have a heart attack if his princess so much as hinted at a pregnancy out of wedlock.

We drink our coffees, and as she finishes her latte, Mia smacks her lips. "By the way, I heard you un-godmothered me."

"Well, Vash doesn't quite fit the penthouse lifestyle. I promise you, give her a week, and she'd end up in Thomas's office or something, leaving a hair-ball on his desk blotter."

"Yeah, well, she's still my fur baby," Mia says before pivoting in that sudden, not-quite-sneaky but disconcerting way she has. "Which is why you need to learn to defend yourself."

Most people would say she's being mean, sucker punching . . . but I know her. I know the way she thinks, and there's a connection in her mind that most people just aren't seeing. And this is definitely another seed Charlotte planted.

"Why?"

"To defend my fur baby!" she exclaims, and then she smirks. "Oh, and you too."

"Ah," I reply, lifting my cup for a refill. "What are you saying, I should get some pepper spray?"

"Pepper spray isn't a good idea. Vashy could get into it and lick the tip or something," Mia says, assured in her correctness. "Can you imagine that poor cat with her tongue hanging out, numb and burning from what she just licked?"

"Probably what Thomas looks like most evenings," I reply, laughing.

She grins, then grows serious. "Seriously, Char told me she mentioned you should learn how to handle a gun. It might not be a bad idea. Hopefully, you'd never have to use it, but just in case. Papa taught me how to handle one. If I were in your situation, I'd at least consider it."

"But I have Vash to protect me," I reply weakly, knowing I'm fighting a losing battle with my besties. "She's a trained scratcher."

She glares at me, compelling me to take this issue seriously.

"Fine," I say, crumbling. "I'll look into it." But I know I'm not going to, still resisting even as I half-promise nothing.

"And you'll take this," Mia says, holding out a folded-over pile of bills. "No arguments, and if you say no, I'm giving it to Charlotte's arms dealer buddy anyway. Take it and make sure you get a quality piece and learn how to use it."

I grumble but take the wad of cash. I still don't want a gun, but this seems like the lesser of two evils considering the big check she tried to give me. I realize she played me like a damn pro, knowing she'd win either way. I'd take the big loan or the money for the gun, but I can't turn them both down.

And I am scared, in denial and full of wishful thoughts that Russell will OD before the next payment is due but fearful about the dangers his presence brings my life. I think about going home late after my Saturday double, the street dark and quiet, no one around but me and Russell hiding around the side of my house.

Or worse, in my house. He's threatened that before too.

"Okay, but I'm giving you a receipt and change on this."

# CHAPTER 8

## Isabella

I T'S FRIDAY, AND BY A MIRACLE OF SCHEDULING AND SHELLEY'S generosity since she knows I have a double tomorrow, I have the full afternoon off.

Taking advantage of it, I drive over to Roseboro Arms, which sounds a lot more like a high-end apartment complex than a gun shop to me.

Whatever. Maybe the name gets the upper echelon of gun buyers who are nothing like me. I get off my scooter and head inside, opening the door cautiously, like I'm going to be greeted with a 'yee-haw' and a hail of shotgun pellets. *I've really got to get my fear of guns under control.*

I'm not quite sure what I expected, but what I find is a quiet, neat little store that looks more like a jewelry shop than anything else with glass cases surrounding the space.

The deep burgundy office-style carpet looks freshly cleaned, and in a surreal twist that must be fate laughing ironically at me, the sound system is quietly playing *Do You Really Wanna Hurt Me?*

"Hi, can I help you?" the man behind the main counter asks, looking up from the magazine he's flipping through.

"Uhm, hi. My friend, Charlotte, recommended I come down here, says she works with a guy named Brady?"

"Brady? That's my little brother," the man says, smiling. "The name's Saul. What're you looking for?"

"Home . . . uh, personal defense?" I reply. "Something I can carry in a purse."

"Well, first thing I'll tell you is that you need to get your permit to carry concealed," Saul says, "but it's pretty straightforward. I'll help you with the forms. Now, let's see what we can do for you."

It's almost dizzying, listening to the man talk about calibers, actions, trigger weights, and more. I give him respect, though, because he's not 'girlifying' it for me. He's giving me the information straight without any of the condescending attitude I expected.

Still, I feel like an idiot. "I'm really not sure—"

"Maybe I can help?"

Even though I've forced myself not to think about him, and my schedule has helped fill in the void, keeping my mind preoccupied, the voice is like cool water on a hot day, instantly quenching my thirst but making me want more at the same time.

I turn, seeing that half-smile on Gabe's face as he looks at me with those piercing eyes. Instantly, butterflies take flight in my belly and my thighs clench together.

With every drop of blood rushing elsewhere, my mouth opens before my brain can filter my thoughts. "You didn't come in Wednesday like you promised. And what're you doing here?"

"Yeah, sorry about that. I had some last-minute business come up, and I got held up out of town longer than I anticipated. I apologize," Gabe says, stepping a little closer. He's just inside my personal space bubble, but instead of feeling like it's an invasion, I want him even closer.

I want to be mad, and maybe I am . . . at myself for getting tied up in a guy I don't have time for and that doesn't have time for me, judging by his trip out of town. But maybe that makes us even? So I let him off the hook a little.

"Well, I didn't give you my phone number, so I can't blame you for not telling me," I murmur, smiling a little. "So what about the other question? What're you doing here?"

"Just shopping. Shooting's a hobby." He shrugs like it's no big deal that he pulls the trigger on a powerful machine that spits out life-ending projectiles. For all my nervousness about guns, the idea of Gabe directing and controlling all that power is sexy.

I can feel the heat on my cheeks and try to cover my dirty thoughts. "Hobby, huh? I guess you know something about guns?"

Gabe chuckles, nodding. "A little. I enjoy target shooting in my spare time. Boring sport to some people, punching very expensive holes in paper . . . but I like it. Thought I'd get some practice in during some down time. What about you? Come here often?" he lets the words ooze off his tongue flirtatiously, but it's with a big wallop of humor laced through.

"Personal defense," Saul injects into our conversation, his own smile not dimming at all. "I was just about to recommend the Glock 43."

"No," Gabe says, his smile never fading but his voice gaining an authoritative edge. "Let's try the Springfield XDM."

Saul nods, always the happy help. "That's a fine choice too," he says to Gabe before turning to me. "Now we just need to make sure you know how to handle it."

I look to Gabe, but he lifts his chin toward Saul. "Let him do the full beginner tutorial. I'll shop around and leave you to learn so you're not distracted." He must see the disappointment mixed with fire in my eyes because he leans close, whispering by my ear, "I'm not going anywhere. I'll check on you in a few. Go get 'em, tiger."

Things are a lot less fun thirty minutes later as I hit the button on the little paper target thing and it rolls in close to me, showing me where I've hit.

"More like where I've missed," I grumble, looking at the three holes in the paper. Ten shots, and I only hit the paper three times? Three friggin' times in ten shots?

I could throw the bullets down the range and hit more often than that.

It's the kick. I know what Saul showed me in the lesson he gave me, but between pulling the trigger and the way the gun seems to jump in my hand, I just feel out of control with each shot.

And the tighter I hold the gun, struggling to control it, the harder it is.

Suddenly, I feel a warm, hard body close to me, and before I can react a strong arm wraps around me, holding my wrists. Then my borrowed earmuffs are pulled down, the cacophony of echoes in the room hitting me full force.

"You're doing it all wrong," a gravelly voice says in my ear as I feel Gabe's body nearly envelop me.

"Well, it's my first time," I say, coating the words with innocence, but my smirk makes it obvious I know exactly what I'm doing. With the flirting, at least, but definitely not with the gun.

Gabe inhales sharply, and his voice is even deeper, his chest rumbling against my back. "Let's start from the beginning. Show me your stance."

He steps back and I miss his warmth. Still, I assume the grip on the pistol the way Saul showed me, and Gabe watches. I can feel his eyes on my body, looking over my shoulders and back, then drifting down my hips and legs before starting back up. It feels clinical, though I hope he likes what he sees.

"Not too bad for a first-timer." His tease is playful, making me smile, and then he lightly asks, "So, what made today the day you purchase a gun? Anything in particular spark this?"

His eyes quickly trace up and down again, though this time there's nothing professional about it at all.

I lower my pistol, setting it on the bench before clipping in a new target. "My friends encouraged me, for the most part. They're concerned about my living alone."

My eyes widen as I realize I just told a strange man . . . a very sexy strange man, that I live alone. *I'm quite literally the too-stupid-to-live girl in every cautionary tale*, I think to myself.

Well, at least he knows I've got a gun. But then again, unless he's the broad side of a barn, he's got little to worry about from me.

"Probably a smart decision in that case," he says pragmatically. "As long as you know how to use it. You know, I think a woman who can handle a gun is . . . sexy."

The way he says it turns up the heat in the firing range by about twenty degrees, and I glance over my shoulder to see him looking directly at me with a dimple-framed smile. "Okay, now what?"

"Reload, and I'll show you," Gabe says, picking up my empty magazine and quickly slipping ten fresh rounds into it. "Oh, and earmuffs. Always shoot safely."

My mind must be twisted, because I swear I can see his eyes twinkle when he says it, but I put my earmuffs back on and send the target to the end of the indoor range. I reload the gun, and Gabe watches, coming around me again and resting his hands on my wrists, his body pressed lightly against mine.

The wanton slut in me begs permission to rub my ass back against his dick, but I refrain, appreciating that he's not using this as an excuse to grind on me like most guys would. Gabe is a gentleman, *something I'm not used to*, I think wryly.

He pulls one earmuff away an inch, his voice muffled against my ear. "Relax your grip. I can feel it in your forearms," he says, and I will my muscles to release.

"There you go. Now, just focus on the front sight. The target's not moving. It's not going anywhere, and when you're ready, squeeze slowly . . ."

He lets go of the earmuff, and I take aim down the barrel of the gun the way Saul showed me, aligning my sights and the target. I take a slow breath and squeeze slowly.

The pistol pops in my hand, and as soon as it does, I can see the paper jerk and a little white hole appear in the black part of the target, the high scoring rings that I've never hit before. Gabe looks and smiles.

"Nice shot. Now, try again."

I'm no Annie Oakley, but this time, I hit the paper nine out of ten times, and best of all, five shots in the middle. I can't help but smile, and Gabe throws his hand up for a high-five, which I return carefully, keeping the gun aimed down range.

"Improvement?"

"Much better," I agree, my shoulders still tingling from where I felt his chest pressed against my back. "Uhm . . . mind showing me how you do it?"

"Sure," Gabe says after a moment. "Can I use your piece?"

I nod, hooking up another target and sending it out while Gabe reloads again.

I step back, expecting the slow, methodical, two to three seconds between shots that I did, but instead, Gabe's an explosion of shots, ten rounds before I can barely take two breaths, his brown eyes going from warm to icy as he jabs the button and reels the target back in.

The paper, which has a few pieces of tape on it from where I've patched holes, suddenly has ten brand-new punctures in the paper, and all of them damn near bullseyes.

"Whoa," I whisper, looking at him with newfound amazement. "Forget buying the gun, I should just bring you home." I slap my hand over my mouth, my eyes going wide.

Oh, my God, did I just say that? I didn't mean it like *that*. Okay, maybe a little, but I wouldn't have said it so boldly if my ovaries weren't exploding like the target paper bits did. Gabe's right, someone who can handle a gun is damn sexy.

Gabe's smile tells me he heard exactly what I said, and what I meant, and those butterflies once again start fluttering like a hurricane in my stomach.

"If you'd like," Gabe answers my accidental proposition but without pressure. "I'm just glad I can help."

"Hopefully, I won't need this, but the strung-out guy down the street has been coming on a little too strong lately."

Shit, I just keep blurting things out that I shouldn't be.

Gabe's jaw clenches. "A neighbor?"

"Kind of. Technically, he owns the land my house is on, a land lease. And he keeps coming by to collect aggressively. He's bad news in general," I explain with a lift of my shoulder. "What're you gonna do?"

"You think he's dangerous?" he asks carefully. His eyes go icy as I tell him how much Russell scared me that morning outside my house, and I can see his hands curling and uncurling. "I'm sorry that happened to you."

"Yeah, well . . . I guess it scared me enough that when Mia and Char said I should come down here, I did," I admit, stepping a little closer. "I mean, there's nothing wrong with learning to defend yourself, right?"

Gabe's eyes are serious as he closes the distance, and if he were to reach out right now, he could wrap me in his arms again. But he just stands there, hands at his side.

"There's nothing wrong with being strong enough to take charge of your own fate," he says, his expression darkening, and I wonder what trick of fate he's trying to control.

Gabe blinks, the iciness melting a little as he reaches up, his hand curling around the nape of my neck as he moves in close enough to kiss me.

But instead, he says softly, "You don't have to give me yours, but I'm going to write down my number. If he gives you any problems, you call me, okay?"

I nod but minimize the situation. "I'm sure everything will be fine. This is just a precaution," I tell Gabe, not wanting to bother him, though secretly, I think that's exactly what I want. After all, he's getting me very bothered. And hot. Hot and bothered, that's me.

Gabe smiles a little, warmth and iciness mixing somehow as he looks at me. It's like he's being warm and intimate with me but could still hand out pain to anyone who's a threat to me. It's the sexiest look I've ever seen on a man's face.

"I insist. Now, let's practice some more."

We try again, and as we keep going, I can't help but get more and more turned on. It's intimidating, the power in my hands, and as I try to shoot, my mind keeps flashing to the brief moments of Gabe popping ten rounds in that circle the size of a grapefruit faster than I could believe.

It was terrifying, but also sexy, watching him in total and utter control of the instrument of death in my hands.

"Remember, relax," Gabe says softly, coming behind me again. He puts his hands on my shoulders and presses them down gently. I hadn't even realized they'd crept up toward my ears. "You're thinking about the results and not the process of getting there. And that's making you tense, throwing you off."

His voice is almost hypnotic, and as his hands start to knead my neck and shoulders, I feel hormones flood my body. I'm turned into Silly Putty under his thumbs, and in my mind, I wonder if anyone's ever made me feel such a twin mix of sensations at the same time.

Scared and attracted, turned on and relaxed, worried and comfortable . . . Gabe's got all of them swirling in my chest, and I feel like there's not enough oxygen in the room.

"There," Gabe says in my ear. "Now, just line up the sights. Remember, you're just shooting a piece of paper . . . and go."

Ten shots, and I feel like a machine.

Breathe.

Aim.

Squeeze.

Breathe.

Aim.

Squeeze.

Ten times the cycle repeats, and when the paper comes in, there are ten holes in the black rings. "Very nice. Very, very nice," Gabe praises.

"Thank you," I reply, grabbing the target.

He takes his turn, hitting all bullseyes again, but I never even look at the target, instead focusing on him. Feet spread wide, hips square, jaw clenched, and eyes narrowed. It's like an action hero popped off the Hollywood screen, especially when he takes the last shot and turns to me with a boyish grin.

He sets the gun down and glances at the clock on the wall. "Listen, I have to go, but maybe we could get together and do this again? Or dinner? Not at the diner, to be clear."

He blinks a little faster, the smallest sign of nerves at asking me out, which I guess is understandable since I shot him down last time. I'm not making that mistake again.

I dig in my bag for a pen and grab my successful target sheet, thinking it might be nice to save as a souvenir of my first shots, but instead scribbling my number on the corner and giving the paper to Gabe.

"Here, take this. You really helped me a lot, and I think this shows that." I smile warmly.

He takes the paper, looking both at the number and the scatter of holes, then back to me. "Thanks. I'll call you soon."

He starts to leave but turns back, and the butterflies in my belly flutter, thinking he's coming back for a kiss. But instead, he tosses me one of his signature panty-melting half-smiles.

"Bye, Bella."

I bite my lip at the name. I liked it when he wrote it, but hearing him say it is even more of a wow. I wave and then he's gone.

Saul steps back into my lane behind me, asking politely, "Ready for me to show you how to break it down for cleaning and safe storage?"

I nod, but the excitement of a moment before is gone with Gabe's exit.

# CHAPTER 9

## Gabriel

THE MORNING IS DOWNRIGHT COLD, A QUICK REMINDER THAT HERE in the Pacific Northwest, autumn comes a lot faster than it does where I was born.

I don't say where I live, because for the past ten years I can't say that I've had a home.

I tend to stick around the corridor from San Fran to Seattle when I'm not on a contract, in the hopes I'll find out something about what happened to Jeremy. But even here, I don't have a home, or even a home base. Just hotels, short-term-lease apartments, and sometimes an AirBnB.

I adjust my hooded sweatshirt as I watch Isabella's house. It's not so cold that my fingers are numb or that the windows fog up.

No, the only thing obscuring my vision has been myself. And that has to stop.

Yesterday, I'd been following her, hoping she might do something 'wrong' on her day off, something that would explain why I've been hired. I'd sat in the gun range parking lot for almost ten minutes, arguing with myself about going inside.

Would she think it was too big of a coincidence and bolt like a rabbit? Or would she be happy to see me?

Ultimately, I'd given in to the curiosity, telling myself that it was possible she'd found out who I am and was getting protection against me. That's something I'd need to know in my line of work, so I'd gone inside, knowing it was more excuse and less truth but happy to justify it to myself anyway.

And I saw her blossom, the confidence she gained as she quickly learned how to shoot turning me on just as much as the warmth of her body pressed against mine.

She was the sexiest thing I've ever had in my arms. From the lean strength of her shoulders to the way her legs spread as she assumed the shooter's stance, and the biggest turn-on was her willingness to stand up for herself against that sleazebag, Carraby. She's a powerhouse, that Isabella Turner.

My brain was torn in half, one side admiring her as a budding marksman and strong person, the other side wanting to pull down the jeans she was wearing, tap her feet a few inches further apart, and fuck her as hard as I could while she bent over the shooting bench.

She makes me want to see if I'm up to the challenge of being worthy of her. I know I'm not, my soul is obviously sullied well beyond what a princess like her deserves, but I want the test anyway.

Even after leaving, I had to go back to my motel room and beat off twice just to give myself enough control to get through the rest of the night.

Which is why I have to get this done quickly. In the gun range, I could feel my self-control slipping, this close to abandoning my mission just to have her at my mercy in another way.

I wanted to bury my nose in the thick flowing locks of her hair, to nibble at her ear and reach around, tugging on her nipples until she creamed all over my cock.

I can't have that happening.

My phone buzzes, and I see it's a message from Blackwell.

*Five.*

The countdown pisses me off. He knows how I work, and the added pressure from him makes me question this whole contract all the more. But I can't back out.

*I'm close,* I text back, wishing I could be certain this course of action is warranted. But am I too close to Isabella already? Too blinded to see the ugly truth?

Sure, I've used my good looks and personality to get close to targets before. Isabella is different, though. She's threatening that line where it becomes more than just my attraction to her body.

Watching her at work, it's painful to see her swallow her pride and do whatever is needed to keep trudging along. I've snuck into her classes, lurking in the shadows in back of the lecture hall, smiling to myself as she gets every answer correct.

It was even more painful yesterday, observing as she emerged from her self-imposed shell, blossoming as she gained confidence with her shooting.

I took pleasure in every smile, every twinkle in her eyes, the times I made her laugh. More than her body, that's what I thought of as I stroked myself last night. Not her ass or her tits or any of that.

I fantasized about her laugh.

I fantasized about being the man who could help her wake up from the hell she's living in.

I fantasized about being the one to rescue her, to whoosh her away somewhere safe and spoil her rotten with attention and love.

And that's dangerous. It's more addictive than any drug her landlord might be on.

With Isabella, I feel pulled in equal and opposite directions at once, and the more I wait, the more I'm ripped in half.

Isabella's door opens, and she comes out, pulling her backpack over her shoulders. She doesn't have a heavy load of books today, so she must have gotten some studying done last night. I hope she got some sleep too, poor thing.

*Shit. I'm doing it again. Too much, too close. Back that bus up, Gabriel.*

She stops, reaching into her pocket and pulling out her phone. She dials, and I'm shocked when my phone starts to ring next to me. I look and see . . . it's *her.*

I slouch down, making sure I'm not able to be seen, and pray nobody in the neighborhood honks their horn. "Hello?"

"Hi . . . Gabe? It's Izzy Turner."

"Bella," I reply automatically, before I can even think about it.

She makes a small, happy noise, and I curse myself inside. I let myself call her that the night I left her a note . . . now I'm using it all the time with her. I've had to remind myself to not even *think* of her that way, but it hasn't sunk in yet.

If anything, it's made the nickname dig itself deeper into my psyche.

"Yeah, it's me. Listen, I know this is stupid, but you mentioned getting dinner and I'm slammed with late shifts for the next six nights in a row, but I'd like to see you."

She hums nervously, and I wonder if she's ever called a guy before. Does she just wait for them to come to her, like woodland creatures seeking out Snow White?

Or is she too busy scraping by to even think about guys?

The thought of her with another guy makes my teeth click together, but she must not hear because she rambles quickly.

"I was wondering if maybe you'd like to stop by the diner? I promise you, Henry's a great cook on more than just the Country Special."

"I'd like that," I reply, twisting inside as I know I'm both lying and *not* lying.

There's half of me that would like nothing more than to share some food and good conversation with her.

The other half . . . wants to run.

Only the tiniest fraction of a percent of me wants to actually kill her, even if I desperately need the information Blackwell has. And I hate that dark, monstrous part of me.

"Great!" she says chirpily, twisting the knife in my gut a little more. I'm actually making her *happy*. "Well, I've got a break at about nine, or if you want to wait until closing time, come by around ten forty-five."

"Sounds good. I'll try to be there at nine for your break and then hang out until you get off, if that's okay?"

Bella giggles, and I swear she sounds happier than ever. "Okay. See you then. Bye."

She hangs up, and I curse myself as moments later, I hear the buzzing noise from her scooter pulling away.

I watch her go and then grab my lockpicks. I walk up to her house, intent on doing what I should have done before approaching her.

I'm going to have to come up with something to tell Blackwell, and fast.

I need an excuse, one way or the other. Something that'll let me do this as I promised I would, or something that breaks my codes and will let me refuse the contract under the already stated terms.

My employers know my rule against innocents, and I'm very thorough in explaining the exit clauses for me and the hiring party. As depraved as it may be, this is a business transaction and I treat it as such.

Blackwell's no different, but at the same time, he's the employer I've least wanted to piss off. Not only is his reach wide, but his offered reward is the Holy Grail I've been searching for. How, then, do I deal with this?

The lock on her back door's a piece of crap, six seconds to pop, and I open the door onto one of the saddest things I've ever seen.

I knew the row of mill houses was in a sad state of disrepair, but from the outside, it seemed like Bella's was one of the better ones. But from my kitchen vantage point, I can see it's a fucking miracle this thing is still standing.

The hardwood floor carries the ghosts of seventy or more years of use. The once-warm stain is worn nearly white where generations of people have walked paths.

The walls are faded, old wallpaper that's so thin I can almost see the plaster and lathe behind it. Whatever color and design it was when it was hung has turned into a washed-out pale brown, with blobs that probably used to be flowers.

The furniture is vintage '70s, a tweed couch with wooden arms and a stained Formica two-seater dinette table.

Everything I see is the same. Old, patched, barely above homeless levels.

But I can see the effort she puts into her home. The spotless countertops, the sheet carefully tucked around the couch cushions to make it less scratchy, and the scent of lemons in the air. It's not much, but she cares for it.

Hate her? How could I hate her? How can I declare her evil?

It makes me want to cry.

Her life's a bad joke, a broken-down house even worse than I expected, a job that works her to the point of exhaustion, and dreams she will likely never reach at the pace she's going. But still, she doesn't give up.

I look around and start to get even more pissed at Russell. How could anyone want to hit up anyone for money for this place?

I'd be doing her a favor if I just burned this whole place down.

I continue exploring, going into what has to be Bella's bedroom.

She doesn't have a bed frame, just a mattress on the floor, but her blankets are spread out neatly and the single pillow is centered and standing up against the wall where a headboard would be. A series of photographs stuck to the mirror with yellowed tape catches my eye.

The mirror is huge but obviously cracked through the middle, or else it would most likely have been pawned or sold long ago to keep the bills paid.

It doesn't take me long to identify Bella in the photographs. Her hair and eyes are still the same stunning rich dark wood color they are now, and I idly wonder how many hearts she broke in school. Quite a few, I suspect.

The oldest photos are of her in much better environs, an

upper-middle-class looking house if my estimation is right, Bella between a man and a woman, with a boy in the background. The woman's obviously her mother, she's got the same cheeks and lean bone structure, but the man's got Bella's hair.

"Her father," I whisper in wonder. I touch the picture of the boy, who's got freckles and is smiling widely. "And brother."

Underneath the photo is a slightly newer one, this time Bella in elementary school with a woman who's not just lean but positively gaunt.

It was taken in this house, although things looked a lot better twenty years ago than they do today. The woman is Bella's aunt, her mother's sister, if my research was correct. The woman looks worn out and exhausted by life, though judging by Bella's age, the picture was taken a whole decade before she died.

I swallow and look down to see a cheap jewelry box, probably empty, but something inspires me to lift the lid. There's a tiny little ballerina inside, but it doesn't turn, either because it hasn't been wound in a long time or, more likely, the mechanism's broken.

More interesting, though, is the small folded piece of newspaper, slightly yellowed with age but carefully preserved, nonetheless. Feeling like the world's most depraved thief, I pinch it between two fingers, fishing it out and unfolding it carefully.

*Local Family Killed in Tragic Plane Crash*

The story's short and rather sad, telling the story of Oliver Turner, his wife, Sarah, and their only son, Roy. Oliver, a successful businessman, was also an avid private aviator and had decided to take his wife and son on a fun little jaunt over San Juan Island to catch the orca that you could see off the coast there.

Unfortunately for them . . . they never returned. Their daughter, young five-year-old Isabella Turner, was the only surviving member of the Turner family because she'd been left behind with a babysitter, according to my intel.

The story finishes with Bella being mentioned almost as a footnote, just a line saying she would live with her aunt.

I carefully fold the paper back up, tears once again threatening me. She's already been through so much, and I feel like a cold-blooded bastard for even accepting this contract. But how could I have known?

Her life hasn't just been a tragedy. It's been a comedy, not the ha-ha kind but the sad, gut-wrenching, sob-inducing kind, where the universe laughs at you while it smacks you around again.

I know the feeling, but I suspect I've barely scratched the level of shit that Bella's had to endure.

I put the newspaper clipping back, leaving her room to check out the rest of the house. There's one other bedroom, and when I open the door, I'm floored by what I see.

It's . . . a painting.

On the wall itself.

The soul poured into what I see makes my stomach clench with emotion. A painting of an airplane soaring over the ocean, the sun gleaming off the silver wings . . . and an island.

There's so much sadness in each brush stroke, the painting done in what looks like poster paint, or maybe house paint. It doesn't really matter. It's the emotions wrapped into every inch of the painting that makes it stunning.

The second pillow that belongs on her bed is sitting in the middle of the room, like she sits in here with the painting a lot. That strikes me as important, the way she takes a few moments for herself in the midst of her busy life. To grieve, to remember, to wish for a different life?

Not really knowing why, I reach out to the painting, wanting to touch the memorial that Bella's painted to her family, but before I can, a yowl from the depths of hell itself rips through the room, and a screaming ball of blackness leaps from the closet next to the painting.

"Holy fuck!" I growl as pain flares through my right hand before I can hurl whatever the fuck it is across the room. Once it lands with a soft thud, I can see it's a cat, green eyes nearly glowing in the middle of a black face, a V-shaped white mark scrunching up as it hisses at me.

My wrist throbs, and I look to see that the cat scratched me pretty badly. "You're lucky, kitty. My reflexes are usually deadlier than that, but I wouldn't hurt you."

The cat meows back at me, like it's telling me that I'm the lucky one, and I back out carefully, leaving out the same door I came in through before heading to my truck.

I have to figure out what the hell I'm going to do about this mess because I've made up my mind and I know it. There's zero chance that I can go through with this contract.

Bella doesn't deserve the ending that's been chosen for her.

And that'd be that, except for Blackwell.

He's already losing patience with my timeline. While I'm known as patient and methodical, we're stretching into the ridiculous levels here.

For an unprotected civilian with no idea of the blind justice they're in store for, a reasonable timeline would've been a week at most. I'm running on three between research, first contact, to today.

I've killed men like Blackwell, protected by security, aware of threats, and risk averse in less time than I've taken on Isabella Turner.

And Blackwell's not a man known for loyalty *or* patience. If I delay too long, he'll circumvent me, probably adding an addendum to include me with whomever he hires for the new contract.

But as I drive, I keep thinking of that painting.

That's why she's sacrificing so much . . . why she's killing herself to keep that broken-down house.

And if it means that much to her, I want to help her keep it too. And more importantly, keep her safe and alive.

# CHAPTER 10

## Blackwell

I SIP MY TEQUILA, MENTALLY BEMOANING THE FACT THAT PEOPLE ARE so predictable. It's a plus for me, really, allowing me to see the chessboard of life and plan accordingly. But sometimes, a bit of a twist would be nice.

I smirk to myself, reaching over to the bar in the back of my limo to grab a lime wedge. I squeeze it into the clear alcohol and shake it around, mixing the sour into the expensive alcohol. "A twist indeed," I say to the empty backseat.

The divider between the driver and me lowers. "Excuse me, sir. We seem to have picked up a tail. Would you like for me to lose them or continue on to your meeting?"

I glance over my shoulder, only seeing the bright round lights of the cars around us on the streets of Roseboro.

Streets that I own, control, and paved. When I came to Roseboro, it was a nothing town, in a depression from lack of employment and in the midst of a mass-exodus of families. Through my skill and nurturing, I've returned life to this city.

*I'm* the reason housing prices in this town have risen every year for twenty years and why the town's high school has grown from a podunk afterthought to one of the biggest and best schools in the entire state.

The reason this town exists is *me*.

And the city is forgetting that. They mock me, with terms like 'Black to Yellow' to describe the workers who leave me to go work for Golden Boy.

Even worse are those who leave to become successful on their own, using the things they learned from me to compete against my company. As if they don't owe me some loyalty for the changes I've brought to Roseboro and to their piddly lives.

I purse my lips as the tequila burns my tongue and gums, holding it in my mouth until it becomes a light numbness before swallowing the sip, having drawn out every molecule of flavoring from the potion. The burn and subtle vanilla and oak flavors help me delay my anger. To focus.

And I have much to focus on.

I finally answer the driver, "Drive around for a bit. I'll be a little late for my meeting, but it's an acceptable delay."

He nods silently, the divider quietly returning to its place a moment later.

*I know you're following me, Gabriel Jackson. The question is why?*

I'd hired him because he's the best in the business, able to adapt and deliver under a variety of circumstances. Silent or bold, messy or clean, the appearance of an accident or message-sending publicity . . . whatever your needs, he can meet them, and according to reputation, has done so with unequivocal success. I'd known his methods are precise, something I can appreciate, but it seems he's getting cold feet.

It can only be because of *her*.

This delay has become untenable, his questions as to my motivation less amusing and more disrespectful, and I'm reaching the end of my patience. Especially as he seems to be more interested in my behaviors than those of his contracted prey.

That's why I have already hired a private investigator to follow Mr. Jackson. Not a competing hitman, at least not yet. But rather a man skilled at being invisible. I like the idea of keeping my pawns compartmentalized, only holding a portion of the bigger picture I readily see.

His reports show that Gabriel's contact with Isabella is perhaps more intimate than I'd predicted, though he did say that Gabriel investigated her home today, so maybe he's not entirely been led astray by her feminine wiles.

Considering that she used tears and a false story to implicate my previous associate, I'm not willing to put anything past the seemingly innocuous Isabella Turner.

"You should hurry, Mr. Jackson," I whisper to the dark night, taking another sip of tequila. "My patience is running thin."

# CHAPTER 11

## Isabella

NINE O'CLOCK COMES AND GOES, AND THOUGH I TRY TO DELAY MY dinner break, I finally sit down in Martha's office to slam a sandwich and fries.

Usually, I sit on the floor or stand at the counter, but with Gabe not being here like he said, I don't want to look pathetic. And I know I'd be watching the door like a hawk, because that's what I did from eight thirty to nine fifteen.

I remind myself that he said he'd 'try' to be here at nine and then hang out until I got off, and that's not exactly the same thing as a sure date. Any number of things could've come up between this morning and tonight.

With a final swallow, I set my dishes in the back sink, straighten my apron, and wash my hands. I slick a quick layer of tinted lip balm on and pinch my cheeks, trying to perk myself up from the disappointment of another dinner alone.

All business, all the time. That's me, and I don't know why I thought for a minute that I maybe could have something else, something lighter and livelier and just for me. I know better. That's not my life.

But Mia used to be all about number-crunching and she had an amazing thing happen to her, so maybe there's hope for the rest of us, my romantic heart murmurs.

Torn between fantasy and reality, I hit the floor again, thanking Elaine for covering my tables.

It's nearly nine thirty when the doorbell tinkles and my heart leaps in my chest. I can feel the difference in the room when Gabe walks in, a smile on his face. "Hey."

"Hey." *Some stellar conversationalist skills I've got,* I think. "Glad you could make it," I greet him, genuinely smiling for the first time all shift, but then I intentionally add, "I already had my break, couldn't wait any longer or Elaine wouldn't be able to cover for me."

He winces, rubbing at his hair. "Sorry. I didn't think it'd be this late, but I got hung up with work and knew you couldn't check your phone much while you're on shift. I'm glad you didn't wait. You need to eat when you can. I was hoping I could make it up to you by hanging out until you get off? Maybe we can do something then?"

His face is open, and it appears he's being sincere, both of which go a long way in my book. Also, he gets brownie points for knowing I can't be on my phone and that I needed to chow down when I could. *He said he'd 'try' to be here at nine,* that same voice hisses in my ear.

I think for a moment, letting him stew a little bit but knowing I've already made up my mind. He's exciting and different, a bright spot in my doldrum life, something just for me. And I'm not going to deprive myself of his yummi-ness, however it comes, however often he stops by, or however long he stays.

Maybe that makes me easy, but I think it makes me human.

So I smile as I push my hair behind my ear and point to a stool at the counter. "Sounds like a plan. How was your day?" I let all my previous doubts and insecurities go, happy to just be here with him in this moment.

*Take life as it comes, Izzy.*

"Not bad. Looking much better now," he says, sliding into a seat at the counter.

He tosses that half-smile that leaves me forgetting that my feet hurt after a long day of running around. Hell, that smile makes me forget how to breathe. And judging by the way it morphs into a cocky smirk, he damn well knows it.

"How was yours?"

"Good, one morning class, then helped my bestie do some house mov-ing before my shift tonight," I reply.

Seeing Mia and Charlotte today for a little while had been great, espe-cially since it was a milestone moment for us. One of our trio is moving up the adulthood ladder by moving in with her man.

Mia had gleefully shown us around her new penthouse home while simultaneously directing the movers, liberally sprinkling 'our house', 'our bedroom', and 'our plans' into the whole tour.

It'd been pretty adorable, actually, but make no mistake, when we got to her precious gaming setup, it was all 'my', 'mine', and 'don't touch' in her occasionally-present Russian accent, even to Thomas, who'd wandered in to say hello.

He'd ignored her semi-joking selfishness like it was their norm, which it probably is, and just wrapped her in his arms and nibbled on her neck, distracting her from telling us *all* about the new TERA game update. He'd winked at Charlotte and me, mouthing *you're welcome.*

I'd been thrilled for her, and even as I stand here on uncertain ground, I'm still happy she's getting her happily ever after. She deserves it.

I bring Gabe a menu, and as he reaches for it, I notice a bandage on his wrist. It's a big one, and I wince. "Ooh! What'd you do, try to get yourself killed?"

Gabe looks at the bandage and chuckles. "Just a scratch. The bandage makes it look a lot worse than it actually is."

I devil him a bit, pretending to poke at the wound. "After your crack gun shot skills, I'd have thought you'd be damn-near invincible. Guess you're human after all, huh?"

He sets the menu down, his bandaged hand going to his lap, and I see something pass through his eyes, but it's gone too fast for me to recognize and label it.

A customer calls for me, and I hold up a finger to excuse myself from Gabe. I head over, taking their order.

As I do, I think back to my conversations with the girls today.

Mia is understandably on the side of love, lovemaking, and generally spreading glittery happiness everywhere. It's a good look on her.

Surprisingly, Charlotte is virtually the polar opposite right now, her sourness coming from the last guy she dated and really liked, who'd ended up as a married father of five.

She'd dropped him faster than he could say, "My wife knows and doesn't care!" So she's reasonably on the side of caution and distrust. Realistically, Char's more likely correct even though Mia spouted off statistics about marriage rates, divorce rates, and some other numerical info I couldn't possibly keep straight.

Mostly, I keep hearing Char's voice, telling me to be wary, slow my roll, and run a background check on Gabe. It's not like I think he's *the one*, but I probably should be careful.

*Keep it flirty and just have fun.*

"It really has been too long," I mutter under my breath, mentally arguing with Mia and Charlotte. To my surprise, Gabe chuckles. I look up, not even realizing that I had drifted back closer to him.

"What's been too long?" he asks, and I can sense the heat to his question.

Even if I'd been talking about too long since I'd had a nap, which I wasn't, I'm thinking about sex now. And to be fair, I was thinking about how long it's been since I've had a partner-accompanied orgasm. B.O.B. has been my sole date for months.

"Oh, nothing," I deflect. "Sorry. My friends are living rent-free in my brain."

"You should charge them. Might help things," Gabe teases lightly, making me laugh and thankfully not pressing for an answer to his previous question. "What are they saying?"

"Well, first, you have to know that one is literally in the midst of her happily ever after and one just got blindsided. So it's all filtered through those lenses." I point to my right shoulder, and say, "Mia here is jumping up and down, clapping and telling me to go out with you, or stay in with you, but to see where this goes."

His eyebrows climb his forehead and his eyes darken, but there's a sparkle of joy in them. "And the other?"

I look to my left shoulder, intoning, "Charlotte is telling me to be polite but recognize that I don't know you, and realistically, you don't give off the vibe of someone staying in town long-term. And she reminds me that I'm not a one-night-stand kind of girl."

I barely hold back offering 'but I could try to be' because for Gabe, I might 'hit that' even with no promises.

There's just something about him that calls to me, body and mind, and I know if I don't at least try, I'll always wonder and probably regret it.

His mouth opens and shuts like a fish, and I'm pretty sure I just dumped way too much information on his shoulders.

The door dings before Gabe can gather his thoughts enough to ask me which way I'm leaning, and I look up as heartburn walks in the door.

Well, not exactly heartburn, but the same delivery driver, along with two other customers behind him.

We're usually not this slammed this late at night, but they just keep coming today.

Seeing my conundrum, Gabe waves me off. "Go take care of business. I'll be here when you get a minute. And I'm staying until you get off tonight."

My thighs clench together with hopeful wishes that he means that in more than one way.

*Shut up, Charlotte, I can be a one-and-done if I want to be.*

Within ten minutes, The Gravy Train's in chaos and Elaine and I are in the weeds. Besides seating the three new tables, two other tables want to add extra orders, and it's so bad that Henry himself has to bring the plates to the counter because we're doing our best to keep the main floor caught up.

"Here you go, ma'am," Henry says, setting a plate down. "Sorry about the wait, seems we've got a packed house all of a sudden. Food's worth it, though." He's trying to be charming and kind, but the woman's having none of his apologies.

I glance over from where I'm writing down Delivery Driver's order, thankfully simple tonight with a double cheeseburger and fries, when the woman replies. "It's kind of hard to mess up a ham and swiss melt."

Henry shrugs and heads back to the grill, but I can see the vein throbbing in his temple and know he's getting stressed out, which isn't good for his ulcer and therefore, isn't good for any of us.

I clip the driver's order to Henry's spinner and scan the floor. Table seven needs refills, which I make quickly and deliver with a smile, promising their onion rings are coming right up. Table twelve is making a waving check mark in the air, so I flip through the slips in my apron and drop it off.

Thankfully, they offer cash and don't need change.

"My burger's fucking ready. You gonna get it or should I do it my damn self?" I hear from behind me. I glance up, and though Henry never hit the bell, Delivery Driver's burger and fries plate is sitting on the warming shelf.

My lips spread in the plastic not-smile everyone who's ever worked customer service has and tell the man, "I'll grab that now." But I don't hurry. He doesn't deserve for me to raise my heartrate one extra beat in hustle for his sorry ass.

"Shitty fuckin' food and shitty fuckin' servers. Lazy bitch."

My teeth are grinding as I move behind the counter to grab the plate, slow as dripping molasses as I check and double-check for accuracy.

*Quality assurance at its fucking finest by Ms. Isabella Turner. You'll get your burger when I'm damn good and ready to deliver it.*

Suddenly, I hear a commotion behind me as hands slap on a table and a voice growls out, "Apologize."

I turn, my jaw dropping as I see Gabe on his feet, his back to me as he stares at Delivery Driver. "What the fuck?" Driver asks, his face going a little white as he looks up at Gabe. "Seriously, man?"

"The people here are working their asses off and doing the best they can. Doesn't matter how much you hate your life, it doesn't give you the right to spread that anger onto these folks."

"Who the fuck are you to tell me—"

"I'm the guy saying you need to find another late-night hangout if this is how you're going to behave," Gabe says, reaching down and 'helping' Delivery Driver out of his seat. "Get out and go learn some damn manners."

For a moment, I'm worried Delivery Driver's going to throw a punch. But I'm rooted in place, something freezing me as I watch him stare into Gabe's eyes. The coldness is back, the same coldness I saw at the shooting range.

Right now, Gabe could hurt this man and not even blink an eye. Tension fills the air as Driver's hand clenches but then relaxes, and he takes a step back, knowing he can't win against Gabe or a roomful of people all sneering at him.

Henry's out of the kitchen again, and behind him is Martha, who's watching from the pass-through to the kitchen with the phone in her hand. My guess is she's already half-dialed 9-1-1 because while she's intimidating as hell, this is beyond even her skills.

"Fuck this. I don't need this place anyway."

Gabe doesn't move as Delivery Driver backs up, stopping at the door. "Hey, cook boy. You should fire that bitch."

He points a thumb my way, making it clear who he means. But then he locks his gaze back on Gabe, anger fraying his control even when his brain knows it's a losing battle. He puffs up, head tilting wildly as he adds to the charges against me.

"Letting people like this asshole get all up in people's faces. Fuck this place."

He storms out, and everyone in the place holds their breath for a second longer. I'm surprised when Martha starts applauding softly. I wasn't sure she'd take too kindly to Gabe taking it upon himself to kick a customer out.

A couple of other customers, including a few regulars, join in, and heat flushes my face as Gabe turns around and gives me a look that has my stomach flip-flopping.

Never has a man looked at me with such possessiveness, care, and more than a little desire. I'm about point-two seconds from running and launching myself at him, ready to ride him like a cowgirl. Luckily, or maybe it's unluckily, Martha gets in the way of my straight beeline to Take-Me Town.

"Thank you," Martha tells Gabe as she comes out, an unfamiliar smile on her face. "Saved me the trouble. I was about to do the same damn thing." We all know that's not the least bit true. Even if she'd wanted to, I don't think Martha, as intimidating as she is, has anything on the fear factor Gabe can inspire. "Though I'd appreciate it if you'd let me do the kicking out next time."

Gabe nods, and Martha hums, satisfied.

Martha turns to me. "Looks like you've got an extra burger and fries. Why don't you give that to your friend as a thank you? Then help us get caught up and get outta here. You've earned it, and Elaine and I can handle this place. We did for years before you came along, honey."

I start to argue out of habit, the running totals of bills versus tips sizing up in my mind. But tonight, I can't seem to care. Martha is right. I've earned this.

A night off to be young, dumb, and broke, as the song says. I've never had that, always too serious, too weighed down with responsibilities, too stuck in could've-beens from my past. So tonight, I'm shrugging all that off. And telling the mini-Charlotte on my shoulder to shut up and let me be a little wanton tonight if I want to be.

I look to Elaine, who nods, eyes darting to Gabe and then the door, telling me to take that man and go.

"Thanks." I shove the cheeseburger plate in front of Gabe, who's sat back down at the counter, promising, "I'll be quick."

He picks up a fry, taking a big bite and talking around it. "I'm here until you're ready to go. Whenever that is." And then he winks at me, like a legitimate, actual wink. That's something I thought guys only did as a cheesy pickup move, but on Gabe, it looks sexy. Like he knows tonight's something special for me.

Heat creeps up my neck, and I know my face is probably a few shades of bright pink as I get to work.

It seems like everyone in the diner is in on the 'Get Izzy Out of Here' plan because every table is beyond easy, asking for refills and a check or saying they haven't had Martha as a waitress in so long, they'd like to request her.

I sneak glances at Gabe, who's shoving the burger and fries down his throat like he wants to be done as fast as possible.

Me too, man. Me fucking too.

Fifteen minutes later, I've helped clear out the main floor and Martha's standing in front of me with a to-go box. "Take this and get out. I'll see you tomorrow."

I take the box, handing it to Gabe to hold while I run to the back. I'm definitely hustling now, elbows damn-near pumping to get to my purse as fast as I can. I take a quick minute to yank a brush through my hair, slick on ChapStick, and pop a mint.

I can't do much about the fry grease-smelling shirt, so I spritz a little body spray on top of it, hoping French fry-lavender is a pleasing combo.

When I come back out, I can feel everyone's eyes on me, but mine meet Gabe's and never waver. I watch as the light sparks in the darkness there, see the slight crinkles at the corners as his smile blooms in slow motion. "Ready?"

"Yep." I mean it to sound cool and casual, but it comes out breathy and dreamy.

His smile turns to a cocky smirk, knowing that he's causing me to lose it. But it's mutual. For all his chill control, I can feel the swirling tension coming off him in waves. And fuck, do I want to swim in that ocean, get pulled under by his riptide, even if it sets me adrift in his wake after he's gone.

He holds out a hand, and I slip mine into it, interweaving our fingers. As we walk out, I almost feel like it's a movie, the diner customers watching out the window as we make our way across the lot.

We stop next to a red SUV and Gabe opens the door for me. I start to climb in and then freeze. "Where are we going?"

"First, we're going right here. Martha told me there's cherry pie and ice cream in this box, so we need to eat it now or the ice cream will melt and ruin the pie. We probably could've eaten it inside, but I was afraid if I didn't get you out of there, we'd never leave."

I laugh, knowing he's right. "And then?"

He moves in close, not touching his body to mine, but so close that I can feel the electricity flowing between us. I tilt my chin up, inviting him, damn-near begging him to kiss me, wanting to taste him and see if he's dark and bitter like coffee or sweet and bright like candy. Maybe a mix of the two?

But he doesn't kiss me, instead using his free hand to cup my jaw. "And then we'll see where we want to go from there."

He's giving me an out. A gentlemanly thing to do, a way to slow the pace to whatever I'm comfortable with. But tonight, I don't want slow and nice. I want . . . Gabe.

"Cherry pie with cream it is," I say, teasingly channeling my inner Jessica Rabbit sultriness.

He laughs, and I'm not sure that's a good thing, but I go with it and laugh back as he helps me into the SUV. He walks around to the driver side, getting in and setting the to-go box on the console between us.

He opens the plastic-wrapped spoon, looking at me only half apologetically. "Martha said you were running short on plasticware, only gave me the one."

Ooh, that sneaky fox. I know there's a whole box of plastic spoons, forks, knives, even sporks in the store room. But in this case, I'm not arguing as Gabe scoops up a mouthful of delectable dessert and offers it to me.

I let him feed me and smile as he alternates, feeding himself from the same spoon too. "It's good, right? Martha's family recipe."

He moans appreciatively, and the sound makes me imagine what he'd sound like slipping into me.

His thoughts don't seem to be as dirty as mine because he asks, "Tell me about you? Who is Isabella Turner?"

The way he looks at me warms me in a different way. Mia and Char know my story, and after working here so long, Elaine does too, but not everyone listens. He seems actually interested, though, not like he's making polite conversation and expecting a textbook 'normal childhood' story.

"Well, let's see. I wasn't born here in Roseboro," I start, looking down. "My family and I lived up near Tacoma, my parents and my big brother. I . . . I lost them when I was only five."

"I'm sorry," Gabe says quietly, but not in that uselessly superficial way. Instead, he looks like he genuinely feels bad for me. "What happened?"

"A plane crash," I whisper. "Uhm, Dad was a businessman. I guess a lot of businessmen have a side hobby, but instead of golf or art or anything like that, he was into airplanes. I only remember little bits, but his home office was filled with models, and he had this Cessna. He'd take us up, fly us over Puget Sound, but I didn't go up often. I was little and Mom was nervous about me touching something I shouldn't. So Dad would let me sit in his lap when the plane was grounded, letting me pretend to fly as he promised that one day, he'd teach me. They left me at home with a sitter that day. Freak accident that couldn't have been prevented. Dad . . ."

I choke a bit and clear my throat to cover it. "He did everything right, did all he could. It just wasn't enough."

I wipe a tear from beneath my eye and look down. "Sorry, that's probably more than you wanted to hear."

I know better than to get too deep into the tragedy of my childhood. Most people don't truly care or they think I should be over it by now. It's always safer to gloss over it and move along, but something about Gabe made me feel safe enough to share. That instinct proves accurate when he doesn't flinch away but instead asks for more.

"I'm sorry, Bella," Gabe says again. "What happened afterward?"

"Well, I was sent to live with my aunt, my mom's sister. She was the only person left in my family who could care for a young kid. She lived here in Roseboro, so I moved here to stay with her. My grandparents were older, but they helped as much as they could. They passed a few years later, and then it was just me and Reggie."

I sigh, looking down as I twist the napkin in my hands. "Reggie was kind. She had a lot of love in her, but not much else. She was my mother's older sister, the wild child of the family. She'd *mostly* settled down by the time I came around, and taking care of me left her with no time for crazy escapades. But she didn't have a diploma or any real skills to speak of, and her body was decades older than it should've been from the years of abuse. So she couldn't work much, and when she did, we . . . well, things were like that old Wu Tang track. Rough and tough like leather. But she loved me, and I loved her. She was all I had."

"Was?" Gabe says quietly. "When did she pass?"

"Three weeks after I graduated high school," I recall. "Pancreatic cancer. Fast and lethal. The hospital bills sucked up all we had, ironically taking the small inheritance I had left from my parents because we'd been too busy working, didn't have time to get it transferred out of Reggie's name. The hospital didn't care that it was really my money, not hers, saying that since she was technically on the account, they were taking their money first. It was all of it."

I can't help but huff a humorless laugh at the memory of the scared eighteen-year-old kid I'd been, begging a guy in a suit to leave me with something as he shrugged his shoulders like there was nothing he could do.

"And that guy I was telling you about?"

"Ah, that guy," Gabe says, his voice dropping to a fierce rumble. "How's he fit in?"

"Reggie bought the house a long time ago and had paid it off with my parents' money to give me a secure place to grow up. But it sits on land that's owned by someone else, originally Russell's parents. Their family bought it back when it was mill housing for the factory workers, I think. They wouldn't sell Reggie the land, but they didn't charge her much for the lease. After she died, they told me they'd do the same thing for me, which was a huge relief. They were decent people, knew that house was all I had left of my family."

I growl, my mood shifting, "But when they died, Russell took over and things went to hell in a handbasket. Russell's the creepy neighbor."

Gabe looks at me sharply, his voice low and protective. "Any more trouble?"

I shake my head, trying to be reassuring. "No. The gun is put away safely, but I can get to it if he gets squirrelly. I really think he's more talk and bluster than action, though." I silently pray that saying the words will make it truer because the reality is, I don't believe Rusty is harmless and mouthy. I think he's getting more and more dangerous as each passing day draws him deeper into addiction.

I can tell Gabe doesn't quite believe me, but he lets it go, surmising with a bit of awe, "But you keep going. You've never given up."

"No . . . I guess I haven't," I admit. "Reggie always taught me that education was the way out, said dropping out was her biggest regret. So I worked my ass off in high school to get good grades while helping with the household bills, and I'm still working my butt off, paying my way through college, semester by semester. It's taking forever, but I'm going to get there." This time, I don't need the universe to hear the truth of the words. I'm going to make it happen myself, no matter what.

"I admire that," Gabe says honestly. "You've fought for everything you have, and when you have what you want in life, you can look back and say you earned every bit of it. Not too many people can honestly say that."

I chuckle, and Gabe tilts his head at the odd response to his compliment. "What?"

"You should meet my friend, Mia. She's got this saying." I adopt her fake Russian accent. "*Don't ask for it, Tovarich. Earn it. Do that, and you'll be rewarded.*"

Gabe's brows shoot together, the question in his chocolate eyes before his mouth forms the word. "*Tovarich*? Mia's . . . Russian?"

I lightly tap his arm, careful not to spill the melted mess of ice cream in the to-go box between us. "Very good. She'd be proud. We tease her that she's pseudo-Russian. Her Papa most definitely is, but Mia was born in the US. Her history is important to her, though, and she has all these 'Russian' sayings and can put on an accent that'd make you think she grew up in Central Moscow. She's a hoot, a rainbow-haired, number-crunching geek who just moved in with her uptight, suit-and-tie-type man."

Gabe hums, smiling a little as he deadpans, "Sounds like a match made in heaven." He finishes with, "Wise words, though."

"So what about—" I ask, but before I can ask about his life story, the light in the parking lot changes. I look over to the front of the diner and see the glowing red 'Open' sign has gone dark. Inside, I can see Elaine, Henry, and Martha peering out the door, smiles on their faces as they very obviously talk about the fancy Range Rover in the lot and its two occupants. "Oh, God, they probably think we're fucking right here in the diner lot," I mumble, burying my face in my palms.

Gabe's laugh is a big burst from his belly, filling the cabin of the Rover. "You make a habit of that? Or have a lot of problems with lot lizards?"

I turn my head, glaring at him. "Of course not. The Gravy Train is a classy joint." I say it with a straight face but can't hold it, and suddenly, I'm laughing too.

"Maybe we'd better get on out of here?" Gabe asks. "Before they call the cops on questionable activities in their parking lot?"

He's still asking, kind and sweet, about our progress even as I sense the need churning in him. But he's got it on lockdown, controlling the wildness I want him to unleash.

"Definitely," I say before my fear changes my mind. I'm not scared of Gabe, not at all, but maybe of doing something crazy just because I want to.

It's not the responsible and future-minded Izzy I've always been. But a bit of untamed joy in the present moment sounds like something I've always needed and pushed aside. Maybe it's not the right time to indulge, with Russell threatening me, school finals looming, and next semester's fees due any day. But maybe it's the conglomeration of those things that makes this the perfect time to let loose for once.

I deserve this. I've earned this.

Gabe starts the SUV, the headlights turning on automatically and the instrument panel glow lighting his face. I can see his relief that I agreed, his desire burning my skin where his gaze touches me. It's a lot to take in, and I inhale, turning toward the window for a moment to let the butterflies in my belly settle.

I see that Elaine's smile is huge now, a knowing look in her eyes, and then she waves goodbye with a nod, like she's proud of me for doing something just for me for once.

I wave back, and as Gabe pulls out of the lot and into the light midnight traffic, I sink into the seat, letting the luxurious leather wrap around me. I've never done anything like this before.

"So, where are we going, anyway?" I ask as Gabe gives me a dazzling smile, his dimples bookending his white teeth.

"It's a secret," Gabe says with a lift of his brow. "A gem of a place I discovered."

# CHAPTER 12

## Gabriel

I SABELLA SITS QUIETLY IN THE PASSENGER SEAT AS I DRIVE, THE TWIN headlights of my 'real' vehicle stabbing the night. I enjoy this Range Rover a lot more than the nondescript throwaway truck I've been using as a work truck, if only for the ride.

It's interesting to see Isabella tense, then relax as I accelerate out of Roseboro. I suspect she's been riding that scooter for so long that she's forgotten what sixty miles an hour feels like as the lights of the city pass us in a blur.

Or maybe her intermittent stiffness is because of me. I have to remember that while I know everything about her, both from her lips and from her file, I'm a virtually unknown entity to her. I'm sure that's weighing on her as much as the speed with which we're racing out of town.

We get to the parking area closest to the secluded spot I found, and I come around, opening the door for her. I help her step down, warning, "Careful, it's a bit of a drop." The words resonate in my head like warning bells, but I refocus on here and now, on Bella.

Looking in the back of my Rover, I grab a military surplus parka out of the back, nothing fancy but something I keep for bad weather . . . although the camo print has proven useful once or twice for surveillance.

Bella smiles as I shake it out flamboyantly, unzipping it and slipping it over her shoulders. "Nice."

"Thanks," I reply, zipping the coat up the front of her, watching as her curves disappear beneath the coat. The oversized parka almost swallows her. She looks . . . adorable, and it makes my heart twist in my chest. "I got it for rainstorms. You know how they can sometimes spring up and catch you unaware."

"Not just weather. Life does that too," Bella says, adjusting the cuffs and zipper, and truer words have never been spoken. She certainly caught me unaware, is still surprising me at every turn. "So, where are we going?"

"It's not far. We'll take the easy route," I say, reaching out and taking her hand.

She pulls me back, her voice sassing in the dimness, "I don't need the easy route."

This woman, challenging me when she doesn't even need to, scared to let something be comfortable because she's so used to fighting for every scrap and morsel she gets, and accustomed to life being hard for no sensible reason.

I shrug like that doesn't gut me and ask straight-faced, "Suit yourself. I guess that means you're an experienced nighttime free-climber then?"

Her eyes shoot wide open as her jaw drops. "A night what? Climbing what?" I can see her backpedaling literally as she takes a step closer to the SUV like she's going to hop back inside.

"The spot I want to show you, it's accessible two ways. One, by the short, easy hiking path I planned. Or two, by climbing up the rock face from the valley below. Your call, just let me know if I should grab my gear. I have two sets. I follow the Boy Scout motto of 'Be prepared.' " I wait patiently, curious how she's going to back out of this because she obviously has no desire to rock climb, especially by the light of the midnight moon.

After the span of two slow breaths, I let her off the hook and offer an easy grin. "Hike sounds best to me. Never know what creepy crawlies might be on the rock face at night."

She shudders, obviously not liking the idea of nocturnal insects or other animals. "Fine. If you'd rather hike, we can do that."

I laugh loudly that she's still not admitting that she can't do the climb but is instead sticking with using me as her out. She glares at me, shooting daggers, but then cracks up too. Our laughter echoes through the trees, disturbing some night fliers, judging by the sound of flapping wings.

Bella steps a bit closer to me and I whisper in her ear, "No worries. I'll protect you from the bugs."

I let my thumb trace a circle on her hand, feeling the soft satin of her skin. She nods and finally, we're off.

Using a flashlight from my gear pack, we walk up the hill, listening to the sound of the waterfall get closer and closer. When we emerge around a bend in the trail, I stop, looking over the scene. We're both silent, taking it all in.

"It's beautiful."

Bella's hand comes to her chest, and I can understand. The moon's broken through the clouds that have been peppering the sky all night, and now it's in its full glory, huge and silver as it shines down on the forest below. The whole scene looks ethereally frosted, not frozen but like it was crafted out of ebony and velvet, dusted with diamonds, and lit from within by the slowly pulsing heart of the forest itself.

"Gabe, this is amazing," Bella whispers, her voice choking. She walks to the edge, gasping again. "I can see most of Roseboro from here!"

I come up behind her, placing my hands on her waist. Even through the parka, I can feel the flare of her hip, the nip in at her midriff.

Part of me wants to pull her from the edge, hold her closer and grind on her until our bodies demand more.

I'm ashamed to say there's a tiny part, fractionally small, that hisses I could do it here, shove her over the edge into the black valley, fast and painless, and that the camo jacket I gave her out of kindness would likely hide her body until I could get safely out of town. That tiny bit even argues that it'd lead to too many questions because several people saw me leave with her tonight, and that'd make me suspect number one in her disappearance.

But even with the automatic response slithering through my psyche, I know it's not happening. I've already made up my mind. I blink slowly, staring into the stars above us.

*Sorry, Jer, I can't. Not her.*

There's no response, but I'd like to think he understands. There's got to be a way. A different way.

"This place is magical," Bella says, breaking into my dark thoughts as she leans back against me, pulling my arms around her. "How'd you find it? Did you really rock climb up here?"

I swallow, inhaling the scent of her hair and holding her more tightly, betraying my contracted word but honoring my loyalty to myself in a way I haven't in a long time. "I did. It's not as crazy as it sounds." I'm hedging. It's absolutely as insane as it seems, but that's why I love it. "Honestly? I've always been an outdoors kind of guy. This place kind of reminds me of when I was a kid."

"I'd like that story," Bella says, rubbing my arm to keep me warm since she's bundled in the one coat, but I think it's also because she's tracing the muscles in my forearm. *Arm porn girl*, I think with a cocky grin she can't see. I flex a bit, squeezing her jacket and popping the muscles for her. Though her eyes stay locked on the amazing view, I feel her legs move like she's trying to subtly rub her thighs together for relief, and heat blooms in my balls.

"Or do you bring all of your conquests into the woods like a wild man?" I can hear what she's truly asking disguised in the joking question. This sweet woman, who never takes care of herself but is choosing to spend her precious time with me tonight, wants to know if this is as special to me as it is to her.

"You're the first," I reply, and I feel Bella's chuckle before I hear it, her back bouncing against my chest. "What?"

"I seriously doubt I'm your first anything, Gabe."

I lean down and bury my nose in her hair before nuzzling her ear. "Point taken. I mean the first here. I just found it a few days ago, and I wanted to share it with you."

What the fuck am I doing?

It's one thing to fail a contract, to go back on my word and refuse it mid-agreement by not killing her. It's quite another to bring my work into my personal life. But unwittingly, that's exactly what I've done. Isabella Turner hasn't been a job for a while now. She's been something else entirely. I'm not sure what it is, exactly, but I want to know everything about her, protect her at all costs, even from herself, and somehow make her every dream come true.

*Nothing big or major or hard about any of that*, I think sarcastically. *Should be able to get that checked off the to-do list in no time.*

But self-recriminations aside, it's the truth of what I want. And I don't have the first fucking clue about what to do about it, especially when the safest thing for me to do is to bail, to hit the highway and just run pell-mell back to a life where every day is the same, a cold existence where my primary focus is tracking down my brother's killer.

Bella looks over her shoulder, smiling wryly. "Does that mean I'm *special*?" Disbelief drips from her tone, like it's the cheesiest of distasteful pickup lines. Like off-brand Velveeta in word form.

One look in her eyes, and I feel my resolve crumble. I'm not going to kill her like I was hired to do, *and* I'm not going to walk away like I should do.

Instead, I answer honestly, from my heart and my gut. "Bella, you're far more special than you realize, more than I dreamed."

I can tell she doesn't believe me. "You . . . you confuse me."

I turn her around, wrapping my arms around her waist again and pulling her tight to me, where she gulps when she feels the rising thickness of my cock against her belly. "Is that so?"

"You're not the first to hit on me at the diner. But usually, they wanted just one thing. You . . . you're different."

I touch my forehead to hers. "You have no idea."

She sighs, and I feel the heated breath whisper across my mouth. I lick my lips, trying to taste her.

Her voice is a hoarse whisper, softly rasping in my ear. "You're right. I barely know anything about you, but I feel like this is right. Tell me about you, Gabe."

It's my own question thrown back at me, but whereas she opened up the Pandora's box of her life story, I can't. Even if I wanted to, which surprisingly, I do, I can't tell her. It's too ugly, too monstrous, and she'd never understand.

So I do the only thing I can. I give her my truth with a kiss, molding my mouth over hers as I truly taste her for the first time and hope it's enough to answer her reasonable request for more from me.

She responds immediately, moving her lips with mine and allowing me access to dip my tongue into her on a breathy sigh.

I run my fingers into her hair, tilting her head the way I want and diving in for more, wanting all of her, wanting to give her all of me in this kiss.

*Jeremy would want this for me. Blackwell can fuck himself. I'll get the information he's holding over my head another way. Or maybe not at all?*

The thought of losing myself in Bella is somehow soft and hazy, a misty dream I hadn't fully considered. But when she mewls under me, pulling a groan from my own chest, I let the fantasy of retribution go in favor of the reality right here in my arms.

*I'm a monster, but on her lips, I taste absolution.*

Forcing my eyes open, I step her backward toward a nearby rock. But instead of pinning her to it, I turn us and lie back on the cold, rough hardness myself, pulling her against me and letting her have some semblance of power. I don't want to overwhelm her, and I'm barely hanging on to the edge of my control with a white-knuckled grip. Her hands come to my chest, finding the sweatshirt and pulling me in for another kiss.

I slip my hands under the thick parka, cursing it for not letting me feel her nipples pressed to my chest. Instead, I find the belt loops of her jeans and move her hips against me, making her slide along the ridge of my cock to let her know what she's doing to me.

"Fuck, Bella."

She bites her lip, white teeth denting the puffy pink fullness and driving me wild. I shift her, spreading her legs around my right thigh and pressing her core to the thick muscle there. Her hips shudder involuntarily at the sensation, and Bella's eyelashes flutter as her eyes roll back.

I can't give her everything, can't take all that I want from her. But I can give her this. A night she deserves, a night to remember. "Ride me, Bella. Use me to get yourself off."

Her eyes snap to mine, timid hesitancy covering desire. She doesn't move at first, so I guide her, feeling her heat even through our jeans. But soon, her instincts take over and she starts to roll against my thigh.

"Oh, fuck, Gabe . . . but—"

"Do it, Bella," I growl in her ear as I reach around and grab her ass, squeezing the firm cheeks and adding to the feelings shooting through her. "Come on me."

Bella resists for a few seconds, but then the feeling of her clit rubbing against my thigh and my teeth tugging on her ear overwhelm her resistance, and the sound that comes from her is the sexiest thing I've ever heard in my life. "*Fuuuck . . .*"

I kiss her neck, feeling the flutter of her heartbeat and letting her have control of what she needs. It's torture, guilt and desire pulsing through me with every beat of my heart. My cock aches. She's so sexy that I can barely contain myself, but the fact that just minutes ago, that dark voice was encouraging me to kill her makes me want to punish myself, deny myself the pleasure I know she could bring me.

Instead, this is for her, and I take my joy from every sound Bella makes as she dissolves in my arms, lost to an ecstasy she so rarely gets in her rough life.

As her hips speed up and her body starts to tremble harder, I encourage her. "That's it. Rub that pussy on me." She moans, and I want to swallow the sound. I keep going, judging that she likes the dirty words pouring from my mouth. "You need this, Bella. Fuck, I need this. I can feel how hot you are, probably messy with your delicious honey. You gonna let me feel you come, then let me lick you clean?"

She loses the rhythm, and I take over, pulling and pushing her back and forth as I flex beneath her. Her hands dig into my shoulders, and then gloriously, her head falls back and she cries her orgasm to the night sky. It's a symphony of sex, and I love every stunning note, instantly wanting an encore.

"Oh, my God," Bella rasps when it's over, and I let her down slowly, the moonlight illuminating her rapturous face. "That was . . ." She searches for words before she meets my gaze, clear-eyed and powerful, demanding, "More."

That I can do.

And while it's faint comfort for the pretenses this began under, I'm going to assuage my guilt by devoting myself to giving Bella as much pleasure as she can handle for as long as she wants me. And I'm going to protect her—from Blackwell, from me, and from herself.

# CHAPTER 13

## Gabriel

IT FEELS STRANGE AND EXHILARATING TO PULL UP IN FRONT OF BELLA'S house *with* her and not to scope out her routine. Bella's almost drunk on desire as I pull her into my arms again, kissing her deeply as she fumbles with the gate latch, giggling as we make our way up the walkway.

I cup her breast over the top of her shirt before we even make it inside. The parka's gone, banished again to the back of my Range Rover, and I feel her nipple pebble under my fingers as I tug, making her moan.

"I fucking need to be inside you," I growl against her neck.

"Let's get inside so I don't give Old Mrs. Petrie a heart attack," she says, glancing over her shoulder to the house across the street. And then she drops her voice low and slow, "And so I can have something softer for my knees."

The naughtiness in her voice draws me with her like she put a leash on my desire and I'm at the mercy of her whims. She unlocks her door and enters, not even reaching for the light switch. I wonder if she's trying to hide the reality of her home from me, like it's something she can ignore if she doesn't turn the light on. But truthfully, all I see is her, even in the dark.

*Besides, you already know what her house looks like, fucking creeper.*

Instead, we walk through the darkness, her fingers wrapped in mine as she pulls me down the hall to her room. The blinds are open, the streetlight shining in, and we're greeted by the same cat who slashed me this morning.

It yowls when it sees me, leaping to its feet, back arched and green eyes glowing with malice. It apparently hasn't forgotten my intrusion into its domain this morning, but Bella just laughs.

"Vash, relax, honey! He's our guest!"

Shooing Vash out of the bedroom, she closes the door quickly, turning and grinning sheepishly at me. "Sorry . . . she's usually a sweet kitty. I don't know what got into her."

"Jealousy?" I ask, lifting an eyebrow. "Pheromones?"

Bella laughs, while inwardly, I remind myself to make peace with that damn cat ASAP. "I guess there are some things you can't charm, huh?"

"I'll work my magic on Vash later. Right now, I'm only thinking about charming you," I reply as I look into Bella's eyes. Even in the dim light, I can tell that she wants this, whatever it is between us.

She made a comment that she's not a one-night-stand girl, and that doesn't surprise me, but she's not asking for more than that right now. I think she probably expects me to be gone in the morning, if not before. But she doesn't realize this is the first step toward something bigger, deeper than just tonight.

She may not realize it yet, but I do.

I don't have it all planned out in my usual way, but I'll figure it out. Just not right now, not when I can feel her body stretching toward mine. And especially not when she reminds me of her earlier demand, "More."

Reaching down, I pull my sweatshirt and T-shirt off, letting Bella see me naked from the waist up. My breath hitches at the contact of her hands on my chest, her palms lightly rubbing through the faint dusting of hair.

"So many tattoos? I want to lick them all," she confesses, or maybe it's a promise.

My cock throbs at the thought of her pink tongue dragging over my skin, and I palm myself, trying to get some relief.

"Lie down," she whispers, pushing me back toward the mattress on the floor. I nod and step back, toeing my boots off as I sit down and she stands above me, her own eyes gleaming in the light.

She strips quickly and efficiently, but the sight of her naked form clad in nothing but dim street light will stay in my memory banks forever. The cool air makes her nipples harden as soon as she has her bra off, and her bare pussy beckons to me. She pulls the clip from her hair, and the dark waves tumble over her shoulders beautifully.

"Fucking gorgeous, Bella."

She smiles, looking pleased at the compliment, and then she kneels down on the mattress beside me, my hand finding her goosebumped skin. "Not yet . . . it's my turn."

She seems utterly confident as I let her lead and explore, her hand making its way to feel my cock through my jeans. I'm already painfully aroused for her before she even touches me, and I groan as she brings me to an impossibly steely hardness in an instant, my balls already drawing up and threatening to spill like an out of control teenager.

"You like that?" she purrs, kissing me as her soft hand slowly massages my cock, warmth divided by just a thin layer of denim.

Pressing her body against mine, her hand naughtily plays with my belt, teasing and tormenting me. Finally, she turns, presenting her pussy to me as she kisses down my stomach, tracing the ridges of my abs and a few of my tattoos with her tongue. She opens my jeans, humming happily as my cock tents my boxers.

I run my hand down her back, caressing her ass as she fishes my cock out. I lift my hips, helping her shove my jeans and boxers off, and then we're bare together, every contact point electricity-filled.

She licks the tip of my cock, making my eyes roll up in my head, and I grip her ass a little harder. It's been more than a little while for me. I've been so fanatical about my quest for revenge that I haven't had time for a woman in my life. I suspect it's been a while for Bella too, so we both have lost time to make up for tonight.

She rains butterfly kisses over the head of my cock, and I fight the urge to shove into the wet heat of her mouth. To keep a restraint on myself, I focus on Bella's pleasure instead of my own.

I bring my fingers lower, between her legs to stroke the soft lips of her pussy, teasing before slipping a fingertip in between. Bella gasps, her lips flaring to cover the entire head of my cock, suckling as I stroke up and down, gathering her wetness on my fingertips before bringing it up to her clit, rubbing her button with featherlight strokes.

"Mmpfh!" Bella moans around my cock, her hips jerking as I find the stroke and pace that she likes best. Her knees spread some more, and in the orange light I find myself enchanted by the gleam of her pussy opening for me as she bucks into my fingers. It's sexy as fuck in its obscenity, a woman taking the pleasure that she wants from me while her mouth and tongue please me back.

I rub my thumb between her lips as I play with her clit, getting it slick and ready before pushing it inside her, where her tight muscles immediately clutch me, almost sucking me in. She's so tight, a slick vise on my thumb as I pump it in and out, guided by the sounds Bella's making. Being inside her mouth and her pussy at the same time short-circuits my brain, and I can't hold back anymore, can't let her be solely in control. I lift my hips, slipping my cock deeper into her mouth, right on the edge of entering her throat.

She pulls back, using her spit and my pre-cum to fist my shaft. "Oh, God, Gabe . . . more," Bella rasps, pushing her pussy back into me as she pumps my cock. "Stretch me so I can take you, and then fuck me."

Growling, I pull my hand back before replacing my thumb with both of my fingers, thrusting them deep inside her and making Bella moan in plea-sure. She bends forward, swallowing as much of my cock as she can while I pump in and out of her, fucking her with my hand as her juices run down my palm and onto the cut on my wrist. Distantly, I realize I lost the bandage somewhere along the way, but I can't care right now.

The slight sting centers me, though, allowing me to focus just on Bella and not on the feeling of her velvety-soft lips wrapped around my shaft or the feeling of her tongue exploring the ridge around the head of my cock. She slurps on me happily as precum oozes out for her to feast on, her pussy gushing around my fingers.

"In my pocket, my wallet," I tell her, not able to wait any longer, and I think she gets my meaning.

I feel her move, reaching for my jeans on the floor. She moans on me when she finds my condom, unwrapping it before pulling off, gasping, "I fucking love Boy Scouts."

"Be prepared, they taught us," I tease breathlessly, adding a third finger to her pussy. "How's that feel?"

"Fucking amazing . . . maybe big enough to not have this kill me." She whimpers as she rolls the condom down my cock. It's tight, but the constrict-ing rim of the condom helps hold back my orgasm as Bella gets me ready before pulling off my fingers and turning around to straddle me, rubbing the head of my cock between her dripping folds. "Are you ready?" I ask her.

I reach up, taking her waist in my hands and helping her as she lowers herself onto my cock, both of us moaning in a sexual harmony as her body wraps itself around my pulsing shaft. She's so warm, her honey-coated walls taking me in and holding me in a perfect embrace. Bella's chest hitches, her breasts shaking as she trembles, wanting more but needing to stop when I'm about halfway inside her.

"Take your time, Princess. I won't hurt you."

The words have so many layers of meaning, more than she could possibly know, and are as much a promise as I can give her right now.

She rides me slowly, my cock sliding deeper and deeper inside her with every rise and fall of her hips until I feel her hips press against mine, and she throws her head back in triumph.

"It feels like you're splitting me in half, but I can't stop," she grunts as her hips take over. I encourage her, reaching up to stroke a stiff nipple, watching as her body bounces up and down on me.

It's the sexiest thing I've ever seen, this beautiful woman getting all the pleasure she can just from me. For once in her life, she's demanding and wanting something selfishly, and I want to give her everything I can, reward her for all the hard times she's gone through, and insure that every day from here on out is better by my side.

I reach around, cupping her ass and helping her. "I have you, Bella . . . I have you," I murmur, more to myself than her, making sure this is reality and not some dream I'll wake up from. I thrust up into her as she comes down, meeting her body with my own as I marvel in the sight of her on top of me.

She's a princess, a queen, and I vow in this moment that I will do what I can to be her knight in tarnished armor.

Bella's hips plunge up and down on my cock, both of us rising together until she pitches forward, kissing me deeply. Her pussy clenches around my cock, and she moans her orgasm into my mouth, gifting me with her release.

It pushes me over the edge, and I hold her tight, thrusting two more times until I explode, filling the condom with hot cum. My body shakes as we fall apart together, her lips grounding me as I hold her safe. And that feels like exactly what I want . . . for her to give me the foundation I haven't had since Jeremy died, and in return, I'll make sure she's happy and secure. In this moment and every other.

We lie together, the sweat cooling on our bodies until she shivers, and I wiggle around to pull at the blankets. I arrange them over us until we're wrapped up like a twin burrito, not perfect but still warm. I grab her single pillow and tuck it underneath my head, pulling her to nestle against my chest with my arm wrapped around her shoulders. "Comfy?"

"Mmm-hmm," she says sleepily. Moments later, she's snoring softly, her body exhausted by all that she's done today. I hold her carefully, close enough to feel her body without waking her while my mind works overtime.

I wasn't kidding about being a Boy Scout, and in my line of work, preparation is key to successful contracts. But I'm unprepared for my current situation and I need to rectify that. I think over what I know.

Blackwell said he wanted Bella killed to send a message to someone else, so she's not the player here but merely a pawn. Perhaps there's a way I can leverage that, offer an alternative path to his endgame?

But from what I know of Blackwell, and that's a significant amount of intel because I don't take contracts lightly, he is not the type to allow an outsider to have input into his chosen strategy. I'm merely a tool for him to use, a resource for a skillset he doesn't wish to employ himself.

So he's not going to let this go, of that I'm reasonably certain. I can put him off for another couple of days, but with the degree of suspicion and impatience he's already fostering, I wouldn't put it past him to line up another hit. And include me in the target roster.

I consider reversing the game. I'm a skilled hitman. Perhaps I should flip the script and take out the threat to Bella . . . Blackwell himself. That'd solve the problem, but it'd be beyond difficult. He's aware of my presence, so the element of surprise is nonexistent. And he's well-protected with enough security that it'd be nearly impossible to get close to him unless I called for a meeting, and doing that would make for a messy exit.

The answer that makes the most sense is to run. Take her with me and leave Roseboro forever. We could do it, start fresh somewhere no one has ever heard of Blackwell. But even as I dream of laying Bella on a sandy beach somewhere exotic where it's just the two of us, I know she won't go. Not even if I tell her the truth, which I need to do regardless. But I know her. If she thinks Blackwell is using her for some reason, my girl is going to put her face to the storm and rage back to protect whoever Blackwell is trying to get at.

Which puts me back at square one. My mind continues to turn, but slowly, the warmth of Bella's body seeps into me, and I drift off. No answers, but all I need is in my arms.

Early in the morning hours, I wake and watch her sleeping. My fitful slumber contrasts with her peaceful exhaustion, and I marvel at the rest of the truly innocent. It's something I can never again have but something I want to protect now. Tracing her back and teasing her to wakefulness, I slip into her once again. It feels like . . . heaven.

# CHAPTER 14

## Isabella

I FEEL THE SOFT TOUCH OF SOMETHING ON MY NECK AND EAR, MAKING me giggle lightly as it nudges me from sleep. Something warm and hairy rubs against my cheek, and I wiggle, wondering how Gabe got so fuzzy overnight.

"Really? I've got morning breath," I say, turning my head away, but a smile takes over my face.

*Meow.*

My eyes flutter open to see Vash curled up next to me, her head tilted to the side quizzically like she's asking me just what I mean. Stretching, I reach over and realize I'm in bed alone, at least human-wise.

For a moment, I think maybe I dreamed the whole thing, conjured it up out of my desire to do something crazy, be irresponsible for once, and to feel Gabe's body against my own. But as fast as I think I made the whole thing up, my body lets me know that last night was real. Very real, and very large.

I stretch out my muscles, loving the way they feel used in different way. This isn't the typical sore-feet and tired calves I wake up to, but rather a whole-body feeling of Jell-O.

*Meow!*

"Vash . . . off!" I grumble, nudging her away. Instead of scrambling, Vash tosses her head and jumps down, confident that she's woken her human up properly and that we're about to get on with the day.

Dammit.

Disappointment floods me as I realize Gabe really has left, and I panic a little, worrying at how stupid I've been.

"Hit it and quit it," I whisper.

I told myself I was going to go with it and have fun, and I did. I don't regret that, but I can't help but have a twinge of something sharp in my belly. More than disappointment, maybe disenchantment? I guess I hoped Gabe was different.

A flash of white on the floor next to my panties catches my attention, and I sit up, realizing that all my clothes are neatly folded, and my bag, which I left in Gabe's SUV, is sitting next to the pile. The white is a piece of cardstock, one I'm familiar with since it's the same cardboard that The Gravy Train uses for their take-home container tops.

This one's been folded in half, though, tented, and has a large *Bella* written on it. Reaching out, I open it.

*Princess,*

*I'm sorry I didn't wake you, but you looked so peaceful and I know you need sleep with your busy schedule. I had to go to work, but trust me, there is nothing I would've rather done than to hold you all morning.*

*I know I promised you a ride to the diner to get your scooter, and I'm sorry I couldn't do that before I leave. But I left you a little something on the kitchen counter to make up for it and make your day a bit easier.*

*I'll see you tonight, nine o'clock sharp, but I'll be thinking about you all day.*

It's signed with a scratchy capital G that I trace with my fingertip. Okay, so he left, but he didn't bail on me. That's a good sign, right?

Touched, curious, and desperately needing to pee, I get out of bed and slip into the bathroom, where I take care of biz quickly before walking into the kitchen. I am floored by what I find.

It's a bag . . . a *big* bag, and while the red and yellow 'M' on the side might not be my favorite restaurant in town, the smell of pancakes, syrup, sausage, and cheese inside has my mouth already watering. I haven't had a real breakfast in too long, and I can't believe he'd do this for me.

More surprising is what I find inside the thoughtfully folded shut bag. In addition to three sandwiches, there's a small carton of milk with *Vash* written on it. It's so sweet of him to think of her, especially considering she wasn't particularly welcoming last night. It's then I see the cup of coffee, bottle of orange juice . . . and a Range Rover key fob. Shocked, I look up through the front window, and it's still there, candy-apple red and gleaming in the morning light.

I press the key against my chest, everything feeling like I'm being broken apart again. It's such a kind gesture, the type of thing I'm not used to people offering. And if I'm honest, the sort of charitable generosity I'd refuse if Mia or Charlotte tried to foist it on me. But from Gabe, it feels different. Like he's taking care of me because he wants to, not because he thinks I'm failing at doing it myself. That's probably fodder for a therapist, or at least a wine-fueled girls' night in, but right now, I'm not examining it too much.

*Take life as it comes, Izzy. And enjoy.*

My body hums happily in soreness from last night, my eyes itchy with tears that I don't want to let fall, and my stomach grumbles for the smorgasbord of food before me. This could be the start of an awesome day.

*Meow.*

I look down to see Vashy rubbing against my legs piteously, and I'm sure she's hungry. Grabbing the milk, I open it and pour a saucer for her. I'll get her food out before I leave.

"Okay, Vashy . . . ten minutes' vacation before we get back to the grind, okay?"

Vash meows again, looking at the bag, and I chuckle.

No wonder Gabe included three sandwiches.

"Uh-oh. Char, I think we have a problem."

My two besties lean against each other, whispering and giggling loud enough for me to hear them as I walk into the cafeteria at Goldstone Inc.

Mia had begged for us to do our weekly lunch on her home turf this time instead of our usual Gravy Train break. She said something about a big project and data this, trends that, and at that point, I'd just agreed to get her to stop talking analytical statistics. I swear, half the reason I went into graphic design was so that I never had to delve as deep into numbers as Mia does. But she loves it, thankfully. Better her than me, I suppose.

"What?" I ask, checking my shirt for stains and that the fly of my black skinny jeans hasn't slipped down. *There's nothing out of place,* I think as I slip my dark hair behind my ear. So why are they still smirking at me? "What?" I repeat.

Mia breaks first, drawling out, "Hey, cowgirl, been riding that pony long?"

I finally get the joke they're telling on my behalf and shove at Mia, a sporting laugh popping free even though I try to hold it back. Mia devolves into giggles and even Char looks damn amused at the tease. "I'm not walking funny," I argue good-naturedly, then pause a minute before asking more seriously, "Am I?"

Char rolls her eyes, turning her nose up. "I am not talking about sex when I'm not getting any. You two can take your hot dicks and keep them to yourselves." She sounds half serious, half joking, and Mia's eyes catch mine.

Before we can communicate via eyebrows, though, Mia smiles widely. "You said 'hot dicks'. I'm thinking you're trying to speak it into existence, girl." She nods sagely, and Char huffs, striding off toward the line of people waiting to get lunch.

We follow, silently agreeing to change the subject because Char seems more than a little touchy. I wonder if she had another bad date? But when we get in line, she's perked up, talking to the lady who just brought out a big tray of rolls.

"You have a Hobart mixer that handles the dough with no problem? I splurged and got a KitchenAid a few months ago, but I would give my left arm to play with a commercial setup."

I have no idea what Charlotte's talking about, and I realize that maybe I haven't been the best of friends with her the way I should be. I'm ashamed to admit that I've been a bit caught up in my own mess to push her to share, especially when she's tight-lipped. But I try to draw her out now. "You turning Chef Ramsey on us? I'm up for any taste tests you want to schedule."

She grins a bit, telling the roll lady thanks before answering me, "I've been playing with some recipes and learning a lot. I really love baking. Cakes, pies, cookies, rolls, breads. All of it. It's a bit magical, adding all these basic ingredients in precise measurements, mixing it properly, all *just* so. But then you bake it, and instead of some boring result, it's beautiful melt-in-your-mouth goodness."

Mia grabs one of the yeasty, golden rolls and plops it on Charlotte's plate, then does the same to mine and her own. "I'll take some melty, yummy goodies too. Hey! You should do that as a job. It's not like you're happy at Blackwell's, so why not? Ditch your job and chase the yellow *biscuit* road to a bakery gig. Or open your own!" Mia claps like she's solved the biggest problem in the world, which honestly, if it were a math problem, she could likely do.

But Charlotte dips her chin, uncertain. "I don't know. It's more of a hobby right now, my sanity saver. Maybe one day." She sounds wistful and dreamy, but a little lost too. I know she struggles with her current job and the overall pall that is the culture at Blackwell's. Bland, dark, heavy with stressful responsibilities, and definitely not worth the amount of work she puts into her role as receptionist and screener.

But I get why she's doing it. If anyone would, it'd be me. It's not like I dreamed of being a waitress one day, but I'm doing what I need to so that the future is a bit brighter. Char's doing the same.

We sit down and each take several bites of our food. It's not as good as Henry's, but I'm mostly happy just to eat a full meal at one sitting, including, wait for it . . . a salad. An actual salad loaded with fresh, crunchy veggies. I could inhale it. But I savor each bite, thinking I should suggest to Henry that we include a salad option on the menu at the diner. It'd likely sell, and if it didn't, I could take the almost-stale lettuce and carrots home with me. Win-win.

Charlotte returns us to the previous conversation, even though she's the one who said she didn't want to talk about it. "Okay, so give us the Beefy McSmiles update. Just hold back on telling us about the magnificence of his hot dick, 'kay?"

Mia grins, pointing with a carrot stick. "You said 'hot dick' again. Preach it, girl, drop to your knees and send that message to the universe."

I save Mia from Charlotte's friendly backhand smack by answering, "He stayed over last night."

Both their eyes jump to me, locking me in place. I want to tell them everything, but at the same time, I want to hold it all tight to my chest. The memory is like a trembling soap bubble, perfect and swirling but so fragile that even a whisper could pop it, letting the magic fly out. So I stick to the bareboned basics.

"He came to the diner, and then we went for a drive, ended up at my place for the night. He left this morning before I got up but left me his car because he'd promised me a ride to the diner today to get my scooter. He's supposed to come by tonight too." I can feel the stretch of my smile, lips spreading ear to ear as the butterflies slam around in my stomach like it's a heavy metal mosh pit.

"Whoa. One taste and he gave you his car?" Char teases despite her protestations that she's not going to listen to commentary about sexual things.

"Izzy, I didn't know you had such a world-class cootch!" She laughs at her own outrageousness.

"Charlotte, please have some manners!" Mia admonishes. "We don't use vulgar terms like that. I prefer to think of it as a perfectly provocative punanny. Much more alliterative."

"Only if she used her punanny," Charlotte volleys back. "What if it was literally a booty call?"

"Hmm, good point. We need more data." They look back to me as they wrap up their comedy routine.

"Enough. You two are crazy. It was *not* a literal booty call," I hiss, trying not to laugh because I don't want to encourage them. I guess I never thought about the weird things we talk about because it was always about Mia or Charlotte, not my nonexistent sex life. But when the spotlight is shining on me, hot and bright, I kind of want to hide like a prudish nun, even though there is nothing puritanical about what I did last night.

Mia slurps from her Coke, her eyes twinkling. "Don't knock it 'till you've tried it." She sets her drink down, asking carefully, "So you're seeing him again tonight?"

"Yes, Mama Mia. He's coming by, and no, I don't know what the plan is. We'll take it as it comes, I guess." It's a reminder to myself more than anything. No expectations, no strings, just enjoy it while I can.

Mia looks to Char, but she holds her hands up, palms facing us. "Nope, I'm out on this little parental lecture. You don't want to know what I think."

I look from one to the other, almost too afraid to ask. "What?"

Mia inhales, still pulling words together as she starts. "Look, when you came in, it wasn't your swaggered walk that sold out what you've been up to. It was the smile on your face. I haven't seen that kind of smile on your face in forever. Like you're actually happy, like the world isn't a giant river of shit you have to slog through." I interrupt, making a disgusted 'ew' face that Char echoes.

Mia ignores us, pointing a blue-tipped nail my way. "You like this guy, a lot. And I love that you are putting yourself out there, and more importantly, putting yourself higher on the priority list. Just be careful, that's all."

Unexpectedly, I feel a sting in my eyes at my friend summing up so disgustingly and eloquently what I'm feeling. Happy, for the first time in a long time. "What if he hurts me?"

Char jumps in. "So what if he does? Just because it hurts, doesn't mean you quit. *Hello.*" She gestures at herself, and I wonder again what her latest dating disaster was, wishing she'd talk with us about it. "Of the three of us, you're probably the most well-equipped with handling some painful shit. Lord knows, you've been through the wringer. So who cares if this is a short-term thing or he disappears back to Albuquerque or wherever? You're having fun *now*. He makes you feel special *now*. You deserve that. And that's worth the heartache you might have at the end."

But the look on her face says that's not necessarily true. I can see the pinch around her eyes, the hurt it causes her to say these things. "Are you okay, honey? You can tell us, you know. Whatever the bastard did, we're on your side. Team Charlotte, all the way."

She smiles, though her eyes shine. "It's fine. Just got a little blindsided, but it's a temporary situation. I'm not heartbroken, more just . . . ugh!" She growls instead of labeling whatever it is she's feeling, and my heart hurts for her.

She shakes herself, flinging off the emotions that have overtaken our lunch and sitting up straight. "Okay, immediate subject change. Mia, you're up."

Mia grimaces, not meeting my eyes, and the mood shifts uncomfortably. I see her swallow and know something's wrong. "What's up, Mia? Thomas kick you out already? You can stay with me, you know?" It's meant to be light, because if I know anything, it's that Thomas Goldstone is one hundred percent head over heels for my girl, Mia.

She smiles, not laughing. "Okay, so I did a *thing*. A thing you're going to be mad about, but I swear it was with the best of intentions. Remember that, 'kay?"

My brow furrows. "What did you do?"

I glance to Charlotte, looking for some insight, but she shakes her head. "Nope, all her. But for the record, I agree that she was right. Just putting that out there, up front."

Mia licks her lips and continues. "So, after we talked before, I told Thomas about how Russell was jerking you around, scaring and threatening you."

My jaw drops, genuinely hurt. "That was private." Shame blooms, hot and acidic as it burns its way through my veins.

She nods, rushing onward before I can get too upset. "I know, but listen. So, I told him what was going on and that Russell had been a prick before but had really amped up his bully routine the last few months. So Thomas looked into it."

I glare at her, feeling betrayed but also wanting to know what Thomas found.

"Remember a few months ago when Russell went radio silent for a little while?" I nod, remembering how wonderful that month had been, but it'd been the calm before the storm, because he'd come back with a vengeance, demanding more than ever. "He was in jail for thirty days, ended up with some major legal fees and interest on some drugs he'd bought on credit. That's why he went so hardcore. He truly needs the money to make good on his own shit. And he's using you to do it."

I'm silent, processing everything she said. It makes sense, but Russell's reasons don't change the fact that I still legally owe him. "Crappy story, but that doesn't change the reality. He's got the legal right to charge me, and I'm going to pay, no matter how hard I have to work, because one day, I'll be caught up." I'm taking Mia's suggestion to heart, speaking it to the universe and hoping fate will help me make it come true.

She rubs at her cuticle with her thumb, showing her nerves, and I realize there's more. "What? Just spill it."

"I paid him," she mumbles under her breath, and I'm sure I misheard her, but then she repeats herself, a bit louder, a bit stronger. "I paid him. The back balance is paid in full, and I set up an account to release the monthly payments on a schedule so he can't hassle you anymore." Her expression is stony, daring me to fight this.

My first reaction is absolute, utter relief. A huge weight off my shoulders, a fear in my belly dissolving, and hope blooming in my heart. Then I realize . . . "I can't let you do that. I can't accept that kind of help, Mia. I appreciate it more than you know, but it's too much." I shake my head vigorously, like that'll make it not true.

She shrugs, like what I just said has no weight at all. "You can't undo it. Thomas helped me set it up so it's all trackable, no cash payments he can say he never got. Russell already took the back payment, so that's a wash. You could stop the monthly payments if you want to, but I'm begging you to let it go."

She reaches across the table, grabbing my hand. "Let me help you this way. I don't want the money back, but if you feel like you need to call it a loan, then wait 'till after you graduate and get settled in a job you love. Then worry about it. I can't sleep another night wondering if that asshole's gone off the rails and hurt you, because he's going to, Izzy. He's losing it, and you're going to be the collateral damage."

Char lays her hand on top of mine and Mia's, the stack of the Three Musketeers ready to tackle the world.

"She's right, Izzy. I know you don't want to hear it, but you need some breathing room, and getting Russell off your ass does that." Her voice is quiet but fierce, brooking no argument. "You're a grown ass woman, and you do a great job handling your own shit, but some problems you shouldn't have to bear on your own, especially when you have awesome friends who are happy to have your back."

I sulk a bit, wishing it hadn't come to this. My head shaking, I try not to be pissed at their ganging up on me, even if it's for a good cause. "I've been scratching and clawing for so long, fighting every step of the way. I won't give up on myself now." They both try to speak, jaws dropping open, but I cut them off. "This is my problem, and I'm going to take care of it."

Charlotte shakes her head, muttering, "Stubborn pain in the ass."

Mia takes the more direct approach, growling, "Your problem, my ass. We may not be blood, but we're sisters." She calms by the slightest margin, pleading, "I can't continue sitting up at night, worrying about you. Do you know that we check in with each other, call The Gravy Train sometimes, all just to make sure nothing has happened to you?"

Charlotte adds to the guilt trip, whispering, "We appreciate that you got a gun, got some training on shooting, but that was before we knew just how desperate Russell is. He's giving me the creeps, honey, and I have a bad feeling about this whole thing. Do what you need to so that you make peace with Mia's help, but take the money."

I look at them both, but they're dead serious. They mean business. And I guess I'd been so lost in my own struggles that I hadn't considered that they might be this worried about me. Hell, at this point, Mia might track Russell down herself and get some of her Russian dad's friends to make a visit. They're teddy bears, but they definitely don't look it.

Letting out a huge sigh, my shoulders sag in defeat. At the end of the day, I know they're doing this because they love me. But my God, they're killing me with this level of kindness.

"Fine," I relent. "But I'm paying you back as soon as I can."

Mia can't even manage to be gracious about winning what I'm betting she thought was a sure loss. She sticks her tongue out at me before saying,

"Sure thing. Your first payment is due the next night off you get, two complete hours jamming in a dungeon."

If anyone else said that to me, I'd probably punch them, but Mia's hardcore gaming addiction means there's at least part of her that's always yearning for hours spent in front of a screen with a controller in her hands. It's not my favorite pastime, but Mia is my bestie, so I've played more than my fair share of her favorite game, TERA.

"Deal, but I am paying you back for real."

Maybe they don't understand, but I have to do this. I can't just take the money. Crossing that line once makes it easier to do it again and again. Before you know it, you're saddled with so many emotional weights on your soul, you just give up.

I can't give up.

I won't give up.

"I gotta go, guys," I say, standing up. "But we're good. And really, thank you. I mean it, I really appreciate it."

Mia and Charlotte stand up too, wrapping me in a hug. I stand still for a moment, and then I give in and hug them back. Tears burn my eyes, and I choke out, "Thanks, guys."

"We love you, you know that, right?" Mia says, holding me at arm's length and obviously concerned she's pushed me too far but willing to do it anyway for my own good.

I nod, knowing she's also right. I might not have any blood family . . . but I've still got two sisters. "I know. I love you too."

Getting in the fancy SUV, knowing that this huge axe hanging over my head is gone, feels foreign, like this life isn't my own. But it is. With good friends and a nice guy, maybe I'm finally turning a corner and going to make some progress.

Maybe, after taking part-time classes for so long that I have teacher's aides younger than me, I can finally graduate. Then I will repay Mia.

"Think of it like a . . . private student loan," I tell myself, and though it's a piss-poor balm on my soul, it does help a little bit as I drive home to get ready for work.

I head inside, making sure to lock Gabe's Range Rover. Vash greets me with yowls for food, as always, and I pour her a bit, relieved to know I might be able to afford her next bag more easily.

The knock on the door makes my heart jolt, hope that Gabe stopped by instantly springing to mind. I rush to the door while trying to not get tangled up with Vash, who insists on winding herself around my legs.

"Vash! You trying to kill me, girl?" I ask, taking a huge step to avoid her tail. I'm still looking down at her loud meow as I open the door. "Hey, Ga—"

"What the fuck is going on? You got some bigshot sugar daddy now?" Russell barks, a distasteful sneer on his face.

"Fuck you, Rusty," I growl, moving to slam the door. But he shoves a dirty, cheap workboot-covered foot in the way, blocking me from shutting the door.

"We're not done," he says, an evil grin splitting his ugly face as he slams his palm to the door.

In a twisted way, I'm just thankful he didn't slap me that hard. That's what I've been reduced to, grateful to not be attacked. I wish I had my gun, even though I fought against getting it in the first place. Right now, I wish it was in my hand because I truly fear that Russell is going to push his way into my house. And then it'll just be the two of us.

And I realize that I'm in bigger trouble than I'd ever imagined.

# CHAPTER 15

## Gabriel

"*JEREMY!*"

*I run around the corner, where chaos reigns supreme. Out of the corner of my eye, I see a black car peeling out of the parking lot, but I'm focused on Jeremy, who's lying on his side.*

*People are screaming, some running, others frozen in place as they pale in terror.*

*And somehow, there's a group gathered around him . . . doing nothing. My brother's lying on the ground, and they're not even helping him up.*

*"Out of the fucking way!" I roar, shoving people aside. Someone grabs my arm, and before I know it, I turn and punch them just so I can break free. It's the next day before someone tells me it was Tiffany Washington whose nose I broke.*

*Jeremy's bleeding all over the blacktop. There's so much blood that I'm not sure how my little brother held so much inside him. I gather him into my lap, letting his head rest on my leg as I look down at him. "Jeremy . . . don't you fucking die on me!"*

*"It doesn't hurt, Bro," he whispers, blood trickling out of the corner of his mouth. "But—"*

*"No," I beg, pressing my hand over the hole in his stomach to stop him from leaking all over the place. But the pool of blood under him keeps getting bigger, and it's bubbling up around my fingers. "Jeremy—"*

*"I love you, Ga—" he says, but before he can complete my name, his body*

*breaks into convulsions. I hold him close, praying it stops, but when he stiffens and a blood-stained breath hits my face, I know.*

*"Jeremy . . . I promise I'll find who did this."*

I wake up in the afternoon dimness, the sun coming through the curtains in sanguine ripples, the dream that haunts my sleep coating my face in sweat. I wipe it away, reminded of how I had to clean Jeremy's blood off my body. He'd soaked everything, and later I found out that both bullets had gone all the way through, one of them clipping his spinal cord, which is why he didn't feel any pain.

Small comfort.

I shudder, sitting up in the cheap motel bed and burying my face in my hands, letting the pain wash over me for as long as it needs to. It's the only way I can face the rest of the day clear-headed.

I remember everything.

I remember watching the ambulance show up, the way they made a big show of trying to help Jeremy at first until they knew it was just that. I remember the look the two paramedics exchanged when they thought I wasn't looking.

I remember the funeral, the way everyone stared at me, the way my parents both seemed to have the light in their eyes just wink out as Jeremy's coffin was lowered into the ground.

I remember everything.

Since that moment, my brother's head cradled in my lap, his last breaths ghosting over my cheek as I pleaded with the Grim Reaper to take me instead, I have never let anyone or anything get in the way of my single-minded pursuit of Jeremy's killer.

I couldn't find out who'd done the shooting the 'proper' way, though I'd tried. The local police proved unable to find the culprit, and the local DA quietly dropped the matter since he was running for re-election and didn't want newspaper headlines about an unsolved murder of a dead teenager messing up his campaign.

So after a while, I turned my back on my friends, my family, my life, and immersed myself in the dark, dirty world that had spawned Jeremy's death.

Along the way, I've gotten plenty of dirt and blood on my soul. It started small, little steps that I thought would get me closer to some kind of answers. But along the way, I got lost. Even with my ethics, my own moral code and rules, the list of my sins is long. More than once, I've wondered if I've become just as evil as the monster I've been searching for.

But I hadn't questioned my life until her. I'd taken this job thinking it was going to be one like so many others, except I would finally get what I'd been searching for . . . the truth. Or at least some real intel that would send me in the right direction.

I wasn't expecting my princess, or this warm buzz in my chest every time I think of her. I pray the feelings I have for Bella aren't just my guilt catching up to me, latching on to an opportunity to feel 'clean' again. Whether she does that to me or not, and she does, she deserves better than to be used just so I don't feel so bad.

I climb out of bed and head to the shower. The hot water pulses on my neck and shoulders, cascading through my hair as I wash, trying to think.

"What should I do, Jeremy?" I ask the steamy bathroom air, trying to get some clarity. "How do I get out of this and do right by her?"

*How should I know? You're the one who's spent years learning how to be a killer. You've picked up a few other skills in that time too.*

Even in my head, my brother's biting sarcasm resonates, making me feel close to him.

I quickly wash and step out of the shower, drying off before checking my shave in the mirror. A day's growth . . . no need for my razor today. Instead, I head back into the motel room and open up my travel bag, grabbing jeans, a black T-shirt, and a red zip-up hoodie to get dressed. Leaving the motel room, I get into my 'work' truck and drive, trying to think about how I can protect Bella.

It's the million-dollar question that's been tearing me up since I snuck out of Bella's bed this morning with no more ideas than I'd had when I fell asleep with her in my arms.

It's a ticking time bomb situation and I have to make a move.

I pull over into the parking lot of a convenience store on the north side of town. There isn't much else around, and it's ancient enough that there are probably no cameras on the side of the building where I park.

Using the privacy, I pop open the console next to me and take out my burner phone. I dial a number from memory, knowing it'll be missed but that my recipient will get the voicemail and respond accordingly.

*"You've reached Larry's Plumbing. I'm out of the office. Leave a message."*

"Hi, I've got a problem with my toilet. The ball float won't do its job.

If you can replace it ASAP, I'd appreciate it," I say, using the necessary code words. "A rush job, if you're available."

I hang up, knowing I just tacked a hefty fee onto what I'm asking, but there isn't much I can do about it. I need help now.

It doesn't even take two minutes before my phone rings. I pick it up. "Hello?"

*"You called about a toilet?"* the voice on the other end asks. I've never met Larry the Librarian, but there are few in the underworld who don't know that slightly nasally voice. I do wonder just how he's able to pull off a front of being a plumber, but for all I know, that's just his damn cellphone line. *"A rush job?"*

"Yes, Larry, I did," I reply. I hear the grunt on the other end. He knows me and recognizes my voice. "I need a supplement."

*"Just a moment,"* Larry says, and a moment later, I hear an electronic beep in my ear. *"Go ahead. The line's scrambled."*

"I need everything you can give me on a man named Blackwell."

He whistles, long and low. *"I can't help you with that."*

"Excuse me?" I ask, surprised. Never in the years that I've been using Larry as my primary information broker has he refused a request.

*"No. As in, if you want to stay topside and not six feet under in an unmarked hole in the forest, you'll drop any inquiry into that man. There are people you should not look into. He's one of them."*

"That a threat?"

*"Just advice. From one professional to another. Goodbye, Gabriel."*

Before I can say anything else, Larry hangs up. I try the number back, but I don't even get the voicemail, instead getting a computer voice that tells me the number I dialed is no longer available.

Shit.

Not even a moment later, my other phone buzzes, and I see it's a text message.

*I want an update.*

Speak of the fucking devil.

"Fine, you want an update?" I ask, starting up my truck and pulling out of the convenience store parking lot. "I'll give you one," I say to myself.

# CHAPTER 16

## Blackwell

THE OFFICE IS CLOAKED IN SHADOW AS I SIT BEHIND MY DESK, waiting and plotting. I tap my hand on the desk, quickly shadow fingering my way through Ravel's *Piano Concerto For the Left Hand* to slow my rising blood pressure.

My father, decades ago, had forced a much younger and more malleable version of me to learn the piano as a means of structuring my thoughts. At the time, I'd hated the hours at the ivories, had pleaded to stop practicing, and the dismissive response my father gave had been the beginning of the end of any positive feelings I had about him.

Coupled with the look of disappointment in his eyes when I didn't perform to his satisfaction, on the piano and in my young life, it'd been enough to eventually make me hate the man. Enough that when he died, I got drunk . . . to happily celebrate his passing.

But still, the lessons stuck, and I often find myself absentmindedly pressing out the broad strokes of notes along a nonexistent keyboard.

The clock chimes eight, and my temper rises a notch. Previously, my guest had arrived early, but now, he is precisely on time. A telling change. While not disrespectful per se, it shows the variance in his feelings about this job, perhaps about me. It's a power move that shows his hand, whether he realizes it or not.

The door to my office opens, without a knock, and Gabriel Jackson comes in, unescorted this time. While that could be seen as a sign of danger, I know that my personal security detail frisked the man when he stepped off the elevator and they'd be in here at the press of a button if I needed them. Still, I won't be careless, considering how Gabriel's reputation precedes him.

"Mr. Blackwell."

My hand stops before the second movement of the piano piece, and I stand up, ignoring Gabriel's greeting to walk over to my wet bar. This is also a power move, one of many I employ regularly, allowing me to stand over my guest and to control the beginning of the conversation more readily. The show of good manners also makes people underestimate the degree of cruelty I am capable of.

I pick up a decanter of tequila, not yet looking at Gabriel. Over my shoulder, I toss, "You're late. In many senses of the word."

"Your security man was extra thorough," Gabriel says as I turn around, adjusting his tie as though my guard had left him disheveled. "I haven't been that violated since my last trip through airport security."

"When someone is as dangerous as your reputation says, it's in my best interests to be . . . cautious," I reply, pouring myself a glass and intentionally not offering one to him. "Have a seat."

Gabriel sits, and I lean against the bar to study him for a moment. Typically, I find that a silent, pregnant pause on my part leads others to shift and fidget nervously, especially when they are well aware they have not met my expectations.

But not him.

Gabriel sits still and patient, but ready, a light tension coiled through his muscles. Unable to wait any longer, I let him have the appearance of the upper hand by initiating. "So—"

"There have been developments," Gabriel says evenly, looking unfrazzled as I sip my tequila. "The job has required more finesse than I expected."

"How so? It should be a rather easy one for someone like you." It's a compliment and an accusation in one. "She's unprotected, unskilled, and slinging slop in a rundown diner. Unless your reputation of handling high-value targets is overinflated, this should've been the fastest contract you've ever completed."

I'm tired of excuses, but at the same time intrigued. I have hired gangsters before, usually as muscle to intimidate someone, but Gabriel Jackson is unique. His demeanor demands further study and a little bit of vigilance.

Gabriel nods, folding his fingers together. "Of course not. But she has very powerful friends."

"Which is why I hired you in the first place," I hiss, setting the tumbler of tequila down on the surface of the bar, realizing a beat too late that my outburst exposes my reasoning for being interested in a podunk diner waitress.

"Tell me why you hired *me*, not a thug, for this contract," Gabriel says lightly.

I scoff, dismissing the request. "I'm not here to stroke your ego."

He shakes his head but continues. "Of course not, but perhaps the answer to your concern is contained in the information you already have." He inclines his head, waiting patiently.

"You are thorough, careful, able to meet specific needs of unique jobs. Your reputation as a cold-blooded killer appeals to a certain type. In particular, it works well for power plays." Hmm, perhaps he is correct. The reasons I hired him and not a Craigslist-advertised hitman are rather apparent. "But the results are not holding to your hype," I finish icily.

"Rest assured, I've earned my reputation," Gabriel replies, still looking unruffled. "If you have any questions on my effectiveness, feel free to ask my former employers. They're all men and women who would stand equal to you in their respective fields."

I've been around a long time. I know a veiled threat when I hear one. And while I'm not normally a man to take threats lying down, I say nothing. The situation has become a bit of a chess match. Luckily for me, I don't play by the rules and am quite comfortable stacking the game in my favor.

However, while I have done many things that normal people would consider evil, Gabriel Jackson is the type of man that one keeps at arm's length when possible.

Besides, he's right. I know Gabriel's former employers, and what he says is the truth.

"Then what are the developments that are staying your hand?" I ask.

"As you're aware, I don't create collateral damage. And I will maintain that professional standard."

"You didn't answer the question. What is staying your hand?"

"Her friends," Gabriel challenges. "You said the job was to send a message to someone in her circle. I suspect you did not predict they would anticipate this sort of reaction from you, and she has been given extra protection." He gives me a hard look, daring me to contradict him. It's on the tip of my tongue to tell him that I know more about Thomas Goldstone that he ever will, but I bite that tidbit back, not wanting to further divulge my obsessive nature with an underling.

He continues at my silence. "Each time I've observed her at the diner, she has had three customers consistently with her. Their presence seemed beyond commitment to the subpar food, so I did some looking. I have yet to identify two of them . . . but one I know. She's a private bodyguard, used to work Secret Service a few years ago."

A small amount of pleasure blossoms that perhaps Gabriel has noticed the PI that I hired to follow him. I'm impressed to some degree. But he doesn't know who the man is or what he's been sent to do. Another play in my favor.

Though my PI hasn't mentioned anyone else in play, but perhaps his vision has been so laser-focused on Gabriel, his intended target, that he didn't parcel out other potential hazards to my plan.

"And this stops you how? You've already said you're not doing the job at the diner."

"I've seen this same woman drive by Isabella's house. It gives me *pause*," Gabriel says, drawing the word out. "Mr. Blackwell, understand this. I'm a professional, not a suicide bomber. I'm a man who has a particular set of skills and rules. If you wanted something done at any cost, you wouldn't have come to me."

"So are you telling me that you cannot complete your task?" I ask, wondering how badly this man is trying to fuck me. I wouldn't be surprised if he turned the whole situation around on me, considering my experience with men in his dark line of work, but he surprises me with his answer.

"Hardly . . . just that we should be careful," Gabriel replies. "It's for your protection as much as it is for mine. I just need time. Mr. Blackwell, I do play a rather effective seducer." His cold demeanor warms in a blink, a charming smile and boy next door joviality replacing his threatening aura.

"So I hear," I say tauntingly. It is a calculated comment, meant to make him feel pinned under a microscope and show that while he may think he has the upper hand in our conversation, he is woefully unprepared compared to a man like me.

His good-natured act disappears, icy frost in his dark eyes as they lock on me.

"Rest assured that I do what I need to so that the job is completed as agreed upon. I have already made initial contact." The words are correct, but they fight their way out, as if he'd do anything to not say them.

Interesting.

The question of whether Gabriel is becoming closer to Isabella as a means to an end or as something else still looms. I consider the options, and her seduction and humiliating end has a certain irony and justice to it that I can appreciate. Fine . . . maybe it will be worth it to see if Gabriel Jackson is actually going to do his job.

I sip my tequila, thinking. To know that Isabella Turner went to her grave degraded and heartbroken . . . that would be a sweet taste of revenge indeed. "Fine. But I want proof. And quickly."

Gabriel nods and gets up. "You can be assured you will get your proof. As soon as her bodyguards relax, I'll make my move."

Gabriel walks to the door, but before he can open it, I call out again. "Mr. Jackson, do not make me lose faith in you. I am not the sort of man you should double-cross."

Gabriel turns, his hand moving so quickly that I can hardly see it before a stainless steel throwing knife embeds itself in the middle of the wet bar, not more than three inches from my hand. "The same could be said about me. You need better security, but *currently*, I'm no threat to you. Goodnight, Mr. Blackwell."

Gabriel leaves, softly closing the door behind him, and for the first time in years, fear makes my hand shake as I set my tumbler down. I pry the throwing knife out of the wood, grunting with effort as the knife's embedded deeply in the antique oak.

The low lights in my office reflect off the muted silvery surface, and in it I can see a warped, wavy reflection of my face. It makes me look like a monster, and after a moment, I set the knife down, pondering the meeting.

First lesson. Gabriel Jackson is not a man to be trifled with. Young, yes. But foolish? Doubtful.

Still, the threats, the lack of fear Gabriel showed . . . they irk me. I'm a man used to having others quake at the very mention of my name. Even those of a caliber to afford hiring Gabriel would not normally go against me.

And yet, Gabriel hurled a knife in my office like it was nothing. Like *I* am nothing.

I need to know, is that the reaction of a man truly without fear, or an act born from fear, the violently desperate reaction of a cornered animal?

The tequila has warmed my stomach, but another warmth spreads through my body . . . the warm fire of anger.

The little shit, daring to threaten me.

Going over to my desk, I sit, my fingers mindlessly tapping out Ravel again as I consider my options.

"Fine . . . I'll give you some more rope," I finally say, opening my desk to search for a very specific phone. One I only use in very specific circumstances. "But only enough for you to hang yourself with if you betray me."

Dialing quickly, I wait as the line rings, bounced through at least two redialing services based off the changes in tone.

I detest using such devices, but in this case, it is as secure as it can be. Finally, after a long period of near-black silence, the line is picked up.

"Yes?"

"Jericho? This is Blackwell."

"It has been awhile. What can I do for you?" the voice says, giving me shivers. And that is why I am using it. If Gabriel Jackson can frighten me, then logically, hiring someone even more deadly, though not quite as *quiet* and certainly not as *ethical*, is the best option.

"I'd like to discuss a potential job offer."

There is silence on the other end of the line, and I wait patiently while Jericho considers his words. "I can be at SeaTac in two days."

"Excellent. I'll meet you there personally. Send me your arrival time."

The line hangs up, and I turn off the phone before putting it away.

My PI will continue to follow Gabriel, perhaps get a read on whether he is being sly or has fallen under Miss Turner's charm. And in two days' time, Jericho will take over this mission if it has not been completed successfully.

That piece of business taken care of, I stand up, reaching into my desk drawer for the small pistol that I keep, just in case.

I have a security guard to chastise.

# CHAPTER 17

## Gabriel

I PULL MY TRUCK OVER TO THE SIDE OF THE STREET, MINDLESSLY pulling off a near-perfect parallel parking job about a mile from the Blackwell building. Taking a few breaths, I go over exactly what Blackwell said, looking for tells, gaps, and information.

The back and forth nature of conversation is sometimes the worst enemy to a well-laid plan, sharing more than intended. Conversing with Blackwell had been more chess match and power posturing than usual, though.

Everything had been going mostly according to plan, and I'd even gotten a bit of insight about his motivation for wanting the hit on Bella. My bluff about security because of her big-wig friends had been just that, a bluff based on the research I'd done and the connections I'd made myself about what in Bella's life could put her at such risk. But Blackwell had all but said that he is using Bella to get at Thomas Goldstone. It seems like an obvious slip of the tongue, which makes me question the accidental nature of it.

But all in all, it'd gone pretty well, I'd even managed to put off his urgency at completing the job, until I'd mentioned using seduction as an effective tool.

*So I hear*, he'd said.

And the game had changed, pivoted on a dime.

In three words, he let me know that he was holding more cards than I'd prepared for.

I'd had to play along, telling Blackwell, the one man I don't want to look too closely at my relationship with Isabella, that I'd already begun a seduction course of action. Of course, the best cover is as close to reality as possible, so in making Blackwell believe I am seeing Isabella in order to complete his mission, perhaps I can distract him from my true intentions.

But that is only a temporary solution.

It's a tangled web of deception, and Blackwell is powerful enough that trying to outmaneuver him is a difficult and delicate undertaking.

I grin at the memory of throwing the blade near his hand. That had been delicate, but not difficult at all, and a show of danger is something Blackwell will respect.

I glance at the digital clock, glowing in the dim light of the truck cab. Eight thirty, just enough time to see Bella for dinner.

Quickly, I pull back into traffic and drive my truck to the motel. I change back into my casual clothes, running my hands through my hair to muss it a bit. Grabbing an Uber, I make my way to the diner.

But this time, as I walk inside, I glance around a bit more carefully. It's part of my nature, especially in my line of work, to be exceedingly careful. But despite Blackwell throwing out a hint about surveillance, I don't see anyone or anything suspicious.

Inside, I simply watch Bella for a moment before she realizes I'm here. She floats around the room as if she's dancing, her tennis-shoe-clad feet barely touching the floor as she does her best to provide good service to her customers. Warmth fills my heart, seeing her work so hard but never complaining, watching as people's blank faces transform into smiles from a conversation with her and the glow she is suffused with shining so beautifully from her very being.

And when she looks my way, her smile broadens. Amazingly, I did that. The man whom most people fear, whom they never want to see darken their doorstep, can bring happiness to this woman. This princess who deserves the best but only gets me.

"Hi, Bella," I say, laying a light kiss to her cheek. She blushes, pink heat beneath my lips for a split second before she pulls away.

"Hey," she says chirpily. "Kinda swamped, but have a seat anywhere and I'll grab you a menu."

I shake my head. "Just order something you'd recommend for me. I'll wait until you get your dinner break and we can eat together?"

She bites her lip, nodding like that sounds excellent. But before she can truly answer, a polite voice calls out, "Miss?" and almost with a click of her heels, Bella is back to work.

I sit down to watch her some more, but part of me is scanning the rest of the diner customers and the parking lot, wondering and thinking about Blackwell's words once again.

At some point, Martha walks up to talk to Henry, and we meet eyes through the kitchen window. She wags a finger, telling me to wait a minute, as if I'm going anywhere. After finishing her conversation with Henry, she comes over, sitting down in the booth across from me.

"I wanted to say thank you again for saving our girl the other night. And by 'our girl', I mean the Gravy Train's. Izzy is one of us, and while your protective instinct is rather chivalrous, and I like that, I'm a bit of a Momma Bear. I'm sure you understand."

I flash her my charming, boy-next-door grin, not for seduction but to charm her, nevertheless. "Of course. I understand and appreciate that you and the rest of the Gravy Train family have taken such good care of Bella. She's not an easy person to take care of, bound and determined to do it all on her own. I admire that about her, but no one is a solitary force. We all need a little support now and then."

Her lips press together, but the edges tilt up so I take that as a good sign. "Not to sound too old-school, but what are your intentions here?" Before I can answer, she adds, "And a short-term fling is a reasonable answer if it's the truth. I just want to know what Izzy's getting herself into so that we're ready to give her that support you talked about when it's needed."

I can't help but find Bella in the room, my eyes drawn to her as much as my heart is. My words are to her, though Martha hears them loud and clear. "I wasn't looking for her, at least not like this. But I found her, or maybe she found me? Either way, the result's the same, I guess."

I shrug, looking back to Martha. "I don't have a lot to offer, no sweet promises of whisking her away to an easy life, or even answers to your questions. Because the truth is . . . I don't know. All I know is that I like her a lot and I want to spend time with her, share the load she carries as much as she'll let me, and make her smile. I don't know if that's enough, but it's all I have."

Martha's eyes look a little glassy, which surprises me. I figured she would be a tough old bird, hardened by life and bitter about love, considering the sarcastic banter she shares with Henry. She swallows, dabbing at her eye. "That'll do, Gabe." She gets up, and I feel like the firing squad is inexplicably letting me go. But she pauses and lays a hand on my forearm. "For now."

I smirk, thinking that perhaps her biting nature is a bit of show and a bit of warning. Carefully, I ask, "Martha? Can I ask you for a favor?"

Her brow raises, but she nods. "Kinda felt like I just gave you one by letting you see Izzy, but shoot."

"I'd like to take Bella on a date. A real one, not just parking lot pie, though the pie was delicious. Is there any chance you could find coverage tomorrow so she could have the night off?"

Martha smiles big and bright at that. "Hell, yes. I can work some magic and make that happen. If, and only if, you'll work some magic and take her someplace nice."

"Deal," I say happily.

"Just one thing," Martha cautions, "you've got to tell her. Good luck getting her to forgo a night of tips for something as self-serving as a date. If you can get her to do that, you'll know she thinks you're really something special."

Martha's words ring in my head as I tell Bella the hopefully good news over the Belgian waffles she ordered for us.

"So, you just asked my boss if I could have the night off? Bit of an overstep, don't ya think?" she challenges. I can see the worry in her forehead, the lines popping out as she furrows her brow. I think she's doing math in her head. X hours times Y amount per hour plus Z in average tips equals . . . a very expensive date.

"It was. In my defense, I simply asked if it was possible from Martha's perspective. If you don't want to, we won't do it. On the other hand, if you do want to go out with me, on a real date where we get dressed up, I pick you up and tell you how nice you look, and we go out for a quiet dinner, just the two of us, then you're free and clear at work." I give her the full-wattage smile, hoping the hard sell was enough.

She laughs, loud and open-mouthed. "Ooh, you're playing dirty. I like it. All right, you got yourself a date." She leans back in the booth, looking toward the kitchen, and yells out, "Well-played, Martha. Guess I'll be needing tomorrow night off."

Martha answers with a wink. "Have fun, you two. Don't do anything I wouldn't do . . . back when I was twenty-five!"

Bella turns back to me, snickering. "That leaves pretty much everything open. Martha once got arrested for protesting by streaking across the football field during the last two minutes of a homecoming game."

I laugh, but fight imagining it in my head. "Ah, the perils of being young and stupid."

Bella shakes her head, eyes wide in horror. "Uhm, this was about five years ago. She was protesting the boys getting away with all sorts of shit under the guise of 'boys will be boys.' She stood right up in front of the judge and said, 'Well, women will be women then too, I suppose.' She didn't even get community service."

"Let's maybe aim to not get arrested at least, though you could streak through the privacy of your own home and I'd chase you straight to the bedroom."

Bella touches the tip of her nose, winking. "I'll remember that."

Her dinner break is nearly over all too soon. She shoves a last bite of waffle into her mouth and wipes her lips with a napkin. "I'd better get back to it. You gonna hang around again tonight?"

I can hear the heat in her tone, the want so blatant and sexy. But I can also see the faint smudges under her eyes. She puts on a great act, a good front, but my girl is tired and needs some sleep.

Plus, I should try to figure out how Blackwell is getting his information before I spend the night again. For Bella's sake and my own.

"Tonight, I want you to go home right after you get off work, take a hot bath, drink a glass of wine, and think about our date tomorrow. I know it's customary for the guy to pick the place, but I'm not all that familiar with Roseboro and I want this to be exactly what you want it to be, so can you choose a restaurant. Anywhere, anything, your wish is my command, Princess."

She sighs out a happy breath, like the mere idea of that sounds blissfully amazing.

"I'll pick you up tomorrow night at seven thirty." I get up, and though we're in the middle of the diner, I can't help but wrap my hand around the back of her neck, weaving my fingers into her hair. I lean down, kissing her softly, memorizing her taste and getting my fill to last the next twenty-four hours.

She's dazed for a moment, and like a proud peacock, my ego inflates that somehow I can kiss her stupid because I'm feeling a bit buzzed on her myself.

She clears her throat and pats her apron. "Oh, let me get your keys for you. Thanks for the sweet ride today, by the way. And the breakfast goodies. I think Vash was swayed by your milk offering."

"That was the intent. To win her over—and the human she lives with."

# CHAPTER 18

## Isabella

IT'S CREEPING UP ON MIDNIGHT WHEN I FINALLY PULL MY SCOOTER IN the gate at home. I do a look-around to make sure Russell isn't lurking around, but it seems clear. Until I get to my doorstep.

There's a brown grocery bag propped against the door. My first thought is a bomb because I watch too much news on the evening shift at the diner. Then my more reasonable brain considers that a bomb is highly unlikely. I mean, aren't those supposed to come in boxes or something?

Still, I kick it with my toe while holding my face as far away from any explosive contents the bag may hold.

It crinkles.

Curious, I look inside. And my heart stops. Literally, jerks to a stop at the overwhelming kindness.

I pick up the bag, unlocking the door and hurrying inside. After locking the door behind me, I spread out Gabe's sweet gift on the kitchen table. There's an industrial-size bag of lavender Epsom salts, two masks, one for my hair and one for my face, a candle, a bag of chocolates, and a chilled bottle of wine.

It's late, and I should fall into bed. But with all this bounty, I can't help but want to self-indulge. Just this once.

So I splurge, doing as Gabe asked and taking a pampering hot bath be-fore bed. It's luxurious, decadent, and just what I needed. And as I slide into my cotton sheets with moisturized skin, dreams of tomorrow pop into my head like bubbly possibilities.

I could get used to this.

I should count my lucky stars that I actually do have some nice clothes. Once upon a time, I used to spend hours thrifting to find deals on clothes that were cute and affordable. After Reggie died and things became much more desperate, clothing had been the least of my concerns, but tonight, I'm glad to have kept some of the nicer things I got on clearance at the Roseboro Thrift.

"Vash, what do you think? Black?"

I hold up the black dress with a long, diagonally-cut skirt, but Vash lifts her chin, clearly unimpressed.

"Okay . . . green? I could add a scarf, maybe?"

*Meow.*

"Critic. Okay, what about the red one?"

She tosses her head, not amused and stalking off toward the kitchen in that way only Vash can. "Fine . . . I'll do it my damn self!" I call after her swishing tail. "It's my first official date in I don't know how long. I'm not going to trust the opinion of a creature that hacks up hairballs anyway!"

I do end up deciding on the red piece, mainly because I've got the best heels to go with it. They were a gift from Mia, of all people, from way back in her crazy single college days when she wanted a wing girl to go out clubbing with, and as I pull on the black open-toed strappy heels, I twirl, sending her another round of thanks.

"God, they feel good," I murmur as I turn this way and that, wishing I had a full-length mirror to see how my legs look. Yeah, I'm just in my best lingerie and heels, so I probably look more like a stripper than anything else . . . but I feel sexy as fuck doing it. "Been too long since I felt like this."

Getting into the dress is a lot easier than it looks. There's no zipper but instead a swath of stretchy fabric that I sort of wiggle and shimmy into until it hits my hips and then tumbles to my knees.

Pulling my hair back, I imagine myself, and finally can't resist going to the bathroom and doing my best to see what I can in the tiny mirror above my sink. I can't see much, but what I can see—

"Vash!"

*Meow?*

"Gonna need you on 9-1-1 duty when Gabe gets here, babe. Because he might just have a heart attack once I get my makeup done."

I start on my eyes. I have dark eyes, so going too smoky on the eyeshadow and liner just makes me look like a raccoon, but I do want to look sultry and sexy. Thankfully, this red dress gives me just what I need, and a swipe of black eyeliner tilted up at the end brightens me up a little bit.

My lips I go deep red, lush and shiny, wanting to draw Gabe's attention to everything I'm saying all night. If he's thinking about what else my lips could be doing . . . well, that's a bonus as well.

I know I've for damn sure been thinking about what his lips could do to me.

Finally, I'm done, and I do my best with my hair, pulling the chocolate curls over one shoulder to trail down over my breast.

God, I feel beautiful.

There's a knock at my door, and I hurry out, doing my best to run in heels. "Who is it?" I ask. I assume it's Gabe, but after Russell's boot-meets-door performance, I'm not chancing it.

"It's me, Princess," a muffled voice says through the door, and I can't help but giggle as I unlock it for him.

"Gabe, I'm hardly a—" I start before all the words in my head dry up.

He's amazing, in a dark black suit that highlights his dark hair and bright brown eyes, his smile dazzling in the dim light of my porch. Forget the date. We're already wearing too many clothes.

Gabe looks me up and down. "You look stunning."

"Uhm, thanks," I stammer, not so smoothly, my heart hammering in my chest as he looks at me with undisguised attraction and appreciation. I've never, in my entire life, felt more desired than I do right now. "You look . . . wow."

"Thank you," Gabe says, half bowing, but I saw his pleased smirk. "So . . . shall we?"

I step back, waving him in. "Do you want to come in? I need to grab my purse."

Gabe doesn't move though. Well, he doesn't come inside. But he leans against the side of the door frame. "If I come in there, we're not leaving. Not with you looking like that, and not with what I see in your eyes right now. And I really want to take you out, treat you right, and show you off in that red dress. Grab your purse, Princess."

His voice is deep and rumbly, nearly a growl of restraint that turns me on, makes me think his coming inside to rip this dress off me is date enough.

But my heart overrules my pussy.

I want to be wined and dined, romanced and wooed. And as frivolous as that sounds, it's the truth. So I leave Gabe at the door, picking up my purse. It doesn't match, but it's the smallest I have and mostly black.

The candy red of his SUV nearly matches my dress, a happy coincidence, but in some small way, it makes me feel like I belong here as Gabe opens the passenger door to help me in like a gentleman. He climbs into the driver seat and begins backing out, asking me, "Did you decide where we're going?"

"I have," I reply but keep some surprises to myself. "Just turn where I tell you to."

It doesn't take long to get to our destination, a slightly worn-down Chinese restaurant in an older part of town. Gabe says nothing as we pull up in front of Golden Dragon, but he escorts me inside, holding out an elbow for me to take and then pulling out my chair for me as we sit down at one of the tables. Coming around, he sits in his own chair, the old green vinyl looking out of place considering the glitz and glam of our clothing.

"I guess you'd like to know why here?"

"I'm curious," Gabe admits, glancing around but quickly re-centering on me. "But I trust your instincts. One, you know Roseboro better than I do. And two, you work in the food service industry, so I'm sure you know where all the good spots in town are, both five-star and hole-in-the-wall."

He's right, but I can appreciate that he trusts me because I know Golden Dragon isn't exactly impressive-looking. "Good point," I reply, wondering just how good my chopstick skills are after so long. "Although it's not just the food quality that brings us here."

Gabe hums, guessing my meaning. "History?"

I sigh, the memories already rolling as I look around the restaurant. "This was one of the few places that I could go with my aunt. Great food that won't break the bank."

Gabe checks the menu, his eyes scanning quickly up and down the four columns. "I'm betting you had the spicy chicken combo platter?"

The eight-dollar special . . . my throat catches as I remember the nights we'd come here. "Good guess. We used to share it. It's nothing fancy, but it was always special when we came. I've had at least a dozen holiday meals here."

"Then let's celebrate it in the way it's meant to be," Gabe says. "Your aunt did what she could, and she did it with love. Whether it's a five-star spread or a single Hostess cupcake . . . it's the company that makes it special."

I blink, looking at Gabe in amazement. The tears are gone, and what's replaced them is a new feeling, honest pride. "How . . . how do you do that? How do you always know what to say? To make me smile. To make me not ashamed."

"Why should you be ashamed?" Gabe asks, looking confused. "From everything you've told me, you're one of the strongest people I've ever met. You should be proud of what you've accomplished and of what you are still trying to do."

"I've spent so much time zombieing my way through life," I reply, trying to explain. I take a deep breath and hold it before letting it out. "And there are still times when I think I'm never going to be free of it. I'll always be 'that poor girl', either because of losing my parents or because of how Reggie and I struggled. But I don't want to live that way forever. I want to live again, to be bright and free. To feel like I did when you and I were in that clearing on the mountain."

"You can do just that," Gabe replies.

I duck my head, not able to meet his eyes for this part despite his assertion that I shouldn't be ashamed. "It's safer, easier to stay asleep at the wheel, to drudge through and follow the plan I set ages ago, with hopes that it'll all be better one far-off, distant day in the future. To live big, to be able to actually see the top of the mountain . . . to do that now, I need a reason," I admit.

It's a big request of him, even though I'm being fairly vague in order to hedge my bets. "If I'm going to wake up, take that risk, I need a reason."

Gabe reaches across the table, taking my hand. "I hear you, and I will happily help you up every step of the mountain. But I want to be clear on something. *You* are reason enough. You deserve to wake up and *own* every second of your life, enjoy them now, not just later when you feel like you've earned it. You've already earned it, Bella. But I would be thrilled to enjoy it along with you."

His answer is somehow even more perfect, though I definitely notice he's not making any undying professions of love, but it's far too soon for that. "I'd like that," I say, his words filling gaps in my spirit I didn't know were there because I've been too busy filling the hole in my belly with the bank account leaking money like a sieve. "It might take a while, though."

"I know."

With a start, I remember my manners. "Thank you for the goodies last night. They were unexpected and wonderful. I definitely enjoyed every second of that bath."

His grin goes lascivious, and his eyes dart downward to where I know I'm giving him a tantalizing glimpse of cleavage. "God, I'm picturing you naked in the tub, bubbles piled up over your nipples and curled tendrils escaping a bun to fall down to your neck, where I could nibble and taste the lavender. Tell me all about it."

There's a hint of cockiness to the order, not bossy but bold, and I'm more than happy to meet it with my own sassiness.

"Well, I got home and thought the bag was a bomb, or maybe a dog-shit surprise, but it was so much better, of course." He laughs at my crazy ideas, urging me to continue with a squeeze of my hand. "It was wonderful. I filled the tub with water all the way to the top, as hot as I could get it, and soaked in the Epsom salts until I was a prune. And like some girl on tv, I ate chocolates and drank wine while I sat there, boiling like one of Henry's potatoes."

"I think my fantasy was of the sexier variety, but I'm so glad you enjoyed them."

The waitress comes by, and I order two of the spicy chicken combo platters. "Ooh, big spender," Gabe teases. "Can we get some of the almond cookies for dessert?"

"If you behave," I tease. "Speaking of, I did the 'tell me about yourself' spiel, complete with tears and trotting out my trauma. You have yet to do yours, so tell me about yourself, Gabe."

I know I sound a bit stiff, like this is a job interview, but if so, he's already got the position. Any and all of them he wants.

"I'm not sure where to start," he says, and I can read the tension around his eyes.

"Just start at the beginning, like 'once upon a time, a beautiful baby boy was born.' Or stick to the basics, like do you have parents? Siblings? Where are you from? What do you do?"

He nods, dropping his chin before answering, "Yes, I have parents, no springing forth, fully grown, from a plant pod. I had a brother, but he died." He swallows. "Not a story I want to relive right now. Sorry."

I bite my lip, sad to see his pain and feel his loss so sharply. "No worries. But I'm here if you change your mind and need someone to talk to."

One side of his mouth lifts in that half-smile he has when he's not sure. It makes him look like a sweet troublemaker.

"As for what I do, I guess you'd say I'm a consultant."

"A consultant? Well, that just clears up everything," I joke, his answer clear as mud. "What do you consult?"

"I'm a systems troubleshooter," Gabe explains, though he again somehow clears nothing up. "Companies or people call me, and I come in and consult with them on solutions. Sometimes the problem's easy, sometimes it's hard. But it's fun."

"And you . . . I mean, where are you based out of?" I ask, and Gabe shrugs. "What's that mean?"

"It means I have enough work that I usually live out of motel rooms. If I were hard-pressed, I'd say I'm a Red Roof guy. I mean, I did three months in Calgary once, nearly six months in New York, but then I've done jobs as quick as two or three days and I'm on the road again. When I don't have work, I'll sometimes use the gap time to relax, take a vacation or something, but other than a PO Box for the IRS, I don't really have a place."

"I can't decide if that sounds lonely or adventurous," I say honestly. "Having never been anywhere, the thought of constant travel is appealing, but not having a home base seems so nomadic. I'm literally fighting to keep the only roots I have, even when it'd be so much easier to let them go."

His face falls, and he shakes his head. "You have the home you shared with your aunt to hold those memories, so you clutch to it, understandably. When my brother died, my family basically fell apart, and the memories I hold of home, history, family, they're all in my mind, in my heart. So anywhere I go, they're with me. He's with me."

He's quiet for a moment, and I can tell he's tortured by the ghosts haunting him right now. Curiosity has me wanting to ask a million more questions, but I can respect that he might not be in a place to share right now, so I redirect the conversation to lighter topics in the hope of lifting his spirits once again.

"So in your vast experience of traveling the world, can you use chopsticks? Because I'm seriously doubting my skills."

His lips curl in slow-motion. "I can absolutely use chopsticks. I have all sorts of skills that'd surprise you."

Something in his tone sounds like he truly believes that, which makes me all the more tingly to see him use each and every one of those skills.

# CHAPTER 19

## Gabriel

WHILE I STOP AT ONE BEER, BELLA ENJOYS HERSELF, WHICH IS just what I want. She deserves to relax, have some fun. There's going to be too much bad shit coming, and maybe this fun night will help her through those times.

"You wanna know my personal record of how many shifts I've worked in a row?" she asks as she sips at her third Mai Tai. "Too many!" she laughs, but then her eyes narrow in thought. "Actually, I think twenty is my record. Can you imagine? Twenty days in a row, no time off at all, serving those big ass blue plate specials?"

"I bet you put some muscles on during that stretch."

"Yeah, right." She snorts but then says proudly, "That was a long stretch, but I made my tuition payment in cash one week before the semester started."

"I have to ask, why stay there?" I ask as I sip at my green tea. "You work too many hours for too little pay. I'm sure you could find something better, even if it was only temporary."

"Maybe I could, but I like it there. I love the people, and Martha works with me. That reminds me of a funny story, actually. Well, it's funny now, looking back, but it definitely wasn't at the time," she says, not slurring her words but definitely getting giggly.

"What happened?"

"It was right after my aunt passed, and I'd been fired from my retail job because I took off two weeks to grieve and plan a funeral. I had no idea what I was going to do for money or even food. I'd applied at a ton of places but just wasn't getting any bites."

Her eyes have gone hazy, her mind faraway in the past, so to bring her back, I tease lightly, "You're right, this story sounds hilarious."

It works as she rolls her eyes, a small smile curling her lips. "Anyway," she draws out sassily, "I was at The Gravy Train and ordered a sausage biscuit breakfast, thought I had the five bucks on me. When I went to pay and looked in my wallet, what I thought was a five was a grocery list. I was dead-broke, literally with just a few cents to rub together, and my bank account was on zero. I was so embarrassed."

"What'd they do?"

"They called the cops!"

My eyes go wide, thinking of sweet and protective Martha and her beleaguered husband calling the police on a poor, broken-down young woman. "No way."

"Hell, yes, they did!" Bella laughs. "But while we were waiting, Henry started lecturing me on looking for handouts and being sneaky about stealing from good people. Somewhere in the middle of his Disappointed Dad routine, he threatened to call my parents, wagging finger and all."

She mimes a stern face, pointed finger rant, then her face softens. "I told him I didn't have any. That stopped him short and he got real quiet. His lecture turned into more questions, and I was too raw to hide anything about Reggie or my situation. By the time the cops got there, he said it was a misunderstanding and gave the cops a coffee each to go. I apologized for the mistake, promising that I'd pay him back as soon as I could, but he put me to work washing dishes that day. He sent me home with a to-go box . . . and ten bucks tucked inside the lid. Within a month, I was waiting tables. So they've always been good to me. They're like family to me, and in a way, I feel like I owe them. They saved me when things were really dark and have had my back with schoolwork and schedules, cheering me on through every final and project."

I nod, thinking about the mental debts we place on ourselves. "I'm glad you have them and they have you. It sounds like a match made in heaven."

Bella inhales, confiding, "I like to think Reggie sent them to me, knowing I'd need someone. Martha and Henry are the closest thing I have to parents now."

Her words pierce the air, and she looks down, clearing her throat. I reach across and take her hand. "It's always good to have folks you can turn to. I wish I still did."

"Your . . . your family's gone too?" Bella asks.

"My parents are alive, out there somewhere." I glance to the window, like my mom or dad might unexpectedly be standing there, but of course, they're not. "But when my brother died, our family did too. We didn't know how to love each other through it, and our grief took us further and further apart. I left as soon as I could, and my parents divorced shortly after that, both of them moving to the other side of the country to get away from the memories. I think seeing each other just reminded us of who was missing. Of the family we'd never have again. We kinda silently agreed to just let it all go to not hurt each other anymore."

"I'm sorry," she says simply. I'm glad she doesn't give me shit for not seeking my parents out, especially considering her past.

It's a complex thing, a parent-child relationship, and though it should have a foundation of love and be sprinkled through with happy memories and hopes for the future, sometimes, that's just not possible.

"The last time I saw my mother, she accidentally called me Jeremy and we both froze," I admit, a story I've never shared with anyone else. "I know she didn't mean anything by it, certainly didn't wish it'd been me and not him, but it was a dagger into both our hearts. I think *not* seeing me, with my similar appearance and my future he'll never have, makes it easier to shove it all down and live on superficially without dwelling. At least that's what I tell myself when I think about reaching out to them and need to talk myself out of it."

Bella reaches out and places her hand on top of mine. "Thank you."

We finish our meal, sharing mostly happier stories and learning about each other. I have to be careful to not divulge too much, which is surprisingly hard. I'm accustomed to lies and half-truths, diversions and distractions. But I find myself wanting to tell Bella everything, ugly truth and all, but that's a danger neither of us can afford. So I stick to lighter times and she seems to follow suit.

By the time we finish, my belly hurts as much from the laughter as the overabundance of spicy glazed chicken and rice, and Bella's cheeks are stained a soft pink.

As we walk out, Bella's good humor and a bit of the alcohol sillies amps up. "I just had a *date*." She does a cute wiggly-ass dance move that makes me think dirty thoughts about smacking that round globe before she teeters a little.

"Whoops!"

"*Had?* It's not over yet, Princess," I correct her, steadying her. "I didn't know you were a lightweight with the Mai Tais."

"I'm not a lightweight!" she protests, eventually standing steadily on her own. "I just haven't had a real drink in like . . . months. But mostly, this is just me being . . . happy." She smiles, looking clear-eyed, and I realize it's true. She's not tipsy, or at least not too tipsy.

"Are you sure I shouldn't take you home, give you a polite kiss on the cheek at the door, and go back to my motel room?" I ask, smirking but serious. "I wouldn't want to take advantage."

Bella blanches and slaps my chest. "If you even think of doing that, I'm going to be so pissed at you I'll sic Vash on you!"

"Ooh, not that! She's a demon beast," I deadpan. "Guess I'd better plan to stay a while, then?" It's not until I say the words that I realize how much I truly want to stay with Bella, not just tonight, but for a lot longer.

A tiny whisper in my head says *forever*, but I quiet it with reminders that I'm not the type of man a woman like Bella needs. Scarred, monstrous, feared, with blood-covered hands and a sin-soaked soul is not the way to reach the mountaintop she wants.

I turn the radio on low as we drive back to Bella's house. She's changed the station, and while The Weeknd isn't my normal cup of tea, the intense sexual beat of *Call Out My Name* supercharges the atmosphere inside my Range Rover. I look over at Bella, who's smiling, biting her lip as she tugs at the hem of her dress, sliding it up her knee and making it hard to tell myself that she's not mine, not for me, because fuck, do I want her, and she wants me in return.

"Gabe?"

"Yes?" I ask, but I see that she's prompting me, my eyes darting back and forth from the road and her creamy thighs.

I clear my throat, reaching over and putting my hand over hers just before she can reach her panties. "If you don't stop, I'm either getting in an accident or pulling over and taking you in the back of this vehicle."

Bella chuckles and takes my hand, placing it very high on her left thigh. "I'm so tempted, but I'll be good and wait." I give us both a taste, a promise of what the night holds by drawing a small circle on her satin skin with my thumb.

When we get back to her place, Vash is waiting for us, yowling in protest when the door opens. "Oh, hush, you spoiled brat!" Bella tells her, feigning a scolding, but the love is apparent. "Go catch a mouse or something!"

I reach down to pet her, hoping the milk offering will have made her friendlier toward me, but she hunches her back and eyes me warily. No hisses at least, so maybe I'm making progress.

Before I can get Vash to come to me, Bella shuts the door and pulls me to her. Cat forgotten, I press Bella against the wall, kissing her deeply as I lift her leg, running my hand up her thigh and under the hem of her dress. Her skin's electric, and as I reach higher, cupping her ass, she moans into my mouth.

"Knew I loved these heels," she purrs as I massage her cheek, pressing her ass back into my hand. "Just the right height."

I growl in her ear, my desire taking over. Last time, I held back, letting her have what she needed . . . but while I've opened up to her tonight, I haven't told her everything.

And that everything is more than she can even guess. It's what drives me, telling me that if I'm going to make this woman mine, then I'm going to make her *mine*.

It's the only way we'll survive.

"Bathroom," she purrs, pushing my jacket off my shoulders to fall to the floor.

I pull her to me, kissing her hard as we stumble toward the bathroom, a trail of clothing in our wake. I'm dimly aware in the little corner of my mind that never turns off that the door to her 'painting room' is shut.

All questions about why are driven from my mind as we enter the bathroom, the tile cool on my bare feet. I step back, watching Isabella strip the rest of the way for me.

The shower head angles over an old-fashioned clawfoot tub, surrounded with a clear plastic curtain that she pushes out of the way. I watch Isabella reach over and turn on the water, and I can't help but give her ass a good smack, making her gasp.

She leans over a little more, and her legs part invitingly, giving me a view of her pussy. "Stay there."

I kneel and bury my tongue in her from behind, my hands pulling her to me. I'm rewarded with a deep moan as I bathe her pussy with a wide, flat tongue, feasting on her essence.

"Yes, Gabe, yes!" she cries softly as I slip inside her. She's sweet and spicy, and I lick furiously, thirsty for her sweet slickness, desperate to drink her down.

Isabella pushes back into my face, her knees quaking when I find her clit with my thumb as my tongue thrusts inside her. Her head drops, a deep moan of pleasure tearing through her as her knees unlock. If it wasn't for her hands supporting her on the high side of the tub, she'd collapse, but I don't let up, wanting to wrench every bit of pleasure from her that I can.

"That's it, Princess . . . give me your come," I growl against her puffy, sopping-wet lips. The sounds coming from my mouth are deep, primal as I suck and lick, my tongue snaking as deep as I can inside while I consume her.

I'm addicted. I'm never giving her up. She's mine.

Isabella's body shakes as she finds the deep release I've been driving her toward, whimpering as her orgasm shakes her, and I pull back, holding her as she trembles. "You're mine," I whisper in her ear, letting my possessive thoughts take weight in the words. "You're mine, and I'm going to show you what that means."

She nods, her legs still spaghetti as we get into the shower. The warm spray feels amazing on my back as I hold Bella close, my cock rock-hard and pressed against her back.

I let her recover, picking up the bar of soap and washing her body, my fingers tracing the curves of her stomach and hips before massaging her breasts.

Her nipples pebble tightly under my slippery fingers, and she turns her head, looking at me with lust-filled eyes. "You . . . I need you, Gabe."

"You have me," I reply, kissing her lips softly at first. Isabella turns around and wraps her arms around my neck as the warm water cascades over us, our bodies slipping together as we kiss again, need building quickly between us. I lift her leg, holding under her knee until her foot finds the rim of the tub as I push her back, pinning her against the tile wall.

"Tell me what you want," I command, looking in her eyes. "Tell me who you belong to."

"You . . . I want you to fuck me with that big cock," she rasps.

My lips smash against hers the second she gets it out, kissing her hard. My hips drive forward, and I'm rewarded with her cry into my mouth as my cock splits her open, swallowed by her tight pussy until I'm deep inside her. Her arms tighten around my neck, holding me still as she adjusts, and I grind against her, letting her feel me until she relaxes, and I feel her nod slightly against my neck.

"Please."

Her voice is soft, barely audible over the rush of the shower spray, but it's all I need as I pull back and start pumping my hips hard, my cock thrusting in and out of her as Bella holds onto me. The slightly curved bottom of the tub and the angle of our bodies mean I can't go full out, but somehow, that makes each stroke even more enticing.

Her pussy squeezes me as our bodies press against each other, her nipples dragging over my chest as I pump in and out of her, our bodies moving not frantically, but with a harmony that grows within the confines of the shower.

"Give it to me, Gabe," Bella grunts in between my strokes, her eyes looking deep into mine. A little hope flares inside me that there are layers to what she's saying, and my cock swells, emotions adding to the pleasure pulsing through me with every slide of my cock in and out of her body.

"You're mine," I growl again, looking in her eyes and hoping she can understand that my two words mean a lot more than just my cock stretching her and setting her nerves on fire. She moans, and my hips speed up a little faster, my toes gripping the porcelain as best I can as the two of us come together, our bodies shaking as we approach the precipice.

Her pussy's a vice around my shaft as the head of my cock rubs over the spots that she loves best, her stomach clenching as I pound her, deep and powerful. Bella tightens, her breath hitching as she's driven to the very edge, and I kiss her hard again, swallowing her cries and biting her lip as I slam into her.

Once again, she shatters, her legs giving out, and she's held up by just my arms and my cock, buried deep inside her perfect pussy. Her convulsions shake through her body and my cock, triggering my own climax. Lost in the waves of pleasure, I growl into her mouth, pulling out at the last possible second to cover her ass with my cream as my fingers dig into her hips, holding her still.

We stay there, frozen in our climax until the water starts to cool down, and I pull back, shutting it off. "Guess we ran out of hot water."

Bella chuckles and nods, getting out. "Take me to bed."

I wake as close to paradise as I've ever been. Bella is nestled in my arms, her soft warmth pressed against me and her lips parted as she snores lightly, squirming every once in a while in her sleep.

She's like this adorable combination of cuddler and gymnast that woke me up more than once as we slept. She'd turn, move, and nearly flip over me at times, all while totally asleep.

Her most recent position has her sleeping with her knees tucked up underneath her, her head turned toward me and her hair half lying over her eye. I run my hand over her back, and she hums, smiling in her sleep.

I don't wake her up, even though the touch of her thigh against my cock is certainly waking *it* up this morning, but I let her rest.

Instead, I watch her, my hand tracing soothing circles on her back until she smiles. "I can feel you looking at me."

"Didn't know I had such a weighty gaze," I murmur, kissing her forehead. "How're you this morning?"

Bella stretches out, turning toward me and half opening her eyes. "I'm pretty sure I'm going to be walking funny again."

"Are you saying I should be gentler?" I ask, making her laugh softly and snuggle against me, but I can feel her shaking her head, almost as if she's embarrassed. "No?"

"I want it every way I can get it," she promises me bravely, nuzzling under my chin. "But before anything else, I need two things . . . brushed teeth and a potty break."

I pull her into my arms, kissing her gently. "Deal."

Bella goes to take care of her bathroom needs while I do my best to make peace with the cat, giving her a bit of canned tuna in her bowl. Vash warily looks me up and down, then struts by like the actual owner of the house she is before starting to eat.

"Yeah, I see you, Vash. I get that you're the boss. Maybe we can call a truce?" She doesn't answer, but her tail waves lazily left to right, so I take it as a sign that she's considering my offer.

I go back to the bedroom and pull on my pants before running my hands through my hair to tame the crazy mess I'm rocking. I'm barely half-dressed when Bella comes into the bedroom, her face freshly washed and looking as pristine and beautiful as an angel. "Bathroom's yours."

"Thanks," I reply, going in and washing my face. Using my finger, I do a quick little rub over my teeth, hoping it's enough to kill the morning breath, and while I do, I hear someone knock on the front door.

I'm instantly on alert, realizing how quickly I relaxed into being here with her and how readily I forgot about the dangers lurking.

As Bella comes down the hallway, I poke my head out of the bathroom. "Hey, let me—"

"I got it," Bella assures me, tugging a long T-shirt over her head and down to brush her thighs. She goes to the door, opening it before I can say anything else.

Fuck.

"Good morning, Izzy. I've come to collect."

I hear the sniveling voice, half bullying and half whining, and my fists clench as I realize who's at the door. Carraby.

"Go away, Russell," Bella says in a tired voice. "We're done, remember? I'm paid up and on a payment schedule. I don't need anymore of your bullshit."

"Bullshit? We'll see how much bullshit it is when I kick you out on the street."

"You're not kicking me anywhere, legally or otherwise." I'm proud of how steady her voice is, so I pause, giving her a chance to handle this herself if she wants to. I'll give her backup if she needs it, but Carraby should be glad that I don't teach him a lesson the hard way.

"You'd best watch your tone. You're paid up, but there ain't nothing keeping me from taking what I really want."

Even from here, I can hear the slimy threat. Money . . . and more.

I won't tolerate any more.

I grab the hand towel, wrapping it around my right hand as I hear Bella say, "You mean like human morals and ethics?"

I take the three steps down the hall to find Bella staring at Russell, her face etched with fury. She's got one hand on the door and one on the frame, acting as a roadblock to keep him from entering, but he's taking advantage of her unwillingness to move back and grant him access by moving in closer and closer.

"You need to leave," I say coldly. I'm measuring the distance from me to Bella, me to Carraby, and Carraby to Bella, already formulating how I'm going to protect her while quickly disabling him. It won't take that much . . . it's just how much I can get Bella to move out of the way.

Carraby looks at me, taking in my shirtless upper body and zipped but unbuttoned pants, his eyebrows lifting. I can see him trying to look more intimidating, and I already know this is going to end badly. He's too out of control, too stuck in a rut of habitual bullying that he doesn't recognize when he's challenging someone better than him. Of course, that's part of my special skill set. I'm an intimidating guy when I need to be, but it's like a switch I can flip on and off.

"Oh, tough guy, huh? Fuck off. This ain't none of your business."

I move closer, slowly and methodically cutting the distance between me and the front door until I lay my hand on Bella's shoulder. I ease her back from the threshold, taking her place. As soon as I do, I pull the door open wide, not wanting it to impede my actions if I have to make a move.

"*She* is my business. You heard her. You're paid up. Leave, and don't come back. I'll be handling any future *discussions* you might need to have."

It's a huge overstep on my part, considering this isn't something I've talked about with Bella, but I need to protect her from assholes like Carraby who will take advantage the instant my guard is down. He needs to learn now not to mess with what's mine, and on a larger scale, that he can't do whatever he wants without consequences.

There's always a bigger fish in the pond, a sneakier fox in the henhouse, and a crueler hunter in the forest.

Carraby looks like he's about to argue more, but instead, he takes one step forward. I let him, even step back as if I'm retreating. It's a ruse, but I'm the only one who knows it.

Quick as a flash, he takes another step, leering wolfishly, and Bella cries out, "No!"

But it's just what I want. As Carraby gets fully in the front door, he unleashes with a short-armed haymaker that barely avoids hitting the doorframe. I let the punch land on my chin, dodging just enough to let him connect but not hurt me.

And now the tables have turned.

He's both come in, effectively trespassing without permission, and assaulted me first. Every legality is on my side. More importantly, though, he's off balance, and I can do any of a half-dozen things to him that would range from inflicting pain to inflicting death, and he can't stop me.

But I can't overplay my hand with Bella here to witness this. So I temper my brutality and grab his shoulders, throwing a single powerful knee to his gut, delighting in the whoosh of air that leaves him as he doubles over.

Not letting him gain any distance, I turn him, wrapping my arm around his neck and holding him in a loose chokehold, darkly growling in his ear as I shove him toward the door. "Leave. Do not come back. Ever. Do not speak to Bella ever again. This is the only warning you'll get, Carraby. Nod if you understand."

His head moves slightly inside my arm, and I take that as agreement, though I know he's only giving in right now because I have the upper hand. This isn't over.

But any further actions will take place away from Bella.

I shove him out the door, and as soon as the pressure is off his neck, he begins blustering, red-faced and yelling nonsense, "Messed with the wrong . . . gonna regret . . . fucking bitch."

I want to follow him, take him to a deserted place in the woods and teach him a real lesson in fear and intimidation. But instead, I use every ounce of willpower I possess and close the door, turning to face Bella.

Hoping she isn't disgusted by me, by my actions and overstepping comments, I await her judgement. It comes as she breaks down and launches herself at me, hugging my neck and wrapping her legs around me. "Oh, my God, what the fuck? I can't believe—"

Her seeming appreciation is broken by a loud 'bong' sound outside. It's the sound of a boot hitting metal, likely Russell's foot connecting with my Range Rover. But that doesn't matter now, not with Bella in my arms, safe and sound. And not flinching away from me after seeing the violence in the one place she considers a sanctuary.

"He's gone. You're okay, I've got you," I say, rubbing her back.

"Thank you," she breathes against my neck, and though I don't say it, I think the same thing back, thankful she didn't kick me out too.

# CHAPTER 20

## Isabella

AFTER A DRAMATIC AND CRAZY MORNING, THE SPELL I'VE BEEN IN, the fantasy Gabe wove around us, shatters. It feels awkward and there's something niggling in the back of my mind that I can't stop prying at.

But I can't figure out what it is.

Gabe drops me off at the Gravy Train for my shift with a kiss and a soft question of whether I'm sure I'm okay. I reassure him that I am, even though I'm not sure myself.

"I'm sorry about Carraby. I didn't mean for that to happen, but I'm glad you're safe. I won't let him hurt you, okay?" He pushes a lock of hair behind my ear, eyes imploring me to believe him. "I'll see you tonight for your nine o'clock dinner break?"

There's something in Gabe's voice that piques the little concern working itself around in my brain, an uncertainty he doesn't usually have. He's not arrogant, but he's always come off as confident.

But maybe this morning bothered him too?

I nod and get out, shutting the door behind me with a deep breath. Fuck. I can't believe Russell attacked Gabe and Gabe had to fight him off.

The scene replays in my head—Russell's leering threats and attack, and Gabe's immediate and powerful response.

As the mental movie of this morning replays again in my head while he pulls out, I see a different side to Gabe. A side I didn't know he had. He threw that knee with the skill and ease of someone who's done it before.

Suddenly, it clicks.

Carraby.

That's the thing that's bugged me this whole time. When I shared my problems, I told Gabe about Russell and his threats, but his last name? I can't remember ever telling him Russell's full name. But Carraby rolled off his tongue like . . . he already knew.

But how? Why?

And what does that even mean?

Memories of Charlotte's words ring in my ear. *You should run a back-ground check, girl. Wish I had, would've saved me a lot of heartache if I'd known who he really was.*

Shit. Is Charlotte right? Only one way to find out.

I run inside and head straight to the back, hollering, "Martha!"

"What?" she exclaims, coming out of her office quickly, her eyes wide and questioning.

"I need your keys. It's an emergency. Please," I say, holding my hand out and bouncing on my toes.

She digs in her purse, grabbing them and handing them over to me. "Are you okay? What's wrong?"

I shake my head, hoping I'm not too late. "I'll explain later, I promise. Cover for me today, please!" I take the keys from her, running out to her silver Toyota. I have just enough time to fire it up before Gabe's bright red SUV pulls through the intersection just down the street, turning left.

I do my best to follow, glad that Martha's car is small and nondescript. More than once, I 'hide' behind other vehicles, wondering what I'm doing as I follow him.

Last night, everything had seemed to be going amazingly well. I'd begun believing that maybe Mia was right and that love, or at least the first tingles of it, can strike when you least expect it. Certainly, I'd felt like this thing between Gabe and me had grown well beyond a one-night stand considering all we'd shared, the stories we'd told, and the multiple times I'd seen his dimpled smile in response to a story I told, even when they were more tragically funny than outright humorous.

And I'd learned a lot about him as we chatted, flirted, and slurped down those delicious noodles. He told me about his job, or well . . . some about it.

He told me about the things he likes and dislikes, and while we didn't get too deep into his family history, he never shirked a single question I had for him.

But this morning, when he looked at Russell, there was something in his face that scared me. I felt like I was looking at a totally different person, someone with the same face and body as Gabe but a totally different soul.

I don't know how I ended up following him. It just seems like the thing to do in the moment. Questions and concerns overlap each other in my mind with my sudden mistrust of Gabe, making me a little crazy.

Am I being irrational? Have I just gone a little cuckoo?

I know it's a bit much, but even so, I don't stop. I don't turn around.

Gabe pulls off the road and into the parking lot at a strip mall, and I follow, watching as he goes into . . . a Walmart?

That seems anti-climatic. I don't know what I was expecting, but my gut is still telling me something is up. And since I'm not really one to get weird vibes, I'm listening to this one, no matter how nonsensical it may be.

So I sit in Martha's car, waiting.

When Gabe comes out, he's got two bags and calmly beelines for his SUV. As he turns, I can see that one bag looks like it's got some snacks in it, while in the other, I can see the clear outline of a rubber mallet.

Gabe gets in his Range Rover, and I have a moment of clarity. Do I stop this madness or keep following? I glance up to the rearview mirror, seeing my eyes bright with worry.

"What am I doing?" I ask my reflection. Relationships are built on trust, but relationships are also built on honesty, and my gut tells me I'm missing something important here. I just don't know.

But when I see the candy-apple red SUV pull out, I know I'm doing this. No matter how weird, how stupid, how embarrassed I'm going to be later when it ends up that I'm overreacting to nothing, I need to know.

I keep sight of him, following as he makes his way to one of the motels in what could be called the industrial section of Roseboro. Not that Roseboro has a huge industrial zone, but there is that chunk of town that's sort of older businesses, I guess.

I park across the street, watching carefully as Gabe goes into a motel room. I'm just about to give up, thankful that nobody caught me going stalker psycho and thinking about how I'm going to explain my behavior to Martha, when the room door opens and Gabe walks out.

But he looks different than he did when he went in. I guess that's understandable. He was still wearing his dress shirt and suit pants from last night before, but looking at him in black jeans, a dark grey hoodie, and work boots . . . I don't know.

There's something off.

It's not like there's anything all that different about what he's wearing from what I've seen before. Almost every time we've been together, he's worn jeans and a T-shirt or something. Last night's fancier dress was definitely the outlier for us both.

But it's in the way he walks as he crosses the parking lot that has me confused.

He looks like he has a purpose. A mission.

And there's no hint of his boyish smile or charming personality. He looks robotic, mechanical.

I'm even more confused when he passes his Range Rover and goes to the end of the lot, getting into a silvery gray Ford truck.

"Wait . . . haven't I seen that truck before?" I murmur as I scooch down in my seat so he doesn't see me. I swear I have, but it's so common a style and color that maybe I'm just mixing it up with another vehicle? I mean, it looks just like Russ—

No.

No *fucking* way.

That time Russell came by, it was right around the time I met Gabe, if I remember right . . . there was another truck just down the block. At first I'd thought it was Russell coming back to bug me again.

But what if it'd been Gabe? Is that possible? Surely not.

Or maybe?

What does that mean, though? Maybe he was just in my neighborhood or knows Russell some other way? That might make sense I guess.

But something tells me that's not the case. Or at least there's a chance there's something else going on. And that's what's making me chew my lip.

I wait until Gabe pulls out of the lot, and then going by my gut, I take a shortcut toward my house. It means hopping on a dirt backroad for a mile, which does a number on Martha's suspension. But it can't be helped, I keep telling myself as my head bounces off the roof of her Toyota. I come up on the back of my neighborhood and park along the curb by the main road in, watching.

The car is dead silent as I pray that I'm wrong.

He could be going anywhere, might need a mallet for any number of things. Maybe Gabe is contracted to fix a problem at a warehouse and is on his way there now? And the truck, maybe he just has a work vehicle and a personal one? That's not unusual.

Even as I try to talk myself into believing that, my tears threaten to spill.

And then the gray Ford truck drives by.

Fuck. Fuck. Fuck.

What do I do? Do I keep following him or call the police? And tell them what? That my kinda-sorta boyfriend whom I've known for all of two weeks is acting sketchy as fuck and I think he's up to something beyond being overly protective of me?

They'd laugh me out of the precinct.

So I follow, still wishing none of this was happening, wondering how it's come to this.

He doesn't stop at my house and instead heads further down the street, turning two blocks up. There's only one house this far out in the neighborhood that Gabe would be interested in, and my stomach drops.

Russell's.

So he is going to pay Russell a visit.

My inner voice whispers, *you already knew that.*

It's true. I knew this was going to end with Gabe beating Russell up. Russell deserves it for sure, but I can't help but feel this is too much. I guess I was hoping the knee to the gut Gabe delivered this morning would be enough to warn Russell off?

I abandon the car, breaking into a jog and ducking through Mrs. Reddington's back yard to cut some more distance off my trek. It's not far, and I'm only part of the way there when I see Gabe's truck, Gabe behind the wheel, parked on the side of the road and waiting.

"What the hell are you doing?" I whisper to myself, kneeling behind an overgrown bush near Russell's house, watching. I know I should approach Gabe, stop whatever he has in mind. On some level, it was my whole purpose of following, but something stops me. I need to see what's going on. I need the truth of whatever this is. Of whatever he is.

My phone buzzes in my pocket, and I see that it's The Gravy Train. I ignore it, I'll make sure to call Martha immediately after. After *what,* I don't know. But I shut it off and keep watching.

It's surreal. I swear Gabe's watching for Russell, while meanwhile, I'm watching Gabe. A little tickle goes up my neck, and I wonder . . . is someone watching me?

No, I'm just paranoid and weirded out by what's going on. But still, I look behind me, scanning the street and bushes.

Suddenly, Gabe's door opens and he gets out of his truck. He approaches Russell's door, but there's something odd about his gait. Like his arms aren't swinging naturally but are stiff at his sides instead. He moves out of my view, but I hear loud knocks, three forceful bangs that reverberate through the still, cool air.

I hear the door open and chance peeking around the corner, staying low to the ground and looking between the branches of the bush. I have a decent view, can see Russell in faded smiley-face boxers, his face bleary and maybe even a little high. He looks at Gabe, who's lifted his hood up, with confusion.

"Who the fuck are you?"

Instead of answering, Gabe grabs Russell by his greasy hair and hurls him backward into his house. I'm so shocked I can barely believe what's happening, and a second later, Gabe's inside as well, gently closing the door to the house behind him.

It's the quiet click that shocks me the most. It's too calm, too premeditated.

Fuck. I shouldn't have sat there and watched.

"Gabe, what are you doing?" I ask, feeling like I'm yelling, but an almost inaudible whisper comes out as I move, leaving the camouflage of the bush in favor of pressing my face to a window.

There's barely a crack in the yellowed curtains, but it's enough to peek into the living room. I can hear Gabe's voice but can't see either of them, just the back of the dingy couch and the wall on the far side of the room.

"You . . . threatened her with breaking and entering, sexual assault . . . you harassed her with propositions of sex," Gabe growls, his voice low but so threatening that I shiver even though I'm outside. "You fucking deserve this."

"Dude . . . what the . . . what are you talking ab–OOOWWW!" Russell replies, his voice rising in a scream at the end. There's a wet thudding sound, and I realize what it is. A rubber mallet smashing down on Russell.

No. No way. Admittedly, I had suspicions that something was off, but not this. I didn't dream it would be . . . this. I guess I'd thought the worst-case scenario would be that he threatened him with it, but this is so much worse.

*Gabe*, my heart cries as it shatters.

There are no other houses nearby. Russell's property is at the dead end of the street and only the mailman comes down here. Besides, I know nobody gives enough of a damn about Russell to check out what's going on, even if they did hear him scream.

"That was your shoulder," Gabe says conversationally before a slapping sound splits the air and Russell starts sobbing. There's the sound of bodies moving, and suddenly, Russell's in a chair next to the window, his movement having shaken the curtain enough that I can see a little more.

Gabe's . . . not Gabriel. At least, not the charming, deliciously naughty man I've known and dreamed about for the past few nights.

This man's . . . ice. His dark eyes are emotionless, his face tense but totally neutral.

He really is like a Terminator. My God, this whole time, he's been this way. Charlotte was right. He has been hiding something.

"Please . . . please, man, whatever you want, I'll—" Russell pleads, but Gabe swings the mallet again, and even though it's rubber, the sound of it smacking into Russell's thigh cuts his words off into another scream.

"Shut up. I've spent days looking into you, Russell Carraby. How you've pissed away your family's fortune. How you take advantage of the few tenants you've got left. You're a waste of oxygen."

There's another *thwack*, and I recoil, realizing I have to do something. "Gabe, no! Stop!"

I stand from my hidey hole, running for the front door. I turn the knob, and it sticks for a split moment, making me think it's locked, but then it gives way to reveal Gabe with his gloved hand around Russell's throat, who's an utter mess. A spray of blood is already splattered on Gabe's face, and the mallet is lifted for what has to be a final blow.

Russell's out, unconscious with his head lolling and only held up by Gabe's grip. Gabe's eyes are deadly, focused and cold.

"No, don't!" I plead as he looks at me in utter shock.

Then Gabe blinks, and while it's not my Gabe, the Gabe I'm used to . . . he's human, at least. I can see the pain flashing hot and sharp in his eyes as his brow furrows.

"Bella? You shouldn't have seen this," he says, letting go of Russell's throat and stepping back as the body drops to the floor. "Fuck, I wish you wouldn't have seen me like this."

# CHAPTER 21

## Gabriel

I CAN FEEL HIS WORTHLESS BODY SLUMP UNDER MY HAND AS I HIT HIM in the chest with the mallet.

I bought the rubber mallet because I knew I wanted to hurt him but didn't want to actually kill him. Handy factoid, the rubber disburses the power of the strike, causing pain but significantly less damage than a normal hammer or bullet would.

I'd already done research on Russell Carraby, even before this morning. As soon as I knew he could be a threat to Bella, I looked into him and then watched and learned.

He wakes up at eleven, still half-drunk, and has a nasty habit of pissing in his own bushes on his way back inside from collecting the mail. He spends his days smoking and playing video games. He mostly only comes out to buy more drugs, steal shit from any store he's not banned from, or to bother the decent people unlucky enough to live on the land he owns.

I'd known he was bad news, but Bella was handling it, and honestly, I didn't want to answer the questions she'd have if I physically jumped in to save her from him. But this morning, everything changed, getting far worse than even I could have anticipated. I hadn't had a choice.

The one knee had been the smallest taste of what I'd wanted to do, and I'd known I was going back for him without Bella there to witness it. Even if it damns me, I'll save her. I'll punish him.

It's what I do.

And anything I dish out, up to and including death, would be warranted and well-deserved by a piece of shit like Carraby.

I'd swear I took the same precautions before approaching his house that I do with every entry I make, but obviously, I was at least partially distracted. Because now I've got Bella, standing in the doorway gawking at me, while I'm over a man whom I just beat unconscious.

And she's looking at me like I'm some sort of monster.

The truth hurts.

"You shouldn't have seen this, Bella," I say, stepping back from Russell and lowering the mallet. "I wish you wouldn't have seen me like this."

"Gabe . . . please, don't kill him," Bella says, her hands coming up in a prayer-like pose at her chin. Oh, my sweet princess, if you only knew how much better your life would be if you'd let me take care of this asshole.

But I didn't come here to kill him, and looking in her eyes, I wouldn't be able to go through with it even if I had.

I sigh, lowering the mallet. "I won't kill him, hadn't planned on it. But he . . ." I shake my head, knowing I can't beat around the bush with this any longer. "Please, I'll explain everything. At your house. I'll tell you everything."

"Why?" Bella asks, her eyes widening as panicked fear pierces her shock. "Oh, God, you're going to kill me." She takes a step back, and I force myself to stay still though every impulse makes me want to chase her and pull her back to me, make her see that I'm doing this for her, that I'll do anything for her.

She looks at Carraby, still unconscious but wheezily breathing through a broken nose. "No . . . no, I'm trying to save your life," I tell her, holding my hand out placatingly. Something in my tone must get through to her because her eyes flash back to me. "I swear, Bella, I'll protect you . . . but you have to understand that you're in danger."

Bella looks at me for a second, then points. "My house."

"Bella—"

"No, Gabe . . . I need a minute to process."

Moments later, I'm parked in front of Bella's house. The front door is open and I can see her sitting on the couch. She's waiting for me. I tried to give her a minute like she asked for, even using Carraby's kitchen to clean up as best I could. But I know she'll probably still see the blood spatter marking me, even though it's gone.

I take a deep breath and get out of the truck, walking up slowly. She watches my approach warily, letting me come in and close the door. I sit down across from her, noting the phone and the gun on the makeshift table between us.

I wonder if she's already called the police. Or her friends, Mia and Thomas. That'd be most fitting since they're the ones who got her into this situation by asking her to interfere in Blackwell's plans. Even if it'd been unwittingly and had seemed like she was only playing a minor part in catching a corporate saboteur at Goldstone.

"Explain." Her tone is fury mixed with fear.

I count it a miracle that she's even here, honestly. And maybe just as much one that I'm here too. This is the point where I should cut my losses and run. But I can't leave her unprotected, because while I'm a scary man, Blackwell will just send someone with less scruples than I have if I leave.

How did I get so emotional about this? And how did my emotions make me so sloppy?

"First, please understand, I'm still the guy who's talked to you, who's taken you out, who's made love to you . . . but I'm more than that too," I admit, watching as she stands to pace back and forth. "It's complicated."

"That's one way to put it!" she says, raising her voice. "I want the truth! All of it. Because the man I saw today isn't the same man I've been falling for!"

The words hang in the air, both of us stopping, and they sting as much as they fill me with wild hope.

She's falling for me? What have I done to deserve that, when I was sent to destroy her?

But maybe it's not too late to be who I was before revenge took root in my heart.

I need to unburden all those hidden lies to find out if it's possible.

"Bella . . . I'm falling for you too," I admit, looking down at my clasped hands, and I realize I'm literally begging her to believe me. "Russell Carraby is a bad guy, more so than you even realize. He's escalating, both in his drug habit and in his threats. I couldn't let that go." I look back up, imploring her. "What if I hadn't been here this morning? He very easily could've pushed his way in here and done . . ." I shudder at the thought of what that vile man would do to my sweet princess.

She finishes my sentence, "He could've done exactly what you did to him. Assault me, hurt me, kill me. But he didn't. You did. And neither of you had the right, him to do that to me nor you to do that to him."

"I know, but it's what I do, who I am. I'm sorry to say that, but it's the truth." I've never been ashamed of what I do before, having trusted in my rules and research enough to know that sometimes, working around the law to punish the truly despicable is the only way. But Bella's eyes light up like she's seeing me for the first time and isn't liking what she sees. At all.

"So you're judge, jury, and executioner all rolled into one?" She means it as an expression, not the actual truth, but I can see that she's starting to get it, realization dawning that my attack on Russell isn't a one-off situation but rather a single repetition of a recurring behavior.

Trying to calm her, I promise, "From the moment we first talked, I knew I couldn't do what I was hired to do." Baby steps to the truth. She deserves it all.

"Which is?" she asks, but I can see she doesn't really want to know.

I clear my throat. No other way to get around it. "I was hired by Blackwell to kill you."

Shocked, Bella stops pacing and shrieks, "You what?"

"From what I have gathered, you were instrumental in foiling some plan of his to discredit a business rival, Thomas Goldstone," I explain, charging on before things spiral any further out of control. "Blackwell's a vengeful son of a bitch, and he wanted to send a message. That's where I came in. But I have a code of ethics, my own moral guidelines, and he damn well knows it. It's why I looked deeper than his initial report. It'd said you were conniving, a key player in this business deal going sour. He knew I wouldn't kill an innocent person."

Bella pales, her hand going to her mouth. "Is Mia in danger? Or Thomas?"

My girl, always thinking of others before herself. Giving to a fault, even when she's the one to suffer for it. "No. At the moment, Blackwell feels certain that they're too high-profile, and eliminating them would create questions that could lead back to him. It's why he aimed for you. Your death would hurt them, but you're an easier target."

Her breath hitches at the description.

"I don't know the specifics, but I did take the job. I did my normal routine, observing you, learning your schedule, where you lived, worked, everything about you. Something felt off. None of what Blackwell said made any sense once I got to know you from afar. I needed to investigate further, to see if I was missing something. So, I approached you."

"And everything from there was just a fucking lie?" Bella asks, her voice rising to a yell. "Was everything just some . . . some way to make it easier to kill me?" She sounds incredulous, like this isn't possibly her life, but it is. And she's in very real danger. I have to make her understand.

"No!" I rasp, standing to face her so she hears me clearly. "Every moment I shared with you just made it harder. Bella, with every time we've talked, from the first moment I touched your hand, I felt split in half. When we went up to the overlook, I knew I could never do it. You're too good, too pure . . . you are what this world needs. Not Blackwell, with his jealousy and his hate. The world needs you. And so I've been delaying, making excuses, putting Blackwell off, trying desperately to figure out a way out of this."

"Why not just walk away?" Bella asks. "Why not go to the cops?"

"Because they're in his pocket," I reply with a dark laugh. "The man's got influence that stretches far and wide." I glance out the front window, remembering Blackwell's words and the suspicion that he has information superhighways feeding all sorts of intel right back to his ear. Particularly ones about Bella and my lack of follow-through on this assignment.

"And walking away isn't an option. At first, it was because he has information I need. Jeremy was killed in a drive by, and I've searched for a decade to find his killers. I've damn near sold my soul just to find out who did that to my sweet brother and Blackwell knows. He claims to know who killed Jeremy. He knew I'd do just about anything to get a lead and preyed on that. It's why I took the job in the first place. But I've given up on that. All that matters is you. But if I don't complete my contract, he'll just hire someone else to do the job . . . and probably add me as target number two."

For the first time, Bella shivers, realizing the danger she's in. "I just wanted to help Mia."

I nod. "I know. You're a good friend, a good person, and I'm trying my damnedest to be a good protector for you."

"Protector?" she scoffs, her eyes going hazy, and I suspect she's picturing the monstrous version of me she saw looming over an unconscious Russell. "Is that what a protector is?"

"I'm not a good man. I was angry at Russell, and even if I didn't go there to kill him, I can't promise what would've happened if you hadn't shown up. I know what I'm capable of, and it's not pretty. The only thing that gives me hope is that you've seen something in me that might be redeemable. I don't know."

"And why shouldn't I call the cops on you? You've been hired to kill me. You've been stalking me. Maybe I should have you arrested since you're the immediate threat."

It hurts, but I hold out my wrists as if she could cuff me right now. "If you wish, I won't stop you. But Bella, I promise that I will give my life to protect you. Yes, I'm falling for you . . . but I'm not foolish enough to think that I deserve your love after knowing what you know about me. But please . . . give me a chance to save your life."

"How?" she whispers. I can see the weight of the conversation taking its toll, the heaviness of what could have happened pressing on her chest as she visibly shrinks before me.

I shake my head, wiping at my cheek and realizing there's wetness there, horror at what I've done to this poor woman. "I haven't totally figured that out yet. One does not simply walk into the Blackwell Building and start recreating the lobby scene from *The Matrix*. Not if they expect to actually get Blackwell."

Bella opens her mouth to say something, then closes it, turning around and starting to pace again. "This is insane. I'm sitting here discussing killing people with a hitman who I want to be my boyfriend, and he's just put my sorta-landlord in the hospital."

"Do you still want me to be your boyfriend?" I ask, glomming onto the one piece of hope in her summary.

But she ignores the question, still lost in her own rehash. "Why not go to Thomas?" Bella asks. In her voice, I hear encouraging tones. She's in shock, but she's at least accepting what I'm saying without dismissing it outright. Belief might still be a little way off, but for now, she's at least listening and taking it in, offering solutions. "You know, the enemy of my enemy is my friend. And Thomas is a friend of friend already."

I consider it, even though it's one of a myriad of possible ideas I've already gone through. "It may come to that. Power for power, but right now, I think it would be like throwing kerosene on a bonfire, and Mia and Thomas would be the ones to pay the price if they jump into the fray. As scary as it is to consider, right now, Blackwell is focused on you, and they are safe."

It's a shitty move to make, because I know she'll do anything to keep her friends safe, even at the expense of herself. But it's the only way I can see getting her to agree with the only idea I've come up with, delay until I can find an angle on Blackwell. I throw the hook, baiting her.

"But I have another idea. Honestly, it's the only way out that I can see right now."

She looks at me through her lashes, not knowing how innocent and scared she looks. It draws out every protective instinct I have. "What?"

"We're out of time. We need to get you out of town, where I can keep you safe until I figure out how to keep Blackwell off you."

"I'm not running!" Bella says, and in her voice and face I see the determination, the spirit that has me falling for her. She's not going to retreat. She's going to take on the world on her own terms, and there's not a damn thing anyone can do about it.

"Bella, I'll do everything I can to protect you. I'll get you back here to your home, to your friends. But we need to get out of town if I have any chance of implementing any sort of plan."

"How can I just leave with you? I have so many unanswered questions. This is crazy."

I walk closer to her, slowly and steadily, giving her time to flee, but she doesn't move. Not even as I push her hair behind her ears and hold her face up, forcing her eyes to mine. "I'll answer any question you want . . . when we're on the road. I can see you want to push me out that door and go to your friends, the ones who have had your back your whole life. I get it, I do. But they don't have the skills I do. And I say that knowing it makes me even scarier in your eyes. You shouldn't trust me . . . but I need you to. Because more than anything else in this world, I don't want you to end up dead."

Bella blinks at the verbal shot, and then her eyes focus, questioning me. But I can't say the words she wants to hear. Not like this, not when it'll seem like a ploy. So I give her another truth. "You deserve all the best things the world has to offer, but the world deserves the very best of Isabella Turner too. Let me make sure that happens. Please."

# CHAPTER 22

## Isabella

I DON'T REMEMBER AGREEING, EXACTLY, BUT I MUST HAVE BECAUSE Gabe is suddenly shuffling around my house to pack my bag. I can't help, frozen and still trying to make sense of the information dump and paradigm shift I was just subjected to. It doesn't work. I'm still so lost.

It feels like no matter which way I turn, there's a threat looming, scary men using me as a pawn, taunting me into running and nipping at my heels to direct my destination the way they want. It's enough to make me want to say fuck it all and run on my own, just ditch my life and start over someplace fresh.

But I can't do that. I have people here whom I love and who love me and a future I've worked hard to secure and am so close to achieving. I won't give it up because some asshole in his fancy tower deems me a beneficial loss.

Gabe stops in front of me, my backpack slung on like he's ready to roll. He puts his hands on my shoulders and looks at me. "Say it, Bella. I'm not kidnapping you, but I want you to come with me. If you can't, we'll find another way. I just don't know what that is."

This is the moment of truth. My decision time.

I don't know Gabe, I realize. I thought I did, and even now, what he shared feels real. But what if it was a ploy? I search his eyes, holding my breath and hoping for some sort of sign.

He takes it as an answer, dropping the backpack to the floor. Running his fingers through his hair, he paces. "Fuck. Okay, we'll stay if that's what you want, but I gotta figure out . . ." His voice fades as he mumbles to himself, eyes going wild before he focuses sharply. It sounds like he's running through scenarios and options for staying here and keeping me safe.

It's what I need. Some small piece of reassurance that he will do what I want, even in a situation that is largely beyond anything I've ever considered, and even if it's not what he thinks is best. I guess I thought he'd shove me out the door regardless, kidnapping me, as he said. But that he is willing to follow my lead somehow gives me peace that what I've been feeling is true and what he feels about me is real.

I bend down to pick up my own bag. "I need to stop by the diner, give Martha her car back, and ask her to watch Vash."

His eyes jump to me, my agreement instantly stopping his play-by-play of possible outcomes and strategies.

He doesn't ask if I'm sure, taking me at my word and moving toward the door. But he stops, one hand on the frame. "We need to assume we're being watched. I chose your school bag so it'll look like you're just heading out for a usual day. But if we look suspicious or angry, basically anything other than the happy couple, it'll rouse concerns."

"What do you want me to do?" I ask, hearing that he's leading up to something.

"We're going to walk outside, kiss goodbye like everything's fine, and get in our vehicles. I'll follow you to the diner, and you need to tell them that this is a vacation or something—like I'm whisking you away, so act happy. And then we'll leave town in my truck."

I take a big breath, realizing just how crazy this sounds. "That's a lot. Martha will know something's up. And don't you need to go by the motel?" I mean it to be more of a sting than it really is, a show that I know something, at least. But it doesn't land, and he brushes the question off.

"I'll get what I need on the road. I do it all the time. Sell Martha on this. Please, Bella."

The kiss outside is awkward, but Gabe pulls me to him and cups my jaw in his powerful hand. If anyone's watching, it probably looks like a sweet, sultry kiss. And for sure, Mrs. Petrie across the street is watching, but if Gabe is right, who else is?

The drive to The Gravy Train gives me time to think, but even without Gabe's influence, I can feel in my gut that this is the right thing to do. If

Blackwell's after me, and I do believe Gabe that he is, this is the best way to be safe.

A single butterfly flutters around in my belly at the thought of being away from my tough life, alone with Gabe and all his terror and his sexiness. And even the fear and questions surrounding this situation aren't enough to contain the slight buzz. It makes me feel a bit pitiful to be excited about something dire, but it's a different sort of fear than not making the rent or having Russell bark and bitch at me.

Russell. Even thinking his name draws up the image of his body slumping to the floor. Is he okay, I wonder, or did Gabe finish the job after I left? A shudder racks through me, but I realize shamefully that even if he did kill Russell after I left, I don't care. God, I'm awful. But Russell has made my life a living hell, scared the piss out of me so many times I've lost count, and is an absolute terrifying waste of a human life. His death would be mourned by none and quietly celebrated by many.

So I don't call the police or an ambulance, even now that I could. Maybe I should do something, but I can live with the guilt of non-action more than I can live with the consequences of Russell taking vengeance for this on me.

The parking lot at The Gravy Train is full, a blessing because it means Martha won't have time to focus on me the way she would if there was no one calling for a refill.

Inside, I wave and smile, feigning that everything's fine the way Gabe said to. "Thanks, Martha. Sorry for the drama earlier, but uhm . . ." I bite my lip, nervous about this part. "I have a huge favor to ask."

Her eyes narrow, but then she lifts her brows, inviting me to ask away.

"Gabe wants to take me away for the weekend, a last-minute getaway." I freeze. "I mean, vacation. A last-minute vacation. Is there any way you could get Shelly or Elaine to cover for me and feed Vash for me?"

"I can do that, but only if you tell me what had you running out of here like your tail was on fire earlier." She crosses her arms, looking every bit the stern mom-figure she's been for me.

I stammer, not sure what to say, and Gabe slips an arm around my shoulders. I hadn't even realized he was behind me. "I'm afraid that's my fault. I was trying to surprise her and might have accidentally let the cat out of the bag, so to speak. She freaked a bit."

Martha smiles like she completely understands that I would do something like that. She reaches for my hands, looking so charmed she might as well be blessing our union. God, if only she knew the truth, she'd be stringing Gabe up by his toenails and she'd use Henry's good knives to destroy the evidence of killing him for being mixed up in this.

"Go, honey. Treat yourself for once. You do so much here. Let us do for you this time." She pulls me in for a hug, and while it feels good to have her love envelop me, I feel bad for lying to her. She turns to Gabe, patting him on the cheek. "You must be something special if she's ditching us for a weekend away with you."

There's a warning in her tone, and I wonder what they talked about the night I saw them talking while Gabe waited for my dinner break.

Outside, Gabe opens the door to his truck, helping me in. I see him scan the lot without moving his head as he walks around to the driver side, just his eyes moving. "I think we're clear. Not sure if that's a bad sign or we're just fucking lucky. But we'll be careful on the way out of town to make sure we're not being followed."

We're quiet on the way out of town, but slowly, conversation starts as my fear fades. It's not that I'm no longer afraid, but merely that my body has burned out all the adrenalin and I'm feeling flat and tired now.

"Tell me how it got to this point," I say.

Gabe scratches at his lip with his thumb, glancing into the rearview mirror for the tenth time. "Like I said, you helped Thomas catch a corporate saboteur whom Blackwell planted. He felt like you were an easier target—"

"Not me, you," I interrupt. "Oh, wait. I just realized something. I don't think Mia and Thomas know Blackwell had anything to do with that whole mess. They thought it was just a single man's vendetta. Well, I guess it is, but they don't realize the man is Blackwell. I need to call them."

I look around for my phone, and Gabe shakes his head. "I left it behind. It's traceable, Bella. You can call Mia from a burner phone if you need to, but I think we need to wait until we figure out the game plan before we get them involved. Can you give me a little bit of time?"

I sigh, turning to look out the window. It feels wrong to not tell my bestie this, but as long as she's safe with Thomas, I can wait a day or two. I still double-check myself again, but as crazy as this all sounds, it also makes sense and feels like the truth. Gabe's truth about why he's here and hanging out with me, so I have to take the leap of faith and not call Mia immediately, no matter how much I want to.

Gabe clenches his jaw, gritting his teeth like he's the one hurting. "After

Jeremy died, I fell apart. It was slow at times, so incremental I didn't even notice, and then I'd take a leap, lashing out at the world."

My head snaps his way. "Tell me," I demand again. And this time, he knows what I mean.

"It started with me asking questions, simple enough but hard, nevertheless. All too quickly, things got violent as I demanded answers from people who ultimately had none to give. But I developed a reputation for a rather in-demand skillset. In a way, I put aside my own mission for other people's, but doing this ugly work let me hide in the shadows, seeking information in a way I couldn't as a regular guy." His eyes leave the road, quickly glancing over to judge my reaction.

"I've tried to maintain my own sense of justice, of right and wrong, by carefully choosing the contracts I accept and doing my own due diligence. That's why I realized that you were an innocent, because I looked into you and couldn't find a single evil thing about you. But I found plenty about Blackwell because I always research my employer as well. It's good to know who you're getting into bed with."

I scoff. "I agree."

But I'm not talking about business arrangements and he knows it.

He reaches over slowly, placing a hand on my knee and squeezing. "You know me. Everything between us was real, is real. There was just another layer you didn't know about then, but now you do."

I want to fall into him, desperate to believe but unwilling to plunge carelessly. "But it's the very foundation we were building on, and now I find out that it's faulty."

He swallows thickly and clears his throat. "Then we'll start fresh and rebuild."

# CHAPTER 23

## Isabella

"B ELLA?"

I look over, where Gabe's sitting behind the wheel of the truck, a worried look on his face. We've stopped for gas, and I guess I haven't said anything in awhile. "Sorry . . . I was just thinking."

"Ah," Gabe replies, starting the truck up and pulling back out. "You just looked . . . I'm not sure."

I nod, turning to him. "How'd you get that nickname? The Fallen Angel?" He's been telling me about his life in bits and bites as we drive, more about his work and 'fall from grace', as he calls it, and about who he'd been once upon a time, before his soul had been stained with his dark actions.

Gabe turns back onto the highway, leading us toward the ocean. "I think mostly because of my name. One of my first contracted jobs was with an Italian guy who was very into the Church. With my looks, it sort of stuck."

I can't help it—it makes me chuckle. "Your looks, huh?"

Gabe looks over, tentatively smirking. "You want to know the only thing worse than someone who's obsessed with their looks? A good-looking person who's full of false humility. It's ironic, really, because I'm the least angelic man, with the ugliest soul. Jeremy was the saint, not me. Don't get me wrong, he was a ladies' man, but he died too young and innocent."

"Tell me about him," I ask as we come around a turn. We're in the mountains, on one of those roads that really should be expanded from the two-lane overgrown logging roads they used to be, with sunlight barely drifting between the trees behind us. "What was he like?"

"Funny," Gabe says immediately, grinning. "That kid . . . I was the older brother, though not even by a full year. But our whole lives, he was the one who was devil-may-care, and I spent . . . shit, if I have any gray hair at all, it's because I spent so much time worrying about that kid."

"What did he do?" I ask, grinning a little. It's helpful and reminds me of the human side of Gabe that still makes my heart flutter in my chest.

"What didn't he do? Have you seen the 'hold my beer' meme? That was him, though non-alcoholic, mostly," he says with a wink. "If he saw someone jump their bike over something, he would be outside the next day, busting his ass and trying it. This one time, just because he saw it on YouTube, he did the flying dive . . . fucking still amazed he survived that one."

"What's the flying dive?" I ask, my imagination trying to picture it, and each picture is crazier than the next.

"He'd seen some college guy do a leap off his roof into a swimming pool, elbow dropping this inflatable zebra or some damn thing. We didn't have a pool at home, but our town's youth center had one. So the next time we're there, Jeremy goes, 'Gabe, keep the deep end clear.' Then he gets out of the pool and goes inside, nonchalant as fuck. I'm wise enough to Jeremy's bullshit by this point. I know I can't stop him, so I just made sure no little kids were in the deep end. Suddenly, the big sliding window to the second-floor game room opens, and five seconds later, Jeremy comes flying out, stretched out like fucking Superman or something. Scared the shit out of me. It was at least a six-foot gap of concrete he had to clear."

"He made it?" I ask, and Gabe nods.

"Biggest, ugliest belly flop ever, but yeah, he was fine. After we got kicked out, we walked home. His chest and stomach were pink and bruised for days. I've never seen anyone with black and blue nipples before him."

He shakes his head, laughing at the memory and making me laugh at the mental image he painted of Jeremy. "Did you two look alike?"

"Jeremy took after our mother more. He had these big green eyes. He could sweet-talk anyone. Like the community center? He somehow got us allowed back in within a week, and by the end of the summer, he'd even kissed Wendy Partridge, the head lifeguard who was pretty much every teenage boy's dream for two summers. I was too serious, too involved in studying and being the outlier to really make the same strides he did."

I squint, trying to imagine Gabe as anything but a handsome charmer. It's damn hard, even knowing what I know about him. "What do you mean, outlier?"

"I guess I was kind of a loner. I mean, I wasn't bullied or anything. You don't bully a guy my size, though I was a bit lankier back then. I just did my own thing. It was me and Jeremy, two peas in a pod, even if he did go out a bit more."

I can feel in his words that he cared a lot for his brother. "You loved him."

Gabe clears his throat. "He was a pain in the ass, but yes, I did. After he was killed and I started down . . . down the path that I've gone in life, I guess I started emulating some of his traits. The first time I had to stand up to a guy with a gun, that wasn't me slickly talking my way out of that shit. That was Jeremy talking through me."

The mountains suddenly stop, and I'm stunned at the sight before me. The highway comes almost to the beach itself, and in front of me, the wild, untamed Pacific roars and rages, crashing against the rocky coastline in gigantic sprays of foam.

Just off shore, maybe less than a quarter-mile, are a couple of rocks that are too big to be properly called rocks but too small to be called islands. One of them, the largest, is almost perfectly domed, ringed with trees and standing in the middle of the sea in front of me.

"This is . . . wow. I didn't expect a safe house out here."

"Well, it's not an actual safe house, but we'll be protected here. It's a rental property, remote and isolated. Just the two of us." His voice goes husky, and I know that there's no way I'll be able to resist him if there's no one around to buffer the heat he so easily stirs up in me.

The rational side of me revolts against the idea, wanting to start over like he said and build slowly and carefully, maybe even wait until the danger passes and I can see if he disappears like fog in the sunshine. But there's another side of me saying that if I'm going out, I'm doing it on my own terms and sexually satisfied.

I'm honestly not sure which side I want to win.

Instead of deciding now, I question him. "If it's a rental, that means there's a record. That's dangerous, right? Blackwell could track us right to the front door."

He looks over, a pleased smile developing, and then his dimples pop. "Good girl. I like the way you're thinking."

Warmth heats my belly and my cheeks, and he continues. "I used an alias to book the rental, so it's not traceable to me at all."

We keep driving, and when we turn off the coastal highway, I can still see the big domed rock. But what takes all of my attention is on the gate in front of us. Large and imposing black iron, but pretty and ornate. Gabe stops at the box and rolls his window down to tap a few numbers on the keypad. It slides open, and Gabe drives a few feet to the other side before stopping.

He gets out, waiting as the gate slides back closed, and then goes over to the mechanical box. He opens it, doing something I can't see, and then gets back in the truck.

"Turned off the gate mechanism and took out the fuse so it can't be turned back on without it. Now the gate won't work electronically, and it's too heavy to manually slide open. We're secure against vehicles because the fence goes around the whole property."

It strikes me that he specified 'secure against vehicles' because that means we're not secure against someone scaling the fence. Because that's an actual risk. Again, I'm struck with how crazy my life has become.

The blooming anxious fear is stopped abruptly as we come through a row of trees to a clearing and the house comes into view.

It's stunningly beautiful, turn of the century styling but updated to be modern. Gabe makes quick work of the front door, and we walk into a foyer with two-story ceilings. A plush rug softens my footsteps as I gawk, spinning in place.

I can't think of the last time I was in a room that was like this. Or maybe never? The walls are elegant, decorated in a slightly Victorian floral wallpaper, and as I look out the big window in front of us, I'm struck by how beautiful the view is. The ocean stretches as far as I can see to the horizon, and the beach beckons.

I realize Gabe is watching me take in the house. "This is what you deserve, Bella. Beautiful things, luxury at your fingertips, and more."

I look away from the view to meet his eyes and shake my head. "This is amazing, but I don't deserve it more than any other person does. All I want is to be safe, to be able to go home to my friends, who are safe, and for everyone to be happy. That's enough."

His smile is sad. "Let me do a run-through. Will you wait here?"

I nod and he disappears. I hear him opening and closing doors and several beeps as he messes with the alarm system. I move to the window, and staring outside, it feels like we're the only two people left in the world.

Moments later, he's back and follows my sightline outside. "I need to check outside too. Do you want to walk with me? We can walk on the beach?" he beckons, the hope that it'll entice me in the gravel of his voice.

I follow his lead out the back door and down the wooden steps to the sand. The beach isn't sugar sand, and while it's beautiful, I can't really see anyone using it for sunbathing. The sand's too coarse, the breeze coming off the ocean and hitting the mountain just a little too brisk. Even in summer, it'd be too cold for a bikini for all but the most hardcore of bathers, and the waves are so wild that every breath of air is tinged with the flavor of salt as the cool mist kisses my skin.

We walk, the sand crunching under our shoes as I listen to the roar of the water, trying to let go of the terror that sneaks up on me and then fades away just as unexpectedly. It's not that anything in particular eases me. It's just not sustainable to live in constant fear, looking over my shoulder. I'm not built that way, jaded and scared of the world. But I get the feeling Gabe is.

We've spent so much time in the past eight hours talking. The thought of his own personal tragedies makes me shiver, and I tug on the sleeves of my sweatshirt to disguise the reason.

I reach over, taking Gabe's hand. His brows lift in pleased surprise, and though his brown eyes stayed locked on me, I turn to look out at the ocean. "I miss my family too. Seems we're both alone."

"You're not alone, Bella. Your family might not be blood, but they're the ones you've chosen and who've chosen you back."

I notice he doesn't make the same correction about himself. Perhaps he truly is alone. The thought makes me sad.

"I try to remember my family, but it was so long ago and I was so little. I'm glad you had your brother for so long, that you were so close. For a long time, I wanted that, would wish that I'd had another year, a month, a week, even a day. To have more memories, but what little I have are faded with time." I look down, digging the toe of my tennis shoe into the sand., "Sometimes, I can't even remember what my mother looked like or what her voice sounded like. I've tried so often."

It's a painful confession, one I don't share lightly or to just anyone.

"The trick is to think of context," Gabe says. "Don't just think of her face or voice. Think of something you did together. Think of a time you had fun together and picture the whole scene. That'll make it come to you."

I close my eyes, and after a moment, it comes to me. "My fourth birthday. She made orange cupcakes with Fruity Pebble sprinkles, just like I asked for. They were so sweet even half of one gave me a stomachache, but I loved them all the same. I can hear her asking me if they were what I dreamed they'd be. I remember her smile when I jumped up and down, yelling yes over and over," I say with a teary smile.

I turn to Gabe, hugging him. "Thank you."

"Always, Bella. I learned that from using the same trick to remember Jeremy."

I shiver, hugging him tighter. When I let go, he takes my hand and we resume walking. "I need to finish the perimeter check. You okay to walk with me?"

I nod, but as we leave the empty beach with sightlines for miles to move into the treed area around the house, I can feel the change in Gabe. He drops my hand, his eyes scanning carefully and occasionally checking the fence line.

I follow along, useless to help, and the one time I try to speak, he gently hushes me with a finger to my lips. He whispers, "Shh, I'm listening for anything in the woods." So I bite my tongue and trudge behind him.

The sun is low in the sky when we get back to the house, the long day taking its toll physically and the emotional roller coaster crashing over me mentally.

Gabe helps me settle on the couch and then moves to start a fire. When he's satisfied that it's going well, he sits beside me and wraps an arm around my shoulders. Too exhausted to be upset any longer, I melt into him.

This should feel wrong. I should be scared of him.

But after everything, both before this morning and after, somehow, this feels right. I feel safe in his arms. Maybe that's stupid of me, but that ship has long since sailed, right about the time I climbed into his truck. Actually, maybe before that, when I let him into my house to explain.

Charlotte whispers in my ear again, *background check*.

But I am where I am, and I don't know that I'd change it even if I could. So I sink deeper and let myself be enveloped by him, even if there's a price to pay.

Even if it's my life.

# CHAPTER 24

## Gabriel

THE ROOM GLOWS IN A SOFT FIRELIGHT, THE FLAMES DANCING IN Isabella's eyes. We haven't said anything for the past ten minutes, just exchanging slow kisses.

They were tentative at first, like she's not sure if this is really what she wants.

So I'm letting her lead for now, knowing that I'm responsible for a lot of our current situation and that Bella is a woman who likes to be in control of her own destiny. This time, I'll let her decide where this goes, even if it's her to one bed and me to another.

But words aren't needed any longer when she reaches up and pulls off her shirt, shrugging it off and freeing her breasts from the simple bra she wears underneath.

Each apple-sized handful sways back and forth as she traces her stomach with her fingertips before lying back on the couch.

"Show me," I whisper, and Bella bites her lip, her hands cupping her breasts before she teases her nipples, pulling on them until her tits are nearly pyramided up from her body and making her gasp in pain and pleasure before she lets them go.

While she kneads her right breast, I run my hand down her body, caressing her soft skin. She writhes, her belly sucking in as I move to the waist of her jeans. She nods, giving me silent permission, and I slip the button free and unzip them, pushing them over her hips. She lifts, helping me get them off, her panties coming off at the same time.

And then she's bare before me.

Beautiful, trusting, good. Too good for me, but I can't stop myself from worshipping her body, tasting her kind heart.

I spread her knees, one to the back of the couch and the other at the edge of the couch, but Bella sets her foot on the floor to open more for me. I can see the gleam on her sweet sex, already puffy and slick with need.

I take her hand, kissing her fingertips and then directing her to her core. "Touch your pussy. Finger fuck yourself for me, Bella," I command, pulling my shirt off as she traces her slit before rubbing her clit with feather-light strokes. She moans, her eyes never leaving me as she slides two fingers deep inside herself, pumping them in and out slowly.

My cock's rock hard, watching her lips cling to her fingers and knowing that soon, my cock will be lodged deep inside her and feeling the same sucking kiss.

"I . . . I can't help it," she mewls, her hips lifting to meet her fingers as she speeds up a little. "Gabe, I need you. Take me. Fuck me, please."

Her words make me speed up, and I stand to strip off my jeans, my cock aching to be inside her. Bella sobs in want as I pause, and she pulls her fingers out, wrapping them around my shaft. She strokes me, coating me in her honey and driving me wild, but I keep a tight grip on my control.

She needs me, needs this, but I can't go too hard on her. Not right now. She doesn't know it, but she needs some tenderness right now, with her heart and with her body.

That I'm even getting the chance to be with her this way is a gift, one I won't waste or cheapen. Already trembling on the edge of no return, I pull my hips back. "Bella, I'm too close. Need to be inside you."

Her breath hitches as I hover over her, holding myself up so I don't put my weight on her. She reaches between us, guiding me to her entrance, holding me still.

"Do you feel that, Princess? That's you and me. No lies, only truth, only us. No matter what," I promise, taking her free hand and entwining our fingers. Bella nods, releasing my shaft, and I press deep inside her, filling her with all I have.

She whimpers, stretched even after her fingers have been plunging inside her. Her fingers tighten in mine, but she doesn't protest, trusting me completely.

I press into her, our bodies grinding together, and I can feel her clit rub against the base of my cock. Her pussy gushes over my shaft, and I pull back, pausing before stroking deeply again, leaning down to kiss her as I push her into the couch cushions.

I pump slowly, relishing every clench of her body around me as I drive into her, pinning her underneath me. I can see the look in her eyes, pleasure and pain and worry and trust swirling in her mind, released in every gasp.

"That's it, Bella," I rasp, speeding up until our hips start slapping together. "Come hard on my cock. I'm here for you."

I pound her, speeding up, but my arms give out, needing to feel her body pressed to mine. I lie over her, hip to hip, chest to chest, my arms wrapping around her. She responds by wrapping her arms and legs around me too.

I bury my nose in the crook of her neck, inhaling her lavender scent as I listen to her moans and mewls in my ear. She gets louder, crying out, and I lift slightly to look at her. Her cheeks are flushed, her eyes widening more and more.

"Right there, Gabe. *Fuck.*"

I pull back and drive hard, hitting a spot deep inside her that lights her on fire, until she shatters with a wail, writhing underneath me. I ride her through it, letting her pussy's contractions push me higher and higher.

I tremble, pulling back and thrusting once more before I go over as well. I pull out as I come hard, my cock spewing over her pussy and belly as I mark her, painting her satin flesh with my seed.

Bella sleeps like the dead, barely moving a muscle save for her parted lips occasionally pursing as she snores softly. Like a creeper, I watch her sleep, unable to relax myself. Even with a nightly check of the perimeter and the alarm, I feel like there's too much at risk, too great a danger to let my guard down.

It's barely dawn when I finally get out of bed, figuring I should go ahead and start the coffee for the day. I am sipping my second cup, looking out over the water, when I hear Bella padding around.

I feel her enter the room, her warmth reaching me even from the doorway. Or maybe it's just that she makes me warm inside, thawing a heart I thought had been irreparable and a soul almost certainly irredeemable.

"I made coffee," I tell her, taking a drink.

"Don't move," she whispers.

Instantly, I'm on alert, turning to look out the window but seeing nothing other than the rising sun in the sky. "What's wrong? What do you see?"

She laughs lightly. "You. Stay, just like that."

She runs off, and I hear her shuffling around before she reappears with her laptop. I only let her bring it because I knew she couldn't get Wi-Fi without my help, and it would help her calm down. "I want to draw you. The light is magnificent."

She sits across from me, telling me how to pose and basically putting me back how I was when she walked into the room. She works quietly, looking back and forth from me to the screen.

"What are you doing, exactly? Is this going to be Picasso-esque and I'll have to smile politely and act like I get the deeper meaning of abstract art? Or are you more a realist and I'm suddenly going to be paranoid about the size of my nose?"

Her smile is soft, but her hand never stops moving. "I'm more of a realist if those are the only two choices, which they aren't. But I've played with all sorts of styles. I love it all—paints, canvasses, pencils, charcoal, and of course, digital. And each medium lends itself to a different feel."

"Is that why you're going to school for graphic design? To be an artist?" I ask, wanting to know everything about her. Not just the dry facts on paper, but the meaning behind her choices, her thought processes as she decided her future.

Her shrug is one-sided so as not to disturb her drawing. "It's a way for me to do what I love and make money. Right now, it's mostly typography-type things. Like I designed the logo, did the menus and boards for The Gravy Train. That was a labor of love, but I also want to do other things. Book covers, maybe, or even video game design? Mia is a major gamer and always begs me to play. The play itself isn't my favorite, but I love seeing how the graphics change and the artist creates the different scenes. It's just like a painting, but digital. I'm not sure yet. I just love art and want to be able to create for a living."

The passion with which she speaks is inspiring, making me wish I had something as pure and beautiful that I believed in. Once upon a time, I hoped that, even in the ugly things I did, I could find some balance. Dark for light, evil for good, make wrong things right.

But I can see the truth now. Bella has shown me that.

And I know that I'll never return to my previous life. I can't. It means I may never get the answers I need about Jeremy's death, and while I'm not sure I can let that go without the retribution I promised, I can feel down to the last shredded tatters of my soul that I cannot kill in cold blood again.

Well, except for Blackwell. But killing him wouldn't be in cold blood. My heart would be pumping fast and hard to have a chance to take him out, my blood heated with fury for the opportunity to insure Bella's safety once and for all.

Bella taps the screen of her laptop a few times in quick succession, breaking my heavy thoughts. "What do you think?" she asks, turning the computer around.

It's me. But not.

She's captured a side of me I don't think exists. Or if it does, it's only in her mind. Is this how she sees me?

It's a profile picture, the sun improbably shining brightly behind me, giving a halo effect. But my expression is dark, my jaw clenched. There's a tightness to my eyes, a sad beauty highlighted by the single solitary tear trailing down my cheek.

I am every bit a Fallen Angel.

But when I look at her, seeing the hope that I like her painting lighting her eyes, I think maybe I could be redeemed. If anyone can save me, it's her. And if anyone can save her, it's me. It's a match made in heaven. Or hell, depending on the outcome.

# CHAPTER 25

## Gabriel

THE LAST TWENTY-FOUR HOURS HAVE BEEN SHEER MADNESS. BELLA and I have cussed and discussed every which way to get her out of this mess. The best idea we've come up with is ridiculous, something that only works in movies.

But considering this whole scenario is pretty cinematic, with the evil hitman who falls for his innocent target and a malevolent villain in a tower overlooking the little people of Roseboro, a good fake death seems apropos.

Oddly enough, my dark background is our best secret weapon. I've seen too much death, know what it looks like, smells like, feels like in those moments, and while staging that with Bella as the victim turns my stomach, it's the only way.

If Blackwell will believe she's dead, and we can hide her away, then it'll give us time to figure out something long-term. That's the point where we're going to need Thomas to step in and use his power in this chess game. A pawn simply can't win it, but Bella can be the strategic move to get the ball rolling.

I finish blending the most disgusting shake I've ever made, pure powdered sugar dissolved in water with a dash of cocoa and an entire bottle of red food coloring. I wasn't sure the internet was right, but even my eye would be fooled by the murky, dark red liquid. Hopefully, when combined with a camera filter, Blackwell will be too.

I pour the mixture into a sport bottle and add it to the bag of supplies. "You ready?" I call out.

Bella appears at the kitchen doorway a moment later, looking nervous. "Yeah, I'm ready. Guess that means this recipe was a solid counterfeit?"

I hold up the blender, tilting it so she can see. Her face scrunches in disgust, and she turns her head away. "Oh, my God, that's so gross. It looks so real!"

Evilly, I stick my tongue out and catch a drip running down the side. She screeches and I can't help but laugh. "Totally edible too," I tease.

She shakes her head, walking away. "Only if you're a vampire!"

We gear up, and with a steadying breath, we set out with a prayer that this plan works.

Thirty minutes later, we reach the summit of a cliff I found on a perimeter check yesterday. It's even more remote than the house, with a view that would warrant it being called a 'lookout point.' Most importantly, the mountaintop gives way to a stair-step of cliff edges off the main ridge.

Taking our time, we get everything set up. Well, mostly, I do while Bella tries to breathe and calm down. There's no need to rush. We need this to look believable, so the beginning has to seem as though I've seduced her completely and we're on a romantic walk through the woods where she suspects nothing.

Right now, though, she looks like there's an invisible firing squad aiming for her. Which, while somewhat true, will not sell our story.

"Relax. You can do this, Bella. We can do this," I say soothingly as I come over, stroking her cheek. "It's going to work."

We've spent hours creating this visual chain of effects, from selfies at the trailhead before we set off on the hike, to the quick video of her ass walking in front of me while I catcalled, telling her to 'swing that ass for me.' Her sweetly shy look over her shoulder had been real, and I want to save it just for me, but it's a puzzle piece in the bigger picture here.

I add a couple of shots of the horizon and the forest below, even taking a 360-degree panoramic that ends with Bella and me together, big smiles on our faces. A few more shots of the happy couple and then it's time to get to the real work of today.

"Are you ready?" I ask, and she bites her lip but nods.

I count down, "Three . . . two . . . one," and hit the record button. "What do you think? Beautiful, isn't it?"

She nods, her voice quavering, but it works for the setup. "It is, but fuck, this is high. I'm scared of heights, Gabe. You know that."

Her voice has just a bit of hysteria to it. I know it's because she's truly getting scared about the intensity of what we're about to do, but it effectively sells the fear of heights she doesn't have.

"Don't worry, I've got you. Come on."

I move toward the edge of the cliff, walking past Bella and showing a view of the forest below us, careful not to show the cliff face with its juts of rock that create platforms below the level we're standing on.

I extend my hand, pulling her to my side and angling the camera toward us. I kiss her, soft and slow, taking my time to help calm her.

"Absolutely breathtaking," I say, bringing the camera close to her again. This close, all you can see is her face, and I can see the wonder and the tremble in her cheek. I want to reassure her, but her reactions look real and are exactly what we need, so I hold myself back.

"You're not filming the view," she scolds me lightly. "Look at the birds flying out of that tree," she says, looking past me.

"Nope," I say, popping the *P*.

"Why are you filming me, Gabe? It's kinda weird." She blushes like she likes it, even as she protests.

"What do you mean?"

Bella cuts her eyes to me, smiling nervously. "I feel like I'm in one of those 'found footage' horror movies. Some monster's going to swoop out of the forest and snatch me or something."

I lick my lips hungrily, ready to get this over with, but don't lower the camera. "Sorry, but the monster's already here."

"Wha—" Bella says, but before she can finish, I grab her by the throat, shoving her down onto her knees. "Gabe, what the—"

I slap her, but it's pulled, and Bella doesn't roll with it, making me stop the video. "Shit . . . Bella, are you okay?"

Bella gets up, nodding. "I'm fine, but . . . that was terrible."

"Okay, let's try again."

"Wait," Bella says, taking my hand.

"This is supposed to be real. Slap me," Bella says simply. "You're barely hitting me, and I'm supposed to go down like you knocked the shit out of me."

I clench my teeth, wondering if I've got the strength to do it.

We start from the top and make it to the strike again, and this time, I don't hold back. Feeling horrible, I growl at her, "Stupid bitch."

Bella falls to the dirt, hard, and blinking in utter shock as she looks up at me. "What?"

The fear is palpable now. The tears trickling down her cheeks are real.

"You thought a guy like me would be with a loser like you? So pathetic. You're just a pawn in someone else's game. Useful, until you're not." The hateful vitriol pours off my tongue, the opposite of everything I believe, but I force the words through gritted teeth, hoping it reads as spite.

"Gabe, why?" she whimpers, and I almost stop, but I soldier on.

It's for a good reason. It's the only way to keep her safe a little longer.

"Gabe . . . please, I—" She's crawling away from me, her hands and knees getting scraped up and snot beginning to run down her face from her continued cries.

I pull my pistol, aiming at her chest. "Don't move," I order her, and she freezes in place.

Stepping closer, I meet her eyes. They're wide and wild as she shakes her head, pleading with her hands outstretched as if she can stop me. "No, oh, God, please . . . no, Gabe."

The shot rings out, a loud crack in the quiet woods, and Bella collapses to the dirt.

I drop the camera face down, cutting the video. Rushing off to the side, I grab the bottle of fake blood and turn back to Bella, who's trying to get up and shaking her head. "Don't move. Stay just like you are so it looks right."

She lowers back to the ground, hissing, "Fuck, that was loud."

I squirt the red viscous mixture on her chest, as if it's leaking from a small but deadly heart hit. "Hurry, we've got to get the timing right."

We talked through the plan from every angle, and one flaw we saw was the camera cut, but there was no other way. We don't have a thousand dollars of Hollywood special effects, and I wouldn't know how to work those anyway. So in order to keep the time stamps lined up, we have to get the video restarted quickly.

My heart hammers in my chest as I see the 'blood' on her.

How close was I to damning myself? How could I have ever considered doing for real what I'm pretending to have done to Bella?

How have I done this for as long as I have? How many souls stain my hands. I know the number, of course, but it's not one I'm proud of. Bile rises in my throat.

I need to atone. It's as good a word as any to get me moving.

Bella smears more of the blood through her hair before lying down in a puddle of it.

Stepping back, the cold side of me takes over, saying it looks good enough to fool anyone but a pro. All bloodied and bruised from the repeated slaps, Bella feigns unconsciousness, her eyes open wide in shock and her breath held for as long as she can.

I take several still shots, showing the damage. I let her get a breath in and then I restart the camera for the next video snippet, showing my booted feet as I roll her to the edge of the cliff using my toes to keep her moving.

At the edge, I bend down, facing the camera myself. "Job complete," I say to the glass circle, all cocky arrogance and ugly indifference to the loss of a human life.

I push her over with a shove of my hand, and she silently tumbles from sight. She'd been nervous that she'd scream, but she holds it in, along with any natural instincts to flail. The result is that it looks like she's already dead and just being dumped into the ravine.

"Bye, Isabella Turner," I say with a wave.

I cut the video again, my heart frozen in my chest as I look over the edge and pray that she hit the rocky platform below us just right.

She's there, but she's still. Too still. Was the drop too far? Did she knock herself out somehow?

"Bella?" I cry out, dropping to my knees to try to descend to her.

She opens one eye slowly. "We clear?" she whispers.

Relief washes through me, and I nod. "Clear."

She opens both eyes then, laying out wide on the rock as if she's sunbathing. "Good, help me get up there. It's a good thing I'm not really scared of heights, but this is really high up."

I toss her a rope, helping pull her back to the top as I coach her about where to place her feet for holds to make the climb up easier. As soon as she has both feet on the ground, I pull her away from the edge and into my arms. "Oh, my God, Bella. I'm so sorry," I say, cupping her face and turning it this way and that to verify for myself that she's okay.

"Hey . . . you look worse than I feel, Gabe. It was just acting. I know you were just doing what you needed to. Are you okay?"

I clear my throat, ashamed. "Yeah. Just some dark thoughts about the kind of man I've become. How do you feel?"

"I'm good. Messy, but good. Let's get this done and then we'll talk."

The image of a blood-splattered Bella, blood actually dripping between her teeth and over her lips, shocks me, and I stumble back, dropping the phone before plopping on the ground. Cradling my head in my hands, elbows on my bent knees, I break.

My mind's overwhelmed, images of the past several years flooding back to pummel me.

"No . . . no," I moan weakly as I see their faces, remember the names. The bodies, the destruction, the ruin I've brought to people.

It's all coming back to haunt me.

I remember the first person I killed, a drug dealer named Guillermo 'Big Willy' Lopez. He'd died with a look of surprise on his face, like he couldn't believe that his time on Earth was over.

I remember the second, Hunter Earle . . . and the third, and fourth . . .

I remember them all, and my self-control breaks. Horror sweeps over me, and I shudder and sob as I'm wracked, unable to control myself.

What have I become? What . . . what have I done?

I feel a hand on my neck and I jolt. "I . . . God, Bella, I'm evil," I force out, hiccupping as my body rebels again. "Everything I've done . . . no matter how bad those people were, it wasn't worth it."

"Come on," Bella says, holding out a hand. "Let's go to the stream we passed. I can wash this shit out of my hair and change out of these clothes, and we can talk."

I nod, numb as Bella helps me up. The stream is only about a hundred feet from where we staged all this, and while it's not huge, it's enough for Bella to dunk her hair and face before changing her shirt.

I sit numbly on a nearby rock as Bella cleans up, and when she comes back, she says nothing, just waiting until I'm ready to speak.

"When I slapped you, and I looked down, I was horrified," I tell her. "Because I remembered the different ways I'd considered taking you out when I first accepted the job and didn't know you yet. And when you sat up, eyes glassy and looking into my soul . . ."

I shiver, hugging myself, and Bella comes around behind me, wrapping her arms around my shoulders. "I'm okay, Gabe."

"But they're not," I protest. "There is no coming back from what I've done. I curse everything I touch with death." I can feel them all around me, like ghosts of my past, whispers of answers I never got and a brother I let down in the worst way.

"You can't change the past. It's come and gone. But what you can do is live your best life for them. For Jeremy, for all the bad people you killed, for me. For yourself." Her voice is quiet but powerful, speaking to the jagged, broken edges in my soul.

"I don't know if I can. I don't deserve to," I whisper. With a swallow, I force myself to look at her and confess. "I don't deserve you. I'm so sorry, Bella. So fucking sorry."

She hugs me again, cooing at me. "It's okay, we're gonna be okay. We're going to get through this, and then you know what you're going to do?"

I shake my head.

"You're going to be the best Gabriel Jackson you can be. Don't dishonor them by forgetting them . . . but don't let their ghosts stop you from living the life you are meant to have. Don't let the past stop you or make you afraid."

She jostles me a bit, like she's going to rattle the pep talk into my brain. It works a little bit, but mostly, it's just this amazing woman loving me. She should be running from me, getting help from just about anyone but me, but against all odds, she chose to trust me to help her. And I won't let her down.

I take her hand, pulling her around to sit in my lap. "Fuck, you are so beautiful."

Her brow crinkles cutely, "What? Uh, I need a shower. That fake blood mostly came off, but still . . . ew."

I look at her. Bare-faced, hair a mess, running for her life, and trusting a monster, she's never been more stunning, inside or out. And she's mine.

I set the truth free, hoping she'll believe it. "Beautiful. And mine, Bella."

Her lips part in surprise, and I dive in, taking her mouth and promising her that I'll fix everything as I explore her with my tongue. I nuzzle into her neck, leaving a line of biting kisses. She tastes sweet and sharp from the fake blood, but underneath, it's her.

My Bella.

Her breathy agreement is a balm to my monstrous heart, giving me hope. "Yours."

# CHAPTER 26

## Isabella

I CAN'T BELIEVE WHAT JUST CAME OUT OF MY MOUTH, BUT AS SOON as I say it, I know I'm right. Forget the scene, forget the dirt and the sweat and the fake blood. Forget all of that.

Gabe needs this.

I need this.

I kiss him hard, taking away any chance he has to protest, and he pulls me on top of him as he lies back on the rock, his hands grabbing my ass and squeezing me through my jeans as our bodies press together.

Like that first time in the woods, there are just too many damn clothes in the way. But as he kneads my ass, his thigh pressing between my knees and up against the zipper of my jeans, I moan into his mouth.

But I want more than a grinding orgasm this time. I want all of him.

I realize that's truer than it should be. I had fallen for him, but when I saw him attack Russell, my heart had shriveled up and retreated in confused fear. And though it's only been a short time, my heart has opened back up to him as we've talked and bared our souls—the good, bad, and ugly. Though his is certainly tipping more toward the bad and ugly than mine.

But I understand what he was doing and who he is. He is going to such lengths to help me and keep me safe, including the whole thing with

Russell. Gabe really does mean that he'll do anything for me. Truly . . . anything.

The weight of that settles me down, emotionally grounding me in him and this moment.

I slide down his body until I reach his waist. He watches, his eyes dark with hunger as I unzip his pants and free his thick cock.

I run my tongue up the underside of his throbbing shaft, and he moans, grabbing a handful of my hair to guide me back where he wants me.

"That's it, Bella . . . fuck, your mouth feels so good on me," he moans, his words disappearing as I inhale him. I can't get enough. The taste, the velvety steel texture, the way he stretches my jaw as I take more and more of him inside me . . . the power I feel.

Here I am with this sexy, powerful, deadly man at my mercy. He's not perfect, that's for sure. No, he's every bit the dangerous hunter, but he's mine. Poor Izzy Turner, the girl everyone made fun of and pitied, who never had a single thing go her way and struggled just to eke by. But that's not who I am with Gabe, and maybe he doesn't have to be the Fallen Angel with me. We can just be Gabe and Bella, ourselves.

I suck him, hollowing my cheeks and bobbing up and down over every inch of his manhood, devoting myself to him. Even as I pleasure him, I can feel the heat building between my own legs.

I look up to him through my lashes, and he thrusts deep into my throat before pulling me off. "Hey, I wasn't done," I protest.

But he pulls at my shirt, signaling me to take it off. I step back, making quick work of the tee and my bra. My nipples tighten in the fresh air, standing at attention and begging for Gabe's tongue, hands.

I glance down to my jeans to work the button and shimmy them off, kicking my shoes off in a mess I'll straighten out later. When I look back up, Gabe is stroking himself as he watches me strip. If I'd realized, I would've done it more gracefully or sexily, but judging by the red, angry color of the head of his cock, he liked my fast stripping just fine.

"Hands and knees, Princess," he commands. It's the first time he's called me that since our painful conversation in my living room, and it feels symbolic that we're back on course, on the same team. Even if the team is Hell's Angels. If that's what it takes to be with him, I'll gladly trade a bit of my soul, darken my spirit to match his intensity.

Dropping to my hands and knees in the soft pine needles, I toss my hair over my shoulder so I can see his approach. Gabe's eyes are on me at first, but as he lowers to his knees behind me, his gaze sinks to my ass and I can see his hand twitch. I arch my back, inviting him, and moan when he slaps my ass, loving it.

"Say it again," he begs, sliding my panties to the side. My wet lips clench as the cool air hits them, and Gabe spreads me open with his thumbs. "Whose are you?"

"Yours."

In a heartbeat, all my breath leaves me in a whoosh as Gabe shoves his thick cock deep inside me in one smooth stroke.

He's huge, and each time we're together it's like being split open, but the initial pain electrifies my body. I feel alive while he pounds me, hammering my pussy as my fingers claw at the rich, moist earth underneath me and I'm pushing back into him, crying out with every slap of his balls on my clit.

I don't need the roughness . . . but I love it and trust him to not go too far. He takes me, completely and fully, and when I clench around him, crying out my orgasm, he grinds deep inside me, letting me ride it out before he starts again.

I can feel each plunging stroke, the throb of his cock and the pulse of his heart as his fingers dig into my waist. He smacks my ass again, and I yelp, loving it and throwing my hair back.

"Gabe . . . please!"

I need him. He needs me.

I am his. He is mine.

Both flawed and scarred, damaged beyond repair, but somehow perfectly matched.

Gabe swells and thrusts hard as he cries out, warmth filling me as he finds his ecstasy. He groans my name, triggering my own shattering. I spasm around him, my eyes rolling up in my head and the shakes coming over me again as I keep him inside me until it passes. I feel Gabe gather me in his arms, holding me close and safe off the forest floor.

"Fuck, Princess." His voice is ragged. "I feel like I'm damning you to hell with me."

I cup his face. "I feel like I'm pulling you out of hell to be with me."

The walk back to the house feels different. Our plan is already in action, and it makes me nervous. I trust Gabe, but even he says this is a risky gamble and the stakes are high. Our lives.

I'd hoped our return would feel more triumphant, like we're taking life by the horns. Instead, I feel like I've grabbed on to the tail of a bull and am just holding on for dear life as I slingshot around.

Gabe kisses my forehead, more sweet than sultry. "Go rinse off and we'll head back. You're sure Mia won't mind our dropping in?"

I give a small smile, laughing softly. "Mia won't mind us stopping in with a moment's notice, but she's gonna flip when I tell her what's going on. But she'll get on board. Probably have a statistical analysis of every angle in five-point-three minutes and a half-dozen suggestions on ways we can proceed from here. It's who she is."

He nods, letting me go clean up while he packs up the house and removes any trace we were ever here.

Alone, I pick up the burner phone Gabe told me to use for the call. It rings and goes to voicemail the first time I call, which I'd expected. Mia isn't the type to answer to random phone numbers. So I hang up and dial again immediately, and she picks up.

"What? I ain't buying whatever you're selling," she says in her fake Russian accent.

"Mia? It's Izzy," I say, and the floodgates of her fury open.

"Where the actual fuck have you been, girl? I called Martha to check on you because I haven't heard anything in a couple of days and she tells me that you went on vacation. Vacation?!" she says incredulously. "Do you even know what that word means? And with some guy we haven't even met, much less vetted? Charlotte is having a fucking cow about this. And not the cute black-and-white dairy ones, but like a big ass, horned monster of a cow. W. T. F. Iz!" She says the actual letters, like double-u, tee, eff, and then finally takes a breath so I can get a word in edgewise.

"I know, I'm sorry. But I've got reasons. Can I come by in a bit? We need to talk."

I hear her inhale, and I'm sure she's got her hand on her chest in worry. "What's wrong? What did he do? I'll fucking kill this Gabe character, string him up by his ball sack, slice and dice him open, and make him choke on his own stomach contents."

"Whoa, no. That is rather . . . descriptive and disgusting. He's fine. He's helping me, actually. But I need to talk to you. And Thomas," I say solemnly.

"Tommy?" she asks leerily.

"I know you have a lot of questions," I interrupt quickly before she can go off on another question-filled rant. "I have even more than you do, probably, but we'll figure it all out soon. We'll be there soon, so be home, okay?"

"Got it," she says, but I can hear the worry in her voice.

# CHAPTER 27

## Gabriel

I KEEP AN EYE ON THE TRAFFIC BEHIND US THE WHOLE WAY TO Roseboro, looking for anything that could resemble a tail. I take an indirect, circuitous route to be sure, and only then do I pull into the Goldstone building's garage, parking close to the express elevator that will take us directly to the penthouse he and Mia share.

When the elevator doors open, Mia and Thomas are standing there waiting for us. Mia and Bella instantly launch themselves at each other, screeches and wails of 'missed you' and 'what the hell' surrounding them as they hug it out like they haven't seen each other in a lifetime instead of only days.

For Bella, I suspect it does feel like a different lifetime. Before, her life was tough, but simple and safe and predictable. Now, it's none of those things.

While the girls have their reunion, Thomas and I eye each other. I know who he is, mostly because everyone knows of the wunderkind who climbed the ranks fast and makes a huge difference in Roseboro. I have the slightest advantage there, because while I know him, he has no idea who or what I am.

But one look in his eyes tells me that's about to change.

It's an odd feeling to intentionally expose myself after so many years of hiding behind masks, ensuring that no one knew the true me. Everyone only seen the part of me I wanted them to, whether it's the ice-cold hunter or the congenial boy next door, both equally a part I merely play and the truth somewhere in the middle.

Scarily, part of me even wonders if the masks have become my reality, so pervasive, that I don't know the difference any longer. Or worse, that this monster I've created is all that I am now.

But for Bella, I'll do whatever I have to. Even if that means exposing my vulnerabilities to the people she trusts.

Because unfortunately, this is a battle being waged on a grand scale. I can handle the smaller moves and strategies, like keeping Bella by my side, safe and sound. But the true threat, Blackwell, can only be handled by working with Goldstone.

I hold my hand out, a peace offering I wouldn't usually give. "Gabriel Jackson. Thank you for seeing us."

Thomas shakes my hand, and in his handshake I get another measure of the man. He's strong and confident enough that he doesn't have to show it off with a crushing grip. "We'd do anything for Izzy. She simply has to ask."

I like him already. He's smooth and direct, warning me and lovingly reminding Bella that she has people, if she'll just open up.

"I'm afraid that's why we're here. Can we sit? The information we need to share is rather involved and upsetting."

"Tell me about this vacation—" Thomas touches Mia's shoulder, breaking her interrogation of Bella. "What? Oh, yeah, we can sit down instead of doing this in the foyer, but we're talking about this, Iz."

We follow Thomas into the living room, but Mia is continuing to monologue the whole way. "Disappears without a call for a whole weekend. Must be some dick to get her to take off work."

But when we sit, Mia really looks at Bella's face and reads that this is bigger than an impromptu vacation, and the scolding jocularity disappears from her voice. "Okay, spill it. What's going on?"

Bella looks to me, so I begin.

"Like I said, my name is Gabriel Jackson, Gabe. But people call me something else too . . . The Fallen Angel."

Thomas's eyes narrow, and I can see his inner alarm bells going off. Somehow, I've actually overestimated and underestimated him at the same time. My research since finding out Blackwell's true motivation showed Thomas to be relatively clean, but you don't get to his level of influence without being aware of the murky waters business often entails.

I'd wondered if my professional name would even mean anything to him, but it seems it does. Smart man, but given what I know of him, he's a good man too and has achieved his success the 'right' way.

He's also incredibly brave, because I can see that he's willing to fight me, if need be, to protect his woman and Bella too, going so far as pushing Mia behind him in preparation. The man's got big brass ones, I'll give him that.

"Izzy."

He reaches a hand toward Bella, and I growl. But before things can turn overly ugly, Bella reaches over to me and entwines her arm through mine, taking my hand rather than Thomas'.

"Thomas, I know exactly who he is and what he is."

Mia peeks from behind Thomas, confusion in her voice. "Okay, for those of us not in the know, can someone tell me why some cheesy nickname—no offense there, Gabe—is making my man go all uber-protective caveman?"

I chance taking my eyes off Thomas, the most significant threat in the room, to look at Mia. "I'm a hitman." She gasps, but I keep the shots going, getting it all out at once. "I was sent to kill Bella but fell for her instead. I was hired by Blackwell."

Thomas drops back to the couch in shock, but he recovers faster than one would expect and his eyes flare back to life, looking from Bella to me to our locked hands. "Start at the beginning and tell me what the fuck you're doing here. All of it."

What follows for the next hour is an uncomfortable and awkward exposé on all my sins and faults. It's painful but necessary as I tell Thomas what Blackwell said about using Bella to hurt him and Mia, revealing the depths and the backstabbing connivery that Blackwell's willing to go to in his quest for power.

Mia moves to hug Bella several times as we both share the story of the last few weeks, stopping at the point of us running away.

Thomas is understandably furious that someone is watching him from the wings, pulling strings and strategizing threats, both with the corporate saboteur and with Bella. "I had no idea. Fuck, why does he even give a shit about me? That makes no sense. We're both doing well in Roseboro. Hell, I thought we were doing well for Roseboro. Sure, we weren't friends, but . . . is he insane?"

"I've noticed that most of my employers are either psychopaths or sociopaths," I reply, finally smiling grimly. "In Blackwell's case, he's a little bit of both, I suspect. Definitely a narcissist."

While Thomas mulls that over, Mia looks to Bella, gesturing to me with a toss of her head, making her purple hair swing. "You sure about this, about him?"

My breath hitches sharply. It's a moment of truth for us, because while I am confident in her answer, there's still that uncertainty, a lack of understanding of why she would choose someone like me when she deserves so much better. "I'm sure. We're . . . together."

Bella looks to me, her eyes shining brightly, and though we still haven't said the words, I can see them in the depths there. I hope she can see the truth in mine too.

I expect there to be arguments, at least a few protests that she's throwing away her life with a criminal. Or even that this is a ploy at Blackwell's behest. Something to pull Bella and I apart. It's what I've come to expect in the world, harsh coldness and indifference.

Instead, Thomas and Mia quickly go into analysis and planning mode, and inside my chest, I feel a warmth build. Is this what trust and friendship feel like? I don't know, but maybe I'm getting more out of this than just a girl and a cat.

"Okay, so we understand why you came to us. We can provide security and more resources—" Mia says, but Bella jumps in.

"We already have a plan. Well, part of one, so Blackwell will think I'm dead. It'll give us some time, we think."

Mia's brows raise so far on her forehead, I think they might disappear into her hairline. "Seriously? Your grand plan is to fake your death?"

She mumbles something in Russian I don't understand, but the eyeroll and palm-to-forehead smack are pretty clear.

Bella nods, clearly used to these sorts of theatrics. "We already filmed it, and Gabe sent the videos and pictures to Blackwell as we came back into town. Gabe has a meeting with him tomorrow."

"Show me," Thomas demands.

I reach into my pocket and pull out my fresh burner phone. I'd already sent the files to Blackwell and to this new phone before yanking the battery and SIM card on the original so that Blackwell couldn't track us on it.

Thomas and Mia watch the videos and look at the pictures, horror dawning on their faces. "Oh, my God, that's awful, Izzy. I can't . . ." she says, looking away for the part where I roll Bella over the cliff's edge. Her face's gone slightly pale green, and I can sympathize with her. Watching it on replay had my own gorge rising. Somehow, the small-screen on the cell makes it look even more realistic, even more horrifying.

Bella gets up and hugs Mia, knowing her friend needs reassurance. "It's okay, I'm okay."

But Mia won't be calmed. She shakes her head, burying her face in her hands. "We got you into this. Fuck, I'm so sorry, Iz. I had no idea."

Bella pulls her back in, not letting go. "You couldn't have known. None of us knew what was going on behind the scenes, and I won't let you beat yourself up for it. I'll sick Vash on you if I have to."

Mia huffs a laugh and hugs Bella back. "Nirvash loves me more than you, and we both know it. Martha said she's fine, by the way."

Thomas and I lock eyes again, letting the girls have their moment of normalcy because we both know it's about to end. When I nod, he clears his throat, his voice deep and resonating as he sits forward, his elbows on his knees.

"Okay, so let's get to work on a plan because it sounds like we need to know our next move when Gabe meets with Blackwell tomorrow."

I appreciate that he doesn't try to stop me on this, thinking that he's going to take over now. There are several things in play, and I know Thomas will have to keep Mia and his business at the top of his mind. But my mind is focused on one thing and one thing only.

My princess.

"Here's what I know," I start as I outline the skeleton of a plan I've come up with. Soon, we're bouncing ideas back and forth, each of us contributing and focused on one goal.

Stopping Blackwell.

The only unknown is what ends we'll have to go to.

# CHAPTER 28

## Blackwell

WAGNER PLAYS OVER MY OFFICE'S SOUND SYSTEM, AND I SIT BACK, enjoying the view of Roseboro after dark. Other than the lights from my sound system and the soft red glow above the door that beckons as if it's the only exit strategy, the only light in the room is the dim glow of the lights filtering up from the city below, which is just how I like it.

I watch the white and red lights on the street below, people skittering this way and that as if their actions have any meaning. Perhaps in some small way, they do. A parent coming home to a child, a doctor going to work, things of that nature. But even then, it is a moment of time, a minor importance in the big scheme of life.

I focus my gaze closer, seeing my own reflection in the glass, and note my austere appearance, the power that surrounds me like a cloud of dominance. I stand taller, broader, luxuriating in my supremacy, my image making the same moves in return.

A legacy. That is something important. Something I will leave, even as I sit here in my tower, overlooking the pawns I move like a master.

Letting my eyes look further out, I cringe inwardly, anger burning deep in my stomach as I see the lights still visible in Goldstone's abomination, glowing brightly like some happy little celebration of the young upstart's arrogance.

I'm coming for you, Golden Boy.

I pick up the tablet in my lap and once again look over the photos I received today, my lips twitching as they try to lift into a smile. But smiles aren't warranted yet. I have too many doubts about their authenticity and the man who sent them to me.

Besides, this is merely step one, intended to be an uncomfortable thorn in Goldstone's side to make him focus elsewhere while I move on to step two. A diversionary tactic.

If this proves authentic, I wonder if Goldstone knows yet. Probably not, but I can still imagine the moment his data-hungry strumpet discovers that her best friend in the world is gone, the screams and tears she'll let loose. I imagine Thomas comforting her, weakly focusing on her loss instead of keeping his eye on the prize.

His company.

When he's distracted, I'll move in and take back what is mine. My rightful place as the leader of this town. More than merely a king, but a creator, the one who designed everything from the infrastructure to the governmental minions who are in place because of my financial support.

I swipe to the next picture. The images are realistic, and on the surface are beautiful proof of her death, and I feel dark excitement bloom in my chest. I zoom in on a blood spatter on Miss Turner's cheek, noting the already purple tint from Gabriel's blow.

I'll admit that I have had serious doubts that the well-regarded Fallen Angel was going to come through this time. He'd seemed rather caught in Isabella Turner's web, but perhaps he's a better actor than I'd given him credit for.

*If* he's authentic.

I watch the video again, enjoying the moment when Isabella realizes the monster she's let in, see the confusion and fear dawning in her eyes.

And for just a moment, I do smile, letting myself celebrate a small victory and feeling excitement for what's to come.

My office phone rings, and I turn around, picking up the private line. "Yes?"

"Sir . . . it's Jericho."

Just the man I was looking to hear from, for he holds the verdict on Gabriel's actions. I lean back in my chair, setting the tablet aside. "What news do you have for me, Mr. Jericho?"

"Your concerns were correct. Jackson has been lying to you."

My hand grips the phone tighter. So much for small victories. But I don't let Jericho hear my disappointment or anger. "I see. And you are certain about this?"

"Yes, sir."

"Fine. Come to my office as soon as you're in town."

"Of course, sir. I'll have options for you when I arrive."

Jericho hangs up the line, and I pick the tablet back up to glance at the pictures again. Too good to be true, a false reproduction of the horror movie result I wished for.

I should've trusted my gut all along.

That a woman of so little importance is costing me this much in time, effort, and finances is ridiculous. I'm regretting not hiring a two-bit thug at this point, one that would've been completely expendable after the job was done. But my penchant for elegance in my revenge was too strong, and now I'm paying the price and past ready to move on to the aftermath of Isabella Turner's death.

But a good strategist knows to keep forces in reserve, to build plans upon plans, with contingencies for every possible outcome. So Gabriel's betrayal is not a crippling blow, but a new opportunity for bigger, bolder moves.

My lips twist wryly as I consider various ideas, from simple to complex, before deciding on a course of action.

He and Miss Turner will be the new assignment. It shall serve them right for their deception, and serve me well for my plans for Goldstone.

The fresh thought of his name makes my blood boil in my veins. Even without knowing it, he's thwarting my plays. How can one man be so lucky?

I may not have Lady Luck on my side, but I have something far more beneficial, unfettered cruelty. And I'm all too willing to acquaint Goldstone with what a true leader of this city can do when he puts his mind, will, and pocketbook to work.

I squeeze the tablet in my hand tightly and then unleash my anger, the device flying through the air and hitting the glass.

I look over, seeing the lights of the city as a starburst effect through the shatter. They add highlight and shadow to my refracted image, giving me a monstrously hideous appearance.

"You have no idea what's coming for you, Golden Boy. But I do. I have so many plans for us."

# CHAPTER 29

## Gabriel

THE PARK'S QUIET, AND ACROSS THE POND I CAN SEE A COUPLE OF basketball courts that are currently empty. It's a weekday, a school day, and it's still way too early for almost anyone to be up for a pickup game.

I approach the bench where Blackwell sits, taking a deep breath to calm myself and do a final scan of the park for gunmen.

*Get it done. Buy yourself time to figure out what you're going to do with this snake*, I tell myself when I'm satisfied it's safe.

Setting my concern aside, I finish my approach, mentally verifying that my gun is tucked away in easy reach, in the false pocket of my light jacket. The jacket is more for concealment than the weather. The early morning sun is shining brightly enough that I don't feel the cold yet.

Blackwell, as always, is well-dressed, this time in a dark suit. I'd feel honored, except I know enough about Blackwell to guess that he never dresses down. I'd bet the man wears three-piece pajamas to bed, with a matching robe for every set.

"Right on time, Mr. Jackson."

It sounds more observational than complimentary or conversational, so I don't respond. I sit down on the bench beside him, angling myself to have an advantage. Though I'm well aware that if this doesn't go off successfully, I'm a dead man anyway, here or in some unsuspecting alley later.

"You know," Blackwell says as he pulls out his phone, turning it over in his hands. I wonder if he's recording what we're saying or if someone's listening in through it. "You've really not done what I hired you to do."

I can hear the threat in his voice, but I knew there would be some strong-arming with him. I have to deal with his skepticism now before it gets out of hand. "You asked me to eliminate Isabella Turner and I did. You have proof."

"I hired you to kill her to send a message to my enemies, to take their hearts from them," Blackwell growls, raising a fisted hand like he's holding an actual beating heart. "I wanted more than pictures."

"If you want to take your enemy's heart, what better way to do it than to actually capture it first before you crush them?" I ask coldly, letting a bit of that side of me out, even though it's now devoted to protecting Bella. "Now he can spend days, weeks, and months being eaten up with doubt and worry. It's more effective than cancer."

"Hmm . . . I have yet to know a cancer that had the side benefits you indulged in."

"It was an effective tactic to get her alone and trusting me," I explain calmly. "She had a difficult life. She trusted very few people. Even before this, she had been betrayed and disappointed by most people she'd met. Getting her to leave her protective detail behind for the day was damn-near impossible, but I did it. And I'm sure that when she didn't return as scheduled, the guards sounded the alarm. And if you think she wasn't terrified, you need to rewatch those videos. Hell, send them to Karakova if you want to really torture Goldstone."

The words turn my stomach, talking about my Bella that way, but I have to add just a touch of sociopathy in order to make this convincing. Blackwell has to actually think I don't give a damn one way or another about what happened, that it's just a job.

It helps, but Blackwell hums anyway.

"Photos and videos are scant proof. I want the body."

"Good fucking luck," I growl, looking over at him. "That cliff was an hour's hike into the woods, and I dumped her into a ravine. I sure as hell wasn't hauling a human body out of there over my shoulder, and I dumped it there for a reason. It's already been twenty-four hours. By now, the body's most likely in some wolf or bear's belly. Besides, the lack of a body is what will destroy Mia, and therefore, Goldstone. A body, a funeral, and a casket lowering into the ground at a place you can go talk to a tombstone give closure of a sort."

It's the painful truth. Visiting Jeremy's grave is a pitiful substitute for him, but it has helped me over the years.

"Without a body, they'll only have questions and get none of that peace. Ever," I continue. "And like I said, when the questions have eaten up so much . . . that is when you do what you want."

It's a bluff, one I'd prepared for. Still, it's a reach, and as Blackwell stares at me, I remember why I'm doing something so dangerous. I remember what I have to live for.

It's going to be the force of my personality and my balls that'll get us through this, hopefully getting us enough time until I can ensure Bella's safety.

"You should know I'm not a man who accepts excuses," Blackwell rumbles after a moment. "If I want a body, I get a body. I should withhold payment."

"Keep your money," I reply with a shrug. "We both know that's not why I took this contract. But if you want to walk out of this park alive, I expect you to keep your end of the bargain and give me the information. And if you think your security men can stop me before I pull the trigger on the pistol I have in my pocket . . . well, try me."

"Is your dead brother really worth that much to you?"

I nod, looking into Blackwell's eyes. It's the first time I've really seen him clearly, not hidden in the murky shadows of his office but in the exposing light of day, and I don't see any humanity in those dead orbs.

Then again, people probably say the same thing about me, or at least they did before Bella brought me back to life. I worry he can see that in my eyes too and deflect.

"You damn well know that's what I've been after."

I'll hand it to Blackwell, he doesn't flinch, though I doubt too many people dare to speak to him that gruffly. Calmly, he reaches inside his jacket, but I'm on edge and move towards my gun.

He smirks and holds up a staying hand. Slowly, he withdraws a small envelope, like the kind you'd put a greeting card in.

He holds it out, and I take it, feeling the data card inside shift around. "This had better not be encrypted."

"It's not." Blackwell rises and puts on a fedora that once again casts his eyes in shadow. "I'm afraid I have a meeting to attend. Don't move from this bench until I've cleared the park, Mr. Jackson. I have eyes on you. Standoff, yes?"

I chuckle, shaking my head. "A standoff only works when both parties give a damn about actually walking away. Remember that, Mr. Blackwell, if you considered welching on your data."

Blackwell purses his lips, and I can't tell if it's in amusement or anger. "I don't think we'll be meeting again, Mr. Jackson. At least not in this life. Perhaps in hell?"

I give him an evil grin, like it's a date I'm looking forward to. "I'm sure you'll be waiting with a proper barbecue and torture rack all ready for me on the outermost ring. Face it, they wouldn't let you into hell anyway."

"Oh?"

"They'd worry you'd take over." I chuckle like it's a joke, though there's more truth than I'd like in the words about the power-hungry nature of his soul.

He tips his hat to me and walks away. After a few moments, I stand up, heading in the opposite direction. I don't know if Blackwell really has eyes on me. The whole idea that you can feel when someone's watching you is just stereotypical horror movie acting, but I'm careful nevertheless. I definitely can't go back to Goldstone's, not now that I truly might have a tail.

So I head to the motel, alone. I hope it was enough, that Blackwell will move on to bigger fish, namely Thomas, who's preparing for him. But that'll only happen if Blackwell bought my bullshit and there's no way to know if he did yet.

What's not bullshit is the data card in my pocket and the feeling inside me, hoping against hope that I'll be able to have my cake and eat it too for once in my life.

# CHAPTER 30

## Isabella

"**S**o, how'd you sleep?"

I yawn, stretching as I pad my way into the 'living room' of Mia's penthouse, rubbing the sleep out of my eyes. "Hard," I admit, smiling as I see Mia looking cute in black pants and a T-shirt from a band she sent me the link to. She calls it 'recommended listening'. I call it 'have an opinion by the next time I see her or she'll shove earbuds in my ears.' Tomato, tomahto. "Cute shirt. And yes, I listened. Starlight was okay, but I liked the older stuff better. And who names their band Babymetal anyway?"

Mia grins, giving a light golf-style clap. "Well done. There's hope for you yet. We'll see if Charlotte does as well on her musical pop quiz too." She's half-joking but mostly telling the truth. I can already foresee an in-depth musical analysis in my future.

For now, she's distracted by bigger fish though. "Gabe's already gone?"

I nod. Letting him go had been hard, knowing that he was walking into a potentially deadly situation. But he'd taken every precaution, leaving extra-early to decrease the chances he'd been seen at Goldstone Tower, carefully tailoring his windbreaker to conceal his gun, and even letting me check everything too, carefully following the steps Saul at the range showed me in an attempt to ease my worries.

It'd worked for a minute, but as soon as he'd left, I'd curled up in bed, terror gripping my stomach in its icy fist. I basically chewed my lip off and picked at my cuticles with nerves, wishing I had a phone to at least check in with him by text message if nothing else.

But the anxiety had worn me out, especially given the stress of the last few days, and somewhere along the way, I'd fallen asleep. It's almost lunch now, and still no word from Gabe. I knew he wouldn't be able to call for a bit in an attempt to make sure everything is clear before we make contact again, but that doesn't assuage my worries.

"When is Charlotte coming over?" I ask Mia, eager for any sort of distraction.

"She should be here any minute. She's bringing a bag to stay too, so we can keep the whole gang safe together. I gave her the bare bones of what's happening but kept it pretty generic since we were on the phone. And I told her to look frantic, scared, and basically freaked the fuck out as she left work, rushed home, and came over. She's no actress, but I think she can fake the tears she'd cry if something had actually happened to you."

I nod, glad we'd gone over including Char, and we'd put together something for her last night in our strategy plan. With Gabe telling Blackwell I had a protective detail, the guards would realize I'm missing in action pretty quickly and report to Thomas. So my girls should be losing their shit and circling the wagons.

And now, my part of the plan is basically to stay in hiding. It's a pretty vital part of the whole scenario, since I'm supposed to be dead and all.

The elevator dings, and Mia shoots me a look. I hop into the pantry, closing the door, just in case. But a second later, the elevator opens and Charlotte comes barreling in. "Someone had better tell me what is going on immediately."

I come out and am swept up in Charlotte's arms for a hug. "Fuck, girl. We always worry about you, but Mia said you're in some real trouble. Not that Russell isn't real, or your school stuff isn't important, but this is like next-level. You okay?"

I smile as much as I can, hugging her back. "Yeah, for now. Though this is all way above my paygrade. I'm having to trust Gabe and Thomas to figure some shit out and set all this right. And you know how much I *love* to depend on other people to handle my life."

The sarcasm stings, but it's the truth. I do wish I could just stomp my way into the Blackwell building, tell him to fuck off in an epic mic drop, and go on with my life.

But it's not that easy, and I have to admit that someone else is probably better equipped to address this strategically. In the meantime, while I stay hidden, I need distraction. I need my besties.

Mia and Char glance at each other and then take action. "Lunch and rom-com movie, stat. We've got you, girl." And then like whirling dervishes, Charlotte pulls plates and glasses from the cabinets and Mia disappears to the media room to get the movie set up.

Char opens the fridge, and I happen to catch a glimpse of the inside. It's stocked full, and I do mean full, of what looks to be the entirety of a grocery store. "Damn, I wish my fridge looked like that! Is that a whole container of raspberries?"

I must sound more desperate than the awe I was aiming for because Charlotte turns around, a frown on her face. "Izzy."

But I cut her off with a hand extended, shaking my head. "Nope. I'm fine."

She presses her lips into a thin line, holding back the argument she wants to make, settling for grabbing the berries and setting the whole bowl in front of me. "Eat."

I don't argue, popping one of the bright fruits into my mouth and moaning at the explosion of sour sweetness on my tongue.

Mia chooses that moment to walk back into the kitchen, grinning. "I'll have what she's having if it'll make me sound like that."

I laugh around a mouthful. "Ha-ha, Sally, but we're not watching you fake an orgasm over lunch."

The movie reference makes them both smile, reassuring them in a small way that I'm okay.

"Apparently, we're listening to you moan and groan, so what's the difference?" Mia teases back. "Speaking of moaning and groaning, I want every dirty detail of your weekend away. And don't you dare tell me that you two holed up in a safe house and didn't get any action."

I shake my head, protesting. "We were scared for my life, on the run. Sex was the last thing on our minds while we tried to figure out a way out of this mess."

My girls look at one another, using each other as a barometer, then simultaneously reach behind their backs and toss invisible flags into the air, Mia whistling loudly. "Calling bullshit on that. Flag on the conversation."

I laugh and give in. "Fine, there was action. But those dirty details are all mine."

Charlotte gives me a friendly pop on the shoulder, making a mock-angry face. "Spoil sport! I'm living vicariously through you."

I rub my shoulder, even though she didn't hurt me. It's just part of the game, and I'm willing to immerse myself in it for a bit to keep myself sane. "Well, I'm just trying to see tomorrow, so you'll have to find your own dick for entertaining stories."

She smirks, weaving her head back and forth. "Fine, no dick tales from you and definitely none from me, then what about the rest of all this? Are you sure about Gabe, about hiding out, about Blackwell not coming after you? What about Russell?"

"I changed my mind, let's talk about the awesome sex," I reply, my forced levity dissolving as I find myself torn between my friends' attempts at cheering me up and the worry about where Gabe is and whether he's safe.

But I realize that right now, I need a deeper conversation than how much meat my man's packing between his legs.

"Actually, I don't know what's up with Russell. He definitely saw Gabe and me together, and Gabe definitely put him in the hospital based on the beating he gave him, so that could come back to haunt us. But I feel like Russell is small potatoes compared to everything else."

"After Gabe told us what happened with Russell, I did a little research online using the town's arrest records, and more importantly, the Roseboro rumor mill," Mia shares, sitting down on a stool. "So word is, Russell doesn't remember getting a beatdown. He woke up, or I guess regained consciousness is more accurate, and got himself to the hospital. Right now, he's claiming he doesn't remember who, but everyone thinks he pissed off the wrong rock slinger."

"Wait, so Gabe's totally in the clear there?" I ask, shocked. Did Russell get hit in the head, or was he really that scared by what happened? No cops, no pissed off Russell? "That's awesome, better than we'd hoped."

"We?" Charlotte says, busting me and returning our focus to the topic she wants most. Gabe.

"Yeah, we," I say, blushing just a little bit. "We might've gotten a weird start—actually, we're still mid-weirdness—but we've got something. He's something . . . special."

Mia coughs, not subtle at all as she says, "Tell her everything."

And for the second time in just over twelve hours, I'm running through everything that's happened in the last few weeks, from both my perspective and Gabe's point of view. It's harder not having Gabe to fill in the parts that he did last night, when he gave me an out in the difficult areas, but I power through it, knowing I need to toughen up and be strong if I'm going to get through this. And that means facing my best friends and admitting that I'm falling for Gabe.

As I wrap it up, Char looks like she's about to be sick. "How in the world am I supposed to go to work in that building, work for that monster, when he put out a hit on my best friend?"

I give her a hug, patting her on the back. "With a smile, that's how. We don't know what Thomas and Gabe are finding out or what we're going to do yet, so in the meantime, you're going to play along. Act like I'm missing, be worried, but try to carry on, and if it gets to the point that you have to pretend I'm gone, we'll put in a plan to cover that. Start with taking a few days off, like you're poking around and worried, also known as laying low and staying safe. Because if he targeted me, he could target you."

She nods, though she looks uncertain. I understand. She doesn't really recognize just how much danger she's in. Until I saw Gabe and Rusty, I didn't understand either.

After a long moment, Charlotte says, "Okay, movie time. Let's do this because I don't think my brain can take any more. I need a fluffy comedy with a guaranteed happily ever after. And then, I'm making us cupcakes. I'm trying a new recipe and I need testers."

"Deal," I say, and Mia echoes my sentiment a half-beat later.

I love these girls. My best friends, who would support me through just about anything, up to and including fake deaths and conspiracies, apparently.

# CHAPTER 31

## Gabriel

I PULL MY HOODIE OVER MY HEAD, EVEN THOUGH THE NIGHT MAKES IT unneeded. But the more generic I can be, the better, and disappearing into the darkness is a definite benefit.

Coming around the corner of the narrow road, I approach the building in front of me, an old industrial-looking place with a sign out front that says Roseboro Textile Services. The drive here had taken me almost an hour, not because of the distance but because of how careful I'd been to lose anyone who might be following. At this point, I have full faith that Blackwell has a tail on me, and while I haven't identified who it is, I'm going to be careful.

I'm a dangerous guy, but I'm far from the only shark in the water.

That's why we're having this meeting here, a place unrelated to either of us and therefore untraceable.

Checking the door, there's a worn title painted on the metal . . . shift supervisor. This is the place.

I don't knock, but out of habit, I stand back and to the side as I swing the door open, making sure I don't stand in the area most people are likely to aim. But no gunshot or threat comes, just a deep voice from the dimly-lit interior.

"Come on in. We're clear."

I step into the room, plain and bare save for a dented government surplus metal desk and a couple of beat-down chairs. Thomas sits in one, gesturing to the other. Closing the office door behind me, I cross the small space and sit.

There's a bit of a silent tension coursing between us for a moment, neither of us used to working with others, at least not like this, when everything we care about is on the line. Finally, he starts. "How'd the meeting with Blackwell go?"

It's the icebreaker we need to get this ball rolling. No accusations, no bullshit. Just focus on the job at hand. "Okay," I say, humming as I think back. "He seemed to buy Bella's death, but he wanted to see the body, not just pictures and video. I told him to go get the damn body himself if he wanted it so bad. He believed it enough to give me the information that was my main payment, so that's something."

I shrug, but my brows knit together.

"What?" Thomas asks.

"It was too easy," I admit, leaning back in the chair as I try to recall all the details of the incident. "Blackwell is slick and smart, and he took me at my word that it was done. Too easy, which means he probably knows something's up."

"Maybe, but those pictures and video were pretty fucking believable. Maybe he wants to believe it enough to not look too closely. Especially since Izzy's not really his objective. I am." I can hear the pinch of pain in his voice. "Fuck, I never should've gotten her mixed up in this."

I toss him a small grin. "Don't know that you would've had much of a choice. I don't know Mia, but if Bella thought for one second that she could help you, she'd do it. No matter the cost."

He nods, seeing the wisdom of my words. "That's true. But look how that's ended up. What do we do now?"

There's a tone to his voice that immediately increases my respect for him. Since our first meeting last night, I've wondered how he, the law-abiding businessman, would react to me, the law-breaking hitman.

Mia, I had no worries. Once she saw that Bella had chosen me, she's been all about the data, about using her skills to protect her family.

But Thomas . . . well, I couldn't know for sure he wasn't just putting on a front for his woman until this moment. He looks at me not as someone who's looking to be told what to do, shirking his responsibility in favor of my voice of experience with the seedier side of business. But also not with disdain or disgust, trying to take over as the mover and shaker he typically is.

Instead, he's looking and talking to me like a teammate, knowing that we both have skills the other can use and that by operating as a single unit with a single objective, we can find success.

Just in this case, success means safety, not profit.

"First, what would you do if Bella *were* actually missing?" I ask him. "That's your next step. Go to the media? Private investigators? Police? Obviously, I'd prefer not to utilize that option, but it could be unavoidable. But what would your instincts be if something really did happen? A big, public spectacle on TV asking for help, or a quiet, behind-the-scenes investigation?"

Thomas thinks, then says without a trace of arrogance, "Depends on the situation. If I thought it was her prick of a landlord, I'd be down there myself with the cops. Something like this, though . . . I'm a man of means, with a reputation and image to uphold. I wouldn't involve the police or the media, not at first. I'd be expecting a ransom note, to be honest. I'd definitely hire a PI."

I nod, agreeing. "Then do that, someone local so Blackwell knows about it quickly to validate that you believe Bella is missing. You and Mia should take him to Bella's house, maybe even to The Gravy Train so it looks like he's investigating Bella's life. But do your best not to freak Martha out, okay? She cares about Bella and I don't want to torture her needlessly."

"And Blackwell?"

We're treading into murky areas, and I measure Thomas honestly. "Do you really want to know the dark plans of evil men?"

Thomas nods. "Firstly, I don't think you're evil."

"I'm not good," I retort. "Maybe just a different kind of evil?"

"Perhaps, but that's an argument for another time," Thomas says. "Second, I'm not the kind of man who sends others to do my dirty work just to keep my hands clean. If we need to do dark acts, then I want to know and want to be a part of it if I can. This is my family involved. I won't sit in the background."

My respect for him increases ten-fold. "Fine. My gut tells me to kill the bastard, though it'd be difficult with the degree of security he keeps. It could also be messy, considering he has to be expecting something." I can see the tightness around Thomas's eyes. "But I'm guessing that's not really your style."

Thomas sighs, looking around the room. "You ever known someone who does the right things for the wrong reasons?" He doesn't wait for me to answer, continuing on with his point. "I feel like that's Blackwell. He has done some amazing things for Roseboro, and for a long time, I looked up to him as a business leader. But where most people would feel good about helping the library get new books, or a Little League team getting uniforms, he sees it as a way to gain notoriety. He gets off on galas in his honor, statues in his likeness, and brass plates with his name on them."

I tilt my head, curious. "Sounds like you know him rather well?"

But Thomas shakes his head, "Barely had more than small talk with the man in all the years we've traveled in the same circles. But you can just sense it from some people, you know?"

"I've gotten pretty good at reading people."

Thomas nods. "Regardless of this situation with Izzy, we need to eliminate this threat. Blackwell lives off the power, the legend he's created in his own mind. I think that's where I can hurt him the most. Take away his influence, make him powerless and inconsequential. Becoming obsolete and forgettable, that's his fear."

It's a good plan, though more of a subtle long game than my style typically calls for.

"You might be right, but here's what I know. There are people who do wrong just for wrong's sake, for the hell of it because it's fun for them in some sick, twisted way. And they're unpredictable, you can't put them in a box or make plans for what you think they'll do because they'll surprise you at every turn. They don't think like you and me. Blackwell's a man who is not going to go quietly into the long night, he's capable of outright evil beyond what either of us would consider. Are you prepared for that? Because what you're describing is a war of attrition."

I pause, letting that sink in. "He's been playing that strategy too, but the game just changed when you became aware of it. And the longer you let this play out, the more dangerous he becomes. If you back him into a corner, step by step, he'll reach a threshold where he acts out in unexpected ways. The slow dance you're both doing will go nuclear. You already didn't see his moves with the sabotage and me, so I'm afraid you don't know him as well as you think you do."

Thomas' eyes tighten, and his fist clenches on the desk. But I don't let up, adding the cherry on top of the bad news. "If you're wrong in this approach, Bella pays the price."

He fires back. "And Mia, and me, and Roseboro. I can respect that Bella is your concern, but as important as she is, this is bigger than her. You waited to come to us with this, knowing you could make moves to set up a better solution. I'm asking you to do the same for me. Let me figure some shit out, see what I can do and how I can situate us to handle Blackwell once and for all."

It's against my nature. Teamwork, delays, slick corporate business deals. I don't want to do any of it, would rather just slash and burn Blackwell to the ground and stomp on the ashes of his life.

And that's exactly why I agree with Thomas's request. I want to step out of the darkness of my grief, my solitary life, my anger at the world that I take out on my victims. They're not innocent, not by any stretch of the imagination, but this is the first step to living in the light with Bella, of creating a life instead of destroying them. My one shot at happiness, and I'm going to take it.

"Okay, but you need to move fast. Because I suspect Blackwell isn't done with you, and you're playing catch-up for plans he's already set in motion."

Thomas dips his chin once and starts to get up, but I hold out a staying hand.

"Wait, I have two things before we call this meeting to a close." It's the smallest of jokes, that a guy like me has some sort of fancy business meeting with a guy like him, but Thomas's lips tilt upward. "A favor and a question."

"Shoot," he says, then grimaces. "Uh, not literally."

I give him the same bare smile. "Blackwell gave me a data card with info about my brother's killers. Do you think Mia would look at it for me? While he said it's not encrypted, I can't be sure he didn't do some other kind of skull-fuckery to it, and computers aren't my thing, but Bella says Mia's next-level genius with them."

He holds his palm out, and reluctantly, I place the envelope in his hand. I want to know everything there is to know about Jeremy's death, but handing over the intel to someone I don't know, don't fully trust is about as crazy a move as I've made since beginning this journey for answers. But it's a necessity.

He slips the envelope into his jacket pocket, the reverse of what Blackwell had done, and the symbolism isn't lost on me. These two men, for all their similarities with business and brains, couldn't be more different at their core. And that thought alone gives me the smallest peace at letting Thomas have the data card.

"And your question?" he asks.

I look around the room and then back to Thomas, who looks out of place in the old, worn out factory. "Why'd you want to meet here? A broke down factory doesn't seem like your style."

He smirks, tapping his temple. "This factory is actually closed, it's been shut down for the past six months and I'm considering buying the building and turning it into a new youth center." He looks out towards the mostly dark factory floor, continuing softly. "There's a group of young men, a boy's home, that I help out at not far from here, though they don't know that it's Thomas Goldstone that is behind it. I don't want attention and accolades like Blackwell. I like to keep some parts of my life private, like my good deeds and my woman. You understand that, right?"

"I do," I say, nodding. "Keep Bella safe for me, please. She's all I have, and I sure as shit don't deserve her, but I need her. She has my heart," I confess.

If I hadn't seen how hard Thomas is hung up on Mia, I don't think I could've told him that. But I saw their love and I want that for Bella and me too.

He leans forward, confiding, "Pretty sure you have hers too, man. She's like a sister to Mia. I'll keep her safe and out of sight while this plays out."

He stands, offering a handshake, and then we step out onto the factory floor. It's not large enough for a basketball court, but it could be other things. "What're your plans for this, anyway?"

"A lot of the boys at the home, they think they've got no chance in life. They don't need a head start, they need to get to the starting line of the race. And while Roseboro High's fine, it still needs improvement. I was thinking here, they could learn all those skills that high school doesn't teach. Coding, basic electricity, wood shop . . . all that cool shit that they don't teach kids in high school anymore."

"A trade school?" I ask, and Thomas shakes his head.

"No . . . or at least, not just that. The kids are going to help build it. Like, one of my first projects for them . . . they're going to build their own gym, right here for this part of the floor," he says. "Come on, I've gotta get this data to Mia."

He looks around the space, his eyes soft in the dim light as if he can already see the youth center in his mind. And then he comes back to the present time, shitstorm brewing and all.

We walk out into the darkness, and before I peel off, I give him a nod. He nods back and climbs into his own truck, driving off into the night. As his taillights fade, I think about what he said.

Good deeds. Doing the right things for the right reasons.

My trust in Thomas grows.

# CHAPTER 32

## Blackwell

THE AIR HAS A CHILL IN IT AS I WAIT ON THE ROOF OF MY BUILDING, looking out toward Golden Boy's abomination of a headquarters and analyzing every nuanced detail. It's what I always do, regardless of whether a strategy is going to plan or not. Only through constant awareness can I make micro-adjustments as needed. Because people are not static, stationary, and predictable one hundred percent of the time, no matter how much I wish it were so.

And it is in their actions and reactions that I find the most interest.

Goldstone has hired a private investigator, is paying an exorbitant amount of money to track down his little fleshpot's friend. So it appears that he does not know where Isabella is and is getting worried. It's the barest hint of a reward for what I've already gone through to see this particular plan to fruition.

But Jericho assures me the pictures are frauds, and that Miss Turner is alive, not rotting in some forest as Jackson vouched. At this point, I believe Jericho over the photos, considering the lack of a body.

So the question becomes . . . if she's not dead, where is she?

Jackson's resources are vast, both personally and in his connections, so he could have stashed her away nearly anywhere, but I suspect he'd keep her close.

That damned woman, drawing men in like flies to a spider.

"Give me a stable firing platform up here and I can have that entire penthouse reduced to ash in thirty seconds," Jericho calls from behind me. That he knows where I am looking is concerning in itself, since I have not told him anything of my issues with Thomas Goldstone, merely giving him the needed orders for Gabriel Jackson and Isabella Turner. I do not like others having information beyond what I choose, especially when it is about me.

But a man of his particular skill set is not to be wasted, so I delve into his expertise. "An interesting proposition, and one I've considered," I answer, sipping my tequila. "I once thought about what it would take to bring a sniper up here."

"A very difficult shot with a rifle," Jericho confirms, squinting and staring into the distance as he analyzes the conditions. "The wind is favorable though. Still . . . a missile would be much better. Larger payload and certain to defeat any sort of bulletproofing he might have on his windows."

"And very visible," I counter. "Even in this town, I can't silence every security camera, every idiot with an iPhone. There would be too many questions I couldn't silence if someone used my roof for destruction . . . even if it would carry with it a certain pleasure."

"Questions . . . is that why you haven't given me a green light?" Jericho asks. "Concern over visibility?"

It's a subtle probe of my intentions, and maybe of my steel. If so, Jericho will find that I stand while others fall. "I have other plans for your target . . ." My lips spread in an evil smile, and I correct myself. "Forgive me, I mean targets."

"Targets?" Jericho asks, lifting an eyebrow. While his outer shell barely reacts otherwise, I know the truth. He's a true sadist, a man who lusts for cold cruelty.

"I want Gabriel Jackson dead. Betrayal and dishonesty are simply something I will not tolerate. But the saying 'two birds with one stone' seems rather apropos. Use the girl to lure him, then kill her in any manner you wish. Dealer's choice," I offer, knowing that by gifting him with free reign, he will shine in his monstrous form of creativity. "However you do it, she will serve her purpose."

I don't explain the impact her pain will cause. I have no need to justify myself to a man like Jericho. And he doesn't need any explanation. His sadistic nature means he will do my bidding in this job happily, though a dangling carrot couldn't hurt. "If you can do it inside two days, I'll give you a bonus that will make it worth your while. Let you relax on a beach somewhere warm for as long as you wish."

"Are there visibility concerns for Jackson and Turner?" he asks. I appreciate his attention to detail, consideration for my specific wishes.

I frown, shaking my head. "Only to the people I want to know of their demise."

"Two days," he agrees. "Consider it done."

As he slips back out the door, I swallow the last of my tequila and look across the entirety of Roseboro to the gold building glimmering in the moonlight once again. Perhaps it's a fortuitous sign, but the moonlight's not pale but ruddy, almost bloody against the tower's surface. It makes me smile.

"Soon, Golden Boy."

# CHAPTER 33

## Isabella

I'M TRYING MY DAMNEDEST TO FOCUS ON A SCHOOL PROJECT, MOVING the text in the layout I'm designing one click to the left and then back, one click to the right. I can't decide which is better. Or maybe I just need a different font?

"Ugh," I tell the empty room, leaning back in my chair and stretching.

If you'd told me a few weeks ago that I could get several days off work to relax, sleep, and do school work, I would've said it sounded like a dream. Add in a stocked refrigerator, endless hot water, a tub that qualifies as half jacuzzi, half swimming pool, and a mattress made by NASA, and I should be feeling like a damn queen.

But the reality of being in hiding is that I'm going stir-crazy. No phone, no internet, and most of all, no Gabe.

Coming to the Goldstone tower would be a sure sign that something's up, so he's stayed away. And even with his burner phone, I understand the security risks. Someone might listen in and catch that I'm alive and well, chilling on the twenty-sixth floor in the penthouse apartment like some spoiled brat.

I wish. I don't feel spoiled. I'm worried.

I get it, we discussed it all. Gabe laid out his concerns, and I put in my own two cents as well, and I agreed to go along with it. But that doesn't mean I like it.

The elevator dings, and I stand, instantly on alert. It's late in the day, but Mia and Thomas should still be downstairs in their offices, working.

Mia had stayed home with me at first, but when Thomas came back from his nighttime meeting with Gabe, the idea of putting her to work analyzing Blackwell was the right move. I feel safer with her jamming on her supercomputers downstairs and finding a solution to this than being with me, trying to figure out which anime she was going to distract me with next.

I don't say anything, quietly peeking down the hall.

"Iz? Honey, where are you?" Mia calls out. There's an odd tightness to her voice.

I come down the hall, hands wringing and not sure I want to hear this. "What's wrong? Is it Gabe?"

She gathers me in her arms, not answering, but she's pale. Tears burn my eyes because whatever she's about to say, I already know it's bad.

"Come sit down, Izzy." She directs me to the couch and sits beside me, holding my hands.

"Just tell me, Mia. Is Gabe dead?" I force out.

She shakes her head. "No, he's fine. Well, I haven't talked to him, but as far as I know, he's fine. But I got a call from the private investigator Thomas hired. He's watching all sorts of alerts and . . ." she swallows, her eyes dropping before they lift back up to mine. "It's your house, Izzy. It's on fire."

"What?" I screech in shock.

It's like a punch in the chest, and I sag into the couch, all the wind taken out of me.

It's nowhere near as bad as Gabe being hurt or worse, but that house is a symbol of my whole life. It's me and Reggie singing carols around a paper cutout of a Christmas tree, it's patching up the backdoor screen again because the squirrels keep coming in to eat breakfast with us, though we both secretly fed them, and talking through the walls at night.

And it's my painting, in Reggie's old bedroom, my memorial to a family I was never able to properly say goodbye to.

It's all I have left. And I've worked so damn hard to keep it.

I stand up, clearing my throat before the tears start. "I have to go."

Mia grabs my hand, yanking me back to the couch. "The hell, you are. The fire trucks are already there, and the firefighters are doing what they can. But this is a ploy, and you damn well know it. It's too convenient. So you're going to sit your ass on the couch and stay here." She's all business, and on some level, I'm glad she's thinking clearly because I'm definitely not.

"Dammit, Mia, my . . . my . . ." I stammer, tears coming to my eyes as I think of what's being destroyed. My painting. Mom, Dad . . . my memorial to a family I was never able to say goodbye to properly.

Vash chooses that moment to wander through the living room, meowing for food. I pick her up, hugging her as tight as her little kitty body will allow me. "Oh, my God, Vash. What are we going to do?"

"You're going to take care of Vash, take care of yourself," Mia says softly, her voice full of love. "That's what matters. I know you don't have much, and what's in that house is so important to you, but they're just things. The real memories, the important things, are right here." She touches my head and then my heart.

"But—"

"Izzy, Izzy. I love you, babe," Mia says, stroking my hair. "I'm sorry, I really am."

I sniffle, and while Mia's hug helps, it's not the arms I want around me right now. "Where's the phone?" I choke out as I set Vash down. "I need to call Gabe."

"Sure, honey," Mia says, grabbing the phone from the side table of the sofa. "Here you are."

It doesn't take long to call Gabe, and he picks up quickly, already knowing the reason for my call. "I just heard."

"Gabe, that was my house!" I cry, but the shocked sadness is beginning to be tinged with anger. It settles me somehow, like a dash of cold water in my face helping me focus. "If this is that asshole—"

"It could be," Gabe says. "But we don't know yet. It might have been something in the house, or it could've even been Carraby," he says, but I can hear that he doesn't believe that for a second.

He sighs. "I think this is most likely a tactic to draw you out, which signals that he doesn't believe the story I fed him. That means you need to stay where you are. The stakes just got a lot higher."

I cringe inside but understand why he's saying that. It's the same thing Mia's saying, and I need to listen to their advice right now while my emotions are pushing me to act irrationally.

"Is there any way you can come over? I know it's dangerous, and it's stupid of me to ask, but I need you. Gabe?"

He's silent for a moment, thinking, and then finally agrees. "It'll take me a little bit to make sure I can get there cleanly, but I'll be there soon."

We hang up, and I tell Mia, "He's coming."

She nods and just sits with me. We must talk, but I'm not really processing anything and couldn't repeat what she says or what I reply.

I don't know how long it's been when the elevator dings again and Gabe comes in, taking Mia's place next to me on the couch and wrapping his arms around me.

I bury my nose in his neck, inhaling his scent to ground myself. I hear Mia excuse herself, saying she's going back downstairs and to call if we need anything. In seconds, we're alone.

Gabe twines a lock of my hair around his finger, whispering in my ear, "I'm so sorry, Princess. Is there anything I can do?"

I shake my head, but feeling him here with me after days apart does soothe some frayed bits inside me. I look up through my lashes. "Can you make me forget all of this? Blackwell, the fake death, and my house. I need to . . . not think about any of it."

His eyes search mine questioningly, his voice soft. "Are you sure?"

"Sorry, it's stupid," I reply, sagging. "I just feel like I'm losing everything."

He tilts my chin back up, looking deep into my eyes. "Bella, you're not losing everything. You have me, and I have you. We'll figure out the rest, deal with Blackwell, and rebuild your house if we have to."

I lick my lips, drawing strength from his steady gaze. "Why? Why are you doing all this for me?"

It's something I've been wondering in the back of my mind all along. Gabe is beautiful, brilliant, and smooth. Why would he want a woman with nothing but dreams?

Gabe's smile is the slow one I like best, starting on the left and moving across his lips until his dimples pop out. "Don't you know? It's because I love you, Bella. I love you with everything I am, everything I have."

Somehow, in the middle of this mess, he knows just what to say to bring everything into focus. "I love you, too."

His slight intake of breath is audible, like he's surprised by my admission, but I suspect we've both known the truth for a while and were just too scared to speak the words, hoping the actions would be enough to communicate the depth of what we're feeling.

But even with the words hanging in the air between us now, I need the action, both to revel in our shared truth and to distract myself from the building storm coming for us.

Our mouths meet, tasting our declarations, though I don't know if he moved to me or I moved to him. I feel him pick me up, his rough hands on my ass as I wrap my arms and legs around him. "Which way?"

"Down the hall, second door on the right," I tell him, licking and sucking on his neck.

In moments, I'm spread on the guest bed, soft cotton beneath me. "I promise you, Bella, I'll do whatever it takes to keep you safe and by my side."

I put my arms around his neck, just holding him and seeing the love I feel reflected in Gabe's eyes.

Every time I'm with him is a new exploration, a way for us to discover not just our bodies but our souls and our hearts. Nothing is truer than this moment, and instead of tearing into each other with rabid passion, clothes flying like a clearance sale in a Marshall's, we lie on the bed, looking into each other's eyes as we run our hands up and down each other's body, memorizing every inch.

"I'm nervous," I admit, feeling goosebumps form on my arms. "It's the first time I've ever said those words to someone who wasn't family. Mia and Char being family, of course."

"Me too," he admits, taking my hand and placing it over his heart. "But I know every beat, every thought, everything I am . . . it's for you."

Gabe cups my face, and I lean in, kissing him softly at first before our kiss deepens, our tongues entwining and our lips caressing each other as we slip and squirm out of our clothes. Finally, I help him slide his jeans off, and our skin presses together, his heat coursing through my veins.

"Lie back . . . let me," he whispers, urging me onto my back and kissing his way down my body. I arch my back, pushing my nipples toward him, but instead, he traces my stomach with the tip of his tongue, dipping into the shallow well of my belly button before kissing lower. He pulls away to kiss up the inside of my thighs before he soulfully kisses my wet pussy.

He doesn't tease me, instead just kissing my lips tenderly, letting his tongue explore my soft flesh. He's driving me crazy, physically and emotionally, with how sweet he's being. But this is what I need right now, and he knows it.

My hips lift, pressing into his mouth as I grind my pussy against his lips and teeth. "Oh, God, Gabe . . . that's amazing . . . oh, God, yes, yes, yes!" I say before my voice leaves me, devolving into a stream of breathy yesses that blend together as I buck against his tongue.

My thighs clamp around his head as I come, and I can feel my body gushing for him. Gabe drinks me down like I'm a fine wine, which only makes me come harder.

He kisses his way up my body to look in my eyes before taking my mouth in a deep kiss to let me taste myself on his tongue. It's a heady combination of the two of us. As we kiss, he thrusts into me slowly, filling me with his thick cock. We move as one, our hips coming together in waves.

My nipples rub against his chest, pearling up, and he dips down to suck on one. But with a groan, he pops off and lays over me, pressing me into the bed with his weight. I feel cocooned in him, surrounded and impaled by everything he is. And I take it, grateful that he is letting me into his heart the way I'm letting him into mine.

The new angle hits a spot deep inside me, and I cry out, "Oh, God, Gabe. Right there."

"Come for me, Princess," he says, and I reach for it, so close to the edge and so desperate to fly. "Come with me."

And that does it. I want to come with him always, both in bed and anywhere life takes us. The thought of our being together forever, however long that may be, considering the threat we're under, is sharply glorious.

Gripping his shoulders as he thrusts deeper and deeper into me, we find our moment of eternity, Gabe crying out his own release as I spasm and clench around him, milking his cum from his balls.

I don't realize I'm crying until Gabe wipes the tears away with his thumb. "Hey, you okay?" His brows knit together in concern.

I bite my lip, nodding. "Yeah, it's just a lot. But with you by my side, I think I can handle anything."

He smiles, dimples popping for me again. "There's nowhere else I'd rather be. I love you, Bella."

I wish I could say his words make the world waiting to destroy me disappear, washing it away with the power of his love. But that doesn't happen. Instead, his vow makes me feel like no matter what is coming down the pipe, I can handle it with him. Hopefully, he feels the same way about my promise.

"I love you, Gabe. Now and forever."

# CHAPTER 34

## Gabriel

THE DARKNESS IS NEARLY PERFECT, WITH A FULL, CLOUDY SKY THAT seems like a blessing, a sign that maybe this stupid move isn't *entirely* reckless. But I wouldn't have been able to say no to Bella regardless.

Wait. Actually, I had said no multiple times, but she'd worn me down, and finally, I'd given in with some rules. And that's how I find myself with a supposed-to-be-dead Bella sitting in the passenger seat of Thomas's work truck as we pull up to her house.

Well, what's left of it.

It's not as much of a burned-out husk as I'd feared, though. From the left side of the front yard, it even looks fine. Or at least as fine as it always was. But from the right, you can see the black char and destruction. The back corner, where the kitchen and living room sat, is basically gone, a black void into the heart of the house yawning open.

I look over at Bella to see how she's taking this, expecting her to be on the verge of falling apart. But the reality seems to have either put her into shock, or she's moving into an anger stage, because she looks fiercely determined in the dim glow of the dashboard lights.

As I park, she moves her hand toward the handle. "No, we talked about this. Stay here until I clear everything."

She nods, sighing and revealing a crack in her brave façade. "I know. I just need to get in there and see what's left."

I rub her thigh comfortingly, making sure the switch on the dome light's off to keep the car's interior dark as I open the door. I don't want to make it easy for anyone to see that it's Bella. The whole point of using Thomas's truck and both of us dressing in solid black with hoodies is so that anyone who happens to see us will assume we're Thomas and Mia coming to check on the house.

I do a scan of the surrounding area, noting all the hiding spots even though I've done this multiple times before while I watched Bella. Then, I was looking for places I could hide. Now, I'm looking for possible threats.

Seeing nothing amiss, I open my door and get out, keeping my head on a swivel. Holding the button on the door handle, I close my door quietly before coming around, carefully walking to avoid stepping on any tree branches or anything else that might make noise. Bella maneuvers herself behind the wheel, poised to crank the engine and run like hell if she has to, and inside, I'm proud of her. She remembers the plan and is ready to jump into action if need be.

As I make the short walk toward the house, I keep my hands in my hoodie pocket, my right one gripping my pistol, ready for action. It seems strangely normal but at the same time silly to go up the two steps to the front door, considering there are gaping holes in the walls and the door itself has been kicked out. But the door frame's still there, so that's where I go.

Glancing back, Bella seems okay, or at least the truck is dark and quiet, so I proceed into the house. It's an odd discord to go inside and be able to see the stars because of the huge holes in the roof. The one good thing? The place is still standing. It's a miracle the fire department had anything except cinders to hose down, as old and dried as this place was.

Once I'm inside, I take my gun out, not worrying as much about visibility behind the few still-standing walls. I check each room, both my footing on the weakened structure and for anything or anyone threatening.

Back out front, I open the door for Bella. "How bad is it?" she asks.

"Not good. There's a lot of damage you can't see from the street, and the whole house has water damage."

She nods grimly, seemingly prepping herself for the horror she knows she's about to see.

Inside, she's silent as she looks around. I keep expecting the tears to start back up, but she must be cried out because her expression stays stoic. Her borrowed black boot kicks out at the ashy remains piled up in what's left of the living room floor. A pile of silvery grey dust puffs into the air at our feet and then falls to the cinderblock-framed ground we can see below since there's no subfloor in this area anymore.

"Watch your step," I warn, pulling her back. "I checked, but I can't be sure it'll hold."

She backs up and moves towards the hall and I follow. I see her take a deep breath, her shoulders rising and falling before she steps through to the guest bedroom. Even in the dim light, I can see her painting is ruined, the sheetrock saturated with water.

"I know it was just a painting," she says, looking at the mess in front of her. "But it meant a lot to me. I painted that right after Reggie died, and it got me through those dark days when I'd lost everyone, everything. It was my therapy, a sign that there could still be beauty in the world, even if I had to make it myself."

She moves to the wall, reaching out a hand to touch the color-smeared and crumbling sheetrock.

"I'm sorry, Bella," I say softly, putting my free hand on her shoulder. "Do you want to see if there's anything salvageable?"

She nods, kissing her fingertips and laying them over the spot where her family used to sit in their plane, memorialized and remembered.

In her bedroom, she squats down in front of the closet, blindly digging deep into the pile of things that have survived the fire. She pulls out a small metal case, about the size of a lunch box, and a sad smile lifts her lips.

"What's that?"

"A memory box Reggie gave me when I first came here," she says, reverently tracing the outside of the box. She opens it and her eyes shine with the tears I've been expecting as she looks heavenward. "Thank you."

She picks up a few pieces of folded paper and some small squares that look to be photographs. Unable to see them in the dark, she lays them back into the beloved box and closes it with a soft snick. "Okay, this is all I need."

I look at her, this woman who has survived her whole life with barely anything but hard times. And when life conspires to take even more from her, she doesn't crumble, burnt and destroyed by the flames. No, she rises like a phoenix. She has only what she packed in her backpack and this metal box to her name, but it's all she needs.

She is gloriously grateful and humble, knowing what's truly important isn't a house or clothes but memories and people.

"You ready?" I ask, giving her one last chance because I don't know when we'll be able to come back here with the dangers lurking around every corner.

She sighs but shakes her head and I step in front of her to lead us out.

I look down the hall before we exit the bedroom, carefully stepping our way back to what remains of the living room. Everything seems clear, but as I come around the corner, a sharp blow hits me in the jaw, sending me stumbling and taking me by surprise.

I don't get surprised. Ever.

My instincts take over, and even though it's damn near pitch black, I blindly turn to fight my attacker. I see a shape, and I focus on that, calling out to Bella, "Run. Go."

I hear the scuffle of her feet and pray she's doing as I said as I launch myself at the attacker. She needs to get out of here, leave me, and get to safety.

In the dark, there's no space or time for throwing blows. Instead we wrestle, slamming each other against the weakened structure of the house. I'd try and use my gun against him, but he's just as skilled as I am, using knees and elbows to blast me rapid-fire style, though I'm giving as good as he is. But I don't have even half a second to reach into my pocket for the pistol, and firing into the dark is a dangerous option since I'm afraid I might hit Bella accidentally.

So I stick to keeping close enough to sense him, laying body shots when I can and blocking his hits as best I'm able. A moment later, I take a sudden knee to the balls, doubling me over in blinding pain.

As I bend over, I reach out to grab the backs of my attacker's legs, taking him down and we scramble across the floor, which creaks eerily beneath the onslaught.

I already know this can't be Carraby, there's no way that pussy could give me this much fight even if he had a nightstick to help him.

So if it's not him, coming to take advantage of Bella's unexpected open-door policy, it's somebody much, much worse. It's something much worse.

"You fucked up, Angel," a disembodied voice says from beneath me. The attacker might be on his back, but I don't have a solid upper hand against him. He's countering my every move, his jiu-jitsu so good I get the sense he's playing with me. Like he knows my next move before I do.

And the fact that he called me by my professional name sends chills down my spine.

But this is life or death, and I fight with everything I have, every dirty trick I learned in my years of evil, because this is for Bella and I know it. I don't care if I never leave this shell of a house, as long as she's safe. I pray she's long-gone by now, well on her way back to Mia's.

I need to give her time to get away.

Half standing, I slam my knee into his kidney and pull back, getting to my feet. If I can't beat him on the ground, then I have to take a chance of fighting him on his feet. My head's still swimming. I've been rocked hard, but I position my body in between my attacker and the door, praying it gives Bella enough time.

My opponent follows me up, and I throw a right jab at the middle of his shape, the smack of my fist connecting with something hard. A small success that I follow up with a flurry of punches to the same area.

He grunts, but in the midst of the flurry, I feel my feet swept out from underneath me, and I'm slammed to the floor, my head bouncing off the floor-boards and making the world swim. I hear a creak beneath me, and I wonder if the fire-weakened structure can withstand much more.

A hardened boot heel slams into my gut, adding to the ache in my balls, and I curl up, protecting my organs and coughing as the hot metallic taste of blood stains my tongue.

"You're really a fallen angel now, Gabriel," the voice says. I look up, and like divine intervention, the clouds part for a moment, letting the moon shine through, the empty roofbeams letting the light in.

It's like seeing the devil come to life.

He's tall, with dirty blonde hair and wearing all black. And fucking night vision goggles. That's how he knew what moves I was making to counter me so well. I'm fighting blind in the dark, but for him, it may as well be daylight in the blackened ruins of Bella's house.

He grins, and as he does, I see the slight pull of a scar by his mouth . . . a scar that is as much his calling card as my good looks.

Fucking Jericho.

He kicks again, my head snapping back, and this time, it's *my* walls that are broken down, the world turning black once more.

# CHAPTER 35

## Gabriel

CONSCIOUSNESS RETURNS IN A PAINFUL PULSE OF RED, FROM floating in space to achingly aware of the hard floor beneath my battered body. But I resist the pain, remembering what got me here.

Jericho.

Bella!

I turn over to my knees, and I lay my head on the floor, fighting back waves of nausea as my body reminds me of the abuse it's taken. I don't know how long I've been out. All I can do is pray Bella listened and drove like a bat out of hell back to Goldstone Tower.

But the gnawing unease in my belly knows she didn't do that. My princess wouldn't leave me, would instead give her all to save me because that's who she is, what she does. She gives everything to everyone while she's the one struggling or in danger.

The fear buoys me, helping me get to my feet even as the world continues to swim in lazy circles. Staggering, I make my way to the doorway, where I lean against the frame for a moment before my eyes start to cooperate and I can see straight again. With a deep breath, I step outside, my heart stopping in my chest at what I see.

Thomas's white truck sits in the driveway right where I left it, letting me know that Bella didn't speed away. More damning, though, is the open driver's side door, hanging wide like a one-winged avian harbinger of doom.

I already know it in my gut, but I run to the truck anyway. The truth won't let me pretend, though. Bella is gone.

The last vestiges of my illusion disappear as I see the nest of wires underneath the steering column and the keys still dangling uselessly from the ignition. He cut the wires . . . I'd left the door unlocked in case we needed to haul ass, but he'd used that against us, cutting the wires.

Jericho's good . . . and now he has her in his grasp.

I slam my fist into the door panel, denting it, but the fresh pain helps me focus. Reaching into my pocket, I pull out my Leatherman and reach further down the wires, finding what I need to hotwire the truck before climbing in. I drive back to Goldstone Tower as fast as the truck will go, but the elevator to the penthouse feels excruciatingly slow, even if it's a direct ride.

Stealth isn't a consideration now, I don't care if everyone from the security guards to the Mayor sees me. Only one man in town would have the connections to hire Jericho, and right now speed is of utmost importance. There's no telling what sick things Jericho is doing to my Princess even in this very moment.

"Thomas!" I bellow as I come off the elevator.

I'm typically a lone huntsman in my line of work, but I'm not so arrogant as to ignore the resources at hand. And I'll do anything to get Bella back. Especially since I have means as extensive and as dedicated as Thomas and Mia available to me.

Thomas comes out of the back wearing boxer briefs, with Mia hustling behind him. A quick glance shows me I've probably interrupted a little couple time, but I'm not here to compare swords with Thomas. Nor am I interested in Mia's body, although he shoves her behind him anyway. As if I'm looking at her when I have Bella.

"What's wrong?" Thomas asks me as soon as he sees my face. "What the fuck happened to you? Where's Izzy?"

"He took her," I snarl, my eyes clouded with rage. "That bastard."

"What? No!" Mia gasps in shock.

"It was a setup," I reply, nursing my aching jaw. "We were getting ready to leave when he jumped us. I told Bella to run, but . . ."

I haven't lost my cool in years, not since Jeremy's death, but I'm a hairsbreadth away from torching the whole fucking city and Mia's trembling like a fall leaf in a windstorm with what I've already said. Thomas stays cool and collected though, all business as he calms the situation.

"Sit, tell us what happened," he says.

I don't sit, needing to pace, but Thomas forces a small shot of scotch in my hand, saying, "It'll help." I toss it back and then manage to relay the story of us taking precautions to go check out Bella's house, how Jericho had been lying in wait for us, the fight and then the empty truck, with Bella nowhere to be found.

Mia gives off a single sob at the end when I tell them about the cut wires, the detail somehow convincing her more than me getting my ass kicked that Jericho is for real.

"What do we do?" Mia asks as she regains control of herself. "Call the police?"

Thomas and I lock eyes, and I know we're thinking the same thing. "No police," I reply, gripping the edge of the countertop. "I'll get her back."

Mia's eyes widen, looking from me to Thomas. "What? She's been kidnapped. We need to call the police."

I know that I'm about to piss off Thomas, but I need to make sure we're all on the same page here. "Mia, do you understand what I do, who I am? Because I'm going to get Bella back, and I do not want police anywhere near this when I do it. This is going to get ugly, fast."

Mia gasps, and Thomas' eyes are tight, but they seem to fully grasp my intentions now, which was my point. Thomas blinks his agreement and I continue.

"This man, Jericho, he has her now, under contract for sure. He's the sadistic type who enjoys his work and has no code other than completing a job. Bella will be like a shiny new toy to him, something to play with and test out her limits."

I swallow thickly, the thought making my stomach roil.

"You know him?" Thomas asks. "Personally?"

"No," I reply with a shake of my head, "only of him and his work. We're, well I guess you'd say we're competitors for the same contracts. But I'm careful about the jobs I accept. For Jericho, it's not about the money or making someone pay for a wrongdoing, it's about sanctioned brutality."

"And he's got Izzy?" Mia sighs, rubbing at her streaked hair. "What can we do?"

"I need your brains and your computers," I tell Mia bluntly. "I need intel."

Thomas raises an eyebrow even as Mia nods, her eyes setting firmly.

"Not to put too fine a point on it, but he did get the drop on you. You sure you don't need help, backup of some sort?"

I shake my head, looking Thomas in the eye. "No. And this isn't up for debate, Thomas. I'm not taking you with me. While you might handle yourself just fine in a bar fight, you're dealing with a trained killer here. This is the point where guys like you *hire* guys like me. And I need to do this job alone."

Mia takes Thomas's hand, solidifying my decision. Thomas needs to stay here for Mia because to some degree, this is still about them, pawns being sacrificed to weaken the King and Queen. Thomas looks at Mia, then back at me. "I fucking hate this."

"I know. And I appreciate the offer, but I can do this. I just have to figure out where he took her."

"Then let's get to work," Mia says, her eyes narrowing as she disappears into the back. She comes out a minute later in some yoga pants and the same shirt before throwing a pair of sweats to Thomas. "My office will be faster."

Mia's basement office is a shrine to all things computer nerdy, and she puts her three displays to work, pulling data as quickly as she can type.

By the time the clock on the wall ticks midnight, we're looking over detailed maps of Roseboro, calculating possible hideout points where Jericho might've taken Bella. Mia's a machine, correlating tax records, population density, police coverage, and more, but even with all of that, there are simply too many possibilities.

"Seven," Mia says, hitting *Print* on her machine. "It's . . . it's the best I can do, Gabriel. If I had—"

"You reduced my load from thousands to seven," I reassure her. "If I have to, I'll—"

That's when we catch a break of the worst sort. My phone dings with an incoming text. It's my burner phone. Only one man, and Bella, have that particular number.

I open it and anger flashes hot and bright-white in my veins. It's a picture of Bella, her hands zip-tied to a chair, her head lolling to the side. Is she dead or unconscious?

"Fuck."

"What is it?" Thomas asks, his jaw clenching as I show them the picture and Mia cries out softly. Underneath the picture is an address, and I note with some satisfaction that it's on Mia's list of seven properties.

The final words are the only possible hope. '*Come and get her*' blinks on and off, with a grinning, laughing animated emoji.

He's enjoying this. The fucker is getting off on torturing her and taunting me.

I stand. "I have to go."

"It's a trap, you know that," Thomas says, surprisingly reasonable under pressure. "And you don't know anything about the building."

"I know, but this is my fault," I reply. "I have to save her."

Mia's brows crinkle and she wipes at her eyes. "Your fault? It's not your fault there's a fucking madman with a weird hard-on for hurting Thomas."

"I knew something was off about this contract from the beginning. It's why I delayed," I admit with a shake of my head. "I should've never taken her from the safety of this penthouse tonight, but I was weak. And while Blackwell wants to hurt her to get at you, Jericho is definitely taking satisfaction in doing this to me."

Thomas's voice is deep, controlled. "You said you didn't know him personally."

"I don't, but I can judge the man by . . . by the way he kills, if that makes sense. My guess is, Jericho's contract is for both Bella and me, because Blackwell will not take kindly to my defection from our deal. But either Jericho or Blackwell, or maybe both, want me to suffer. I was unconscious on the floor, Jericho could've just taken me out then, walked outside and double tapped Bella, and the job would've been done. But he didn't."

I imagine that scenario, my Bella splayed out in the grass, dead in the dark night, and pray that whatever Jericho's doing to her now doesn't make a quick and easy death a preferable, peaceful option.

I think about what I know of Jericho. Despite his sadism, and his reputation for cruelty, he's also known for his detailed planning and precise execution. It's why he's often hired to extract information, because by the time he's done having his fun, his victims will spill their guts just to get a final release from the pain he's put them through. Though sometimes he's hired simply for the torture aspect, no information needed, his depravity simply providing a painful death to the target of his contract.

Evil. That's the only word to describe him.

"Gabriel?" Mia asks, and I clear my throat.

"We're not friends, or even colleagues, but there's a certain level of respect given to other pros. By taking the contract against me, he's saying that

I've betrayed the profession, and he'll want to back it up. But he wants to draw this out for his own pleasure, torment me by getting at Bella. That's the only reason he would've taken her and left me, to make it hurt because he's a cruel bastard. And once he's had his fun, he'll kill us both to complete his contract."

I say it matter-of-factly because if I'm going to make this work, I have to get in touch with the cold, heartless side of me again. Discussing hits for hire is par for the course for that part, even though this contract is as different as can be.

But Thomas and Mia look horrified at my casual discussion of death.

"Oh, my God, I'm going to be sick," Mia says, her hand covering her mouth. Thomas rubs her back soothingly.

"I'll be in touch as soon as I can," I say at the door. "Mia, if you can, I need you by the phone, ready to send me information."

"I can do you one better," Thomas says, reaching over and swiping a tablet computer from a docking station next to Mia's desk. "This is tied to her systems, a little gadget we worked up for business trips. She types it, it'll pop on your screen."

"Good . . . then I need any information you can gather in the next ten minutes," I reply. "Video feeds, traffic cams, anything. And I'd suggest you stay here. If Blackwell is escalating, who knows if he still considers you off limits."

Thomas purses his lips, nodding. "I'm trusting you to take care of Izzy. You can trust me to handle Blackwell."

"If I fail . . . turn this place into a fortress," I advise him. "At least until you can get out of town."

The drive to the address Jericho gave me is quiet, the tablet beeping from time to time as Mia sends me information. I use every beep as a chance to separate myself, to shut down my humanity and to become the cold, relentless killer I know is inside me. My emotions close off, my heart slows, and my blood ices.

I become the Fallen Angel once again.

No . . . I must become more. Or is it less? More monster, less man, more evil, less salvageable.

Because tonight, I cannot stop. Not until Jericho is dead.

I only hope that I can come out the other side of tonight with Bella and my soul intact.

# CHAPTER 36

## Isabella

T HE FIRST THING I'M AWARE OF IS THE CHILL. IT SEEMS TO BE
everywhere, on my skin, in my bones . . . even my hair feels chilly
somehow.

I try to reach up, needing to wipe the tears leaking from the corners of
my eyes. But when I go to lift my hands, they don't move and I realize I'm tied
to a metal chair. I fight the restraint, but I can only wiggle a little bit before
chafing my wrists. The same is true for my ankles. Blinking until I can see, I
look down, seeing that both are bound with plastic zip-ties.

Shit.

"Hello?" I murmur, my mouth tasting like chemicals. My mind's fuzzy,
but I have a vague memory of a cloth over my face and darkness.

I look around the room, trying to figure out where I am. I can't see
much. The lights are so dim that I can't see the walls of the room, so I try
again. "HELLO!"

The sound bounces off the walls, echoing and reverberating loud enough
to make my ears ring. Well, at least I know that wherever I am, the room's
not that big.

I wince, wishing I could put my hands over my ears, but all I succeed in
doing is making my forearms hurt.

"It won't help you," a voice with a slight accent that I can't place says from the darkness. "You can scream until your voice gives out. Nobody will hear you. This building is a mile away from anything."

"Who . . . who are you? What do you want?" I ask, trying to keep the fear out of my voice, but the tremble is obvious.

The lights suddenly brighten, and I see where I am. Or at least, I see where, but that doesn't mean I understand.

It looks like an office, the sort of place you'd find in a mechanic's shop or something industrial.

I can't tell anything else because every surface of the room is covered in plastic drop cloths, the kind you get when you're painting a room and you know you're going to make a mess. Thick ones, too, slightly opaque clear plastic that covers every wall, the window, which I can tell is there only because a dim light shines through it, the floor, the door . . . looking up, I can even see the ceiling is covered in plastic.

The idea of being surrounded by so much plastic chills me to the bone, bringing to mind all sorts of images from the worst of the late-night horror movies.

But then I sense someone behind me, and slowly, a tall blond man, his hair neatly styled and his face looking cold and aristocratic, walks around me, coming to a stop directly in front of where I'm sitting.

He's dressed all in black, but where Gabe and I were wearing jeans and hoodies, this man is wearing slacks and a button-down dress shirt. And black leather gloves, filling my heart with a sick, desperate feeling of dread. He tilts his head, lifting an eyebrow, and after a moment, I realize he expects me to speak.

"Who are you?" I repeat.

"My name is Jericho," the man says. "And you're Isabella Turner."

He smiles, and another chill goes down my spine. It's the smile of a man who would have no qualms about ending my life. My heart stills in my chest because in his eyes I see no mercy, no humanity.

It's even worse than seeing Gabriel when he was ready to kill Russell.

"You amuse me," he says, but his face shows no sign of joy. "So please tell me, how did such a worthless thing happen to create so much drama? I don't understand it."

He brushes the back of a finger along my cheekbone, and I recoil, trying to get away. "No," I say, shaking my head. "Don't touch me."

From somewhere far away, I hear my name. "Bella?"

I can't pinpoint where it's coming from. It's muffled by either the walls or the plastic, I don't know which. But I know who it is.

It's Gabe! He's come for me. *Thank God*, I think. But then I see the glee on Jericho's face and I rethink my hope that Gabe can save me.

"Gabe! Run!" I shout, wanting at least one of us to get out of this and strongly doubting there's any way I am leaving this room alive.

Jericho turns back to me, his eyes alight, and I realize just how dead inside he looked before. But this . . . this look is so much worse. "Ah . . . he was a little faster than I anticipated. I'm not done setting the scene for him. Too bad, but we will continue this conversation later. Time to get to work."

I've heard the saying that if you love what you do, you'll never work a day in your life. Watching him hustle over to the desk, I suspect that's true for Jericho. He loves his work, as twisted and awful as it is. And I'll be the one to pay for that bloodlust. Me and Gabe, if I can't get him to leave me.

Jericho picks up something from a toolbox on the plastic-covered desk. At first, I can't see what it is, but then he turns and shows me, the anticipation part of the terror he's after. It's a pair of pliers, just like the pair I've used at The Gravy Train for helping Henry in the back with minor repairs, but these have sharp blades. He clicks them together, mimicking the movement with his mouth, teeth chomping at the air.

"What's that? What are you doing?" I say, my voice stuttering with fear and my eyes wide.

He doesn't answer, coming closer step by step, and I thrash in the chair. But he's got me trussed up tightly, with my feet off the ground, and the chair's hard to tip over. All I do is abrade my wrists and slam my shoulder blades into the back of the chair hard enough to make me scream.

Jericho grabs my left hand, and though I try to pull it away, it's locked in place by the zip-tie restraint. He runs the cold metal down the back of my fingers, sending shivers through my whole body.

"No, no, no—" I plead, not even fully grasping what he intends but knowing it won't be good.

"Eeny, meeny, miny, moe—"

My cry turns to a blood-curdling scream as Jericho, in a blur of speed, fastens the pliers onto my pinkie finger and twists it to the side.

The pain is instant and overwhelming. "Aaaaaahhhhhh!"

Tears run, and a new level of terror fills me. Fear of the unknown is one thing, but this is the first step of destruction in Jericho's plan, and the reality is beyond anything I've ever known. I thought I knew pain, emotional devastation from the losses I've suffered, and even physical discomfort from hardship. But this is sharp and bright and hurts so fucking much.

"Delightful . . . I love that sound," Jericho says conversationally. He bends closer, as if inspecting his handiwork. I can't help but look too, even though I desperately don't want to.

I'm half-expecting to see my finger dangling loosely, but instead I find it's not there at all. Jericho cut it clean off from my palm and the room spins as I feel faint at the sight. Even through the dizziness, I swear I see the flash of Jericho's tongue as he licks his lips, delighted at the rivulets of blood running from the gnarled nub where my finger used to be.

"Bella!"

I hear Gabe, his footsteps pounding. My courage, telling him to go, evaporates in the fiery pain, and I look around wildly, trying to find him, shamefully wanting him to save me, help me, rescue me.

In a haze, I see Jericho's anticipation. He's ready, setting the pliers down on the desk and opening a drawer in order to withdraw a pistol. And for a split second, I can think clearly.

"No! Leave me, Gabe. He's going to kill us both. Please, I love you. *Go!*" I struggle against the chair again, trying to get free or at least away from Jericho.

A shot rings out in response, cutting off my words. It's loud and piercing, echoing in the empty space, but it sounds close. Really close.

Jericho grins, finally truly happy. "Showtime." His voice is robotic and cold, his countenance even more menacing as he inhales, spreading his shoulders wide.

He moves behind me and the plastic rustles. I look over my shoulder, and he's gone, disappeared into the space beyond the plastic room he's created for me.

"He's coming, Gabe!" I cry out, choking on tears and fear. "Run!"

My words are too late, though, as a pair of gunshots cuts me off. My heart's in my throat, terror that Gabe's been shot evaporating as I hear a scuffle start out of my sight. I don't know where they are because everything echoes, but I can hear the smack of flesh, the grunts as the punches connect, and the sound of their bodies banging against what I can only guess are walls and furniture outside the plastic.

My brain is a useless blob of jelly between my ears, and my chest aches from holding my breath until instinct takes over and I breathe again. I jerk against my restraints, and at first I think I've got nothing, but then I feel something . . . slip.

Blessedly, my mind focuses and I repeat the motion, wiggling my hand back and forth, to see what's giving way. The blood is helping my wrist slide between the plastic bracelet and the arm of the chair, lubing the tight fit a bit.

I've got the smallest space to pull my hand through and the thought of pulling my pained hand through that pinching gap already has me moaning in fear, but as I hear another thud from the fight outside, I put it aside.

I can do this. I have done some ridiculously difficult things in my life, been through hell and come out the other side, and can tackle any obstacle in front of me and conquer it. I'm a strong woman, and I won't sit here and wait for someone else to do what I can do myself.

And Gabe needs me.

Renewed, I don't thrash my whole body, but instead focus on just my left arm. I pull back slowly, lifting as I do to try and slip through the small space, but the only feeling I get is my wrist screaming as the nylon tightens like a vice around my bones.

I yank, twisting left then right, and the chair tips up again, this time almost overbalancing me to the point of falling over. But I'm so close, I can feel the increasing give in the zip-tie.

I think it through and fold my thumb across my palm, making my hand as narrow as possible. Taking a deep breath to prepare myself, I jerk hard and pain flares through me.

The chair falls from the force of my pull, crashing to the floor and knocking the breath out of me, and for a heart stopping moment, I think I've failed. But then I realize my hand is loose, bloody and disfigured but free.

Oh, my God! It worked!

I can't do the same to my right hand though, so I look around. The desk, with its tools, is just four feet away, but it feels like four miles as I claw my way towards it, dragging myself by one hand, each grip on the floor making me grunt in pain. When I get close enough, I look up at the toolbox above me.

I grunt as I reach up, grasping for an edge of the metal box. With a yell, I shove the whole box off the edge of the desk, and the contents spill onto the floor next to me. There, right in front of me, is my salvation . . . a pair of wire cutters.

I shiver suddenly, wondering what Jericho had in mind for me with this tool, but I don't have time to ponder it now. Instead, I use the tool to cut my right hand free, and then both legs, and get to my feet.

*I have to help Gabe*, I think, pushing my way through the plastic in front of the door. It's still dim in the space, but outside, the office is more of a warehouse area with high tracks of faint yellow light.

I follow the sounds of their fight, grunted words becoming clear as I get closer.

"Should've just done your job, Gabriel," Jericho says. "She's just a contract."

"No, she's not," Gabe replies in a growl, like he's hurt. "She's mine."

I move closer, seeing the fight firsthand as they jockey for position. They're both bleeding, tangled in a pile on the concrete floor as they roll back and forth, short elbows and punches emerging from time to time to thud into the other's body before doing it again and again.

I want to scream for Gabe, but he doesn't need a distracting cheerleader right now. He needs actual help. I'd love to think he could handle this completely on his own, and the truth is, maybe he can. I've never seen him truly in action like this. But I can't stand by uselessly when the man I love is fighting for his life. And mine.

Seeing a broomstick against the wall, I grab it and risk getting even closer, ready to whack Jericho as soon as I get an opening. Suddenly, Gabe, who's on the bottom, elbows Jericho's neck, giving me an opportunity.

I wind up, swinging for the fences, and the broomstick cracks off Jericho's skull, shattering into three pieces but failing to knock him out.

Jericho turns his head, like some Terminator machine, staring daggers at me, and grabs the remains of the broomstick.

"Steel plate . . . skiing accident," he says, pointing to his head before tossing me aside. Gabe yells in fury as I go stumbling, but fortune smiles on me as I bounce off a water cooler and see a dark shadow on the ground. I bend down quickly and see if the spot is what I think it is. Thankfully, I'm right, and my right hand wraps around the cold metal of a gun.

Whether it's Gabe's or Jericho's, I don't know. But I check the safety and see the little red line on the safety, just like Saul taught me at the gun shop.

"Stop. Step away from him," I bark, praying my voice sounds more badass than I feel because my knees are seriously knocking.

Surprisingly, they shove off one another, actually doing what I said,

Jericho getting to his feet while Gabe rolls to his knees, his hands out to me. Jericho, on the other hand, seems more intrigued than anything else.

"Come here, Princess. Let me have the gun," Gabe coos instead. "You don't want to cross this line. Trust me."

To be honest, that sounds like the best idea. Of the two of us, he's definitely better equipped to handle Jericho and a loaded weapon.

But as I reach toward him, Jericho lunges for us.

I don't think. I don't have time. Whether I'm the target or bait, I don't care. I just react in self-defense, my hand squeezing the trigger just like I was taught. Somehow, the pop of the pistol sounds quieter in here than it did when I practiced, and Jericho's body jerks once, twice, and a third time. He stumbles, his left hand going to the hole that's appeared in his chest, and he looks at his hand in total shock before he collapses to the floor.

"Oh, my God, did I kill him? Did I just kill a man?" I whisper as Gabe gets up and takes the gun from me, gathering me into his arms.

I can't . . . no . . . what? My mind fogs in disbelief, and the world starts to spin.

I can just make out his face, his eyes wide with shock, fear, or maybe anger? I don't know, but I can't focus to decipher it right now.

Instead, I collapse into Gabriel's arms as everything goes black.

# CHAPTER 37

## Gabriel

I HOPE THAT WAKING UP THIS TIME IS A COMPLETELY DIFFERENT experience for Bella. There are no zip-ties and chair, no Jericho and plastic. Instead, she's cocooned in the soft fluffiness of memory foam and Egyptian cotton, her head cradled on two down pillows that I've wanted to adjust but haven't for fear of waking her.

She makes a small noise, and I lean in close, worried she's in pain. Her lips twitch, and I can see she's having a nightmare, so I reach out, laying a hand on her forehead. "It's okay, Princess, I've got you. Welcome back."

She tries to make words come, but her throat seems to be scratchy and dry because she swallows a few times. I hold a glass of water with a straw in front of her and she sips gratefully.

"Not too much at first," I warn, and she slows down her gulps. "You've been out awhile . . . don't want to upset the stomach."

The bit of water eases her throat and she blinks, still a little groggy. "What happened? Where am I?" she asks, but then looks around. "Mia's?"

I grimace, focusing on her first question. "What's the last thing you remember?"

She blinks again, remembering, and I can watch the play of emotions across her face like a movie. The house, the fire, Jericho knocking me unconscious and kidnapping her. I see the fear, fear I had to be dead if I was letting Jericho take her, the fear she must've felt when she woke up in the plastic-covered room, the fear of seeing Jericho and me fighting.

And the gun.

"Did I kill him?" she asks tentatively after a moment. "There's a piece of me that hopes I didn't, that hopes I just hurt Jericho and we got away. There's an equal part of me that hopes I killed the fucker and that we're safe."

I nod slowly, stroking her cheek. "You were protecting us. You did what you had to do, Princess, and I don't want you to doubt for a second that if you hadn't shot him, he would've killed us."

I speak to her gently, unsure whether she feels guilty or remorseful over what she's done. Killing someone is not something to be taken lightly, and I can still remember vividly the first time I took a life.

There are times I wish I'd had someone I could trust to help me through the change it wrought upon my mind and my soul. So if I can be that for her, I will be.

She looks pensive, as if she's teasing through her thoughts, looking for any sign of doubts, and I can't read her expression to know what she's feeling. "Do you feel bad about the people you've killed?" she asks bluntly. "Any of them?"

I jolt, surprised at the question. "Bad is maybe too generic of a word. I don't feel guilty. They were all just like Jericho, not trained killers per se, but still people the world's better off without. I made sure of that. If I regret anything, it's that the situation ever came to that. I hate that they wasted their lives doing something that got them killed. I'd say I feel tainted, with a better perspective of what life should be. Does that make any sense?"

Admittedly, it's not the smoothest monologue in history. I've never tried to put my feelings about my work into words. It was safer to just keep it inside. I didn't have anyone to talk about it with, anyway, and was always able to justify my actions with thoughts of catching Jeremy's killers.

Even when the contracts moved beyond things that would help me with that mission and were more about taking out my anger on the world in a violent, destructive manner, I found some reason to make it okay on the surface.

Deep inside is a different matter. I know I'm damned and made my peace with that long ago.

"I know. I don't regret killing him, even if it was awful. Because the worst part of it all was the fear that he would kill you. He was excited about the idea, like a high he got from the anticipation, the torture, the experience of it all."

She shudders before continuing. "When he heard you, Jericho's face went from dead and impassive to hungry and eager. When you came in to rescue me was the only time he came to life. But, now what? Am I going to get in trouble?"

"I took care of it," I reply softly, knowing that even if I hadn't, I would have protected her. She would never have gone down for killing Jericho, even if I had to cop to it myself. In this particular case, though, that isn't necessary. "There will be no questions, no cops, and no one looking for Jericho. He was as alone in the world as I was before you. No one will miss him."

She frowns, looking down at the comforter. "That's sad."

Her words touch me. She can become strong and tough . . . but there's an inner essence of purity, of goodness, that will never be shaken. I swallow, my throat tight as her eyes lift back to mine.

"Do I want to know how you 'took care of it' or will that just give me nightmares?"

I lift one eyebrow, giving her a moment to decide for herself, and she shrinks a bit. "I don't want to know. At least, not now. Maybe one day."

I give her a soft smile, brushing her hair back and pressing a kiss to her forehead. "Anytime you want to know, I'll tell you everything. Or if you never want to know, that's just as fine."

Honestly, I selfishly hope she chooses the option of never knowing. There's no benefit to her knowing the dirty details of how I used Jericho's own plastic tarps to wrap up his body, minus one key piece. She doesn't need to know how I used Thomas's truck to haul Jericho's body out to the woods, where I implemented the same plan I'd originally had for Bella. The specifics of what I did won't give her anything but nightmares. I'd spare her those, as long as she trusts that I handled everything with the skills I've developed for years.

I made sure this body dump was my cleanest ever, with no possible signs of what happened, who did it, or where. One, because I want to make sure she is never implicated as the one who pulled the trigger, and two, because I want us to both get away scot-free so we can be together.

"What about Blackwell? Isn't he just going to send another hitman? This is never going to be over, is it?"

I wish I could spin her a tale of sunshine and rainbows, of happy endings and chocolate cookies. But I can't. "There's no way to be sure. To a logical man, he shouldn't. He went after you to try and get at Thomas indirectly since Thomas is too public, too well-protected. It was about the element of surprise. Now that Thomas knows, the costs of striking again is high, especially when Thomas is preparing for war. Blackwell has bigger fish to fry, the one he truly wants."

"Are you saying I'm a little fish?" Bella asks, trying to deflect her worry with humor. "The kind you throw back when you catch them?"

"Well, I'm not throwing you back, for damn sure. But I'm feeling like I'm the one hooked on your line." I lean in, kissing her neck before nibbling softly.

She pulls her hands out from beneath the comforter, beginning to reach for me, but stops when she sees the bandage on her hand. "Oh, my God, I forgot that part. Or blocked it out. My finger!"

She touches the thick white bandage wrapped around her palm and over where her left pinkie finger used to be. "It's numb."

"I'm sorry, Princess. Thomas had a doctor come in to clean and stitch it. The doctor said you'll be fine but need to take antibiotics for a couple of weeks. He gave you a mild sedative to do the stitches, that's why you were a bit groggy."

"Yeah," Bella says before she sniffles, looking at her hand. "I'm sorry. I know it's stupid to cry when things could've been so much worse. But it's my hand. I'm an artist, for fuck's sake."

I kiss her bandaged palm and then her right palm. "Bella, you're right-handed. You can write, draw, paint, and more. The only thing you're going to have problems with for the next few months is typing. I'm sure your geeky buddy will hook you up with some *Star Trek* voice typing program if you ask."

She rewards the silly joke with a watery smile, sassing slightly, "So you're saying I'm overreacting?"

"I am way too fucking smart to ever say that," I reply with a chuckle. "But what I am saying is that sometimes, we fixate on small things when the big things are scary. I just want you to know that you're okay, you're safe, and you're with me."

She snuggles into my arms and I hold her tight. "I almost lost you, Princess. I promise that will never happen again. I love you."

"I love you, too. I don't want to lose you either," she says pointedly.

I know what she's asking, if I can give up my mission to find Jeremy's killers for her. The danger and risks of going after the men who would take his life so casually could result in me losing my life.

Once upon a time, that was a reasonable loss. I would have happily died if I could take them out with me, one big blaze of glorious vengeance for Jeremy. But I can't do that now, won't do it to Bella.

She's lost so much, and for whatever crazy reason, she's chosen me as one of her people. I won't make her feel that loss again for any reason if it's within my power.

"I already told Mia to delete the data card," I whisper softly. "Jeremy will understand."

Bella blinks, stunned before she cups the back of my neck with her good hand, pulling me towards her. She lifts up to kiss me, and I can feel the heat building inside her the same way it is in me. Reluctantly I resist, looking in her eyes.

"Bella, you need to rest, recover. Your hand—"

"I can keep it off to the side," she says, biting her lip. "I feel okay. As long as you don't touch my hand, I'm good. And I need this. I need you, Gabe. I thought you were . . ."

Her voice cracks, and I roll her back carefully, pinning her beneath me with her arms over her head on the bed, out of the way. She instinctively spreads her legs, cradling me between her thighs.

"I'm right here, Princess," I say, grinding against her. "We're both safe, together."

She nods but her eyes still look anxious.

I reach between us, lifting her T-shirt nightgown up and her panties down before pulling my hard cock out of my boxers. There's no need for foreplay. That's not what this is. The reassurance she needs is that she's alive, I'm alive, and that she's still everything I need.

Right now, I need to remind her that she is mine, imprint myself onto her, no, *into* her very cells so she feels me even after my cock leaves the heaven of her pussy.

I push into her slow and steady, letting us each feel every inch as I open her, spreading her soft folds and velvet walls, forcing them to conform around my thickness.

Each stroke is a vow.

Each retreat is a promise to always come back.

And as we come together, we pour our love, our hopes, and even our dreams into each other, along with our sticky cum, in beautiful and carnal bliss.

# CHAPTER 38

## Blackwell

"**S**IR, A PACKAGE HAS ARRIVED FOR YOU," MY SECRETARY SAYS, HER voice quavering. She knows about the extra security, although she doesn't know why. She just knows that I've placed a dozen security guards between the lobby and my door at various places, and each of them carries a gun.

I'm taking no risks when it comes to having two hitmen in town, both well skilled in their respective styles. Especially since I'm certain Gabriel Jackson would like nothing better than to get close enough to make me his next victim.

"Bring it in," I snap, not having time nor patience for her mousy pussy-footing about.

Three days.

After a deadline of two days, I've been waiting for three days since Jericho promised me my proof. Three days since I've had to place myself in this prison that's my own home and office.

"Sir, the package has specific instructions that you have to sign," my secretary says quietly. "Should I have them bring the box in here?"

A chill goes down my spine, and I force myself to slowly nod my head as a courier brings in a nondescript cardboard box. On each side are red stickers that say *Fragile, Handle With Care*, and the top is sealed with plain brown packing tape. "Sign here please, sir?"

I take the clipboard and see that the package is marked *Gift*, but there's no other information. I scribble my name, and the courier leaves like he wants to be anywhere but here, already ignored as I look at the box.

"Is that all, sir?" she asks, ready to go just like the courier.

"No. Open it," I tell her.

"What?" my secretary asks, shocked. "Open it?"

"Yes. Open it!" I growl. "Are you deaf as well as stupid?"

She swallows and shakes her head, taking the knife from my blotter and starting to cut the tape. Already, I can imagine an explosion, a bomb or something being sent by Gabriel Jackson. It's not his style, but my mind still wanders, contemplating scenarios.

Or perhaps this is finally my proof from Jericho?

The options are endless and therefore too unknown to open the box myself. But my secretary is disposable, with others lined up to fill the financially beneficial role.

"Oh, my God!" she screams, backing away. Her face loses all color. "Oh, God."

Before I can ask what's in the box, she turns, retching blindly before fleeing with staggering steps as though she's drunk. I watch her go, then turn my attention to the box which sits, the flaps open, the plastic that was used to pack the object inside exposed as well.

It's with almost a sense of inevitability that I cross my office, nudging one cardboard flap aside to look down into the plastic-wrapped face of Jericho.

There's a piece of paper in there with him, and my hand is steady as I reach in, unfolding it to see the typed note inside.

*You once told me you prefer a body as proof, so consider this confirmation of death. And you seem to be rather fond of sending messages, so here's one for you. If you come after the people I care about, the Fallen Angel will have one last target . . . you. Besides, I think you have other things to worry about.*

Underneath is a symbol that looks sort of like the letters V and A combined . . . but I know what it is. It's the symbol of an archangel.

It's the symbol of Gabriel.

*Well played, Mr. Jackson.* If I weren't angry with him, I might be impressed with his gall.

His implication that Goldstone is focusing on me should be a threat, but truth be told, it excites me. A worthy opponent for me to win against.

Let the games begin.

# CHAPTER 39

## Isabella

I T'S BEEN QUIET FOR A FEW DAYS, AND AS CRAZY AS IT SOUNDS, I NEED to live my life. I refuse to be shut away in Mia's penthouse, no matter how castle-like it may be, any longer. There's only so many video games, so many hot tub baths, and so many rides one can take on a spin bike before your cabin fever gets out of control, and I've done all of this before.

It helps that Gabe has told me that I'm his new full-time gig. A protection detail, he calls it. I say he's my bodyguard when I'm feeling friendly, my babysitter when I'm a little on edge from the lack of fresh air.

Thankfully, he's agreed to let me out today, so I grab my backpack, double-checking that everything is inside.

"You ready, Princess? Your chariot awaits," he teases, flashing me the double-dimple smile I love so much.

He's been amazing, helping me calm down when I have a bit of a flashback or worry about what could happen next and using all of his imagination to keep me entertained in a myriad of ways when I'm feeling bored.

I'm not ashamed to say that Mia accidentally walked in on just one of those imaginative distractions yesterday morning. But being Mia, she just offered a hooting cheer and even clapped before closing the door. Thankfully, it'd been mostly my ass she saw, and nothing more . . . revealing. If she'd seen Gabe, the possessive bitch in me would've had to get her for that.

I lift to my tiptoes, and he stands tall, making me work for it. But I gain enough height to kiss him, rubbing a small circle with my thumb over each dimple. "Let's go," I say, ready to get my life back.

We take Gabe's SUV to the school, and I sit while he does a preliminary check of the parking lot before letting me out. It feels ridiculous. I'm not some celebutante fake royalty, but considering the outlandish story my recent life tells, I'll take it.

He opens my door, helping me out. "Which way first? I did a walkaround of campus yesterday, scouting weak security areas, hiding spots, and risk points, but I'd rather follow a spontaneous route to check in with teachers so that no one can lie in wait."

I waggle my eyebrows at him, adjusting my backpack just a little tighter to make my boobs stick out some more. "Talk security to me again. It's so sexy."

"Princess, don't distract me or I'll just throw you back in the car and fuck you right here," he growls, his hands still by his side as he maintains his control physically even as his voice slips a little. It's hot as hell, knowing that I can affect him while still driving him to such depths of dedication that he'll resist kissing me here. I'm sure he'll take it out on me later, though.

He continues. "And that wouldn't be safe for either of us because fuck knows, I'd be watching my cock slip in and out of your pretty pussy and not looking for threats." He knows exactly what he's doing, teasing and turning me on with his filthy promises.

My smirk is pure devilment, and my words are a purr. "I feel like you mean that to sound like a bad thing, but it sounds like a risk I'm willing to take."

It's not, and we both know it. Neither of us are gambling that big when the stakes are this high, but the tease is enough to promise later games.

Gabriel chuckles. "You're full of shit. But if it's a public fucking you're after, I'll shove you up against the penthouse window when we get done with our errands. Now where to?" he growls.

I grin, feeling like I won the verbal sparring and got a promised prize for tonight. "Fine, let's go see Professor Daniels first."

The meetings with my professors go surprisingly well. The first time I'd explained that I'd had a family emergency requiring some security measures that kept me off-campus had been awkward. But starting with Professor Daniels, I'm repeatedly assured that Mr. Goldstone had made it clear that he appreciates the university's assistance in keeping his inner circle safe.

My jaw keeps hitting the floor, shocked at just how understanding everyone is, but when I'm told I don't even need to turn in the assignments I'd missed, I balk.

No way am I going to let that fly. I've worked my ass off to get where I am, earning every single class with hours of slinging food and every single grade with hard work. I tell each of my teachers that I appreciate the senti-ment but that I've done the assignments and want the grades deserved by the caliber of my work.

Everyone is willing to accept that, except for Professor Foster, but she's always a stickler, so I'm all too happy to take the late grade, since at least she lets me turn in the project I'd completed, albeit at a ten-percent penalty.

After completing the school check-ins, I have to do an even scarier one. The Gravy Train.

"Martha and Henry are going to have my hide for being gone so long without a word, especially after unexpectedly going on a 'vacation' and leav-ing them stranded," I say with a cringe.

"I think you'll be surprised," Gabe says as he walks me across the park-ing lot.

He's right. When I go in, there is only love. Martha almost drops the tray she's carrying, and Henry runs out from the kitchen, still holding his spatula.

"Izzy, you'd better get over here and give me a hug!" she says, not giving me a chance as she wraps her arms around me on one side and Henry takes the other side. He's muttering something about me making his ulcer hurt, and I can't help but smile, having missed his grumbles.

Elaine stands back, waiting her turn, and then hugs me too once Martha and Henry let me go. Seeing my bandaged hand, she steps back, looking at it carefully.

"What the hell? We were betting he swooped you off to Vegas to get hitched, but this don't look like no wedding band."

She gives Gabe a hard look, but before she can consider fetching one of Henry's knives for Gabe's balls, I hug her again.

"No, no . . . it's fine. I am fine. Just a little drama, but I'm all good. No Vegas wedding either," I protest. "If that happens, I'm gonna do it right. In a real church, with you all there."

"And Elvis?" Elaine asks before calling over her shoulder, still eyeing Gabe. "Pay up, Henry. Told you our Izzy wouldn't get married without us."

"Fine." He digs in his pocket, pulling out a ten-dollar bill and holding it up for Elaine to take. She stuffs it into her apron pocket, earning a 'harrumph' from Martha. Henry shrugs and looks me over. "All right, then, girl. Tell us what you've been doing and what's happening now because my ulcer has been flip-flopping between worried and excited. Both hurt like the dickens."

I give them a very edited, very short version of the last few days, making the getaway seem like the vacation I told them it was from the beginning and then the stayovers at Mia's more girls'-night-in than safety concerns. I can't mention Jericho or the danger. It wouldn't be safe for them or for me, really.

"We heard about your house," Martha says sadly as Elaine tells a customer to hold their horses and holds a finger up in the universal sign of 'in a minute'. "You okay?"

"It's almost a total loss, given the fire and water damage," I admit. "It was so old, it practically needs to be rebuilt. I'm just staying at Mia's for now."

It hits me as I finish—I'm homeless, for all intents and purposes.

Thank God for good friends. I've put them off so many times over the years when they've tried to help me, hidden how dire my situation was time and again, but when I need it, they step up to help without hesitation.

Gabe speaks up. "Doesn't matter," he says quietly. "I've already talked with a contractor, and even if it means a total razing and rebuild . . . we'll do what it takes." His eyes go soft, his gaze loving. "This beautiful Princess isn't going to be without her castle for too long."

My jaw drops. Henry smiles proudly. Martha and Elaine have matching shit-eating grins.

Martha whispers loudly to Elaine, "Told you he was one of the good ones."

I can't look at them, too hung up on the bomb Gabe just dropped. "What are you talking about? I can't afford to have some contractor rebuild my house."

Gabe brushes a thumb along my bottom lip, not giving a shit about the crowd watching the intimate gesture. "I was going to save this for later," he whispers in my ear, "but I couldn't hold back. It will be rebuilt . . . and it's not quite *your* house anymore."

I flinch at that, fiercely saying, "The hell it's not. I worked my ass off to keep Reggie's house, and it'll be mine until the day I die, even if I have to work my fingers to the bone to keep it."

His smirk is maddening until he continues, "I meant that it's not your house. It's *our* house, Princess. I know that's where you want to stay, and I want to stay by your side, so I'm moving in."

I blink, my anger dissipating instantly. "You want to move in with me?" I ask incredulously, giddy delight forming in my belly. Then, because I can't help but tease him, I say sassily, "I didn't ask you to."

He leans forward and whispers hotly in my ear, "Do I look like the kind of man that waits to be asked for shit? You're mine." Then he stands back up, gives me a look that dares me to disagree and declares, "I'm moving in with Bella."

I study his face, looking for any sign of uncertainty and find only love. I see my home, not the four walls I've always felt kept me in touch with my past, but my actual home in Gabe. A future for us. Wherever that may be.

*He* is my home.

But that he knows how important my house is to me lets me know, without a doubt, that he gets me. And with him having traveled for long years, I'll do whatever I can to make my house as much his as it is mine. And to hold his heart as dearly as he holds mine, in a safe haven.

"We're living together," I say, agreeing.

"Does this mean you're leaving us?" Henry asks cautiously and I wonder if he realizes he's rubbing his belly.

I shake my head, "Never. This is my second home."

It's been a long road, and I've been alone for a lot of it, beaten down by life again and again. But I have a good circle, supportive people who help me even when I don't want it, love me even when I'm too busy hanging on by a thread to give much back, and who would do almost anything for me.

I look to Gabe. Actually, he would truly do *anything* for me. Even kill. And rather than being scared by that, it gives me peace, hope, and makes me feel loved.

# CHAPTER 40

## Gabriel

"A TOAST," THOMAS SAYS, RAISING HIS GLASS OF RED WINE, AND WE all follow suit. "To a growing circle of family."

He looks around the dining room table, making eye contact with each of us, Mia first, followed by Charlotte, Bella, and lastly, me. Our fivesome has become rather tight-knit over the last couple of weeks.

Bella and I are both living in the guest room, but that's going to end when our house is ready.

The contractor showed up with a big fucking crew, and they've been working their asses off to finish ahead of schedule and earn a nice bonus. With Thomas paying for the rebuild as an apology for getting Bella mixed up in all this, I put up the rush order bonus, and Bella has decided to be okay with that after I'd promised her we'd christen every room and surface in the house.

And I plan to keep my word.

"To a day well-lived, a night well-slept, and a life well-loved. Cheers!" We lean forward, clinking our glasses to one another's and sipping.

After a few bites of delicious chicken and rice with asparagus, conversation begins again. The girls especially always have something to say, and Thomas and I have learned to have near-whole conversations with our eyes and eyebrows in response to their antics.

"But for real, I told my boss that I'd be happy to pick up his dry cleaning, but only for the next two weeks," Charlotte says, her voice tapering off in excitement, begging us to ask for more.

Mia's fork clangs to her plate as she realizes first what Charlotte is saying, "You quit your job!"

Charlotte nods, "I did. I'm so glad to be getting out of there, especially with all the nerves that every meeting was going to be a surprise firing squad of Blackwellian design. I've never been so happy to be the invisible girl at the front desk everyone ignores. But I got the business loan, put in an offer on the location I fell in love with, and I'm doing it. I'm opening my own bakery." She looks to Thomas, "Thanks again, partner."

Thomas shakes his head. "Nope, read that contract again. I'm not a partner and don't want to be involved in any way. I'm just a silent investor in a business owner I believe in. Especially if you add a delivery service for my orders. I'm seeing quarterly Bundt cake meetings at Goldstone, birthday cakes for the boys at Roseboro Boys' House, and some cookies for the veterans' monthly meetings."

"Deal," Charlotte says, and we all congratulate her.

Going by the few samples and trial runs of recipes she's brought by The Gravy Train, she's an awesome baker, and I'm looking forward to eating more of her creations. And being a taste tester.

She talks a bit about her plans for the space she's found, a supplier of Belgian chocolate she discovered, and then she turns to Bella.

"And I need to hire you to create my logo, business cards, menu boards, and whatever else I haven't even thought of yet."

Bella beams. "Really? You want *me* to do that?"

Charlotte rolls her eyes, "Duh, of course. You're the best graphic artist I know. You're also the *only* graphic artist I know, but don't let that dilute the compliment." More seriously, she says, "Just let me know the going rate, or maybe the friends and family discount rate?"

I lean over to whisper in Bella's ear, and she turns to me, a smirk on her face. "You sure?"

I nod, and she looks back to Charlotte. "My security detail has advised me that my fee should be . . . a weekly muffin and coffee for each of us when we stop by to visit."

Charlotte jumps out of her chair, throwing her hand at Bella and then me for a shake. "It's a deal, no backsies."

"I might be able to use the designs as a showcase for my final project too, if you don't mind? Two birds, one stone," Bella says thoughtfully.

Mia interrupts, sarcastically adding, "I'm sure your showing the bakery's logo and menu to a big group of hungry college students and professors will be a huge inconvenience for a new business owner. Huge." She holds her hands far apart and then moves toward her mouth like she's devouring a whole cake by herself. Her grin is visible even behind her hands.

"How's school going?" Thomas asks Bella, ignoring Mia's weirdness as she talks to the imaginary cake she's still pretending to eat.

"Good, turned in all the assignments I missed, even the ones Professor Daniels said I didn't need to." She rolls her eyes and Thomas laughs. "Everyone seems adjusted to my shadow here, and I've scared off all the girls who tried to talk and flirt with him."

The last part is growled, making me laugh as I remember Bella damn-near licking me to mark her territory when some blonde kept inviting me to her study group despite my telling her repeatedly that I'm not a student.

"Just maintaining surveillance on my most valuable possession. Where she goes, I go," I say, resting my hand on the back of Bella's neck and rubbing small circles with my thumb.

Mia's accent appears again. "Newsflash—it's 2019. She's not your possession."

Bella's eyes lock on mine, and I can see the heat there mirroring my own. She doesn't break our eye contact, but she tells Mia, "Shut up, Mia. He didn't mean it in a bad way. And I've heard some of your stories, so you have zero room to talk."

Thomas clears his throat uncomfortably. "Before you two run down the hall to have sex in my guest bedroom, I did have something I wanted to give you, Gabe."

His all-business tone wakes me from the spell Bella is weaving around me. Reluctantly, I turn to him, one eyebrow raised and my other hand on Bella's thigh.

"Mia finished going through the information on the data card," he says quietly. "I know you asked that we ignore it, but we thought you'd like to know anyway."

I swallow, and Bella lays her hand over mine, squeezing it supportively. "And?" I ask both Mia and Thomas.

"There were two main names on the card you gave me. One, Joe Ulrich, you don't need to worry about. He's dead. But there was a full life history and background check if you want to see it."

"Dead?" I ask, lifting an eyebrow. "How?"

"Auto accident. His Harley hit an ice patch in Colorado and his head bounced off a Winnebago, with no helmet. The report includes pictures and the autopsy, if you're curious. Also shows there was a false bottom in his gas tank, and he was riding with two kilos of crystal meth, so nobody was really crying over his death."

I nod. "What about the other?"

"Steven Valentine," Thomas says, more cautiously than before. "He's still around, changed his name though. Now he goes by Simon Bulger. You might have heard of him?"

I shake my head, and Thomas continues. "Butcher Bulger?"

I blink, surprised. "Yeah . . . head of the Devil's Forgotten Demons."

Thomas looks to Mia, who likely read the data card information first but is letting Thomas be the bearer of the bad news. "It looks like both were bikers before the incident with your brother. The intel says they might have been probies for the hit."

I scrub at my mouth, the five o'clock shadow rough under my palm as I think. "I don't work with bikers. They usually handle their own shit and don't have a need to outsource, but I've dealt with them a time or two. Before they allow a probie to get patched, they have you do a crime and turn the evidence over to the club to hold over you. So Jeremy's death . . ."

"I don't know," Thomas says with a shrug. "But Bulger's still around. The file included his last known whereabouts, but he's in the wind right now, hiding out with his motorcycle brothers as security to distance himself from recent club shit. The FBI wants him on a list of warrants longer than my arm."

"Thank you," I tell him honestly.

Thomas's head tilts and his face is carefully blank. "What will you do with this information?"

I pause, thinking how to say this even as everyone at the table holds their breath impatiently. "Before, my answer would have been easy," I finally answer. "I would have gone to war with all involved and left a river of blood behind me, retribution and revenge mixed with savage bloodlust, my reputation for preciseness be damned."

And still, no one breathes. "And now?"

"Right now, my only concern is making sure that Bella's safe and that

Blackwell doesn't go fucking around in her life anymore. I have to believe Jeremy would understand that."

Bella's smile is sad but understanding. "He'd want you to live, not be dragged further into the dark. You've spent long enough there."

I give her a kiss, sweet with emotion and salty with the few tears she can't hold back, knowing that I'm choosing her over everything I've lived for over the past years. It's one thing to say I'll do that when the opportunity to make my brother's killers pay is a hazy, indecipherable possibility. It's quite another to choose a life with her when the other option is so readily laid out before me.

But still, I choose her, and I'd do it time after time.

Mia and Char croon in sync, "Aww, he loves her."

And I can't help but smile at the blush that washes over Bella's face. She's not used to being the center of attention, even with her friends. I think she's been hiding, to some degree, most of her life. She says she's been 'asleep at the wheel', just going through the motions like a hamster on a wheel because she had to keep on keepin' on or risk the house of cards she lived in falling to pieces.

But she's slowly relaxing into our new reality, where there's food in the refrigerator, the bills are comfortably paid, and she doesn't have to work herself to the bone just to keep her head above water.

I appreciate all the things her friends have done for my princess before I met her, sneakily helping when they could, checking in on her, and just generally being her best friends.

"You guys are second on my list because Bella cares deeply about all of you. Bulger's dropping down on the list to at least third."

It's a hard thing to say, but I'm a hard man. I have made decisions to end others' lives multiple times, but this time, I'm deciding to live mine.

I do think Bella is right. Jeremy would want this for me, would be happy I've found someone, and I daresay, I think he'd like Bella and the way she keeps me panting after her like a horndog.

*Never thought I'd see the day,* Jeremy says in my mind, miming a whip. *Pussy whipped fucker.*

I grin, mentally talking back. *Oh, but what a pussy it is.*

Even saved, I'm still no Prince Charming with sweet words, but Bella never seems to mind my dirty thoughts, especially when I share them with her.

Before I get a chubby at the dinner table, though, and sweep her off her feet to run to the guest bedroom, I try to focus back on the conversation around me.

I ask Thomas, "I'm doing my part to keep Bella safe, but you said you wanted some time on the Blackwell issue. Any updates or anything I can do to help?"

I'd truly wanted to kill Blackwell myself, rush into his fancy tower and take him out. Or wait for him to come out and kill him in the streets of the town he thinks he owns.

But the reality is, since I sent him Jericho's head, he's gone hermit, virtually living 24/7 in his tower, rotating between his office and his apartment there. And always with a full army of security. It wouldn't be the most difficult assignment I've ever taken on, but I don't trust Blackwell to not have some type of plan to sell me out if he were to disappear or die. He's a smart man, knows I'm here and gunning for him, so it would behoove him to plan accordingly.

So I've had to back off and wait in the wings while Thomas wages war in a very different style from my own.

Mia answers, "Definitely making progress. I've been doing a full analysis of Blackwell holdings and investments, evaluating which legs of his business hierarchy are most vulnerable, either financially or personally. I found several options for strategic takeover or flat-out destruction."

She begins talking in facts and figures, and I lose the train of her thought process around the fourth decimal point of a percentage of some company's quarterly profit-loss report.

Thomas smiles at her like she's reciting romantic prose or filthy sex talk, neither of which makes any sense to me because math is basically the ninth ring of hell to me.

Finally, he takes over and I understand what he's saying. "Long story short, I made a successful hostile takeover bid for Danver's Aluminum this morning. They're now under the Goldstone umbrella."

"And that matters why?" I ask.

Thomas takes his turn then, launching into some story about how his company had bid on the contract for Danver's years ago but had lost out to a Chinese consortium, effectively making Danver's go commercial instead of keeping their military contracts.

Mia found out that Blackwell has a considerable share in the company, likely directed their decision away from Goldstone, and was in fact double-dipping in profits by also holding a voting percentage of the corporation in China that buys the airplane parts. It's like a complicated version of a shell game, shifting monies in and out of the country and companies to maximize the profit margin.

"But now, I own the majority of Danver's, and the first order of business is to cut all ties with foreign entities and reapply for the military deal," Thomas wraps up.

"Other than the contracts, this doesn't sound like you're waging war on Blackwell, but rather like business as usual for you," I argue. "We need to act quickly to keep us all safe."

Thomas's lips press together in a thin line. "I disagree. Blackwell has waged a years-long war on me and my company, going so far as sending in spies and trying to kill my family." He looks at Bella, who jolts at the label before her eyes soften.

He tells me, "Your style is swift, decisive, and that's warranted in certain situations. Hell, if you get the chance, take him out, for fuck's sake. But in the meantime, I need to play this smart, be methodical. Taking back a company that he actively worked to keep from me is a strategic first move, a sign of what's to come."

Thomas's voice has gone cold. "Blackwell will be destroyed one way or another, but his legacy, the thing he covets most, will also be decimated. That's what I want."

Char raises her hand like we're in elementary school, telling Thomas, "You realize you sound just as maniacal as he does, right?"

Mia defends Thomas. "But he's doing it for the greater good, not because he's an asshat in a tower with a narcissistic God complex. Like some Evil King of Roseboro."

Char laughs. "Fair point."

Thomas looks at Mia, and she sighs. "There is something though, Charlotte. We think you need security. Thomas and I already have it here in the tower, and take guards with us when we go out. Izzy has her own personal protection in Lover Boy over there who follows her everywhere she goes. Gabe is right that we don't know what Blackwell is plotting next, and the last thing we need is him coming after you the way he did Izzy."

Charlotte shakes her head, and though I already agreed with the plan to get her a guard of some sort, I let Mia and Thomas talk her into it.

Thomas adds, "The bakery building will have a top-notch security system, including cameras. But that won't keep you safe in the moment if something happens, won't protect you on the way to work and home, or anywhere else you go."

Though the rest of our dinner conversation has flipped between lighter and heavier subjects, this moment is what truly sets the tone. Acknowledging the elephant in the room with us, the very real risk looming over each and every one of us, but none more than Thomas. The pressure that responsibility adds to his shoulders must be back-breaking, but he withstands it like Atlas, only fighting to keep those around him safe from an unpredictable adversary he never saw coming and that will stop at nothing in his plan for destruction.

"I'll think about it," Charlotte yields. But looking at Thomas' eyes, I can see that whether Charlotte agrees or not, she'll have a protective detail. I make a note to give him a short list of possible options, good men that will blend into her daily life without notice, but can be deadly and decisive when needed.

Changing the subject, she adds, "And on that note, can I suggest we revisit the taste testing of my recipes? I have a Kahlua-infused chocolate cake with coffee frosting and shaved coffee bean garnish I'm dying for everyone to try."

Bella holds her belly. "Good lord, Char. I will never sleep again if I eat that."

But I tease, "I'll stay up with you and keep you busy, Princess."

The blush on her pale cheeks and the way she bites her full bottom lip tell me she likes that idea almost as much as I do.

# CHAPTER 41

## Blackwell

S ILLY BOY.
He thinks he's making strides against me, playing at buying companies like this is some game of corporate Monopoly. As if hitmen are the worst I can sic on his pathetic life. Using the Fallen Angel had been a calculated move, and while I'm disappointed that play didn't come to the preferred conclusion, it was but one of my planned attacks.

The Golden Boy has no idea what he's up against, the depths I'll go to demolish him and insure my rightful place as the creator of Roseboro for all time.

Especially now that he can sense the target I've had on his back for years. I pray to any god that may be listening to a monster like me that the laser dot burns him hotly, feels weighty with the very real threat I wish to carry out.

He may not be a worthy adversary, not remotely on my level, but no one truly is. But as far as I'm concerned, the game just got interesting.

He's waging a war, thinking like the business man he has always been, from point A to B, with possible sidetracks under consideration. I'm plotting nuclear destruction of his entire existence, a devastation he could never fathom and could certainly not recover from.

*And plans have already been set into action,* I think with a pleased smirk.

My messy to his neat. My chaos to his order. My sovereign reign to his democratic leadership.

My strength to his weakness, the one he doesn't even know he has yet. But I'll be sure to remedy that. As soon as the last puzzle piece falls into place.

# EPILOGUE

## Gabriel

I UNROLL THE HOSE, PULLING IT TO THE FRONT YARD AND SETTING UP the sprinkler to water the newly planted sod and flowers. The house is looking good. It looks like a home where people are proud to live.

The door across the street opens and Mrs. Petrie steps out slowly, lifting her hand in a wave. Her lined face lifts. "You coming over here next, Gabe?"

"Yes, ma'am," I say, already heading out of our gate and crossing the street to hers. "I'll get your sprinklers all set up."

It's not a role I ever thought I'd be in—helper, friend, savior, especially not when my soul was destroyed so long ago—but it's growing back from the tatters, seeds taking root and blooming just like the rosebushes Mrs. Petrie begged me to plant because they reminded her of her own mother.

Shortly after I moved in with Bella, Russell came poking around again. He'd been high and more desperate than I'd ever seen him, and that's saying something. He'd fallen to his knees on the porch, begging tearfully for money, saying even a few bucks would help. At first, I'd thought it'd been so he could buy more drugs, but the truth had been so much worse.

We'd denied him, and then he'd gone after Mrs. Petrie. I'd defended her too, telling him to get off her porch. I'd intervened and protected the small group of people all up and down the street since I was the only thing Russell seemed to be scared of in his panicked mania.

He got desperate enough to rob a store in town, and his sins finally truly caught up to him, something I can understand and pray never happens to me.

Any loyalty the cops felt to Russell's parents had been worn away by his continued bad behavior, and they'd arrested him. Russell put up the last thing he owned as collateral for the bail and attorney fees, his house and the land the mill houses sit on. But before he was bailed out, he was killed by another inmate.

The typical thinking is that dead men don't pay debts, and Russell was in deep to his dealers and loan sharks. But the consensus is that they were more afraid Russell would rat them out to lessen his sentence, and the money and Russell were acceptable losses in that equation.

When he died, the land and Russell's house went to auction and I bought them for a steal. So now, Bella and I own the land for the row of mill houses, and we treat our neighbors properly.

The fees have dropped to a bare minimum, the sense of community has returned, and the homes are slowly but surely being updated and cared for. I help out where I can and act as landlord for Russell's house, which we've converted into a rental property after renovating it.

"All set, Mrs. Petrie. I'll be back in a couple of hours to shut it off and put everything away," I call out to her. She stays on the porch, not able to come down the steps very much anymore. When I come back, I'll be sure to sit with her for a bit and see if she needs anything from the store this week.

But for now, I go back across the street because my princess is sitting on her throne on the small porch we added. Okay, so it's more of a porch swing than a throne, but she looks regal in her purple tank top and denim shorts, one bare foot lazily pushing the swing.

I sit down beside her, throwing my arm along the back of the swing, and Bella snuggles in closer to me. I reach down and pet Vash, who's sitting in Bella's lap. The ornery cat has finally decided I'm an acceptable food-giver and will usually let me pet her as long as Bella is around.

Bella sighs happily, a soft smile on her face that makes me feel warm and fuzzy inside, which is a feeling I thought I'd lost the ability to experience. Her voice is music to my ears. "You saved me, you know. Hunted me down, woke me up, and brought me to life."

It's maybe a bit dramatic, but it's also a bit true. "Maybe, but you saved me right back, from loneliness and dark hatred, by bringing in your light and stubborn hope that everything would be okay if we just kept fighting for it."

"With a smile and a song, and some hard work," she says, then whistles cheerfully. I told her once that she reminded me of Snow White, with her dark hair and pale skin, and her endless optimism and kindness, even when life had been cruel and most folks would've fallen into bitterness, so now she likes to quote the movie to me. Thankfully, she doesn't sing the songs often. For a Princess, she's not the best with staying on pitch.

"I love you, Princess," I say, not her Prince Charming but the hunter who stole her away to save her. "Let's go inside."

I scoop her into my arms, Vash jumping down and following us like Bella is the damn Pied Piper. I carry her through the new cozy living room, with warm wood floors and cream-painted walls, to our bedroom. Bella had dreamed of a canopy bed, but the room is too small, so she'd settled on a scrolled iron headboard with fabric layered behind it.

I toss her to the bed before ordering her, "Naked. Now."

I follow my own command as well, and she grins, hurrying to beat me as she says, "I love you, too." Then she turns over, getting on her knees and elbows, her hands gripping the ironwork. Her left hand is fine now, healed with a pink scar I always tell her makes her a badass, but mostly, she doesn't even seem to think about it anymore.

"Fuck, Princess," I growl, my voice rough as sandpaper as I look down the line of her curves, from her heart-shaped ass to her narrow waist, with her dark curls curtaining over her back. I kneel behind her, laying kisses down the bumps of her spine until I bite the apple of her ass.

She arches, pressing herself to my mouth, and I lick her, tasting her sweetness from behind. I use my thumbs to spread her slick lips open and dip into her, fucking her with my tongue the way I desperately want to fuck her with my cock.

I swirl around her clit until her hips circle too, chasing me and the pleasure I'm layering on her with my tongue, my hands, my words.

Finally, I give in and stay where she wants, flicking my tongue over her clit in rapid flutters and pressing two fingers along the front velvety wall of her pussy. Her cries tell me she's close, and I take her right to line and then . . .

Stop.

She whines, bucking her hips and begging me to finish her off. "Gabe," she says, turning the single syllable into at least three.

"I'm going to edge you, take you to the point where you're about to come over and over, but you're not going to come until you're impaled on my cock and I'm filling you with cum." I let every dark and dirty thing I want to do to her color the promise.

She nods, looking back at me over her shoulder with fire in her eyes.

I keep my fingers deep inside her and kiss my way back up the round globe of her ass, enjoying the way she wiggles in need, fucking herself on my hand. Flattening my tongue, I give her a long, slow lick along the crease of her ass before diving in and teasing the tight pucker.

She jumps in surprise, but the noise quickly turns to a moan. "Oh, my God, I've never . . . I didn't know." And then she spreads her knees a bit more, giving me greater access as she arches.

I lick her, then spread her slick juices up to her asshole, tracing the edges with both my fingers and tongue as I give her a chance to relax into it. I slowly start to push my finger inside her ass, lazily licking her clit to keep her climbing toward that peak I won't let her fall off of, at least not yet.

"That's it, Princess. Let me inside this sweet ass. One day soon, I'll fuck you here and claim you completely."

Her whole body clenches tight, and I retreat, smacking her ass. "I think you like that idea, don't you? Remember, you don't come until we're coming together."

Her breath is coming in harsh pants. "I can't, I need—"

"What? What do you need?" I'll give her anything she asks for, but I'm hoping I know her answer because all this teasing her has me on the edge too.

"You," she moans. "Please."

*Thank fuck*, I think, lining up behind her. I rub the head of my cock along her lips, covering myself in her cream and bumping her clit before I notch myself at her opening and slide in, one agonizing inch at a time. Any faster and I'd come instantly from her slick pussy taking me in, but the slow pace is driving us both mad.

I force myself to give it to her slow, but I succumb to the need for roughness, slamming into her so hard and deep, I bottom out with each individual stroke.

She cries out with each thrust, bouncing and rebounding off my hips, so I grip her waist, holding her in place. "I can't wait anymore, Princess. You ready?"

Her eyes meet mine, pupils wide with lust, but I can see the deeper meaning there. "Ready for anything with you," she says quietly, and her devotion to me is blessedly obvious.

How a soul as pure and sweet as hers can accept one as stained and sullied as mine, I'll never know. But I am so fucking grateful for it.

I can't promise her I'll never do anything wrong, anything violent ever again, but I can promise her that I will always act with her love and her future in mind.

So I slam into her faster, giving us both what we want.

"Now, Bella. Fucking come with me right now."

And we detonate, the two of us creating something beautiful, something neither of us thought we'd ever truly have.

Love.

Her, because she didn't trust the permanence of life.

Me, because I felt I didn't deserve it after letting my brother down.

But both of us were wrong. We deserve love. We have love. From and for each other.

# EPILOGUE

## Isabella

I DON'T KNOW IF I HAVE EVER BEEN THIS NERVOUS. I LOOK IN THE mirror on the back of the door, even though I've already checked my outfit three times. It's not like it matters. No one is really going to see me, but it does matter. It's a sign of how important I'm taking this meeting.

So I look at my dark-wash jeans, low-heeled boots, and lightweight cotton shirt. The neckline is wide, showing my collarbones and framing the necklace Gabe gave me for passing my finals. I'd told him it wasn't necessary. I mean, I've passed every test I've ever taken without some promise of a material reward, but he'd insisted.

I swear, I half think it's a tracker for the rare occasion he lets me go out without him escorting me. But I don't mind. It's a beautiful necklace, and I love having him with me as much as possible, especially when there's still a question about what Blackwell's next move will be.

Gabe's head pops around the door frame. "You ready?"

I nod, biting my lip nervously.

"You look beautiful. He's going to love you. No worries."

I'm a bundle of nerves, and Gabe is as cool and calm as can be as we get into his SUV and he drives. I lose track of the turns, finally relaxing a little and singing along with his deep baritone to some old rock tune on the radio.

He turns through a metal archway covered in flowers, parking and coming around to help me out. We walk through the rows of stone, Gabe's hand in mine leading me. He knows exactly where he's going, like he's been here many times before.

And then he stops, and I look down, following his eyes.

"Hey, brother, got someone I want you to meet. This is Isabella Turner, my Bella. I think you would have really liked her." He speaks casually but switches in and out of both past and present tense. He probably doesn't even realize he does it, both living with Jeremy in his past and carrying Jeremy with him in his heart in the present.

I smile softly. "It's nice to meet you, Jeremy. I've heard a lot about you."

And there, under the bright sun and swaying trees, I listen as Gabe tells our story to his brother. He apologizes for not following through with his promise of revenge but finishes with the belief that he's doing the right thing, and Jeremy would've wanted that.

"Besides, as much as I love you, man, I love her too. And she's got something you don't have . . . a pussy that sucks me in like a damn vise."

I gasp, shoving at Gabe's shoulder. "What the hell! You were being all romantic and then you go and say something crude like that."

Gabe gives me the grin I love, slowly growing until his dimples pop and he's already halfway out of trouble. "That's how brothers talk, Princess. It's not like you thought I was some sweet Prince Charming."

He leans in, whispering in my ear even though there's no one around us in the cemetery. "And you wouldn't like me if I was."

"Fine," I say, rolling my eyes. "But you're my not-so Prince Charming, so let's keep the talk about my pussy to a minimum with other people."

He narrows his eyes. "That mean you're not talking about my cock with Mia and Charlotte either?"

I freeze, remembering how I'd just told them about our successful mission to christen the whole house. "That's different," I say, knowing it's not at all.

"Innocent, sweet, good girl, my ass," he says, but I giggle because he squeezes a handful of my ass as he says it.

I look to the rounded concrete engraved with Jeremy's name. "You see what I put up with from this brother of yours? But as much of a danger to my good name as he may be, I love him too."

A big wind blows through us, warm and swirling, and a white flower drops from a tree beside us. Gabe picks it up, moving to place it behind my ear, but I take it from his hand. Walking over to the tombstone, I lay it on top. "We'll be back soon, Jeremy. It was nice to meet you."

And then we go home.

Together.

# VOLUME 3

# HAPPILY
# NEVER
# AFTER

# PROLOGUE

## Lance

*One Month Ago*

MY DRESS WHITES FEEL OVER THE TOP, BUT I PROMISED MY FATHER that I'd wear one of my dress uniforms for my homecoming, and since it's the last time I get to wear this high-necked, choker-collared thing, I might as well please him.

I chuckle as my taxi driver glances back at me for the fourth time since he picked me up from the airport in Portland. "Mind if I ask you something?"

"Go ahead," I reply, watching the highway roll by. We come over the bridge and around a curve, and there it is. Roseboro. My new home, apparently.

At least, temporarily.

"That's a SEAL trident on your chest, ain't it?" my driver asks, and I look down at my left chest, where the gold badge sits above my dual lines of other medals and pins I've picked up over the past ten years. "Were you in the Teams?"

"I was. I'm on terminal leave. My time with Uncle Sam is over." It doesn't sound real to say it, and the words sit hollowly in my heart.

"Oh. Mind if I ask which Team?" the driver asks.

I force a laugh. "You know the old line, don't you? I could tell you—"

"But then I'd have to kill you." My driver laughs, nodding. "Yeah, I'm old enough to remember that movie. I was a Marine myself. You boys were the only squiddies we really respected. If I can ask, why're you leaving? That's a Lieutenant Commander's board on your shoulder there. Most who get that high are lifers."

I clench my jaw, looking out the window unseeingly. "I . . . lot of memories. I've done my bit, and now I've got family matters to attend to," I reply honestly. "Guess it's time to handle the hard fight now."

He hums, likely hearing that there's a lot more to the story but respecting my privacy. I'm sure he had similar issues when he came home from his tours with the Marines. You can't just fall back into civilian life. There's an adjustment period where you lock up your reality in 'the sandbox' and acclimate to life stateside.

The rest of the drive goes quickly, and we barely skim the edge of Roseboro. I'm slightly disappointed. I wanted to see my new 'home town', but I'll have time for that now, I guess. *Home.* Doesn't sound right, doesn't feel right. But hopefully, it will. It's not too long before we're pulling up to a gated road.

"Whoa. Is this the right address?" At the driver's nod, I pick up my phone, telling him, "Okay, then. Let me get us buzzed in."

But the call isn't necessary because the gate swings open as soon as he starts to roll down his window. He glances back at me in the rearview and I offer a shrug. I don't know any more than he does at this point, having never been to this house.

The Jacobs manor on the outskirts of Seattle is big, of course, several acres overlooking a golf course and surrounded in the distance by tall trees and mountains.

I grew up surrounded by plenty of luxury, but this is a whole different level of flashy and fancy. One I'm not familiar with anymore, at least. I've spent the last decade living in whatever quarters the Navy afforded me, small bachelor officers' quarters or sharing claustrophobic quarters aboard ships. I doubt my last bunk would even qualify as a closet in this place.

"New family house, I guess. Things have changed while I've been gone," I lamely say, scanning the front of the house. "A lot."

The driver sounds sad, humming as he slowly makes his way up the driveway. "It always does, but whatever you missed, you'll catch up. The only easy day was yesterday, and besides, you can't quit. You ain't dead."

His reminders of the famous SEAL mottos are a kind admonishment to get my shit straight. No time for whining and wondering.

He parks in the big circle drive in front of the large mansion which gleams a mellow greyish-brown color in the fading sunlight. I get out, and the front double-doors both open, revealing a man in a black suit and a woman in a slim-fitting black dress and tights.

"Welcome home, sir," the butler says. If I remember correctly, his name is Hamilton. My childhood butler, Wilfred, retired when I went to college, and I haven't been home often enough to remember the new staff's names. "Your family is waiting for you in the great room. Mariella will show you the way."

Okay, the great room. Guess we're too fancy to call it a living room or a dining room these days. Fuck, how much has changed since I was last here? I try to remember my last trip home, but I'm coming up blank. Two years? Maybe more? I know my parents came to Virginia to see me about a year ago, and we'd talk on Skype when I had clearance to do so, but it's been a while since I've been home. Even then, it was Seattle, not *here*.

I turn to get my bags, but the driver already has them unloaded and Hamilton is directing him on where to leave them. The sea bag looks comfortable and familiar on his shoulder, as does the cocky grin he flashes me. "Welcome home, sir," he offers. "Oorah."

"Hooyah!" I respond, and I swear Mariella jumps a foot in the air at the sudden bark. I can't help but grin a bit too. Maybe this won't be so bad, I hope.

At the door, Mariella stops and stares at my shoes. I don't look down, knowing they're in pristine condition, having polished them myself this morning before dressing. "I'm not supposed to say, sir, but it seems prudent—"

"I know my parents," I reassure her, and she looks up through her lashes. I press a finger to my lips. "I'll pretend I'm surprised. How's this?"

I fake a look of shock, my brows lifting, eyes wide, mouth open in an O, and her shoulders bounce as she holds back the laugh. She's innocent and fresh, and as young as she is, probably new. She doesn't want to get in trouble, and I understand.

"Very good, sir," she agrees and then opens the door once again, leading me inside.

The great room is at least deserving of the name, large and high-ceilinged with fluffy couches and plush rugs. My parents jump out from behind the tall-backed chairs at the same time a remote-controlled banner unfurls to read *WELCOME HOME, LANCE!* I do my best to grin in shock, but I'm not sure my mom buys it.

"Hey, guys, it's good to see you too," I greet them, hugging them both at the same time and then shaking my dad's hand. "It's been awhile."

"I'm just glad to have my baby home," Mom says, pulling at the hair at the nape of my neck. "Dear Lord, Son, I thought they required military men to have their hair high and tight? What is this mess?"

I duck away from her touch but don't miss the look of loss on her face. But I'm not a kid anymore, and having my mommy pet my hair isn't quite my norm. "We've been through this. The Navy lets SEALs have more leeway, and I'm within regs . . . barely," I confess. "Starting tomorrow, I think I'm going to grow my beard back out too." I rub at my stubbly jaw, the day's growth barely a beginning to the scruff I wear in my rare off-times.

"A beard?" My mom gasps. "Bishop, say something—"

"Oh, hush, Miranda. He'd look fine with a beard. Like that Thor boy from the movies," my dad admonishes, and I'll admit I missed their banter. They're good together, an example I'd be proud to try to live up to, even if that's not remotely on the horizon for me right now. Primary target: the family company.

Speaking of family . . . "Where's Cody?"

Mom and Dad exchange glances, and I see a crack in their façade. My little brother, Cody, has always been the hellion of the family, and while neither of my parents were happy I enlisted, I get the feeling that Cody has more than once made them consider military school.

When we were kids, I tried my best to keep a handle on him, but with the age gap between us, I was caught up in my own life. Still, I tried my best, and when I left, I figured he'd grow out of it like most kids do.

But that was when he was younger, a teenager out to test every limit. He's a man now, already mid-twenties, and he should be well on his way to being an upstanding citizen, working at Jacobs Bio-Tech or striking out on his own and independently self-sufficient.

I get the feeling that's not at all the case. With as little free time as I've had since joining the Navy, I haven't been able to keep up. Too many rushed calls with that stupid ten-minute timer in the corner of the video screen, too many rushed emails filled with platitudes and little else. I've fallen out of touch with my little brother, slowly but surely losing what closeness we once had.

But I figure my being here will be good for us both, and I'm looking forward to rekindling the brotherly relationship we had when we were younger.

"He's taking care of some things at the new headquarters," Dad finally says, but I can tell he's hedging. "Maybe he can give you a tour?"

But it sounds like an empty offer, no real promise for follow-through. I let him off the hook, even as I make a mental note to do some serious follow-up on what the hell is going on with my brother. "Sounds good, Dad. If you don't mind, though, I want to get in civilian clothes and get the lay of the land first. Maybe clean up my sailor-worthy language before you put me in a corner office."

I grin and Dad looks relieved. "Deal. Of course, take all the time you need to settle in. Relax some. In fact, your mother—"

"Would love to introduce you around town," she takes over, finishing Dad's thought as she links her arm through my elbow. "I've met some nice people in Roseboro. It's feeling like home already for us, and I want it to feel that way for you, too. Some of my new friends even have daughters around your age."

She says it so casually, like there's not a myriad of innuendo and plans tied up in those words. I can virtually hear the wedding bells she's ringing for some unknown bride and me.

"Mom—" I start before shaking my head. How do I get through to my parents that I don't want a set-up life? It was part of the reason I left to begin with. And the Navy taught me discipline and duty, how to stand for myself, lead others, and complete missions according to protocol. I'm not coming home to be babied and led around by my nose like a good little boy.

I almost chuckle at the thought of my mom, who tops out at a solid five-five and maybe a buck twenty-five, trying to force me into anything. But it's not my height and weight that make it an unfair battle.

In fact, quite the opposite. *Though she be but little, she is fierce.* I don't want to disappoint her. So I'm better off making this clear from the start so she doesn't have any hurt feelings later.

"Mom, I'm not looking to date, not looking to get married right now. And when I do, it'll be a woman of my choosing, not because she's Joannie-from-the-club's daughter and quite lovely." I fasten a fierce look on my mother, silently ordering her to stand down.

Strong men have wilted under the weight of my hard stare, but my mother? She simply huffs and flips on her mega-watt smile, the one that

LAUREN LANDISH

matches my own. I swear she could stare down a pissed-off Admiral and have that same smile on her face as he crumpled at her feet. "We'll see, dear. I just want you to have friends. And you can't blame a proud mother for wanting to show you off a bit, now can you?"

Oh, I can. But we both know I'm gonna smile and wave like a damn pony from time to time, but I draw the line at dating at her behest. A man's gotta have limits.

Dad breaks the staredown, clearing his throat. "How about the nickel tour of the new house? We set you up on the east side since we figured you're used to being up with the sun."

Dad beams as we walk, talking about the house and the company interchangeably as I store every nugget of information away.

There's something going on. Dad virtually begged me to come home, which I would've ignored, but then Mom wrote me a letter telling me how stressed Dad has been.

Now that I'm here, they're all rainbows and unicorns. Except about Cody. They were obviously jumpy about that particular topic.

I'll get to the bottom of things, fix what I can, and go from there. I'm a mission-oriented man, not Dad's business puppet, poised to take over whenever he deems me fit, not Mom's chip to bargain off as the matchmaker of the year, and not my brother's keeper.

Though that one may be up for negotiation if he needs me.

# CHAPTER 1

## Charlotte

*I*'M DOING IT! *I*'M ACTUALLY GOING TO FUCKING PULL THIS CRAZINESS OFF. Looking around the grand opening melee of my new bakery, *Cake Culture*, is the biggest rush I've ever had. A dream actually coming to life before my very eyes with frosting, sprinkles, and cute pink awnings edged in chunky glitter to look like sugar.

A dream come true is something a girl like me doesn't get very damn often, and I'm going to enjoy the moment.

"Charlotte, move your ass!" my best friend, Mia Karakova, barks. Her blonde and blue ponytail flips as she whips her head around to give me a very pointed look. If I'm not careful, she's going to start cursing in Russian, which is how I know the shit's really hit the fan.

Apparently, I'll have to take a celebratory moment later. Instead, I do as she *requested* and haul out another tray of cookies. It's the least I can do since she's helping me out today. She didn't volunteer, more like I volun-told her to be there to smile and wave at the masses.

I figured her presence would be a goldmine of publicity since she's all over the society pages now that she's engaged to Thomas Goldstone. As in, *the* Thomas Goldstone of Goldstone Inc. and Goldstone Health, and basically the biggest poobah in all of Roseboro. Up to and including being a silent investor in the cakery of my dreams.

So if she wants to boss me around a bit, even though technically, I'm the boss, I'll jump to it. Because she's right, we are hopping like mad in here.

Helping the next customer, I tally their purchases, making sure to use the names I came up with. Branding. It's all about branding. "Okay, so one 'What Is That, Red Velvet?', one 'Crazy for Cocoa-Caramel Swirl', and a 'Peanut Butter Bomb Diggity'? That comes to nine dollars even." The customer hands over a ten, telling me to keep the change with a wink.

He's cute, but I'm on a no-men kick so I give him my customer service smile and offer, "Have a nice day!"

Trixie Reynolds, my new assistant who's been a lifesaver as we prepped to open, slithers up next to me. "Ooh, that one was a Mr. Hottie Tottie, girl! Why the Elsa freezing the world routine?"

I raise an eyebrow. Trixie knows I hate that damn movie. "You know the drill. I'm married to my cakes right now. It's all I have time for as a new business owner. Besides, I'm a redhead, not a blonde." I flip my slightly Elsa-ish braid over my shoulder, letting it fall down my back.

She tsks, stage whispering, "I think your cake is exactly what needs to get drilled. Maybe yank that cake pop stick outta your ass too." Ouch, harsh much? But she says it with a smirk and a twinkle in her eyes, and I feel the teasing giggle bubbling up. I can't help it today.

"No happily ever afters for this chick. I'm work, work, working my way to the top," I sing-song in my best Rihanna impersonation, which basically sucks because I'm an awful singer.

The fact of the matter is, I used to date. A lot. I kept searching for Mr. Right but settled for Mr. Right Now more times than I probably should've. Not in a skanky way—a girl's got standards, but also, a girl's got . . . needs. So a 'friends with benefits' here, a 'date who couldn't carry a conversation but was smoking hot and offering to lick me off' there, and even some serious relationships that didn't stand the test of time, all add together to make me disillusioned. Especially after some epically plot-twisting losses. As if I would seriously believe that he was separated from his wife, the one I didn't even know about? Yeah, guys can be asses.

And I'm not playing those games anymore.

Maybe never again.

Mia interrupts, loudly proclaiming over the crowd, "And you get a cookie, and you get a cookie." She's handing out my Grandma's Secret Recipe

Chocolate Chip Cookies like Oprah, and people are literally screaming with outstretched hands to get one of my masterpieces.

It's almost enough to bring a tear to my eye as I scan the crowd.

But as I do, I see a table by the door that stops my happiness on a dime. Full stop. *Errrrrkkk.*

A single guy, sitting at a table alone, nursing a cup of coffee and the same muffin I gave him almost three hours ago. Steven.

My damn security guard. Well, you can't tell he's my security guard, not with the plain, unassuming polo shirt and jeans he's wearing. But his skills are just as deadly as his fashion is boring, and he's the only person in the shop not looking like they're having fun.

If people really knew what Steven and his compatriots were doing, I'm sure they'd have a simple question. *Why would I need security for the grand opening of my cake shop?* The answer's as simple as it is complicated. I need security because of a mental-gymnastics domino effect. I'm friends with Mia, and she's engaged to Thomas, and Thomas is the biggest rising star in the Pacific Northwest and soon to be the richest man in Roseboro, a fact that pisses off my former boss to no end.

Blackwell. The name so chilling, so powerful, that like Madonna or Hitler, you only need one.

I worked as a receptionist and screener at Blackwell Tower for over two years. Hated every last soul-sucking minute of it, but it'd been a necessary evil to pay the bills even after I'd let go of the hopes of learning about running my own business.

Everything was fine enough, right up to the point Blackwell went batshit crazy and tried to take out Thomas, hitting him from every angle and playing dirty by sending a hitman after Izzy, the third musketeer to Mia and me.

Luckily, she's a fucking goddess and ended up sweeping her hitman off his feet. Yeah, Mia got the happily ever after with Thomas and Izzy got the happily ever after with Gabe. But now we're all on edge, wondering what's next, waiting for that big size-twelve shoe to drop, and jumping at shadows.

So Steven sits, one of my constant guards, my just-in-case insurance. He's so invisible in his blandness that the man's damn near a ninja, something I can relate to from my corporate days. But he thrives in his obscurity, whereas I just want to be seen, for a change. For something other than my red hair, which is what always gets attention first.

*"Is it natural?"*

*"Yes, it is."*

And that's where the often-repeated conversation divulges. Women have been as bold as to ask for a snip to take to their stylist to color-match their own tresses. A bit intrusive, but complimentary in a weird way. Men go straight south and ask if the carpets match the drapes, demanding to see my fire crotch. As if.

And again, why I'm on a no-men kick.

The double-doors to the back swing open, and Izzy steps through, already donning one of my polo shirts with the logo she created for me. It's pink and black striped to mimic the awnings out front with white bubble lettering that looks like frosting. Totally adorable, and her best graphic design work, if I do say so myself. She's got a tray of cherry pie tarts in hand, and the crowd oohs and ahhs at her timely entrance. I think I even hear stomachs growling in want.

"I've got five mini cherry pies, the perfect mix of Ranier and Black Tartarians so sweet and juicy that we don't even add sugar to the filling. Better get in line," she announces.

More than five people instantly stand in front of her, and Gabe points very clearly from beside her while declaring, "Not here. Over there."

He's indicating the line at the register, shooing people away from Izzy. Steven is my guard, but Gabe is Izzy's and he takes his job seriously. Like *deadly* seriously.

Izzy smiles at him like scaring my customers is the sweetest, most romantic thing he's ever done, and I force down the bile.

Okay, it's not disgusting. It's devoted, dedicated, and maybe I'm jealous. But I'm also really happy for my besties for finding guys who fit them so perfectly. Though who would've predicted the geek and the boss, that's Mia and Thomas. Or the innocent and the monster, that's Izzy and Gabe. Not sure where that leaves me, the cynic?

That's right. Busier than an air conditioner repairman in Hell with summertime coming on.

Izzy brings the tray up front, and Gabe goes to take a seat by the door with Steven. The two almost never talk when 'working', but they share a comfortable, if intimidating, silence. "They're gonna scare folks from even coming in the door," I lament to Izzy. "Seriously."

She grins, shaking her head. "Uh, not to brag, but have you seen Gabe? He's like every woman's wet dream. You'll have people coming in just to stare at him. Maybe we should put him in a polo and have him hold samples outside?"

She tilts her head like she's considering that idea, or maybe fantasizing about it, so I tell her no way before she gets too invested. Gabe, who's got hearing like a dolphin or something, flashes me a dimpled smile from across the room, mouthing, "Thanks for the save."

I ring up the next customer, who buys all five pies for herself, drawing a groan from the masses. "More on the way!" I promise them and shoot Trixie a look. She salutes then tucks a lock of wavy blonde hair behind her ear like she means business.

"On it, Boss. I know there are two more trays just getting that last bit of browning in the oven. Y'all just hang tight, and we're gonna have you scooping up cherries and declaring them finger lickin' good."

I smile. She's a bit of a wild child and I never know what'll come out of her mouth, but Trixie's a great worker and doesn't mind if I pay her bonuses in product. Lord knows, I need every shiny dime that rolls in this place to keep it running since I'm at the investment stage, not the profit-turning stage.

Yeah, I've got Thomas backing me, but that doesn't mean I'm going to act a damn fool over things. I plan on paying him back every dime, with interest.

But today is going better than I'd possibly hoped, and I'd hoped so big it scared me. That's what goals are supposed to do, scare the bejesus out of you so you work for them. And now, as long as these customers keep coming back, maybe this venture will be bigger and better than my wildest imaginings. I cross my fingers and knock on the wooden counter by the register for luck.

I'm not superstitious, but it couldn't hurt.

We work for hours, Mia, Izzy, and Trixie each having my back and stepping in to help almost before I even know where to turn next. It's awesome and amazing and a solid step in the direction I want my life to go. Customers are happy, deliriously sugar-high and groaning their delight as they head out the door, until finally, it's closing time.

Trixie heads to the back to start prep work for tomorrow's hopefully just as big rush, and Izzy and Gabe head out so she can get some studying done. I don't know how she does it. I'm ready to collapse, but she was rambling on about a test she has in two days and how she has her study time allocated by chapter between now and then. Gabe watched her like she was discussing the cure for cancer, not graphic design.

As Mia and I wipe down tables, she says, "Today was great! How do you feel?"

"I feel like I'm fizzy on the inside, like my skin is too small and I just need to jump out of it for a minute and shake off the energy like a dog." I grin huge and wide, probably looking more than a bit crazed, but I think she gets it.

She always gets me.

"So, I have an idea I want to run by you." She drops into her fake Russian accent, which sounds vaguely threatening even when she says nice things. Her father, who is actually Russian, suffers the same affliction except his is pretty permanent. Even when he says, 'I love you', it almost sounds like that's something to fear even though he's the sweetest man you could ever meet. "And you can say no, but I strongly urge you to say yes."

"Hit me," I say, fearing nothing right now because I'm on top of the fucking world.

"You know how Thomas has the gala next weekend?" she says casually, like a big gala is just par for the everyday course.

"Yeah, the charity one, right? To see if that bio-tech company can help with the pro-bono stuff Thomas is doing at the hospital?" I say, not sure where she's going with this.

Mia had wanted Izzy and me to attend as her friends, but Thomas had squashed that as a needless security risk. Too many out-of-towners, too many unknown 'plus ones', he'd said. Mia had argued that Steven could go as my date and Gabe as Izzy's, and we'd be just as safe as any other time, but I'd taken Thomas's side, not wanting to hobnob with the rich and fancy, anyway.

I've had more than my fair share of that mess, and I'm not looking for a repeat performance if I can get out of it.

"That's the one! I need you to make a cupcake tower!" she squeals, like it's the best idea in the history of ever, even clapping and jumping up and down a little bit. Her eyes are big and round, like one of her favorite anime characters, silently begging me to see the brilliance of her idea.

"What?" I ask, not catching on at all. "You want a cupcake tower?"

She settles, clicking into business mode like she wasn't just a giggly fan-girl. Albeit, a fangirl of my cupcakes, so I'll give her some leeway. "It's a per-fect opportunity to highlight a new business in Roseboro to people who can use you for corporate functions, weddings, their kids' ten-thousand-dollar birthday parties, and more. Your cupcakes in the hands of the people who move and shake things in the area. It's perfect."

"As long as they like them!" I say, shock and doubt worming their way through my veins. Moving and shaking is really close to making or breaking, and my confidence is waning a little in the post-work adrenaline crash.

Mia rolls her eyes like I've lost my damn mind. "Duh, of course they'll love them. Have you tried your spice cake?" She grabs a mini-cupcake off a tray and shoves it in my fish-gaping mouth.

True. It is a good cake. I'd worked that recipe over for almost two weeks straight, batch after batch, to get the perfect balance of spice and sweet. Around the delicious mouthful, I argue, "The gala's in eight days! You already have caterers that were booked weeks ago. I can't just waltz in there like that."

She scoffs, waving off my worries. "Uh, yeah, you can. It's my party and I'll have cupcakes if I wanna." She feigns being a petulant, entitled brat rather well, considering I know how down to earth she truly is. "Look, I'm nervous. This is a big deal for Thomas, and I need a friendly face there. And it really will be good for *Cake Culture*. Say you'll do it."

I consider her proposal long and hard. It'll be long days and some even longer nights, and . . . oh, who am I kidding? I don't think at all. I already knew I was going to say yes as soon as Mia asked and am basically fist-pumping inside my brain while simultaneously trying to decide on which flavors to highlight.

"Okay, on one condition," I negotiate. "I'm not going as a guest. I'll go as the baker and stand by the tower to answer any questions, hopefully make good impressions with the cupcakes, and represent the business." I add a snooty lilt to my voice, tilting my nose into the air. "Not as a fancy-dressed Roseboro elite."

Mia pushes at my shoulder, grinning. "Hey, that's me you're talking about. I'm a designer-dress-wearing boss bitch, but I'm not snobby like that."

I grin evilly, shaking my head as I look her up and down like a finishing school director. "No, and that's why you'll never fully fit in with that crowd." Her jaw drops at the jab, but then I explain, "You're way too good for them, and that's why I love you, honey."

Eight days later, my face is basically stuck in a smiling expression. My mouth is pretty much stretched wide, teeth flashing, eyes watering with happy tears after the past week.

The grand opening wasn't a fluke, and I've started to notice regulars who are coming in for their morning coffee and muffin, then returning for their afternoon sugary pick-me-up treat.

I'm doing it! I'm actually succeeding with my bakery.

Trixie puffs, brushing a lock of hair from her face. She's just as meticulous as I am about keeping her hair pulled back when we're baking, but right now, the baking's done. Instead, she's helping me get dressed in my apartment on the second floor above the bakery.

The apartment's still a bit of a mess, boxes here and there because I've spent every waking minute of the last few months downstairs, getting the bakery ready for business. Priorities in order . . . check. Trixie didn't seem to agree as she sidestepped her way to my bedroom though.

"Is this everything?" she asks. I can see her cringe though she tries to hide it.

I look to Trixie, with her long, permed blonde hair, miniskirt, booties, and layered tank tops. I rarely see her out of uniform, but I'm sensing that her personal style is circa-1994 in a cool way that only the young can pull off. Actually, she's pretty close to my age, mid-twenties, but I could never pull off her bold style the way she does.

I glance to my closet behind her, where my wardrobe goes from business chic pencil skirts and button-up blouses to casual jeans and T-shirts. There's virtually nothing in between. I've never needed anything else, and my yoga pants are folded in my drawers.

Trixie hums, flipping through the hangers and examining clothes. "Okay, so no Office Barbie attire. Too uptight. No store logo shirt. Too casual. Definitely not jeans." She gets deeper into my closet, and I can't even see what she's looking at anymore.

"Aha!" she exclaims. "Found it!"

She pulls out a pale blue dress from somewhere in the pit on the left side of the generous closet. I don't remember even buying the dress, but the tags are still dangling off the side. It's gorgeous, though, and I wonder what was going through my mind when I bought it.

"Put this on," she orders.

"Shouldn't I wear black? You know, to blend in like the caterers and wait staff?"

Her eyes narrow, her forehead crinkling in frustration. "Do you want to *blend* in? Or do you want to make sure *everyone* remembers the hot ginger who puts the spice in Roseboro's *Cake Culture*?"

Decision made, I grab the dress and run into the bathroom to pull it on. I can't see in the mirror, at least not the full effect, so I step back into my bedroom. Trixie gasps and does a little finger twirl in the air, and I follow her instructions, pirouetting in place.

"Yep, that's the one. Check you out, Miss Thang."

Standing in front of the mirror, my jaw drops. I don't know when or where I got this dress, but I'm reminded now why I bought it. It's perfect, like it was custom-made to fit me. The cap sleeves make my shoulders look dainty but strong, the waist sits at my narrowest part, and the bottom flares out in a circle to hit a few inches above mid-knee. It's demure and conservative but stunning on me with my red hair and blue eyes.

"Wow," I say breathlessly, not feeling the least bit of embarrassment at my own reaction to how amazing I look.

Trixie beams. "Put these on."

She bends down, lining up a nude wedge heel for me to step into. Once I do, she buckles the straps around my ankles. "Are these comfy enough that you can stand in them for hours on end?"

I nod, cocking my toe, and she grins wider. "Good. You're wearing them either way, but I wondered if I needed to set you up with a foot soak for when you got home tonight."

I can't help but giggle at her craziness, but when I turn back to the mirror, the laugh catches in my throat. The heels are the *piece de resistance*. I look good. Young and carefree, but also pulled together, like someone who knows their stuff and is damn proud to show off.

*I'm gonna be proud to show off my cupcakes,* I think happily.

Trixie helps me load the huge plastic storage boxes of cupcakes into my newly purchased used minivan. No one ever wants to drive a minivan, but sometimes, they make the most sense. Like for cake deliveries and as a big, moving billboard for a fledgling company.

Once onsite, I look for Mia, but the caterer tells me that Mia has already come downstairs, issued directives, and disappeared back upstairs to get ready. She happily lends me a worker to unload the boxes, though, and then I get to work putting everything on the tower so that everything is perfect.

It's huge, five feet tall on top of a table, with five layers, each holding a different flavor.

The overall effect is eye-catching, and the smell of sugary goodness will hopefully draw them close enough to sample my wares.

Tonight, nothing can stop me. I'm ready to let the spotlight shine on *Cake Culture*, and maybe me too. But only as the baker. I still don't want to do any of the social *Hunger Games* that I know will be going on tonight.

After a couple of hours of people milling around and happily sampling the five flavors of cupcakes I brought, a dark shadow falls over the night in the form of my family.

I haven't had the best of relationships with them, and to be honest, I'm surprised they're here. Thankfully, I see them before they see me, but it's not like I can leave my post. These are cupcakes, not canapes.

"Oh, my gracious, these are just divine! What's your secret?" the lady in front of me implores, and I tick my eyes back to her, though they desperately want to look over her shoulder again and see if my dad, stepmother, and stepsister are making their way over.

"Grandma's love," I say quickly, repeating the semi-honest answer to the often-asked question. "And quality ingredients sourced from fair-trade suppliers. The vanilla is from Madagascar, the chocolate from Ghana."

"Well, wherever you're getting it from, it's what you do with the ingredients that truly make it special. Well done. May I take a card?" she asks, already deftly slipping one into her clutch purse.

"Of course. Thank you for the compliment. *Cake Culture* would be happy to help with any of your bakery needs, personal or professional." It's another growth opportunity, a network connection created, a baby step toward future success.

The bubble pops nearly instantly, though, as the woman steps away and another takes her place.

My stepmother. Or *stepmonster*, as I like to call her, but only in my head because to do so aloud would only enrage her and drive me further from my father, which I don't want.

I might be his little girl, but we both know that she holds his reins, and she'll happily snap them tight and try to take him away with nothing but an evil smile.

"Hello, Priscilla," I greet her. "Lovely to see you." Ice crystals form on the crisp ends of each word, but she can't fault me for manners, at least.

"And you as well, darling," she says, with saccharin twisting through her politeness. She's sweet-looking on the surface, as always, but I know the truth. She's as deadly as a coral snake, and her grin's just a front. Those pearly whites are ceramic-capped knives ready to slice a chunk off anyone who gets in her way.

Pity my father never sees that.

He only sees what she wants him to see—her still-stunning beauty, perfectly-dyed raven-black hair not hinting at the grey I know she has in streaks, cool grey eyes that miss nothing, designer clothing selected by her personal stylist, and a Botoxed mask of pleasantness she can pull on at will. She's not natural, but she's still a head turner.

But I've seen beneath her façade to the real person. She's manipulative, opportunistic, narcissistic, and spiteful of my existence as a sign of my father's former happiness with my mother.

"What brings you to Roseboro? I thought you were sticking to the upper echelon of Portland these days?"

At least that's what I'd been hoping since I rarely see them out this far from the urban culture centers that Priscilla likes to run in.

As if on cue, my stepsister, Sabrina, glides up next to her mother, eyeing me as if I'm a glob of gum ruining the bottom of her red-soled shoe. "Special circumstances, you see."

It sounds like a brag, but I'm not sure what she's boasting about. If anything, at this party in particular, I have a bigger in with the host than she does. I don't think my family's ever had business dealings with Thomas Goldstone, while I'm sort of second-level besties with the big man. I just don't care to use my friends that way, unlike some people.

"Would you like a cupcake? I've got red velvet, lemon custard, vanilla, chocolate, and spice cake. Something for everyone."

I don't bother giving them the cutesy names I agonized over for each flavor, like 'What Is That, Red Velvet?' as an honor to the famous line from *Coming to America*, or 'Tell Me What You Want Spice' as an ode to the Spice Girls. For Priscilla and Sabrina, I stick to the bare-bones basics in the hopes that they'll shoo away faster.

Priscilla looks down her nose, sniffing a single time. "Well, it does smell nice. I'll give you that."

Sabrina looks at the tower longingly, and I can almost see her debating flavors in her mind, but one nudge from her mother and she pastes the smile back on her face.

"No. I've been following a strict juice detox plan for the last two months.

I've never felt better, and my hair and nails are perfect now." She holds her hands out, inspecting them before she twirls a lock around her finger.

Priscilla clears her throat, and Sabrina pops back into position, hands at her side, no fidgeting, chin lifted, back straight, and shoulders down. It's the perfect mimicry of Priscilla's own practiced stance.

"Congratulations," I say, but the devil in me can't help but torment her a bit. It's warranted after living with her and Priscilla for my formative years and putting up with their constant barrage of insults and putdowns. "There is some lemon juice in the lemon custard, though, if you'd like to try that? Fluffy, melt on your tongue sweetness with a bright spot of custard that delights your taste buds and makes you want another bite. The frosting is thick and rich, decadent, and sinful. Would you like?"

As I describe the yummy cake, I swear Sabrina's eyes have glazed over like I'm whispering sweet nothings in her ear. The best part is that I know she won't eat one, but she'll be fantasizing about how good it would've been for days.

Evil, I know. But I feel justified. Sabrina was never the worst offender, though. That honor was all Priscilla. Sabrina's more a clueless socialite, always doing as she's told and never having to work for anything other than maintaining her beauty.

But that was enough for her to get in a fair share of barbs back in the day as she compared us, and not surprisingly, I always came out the loser in her estimation.

Priscilla steps in front of Sabrina, literally putting herself between her and the cupcakes as if she doesn't trust her to not stick her tongue out and lick one. "So, Charlotte, tell me about this bakery of yours and why you're here as the *help*. I don't understand why you would choose to leave a stable position with so much opportunity at Blackwell's. It's the best place in Roseboro to work, as I understand it."

I roll my eyes, knowing as soon as I do so that I might as well have waved a red flag in front of a bull. Rookie mistake, but I'm out of practice in dealing with her. Ten years ago, I could have smiled my way through a lie detector test because of her. "Working for Blackwell was fine until it wasn't. Now I'm chasing a dream and doing quite well with it."

Fine. That's an unlikely description. Blackwell Tower is run like a slave shop from the bottom up. The whole monolith is a twenty-first century feudal kingdom, with a king who's gone mad.

She sneers, obviously not impressed, and I'm not inclined to tell her what a monstrous villain Blackwell is. It's not like she'd believe me, anyway. Who would believe that he hired a hitman to kill Izzy and placed a spy inside Thomas's own company to try to maneuver him to a losing position? And she certainly wouldn't believe that the guy in the black suit leaning casually against the wall and holding a soda water is my guard because we don't know Blackwell's next move.

She wouldn't hear a bad word about a man like Blackwell, whom she practically worships because of the clout he's carried in the area for decades. It's power she's aspired for her entire life and never had. She wouldn't believe anyone could care about my existence, or lack thereof, enough to warrant protecting my life.

But there's one man who would. My father.

"Where is Dad? I saw him come in with you," I ask, focusing our attention on the one thing we have in common. Abraham Dunn.

We scan the crowd and see him at the same time. Priscilla smiles, and while I'd like to light up at the sight of my father like I once did, he doesn't look well and worry blooms in my belly.

He's lost weight, going from lean to almost bony. His suit hangs on him, though I know it was custom made for him. I wonder if nearly twenty years of Priscilla's money grubbing and social ass-kissing have finally worn away at him the way they did me. Once upon a time, we were two peas in a pod, kicking back with a Mr. Pibb and talking about our day.

But Priscilla put a stop to all that, and she's been driving the wedge between Dad and me deep.

And he doesn't even see it, sadly.

Suddenly, someone calls Priscilla's name, and we turn from my father to see a family approaching.

Priscilla steps away from the table, Sabrina following like a dutiful puppy, to greet the newcomers, a pleasant-looking man and his wife.

Suddenly, my heart stops in my chest because next to them, several inches taller than his father and looking like sex in a tuxedo, is the most handsome man I've ever seen.

A tiny part of my brain stores away the idea of calling a chocolate and vanilla cupcake 'Sex In A Tuxedo', but the bulk of my grey matter is chanting, 'hubba, hubba, hubba.'

He stands out, his white jacket pristine as newfallen snow in the sea of blacks and charcoal grays, a shining beacon of light . . . almost like a prince. "Holy shit," I whisper.

Steven is at my side in an instant, his voice low and insistent. "What's wrong?"

I don't look at him, don't bother scolding him for being intrusive, which is against our I-don't-see-you deal, instead asking, "Who is that?"

He follows my sightline and answers, "Lance Jacobs, eldest son of Bishop and Miranda Jacobs. Heir apparent to Jacobs Bio-Tech. Are you okay, Miss Dunn?"

I'm about to tell him I'm fine when I see the way Sabrina and Priscilla are eyeing Lance. Like a piece of meat. Like a goldmine. Like a stepping stone to a richer future. And my blood pressure goes up a few notches.

Fuck.

Really, Fate? The one guy who makes my heart race, my body pulse, and my mind think about *things*, some sweet and some not-so, and he's already in Sabrina's clutches?

Well played. Well fucking played.

# CHAPTER 2

## Lance

"A WHITE JACKET?" I ASK HAMILTON, WHO'S HOLDING UP SAID ITEM for my inspection. "I just spent a decade in the Navy and now I'm supposed to wear a *white* jacket for this fucking gala? Are you trying to screw with my head?"

"Mister Jacobs felt that it would be good for you to stand out at tonight's proceedings," Hamilton says, unperturbed. He's been with the family long enough that he's comfortable, although he and I have just started to get on the same page since he was hired after I enlisted. "If you wish, I can—"

"No . . . no, Hamilton, I know you're just doing your job." I sigh, adjusting my black bowtie before holding my arms out. "At least it doesn't have that high choker collar that my dress whites had."

"Of course, sir," Hamilton says, helping me with the fitted jacket. "And you'll get to wear black pants as well. Better for any potential messes or confusion with a groom cake topper."

I chuckle at his dry humor, glancing into the mirror to see his straight face. Honestly, it's hard to tell sometimes when he's being serious and when he's joking. In the month that I've been home, I'm just starting to get back to 'the block,' as we used to call it in service, and I know I've got a lot on my mind.

Mostly, it's the company. Dad's basically wanted me to shadow him from sunup to sundown, doling out tidbits like he's dying tomorrow and wants to download his brain into someone to keep the lights on. After making sure that wasn't the case, that his health problems are nothing more than bad gas and needing a week's vacation in Hawaii or something, I've been focusing on handling my own transition.

Beyond that, it's Cody. I rarely see him, though he supposedly lives in this same gigantic house. I've stopped by his office at work, but he's constantly *unavailable*. We've scheduled dinners for which he's no-showed, and other than a handful of empty promises when I happen to catch him in the kitchen, I've had zero chances to figure out what's going on with him.

I'm almost certain he's only using the house as a laundry station and occasional drive-thru meal option, mostly staying in town somewhere.

Ever the rebel and quintessential playboy, I imagine he's got a girlfriend in town where he stays, one whom maybe he isn't comfortable having around the family. But that's supposition, not solid intel.

But why he'd hide someone away, if there is, in fact, someone, is concerning.

And Cody's work ethic, or lack thereof, I'm beginning to suspect, is also worrying. Was he unavailable because he was head-down, working hard, or not even in the office? Both are equal possibilities.

But if he's working so diligently, why would our parents be so concerned? The scale tips away from Cody's favor.

"Sir?" Hamilton asks, interrupting my thoughts. "Your cufflinks?"

"Of course, thank you," I reply, taking them from him. They're one of my personal mementos of my time in the Navy, small gold shields with the Navy crest engraved on them.

On a personal level, it's probably the most annoying thing about living a life of luxury again. For a month, I've never had to wash a pair of socks or even pick them up off the floor. I know Mariella feels insecure because there's so little she can do in my room, and no matter how many times I explain to her that years of Navy life means I'm used to cleaning my own stuff, I think she's worried that I don't like her.

"Hamilton?"

"Yes, sir?" he asks, looking professionally interested.

"Tonight's event . . . what can you tell me about the movers and shakers in Roseboro?"

"The biggest of tonight's attendees will be the host, Thomas Goldstone," Hamilton says, his eyes tightening in approval at my question. "Your father is working with his company on some projects, and he is one of the richest men in the Pacific Northwest. You've seen the large gold tower in the middle of downtown?"

I nod, recalling what I've read both online and in internal reports about my father's dealings with Thomas Goldstone. "Who else?"

"Abraham Dunn, sir. He's more from the Portland area than Roseboro. I know very little else of him, other than that your mother is pleased to see his wife and daughter again."

Isn't that the truth? With Dad trying to info dump my brain, Mom has kept to her promise of trying to match me up despite my protests. She's being sneaky and subtle about it, or at least she thinks she is, but I'm on to her games. Especially when all she's talked about is the charming, beautiful Sabrina Cohen, daughter of Priscilla Dunn and stepdaughter of Abraham Dunn, who's an up and coming player in their society circle.

I swear, according to Mom, Sabrina is more beautiful than Miss Universe, farts rainbows, and has been known to help nurse baby birds with broken wings back to health while working on world peace. I believe exactly zero-point-three percent of her assessment.

I finish getting ready, dismissing Hamilton to do the final tweaks myself, and then head downstairs where I see Cody in the great room, his tie loose around his neck as he pours a three-finger scotch.

"Cody, would you pour me one too? I'm not sure I'm ready for this dog and pony show tonight. You?" It's an olive branch, a way to connect with the brother I fear I no longer know in the least.

What happened while I was gone?

He hands me a crystal tumbler, equally filled as his own, though I know I can't down that much. I'm not a lightweight by any means, but we're going out and it'll be a full night of champagne, tiny appetizer bites, and banal chatter. It's more dangerous than a firefight in Fallujah.

I need my wits about me.

Cody tosses half the liquid back in one shot, swallowing easily and sighing loudly.

"You okay, man? I've been trying to catch up with you, but I keep missing you," I say, eyeing him. He looks bright-eyed, red-faced, and I wonder if that's his first drink of the night, or perhaps his second or third?

"Been working my ass off, as always, not that anyone notices. I could use a bit of relaxation," he says, tossing back the other half.

"Maybe try something less liquid for relaxation? Running, meditation, massage, maybe sex?" I venture, feeling him out to see if he's got someone.

He scoffs, setting his tumbler down just a little too hard. "You don't have a damn clue, do you? You have no idea the stress I'm under."

I can't hide the incredulous look as it washes over my face. "I don't understand stress? Seriously?"

I really don't get it. I can't talk with him, or anyone, really, about the specifics of my missions, but he's being ridiculous. "I've been responsible for a team of men on dangerous missions, have literally held a man's head in my lap, promising he was going to be okay even though I could see his leg was blown off, and so much more. *That's* stress. A project at work is pissant shit."

It's not the way I hoped this conversation would go, but I can't stand by and let him wallow in the self-pity party he's obviously started. Maybe a reality check will do him some good.

But of course, it doesn't. Nobody wants to compare trauma and drama, least of all, me.

"Oh, fuck you, Mr. All-American Hero GI Joe," Cody snarls. "You left and Dad put all of it on me. I've been handling it all, but is that enough for the old guy? Of fucking course not, so here you come to save the day."

I can't help the teenage eyeroll that comes out of habit from my younger days, but I try to offer a more adult pragmatic commentary as well. "Cut the problem child bullshit, Cody. If you need help at work, let me help you. If you don't want help, then fix whatever's wrong. Because something's wrong."

I pour the scotch down the drain of the wet bar, a tight restraint the only way I manage to not pointedly shoulder bump him out of the way like we're stupid kids again. If I'm asking for more from him, I have to demonstrate it first. *Be a leader by example*, I remind myself. "A man controls his vices, not the other way around. Perhaps you should have a water before we go?"

Cody looks like he's about to smart off again, but Mom and Dad come in, dressed to the nines, of course, and Cody bites back whatever he was going to say. "You look lovely, Mom," I say, kissing her cheek. It's not a lie. Mom's always been beautiful to me.

Mom preens while Dad looks between Cody and me, but none of us says a word about the discussion we were just having. There are better ways to get him to pull his head out of his ass than calling him out in front of Dad.

The ride to the Goldstone building is quiet, Mom and Dad pointedly not saying anything about Cody's scotch breath while I try to focus on anything but the fact that I'm walking into a setup. Mom will be in her element at this thing, and I'm predicting she'll drag me around for introductions to everyone in the room.

The lobby of the building is modern and beautifully elegant, a large section of glass leading into an atrium of sorts where the gala has been set up. There's a DJ and dance floor area, a swath of tables where I'm sure business deals will be discussed tonight, and a pleasantly large spread of delicious foods. I'll hand it to Thomas Goldstone. He knows how to throw a party.

Everything is glitz and glam but not arrogantly so. I ask an hors d'oeuvres waiter what he's passing and he tells me it's PNW salmon on a round butter cracker. He laughs when I ask him if that's the same thing as a Ritz and affirms that not only are they Ritz, but generic Ritz at that. I pop one in my mouth and groan at how good it tastes. I learned in the Navy that it doesn't take brand names to make it good. In fact, the best chef I've ever met didn't graduate from Le Cordon Bleu but from Naval culinary school.

It makes me wonder about the man, and more than what I've seen on paper. He's a billionaire but doesn't seem to suffer the affliction of entitlement so many of his wealth do. I'm interested whether I'll get the opportunity to meet him tonight.

On the other hand, my first meeting with the Dunns goes about as I expected. Mom and Priscilla Dunn compliment each other's dresses, discussing the upcoming resort season. For real, as if it matters that you get your tan in Hawaii or Catalina.

My first impression of Abe Dunn seems more shark-like than presidential. I don't want to brand the man too quickly, but I get the feeling any business deal he's a part of is substantially slanted in his favor. But overall, they seem cut from the same cloth as my parents, just a bit lower on the totem pole and ambitious, which isn't necessarily a bad thing.

Ambition is what fuels hard work, and hard work is what gets you to new horizons.

Sabrina, though, is everything my mother said she was and everything she didn't say too. She's beautiful in a vapid, bland way that seems almost repetitive in the room of socialites. Same heavily highlighted hair, same black dress with a slit up the thigh, same pink glossed lips, same willowy frame. Just same, same, same.

I could turn around and see five women just like her, and odds are I'd find another named Sabrina too. Mildly, I wonder if they manufacture them in a factory somewhere.

Cody interrupts the discussion of the latest tax implications of trade embargos, and I could kiss him for it. "I'm going to get a drink. Anyone need anything?"

I raise a finger, eager for the interruption. "I'll come with you."

Not surprisingly, Sabrina volunteers too. But we're mere steps away when I feel Dad's hand on my shoulder. "Lance, could you stay? You'll want to hear this. I'm sure Cody can fetch you something."

I see a spark flash through Cody's eyes and feel the shot myself, though I'm not sure Dad intended it to be such a dismissive hit. Cody's your son, not a Cocker Spaniel.

"Sure," I tell him, apologizing to Cody with my eyes.

He walks away, and I doubt that I'll see him again tonight. Although I'm not one for self-pity, after that dismissal, I wouldn't be surprised if my brother channeled Achilles sulking in his tent . . . at least until someone catches his eye.

Sabrina returns to her mother's side awkwardly, and I to Dad's.

Before the conversation begins again, Thomas Goldstone takes the podium, tapping on the microphone. He's wearing a classically fitted tux, tailored but not clingy. Even in the formal attire, though, you can tell he's a fit man. I've learned how to assess people's skills within a few seconds of seeing them.

The DJ stops the remixed Korean pop song he's playing and Thomas speaks. "If I could have everyone's attention? Thank you for coming tonight."

His voice carries across the room and stops all conversation as eyes turn to him. Every glass lowers, every mouth closes as he looks out on the room, not as a tyrant, but with just the pure force of his charisma. He's commanding, I'll give him that.

Thomas holds out his hand, and a gorgeous woman with blonde hair joins him. She turns to look at him, stars shining obviously in her eyes, and I correct myself. She's blonde, but there are a few chunks of purple and black woven in stylish streaks throughout her hair. She's wearing a purple dress and some platform-style boots that look straight out of anime, or maybe anime porn. If I'd ever seen such a thing, which I most definitely would never admit to.

Thomas kisses the woman on the cheek and I realize this is the fiancée number-cruncher I'd heard so much about. The rumors are true. By looking, they don't match in the least. But anyone with eyes can see they're in love.

"First, how's the food?" Thomas asks, smiling. "If you haven't already, check out the cupcakes provided by the wonderful bakers at *Cake Culture*. Charlotte, they're delicious. My only complaint is that I'll be up all night on the bike to work off the half-dozen I've already eaten." He pats his flat belly and the crowd laughs, and then he points to a tall tower of cupcakes I hadn't noticed before. "Save me another chocolate one though!"

Everyone laughs again, and he goes on to thank the caterers, DJ, and event planner by name. Slick and impressive. He doesn't have to hand out credit, but in doing so, not only does he give a boost to the local businesses supporting him, but they're going to be more loyal to him in the future.

"Again, thank you all for coming to our Charity Gala. I'm sure you're thinking, '*Hey, Goldstone 'charity' is pretty vague. Why are we here?*' Let me explain. To me, charity is not simply writing a check and donating money. It is the seed that grows into hope, and every person has seeds they can sprinkle around their community, their city, their world. Those seeds can flourish, creating hope big enough to truly affect change. Now, some of us have more seeds than others."

He pauses to look around the room, making sure everyone gets his meaning. Obviously, the attendees tonight are all wealthy, pillars of the community, both old money and new money.

"I look around this room, and I see a lot of potential. By using those seeds in truly influential, intelligent ways, we can create an entire movement of hope. For Roseboro and beyond." He pauses dramatically, letting his words sink in.

He's a good speaker, with a voice and manner that make you feel like he's not talking to a crowd but instead talking to you individually. But my bullshit meter is going off because he still hasn't discussed any specifics yet. I hope he's got something more than a 'give because you can' card up his sleeve.

"After several long discussions with my wonderful fiancée, Mia, and then several more with my legal team, I've come to two conclusions. One, everyone has their cause that inflames their passion, that they feel is important to the world. The second is . . . I can't do it all. So I'm issuing a challenge. A challenge to each and every one of you to join in a new Hope Initiative. Gathered in this room are not just the business leaders of the Portland-Roseboro-Seattle corridor, but community leaders, activists, and more. As much as we've already done to make our communities great, we can do more. We need to work together, discuss, debate, coordinate, and make things even better."

The crowd looks around at one another, and I do the same. Looking closely, I can start to spot the differences. Not everyone is at home at this event like Mom and Dad. I can see the starry-eyed looks from folks in rented formal clothes who definitely don't do galas like this on the regular. It makes me smile to see their excitement, remembering when I thought these things were a fun night of fanciness, not a dreary responsibility.

"Tonight, we begin a competition, though that word seems not truly in the spirit in which I hope to proceed. Let's call it a . . . show-off show. Over the next three months, every business, group, and team in the region is challenged to come up with an innovative, impactful way to reach a portion of our community that needs help. You will implement it, work it, and report on it. At the end of three months, the winning project will be funded for the remainder of the year and receive a three-year grant of one million dollars per year afterward."

The audience responds, a wave of people murmuring to their neighbor about Thomas's announcement before an excited buzz starts to fill the room.

Thomas thanks everyone once again and leaves the podium. Media pushes forward, trying to get to Thomas and Mia, who smile congenially and answer questions.

"Wow," Dad says.

"Impressive," I agree. "The man's putting his money where his mouth is."

Abe stands a bit taller, like he's trying to impress my dad. "It must be nice to do business with the Goldstones. You're partnering Jacobs Bio-Tech with him, correct?"

But before Dad can reply, a redhead bumps his elbow, sending him jutting forward. Priscilla catches her husband as the redhead exclaims, "Oh, Dad, I'm so sorry! I just wanted to say hello and see if you'd like a cupcake?"

A cupcake? Ah, this must be the talented Charlotte that Thomas spoke of.

She turns to us, and my mouth goes dry. Forget the dime a dozen Stepford debutantes . . . this is a *woman*. "Forgive the interruption. So sorry."

She's blushing, pink turning her fair skin bright in blotches on her cheeks and chest. A chest that, I'm not afraid to admit, I'm drawn to admiring and exploring, wondering just how far that blush spreads over the lush mounds hidden beneath her dress.

"Charlotte, how clumsy can you be, girl?" Priscilla hisses, clearly not pleased.

Abe pats his wife's hand, clearing his throat. "I'm fine, dear. So good to see you, honey." He leans forward, kissing Charlotte on the cheek and introducing her. "Mr. Jacobs, my other daughter, Charlotte."

She extends her hand to my father for a real handshake, not the limp-wristed kiss-it shake most socialites offer. But when she steps out from behind Mr. Dunn to fully join our circle, I get my first chance to look her over from head to toe.

She's more than just a woman. She's absolutely stunning. Her deep red hair is in a braid, with loose ends escaping the plait over her shoulder, her blue eyes sparkle in the neon strobe lights the DJ turned on, and she's wearing a simple blue dress that doesn't remotely fit the dress code for a formal event.

She looks ready for a date, not a gala. But the dress is doing amazing things for her, highlighting every curve and valley, making my palms itch to trace them myself.

Sabrina speaks, though it honestly feels like she's murmuring from the far end of a hallway, as enraptured as I am with Charlotte. "Charlotte, seems your little cakes are popular. Well done."

I can't decide if she's being snarky or congratulatory. There's not enough to her tone to decipher. Or maybe not enough to her period to have an opinion one way or another.

"Thank you," Charlotte says, but there's no warmth to the sentiment. In fact, she sounds rather cool. I can definitely read her.

Charlotte's eyes move to my mother, whom she also offers a handshake and introduction. Then her eyes meet mine . . . and time stops. At least for me it does, and I think for her too.

In all my life, I've seen so much of the evil, ugly, dirty side of the world that I've only kept my sanity by being a firm believer in the existence of a balancing force. That for every evil, there is an equal good. And while I've never felt it before, looking into Charlotte's eyes, I swear that I can see the world brighten a little. She's . . . what the world is meant for. She's what I spent all those years fighting to protect—the few, the good, the innocent and beautiful.

A smile tugs at the corners of her mouth and her eyes lower, almost as if she's shy.

I extend my hand, wanting to touch her if only to prove that she's actually real and not some divine being walking among us mere mortals. "Lance Jacobs," I say, noting that my voice has gone a bit husky, so I swallow thickly. "A pleasure."

She smiles back. "Charlotte Dunn."

The moment our fingers touch, I swear a spark jumps between us, and Charlotte seems to feel it too, judging by the speed with which she yanks her hand back and the way her eyes suddenly widen.

"Very nice to meet you," I reply, my voice laced through with a sexual desire that is pure, animalistic, and absolutely authentic.

My dad clears his throat, and the prattle between my parents and the Dunns begins again. I ignore most of it, tossing in uninterested non sequiturs from time to time, but mostly watching Charlotte.

"You know, Lance, I finally realize who you remind me of," Sabrina says, putting her hand on my forearm. It feels like she's marking her territory, but I'm most definitely not hers in any way. "You look so much like Charlie Hunnam that it's eerie. With those movie-star looks, although I'm not sure about the beard—"

She reaches up to touch my face and I pull back, utterly done with Sabrina's attempts at seduction. "Excuse me . . . I should visit the men's room."

It's a pretty weak excuse, especially since I've been eye-fucking Charlotte for the past five minutes. I don't miss the twin scowls from Priscilla and her daughter, but I couldn't give a damn right now.

I give Charlotte a pointed look as I leave the circle and enjoy the way her eyes widen in surprise. But from across the room, I watch and moments later, she makes her excuses and moves away from our parents.

I'm feeling pretty good about our chances as she moves through the crowd toward me, and a wild hope builds in my gut. Maybe my mother was on to something, after all. She just had the wrong sister.

But Charlotte takes a jaunt to the left, skipping me over in favor of heading back to the cupcake tower. She begins talking to Mia, not even once looking for me, and I can't help but feel a twinge of disappointment.

I head to the bar, assessing my next move. And once I have a scotch and water in hand, I turn to find her again. Instead, a man to my right intercepts my attention. "Jacobs?"

I turn, surprised to see Jonathan Goldstone, an elite Air Force Pararescue Jumper who saved my ass in the hairiest shitstorm of my entire service. One of those situations that imprints itself on your soul . . . and now the man's standing beside me, a grin on his face.

"Goldstone? Wait, are you one of *these* Goldstones?" I ask, only now putting it together. It's not a common name, but not exactly uncommon either, so I'd never connected them.

He laughs, offering his hand, and we shake. "Yep, though our branches are a bit spread on the family tree. Second cousins, I think, or cousins once removed? Not sure how that works, but our dads are related somehow. What brings you here?"

"Jacobs Bio-Tech, my dad's company, is partnering with Goldstone Health. I'm back to help with the family empire, I guess."

Jonathan takes a sip of his drink, clear and smooth, so it could be water, vodka, or tequila, for all I know. "Thought you were a lifer for sure. Especially after that op, and you stayed in. I still remember the way you guys looked when we HELO'd in with med support. Like we were the second coming of Jesus, there to save your asses." He spreads his hands wide, chin lifted and eyes looking heavenward, his voice sounding like a choir. "Aaahhhh."

I smirk, never letting an Air Forcer get one up on me. "That's not exactly how I remember that going, but I'll let you keep your fairy tale. I'm out now. You? Figured you'd still be fighting the good fight."

He shakes his head and finishes his drink. "Nope, after that Kandahar op, I was rotated back to training cadre. The brass thought I needed a break after the dust settled. I found my heart wasn't in it, and going back to the Jumpers didn't quite fit either, so I got out. Work the private sector now, security, surveillance, and investigations mostly. I could hook you up if you need a second career opportunity?"

I take a sip of my scotch, wishing I could take him up on his offer. I know I'm back home for one reason only—my family company. But dealing with their drama seems so pointless and useless when there are such bigger issues in the world. It'd be nice to work with other people who've seen the impact on a broader scale too, not my brother whose biggest concern is an arbitrary deadline. *Deadline?* I think. *No, a real deadline is making pickup before the bad guys actually kill you.*

"That sounds intriguing, but I can't take you up on that now. Family shit. You understand?" I say, and Jonathan nods. "But thanks for the offer. I'll keep it in mind, if that's okay?"

He hands me a business card and I'll admit to being impressed by the heavyweight, embossed white cardstock. The engraving is a discreet, professional black *Jonathan Goldstone—For Personal Matters* and lists a Seattle phone number. "Very spy of you," I tell him, slipping the card into my breast pocket as Jonathan tilts his head, not saying a word.

I wonder what exactly it is he does. I know a lot of guys go the mercenary route after getting out, and while Pararescue has the skills to do that success-fully, Jonathan doesn't have the personality or vibe that screams soldier for hire. He's still sharp as a tack, but there's the same look in his eyes I saw years ago. He wants to save a life, not take one.

After shooting the shit a bit more, he excuses himself, and I make an immediate beeline for Charlotte. I didn't forget about her while I caught up with an old buddy and actually used the time with Jonathan to watch her more, seeing her light up as she talks about the cupcakes to people as they try to decide between the delicious-looking treats.

I approach the table like I'm being drawn to her by gravity, locking Charlotte in place with my gaze. I swear the crowd parts for me to get there faster, and as I get close, Charlotte's eyes turn to me, and she freezes, unable to look away. Part of her looks like she's scared, wanting to be saved, for some-one to pull her away. From me.

But I'm the one interested in sweeping her away, and I certainly won't let someone else get in my way now that it's just the two of us.

*Careful, man. Don't scare her.*

"Hi again. I hear great things about your cupcakes. Which do you rec-ommend?" I ask politely, giving her a moment to catch her breath. Because I can see that she's not breathing, her lips parted but nothing moving past the pink fullness.

My words unlock her, and she smiles, transformed into a sassy spitfire right before my very eyes. "They're all quite delicious. Just depends on what you're in the mood for."

I can't help the obvious punchline, looking at her hair as I ask, "Do you have any *red* velvet?"

A laugh bursts out hard and loud, and she slaps her hands over her mouth. "Oh, my God, does that kind of shit actually work on women?"

I smirk. "You'd be surprised. Though I'm a little rusty. I was a little busy over the past few years in the Navy."

Her left eyebrow jumps up. "First swing, cheesy. Second swing, guilt trip with the soldier gambit thrown in. You're about to strike out, Mr. Jacobs."

I like her. I like that she's calling me on my shit, though my 'guilt trip', as she called it, wasn't intended as such, but rather as an honest explanation for my lack of game. "Maybe I should just play it safe and ask you to dance then? Harder for my mouth to get me in trouble there."

I point back at the dance floor with my thumb, noting the crowd that's dancing to a 90s hit and getting low, low, low with their apple-bottom jeans. It's an odd disconnect for the upper-crust tuxedo and gown group, but somehow, it feels comfortable.

But Charlotte shakes her head, popping my bubble. "As much as I'd like that, I'm not here as a guest. I'm working." She gestures to the huge tower of cupcakes.

But like an angel sent from above, Mia shows up at Charlotte's side. "Hi, Mia Karakova, and you are?" I swear I hear her mutter under breath . . . *besides talking to my best friend.*

"Lance Jacobs. Nice to meet you. Thank you for inviting Jacobs Bio-Tech to tonight's gala. The Hope Initiative sounds like an innovative way to implement real change." See, with other people, I can pull some slick shit together. I've been by Dad's side and a military officer. I have a brain in my head that can carry a conversation. Except when all the blood is rushing south, like it does with Charlotte.

Mia's face brightens, and I realize just how threatening her previous scowl had been. Apparently, I passed a test. She talks a bit about the goals of changing Roseboro for the better, and I listen politely, though my eyes are basically burning holes in Charlotte's dress the whole time. Charlotte is blushing, and I swear almost twirling in the dress, giving me different angles from which to appreciate her.

"How do you know my girl, Charlotte?" Mia asks, breaking the mutual eye fuck Charlotte and I are participating in.

"We just met. Our parents seem to know each other," I reply. "I was asking her to dance as you came up, but she seems to think she's unable to leave her post."

Mia whirls on Charlotte, virtually shoving her my way. "Go, scoot, get your groove thang on, girl. I'll hand out cupcakes like I did the cookies."

Charlotte laughs, slightly nervous, but I can hear her desire. She *wants* to dance with me. "Should I warn Thomas that you're about to get on the table and start chunking cupcakes? One for youuu . . . and one for youuu . . ." She drawls out the words, feigning tossing a football. "Gonna have frosting everywhere."

Mia's response is a finger pointed at Charlotte and a shaking head. "Don't you dare warn him."

I sincerely hope she's kidding, but either way, I'm taking the opening. Taking Charlotte's hand, I lead her to the dance floor and we begin to move.

It's a fast song, something I've never heard before, so I can't take her in my arms, but I do let one hand trace down to her hip as we sway in time with each other.

I feel like there are eyes on us from every corner of the room. When I take Charlotte's hand and twirl her, I do chance a glance toward our parents, and while our dads are deep in conversation, our moms are diametrically different in their responses.

My mom looks like she's floating on air, hands clasped beneath her chin, and I can almost feel her hopefulness that maybe I'm not a lost cause for grandchildren. Priscilla, however, looks like she would kill me with her bare hands, painfully and slowly. Sabrina stands at her side, looking petulant, with her bottom lip actually poking out in a toddler-worthy pout.

But none of that matters when the music changes and I get to pull Charlotte in closer. "Tell me about you, Charlotte Dunn."

I don't know how much time we have, and I want to know every single thing she'll share.

She looks at me like I've lost my mind, her body still pressing against me. "Why? I'm just the redheaded stepchild. Pretty sure you're supposed to be fawning all over my stepsister, Sabrina."

I smirk, purposefully keeping my eyes locked on Charlotte's baby blues. "I think I'm right where I'm supposed to be." I twirl her, watching raptly as her dress flares out slightly. "Why cupcakes?" I ask when she's pressed against me once more.

"Why *not* cupcakes? They're delicious little bites of happiness." Her smile is genuine, and I mirror it, infected with her obvious excitement. "But I don't just make cupcakes. I also makes cakes, cookies, pies, and muffins. Basically, if it's baked, I make it. *Cake Culture*, that's my bakery, is still in the baby stages with the same type of long hours and singular focus as a new-born. But it's my everything. God, I do sound like a new mother. Wanna see pictures?" she jokes.

"Sounds like a labor of love. I admire the commitment and guts it takes to open a new business," I reply, impressed with her.

"You have no idea. I quit my job for this and put every single penny I have into it, plus some, to get it off the ground. Scary as fuck, but so far, so awesome." As she speaks about her bakery, I can feel her relaxing in my arms, the passion for her work palpable in every word.

"I'm in somewhat of a similar situation. For a long time, I figured I was a career Navy man, but plans change and here I am. Back home for the family."

We continue talking, but the words start to drift off as the DJ rolls into another slow, sexy, damn near pushing the line for a gala like this song. This one has a thick baseline, and when he changes the strobes to a deep red and blasts the fog machine, the whole dance floor's vibe changes to something hot and sultry.

I expect Charlotte to pull away from me at any moment, but she doesn't. Instead, she links her hands behind my neck and moves in even closer. I know she can feel my cock thickening in my slacks, but I'm not willing to pull away from her, even to be gentlemanly. It's been too long and she feels too good.

I slide my hands around her lower back, pressing her against me, pinning my cock between us, and Charlotte gasps, her eyes popping to mine. "Holy shit."

I can see the lust burning in her eyes, can feel the heat racing along her skin. "Won't say I'm sorry for being so affected by you. You're a siren, Charlotte, luring me in with every word, every curve, every . . . thing."

I see her soft smile, pleased that she's responding to me just as much. We move like that for an eternity, or maybe it's minutes. Either is just as likely because I'm living fully in every moment I'm touching her.

She spins in my arms, putting her back to my chest, and she guides my hands around her waist, placing her own over mine. From this vantage, I can see the rise and fall of her breasts, even in the conservatively scoop-necked dress. I wonder if her nipples are pebbled beneath it and go in for a closer look.

Pressing my lips to her neck, I breathe her in. Sugar. Vanilla. Sweetness but with something deeper, darker too. Whispering in her ear, though no one could hear anything I say over the music, "You are making it very hard to control myself. We're in a roomful of people, some of whom are likely well aware that your lush ass is cradling my hard cock right now and that I desperately want to slide my hands up a few inches to cup your breasts and tease your nipples."

I'm being aggressive, more so than I usually am, but something about Charlotte calls to a baser, primal level of me. And to be honest, she's not shying away from it. In fact, I can feel her arching, pressing her ass against me and lifting her chest like she wants me to feel them too.

I'm contemplating asking her to ditch this gala and find the nearest horizontal surface—or hell, a vertical surface, anywhere without an audience including our parents—when a man in a black suit interrupts.

"Sorry, Miss Dunn. Miss Karakova needs you immediately." Something about the man seems familiar. Not that I've seen him before, but in his stance, his speech. He's former military, I'd bet my trident on it.

I wonder if he's one of Jonathan's guys, which would make sense that Thomas would hire family for his security detail.

His words break the spell, and Charlotte-the-Siren disappears in favor of Charlotte-the-Cupcake Genius. Unfortunately for my aching groin, while she's just as beautiful, she's focused on something besides our bodies right now.

"What's wrong?"

The man's eyes flick toward the tower, and I see that Mia is indeed on the table, handing out cupcakes like a birthday party mother, forcing two and sometimes three to everyone within reach. Even from here, I can read her lips, "Sooooo goooood."

Charlotte lurches away, already having forgotten me. But she only gets a few steps away before I grab her hand, stopping her flight. "Charlotte?"

She smiles, but it's tinted with regret at the edges. She steps back to me, pressing her lips to mine. She's soft, sweet, and gone too soon. "It was really nice meeting you, Lance. I've gotta go, sorry!"

She disappears into the crowd, and I'm left wondering what to do. I struggle to see her red hair through the sea of black sequins and tuxedos, but I lose her. For a moment, I sag, looking down at the red carpet that only reminds me of her.

Something glints against the red, and I bend to pick it up. It's a small bracelet with a C engraved on a tiny circle, like a monogram. It's not fancy, more a simple gold micro link, but I know as soon as I pick it up that it's hers.

The lights flash, making the metal gleam, and I wrap my fingers around the memento, remembering how she felt pressed against me, how her eyes lit up when she spoke, and how her sassy mouth made me want to taste her teases.

Damn it. I'm going to have to tell my mother she's right, and she's never going to let me live this down.

I do want one of Abe Dunn's daughters.

Just not the one she expected.

I want Charlotte Dunn.

# CHAPTER 3

## Blackwell

"**Y**OU HEARD THAT RIGHT. THOMAS GOLDSTONE, THE GOLDEN CHILD *of Roseboro, laid out a very daring challenge to the community,*" the idiotic talking head blathers on the screen, grinning widely.

"*And he backed his words up with substantial financial support. It'll be exciting to see what ideas will come of this over the next three months. We'll continue reporting as progress is made by the various teams that are already forming. Reporting from the Goldstone Building, this is Trevor Olliphant, Channel 5 News.*"

It's hard not to slam my fist down on my remote with disgust as I turn off the television, growling. Yet again, I've been upstaged by Thomas Goldstone. Not that I've made any large public moves lately. No, my chess game is better played in the shadows, strategic moves hidden by layers of players who only know a portion of my greater plan.

Unfortunately, my plan hasn't gone accordingly, as of late. My agent inside Goldstone was discovered, and while my name didn't come out of it, it was still a setback.

Then my idea to hit Goldstone's weakness, his bleeding heart, resulted in Isabella Turner seducing the hitman I hired. That hurt even more, because now Goldstone knows I'm coming for him. And a prepared enemy is always more dangerous than a surprised one.

To some people, that would be more than enough to send them scurrying

in defeat. But this isn't a game. This is war. And war is a long game, a culmi-
nation of many moves that result in a win on a broad scale.

The history of warfare is filled with stories of men who would hit, get
beaten, retreat . . . and eventually emerge victorious. George Washington lost
more battles than he won, yet he was the Father of the United States.

And my next plan will be my Yorktown, where I will destroy in one maneuver not just the Golden Boy, but his woman, her friends . . . and everyone
who might doubt me in Roseboro.

There will be no doubt who the king of Roseboro is when I'm done. I
built this city, and it will remain mine. *In aeternum.*

Still . . . the 'Hope Initiative'. What a joke. I've already heard about certain
community groups and organizations who are planning and implementing
a mere twenty-four hours after Goldstone's announcement. The sheep are
practically tripping over themselves to try and get lined up to play Goldstone's
little lottery.

I've also heard gossip questioning why Blackwell Industries wasn't at the
gala. Not that I was invited, which makes me smile. Goldstone's finally realized what he's dealing with, and while he's not being foolish, he's not inviting
the wolf into his hen house. It makes things tougher, but the thrill of having
a worthy adversary is at least rejuvenating to my old bones.

My company won't be participating in his Pollyanna schtick either way.
Simply put, I won't entertain such idiocy.

There's a knock on my office door, and my new secretary opens to reveal Chief Frank Harris of the Roseboro Police Department. "Mr. Blackwell,
your—"

"Show the Chief in," I interrupt her, standing up and giving a rare, true
smile. "Frank, it's good to see you again. What brings you by?"

He gives a polite nod as he comes in. "Custis, how are you doing?"

"Do you really want me to answer that, Frank?" I ask, coming around
to offer a handshake. He's the only person to use my first name, or at least to
do so and not suffer consequences. But he's earned it, and I do have a certain
fondness for the man.

Harris and I have been acquaintances for nearly thirty years, when I
identified a smart, capable, but not totally honest police sergeant who could
be very advantageous to me.

Over the decades, I've carefully nurtured our relationship, making sure
that Frank's been placed in the right opportunities. Never overtly, of course,

I don't want his good reputation within the community to be tainted with the scent of scandal, but when subtle pressures could be applied or information slipped to the Sergeant, then Lieutenant, then Deputy Chief, that could prove helpful to him . . . well, they were.

Frank, of course, isn't totally innocent. He's looked the other way plenty of times over the past thirty years as my plans have gone down, but in his mind, the net benefit to Roseboro far outweighs my . . . methods.

"I'm not too worried about how you're doing, more like *what* you're doing. The whispers and the names that I've heard around town over the past few months have . . . concerned me," Frank says, sitting down, and I do the same. "But I heard something that might prove even more worrisome to you. Figured you'd want to know."

"Oh?" I ask, tenting my fingers.

"There's an investigator in town, a new one. And he's looking pretty hard at you." He delivers this news like it's near-catastrophic. He is obviously surprised when I don't react accordingly.

"So?" I ask instead, unperturbed. "I've had plenty of dogs come sniffing at my door. They get shooed away easily enough. That's your job, isn't it?"

"Not when they're hired by Thomas Goldstone," Frank replies. He's one of the very few who knows of my hatred for the Golden Boy, though he doesn't really understand why. Frank is a resource, and while I have a certain grudging respect for his skills, accomplishments, and contributions to me and to Roseboro . . . that doesn't mean I'm going to share my thoughts on the matter.

"Then deal with it."

For the first time in a long time, Frank shakes his head in refusal to one of my requests. "As much as I'd like to run this guy out of town for you, Goldstone has everyone at City Hall swinging from his balls right now. Hell, he's reaching all the way to both state houses. I try and get in the way, I'm just going to get run over by the Goldstone freight train and they'll just bring in some Feds or Staties. No offense, Custis, but I'm not going to play Sancho Panza to your Don Quixote."

I purse my lips. "And do you at least know who this private investigator is?"

"The word I'm hearing is it's some relative of his. But I can't be sure, and the one name I've got . . . he's bad news, Custis. I'll put it bluntly. I've covered your shenanigans for thirty years, and you've done right by me for it. But if this investigator is able to connect you to some of the things that you've done—"

"I understand," I reply, leaning forward though I know it's a pressure move against someone I consider to be on my side. "If it helps you, Frank, I don't blame you for wanting to cover your own neck."

"It's not just my neck. It's this whole city's!" Frank protests, his hand half clenching before he remembers his place. "Dammit, Custis, I know you're a ruthless son of a bitch, but you've done a lot for Roseboro. I remember what this place was before you arrived, a two-bit suburb, not even worth stopping for gas in. Half the folks were commuting to Portland for work, the other half were on food stamps, drinkin' down at the Mellow Tiger every night, and . . . this town was nothing. You made it better."

"And yet it is Thomas Goldstone's ass that they kiss," I remind him subtly. "Frank, I want this problem taken care of. Remember, if I'm taken down, the fallout will not be simply confined to this tower."

Frank pales but nods. "I'll see what I can do. I'm the police chief, but there's a limit to how far I can stretch the law and keep the spotlight off both of us."

"I understand," I reply, nonplussed. "Keep me updated."

Frank gets up, reaching down to pick up a small brown bag that I noticed he brought in with him. "Here, Joan wanted you to have this."

"Thank you," I answer, knowing what's inside. For some reason, Frank's wife, a woman with a blinding smile and a sweet disposition, thinks I'm just an errant soul who needs a little more love and affection. Adopting me at arm's length, for thirty years, I've put up with her misplaced affection, even though I can barely stand her.

I open the bag, my stomach curling in disgust when I see it's a sugar cookie, carefully iced and decorated. I grit my teeth, not wanting to smash it under my fist until Frank is gone. The woman is always trying to get under my skin with some sugary message of friendship, a relationship that does not exist no matter how many times she invites me to dinner.

At the door, Frank turns. "I'll be in touch."

He leaves, and I carelessly toss the brown bag and cookie to the trash, my mind turning to each chess piece in play, each potential move I can make.

An investigator, funded by Goldstone himself and possibly related to him. Seems he's not content to passively see what happens now that we both know the game is underway. My head start is hard-earned, through blood, sweat, and tears. Not my own, of course. Like any Grandmaster, I've sacrificed pawns along the way.

Perhaps it's time to unleash another weapon. I have them in so many places already, sleeper spies ready to do my bidding here, instigate and interfere there. Machiavellian, of course, but by keeping the pulse on every corner of Roseboro, I can direct this town in any way I see fit. For its betterment, and my own.

The stroke of genius hits me, a cherry on top of my other plans, so to speak. With a smile, I pick up my phone, dialing a number I have only called once before.

The answering voice is filled with nerves. They obviously remember who this number belongs to. "Hello?"

"Proceed. When you have things in motion, call this number." I hang up, imagining the click and dead air in the other party's ear and their fortifying breath as they prepare to do as told.

"Soon, the world will see your true worth, Goldstone. And mine as well."

# CHAPTER 4

## Charlotte

There's something Zen-like about baking. Maybe it's the ratios, or the constant humming of the machines I use, or the repetitive nature of rolling and shaping pastries? But there are times, especially in the early mornings when I'm getting the fresh batters together for the morning rush, when I love just being alone and letting my mind wander.

This morning, mine wanders to only one thing . . . my bed.

I'm beat after the late-night gala. Cleanup duty had been fast, mostly because I'd been hoping I'd see Lance again and we could pick up where we left off. But I didn't see him the rest of the night.

Except for in my dreams. And holy hell, were they hot.

I'd imagined we'd snuck out of the gala and into a private alcove in the hallway, where he'd shoved me up against the wall and kissed the very breath out of me. I'd dreamed he pulled the thick cock I felt out of his tuxedo pants and I'd held my dress up for him to get access to my slippery pussy.

I loved the thought of him pounding me so hard, right there where anyone could've caught us, that he'd had to cover my mouth with his hand to keep us from being discovered because of my orgasmic yells.

And I'd felt ridiculously satisfied when he'd pulled out and iced my cupcake.

Shit. Somehow, over the past few months, thoughts of baking filter into everything, even to my dirty thoughts and fantasies.

But I'd woken up this morning in a fog, one filled with lust, excitement, and okay, some exhaustion at the early hour. Baker's hours start well before sunrise, after all. I'm the one who wakes up the roosters for the farmers.

The back door of the bakery opens, pulling me out of my reverie, and I look over my shoulder to see Trixie coming in, her jacket wet. "Whoo! The heavens are getting ready for a circle jerk up there!"

"That looks like rain," I deadpan, wiping my hands on my apron. "It's been a while since my last hand job, but I remember some things."

She grins like she's storing that info away for later dissection and then flips into a 'television preacher voice' straight out of the 90s. "Ah, but you don't understand the heavenly seed!" Trixie teases, taking off her neon color-blocked windbreaker and rubbing at the dark spots of water on the sleeves. "When the seed falls upon the Earth-ah, the heavenly seed-ah, takes root! The Earth, having been made pregnant-ah, bears forth-ah, the fruits! Let's raise an offering!"

I can't help it. I laugh at her antics. She's such a weirdo. "Then why don't you have a pine tree growing out of your hair? You telling me you're not fertile soil?"

Okay, so I'm a weirdo too. It's why we fit together so well after such a short period of time. Yeah, it's a lot of intense, long-houred, early morning work, but for someone I met only months ago, Trixie and I are almost thick as thieves.

Trixie thinks for a second and must not come up with any witty reply because she sticks her tongue out at me. Like the mature woman I am, I do the same but add a set of crossed eyes to the insult.

And then we're both laughing way too loudly and crazily to do anything else.

"Well, you're in a good mood this morning. That must mean the gala went well?" Trixie asks as she washes her hands and puts on her own apron. She'd stayed back to close up the bakery and do the evening prep while I went last night. I don't know what I'd do without her.

"It went more than well!" I almost squeal, tossing a ball of dough to the floured table in front of me. As I start to roll it out to the thickness I want for sugar cookies, I tell her all about Thomas's declared love affair with *Cake Culture* and the Hope Initiative. Last but not least, I tell her about meeting Lance.

As I describe him, her eyes get bigger, her jaw drops open, and I swear I can see sprinkles shooting out of her ears as I describe him. "So, some former military family type who's hotter than cakes fresh outta the oven damn near makes you have an orgasm in the middle of the dance floor, and then you run off and don't find him again to make him finish what he started, when I know damn well how long it's been since you've had a male-facilitated big O? Damn, Cinderellie, you'd better get to brushing that mop on your head before Prince Charming comes hunting you down."

I laugh and then freeze, another silly thought going through my head. "Oh, shit, does that make Mia my Fairy Godmother? Do not tell her that or she'll probably buy a damn wand and go around bippity-boppity-booing everyone on the head in a Russian accent and end up with assault charges."

Trixie's smirk is prep for the zinger I know she's about to unleash. "Uhm, excuse me, but if you'll recall, I'm the one who got you all gussied up and took care of matters so you could shake your tailfeathers at the ball. *Pretty* sure that makes me your Fairy Godmother. What's that gig pay?"

I shrug and hold up a limp, unbaked sugar cookie. She flashes me a thumbs-up, grinning. "Deal. You drive a hard bargain, Cindy."

The oven timer dings, and she turns it off, grabbing hot pads to pull a tray of morning muffins out. She places each fluffy Blueberry Hill Delight on the tray for the bakery case and I remind her, "Hey, can you pull one for Steven? And get his coffee too?"

She nods, plating one of the huge muffins, but before she heads out front to deliver it, she turns to me. "What's the deal with him again? At first, I thought he was like a super-overbearing boyfriend, but then you said he was security. Uhm, something worrisome about the bakery business I don't know about?"

I sigh. I haven't told Trixie about all the mess with Blackwell. She just knows that I used to work there before opening *Cake Culture*. Since most of the story isn't mine to tell, I've been hesitant to share that even though we've told each other all kinds of other stories.

"Long story short, Thomas is protective of his investments, and of his friends, especially Mia's besties. Steven and the boys are just a safety precaution, for the business and for me. So be nice to him. Lord knows, he must be going stark-raving mad having to listen to us all day, every day."

Trixie gets a twinkle in her eye, and I swear I can see the hamster in her mind running faster with ideas on how to spice up Steven's days. But she smiles sweetly, too sweetly, and says, "Sure thing, Boss. Nice to Security Steven and his boys. One muffin and coffee coming right up."

She adjusts her boobs through her shirt, making me wonder if she means an actual muffin or something a little more suggestive. She even wiggles a bit as she goes through the double doors, and I'd bet my favorite mixing bowl that she's out there flirting her ass off. Spicy and sweet, that one.

I finish the cookies, setting them in the oven and traying the chocolate chip muffins I made earlier. When I swoosh through the double doors myself, Trixie jumps like she was busted and I realize that she was taking a picture of Steven.

I smirk, figuring she's stashing one away for the spank bank or maybe sending the hottie shottie to a friend for some girlish oohs and ahhs. "You good?" I ask, though I suspect she's more bad girl than good girl.

All-business Steven could probably use a bit of shaking up, Trixie style.

"Yep," she says, popping the P. "Just checking Tinder one more time before the day gets underway. Swipe city, ya know?"

She says it just a little loudly, and I wonder if she's trying to communicate that she's single and ready to mingle. I chance a glance over my shoulder, but Steven is looking out the window, eyes scanning left and right up the empty sidewalk as he sips his coffee. Trixie sighs.

"Can you make sure everything's ready out here? I'm going to grab the rest of the goodies for the case." I head to the back, leaving Trixie at her post.

Busting through the double doors, I stop at the sight before me. Flour-covered stainless steel prep table, two huge wall ovens filled with treats I made, a stack of boxes with my logo on them, and a whiteboard with all this month's special orders written out. Honestly, it looks like a barely-controlled bomb's gone off, and it's barely seven in the morning.

I never would've thought this would be my life. Didn't think I had the courage to chuck away everything I knew.

My normal life before the bakery was nothing like this. But what's normal?

Normal's boring. Normal's stagnating. Normal's sitting on your ass in a cubicle in a job you hate just so you can say you've got health insurance and a 401(k).

Normal's dying . . . just doing it slowly.

"So fuck normal," I tell the empty room.

This is my new normal. Risky, adventurous, something I'm passionate about, and something I can give to the world to make their day a bit better. Because sugar definitely makes everything better.

I take a couple of trips back and forth and am just loading up the last tray when I hear a loud knocking on the front door. Trixie pops her head through the door. "Hey, Char, you definitely want to take this. It's your stepsister, I think? Expensive dye job with streaky highlights, looks like she smelled something rank? Steven's about to go Judge Dredd on her ass."

"Shit," I reply. "I'm coming. Can you take this last tray, and maybe serve as a witness in my defense at the trial?" I roll my eyes, but I'm half-serious because I already know this is going to get ugly.

Up front, Sabrina is raging, slapping a palm against my freshly-applied logo, and Steven is standing wide-spread with his arms crossed in front of the door.

"I got this, thanks," I tell him before hollering through the door. "Stop banging on my door so I can unlock the damn thing."

She waits, but I can see her foot tapping, which makes me go even slower.

As soon as she hears the lock click open, she jerks on the door, finger pointing in my face. "What the hell are you thinking, bitch?"

"Good morning to you too, Sabrina," I reply, and while I sound sweet, we both know I'm faking. "What brings you by this morning? Need a coffee and muffin?"

"You know why I'm here!" she hisses. "Lance is *my* man. Mother already set it all up, so you can just crawl back to whatever basement you came out of and leave him the fuck alone."

A hilarious joke about Mia being a basement dweller who got the hottest bachelor in the city almost works its way out, but Sabrina wouldn't understand the beautiful irony of it so I let it go and focus on the rest of her statement.

"Sabrina, last time I checked, you can't call dibs on someone. It's not like you can buy him at an auction. And if we're going by childhood rules . . . *I licked him, so he's mine.*"

I know, even as I say it, that I'm poking the bear, but it's so fun to finally be at a point where I can get a rise out of her and give it back. I shrank under her insults and superiority complex for way too long. So what if I didn't actually lick him?

Sabrina sputters, a quiet squeak of affront passing her perfectly painted lips. Yes, at seven in the morning, she's already fully coiffed. Unlike my messy hair, bare face, and polo and jeans uniform covered with a floury apron.

"Whatever Priscilla might have told you," I say, because I *never* call Priscilla anything resembling Mom or Mother, "Lance is a grown man and can flirt, dance, and date anyone he wants. I know you'd hoped it'd be you." I fake a *tsk* and shake my head sadly, looking her up and down. There's nothing out of place. She's the perfect socialite, but I make it seem like it's not remotely up to muster. "But Lance seems to have felt otherwise."

Sabrina seemingly gets over her initial flashy rage and reverts to her training, which has been drummed into her head since birth, I suspect. She sneers, every snotty stereotypical bitch come to life before my very eyes. "And you think he'd prefer someone like *you* instead?"

She returns my head to toe appraisal, and where I used to cower, hoping she wouldn't fixate on any one thing to torment me over, now I stand proud. I've grown over the years, stronger in many ways because of the hell Priscilla and Sabrina put me through. Even my comfort in my own skin was shaped by their constant criticism.

I still remember the last time Sabrina scanned me this way. I was sixteen, she was eighteen, and she'd had a glint in her eyes as she told her mother that the baby hairs around my hairline surely showed my lack of basic hygiene.

It'd brought on World War III, with any and all body hair as the evil enemy. I'd been so young, still so innocent, that when the waxer started ripping off the strips, I'd cried, not understanding what was wrong with peach fuzz on my arms. I'd been mortified at the full bikini wax, though, feeling intimately violated. It wasn't until years later, when I finally got waxed by my own choosing, that I realized the first waxer had been intentionally and insanely rough, likely at Priscilla's behest.

But none of that matters now, not in my new and improved self-image. I may still have insecurities—*who doesn't?*—but I can see that Priscilla and Sabrina used every trick in the book to keep me small for my whole childhood.

I don't think they're jealous of me. It's more just that they used me to make themselves feel bigger.

In some ways, I don't even fault Sabrina for it. She doesn't know any better, having been raised and shaped by Priscilla. But she's a full-grown woman now, and she needs to get a grip on how the real world works.

"Judging by how he ditched you and swept me away on the dance floor, I'd say yes, he'd prefer me. The bigger issue is that neither you, nor your mother, can control others the way you think you can," I explain patiently but evenly. "And stomping your foot or throwing money at problems doesn't work. Come on, Sabrina . . . *do better* than your mother."

It's wishful thinking that she'll hear the slight encouragement, but it's all I can give the person who made so much of my life hell.

"Seems she did pretty well with Daddy." She lifts her chin, haughty and snarky at the same time.

She knows I hate it when she calls my father *Daddy*. He's not her Daddy. Hell, he's barely even mine anymore. Once upon a time, he was on my side, a fun guy who helped me, loved me. That man was Daddy. But Priscilla ate away at our relationship too, under the guise of guiding me into womanhood, something my dad basically got super-nervous about. And now he's simply Dad and has been for a long time.

My face falls as her shot hits a bullseye on the button she loves to push, and she knows it, her eyes lighting up. She hair-flips, walking toward the door like the victor she is, but she tosses over shoulder, "Don't forget your place, Charlotte. Make your little cakes and cookies." She smirks as she looks around the bakery. "But leave Lance to me. He is *mine*."

The jingling bells sound like a death toll as she walks out, the silence heavy as Steven and Trixie stare at me, having seen the whole showdown.

"Miss Dunn?" Steven asks softly. "Would you like me to put her on the *persona-non-grata* list?"

Trixie interrupts, clucking her tongue. "Uh, no. I'd like you to put her on the shoot-on-sight list, capiche?" She hurries around the case, wrapping an arm around me as she hustles me to the back, muttering the whole way, "*Security Steven*? He just stood there and let that bitch rail you over. Useless."

Guess Sabrina ruined Trixie's crush, along with my crush on Lance. A morning well-spent in her books, probably.

# CHAPTER 5

## Lance

I've never been a man to daydream much. I've seen too many things. Dark, horrible things. Things that scar a man's soul. Things that can give the most hardened badass nightmares for the rest of their existence.

So I don't daydream because those are the memories that take the opportunity of a wandering mind to force their way to the forefront.

*"Sir?" he asks me, and I know he wants the truth I can't give him. Not now when hope is all he has to hang on to. I won't take that away.*

*"It's just a scratch," I tell the badly wounded man. "You're gonna be on your feet in no time."*

*"Bullshit, sir." His brown-smudged face is covered in the very dirt he's talking about through choked swallows. Sweat and tears run rivers through the filth, making mud on his cheeks as the beat of the chopper blades fills the air.*

*A sudden burst of adrenalin shoots through him, and he grips at my shirt with surprising strength. "Don't die out here like me, man. Go and live your life, not someone else's. I should've been home with her."*

*His eyes swirl, unfocused on the shades of brown around us—brown dirt, brown buildings, brown uniforms, only the bright blue sky a relief. His voice is getting weaker. "Do one thing for me?"*

*"You can tell her yourself," I reply, knowing he's thinking about his young wife and the baby daughter he hasn't even met yet. He could have taken leave. I would have put the paperwork through in record time and the Commander would have*

*stamped it no problem, but he didn't want to leave his brothers holding the bag on this shitstorm. Now, he'll never meet the babe.*

*He smiles, taking my hand. "Just . . . tell her about me?"*

*"I will," I promise, knowing that I'm admitting the truth . . . but I think he deserves to hear it.*

*His smile is pain-filled. "It was an honor, sir."*

*Tears burn my eyes, and I clasp his hand tightly. "The honor is mine."*

*He tries to say something else, but before he can, his breath hitches twice, the last exhalation exiting his lips without the heroic battle cry of a movie or the dramatic swell of music you grow up expecting. Instead, it's like a sigh, a tired, exhausted man at the end of his labors, setting down his load for a final time, never to pick it up again.*

*"Hooyah." I fare the body well just as the chopper starts to descend. Thirty seconds later, we're on the deck, and I have to let him go. There are other men under my command, under my care. And right now, they need me.*

*But I take one split second to look to the sky, promising that I'll tell that little girl all about her father, the man who faced death with honor and died as a hero.*

Back in my bed, I shake my head, fighting the memory down and locking it in the box with so many others. I breathe slowly and deeply, remembering where I am. It's weird to even think about this as a bed. I'm so used to a *rack,* or a *bunk,* that even the term 'bed' feels foreign. But there's no way anyone would ever call a king-size memory foam mattress like this a rack.

I flop onto my side, and a sparkle on the bedside table catches my eye, along with the alarm clock. I'd purposefully not set it, hoping for a little extra shut-eye after the late night at the gala. Seems instead of my usual six AM wakeup for PT, I've managed to sleep in until almost seven thirty. Not bad for a civvie.

But the gold bracelet is what changes my mood from the dour dredges of my dreams, transporting my mind to the happier memories of last night.

I pick it up, holding the dainty bracelet in my hand and remembering the redhaired spitfire who wore it and the way she set me spinning. She's taking the world by storm, making her own way, despite her family and the odds against her. That takes guts.

And sometimes, guts are enough. Whether kicking in a door when you know there are half a dozen men on the other side ready to fill your body with bullets, or standing up to everyone and everything else to open a simple bakery . . . guts are guts.

And Charlotte Dunn has them in spades. I remember her smile, her sass, the smell of her skin, and the surprising feel of her lips on mine. She's the kind of woman my buddies and I would dream about back in BUDs, a fantasy woman who would make all the hell we were going through worth something. A scarlet angel, strong and innocent and ready to soothe our souls and tell us everything would be okay, despite the violence and ugliness we'd wrought.

A voice in my head says to me, *she's no angel.*

But I can't help but think of the way she moved against me, her lush curves dimpling beneath my grip, her ass cradling my cock as she arched, asking for more. And now, like last night, I'm rock fucking hard again.

I stare at the bracelet, a link near the clasp broken, and imagine her wearing it once again as her soft hands wrap around my shaft, the light twinkling as she works me up and down. I can't help myself. I slip my hand beneath the sheet and palm my thickness. A few massage strokes later, I'm delving into my underwear, pulling my cock and balls out and kicking the sheet out of the way.

I hold the bracelet, eyeing it as I jack myself with long strokes, mentally replacing my hand with hers. I rub over the head, wishing it were her lips, and the thought of her sucking me has me damn near the edge. A filthy thought takes root, and I wrap the delicate bracelet around the crown of my cock, just below the ridge. I thrust into my hand, careful to not break the bracelet further, and watch the monogram charm dangle against my skin, faster and faster in time with my heartbeat. I can barely breathe as I come in spurts, white-hot jets covering me and the gold links as I spasm, growling her name through gritted teeth, "Char . . .lotte."

Spent, I carefully unwind the links from my cock and wipe them on my underwear, promising myself to clean it properly. I wait for my breathing to return to normal, thinking sweeter thoughts about Charlotte but wondering if she went home hot and bothered last night too.

I'd wanted to track her down, but family obligations had gotten in the way, and I'd had to help a tipsy Cody into the family limo.

But today is mine. And so is Charlotte.

I get out of bed, energized by the thought of tracking her down to continue our conversation from last night. I shower and dress in a Navy PT shirt and shorts, taking a minute to soap and water wash Charlotte's bracelet before placing it into my sock drawer for safekeeping while I work out.

I find Hamilton in the kitchen, a carafe of coffee in his hands. "Mister Lance, good morning."

"Hamilton, I don't suppose I could convince you to not call me Mister Lance, could I?" I ask, smiling and taking an offered mug. "I mean, I couldn't like, slip you a fifty once a week or something, or duct tape your shoes to the floor if you don't stop?"

"Hardly, sir. And duct tape would just damage my shoes. But I would enjoy the cat and mouse game. It would provide an entertaining diversion from my day to day duties. Beware, though. I would retaliate." He narrows his eyes, which would probably be threatening if he wasn't grey-haired and so thin a strong wind could knock him over.

I laugh, nodding. "I learned long ago to never, ever mess with someone who is involved with laundering your underwear. Not every threat is so easily seen. The most dangerous opponents aren't the bigwigs but the little guys because they've got nothing to lose."

Hamilton nods, like I'm saying something quite wise, even going so far as to rub his nails on his lapel, like he's buffing them proudly at what he's capable of. "A wise lesson, sir."

"So, what's Chef whipped up for breakfast?"

"I'm afraid it's her day off, but I'd be happy to, ahem, *whip* you up an omelet, if you'd like. I'm quite adept, making them for your father regularly."

"I think I'll just grab some toast. No worries. Where is dear old Dad this morning? Figured he'd still be in bed after the late night." I glance around, listening and not hearing evidence of anyone but Hamilton and me.

He moves closer, almost whispering, "I'm afraid Mister Jacobs had a rather late evening, filled with discussions with Mrs. Jacobs. You might do well to make a run for it, but if you'd rather chance it, he's on the back patio. Wanted breakfast by the pool today, sir."

I wonder what my parents could've been up to all night. Well, I don't *wonder*, because I don't want to think about my parents having sex. I'm still partially convinced that I was delivered via stork and Cody was a medical experiment gone wrong.

But the conversation part of the evening is interesting. They're probably celebrating my interest in Charlotte, my mom strutting around like a peacock that she was right and already planning a wedding and baby shower.

I make a quick slice of toast, adding a dab of peanut butter for some protein, and head out back. Dad is by the pool as Hamilton said, his plate empty and eyes staring sightlessly at the rippling water. His face is stormy enough that The Weather Channel could make a report about it, probably give it an old-school name, like Storm Bishop. I smirk, laughing at my own joke of Dad's unusual name.

"Good morning, Dad."

He doesn't even look to me, just points to the chair across from him and says sternly, "Sit down. I want to talk to you."

"Sure," I agree, surprised at the tone but not wanting to start the morning with a fight. Based on his mood, his late-night conversation with Mom must have been about my brother, not me, and I wonder what the hell Cody did now. He was fine when I laid him in bed, still in most of his tux because I was only taking off his shoes and jacket. "What's on your mind?"

Dad takes a sip of his coffee, not seeming to stall but more as a power play. Against his own son? What the hell is going on?

"Your behavior last night was . . . embarrassing. Honestly, something I'd expect from your brother, not you. The way you treated Sabrina Dunn . . ." He tapers off, tsking under his breath like I'm a disappointing wayward child.

I pick up my toast, taking a bite as I digest his words. I'm not going to be baited into backing down like I used to, because I'm not the little boy he once knew.

I realize with a start that he doesn't know me at all. I've been gone for years, only able to make quick trips home for holidays and the occasional leave. He hasn't been able to bear witness to my growth as an officer, as a man, as a human being with his own wants, needs, and plans. That's going to change.

"I made it abundantly clear to both Mom and you that I had zero interest in being fixed up. I turned down setup after setup as you two tried to get me to meet every debutante you thought met your standards, but you refused to listen. Instead, you kept setting me up and somehow expecting me to sit down like a good little boy and do as I'm told. That's not who I am. That's not who I've been for a very long time now. And I won't let you and Mom box me into something I don't want." I lean back, having said my piece.

"You didn't even give the girl a chance!" Dad complains, and I can hear my mother in his words. I thought she'd been happy watching us dance last night, probably feeling victorious this morning. But I guess not.

Apparently, my shunning a vapid bitch was way more worthy of late-night discussion than Cody's overindulgence. "She's a fine young woman from a good family. She's a good match for you."

"In other words, she's willing to lie back, take enough doses of jizz to get her knocked up two or three times, be arm candy otherwise, and spend money like it's water the rest of the time," I rumble.

I swear I think my father's heart just stopped beating, "You will not use such crude language. It does not befit a Jacobs."

Realizing I might've been a bit crass, even if what I said is true, I take a breath. "I'm not looking for that type of woman, or any woman." Even as I say it, Charlotte's face floats through my mind. "I came home to help our family. That's it. Anything else is on my own, not your concern, and not Mom's either."

"I can't accept that, Son," he argues, shaking his head. "I've spent my whole life taking care of this family, and to be honest, I can't keep doing it by myself. I need you to step up, lean in, and pull your weight so we can keep it going. This isn't the Navy, Son. There isn't a constant line of people who will kiss your ass. This is the real world, and it's a reality I think you've lost touch with."

"Out of touch with reality?" I ask, my pride pricked and my anger rising a little. "Dad, I hate to tell you, but I've been learning more in the past ten years than you seem to realize. I was learning what true sacrifice is, what leadership should be. You think I was dicking around, playing cops and robbers or something?"

It's hard to talk about, and my words falter. I don't know if I'll ever be able to tell him how I was learning lessons he'll never understand, lessons engraved in blood, sand, and cordite. And those lessons tell me that his expectation that I'd come home, fall into line, marry the idiot of his choosing, and start popping out babies is not the way to success.

Dad sputters, seeming lost at my words. "I'm not trying to hold you back. I'm trying to help you move forward. I'm sure you did learn a lot in your service, but I know a thing or two myself. Things that I had to learn the hard way, because I found out almost too late that family is everything. I sacrificed too much to the office and missed too many days with you, your mother, and Cody. Lance, I want you to be happy. And everything in my experience, my heart, my gut, tells me you need a wife and kids to do that. Something to ground you when the going gets tough."

I sigh heavily, knowing he's not evil, just a man who's probably getting the first real sense of his own mortality. But I've understood mortality in ways he never has, both by taking lives and having men die in my arms when their lives had barely even started.

"Dad, I'm not saying I'll never get married. I'm just saying let me do it my way. I want someone . . ." I pause, not sure what I want because I've never had to put it into words because marriage always seemed like a far-off, nebulous idea.

"I want a wife who is smart, capable, a partner who is damn well ready to support me but can also pick up the reins and lead herself if something happens to my ass."

I see a handful of women's teary faces flash through my mind. Not every guy I knew in the service was married, but I've been to enough funerals to see the power it takes to be a military wife, always wondering and worrying and one day, getting the call you prayed would never come. But those women, with black clothes and ramrod-straight backs, served their country just as well as their husbands, who made the ultimate sacrifice. I need someone that fierce and fiery.

Dad gets up, his words clipped. "Be that as it may, we have a family dinner with the Dunns next week. Abe, Priscilla, and Sabrina," he says, pointedly looking down his nose at me, well aware that he's leaving Charlotte off that list.

He hasn't said one word about her in this whole tirade, but I can tell just from that look what he thinks of her. "And you will attend, you will be polite, and you will smooth things over with them for your egregious behavior, especially the so-called *dancing* you engaged in with Charlotte."

Without giving me a chance to reply, he brushes past me and goes into the house, already yelling for Hamilton. I watch him go, my fists clenching at my sides.

*What the hell just happened?*

I told them both I wasn't interested in dating. Honestly, if Dad's so worried about me finding someone, why isn't he excited about me showing interest in Charlotte? I told Dad specifically that I wasn't interested in Sabrina, but he expects me to sit at some family dinner like some sort of an arranged marriage? Fuck that.

I take a step toward the door to chase Dad down and tell him in no uncertain terms that I'm not smoothing things over with anyone, least of all the shallow, gold-digging Priscilla Dunn or her brainless daughter.

But then I remember Charlotte.

And I realize that I don't have to go full-frontal attack on whatever this deal is my parents are planning. It's not like they can force me into liking someone.

Especially when my interest already lies elsewhere. I'm doing things my way, whether anyone else likes it or not.

I smile to myself, decision made. I yank my shirt over my head, kick off my shoes, and execute a perfect dive into the pool. I hold my breath, powering through lap after lap underwater, wanting to keep my skills fresh. But I finally emerge, taking in oxygen carefully as I recover.

To hell with it. I've got plans today. I'm going to track down Charlotte Dunn. And maybe eat a cupcake.

# CHAPTER 6

## Charlotte

"**C**AN I GET ANOTHER DOZEN OF THOSE CUPCAKES I SAW ON TV?"
It's a question I've heard time and time again this week, ever since the news showed footage of Thomas and Mia's gala, complete with the *Cake Culture* cupcake tower. As I box up what we're calling the 'Tower Pack' with each of the five flavors from the gala, I shiver as I think of what it all means.

Most bakeries work for years to get this type of promotional notoriety, struggling just to keep the lights on before they're well-established. And that's if you're good. Because no matter how Instagram famous you may be, nothing will make up for crumbly cupcakes and dry pie.

You've gotta have skills, and I'd like to think that I do.

But you've also got to have a bit of luck and good fortune on your side, because the truth is, *everyone* has that grandma or aunt or neighbor who makes the best cake, the most badass cookies, or a mouth-watering pie. And you've got to get them in the door to try yours instead.

So I'm counting my lucky stars that Thomas's bit of magic has proven beneficial, and my culinary skills are exceeding the expectations of the customers. *The new and repeat customers*, I think with a shimmy-shake of my ass in my increasingly tight jeans.

Okay, the saying, 'Never trust a skinny cook,' might end up being true if I don't stop experimenting and sampling my own creations.

The lady eyes the box of goodies as I hand them over, and Trixie whispers from beside me, "That's the third time this week that lady's been in. She's a realtor and is putting your cupcakes out at every open house. Pretty sure she's eating one or two for herself, too, because she told me her favorite was the 'Black As Your Soul' and that's not in the tower box she keeps buying."

I grin, thinking of the prim woman devouring one of my creations, her favorite being a dark chocolate cake with bittersweet chocolate frosting infused with coffee. It's rich, dark, and decadent, and one of my favorites too because the coffee, chocolate, and sugar give a pick-me-up like no other. It's practically a Red Bull in a wrapper.

Trixie eyes the woman and then cracks up. "If we keep this up, we'll need to open a Planet Fitness next door. For our customers and ourselves." She pats her own slim ass, with nary a pinch of cupcake-given fluff.

"Oh, hush. If anyone's going to need a few days on the treadmill, it's me," I huff, but I'm not really concerned. I eat healthfully and work hard, and around here, that's workout enough between the cardio I get running back and forth and the strength training I get picking up the heavy trays and pans. Just need to stop sampling the merchandise.

Trixie reads my mind, quipping, "We are working our asses off, and with all the batter we're stirring, our forearms are gonna be as jacked as a fifteen-year-old who just discovered *PornHub*." She flexes, turning her fist one way then the other and showing off her tiny biceps.

"You're such a goof," I tell her, laughing way too hard. Oh, God, I think I just snorted a little. Trixie's eyes go wide with laughter, and I rush to change the subject before she can start calling me a piggy. She wouldn't do that, probably, but I've got trust issues from Priscilla and Sabrina, who would take full advantage of my doing something so uncouth.

"I've been thinking about the Hope Initiative," I say, hoping it's a big enough distraction. Or that another customer will walk in, but we're in the afternoon slump, barely thirty minutes till six o'clock closing time.

"Hate to tell ya, but I think everyone in town's been thinking about it. That's some serious dough, and I say that as an expert in dough and the lack thereof." She starts out silly but ends the statement a bit more seriously than her usual cheekiness as she wipes the counter down.

"You planning anything?" I ask cautiously, wondering if she's open to sharing. I've learned a lot about her in our time working to get the bakery open, but I can tell she holds some things back. I get the sense she's not exactly proud of where she comes from. "Maybe we could work on something together?"

"Kids, maybe? Or old people?" she says aimlessly as we both move to wipe down tables. "Or maybe kids and old people together?"

"Sugar Daddies are kinda gross, and not exactly a community service," I say, hoping to brighten her back up with a joke that sounds more like her than me.

She smiles, but it's weak. "No, like kids visiting nursing homes, talking to the people who don't have family to visit. Or maybe a subsidized preschool at a nursing home, and the old folks can play cars and do puzzles with the kids. Kind of a grandma-on-demand deal."

My brows go up. "Those are great ideas, Trix."

Her smirk is more in line with what I'd expect from her when she teases, "You thought I'd suggest massage parlors for PTSD sufferers, or something equally awful, didn't you? *A happy ending every time* could be the slogan." I bust out laughing, my belly hurting from how crazy she is, which only fuels her fire. "Or what about a scholarship for strippers? You know, they always say they're going to college. We could help them actually go."

"You have such a dirty mind," I say, and honestly, it's a compliment. I love how twisted her sense of humor is and that she gives zero fucks to the appropriateness of the shit that comes out of her mouth. We move to the back, laying pans and mixing bowls in the sink and starting our closing cleanup routine.

She shrugs. "I half-mean that one. Where I grew up, most of the girls I went to high school with ended up working on their backs. Whether that was as a stripper or because they married a guy with a halfway reliable salary, it was the same result either way. Hard to get out of the trailer park when you have no skills other than the ability to spread your legs."

I stop, looking at her. "That's awful."

Her look is sad. "Just the reality. I didn't grow up in Roseboro. I grew up in the panhandle of Oklahoma. Our only claim to fame is that our county touches four other states. We were so far out there that we had to take a forty-five-minute bus ride to Boise City to go to school because picking everyone up with miles between the few bus stops made it take forever. Made for long days, and most kids just dropped out. I mean, why get some fancy diploma when you're going to scrape by, anyway? Nobody who could afford to hire you out there required the piece of paper."

I take a long moment, trying to imagine the type of childhood she's describing. Mine was far from perfect, really far. But at least I always knew I'd have a roof over my head, food on the table, and an opportunity to learn. "I'm so sorry. How'd you end up getting out?"

Her laugh is ironic, and she shrugs. "Because school was my only outlet. It got me out of my house, and I would've ridden that bus twenty-fucking-four-seven if it meant not being at home with my dad. He . . . did his best when I was little, but he was stuck too and took that out on my mom and me as I got older. My desperation actually meant I got good grades, high enough to be valedictorian, which isn't nearly as impressive as it sounds. Being number one in a graduating class of twenty isn't all it's glammed up to be. But it got me a scholarship for an associate's degree in business, and I worked my ass off and got an internship in Seattle. The whole town pitched in to buy my one-way plane ticket."

She smiles like that's a good memory, at least considering the rest of her life story. "That's how I ended up in Roseboro. After the internship ended, I couldn't afford to get back to Oklahoma, and why would I go back there? Seattle's too rich for my blood, so Roseboro it is."

She shrugs like it all makes perfect sense, and in a roundabout way, it kinda does. Maybe it's why we understand each other so well. We come from very different backgrounds, but both of us had to claw our way out of our youth for a better future. And now we both have one.

I make a mental note to give her a raise as soon as I possibly can, though she already carries the Assistant Manager title. Of course, there's just me and her right now, but she deserves the title for all she does.

She seems weary from the heavy share, so I try to give her an out back to our previous conversation. "Still not sure a stripper scholarship is the direction we should go for the Hope Initiative. But maybe something as impactful, education or vocational training to give marginalized people a better tomorrow?"

She nods, dipping her hands into the sinkful of sudsy water. "Let's think on it, maybe come up with a few different ways we could meet that objective."

I can hear the business education coming out, and where before, I'd written it off as no big deal because she sounds like most people I talk to, I can hear just how hard she worked to even the playing field when everyone else had a head start from her humble beginnings.

We get to work, Trixie washing dishes as I mix dough for tomorrow's breads. She's got music blaring, singing along like she's under the spotlight at karaoke night. "Oh, baby, baby . . . how was I supposed to know . . ."

A knock rattles the back door, and we look at each other. I almost go answer it out of habit, but then I remember the rules and pop my head out the front. "Hey, Steven, you expecting anyone? Someone's at the back door and all my deliveries already came."

He's up in a flash, opening the door a small crack with a hard look on his face. He questions whoever's out there but doesn't seem concerned, and then he opens the door wide and I almost drop the big wooden spoon I'm holding like a weapon rather than the mixing utensil it was intended to be.

Lance Jacobs.

He's standing in the back alley behind my bakery, looking good enough to eat. He looks different from before, but no less gorgeous in blue jeans and a white T-shirt, his hair mussed and his scruff glinting in the waning sunlight.

"Hi, the sign out front said you were closed, but I figured you'd still be here." He looks at Steven, a question in his eyes. "Is it okay if I come in?"

I'm still a bit stuck on how hot it suddenly got in here. I need to turn the air conditioner on if Lance is going to come around. My mouth opens and closes but no sound comes out, so Trixie answers for me.

"Hell yes, boy. You can make deliveries to Charlotte's back door anytime."

My eyes widen and my cheeks flush pink, and I know they're splotchy. I'm not one of those girls who blush prettily on the apples of their cheeks. Nope, I'm a ginger through and through, and my blush is more of the mottled feverish variety. But I suspect Trixie knows exactly what she said, and what it sounded like she meant, because she's grinning widely.

I shake my head, waving him in. "Please, come in. Of course."

Lance grins a smile that tells me he was expecting that answer. Cocky.

But that reminds me of his cock, and I blush anew. Lance looks at me like he's reading my mind and liking what he's seeing.

Trixie interrupts the stare fest Lance and I engage in, shoving Steven toward the door. "So, I guess we'll be going if that's all, Boss Lady? Although, these dishes still need to be done. If you want me to stay and wash them all, I can do that?"

She lets the question hang, and Lance picks up what she's putting down. "I can help with the dishes and mop floors, whatever you have on your agenda for the evening."

I shake my head, genuinely confused at why he would want to work with me tonight. I mean, it's not like doing the dishes is sexy or rolling out dough for cookies is fun for most people. Me and Trixie are the weirdos like that. "Why would you do that?"

His shrug communicates the duh even better than his sweet words. "Because then I get to hang out with you."

"Oh, okay, but, uh, no funny business in my kitchen. This is my livelihood." I don't know if I'm reminding myself or him.

"No baby batter in the muffin batter," Trixie sing-songs, and I swear Steven chokes on his own tongue.

"Miss Dunn, if you're in for the evening, I'll clock out and street patrol will remain in place overnight. Mr. Jacobs has already been cleared. Are we good?" Steven says, his voice low and controlled.

I nod, not bothering to look Steven's way so I see the questioning look on Lance's face at the automaton summary, but I'm too far gone, ready for Trixie and Steven to get the fuck out. But maybe that's a bad idea because I'm afraid I'll jump into Lance's arms point-oh-two seconds after the door locks. But still, I nod. "We're good, Steven. Thanks." Distantly, I hear them both leave.

And we're alone.

I half-expect Lance to rush me, pin me against the table, and pick up right where we left off, but he surprises me by coming over slowly. He pushes a wayward curl behind my ear and plants a soft kiss to my lips. He tastes like mint, and I like the idea that he primped a little for me, like his showing up here uninvited and unannounced was as big a deal for him as it is for me.

I don't have guys chase me down. At most, they swipe right, I swipe right, we show up for drinks, maybe dinner, and that's that. Occasionally, we scratch an itch, but it feels like Lance is putting forth effort. For me.

"I missed you," he whispers, the words vibrating against my lips.

I chuckle. "It's been three days and twenty-some-odd years before that. I don't think you can miss someone you only met once."

*Shut up, Cynical Charlotte.*

But Lance's mouth lifts on the right side like he can read my thoughts, and it makes him look so kissable I'm tempted to lean in for another peck. "Oh? So you're telling me you walked away and haven't given me another thought?"

I shrug noncommittally, inwardly smiling at the first step in this little dance. "Work's been busy. New business owner, you know." But we both hear the lie. I've been thinking of him and he damn well knows it. But I know he's been thinking of me too, so I turn it back around on him before he can call me out on it. "What took you so long to track me down?"

"This." He reaches in his pocket, pulling out something in his hand, and I almost make a joke about having a rocket in his pocket, but I'm glad I held it back because he opens his fist and reveals my bracelet. It's nothing too expensive, just a pretty trinket I bought at the mall years ago on a whim, but the way he's holding it, it could be as precious as a Cartier original.

"It took me a day to find someone to repair it since I don't know the city, and then it took the jeweler two days to fix it. I just picked it up an hour ago and got here as fast as I could."

"Thank you," I stammer, my breath gone at the kindness. He reaches down, lifting my hand in his strong but gentle touch, draping the bracelet over my wrist and attaching the delicate fastener. His touch is electric on my skin, paralyzing me. "Really, it's not that big of a deal, but thank you so much."

"I think it was a rather *big* deal," he says, and I can see the tease at the crinkly corners of his eyes. He's not talking about the bracelet anymore. Well, two can play that game.

"So were you thinking you'd roll in here with my bracelet and I'd be so thankful, I'd just hop on the nearest table and leave butt imprints in the flour?" I ask, aiming for sassy but failing because honestly, it doesn't sound like a half-bad idea. "The health inspector might have an issue with that."

Lance takes a step forward, and I mirror him, moving backward until my ass hits the sink counter. My breath is coming in pants, and I'm scared. Not of him, but maybe of what he could do to me, in a *good* way. A really good way.

"I just felt like we didn't get to finish our conversation, and I wanted to see you again. And now it seems"—he pauses, looking around, and I'm expecting a line about our being alone at last, but he goes another way—"you're in need of a dishwasher. Good thing the Navy taught me how to wash a dish or two."

His smile is charming and silly, the heat still there, but it's underneath the lightness. He reaches behind me, dipping his fingers into the suds Trixie left behind and then blowing the iridescent bubbles off his hand. My dirty mind chants, '*Blow me, blow me, blow me,*' and that's not even really a thing for women, but the need in my veins doesn't seem to give a single fuck because it's racing hot from my head to my toes.

"Well, I guess you could put those muscly arms to good use for something. I do have some dishes that need washing, a floor that needs cleaning, some inventory to put away, and about a dozen things to prep for tomorrow." I wish I were lying. Or that I could just let someone else do the work and disappear upstairs with Lance for some crazy, flour-dusted sex.

But *Cake Culture* is my baby. And I won't half-ass it, even for a piece of ass as hot as Lance Jacobs.

He steps back away from me, and I miss his warmth, even in the heated kitchen. He claps loudly, like the decision's made. "All right, dishes . . . on it. You . . . baking or whatever it is you were doing with that spoon when I came in."

And just like that, we're teammates, working toward a common goal.

The work passes by quickly, with each of us sharing a bit about our families since that's what started this whole thing last night.

He tells me how he's worried for his dad and about his brother but doesn't know what to do about it yet. I tell him how I miss my dad but gave up long ago ever figuring out what he sees in Priscilla. We bond over our mutual distaste for stuck-up, entitled brats like Sabrina. It's a bitchy move, but my assessment of him goes up by four degrees when he imitates Priscilla's 'smelled something bad' face and Sabrina's blank stare spot-on.

We even talk about his time in the military, with the standard 'I'd tell you but I'd have to kill you' punchline.

He doesn't get it when I tell him that he should tell my friend Izzy's guy that joke and see what happens. But I don't explain, just laugh and shrug it off like Gabe's a scary guy. I mean, he is. But only for things that threaten Izzy these days.

I think.

Before I know it, the kitchen is spotless and there's not a single thing I can do to keep him here. At least, not downstairs. I know plenty of things I could do with him upstairs, but I'm not sure that's a good idea.

As amazing as he seems, I have a lot on my plate and so does he. Add in the family shitstorm our dancing caused, and this seems like a recipe for disaster.

I snort at the joke in my own head and Lance tilts his head. "What?"

"I'm just a little punny in my head sometimes. Who knew baking had so many double-entendres and dad jokes tied up in it?" I chuckle, shaking my head.

"Like Trixie's baby batter?" he asks, laughing.

"Oh, God, that's nothing. You should hear her talk about her muffin, her cupcake, her loaves. And the frosting jokes? Enough to make me not want to eat a glazed donut or toaster strudel ever again. Or cream filling. Cream pies. Cherries. It goes on and on . . ." I trail off, lifting a shoulder. "It's a baker thing. You wouldn't understand."

We both bust up in laughter, and the unspoken pressure of 'what now' floats away like the soap bubbles down the drain. "I'd like to see you again," Lance says confidently.

I want to say yes. Every cell in my body, especially the red blood cells singing through my pussy right now, want to say yes. "I can't," I say, forcing my brain, and not my body, to do the talking. "I'm focused on work right now, and it sounds like you are too. But this was . . . nice."

*Nice? What the hell, brain? Come up with something a little less blah next time, please?*

My brain shoots back, *I'm working on low blood flow here. Give me a break.*

Lance bites his lip like he knows exactly what I mean by nice, and it's not just merely pleasant, for damn sure. "It was nice."

How in the hell he makes the blandest word in the English language sound like sex talk, I'll never know, but I don't analyze it too long because he plants his lips on mine.

He cups my cheek, fingers diving into my hair, and the kiss ignites. Tongues tangle, breath mingles, eyes close. And holy fuck, Lance can kiss. I swear I feel him everywhere, but he's not touching me except for the kiss. I want him to touch me . . . everywhere.

But he pulls back, smacking satisfiedly like a cat who got the cream. *Fuck . . . cream . . . yes, please.*

"Nice," he says simply, and then he moves to the back door. "Lock this behind me, Charlotte. Okay?"

The slam of the heavy door sounds like a death knell. What did I just do? *Come back,* my body cries. *Stay strong,* my brain argues. The battle goes on long enough that I know it wouldn't do me any good to chase after him. He's gone.

I flip the lock and then the lights before heading upstairs. I trace my lips with my fingers, still feeling the lingering burn of his kiss.

# CHAPTER 7

## Lance

I THINK SHE FULLY EXPECTED ME TO GIVE UP THAT EASILY.
Like hell.
I survived a training course that has a ninety-seven-percent attrition rate. I went through a week where I got five hours of sleep *total*. I ran three miles once on a sprained ankle because I had men's lives, and mine, on the line.

So Charlotte's getting a bit of cold feet, when the rest of her is so blatantly hot for me, doesn't scare me off in the least.

It makes it . . . interesting.

I want to see how far she'll push herself to hold back from me, hear more of her silly puns, and learn every single thing about her, from her thoughts on the future of the world to where she's most ticklish. A big spectrum, I know, and that's why I'm guessing it'll take a lifetime to get it all in.

*Ha, get it all in. Fuck, she's already rubbing off on me.*

I snort. *I wish she'd rub off on me.*

But her thinking she's an easy pass, and that I'd just get on with my life, must be why her eyes grow to dinner plates when she sees me bright and early the next morning.

"What are you doing here? I thought we agreed . . ." she stammers.

My smile is cocky as shit and I know it. "We did agree that things were nice. That's why I figured I would hang out a bit today. Enjoy a nice *muffin* now and a nice *cupcake* later, maybe one with *loads of cream filling.*"

I let every filthy thought in my head coat the puns she tossed at me last night. Two can play this game, Charlotte Dunn.

She looks a bit pink, the splotches faint but rising. They're not classic blushing beauty marks, but that makes them even hotter to me. They're authentic. "But don't you have to work?"

"I am working. I don't exactly have a corner office, or any office, really. Been mostly working at a conference room table to get caught up on the business, and I'm thinking that table over there has a much better view," I say, pointing to a round table in the corner. "So, you think maybe I could sample your muffin now?"

Fire lights her eyes, and I await her devilment with hope. This is the sassy spitfire who draws me in even as she tries to burn me down.

She pauses dramatically to get my hopes up intentionally. "Today's special is a cinnamon apple pie combination. The cake is a bit spicy, a bit sweet, with a warm, gooey apple pie filling you want to lick out and savor. I'll let you in on a little secret, too—if you ask *just* right, we'll lay a drizzle of glaze on top or it's good with a big scoop of vanilla ice cream too, just melting into the cake, covering it in sweetness."

Fuuuuuck.

Her words have me rock-hard in my jeans, throbbing stiffer than I've been in days. And it has absolutely nothing to do with food and everything to do with the way her tongue curls and her lips purse as she seduces me, knowing damn well what she's doing and doing it expertly.

She's way better at this than I am.

I swallow, or maybe it's more of a gulp, but I step closer. "Sounds like something I'd love to eat every morning, just to start the day off right with that flavor on my tongue, lips, or running down my chin."

My voice is quiet, husky, and dark, and I can see Charlotte's breath catch. Smooth? No, but it works because it's passionately honest.

"Girl, if you don't run your ass upstairs with that chunk of man right this second, I'm liable to shove you to the ground and take him upstairs myself," Trixie says from way too close.

Shit. Neither of us had noticed that we have an audience now, but Trixie is smirking so much I think her face might crack. The same guy is sitting by the door, and I swear he's fighting a smile too.

For a split second, I can see Charlotte consider doing exactly what Trixie said, but responsibility reigns and with the slightest shake of her head, she steps back. I don't hide that I adjust myself, wanting her to know how much she gets to me and not giving a shit about the rest of the eyes that see.

"I'll just sit over here and work. Don't let me bother you, and I'll take a muffin whenever you've got it ready." It's a promise as much as a breakfast order. I'll wait for her, but I'm not going anywhere.

I sit, opening my laptop and getting to work. The bakery starts to get busy, and before I know it, Trixie and Charlotte are running around like mad.

At one point, Trixie delivers my cinnamon apple pie muffin, whispering that Charlotte didn't trust herself not to sit on my lap and ride me like a pony if she came any closer. My guess is that's Trixie's take on the situation, not Charlotte's actual words, but when I glance up, Charlotte is watching me closely from across the room.

I take full advantage of her attentions, picking up the muffin she made with her own hands and inhaling deeply, savoring the rich smell that I can imagine is the same as what she smells like in her most secret of places before taking a huge bite.

Trixie chuckles from beside me, but it's Charlotte's reaction I'm looking for. I see her shift behind the counter, pressing her thighs together as her mind goes to the exact places that I'm going, distracting her with the fantasy. I give her a wide grin, cheeks stuffed full like a chipmunk, and hold up the muffin in praise.

We all resume our dance, me working on my laptop, Charlotte and Trixie feeding the hordes of people coming through the door, and the security guy holding watch by the door. Steven, she called him, and it makes me wonder what he's doing here.

It's not unusual for people to have security or bodyguards in our level of social circle. Hell, my parents' driver is trained and could safely pull off a movie-worthy car chase scene in a Toyota Corolla. He's that good.

But the Dunns aren't exactly at a level where I'd expect possible threats warranting a full-scale guard worthy of a royal. Thomas Goldstone would warrant that type of treatment in Roseboro, but not many others.

But there sits Steven, discreet enough that he doesn't disrupt business, but it's in his subtle movements that I realize he's well-trained and situationally aware.

It causes me to look around a little more closely. The front windows to the street look a little thicker than I'd expect and with that slight difference in the diffraction of light that makes me suspect they're polycarbonate. If so, that means they're bulletproof, which worries me.

And Steven mentioned street patrol. Whatever other issues may surround the business, someone feels Charlotte deserves 24/7 security, and that worries me even more.

It's an intense amount of coverage for almost anyone, but certainly for a baker, even one as gorgeous as Charlotte. I'll have to ask her about it, make sure she's okay or if there's anything I can do to help if she's not. I've got some skills of my own, and they don't just extend to sucking the filling out of a muffin.

My attention is drawn back to the woman sitting across from me, who's been rambling non-stop since she sat down ten minutes ago. Kelly Washington, she'd said her name was. She's my third seatmate of the day because *Cake Culture* is frantically busy and there's not an empty seat in the house. Even Steven has a tablemate, although he looks like he'd rather share the table with a rabid Rottweiler.

"So, anyway, after I had a single bite of the cookies here, I knew this was my new favorite treat. I told our pastor that he needed to get these cookies for the post-service social every week because if people knew they were getting this kind of goodie, they'd come for the service. He's a great speaker, you see, and more folks need to hear the good word . . ." She continues babbling in one long run-on sentence, and I'm not sure if she's hitting on me or trying to recruit me to her church. I'm hoping the latter because she's probably a few years older than my mom, and I'm not into being anyone's cougar cub.

I let her ramble on, smiling politely but mostly watching Charlotte. She's slammed, or what's busier than that? I don't know the proper food industry slang, but it's what *Cake Culture* is. Charlotte and Trixie are bouncing around like rubber balls, rushing between serving the line and scurrying to get more from the assembly line they've got back there. Every time Charlotte comes out with a fresh tray, people cheer like she's bringing food to the starving, which maybe they are, I guess, because then they descend on her like it's Shark Week, begging to buy each and every morsel.

It's a miracle those two haven't buckled under the pressure, but they both have genuine smiles on their faces, not fake customer service ones, like they're enjoying the madness. And the well-oiled machine they're keeping in motion means that every customer walks away with a treat and a smile on their face.

It's impressive, but I can see the strain. They're running at full capacity, and all it's going to take is one pebble thrown in the works and they're go-ing to have problems.

Charlotte disappears to the back to turn off the beeping alarm of the oven, and Trixie continues helping the swirling line of customers. Suddenly, I hear some grumbles near the front of the line.

"You're buying them *all*?" A man's voice shouts out grumpily. "That's not right, and I promised my kid."

"Too bad, so sad," a woman's voice taunts, not helping matters in the least.

Aaaaand . . . the pebble is tossed.

The glob of people moves a bit, almost the swirl of a mosh pit before things go bad, and I can see Trixie's eyes widen in surprise and a bit of panic. She's losing control, and a crack under pressure for a new business could be the kiss of death.

Not on my watch. I leap into action, standing up and letting out a shrill whistle that can and has stopped entire troops of men.

Everyone freezes, turning to look at me.

"I know these treats are the best thing this side of heaven, but *no one* is fighting over frosting. Understood? If everyone could line back up, you'll be served as quickly as possible. Everything here is delicious, and there's more on the way from the back."

I make my way over to the bakery cases, slipping behind to stand next to Trixie. She starts to protest and then seems to think better of it. "Okay, Commander Cookie, take your shot, but if Char kills you, I'll cover for her and you were *never* here. Wash your hands. You do the boxing and I'll do the register."

I nod, doing as she said and donning the white half-apron she tosses my way. "What can I get you?" I ask the next customer.

I'm on my sixth order in four minutes when the door opens and Charlotte sticks her head out, her eyes going wide when she sees me boxing up a six-pack of red velvet cupcakes along with a French silk pie. But she also notices that the line's now at the register where Trixie's being held up more by the credit card machine than anything else, and she seems agreeable, or at least not murderous.

"Chill yourself out. Go make magic back there," I assure her, giving her a thumbs-up. "We've got this."

The rush lasts another hour, and when Charlotte brings out her third big tray of cookies for the case, she jerks her head toward the back. Saying nothing out front, I follow Charlotte into the back, where she turns on me. "What are you doing?"

"Trixie was drowning, and you were being sucked down at the same time," I explain easily. "You can't say you weren't, and look at this kitchen. That sink's full, and you're going to be here until one in the morning cleaning up at this pace. Then what, up at four to start cranking the next set of cupcakes?"

Charlotte looks over at the mountain of stuff in the sink and sighs, nodding. "I can't have you out front though. You don't have a food handler's license or health certificate or any of that stuff. Health Department comes through here and my ass is grass."

I make a mental note to look into what it would take to get the paperwork she's talking about. It's not that I want to be a baker, or a bakery worker, but I want to spend time with Charlotte and this is where she is. So if being legal to throw some cakes in a box is what it takes, I'll get that piece of paper.

"Fine, for now. I'll just help out by cleaning up back here so you don't have to stay so late tonight," I retort, walking over to the sink. "Unless Roseboro has a dishwasher's certificate?"

She bites her lip like she's going to stop me or maybe like she's going to jump me. I'm okay with one of those options. But eventually, she just shakes her head, chuckling. "Have it your way. Thank you."

She disappears back to the front to help Trixie.

It's weird, but her letting me wash the dishes feels like a victory. I can tell she's not someone who asks for help often, so I feel like she's letting me see behind the curtain a little bit. *Progress*, I think.

For the next hour, I scrub, scour, and rinse plates, silverware, and big baking pans, sending them through the industrial machine just like Charlotte showed me last night. I didn't plan on ever using the teaching session again, but I'm glad to help her if this is what she needs.

Besides, it keeps me distracted from the shit with my family. The hours I spent working this morning helped me get a better handle on things, but I'm basically reviewing the last ten years of Jacobs Bio-Tech.

Before I left, I had no real idea what Dad did. He mostly seemed like a paper pusher and handshaker to me, which is why I wanted out of that gig. I didn't want to be some boardroom suck-up or pampered prince who gets handed the keys while his ass shines an office chair.

I'd wanted adventure, to see the world, to make a difference, and though the bio-technology that my family company creates makes life better for some, it didn't appeal to me. So when it came time for college, I bounced my way across the country.

Florida was where I ended up, and for two years, I was a party guy in a party school. But one day, I saw a Naval ROTC booth, and all that changed. I earned my commission, went straight to the SEALs, and I found a home for a long time.

But now I'm back and woefully out of touch with Jacobs Bio-Tech. I'm remedying that, getting in deep and engaging with everything a decade of Naval professionalism has taught me, but shit, it's so boring and dry. Not that dishes are exciting, but at least they're wet.

I smirk at the pun, thinking that Charlotte would like that one.

Every once in a while, Charlotte makes a trip back to start another round of baking. As I work, I can feel her eyes on me, and I watch her too, entranced by the way the sweat-darkened hair at the nape of her neck clings to her skin and the way her muscles flex as she lifts a heavy bowl of cake batter to pour it into the floured pan.

It feels like we're dancing again, but instead of being body to body with only the thin layers of fabric between us, we've got space and stainless steel. And instead of pulsing music, we've got humming machinery. It's a seductive tango, and I can see that she's as affected as I am.

It's almost closing time, and I'm betting Charlotte is ready for a repeat of last night, maybe an extended version where we head upstairs after all her prep work is complete. It's tempting, so very tempting.

But I don't want her to think I'm only helping to get in her pants. Oh, I want in her pants for sure, but I want more than that too.

So I take a look around and do as much as I can to get her set up for the work she needs to do tonight—a stack of mixing bowls ready on the prep table, a set of spoons and spatulas nearby, the ovens preheated, and I order dinner to be delivered for her, Trixie, and Steven in two hours.

I step back out front, pleased to see near-empty cases, tables full of happy cake eaters, and a smiling Charlotte. I step behind the counter, close enough to put my hand on her lower back where no one can see, but Trixie notices and suddenly becomes very invested in cleaning on the other side of the room.

"You are amazing," I tell her honestly, murmuring into her ear so I can smell the sweetness that surrounds her.

She smiles even bigger, and I love that as happy as she is about her fledgling business, she's happy to see me too. "You're pretty awesome your-self." She shoulder checks me, flirting.

"The kitchen is spotless, I've got you all set up for your work after you close, and dinner will be here shortly." I press a soft kiss to her temple, not quite goodbye, but she senses that I'm leaving.

"You're not going to stay and help me tonight?" she asks, and her cheeks get splotchy as she realizes that she's admitting she likes me being around. "I mean, not that I expected you to just suddenly become my helper, but last night . . ."

I lower my lips to her ear so that only she can hear, my words a silky ca-ress of her ivory shell. "Last night was so nice I stayed up for almost an hour when I got home replaying every minute of it in my mind and jacking off to thoughts of you bent over your prep table."

I hear her intake of breath and I continue, "So tonight, do what you need to do as quickly as you can, and then . . ."

It takes every bit of restraint I've got to give her the order she needs, not the one I want. "And then go to bed because I'm hoping you were up a little extra-late last night too. You're running yourself ragged, and I won't be the cause of your burning out too soon. I've got a vested interest in making sure you keep baking."

Her eyebrows lift, and she glances over her shoulder. "To make me happy?"

Hope and romanticism are woven through the words, but I can't help but lob the ball she setup so perfectly. "To keep my belly happy. I'll be back in the morning for breakfast. I'll expect my table to be available and the muf-fin of the day to be hot and ready for me."

My voice is barely a rumble, a promise only she can hear.

Laughter flashes in her eyes, and she turns to face me squarely. "You are smoother than buttercream frosting, aren't you? I think you could read the phone book and make it sound like the dirtiest of bedroom talk."

I lean down until my lips are a fraction of an inch from her ear again, whispering, "Aaron Abernathy, Allison Ackard, Amber Ada, uhm . . . that's all the A names I can think of. I'm much better when I get to the Os, though."

She doesn't laugh, instead sighing blissfully. "I think I just want you to say my name."

"Trust me, I did. Every time I've come since the gala, I've had your name on my lips. Sweet dreams, Charlotte."

I want to kiss her fully on the lips, not giving a single fuck about the room full of people or that this is her place of business. I want to publicly claim her even though we're still doing this dance around each other. Let every single person in here know that I'm the lucky fucker who gets to frost her cookie and fill her Twinkie.

But I don't. This is her place, and I want to show her that I respect her as not just a woman, but as the baker and businessperson I know she is. So I can't . . . not in front of her customers.

Fuck. I've got to get out of here or my attempt at being the good guy is going to fail miserably because I'm at the end of my rope, about to drag her upstairs to fuck her right now. I'm not a total shit. I'd feed and listen to her talk about anything she wants to talk about for hours after, but we'd definitely end up fucking all night. I can feel it in the sparks floating between us.

"I'll see you in the morning, beautiful."

Grabbing my laptop and bag, I make a beeline for the door. Steven gives me a smirk, recognizing the gait of a man trying to walk with a boner hanging thick between his legs. Fucker. He gets to stay, but at least he doesn't seem interested in Charlotte at all beyond his job. Again, I meant to ask her what that's all about.

Tomorrow, maybe?

# CHAPTER 8

## Charlotte

"HOW DO I LOOK, TRIX?" I ASK, COMING DOWN THE BACK STAIRS into the bakery.

"Dayum, girl, you look good enough to eat!" she says, biting at the air. "You sure you don't want me to make myself scarce today? I think you and Lance could handle everything just fine without me."

Today's technically my day off, or at least the one day *Cake Culture* is closed. With just me and Trixie working here, we need Wednesdays to bake all day and prep for the weekend's special orders. Today, we're making a huge multi-tiered cake for the Fredricks wedding, a monstrosity that could take more than a day to finish.

At least we don't have any custom birthday cakes on the schedule for the day too. I try not to worry about that because the wedding order is big enough to float my custom cakes budget for the month.

I shake my head, feeling my bouncy ponytail brush my shoulders. Reaching up, I adjust the white scarf tied around the elastic, which I maybe chose because I know it pops against my red hair, something I consider my best feature. "No, please. You have to stay. That's like a direct order. If you leave me here alone with him, nothing will get done but *me*."

I hate to say that, but it's the God's honest truth.

Lance has spent the last the three days coming in like clockwork. I swear, yesterday, Trix yelled out 'Lance' like he was Norm coming into his favorite bar. He works at the table in the corner, staring sexily at the computer screen and eating my muffins. Sadly, an actual muffin, not the one I'm getting desperate for him to dive into.

But when we get extra-busy, he'll pitch in and help. And he's got the back cleaned and set up for me every day. But before I can do much more than say thanks, he leaves, and it's driving me nuts.

I'm so horny I actually proposed a new cupcake called 'Nutz for Nutz' to Trixie, totally oblivious or maybe wanting the double-entendre of the almond cupcake with butter cream frosting covered in almond slivers. Thankfully, she'd advised that maybe I wait and see if I still think that's a good idea after I get laid.

Unfortunately, no laying has happened here. He kisses me when we're in the kitchen, hidden behind the big double doors, and I damn sure kiss him back, but that's as far as things have gone and I'm about ready to make a move myself. And today is going to be hard to hold myself back because he said he'd come and help me all day.

Seriously, there is nothing sexier than a man cooking, except maybe a man who cooks because he's doing it for you.

I turn around, looking at myself in the convex security mirror over the register. I check my lip gloss, and Trixie sighs.

"Not sure I understand why that's a bad thing. Girl, get you some while the getting's good."

"I know, but I've done the dreaming of Mr. Right and settling for Mr. Right Now. I feel like I need to be focusing on the bakery now, not out gallivanting around with some guy."

She rolls her eyes and turns back to me. "I don't know if you've caught on to this, but that boy is plum crazy for you. Hey, wait . . . write that down for a fall flavor. Plum Crazy. I'm thinking muffins, maybe streusel-topped or sugared? No, with ginger."

She taps her head, like she's a slightly demented genius or something. "What was I saying again? Oh, yeah. Lance is gone for you. He's just slow rolling because you're scared and he's respecting that. I don't know if that makes him your Prince Charming or some shit, but it'd definitely make for some good times away from the stress of the bakery. All work and no play makes Charlotte run out of batteries faster than an industrial mixer."

I laugh. She's gone too far with that one. "The mixer is plugged into the wall. Actually, so's my favorite friend."

Trixie's jaw drops so far she gets a double chin that she doesn't actually have. "Your vibe plugs into the wall? Hell, how much horsepower that thing get? Giddy fucking up and yeehaw!"

Thankfully, she doesn't say anything else because there's a knock at the back door. "Who is it?" I say, pointing a warning finger at Trixie, who blinks at me with a look of pure innocence on her face that's about as authentic as a Hostess cupcake.

"Lance Jacobs, reporting for duty, ma'am." I hear him report, military-style, through the thick metal door.

I won't say that his official, powerful-sounding voice has no effect on me because that'd be a bald-faced lie.

I open the door and Lance steps inside. He's got on a T-shirt and jeans, both of which hug his muscles deliciously. I'm not usually a biceps girl, but something about the way the sleeves are straining over his tan, toned bulges makes me want to bite them. And then he turns, setting a bag down on the table, and I change my mind. *Mmm, dat ass.* I want to bite the apple of his ass.

"Sorry I'm late," he says, and then he looks at me, totally catching me eyeing him. His eyes light up, one brow raised like he's saying *busted* without a word. But when I bite my lip, his eyes darken.

Trixie clears her throat, not ashamed at all. "Uhm, not to interrupt the eye sex you two are in the middle of, but that bag has a bow. Is it a present? I love presents, but it's probably for Charlotte, right? That's okay. I like to watch other people get presents too. Open it!"

His grin blooms like the sun popping out from behind a cloud on a summer day. "It is a present. One for everyone, actually."

Trixie jumps up and down like a little kid, clapping, and I remember what she told me about her childhood and I'm guessing she probably didn't get many presents.

"Go ahead, Trixie. You can open it," I tell her, and she doesn't have to be told twice, grabbing the bag from the table and tossing the tissue paper into the air.

She pulls out an apron, then another, then a third. Each one has the *Cake Culture* logo on the front, each in a slightly different shade of pink.

She spreads them out and then hands me the darkest one, and I see it says, *Sweet Scarlet* on it below my name. She holds hers up to her chest, and I see the pink embroidery emblazoned says, *Not for Kids.* The joke is good, and very apt. Trix aren't for kids, and neither is Trixie.

The last one, she holds up and then laughs hard. It has Lance's name and below reads, *Commander Cookie*, making Trixie laugh. I look from her to Lance, missing something.

Trixie explains, "When he stepped up to help, I called him Commander Cookie and told him not to mess anything up."

He laughs too, taking the apron from Trixie but pointing out, "Actually, she said that if you killed me, she would be your alibi. It was appropriately, threateningly protective."

I slip the apron over my head, tying the strings around my waist. "This is very sweet. Thank you." I press a friendly kiss to his cheek, but my face flames anyway. "Okay, we've got work to do, troops. We'd better get to it, or this wedding cake might be my first and last."

There's no argument, just a feeling of unity as Trixie and Lance tie their aprons on and we get to work, using the forty-quart industrial mixer to draw the batter together. The only hard part is that since the bride wants a white-white cake, we can't use any yolks at all, and just to be extra-sure, I'm using a very special type of butter as well that is almost white too.

I've tried using other methods, including one recipe that had me using coconut oil, or one that used lard, of all things, and while they did make a whiter cake . . . frankly, lard cake is something that *nobody* should eat.

"Okay, so the plan's for two hundred servings," I relay, "and the couple wants a really big bottom layer, so we're going to do two twelve-inch rounds on the bottom, then a ten, eight, and six. They've got their own porcelain topper, so we just need to have a smooth surface with ruffled edges up there to prep the top."

"Two hundred servings?" Trixie asks. "There's no way they've got two hundred guests coming to their wedding, right? I mean, that seems like a lot. I don't even know two hundred people!"

I spray down another one of our cake rounds. "I don't care if they have ten people show up. If they order a huge cake, they get a huge cake."

Lance looks into the mixer, watching the dry ingredients blend. "Biggest wedding I've been to was five hundred guests, give or take."

Trixie and I look at each other, whispering simultaneously, "Holy shit."

"Can you imagine how big that cake was?" I ask Trixie, who shakes her head. Hell, the payment on that would probably float me for months. Raising my voice, I look up at Lance. "Who was it?"

"Navy wedding. They met on board the *Reagan*, so they invited a ton of the crew. It was nothing like this cake though. Just a normal wedding cake and a ton of sheet cake."

The timer dings, and I go over to the mixer, shutting it off. I fill the cake pans with the white liquid, praying my hardest that Trixie doesn't make any cum jokes right now. But when I glance over, she's looking back and forth from Lance to me, missing the opportunity.

She fills two of the smaller rounds while I get the big twelve-incher, and then we get the spring forms into the preheated and waiting oven.

"Next, let me show you how to make buttercream because we do it in small batches," I explain to Lance once the timer's set. I take two pounds of butter and hand him the big chef's knife. "First, cut this into chunks about an inch wide. Don't worry if it's not perfect."

Across the room, Trixie hums tunelessly, a bit of an upgrade from her usual 90s hits redux, and then says, "Tell us about you, Lance."

It sounds like she's interviewing him for something, but I'm interested to hear his answer. He told me the basics already, but I'm hungry for more.

He keeps cutting butter but answers, "I was born in California. That's where my family's company used to be headquartered. It was Jacobs Pharmaceutical then. Went to Florida, graduated, went military, much to their absolute *not*-delight, worked my ass off and got my MBA degree while I served, and became a SEAL. Along the way, I got to travel, see the world, in both good and bad ways, and basically grew up. Now, I'm home, seeing if my next step in life is with Bio-Tech."

"Why'd they change names?" I ask, taking the butter cubes and putting them into the smaller mixer.

"When my dad realized that pharmaceuticals is a crapshoot and bio-tech is *the wave of the future*," Lance says like he's heard the phrase from someone else, maybe his dad. His accompanying shrug tells me there's more the story, or to his feelings about the change. He doesn't say anything, though, as he finishes the last of the butter, handing me the cubed-up pieces on the cutting board. "Okay, now what?"

I drop them in slowly, watching it swirl for a moment. "Add three droppersful of this vanilla extract," I say, watching him do as I instruct. "Then we'll slowly add powdered sugar. For each batch, we're going to use about four cups, but it's more art than science so we go by texture. We're looking for fluffy peaks. Think Bob Ross, happy little clouds."

Lance watches, his eyes intensely taking in what I'm doing, and minutes

later, I add my secret ingredient, organic cream for the richest, smoothest texture possible. A pinch of salt for balance and the first batch is done. "Okay,
now we scrape all this into a big container for storage and repeat for the next
batch, and the next, until we've got all we need. Got it?"

He nods and opens the refrigerator, grabbing more butter. I like that he's
a fast learner, confident but willing to be taught.

"How about you two? What led to baked goods heaven?" he asks as he
starts cutting again.

Trixie goes first as she pulls the first batch of smaller cakes out of the
ovens for testing. "My high school was tiny, very few options for classes, especially back then. I could take keyboarding, which I already knew how to
do, or home ec, where you got to eat what you made. It was pretty much a
no-brainer, especially since cooking days usually meant I got more to eat in
one meal than I usually got to eat in a day."

She pauses, checking off our progress on the job board on the wall,
thankfully not seeing Lance and me lock eyes, the sad realization of just how
fortunate our privileged upbringing was. I certainly never went hungry and
I sincerely doubt Lance did either.

"Turned out I was pretty good at it, so when I was out here and my business internship ended, an assistant manager gig sounded pretty sweet. The
business of baking, if you will." She looks back and smiles at me, and I feel
warmth flow through my heart. I'm so glad we found each other.

"Your turn," she says, like she wants the focus off her.

"My grandmother," I tell Lance, then explain. "She's how I found baking. When my mom died, my Dad was lost a bit. I don't remember much. I
was little. But I was excited when he married Priscilla. I didn't know her well,
but I thought having a sister would be like a sleepover every night. But . . .
well, you've met them."

Trixie and Lance both scowl, nodding. Lance gets the butter whipping,
and I stand back, watching him work as I talk.

"So Dad would send me off to my grandmother's at least one or two
weekends a month and quite a bit of time each summer. I always thought it
was because he knew how awful they were to me, but looking back, I think he
was just keeping my connection with my mom's family strong. And Grandma
Winnie took full advantage of our time together. She taught me everything
she knew, from gardening and canning to baking and sewing. Though the
sewing didn't stick. I always bled all over everything because I couldn't get

the hang of the needle." It wasn't that I couldn't push the needle, but I was the kind of person who always, somehow, would push it through into a waiting finger on the other side, no matter what I did.

I smile, remembering her patiently helping me, her wrinkly hands over my small ones so I could cut things safely in her kitchen that always smelled of pine cleaner and baking bread.

"I went to college here in Roseboro, worked at Blackwell for a while, but it was basically hell, so when Thomas offered to help me get started on my dream, I jumped at the chance. And here we are."

Highly edited, but I'm not sure if Lance is ready for the deeper story. Hell, even Trixie doesn't know much more than the surface. Meanwhile, Lance has his butter just right.

"Okay, ready for the powdered sugar," I say, looking into the mixing bowl of the second batch. "Nice fluffy peaks."

Trixie goes into the supply closet and then comes out with a look of horror, rambling fast. "Oh, no, sorry, Boss. We're out somehow. I'll tell you what . . . I'll run over to the mega warehouse store over by the highway and get a big bag or two, and grab the rest of the things on the shopping list. I'll be back before you know it." She pauses. "Or in about an hour."

She emphasizes the time and then is gone in a flash.

Lance and I look at each other, and then we both laugh. He wipes his eyes, turning off the mixer after he's done. "That was some awful acting on her part. She could've just said, 'Hey, I'll leave you two alone,' and then bounced."

I shake my head, knowing exactly what she pulled. "No, she couldn't, because I full-on Boss ordered her to stay today so she had to come up with an excuse. And I know it's an excuse because we order out supplies from a delivery service, and we just got restocked yesterday. Even the warehouses don't carry fifty-pound industrial bags of sugar." I point to the bottom shelf of the rack where we prepped all the things we'd need for today's work. "See?"

Lance sobers, his face looking a little guarded for once. "You didn't want to be alone with me? I can leave if you want." He wipes his hands on his apron, stepping away from me.

I blurt out unceremoniously, going by gut instinct, "I didn't want to be alone with you because I'm about to drag you upstairs and fuck you six ways 'till Sunday. And I'm doing everything I can to *not* do that. I purposefully didn't shave my legs, I have on my worst granny panties, and I was hoping for a chaperone. Because I have to finish this cake today. It's a big deal. A really big one. So I need you to man up here and *not* fuck me, okay?"

I slap my hands over my mouth, stopping the word confetti. I can feel the heat on my face, and I mostly want to sink into a big puddle on the floor.

Lance's guarded look turns cocky and then serious again. "You really know how to take a guy on a roller coaster, don't you? I literally just went from 'mayday, mayday' to 'fuck, yeah' to 'Responsibility Rick' in one monologue. I'm going to do my absolute best to focus on the last part of that and not the image of you in high-waisted cotton briefs because right now, that sounds damn near as sexy as a thong. Fuck, do you wear thongs?"

His eyes trace down my body, focusing tightly at the apex of my thighs, and he shakes his head. "Wait. Don't answer that. Do not answer that right now." He adjusts himself and takes a big breath, like he's shielding himself for battle. Against both our urges. "Tell me what's next. With the baking, with the cakes. Please, talk about cakes."

I remember how much he liked when I talked about the muffins, but I don't think either of us could stand the tease right now, so I keep it professional. Well, as professional as I can when I can feel my nipples pebbled up beneath the apron he gave me and my panties getting wetter with every step.

The first round of cakes is cooled, the frosting is ready, and oh, this is going to be bad. "The next step is dirty frosting," I say, the colloquial term sounding more sexual than it ever has before.

He groans, looking to the ceiling. "Are you shitting me, Char? Dirty frosting? Are you trying to drive me insane?"

His voice is a rumble that I can feel even from five feet away. Shrugging apologetically, I shake my head. "That's really what it's called. Let me show you."

He moves closer, coming to stand next to me, but I can hear him muttering, "Yeah, show me your dirty frosting. Why the hell not?"

I can't help but grin a bit. "I swear, I'm not trying to poorly seduce you. I really do need to finish the cake. Dirty icing is a sort of glue that holds the cake layers together, and to get the right shape for the decorative work that I'll do later. We've got to get the bottom layers down, like the foundation of a building, and then the other layers will sit safely on top." The drier explanation helps tamp things down a half-notch, thankfully, and we get to work.

But even though a twelve-inch round is a giant piece of cake, it's not a lot of space to work, and Lance and I are forced tight together. Time after time, his arm brushes up against mine as we undo the latches on the spring-form pans and take the cakes out.

"Okay, now lift carefully. We don't want to crack the layers."

I feel a slight pressure against my left breast and realize that Lance's muscled forearm is touching it as he carefully rotates the ring of the pan like I showed him. It's side boob, but my nipple doesn't seem to mind because it perks right up, sending a thrill through me. His eyes are focused on the cake, but my attention is totally on what he's doing to my body.

"How's that?" Lance asks, his eyes cutting to me, and he realizes where his arm is. "I . . . I'm not going to apologize for that."

"I wouldn't want you to," I murmur, taking a shaky step back. "Okay, what we need to do next is get the bottom layer. It's going to be our base."

I get the flat cake knife, and we transfer the cake to the frosting turnta-ble, aware of every moment of Lance's eyes on me. Still, we work together well, and I have to grin as I grab the bowl of buttercream. "Okay, now the part that'll get you all hot and bothered . . ." I say, not sultry because we're al-ready too close to the fire, but playful and teasing. "Playing with my cream—I mean, the buttercream."

He rolls his eyes, but I can see the dirty thoughts behind his baby blues that are darkening fast even as he tries to keep focused. "So, what's first?"

"First, let's get a big dollop in the middle, and we'll use this cake knife to spread it out. Don't manhandle it, but don't be too gentle, either."

"A little roughness is okay. Got it," he deadpans, but I swear it just got hotter in here.

My voice is a bit shaky, but I power on, flipping one cake as I attach the two layers. "Always try to keep a flat surface up, other than your bottom layer," I hint. "It makes decorating and frosting easier. The light domes in the cakes will be filled with the dirty frosting like a wall spackle."

I show Lance what to do, and after a quarter of the cake, he takes over, carefully using the turntable to get the sides smoothed out. "Well?"

"Not bad," I admit, stepping in and checking carefully. "I might just feel better about this afternoon now."

"What's this afternoon?" Lance asks. "More of this?"

"I wish. No, I'm gonna leave most of this in Trix's hands to get the first pass done. She'll get the fondant on the bottom layer as well. But I've got a meeting today . . . with my father. My presence has been requested."

Lance clucks his tongue, humming. "You don't sound happy about that."

"I'm not," I admit. "I've been basically summoned. I'm sure it's about the charity ball. I figure I'll get my ass chewed out for the way I behaved with you. I'd bet the entire fee for this cake that Sabrina whined to Priscilla, who then whined to Dad, and now it's up to him to reinforce the threats."

"Threats?" Lance asks, instantly on guard, and I can see the warrior in him stiffen at the word. I half-wish I could take him with me tonight and let Dad try to bully me into leaving Lance to Sabrina with him standing right there.

I tell him about Sabrina stopping by the bakery, and he laughs. "So I'm just a slab of beef with a wallet, that about right?"

"And social standing, don't forget that," I add, knowing that climbing the social ladder is just as important a factor for my stepmother and stepsister.

"I get it," he says quietly, his hands reaching out and pulling me close. "Your stepmother is playing matchmaker and my mom is playing match-maker. They think they've got it all figured out. But they forgot one import-ant detail. The biggest one, actually. I make my own choices, and I'm already interested in a woman."

"And who might that be?" I ask coyly, the beatdown little girl inside me wanting to hear him say that he's picking me over Sabrina. It's stupid and a bit broken, but when it was between the two of us, there was never a question. Sabrina got everything, and I dealt with whatever scraps were tossed my way.

But Lance is not scraps, not by a mile.

He draws me in, his hand cupping my cheek and his lips so close to mine I can feel our bodies pressing together again. "Here's a hint . . . if I were going to choose Sabrina, I'd be wearing a suit and tie and be in an office at Jacobs Bio-Tech, not in the back of a bakery looking at the most charming streak of frosting on the tip of your nose and wondering what it would taste like to lick it off your skin."

Our lips are barely an inch apart, and I want him so badly, it's me who starts to close the distance when suddenly, I hear the sharp sound of a tail-gate being dropped open and a second later, Trixie comes in the back door. "Whoo . . . sorry, should I come back later?"

"Crap!" I growl, slapping Lance's chest to hide my embarrassment, "You weren't supposed to frost my nose, you clumsy oaf!" My acting skills are even worse than Trixie's, though, and no one is fooled, least of all Trixie.

"Hmph, frosting her face already?" Trixie teases, her eyes twinkling, and I blush even deeper. "Kinky."

"A gentleman never tells," he quips, wiping my nose with a paper towel.

"Well, does a gentleman help a lady unload heavy bags of sugar we don't even need after she gave you a solid hour and a half of alone time?"

I knew she was making shit up to bail on me and leave us alone, but a glance at the clock sends a jolt through my system. She's right. It has been a while and I'm behind schedule now.

I can't let this cake get away from me or I'll be up all night decorating it. Lance presses a soft kiss to my cheek, but I'm already head-down in work mode.

# CHAPTER 9

## Lance

I BRUSH MY HANDS OFF ON MY APRON AND FOLLOW TRIXIE OUT TO HER truck, parked in the side alley by the bakery. She grabs a cardboard box of supplies and motions for me to take another.

"Seriously, I left you alone with her for that long and you were *just now* making a move? What is this, amateur hour? I figured you military types would be all '*target acquired*' and dive right in. Charlotte needs a good fucking, for damn sure," Trixie says, needling me.

I grin at her bluntness and heft a bag onto my shoulder. "Me too, but I want more, and I respect that she's got other priorities right now. Besides, target acquired is some tanker shit, not SEAL."

Trixie's brows furrow, and she side-eyes me through slits so narrow you can't even see the color of her eyes. "You one of those romantic gentlemanly types?" I don't answer, not willing to open the curtain around my heart to just anyone, and she hums, like she's trying to decide. "Hell, maybe I need to up my estimation. I was just happy for her to get a little sumpthin'-sumpthin' and for a warm body to help with the busy times."

It's a friend evaluation if ever I've heard one. She might as well have asked me my intentions with Charlotte. But I'm a man of action, not words. At least not words with Trixie. I'll save whatever sweet talk I have for Charlotte herself. So I heft the bag a little higher and make a move toward the door, giving Trixie a wink instead of an answer. She smirks in return like she's got my number, loud and clear.

Back inside, Charlotte has turned into a drill sergeant. "Trix, honey, we've gotta get our asses in gear. I need these dirty-frosted, refrigerated, and ready for frosting ay-sap." Every word is sharp and crisp, and I have to smile. I know that tone.

"On it, Boss," Trixie replies, haphazardly saluting and clicking her heels together.

"I'll get the rest of the supplies while you two get to work."

It seems playtime is over for us all. Outside, I grab a bag of flour, slinging it over my shoulder and carrying it inside. Charlotte looks up, a grateful look on her face, and she jerks her chin toward the supply closet. I nod and put the big bag on top of the stack of three others. Charlotte was right. They had plenty of supplies.

I head back out for another load and the blistering sun glints off a window across the street, grabbing my attention. There's a big, black Suburban sitting at the curb, angled just right to keep watch on the bakery.

I remember that Steven's not here, so this must be the overnight or off-day guard. Questions I've been squashing down float back to the surface.

I walk across the street, holding my hands out at my side to show I'm no threat. Well, I'm still a threat, but I'm unarmed, at least. And I'd bet my right hand the guys in the SUV are packing, so I err on the side of caution, hoping I don't get shot in the street based on a misunderstanding.

The window rolls down with a smooth whir. "Good day, Commander Jacobs. Can I help you?"

The guy knows who I am. Not sure if I think that's invasive or thorough. But I can see that they're professionals, though they're in jeans and generic black polos.

"Who are you? Name, rank, serial number?" I deadpan, well aware that the Geneva Convention doesn't hold sway here.

"Need to know only, sir," the driver says, putting his forearm on the window sill purposefully, and I see the trident tattoo he's flashing me. "No offense."

"None taken," I reply, nodding my chin toward him. "What Team?" It's the question he wants me to ask, and an answer will at least give me something to go on.

"Four," he says with a smirk.

"Did you like San Diego?" I ask, and he laughs. It's an easy check for 'fake' SEALs. The even-numbered teams are in Virginia.

He shakes his head, his grin growing. "The East Coast is beautiful this time of year. You ever been?"

"Nah, Team Three. I fucking loved San Diego."

It's not a perfect check. There's enough information on the internet that people can fake being a SEAL halfway decently, but it's a start and lets me know what kind of guys I'm working with here.

"Can you give me anything? Charlotte doesn't quite seem the type to warrant the royal treatment." Well, at least not with security. I could give her a damn fine pampering like a princess.

The driver looks to the passenger, who shrugs. At least I know who the high rank is of the two now, and my hard look returns to the driver, who's clenching his teeth like he wants to say more, but he barely gives me a crumb.

"It's a security gig, sir. For Miss Dunn's protection. That's all I can say."

The look in his eyes says that's all I'm going to get. But I try once more, laying my cards on the table, so to speak.

"I'm here daily, along with Steven. And inside, when he's gone in the evenings sometimes, hopefully more often, if she'll have me." I glance over my shoulder at the pink and white awnings, the glass letting me see into the dining area of the bakery, but my eyes track to the covered windows upstairs, hoping that we'll eventually get to that point. "If there's anything going down, I can be a resource. I'll protect her. Even if you can't tell me what's going on, can you tell me if I should be armed?"

The driver presses his lips together. "If you'd like. Won't be needed though. We'll do our job."

I nod, offering him a handshake and then reaching across to shake the passenger's hand as well. I walk back across the street, feeling their eyes on my back as I grab the last bag and take it inside.

I've got no more answers than I had before. In fact, I might have even more questions.

# CHAPTER 10

## Charlotte

*W*HAT IN THE HELL AM *I* DOING?
I ask myself the question repeatedly on the drive over. I wish the drive were longer so that I could put this off as long as possible, but on the other hand, it might be better to get it over with. Either way, the thirty-minute drive to Dad's house goes by before I know it.

I say 'Dad's house' but really, I mean Priscilla's house. She's the one who picked it out, who 'convinced' Dad that it was just the house to have even if it was too much money for our family, and who decorated every room.

Still, I grew up here for so many years, I even have a room on the far end of the hall on the second floor, overlooking the front yard. Not the gorgeous garden in the back yard, of course. Sabrina got that one because it had the view and the bigger closet.

But this house has never been home to me.

Once upon a time, I'd hoped that Dad would come to his senses and see what a bitch Priscilla is and how shitty Sabrina treats me.

But he was always so busy with his work, mostly to pay for Priscilla's lifestyle. So before too long, the pecking order was established. Priscilla was the queen of the household, Sabrina the pampered princess, and I ranked somewhere . . . lower.

I feel like in a lot of ways, Dad just didn't know what to do with a daughter. The little time we had, just the two of us, certainly was more tomboyish than anything else. So he left me to my own devices with Priscilla, hoping for and only seeing the best.

To her credit, Priscilla was good. I can see that now in hindsight. Her criticisms were always couched in a way to make it seem like she was helping me . . .

*"Oh, dear, your hair is so unfortunate. Those curls are just as unruly as you are, poor girl. Let me fix it."*

And then she'd yank and pull, ripping my hair from the root and scraping my scalp with the cheap plastic brush she kept just for me, until it was smoothed into a bun so tight it gave me headaches. She'd spray it with hairspray, making sure to get it in my eyes so they burned and watered. I learned not to jump or cry out because then she'd slap her hand on my shoulder, her nails digging in as she ordered me, *"Sit still and quit squawking like a crybaby."*

Dad never seemed to notice, the few times he was around. If anything, he'd simply smile and tell me my hair looked nice when Priscilla prompted him, proving once again that she had him fooled. Or he'd say that he was glad I was growing up into a young lady, like jeans and T-shirts were somehow the devil's garments.

Over the years, Sabrina couldn't help but learn at her mother's side. Her snide remarks and blatant role as the favorite made me an unwanted guest in my own home.

I pull into the driveway, looking at the house. It's not the nice, comfortable family home I'd lived in when my mom was still alive so long ago, though I only remember it from looking at pictures so many times.

Then, Dad was a man who made a six-figure salary and lived a five-figure lifestyle. Now, he's worked his way to a seven-figure paycheck but lives like it's eight.

This monster of a house is one sign of that, pretty unless you grew up here. Six bedrooms and seven baths, a pool out back surrounded by flowers and statues. The brand-new BMW sitting out front is another sign of Dad's indulgences, this year's model because Priscilla gets a new one every year on her birthday. Black every time, just like her soul.

Sighing, I get out of my car, the very sensible eight-year-old Volkswagen that Dad got me as a high school graduation gift. It's been a damn good car, and I have zero need for anything newer, and Dad quit offering when I refused after college. With Priscilla taking advantage of his money, I refuse to do the same.

I ring the bell and a second later, it opens. Dad looks like he's just come home from work, which is likely the case. His suit and tie are still pristine, though I'm sure he's spent the day at the office. "Charlotte, come in."

Uh-oh, the Disappointed Dad routine has already begun.

I close the door behind me, following him into the living room and sitting down like he does. I look around at the latest décor. It's straight out of *ELLE Décor*, probably last month's issue, so it must be Priscilla's latest update.

The chair beneath me is uncomfortable, but even worse is the discomfort between me and the man I still hold out hope for. Hope that he'll hug me, apologize for the suffering I've been put through, and hand me a Mr. Pibb once again.

Instead, he draws out the moment until I start fidgeting. "Where are Priscilla and Sabrina?" It's a rookie question, and I know it'll only highlight the gaping distance between Dad and me, but the desire to know if I'm going to get taken out from behind is hard to resist.

"Out. I wanted this to be just us." Like the silly little girl I still am inside, that hope starts to blossom. But it's quickly squashed when he looks at me harshly. "How could you do that to your sister?"

"Sabrina isn't my sister, just like Priscilla isn't my mother. We've had this conversation," I say, disappointment making me roll my eyes. I'm sure to him I seem petulant and immature, but really, it's a conglomeration of frustration over the fact that he never sees the truth.

"We have. So let's have a different one." His tone is distant, professional, as if I'm an employee in his company, not his daughter. "Priscilla has worked very hard to cultivate a relationship with the Jacobses. And to present Sabrina as a good match for Lance Jacobs. I am embarrassed that you would interfere, slotting yourself into a position created for your sister. Your behavior at the gala was grossly unacceptable."

"My behavior?" I sputter. "You think *my* behavior was unacceptable? But Priscilla conspiring with Mrs. Jacobs to marry off their children, with zero regard for whether Lance is actually interested in Sabrina, is perfectly fine? Like we're in medieval times, marrying for land boundaries. If you'll remember, I was nothing but polite when I met them. Lance followed me, at the gala and at the bakery."

*Shit.* I didn't mean to say that. I don't want them to know that Lance is hanging around and helping me at the bakery. It feels like it's private, between me and him. Maybe Dad won't notice? I cross my fingers and toes, praying that he's too riled up at my hinting at the horror of an arranged marriage in this day and age.

"Speaking of the bakery, I still do not understand what prompted you to give up such a promising position for drudgery."

Well, one crisis averted in favor of another. "Dad, working at Blackwell was never going to be what I thought it was, or the lessons you said I'd learn at a big company. I wasn't learning anything, and it was . . ." I freeze, the word 'dangerous' on the tip of my tongue. But I can't tell him about Blackwell's attempts to hamstring Thomas, can't tell him about the SUV parked outside even right now because my security followed me here. "It was a dead end."

"Hmph."

I punt, changing directions. "I love baking. And *Cake Culture* has been a roaring success. I'm working hard, but I love it. I've learned so much, building something great from the ground up. I thought you'd be proud of me for that."

"I have always been proud of you, upset at your teen rebellion, occasionally, but proud of your work ethic. This step is too far, though, Charlotte. Working before dawn until late at night, requiring a singular focus. You do always pick the hard way, sometimes just to spite everyone around you." He sighs, like my bakery has anything to do with him, Priscilla, or Sabrina. "But why struggle when there is an easier path? You could've worked your way up at Blackwell, worked for me or one of a dozen companies . . ."

His voice trails off, and though I know the definition of insanity is to do the same thing and expect a different result, I explain what the bakery means to me again for the hundredth time. "I love it, Dad. It's my heart and soul, hard work, and creativity in each of those baked goods. I've taken the lessons Grandma Winnie taught me, the recipes she shared, and improved upon them. I'm succeeding. Yes, it's hard and takes more time than exists in a twenty-four-hour day, but I love it."

I beseech him to understand, pleading with my eyes.

His gaze locks on me, and that stupid hope tries to rise again. His answer is a mixed bag, though. "Fine. If you're so staunchly sure that this is the path you want to traverse, I'll support that. Not financially, of course. But you have my blessing." He pauses long enough for my brain to celebrate his support and scoff at his unneeded blessing to do whatever the hell I want.

"But if you want that, you need to step aside and let others, who choose differently, have a clear path. You will leave Lance to Sabrina. She needs a good man, one who can take her in hand and deal with her high-strung personality. Priscilla has worked hard to make this happen, and you will not interfere."

"Dad," I say, my jaw dropping.

He shakes his head definitively. "We are hosting a family dinner with the Jacobses on Sunday. You will attend, you will obviously rebuff any advances from Lance, you will redirect positive attention to Sabrina, and you will be pleasant to Priscilla. She's been a good mother to you, and as your father, I need this from you."

His laundry list of to-dos is laughable, but the rest sticks in my craw. A good mother? Priscilla? She turned my family inside out, made my life a living hell, and took my Daddy away from me.

I shake my head, the mirror image of his earlier movement, and his lips quirk. "You are the spitting image of her, you know?"

My heart stops, and for a moment, I think he means Priscilla, which is the worst insult he could ever give me. But he continues and my heart cracks wide open.

"Your mother was a stunner, had me wrapped around her little finger." He doesn't often talk about Mom, but the idea that both women in his life have had him at their beck and call is an uncomfortable comparison between the woman I hold in the highest regard and the one I hate with a vehemence bordering on unhealthy.

"She is the reason I succeeded in those early days. I was young, foolish, and slacked off too much, but she would sit me down and make me study. Later, when I had all these pie-in-the-sky dreams, she'd force me to make a step-by-step plan to make them a reality. She taught me how to work hard and see a goal to fruition. My company, my everything"—he looks around the house that Priscilla designed—"it's all because she loved me and saw something in me. In you, I see both of us. Your mother's focus and my dreams. Hopefully, the very best of us both."

He smiles softly, and I see my Daddy for the first time in years. "Thank you. That means a lot to me," I confess.

He stands up, arms open wide, and I stand up too, never too big for a hug from the man I miss desperately. He feels smaller in my arms than I remember, the giant of a man suddenly more human, more flawed, and I realize that he's doing the best he can. I might not like it in the least, but he's choosing his life every day the same way I am. He doesn't understand my bakery and I don't understand his wife, but we can still love each other in spite of the differences in opinion.

"Sunday, Charlotte." His tone broaches no argument.

I nod but push back slightly to meet his eyes. "I'll come, but Priscilla and Sabrina are wrong in this. Lance isn't a car they can buy. He's not a horse they can choose as a stud. He's a man, one with his own opinions. You'd do well to remember that."

He presses his lips together, nodding. "As would you. Sabrina is a beautiful young woman whom any man would be fortunate to call his wife. Don't interfere. Don't risk yourself when you say your focus is devoted solely on *Cake Culture*."

He presses a quick kiss to my forehead like he did when I was little, and I turn to go before the tears burning at the corners of my eyes can spill over.

That he knows the name of my bakery is a small feather in my cap, a sign that maybe he has been listening. But as I get into the car for the drive home, I know I'm going to this dinner, not because I'm doing it for him. And certainly not for Priscilla or Sabrina.

I'm going to dinner because Lance deserves to have someone sitting at that table who's on his side. I don't know what we're doing beyond the fact that he basically makes my ovaries twerk like they're backup dancers in a Nikki Minaj video, but I know that he shouldn't get ensnared in Sabrina's scheming web, even if it is gold-encrusted.

Sunday dinner, it is.

# CHAPTER 11

## Lance

*G*OOD LUCK TODAY, NOT THAT YOU NEED IT.
        I consider adding a tongue emoji to the cake one I include on the text to Charlotte.

Today's her big day with the wedding monstrosity we've been working on. Purely by necessity, I've been helping more in the shop because of it. In addition to helping with cleanup, I've been running things from the back up front and pulling trays out of the ovens while Charlotte does the finicky decorations needed on the four-foot-tall wedding cake. Still, I want her to know I'm thinking of her, so I click *Send*.

*She says* \*~\*Thank You~\*~. *You should see the heart emojis popping out of her eyes right now. But for real, she's busy. Leave us alone.—Trixie*

I appreciate that she took the moment to reply, even through Trixie, knowing that they're likely swamped. Charlotte told me that she'd spend a chunk of time getting the cake set up and that Trixie would be running the shop today, but they'd both denied my offer of help, saying they had it well in hand.

I feel surprisingly adrift without a plan to go to the bakery like I've been doing every day. It's just not as meaningful to me without Charlotte there. But I have been working on the information download for Jacobs Bio-Tech, going through files and familiarizing myself with almost a decade of data.

Honestly, the company seems mostly to be headed in the right direction, which makes me question why I was needed home so desperately.

Research seems to be on the cutting edge, a ballsy risk, but one that makes sense for the industry. Payroll doesn't seem excessive, and while the marketing materials I've looked at seem a bit dry and boring, that's not my area of expertise.

All in all, I'm mostly impressed with what Dad's accomplished in his quest to make the family company thrive. I can see his blood, sweat, and tears in every facet.

Maybe that's what made him ask for help? The sheer volume of work he's been shouldering has to be wearing on him, even with Cody's help. And while he's in good shape, a man pushing sixty might not have the same energy as a younger man.

Of course, I can see Cody's touches here and there. He's done some project management on some new designs that look good. They're nothing groundbreaking, but they were completed on time and the financials on the results seem to be good, at least to me.

But the progression of his responsibilities does seem lacking. I wonder if that's his own preference or Dad holding him back.

Needing to clear my head, I throw on athletic shorts and tennis shoes and make my way to the home gym Dad installed when he built this place.

In some ways, I'm still adjusting to civilian life. Instead of clean, beautifully lubricated and maintained equipment, part of me still looks forward to a workout where there's sand in my shirt, rough metal digging into my hands, and saltwater stinging my eyes. Still, it feels good to move, to challenge my body and push myself.

No, desk life is not for me.

Finishing up with my favorite machine, the Jacob's Ladder, I swipe at the sweat running down my face, then toss the towel around my neck for my cooldown stretches. It's only because I'm changing positions that I see Cody pause in the doorway. He's dressed like he's here for a workout too, but as soon as he sees me, he turns to walk away down the hallway.

"Cody! Wait, come back," I call. In the hallway, I can see him look upward and sigh, like he's stuck between a rock and a hard place. But he does come back.

"Fine. But I'm not talking business with you. This is my escape from that shitshow, so don't even try it, Mr. All-American Hero, come to save the fucking day."

Bitterness drips from every word as he steps onto the treadmill, which surprises me.

Once upon a time, we were close. Well, as close as we could be with the years between us.

When I was off to the military, he was still in high school, so the years before that had us mostly interested in different things, but I'd always had a soft spot in my heart for my little brother. I hope that we can find some common ground again, now that we're both adults.

"We don't have to talk business if you don't want. Trust me, the SEALs were a lot simpler than that corporate jungle. Wasn't perfect, but I had sun, sand, and could wear a T-shirt for half my damn job. But when Dad and Mom said they needed help, here I am. Woof, woof," I say, letting Cody know that being caught up in Dad's games isn't sitting well with me either. I want Cody to drop whatever burr he's got up his ass about my being here.

He smirks, shaking his head. "You can stop the woe is me sacrifice act, Lance. At least you get to be a fucking Goldendoodle, coming back all decorated and welcomed and shit. I'm like the chihuahua that gets shoved off to the side, no matter how much I bark. Yip, yip, yip."

The joke is harsh, but he sounds funny, and I can imagine him bouncing around like a tiny dog that thinks he's the fiercest beast. I can't help but laugh, and after a minute, he does too. Cody's laugh is rough, though, like he hasn't done it in way too long, and I wonder just what the hell went wrong here for him.

"Fuck, that feels good," I say, wiping the salty combination of sweat and tears from my eyes. "I missed you, brother. I swear, I went away and you were this gangly kid with his head down in school work. Before I knew it, you were a man who was making your own way. I feel like I don't even know you now, like maybe you don't even like me anymore."

It's a big confession, one that might send him stomping out of here when I barely forged a crack in the wall between us, but I'm a gambling man. And if anything, I think it'll give Cody an opening to dump all his venom on me. I'll take it because then I'll know what I'm dealing with, at least.

"Like you give a single, solitary fuck about what I want or like?" Cody asks, snorting derisively. "First off, I'm not walking my own path. I'm walking the one Dad wanted you to follow. So when the prodigal son returns, you get set up for the good life, and once again, I'm reminded that I'm a poor substitute for you in every way."

"Substitute? You were never . . . Cody, you've always been an important part of this family. And from what I can tell, you've done a great job at Bio-Tech." He scoffs, but I soldier on. "I'm honestly not sure why I'm needed here. It seems like Dad's stressed to the max and you and he are damn near at each other's throats, but from what I can tell, the company is okay."

"You have no idea, do you?" he shakes his head, rolling his eyes. "You're so fucking clueless you don't even know what you don't know."

"Fine. Fill me in then, Cody. Tell me what the hell's going on!" My voice raises in frustration.

He snarls, years of anger bubbling to the surface and overflowing in a rage-filled rant as he starts pacing back and forth, letting it out maybe for the first time ever. "You want to know what happened? Fine! You happened! You ran off to go do your own shit and never cared what I had to do back here. You think I wasn't a substitute? They compared every single thing I did to what you would do and I came up lacking each and every time. So I tried to do better, be better, and fill in the gaps you left behind. You didn't want the family business, so I joined right up. You wanted to see the world, so I stayed right here at home. I've done all the things you weren't willing to, worked my ass off as a junior executive, paving the way to a life I thought I wanted as a VP. I figured eventually, he'd have to see that I'm just as good—" his lip curls, and he points a thick finger at my chest. "No, *better* than you. Because I'm willing to do what the family needs, not run off on a whim."

He turns to leave, but I can't let it end like that. He's said his piece, but I've got one of my own, so I yell back, stopping him in his tracks. "You think I ran off on a whim? My whole life has been plotted out for me, expectation on top of responsibility, with zero concern over what I wanted. So yeah, I got out. And you could've done the same, but you *chose* not to. Now, I get lured here under false pretenses, all because they've decided I should be ready to settle down. I'm not back for five minutes before they're pairing me off with a socialite who has more ass than brains, and her ass is *flatter than a fucking crepe*!"

I cringe, the food pun rolling off my tongue and not having near the thorny emphasis I'd intended. Cody looks angry, but then an incredulous grin washes over his face. "A crepe? What the hell kind of military slang is that for a piece of ass like Sabrina?"

"Sorry, I've got a bit of baking on the mind," I say, shaking my head.

The tense stalemate is broken by my unfortunate slip. "Ooh, I know what's got you thinking about cupcakes and popping cherries."

I shove at Cody, feeling good again as we laugh. "Leave Charlotte out of this."

He pushes back at me, and for a minute, I swear we're kids again. We're not really trying to hurt each other, but we end up bear hugging, mock-wrestling in the hallway. I'm better than him, trained in ways he's not, but I let him get in some pushes, rolling up and down the hall and banging off the walls.

We both need to burn some of this testosterone out because we don't need to fight for Alpha, not in our own family. Neither of us is out of shape, but between the pretty aggressive wrestling horseplay and mouthy taunts, we're out of breath quickly and both flop to the carpet, laughing. I'm spread-eagle, leaning back on my hands, and Cody is laid out on his back, staring at the ceiling.

"They'll never go for it, you know that, right?" he says and then turns a side eye to me. "Charlotte won't happen."

He sounds resigned, like he's used to Mom and Dad getting their way. And I guess with his way of dealing with them, they always have.

But I've always handled their intrusiveness a bit differently, and I have no problem saying, 'fuck it all,' and walking away. Even though neither of us, my parents nor me, truly wants that.

"We'll see. She's not why I'm here. I'm here for you, man. Dad too. Tell me what I need to know. I'm on your side. There's got to be more than what I'm seeing in the spreadsheets and quarterly reports."

I get that Dad probably wants me to take over, but Cody seems a reasonable, if not good, heir to that responsibility.

Which would leave me open to whatever life I wanted, maybe even a return to the Navy.

I imagine that life once again taking over my every moment, a simpler life in some ways, one of mission-oriented focus.

But that image blurs in a red haze, one that clears and focuses into a certain redhead with fair skin that blushes in splotches, blue eyes that enflame me, and a sense of humor that makes me feel lighter than I have in a long time. Another kind of mission . . . but one just as important.

Cody, not privy to my thoughts, gets up after a minute and goes into the gym again, and while I know Dad feels like Cody isn't pulling his weight, I can see the heavy weariness Cody wears. Whether real or imagined, the expectations are drowning him.

"Cody."

He stops at the door and turns back, his eyes cold and hard again.

"Look, Lance, I know you're not doing it on purpose. But just stay out of my way. This will be my company. I've worked for it. Fuck knows, Dad didn't give me a damn bit of it just because I share his name. I've earned this, and I won't let them hand it to you just because you're their favorite."

He closes the door, and while I'm tempted to go back into the gym and settle this, I know this isn't the time. Despite our playfulness, he's still angry deep down. That anger is going to bring things to a head between him and Dad sooner or later. I only hope we can all survive the fallout. We've been a mostly happy family, or at least Mom and Dad have always had our best interests at heart even if I didn't agree with their methods. But I'm afraid this meddling is going to cause irreparable damage to our family if we don't change course.

# CHAPTER 12

## Charlotte

I HAVE NEVER BEEN SO NOT-HUNGRY FOR DINNER IN MY LIFE. BUT I'M here all the same. I spent extra time on my hair and makeup and have on a lovely A-line floral dress I've worn a few times, but never in front of Priscilla.

That I'm even conscious of that irks me on a cellular level because I couldn't care less about who sees me wearing what, but I don't want to give them ammunition and start the night off at a loss.

The door opens after I ring the bell, and Sabrina appears, looking gorgeous. I'm not a troll by any stretch, but to myself, at least, I'll admit that Sabrina is a beautiful woman. On the outside.

Her freshly-highlighted hair sheens, falling in a smooth sheet down her back. Her blue eyes are played up, her full lips blood-red. Her designer-label white lace sheath dress looks nearly bridal, save the low V-neck that highlights a full cleavage. Her heels give her a height advantage of several inches, all the better to look down on me from upon high.

"Well, don't you look *pretty*," Sabrina says, her tone relaying the opposite. "So . . . ladylike."

*Like she knows the first fucking thing about being a lady.* But I remind myself for the tenth time since I left home that I'm going to be on my best behavior. For Dad and for Lance. "Thank you, Sabrina. You look lovely as well," I say civilly, my tone bland.

"You don't have to fake being nice. No one is here to see it yet, since *my* man isn't here yet." The smile on her face is venom-filled, like she's daring me to disagree with her decree.

*Ooh, bitch, if I weren't...*

Well, there goes my promise to Dad. It's hard for me to hold my tongue and not tell Sabrina that Lance has been hanging out at the bakery, working oh-so-close and oh-so-late with me, sneaking in kisses here and there. I imagine doing it and the look on her already Botoxed face.

But I'm not going to lay any traps for Lance. I'm here to help him through them. He'll have enough to traverse tonight without my laying it all out there before he even gets here.

I head into the living room, noting that there are already a few subtle changes to the décor. The artwork over the fireplace is a new, and likely expensive, abstract in swashes of pink and gold, and the pillows on the couch are woven through with metallic threads, giving everything a gilded appearance.

Priscilla doesn't acknowledge my entrance, but Dad gets up, kissing my cheek. Though it's more polite manners than affection, it renews my resolve to behave and keep my tongue in check.

Thankfully, it's only moments later that the doorbell rings again, announcing the Jacobses' arrival.

Mr. and Mrs. Jacobs come in, looking elegant. Mr. Jacobs wears a finely-tailored suit in a deep charcoal grey, and Mrs. Jacobs is in a knee-length pale grey dress with an architectural portrait collar that makes her collarbones look regal.

After handshakes and air kisses—yes, for real, and prompted by Priscilla, of course—Sabrina can wait no longer.

"Where's my Lance-y?" Her voice is practically an octave higher than usual, making her sound childish. In my gut, I feel something churn, and I know I'm going to be scarfing an extra cupcake tomorrow to make up for a very lightly eaten dinner tonight.

"Lance and Cody elected to drive over together. I believe Cody said something about showing off his latest modification? Something to do with speakers, I believe, but I'll admit to being a bit befuddled by his love of loud music. Must be a young man thing. It simply hurts my ears," Mrs. Jacobs says, laughing lightly at herself. "Likely just an excuse for some brother time. I'm sure you understand."

She looks from Sabrina to me, and I have to bite back my reply.

*Oh, sure. Sabrina and I are the best of buds. A regular Obi-Wan and Anakin, we are.*

I blame my geeky metaphors on Mia, the ultimate geek who's forced me to watch more Sci-Fi, both animated and live-action, over my lifetime than I'll ever admit.

A house staff member comes in, holding a tray of white wine, which we each take gratefully. I almost drink it as a shot, needing the fortification, but I manage to sip slowly and politely.

"So, what does Cody do?" Dad asks Mr. Jacobs. "I must admit, I've heard so much about Lance"—he looks to Sabrina—"but Cody's a bit of a mystery."

He looks at me, like he's giving me permission to go after Cody Jacobs as long as I leave Lance alone.

"As he likes it," Mrs. Jacobs says, gripping her glass a little tightly. "He's an executive VP for Jacobs Bio-Tech, began there while still in college, in fact, and has never worked anywhere but the family business. He's a home-grown exec, you see."

There's a bit of pride in her tone, but simultaneously, she makes it sound like Cody only holds his position because of his name. It's a delicate balance I suspect she's perfected through many tellings.

It does make me wonder, if Cody is already here, working under Mr. Jacobs and being the good little silver-spoon boy, why they're so hellfire-bent on bringing Lance back and marrying him off. It seems any desire for grand-kids and a legacy could be well fulfilled by the younger of the two Jacobs sons. Probably with a greater degree of ease and control than they seem to have over Lance, who is a man who does whatever the hell he wants.

*He hasn't done you yet, and he definitely wants you. You want him too.*

I don't get a chance to uselessly argue with myself because a fast tap-tap-tap sounds on the door. A moment later, Lance and Cody enter, and the temperature in the room jumps about ten degrees.

Cody, for his part, looks every bit the carefree playboy. His suit is expensive but not fresh-pressed, his jaw has at least a day's worth of stubble glinting along it, and if I'm not mistaken, his eyes look a little red as he flips his sunglasses up onto the top of his head.

"Sorry we're late," he says, not looking the least bit sorry.

Lance has the wherewithal to look sheepish, but he's the opposite of his brother in other ways too. His scruff is well-kept, trimmed neatly, his hair not compulsively styled but neat and tidy, and his navy suit is pristine, highlighting the blue of his eyes to perfection. "Yes, our apologies."

"That's okay, Lance-y, you're just in time for dinner," Sabrina says, and I fight to hold back the hip-thrusting victory dance when I see his eyebrows shoot up at the nickname.

Lance doesn't respond, just makes his way to my dad, shaking his hand, then Priscilla's, and then Sabrina, who looks disappointed he doesn't kiss the back of her hand. Suddenly, we're face to face, his eyes burning into mine.

"Charlotte." His voice is deep, the timber making all the hairs on my arms stand up.

I try to warn him off with my eyes but probably fail since his hand is still wrapped around mine long after is proper. "Nice to see you again, Lance."

My voice is purposefully neutral, not hinting that not that long ago, we were *this close* to making out over a wedding cake. Hell, not even letting on that we've seen each other since the gala.

Priscilla notices something, though, and claps, saying sharply, "Dinner." She plasters a fake smile on and gestures with her hand. "I mean, right this way, please."

She leads us to the dining room, and oh, my God, there are place cards noting who's to sit where. Seems Priscilla isn't leaving anything to chance. Dad and Priscilla take their natural places at the ends of the table, Mr. and Mrs. Jacobs sitting at Dad's right and left. Lance is sandwiched between his mother and Sabrina, I'm between Mr. Jacobs and Cody, who at least also looks like he doesn't want to be here.

Lance looks like he's preparing for the Spanish Inquisition and reaches for his water glass almost immediately. Meanwhile, Cody is looking across the table, blatantly staring at Sabrina's cleavage. Not that she notices, because as soon as she sits down, she's practically rubbing her tits against Lance's arm, damn near climbing into his lap right here at the table.

Dinner is served, something pretty on the plate and likely delicious, but I don't taste a thing. All my attention is on the conversations going on around the table, both verbal and nonverbal.

"So, Lance . . . what's it like being a real American hero SEAL?" Priscilla purrs.

Like she was prompted, Sabrina leans into Lance. "Yes, Lance-y. You're so brave, rushing into danger like that. So strong and powerful," she simpers, squeezing his biceps.

Okay, so she's not wrong, exactly. Lance is all those things, but the needy, worshipful way she compliments him rubs me wrong. To help, I glance over, where I'll give Cody credit, he seems to see through Sabrina's charade because he's rolling his eyes so hard they might get stuck that way.

Lance ignores Sabrina's manicured hand and looks at Priscilla instead. "If you want to know the truth, I spent most of my time in combat, scared out of my wits. 'Courage is not the absence of fear, but rather the assessment that something else is more important than the fear.' That's the mission."

Sabrina interrupts, "Ooh, you're so smart. That's brilliant."

"FDR seemed to think so," I say under my breath, and Lance looks at me, a smirk on his face that I caught the famous quote that Sabrina seems woefully unfamiliar with.

"Are you a presidential fan, Charlotte?" Lance asks, and four sets of parental eyes turn to me, plus Sabrina's glare.

"Oh, uh, not particularly. I just bake," I say, trying to avoid making myself sound small and unfortunately failing. I have more experience with that than I care to admit, and with Priscilla's narrowed eyes, I revert more easily than I'd like.

"How is the bakery coming, dear?" Mrs. Jacobs asks. "I heard your cupcakes caused quite the stir at the gala."

I dab at my mouth with my napkin, smiling a little as Priscilla scowls. "Thank you, Mrs. Jacobs. Thomas and Mia really helped me get the word out, and business has been going better than projected. I've got quite a few regulars already and a rather large wedding cake custom order going out this weekend."

"Way to work those connections, dear," Priscilla quips. "You certainly need them, considering you won't be getting any real recognition when people can buy a cake at Albertson's. Not like they give Michelin stars for baked goods, though yours are good, I suppose," she jokes, laughing lightly like she's teasing, but the only person who laughs with her is Sabrina.

I'm at my max, the threshold for bullshit about two feet ago, and now I'm swimming through it to wrangle my hands around Priscilla's neck, not literally, but figuratively, as I respond.

"I don't use my friends that way and don't choose them based on what they can do for me like a narcissistic user. Mia has a quote I think you'd be interested in. 'Don't beg for it . . . earn it. Do that, and you'll be rewarded.' And *that's* what I'm doing. Not trying to *suck up* to people to get my way up the social ladder."

My emphasized words, combined with my pointed look at Sabrina, sends a very clear message. It isn't missed as Dad slams his napkin on the table, the sound sharp before he barks. "That's enough, Charlotte. Once again, despite our conversation, you can't seem to understand proper decorum. Priscilla put on a lovely dinner so Sabrina and Lance could get to know one another, and all I asked is for you to not interfere. But you sit here and insult them. I'm disappointed in you. Apologize now, young lady."

I can see the twitch at the corners of Sabrina's lips, her delight that I'm getting reamed out. I guess this time, she didn't really do anything to me. It was Priscilla who insulted my bakery, but I threw them both under the bus as fast as I could. It's deserved time and time over, but I look like the bitch right now.

"My apologies," I offer the table, my head held high and my tone saying I'm anything but.

I hear Cody murmur beside me, "Best part of the whole night, hands down."

I'm encouraged by Cody's words, but it's the look in Lance's eye that pleases me the most. His hot gaze bores into me, making me rub my thighs together for relief because I can feel the dark promise in his eyes.

Conversation begins again, pointedly veering away from anything that I can contribute to.

Mrs. Jacobs and Priscilla discuss upcoming events on the social calendar for the season, including the value in going with a staunchly respected designer for gowns instead of gambling on a new uprising hotshot. Priscilla devours every word like they're gospel, and maybe to her, they are.

Mr. Jacobs and Dad then move to talk about Roseboro and the move of Jacobs Bio-Tech to town. "It's been an exciting change," he says, "though I may feel differently when the winter snow hits."

Dad agrees, sipping his drink. "It takes getting used to, but Roseboro is worth it. The town has changed a lot over the last twenty, thirty years. While we're not quite in Roseboro, I've of course kept my eye on things. It's quite exciting."

Their talk turns to Blackwell and the changes he's brought to town, and then to Thomas Goldstone and the changes he's bringing along with the partnership with the bio-tech company.

Sabrina interjects. "Mr. Blackwell has done such great things. It's a pity Charlotte couldn't keep her job there." I have intentionally kept my mouth shut, letting all the attention drift away from me, but Sabrina couldn't resist the opportunity to cut me.

Mr. Jacobs turns to me, lifting an eyebrow. "Oh? You used to work at Blackwell? Why'd you leave?"

I nod, looking at Dad. "I did. I decided to pursue a dream and left."

I'm leaving off *so* much to that decision, but I don't want to push it considering my earlier outburst.

Dad frowns, shaking his head as he explains to Mr. Jacobs, "You remember what it's like to be young, taking the more difficult path despite every advice to the contrary? I'm afraid she has the best and the worst of both her mother and me, and she refuses to see sense from a voice of reason and experience."

It's not the harshest thing he's ever said and mirrors the way we'd left things the other day, but this feels more patronizing. I can feel myself shrinking in my seat, and I bite my lip to keep from saying anything else.

Lance suffers no such need to keep quiet, standing and tossing his napkin to the table, similarly to how Dad did earlier. "Seriously? Do you hear yourself?" He looks at Dad as if he expects an answer, but Dad merely looks back in total shock. After a moment, Lance expounds. "Charlotte left a job to chase a dream, one that I've seen her work hard at and she's flourishing with. Yet you continue to downplay her success, all the while, playing up a daughter whose sole 'work experience' is sitting still for the amount of time it takes to have her extensions attached in the salon chair."

Sabrina lets out a weak sound of offense, but Priscilla's is loud. "Why, I never!"

Lance turns to Priscilla, a look of disdain on his face. "You're right. You never. But I do. *I see you.* Every snarky comment, every jealous look."

Priscilla has the gall to look offended, like she doesn't know exactly what he's talking about.

"Lance, please!" Mrs. Jacobs exclaims, but he whirls on her next.

"Mom, I understand that you think you have my best interests at heart, but back off. I'm a grown man, and I'm not marrying someone because you've deemed them an acceptable match or worked some backroom deal with Priscilla. What you think you're getting out of this, I don't know, nor do I care. I'm here and I'm home, but not for this circus."

He thrashes his hand around, gesturing at the table.

Lance pushes his chair further back, stepping away from the table and taking a few steps toward the doorway.

"Lance, I demand—" Mr. Jacobs starts, but Lance doesn't give him a chance to finish his sentence.

"You'll demand nothing of me, Dad. You're asking me to help with the family company, and I've done so, in spite of my own career and despite there being a Jacobs son ready and willing, and from what I see, more than able to take over the company mantle."

The only people at the table not sputtering are me and Cody. We both have huge shit-eating grins on our faces, and I'm guessing similar wishes that we could've said all that ourselves.

I guess he's said everything he's had brewing up, because Lance moves to the doorway but pauses to glance back once more. His eyes meet mine again, challenge sparking in his baby blues. "You coming, Red?"

My smile falters, my jaw dropping as I look around the table. Shock, fury, and even Cody's still-growing smile greet me. I should do as I'm told, sit still and not make a fuss, like I've done so many times before.

*Fuck that.*

I get up, dropping my napkin to my chair. "Yep, let's go."

# CHAPTER 13

## Lance

O N THE FRONT PORCH, CHARLOTTE SAGS, AND WE CAN HEAR SABRINA whining loudly inside. "Mommm, get him back! Charlotte can't have him!"

"Oh, my God, oh, my God. What the hell did I just do? What did you do?" she says, eyes as big as dinner plates meeting mine.

I can see the fear, and I hate it. She's strong, sassy, and badass, not this scared and quiet mouse they try to get her to be. "It's all right. I've got you. There's just one thing."

"There's more?" she says, starting to breathe again.

I nod, a grin spreading on my face as I take her hand. "I rode with Cody. Is your car here?"

She adds a couple of inches to the space between us and I can see the fire relighting in her eyes. "All that, a massive hair-flip out after telling everybody off, and now we're going to have to do a walk of shame out of here as we call for an Uber?"

I blanch. "I didn't think that far ahead. I just couldn't sit there and let them manipulate me like that and put you down that way. Of course, if I were solo, I'd just do that whole walking against the wind shit. Stalk off like a badass."

She smiles, breaking the tease. "My car's over there." She points to a black

VW, pulling me that direction as she takes my hand. It feels casual, comfortable, like her hand has always belonged in mine.

We get in, and she pulls out of the driveway carefully, waving to the SUV across the street I hadn't noticed when we came in with Cody's music blaring louder than a firefight in the dead of night.

It's probably a good thing she's driving. I would've peeled out, tires squealing just to emphasize my points further with our families still inside.

The drive to the bakery is quiet, and though I don't want to assume, I'm hoping we continue this attempt at running away right up the stairs to Charlotte's apartment. She parks and reads my mind, waving at the SUV once more before opening the back door and leading me up the back stairs.

I get the vaguest impression of a small apartment before I make my move, pressing her up against the door she just closed. "What are you doing?" Charlotte asks, her chest heaving as she tries to catch her breath.

"This," I say before moving in to kiss her deeply. She resists at first, but her hands don't push me away, instead weaving into my hair to pull me in tighter. She opens her mouth, and I claim her, feeling like we're on the same page. I press closer, pinning her between the door and my body, and she arches her back, pushing against me, hungry for more.

I trace my hands down her side, brushing the sides of her breasts before gripping her hips and lifting her. Her hands lock behind my neck, her legs going around my waist, her pussy centered over my cock. I can feel her heat, and my control slips.

"Where?" I demand.

"Down the hall, on the left," she mutters between kisses.

I move across the living room and into her bedroom before letting her slide down, never losing contact. I tug at her dress, finding the buttons on the back and fumbling with them. "Are you trying to torture me?"

She chuckles, her hands running down my chest to my belt. "I wasn't planning on needing it off in a hurry."

I pause, her words not dimming my passion but putting steel back in my self-control. "Do you want to slow down?" Even as I ask, I kiss her neck, praying she doesn't ask me to stop again.

She shakes her head, getting my belt undone and moving on to my slacks. "Fuck, no. If you can't get it, turn me around and push the skirt up."

Now I'm the one disagreeing, even as the image fills my mind. "I want to see you, all of you."

As if it's choreographed, we each reach for our own clothes, her getting the rest of the buttons undone and dropping her dress to puddle at her feet. I yank my button-down shirt over my head after only undoing a few buttons and then drop my slacks down, kicking my shoes off at the same time.

She's glorious, a scarlet-haired angel in a satiny cream-colored bra and panties that look almost golden against her pale skin. My cock, which is already rock-hard, twitches, and Charlotte hums as she gets a good look at the bulge in my boxers.

"Gorgeous. Come here," I growl, grabbing her hand and pulling her back to me, but she reacts quickly, keeping a hand between the two of us. She cups my cock, hesitantly at first but growing confident as she explores my length through the thin layer of cotton.

"This is . . . wow."

We tumble to the bed, our mouths never leaving one another. She cradles me between her bent knees, and I run my hands up her thighs, massaging the perfect twin globes of her ass. The sound of her moans drives me lower, and I start kissing down her body. She whines as I move away and she loses contact with my cock.

"I want you." She pouts.

I ooze precum, already on edge at the needy sounds coming from her lips. "You'll get me, I promise. I'm not going anywhere, but I need to taste you."

She arches as I lower myself, pressing my lips to the fullness of her breast escaping from her bra. She reaches behind her back, undoing the fastener quickly and taking her bra off completely.

Her tits are snowy white, and I cup and press them together before burying my head between them to kiss and suck on her skin, enjoying the way it pinks up beneath my lips and teeth. I lick and suckle at first one rosy nipple, then the other, as I run a finger up the inside of her leg to the flat of her panties over her slit.

Her lips cling to the damp satin, outlining the narrow valley between, and I stroke her with my fingertips, learning her body by her responses. Charlotte's moan when I find her engorged clit is held back as she bites her lip, but her hips lift up to my touch, begging for more. I focus my attentions there, rubbing her clit through the now-soaked fabric and sucking hard on her nipple, giving her occasional nips that make her arch anew.

Her fingernails scratch at my back, urging me on. "Fuck! Oh, *fuck*!"

Her whole body quivers beneath me, muscles tightening and spasming. "I'm gonna . . ."

"That's it, Charlotte. Come for me. I've got you," I tell her supportively, my breath hot on her cleavage.

She rides the wave back down, her eyes peeking open to stare at me in wonder as a smile breaks on her reddened lips. "Holy shit, I never come that fast."

Part of me wants to preen and puff up like I did something awesome, but mostly, I just want to make her do it again and again. This time, I want to taste it, and the next, I want to see the convulsions of her pussy lips hungrily sucking my cock deeper inside her waiting body.

"I want more," I say. "I want it all."

She nods, agreeing, so I push her legs open and drop to my knees beside the bed. I tug her panties down, and she wiggles to help me get them off. She's fully nude before me, and I let my eyes drift up her body to see just how stunning she truly is.

Her hair is spread out like a burning halo, her wide blue eyes watching me in lusty anticipation, her body curvy and built for sin, all framing a pretty pink pussy that's already gleaming, messy with her cum. I can't help but lean in, inhaling her sexy scent and pressing a soft kiss to her bare mound.

My cock twitches, a fresh drop of precum releasing as her sweet taste hits my tongue. I could drink from her morning, noon, and night and still be thirsty for more, but she reaches for me. "Fuck me," she pleads, her eyes begging. "I need you."

"Yes ma'am," I say, teasing as I move up her body, lining my cock up with her entrance. I push slowly, giving her just the tip to let her feel me before I enter her, coating myself with her honey as I rub my thumb over her clit.

"*Yes*," Charlotte purrs. She tilts her hips, and I dip in deeper, feeling her tight walls fight the intrusion.

Our eyes lock, and I watch her every movement for any signs of pain or discomfort as I thrust in inch by inch, pausing to pull back and slip in again. With each stroke, I open her a little more, stretching her. "That's it, take me. Relax and let me in, Char."

She nods, biting her lip. "Feels . . . like . . . you're splitting me in half," she gasps out. But when I try to retreat so I don't hurt her, she locks her feet behind my back, keeping me in place. "More."

Carefully, I start thrusting faster, letting my thick girth fill her. I can't believe how tight she is, but maybe it's been that long for her or maybe she hasn't had someone my size before. Whatever the reason, it's enough to drive us both to the brink faster than I'd imagined.

Her breasts bounce as I start to pound harder, careful not to bottom out but still plunging deep into her pussy and deeper into her soul. Suddenly, she opens up, and I slide all the way in, our hips clapping together. We both freeze as she cries out, but the sharp gasp turns into a moan of delight. "Oh, my . . . fuck!"

I grin, kissing her hard and staying in place. "Good girl, Charlotte. You ready now?"

Her answering smile is pure joy with a hint of challenge as she unlocks her legs and grabs my ass, a cheek in each hand as she guides me. I let her lead for a moment, but she quickly becomes overwhelmed, letting me take over the pace. "Fuck, you feel good. That tight pussy squeezing my cock. I'm already ready to blow. I need you to come with me."

She cries out, bucking and fucking me back as we chase our orgasms with the same intensity we're chasing our futures, not giving a single thought to anyone or anything else. It's us, together in this moment, needing only each other.

My balls slap against her ass, and in the back of my mind, I can hear something telling me that this is my future, right here, buried in the heaven of her slick pussy. She cries out, and I lean over her, pressing our bodies against each other, wanting every point of contact I can get.

Her body contracts, curving beneath me, and she calls out my name before burying her tiny teeth in the muscle of my shoulder to silence herself. The sharp bite of pain sends me over, and I bellow, exploding to fill her with shot after heated shot of my sticky cream, claiming her deeply.

When the waves pass over us both, I hold her in my arms, staying inside her as she flops to the bed beneath me, spent and exhausted. Eventually, we both open our eyes, matching smiles on our faces. "You've got a mark on your shoulder," she says apologetically.

I shrug, not minding it. I could wear her mark happily. "You'll probably be walking funny tomorrow."

She wiggles a bit, and I can feel my cum leaking out around my cock, covering us both in the creamy mess. "I think I'm good."

I raise a brow, smiling a little. "Is that a challenge?"

She grins, clenching herself around me. "Didn't mean it to be, but feels like certain parts certainly took it as such."

I flex, pulsing my hardening cock inside her again, ready for round two.

Hell, we've already broken plenty of expectations today between both our blow-ups with our families. The least I can do is burst through every single one of her expectations about being with me and surpass each and every one, tonight, tomorrow, and for however long I can keep her here before she needs to disappear back downstairs for her early morning call to work.

I roll her over, seating her on top of me. "Ride me, Red."

# CHAPTER 14

## Blackwell

"Are you sure, sir?" my driver asks, holding the keys out to me despite his concerns. He's more than just a driver, of course, highly trained in many useful arts, although he spends the bulk of his days making my armored Cadillac Escalade perform like a vehicle one-third its size.

But tonight's work needs to be done . . . alone. It's a turning point, for me and for Roseboro. The game has been changing slowly, amping up in increments. But tonight begins the final moves. The plans that will ensure that my mark is indelible.

"Quite sure," I reply, removing my tie. In addition to leaving no witnesses, I will be sure to leave no trace evidence either. Not that anything pointing toward me would be a problem, not in a city where I own the police. "I assume it handles as a normal vehicle?"

The driver dips his chin once, acquiescing to my demands. "Yes, sir. It requires more time for braking and slowing down for sharp turns, but that's mostly due to its center of gravity, not the security modifications you require."

I get in, tossing my tie and jacket into the passenger seat before pulling out of the deserted lot. Despite my driver's warnings, the Cadillac handles like a fond memory of my youth, when cars were truly land ships and a Cadillac was the king of the asphalt seas.

Things have changed since then, some for the better and some perhaps not. But my reign at the top of the food chain is one of the best progressions from my younger days.

Approaching the house, I scan the road around me. Everything is quiet, all of suburbia sleeping soundly in their beds, not knowing that hell has come for them.

No, not them all. But one in particular.

I've let him live, thinking he might be useful in the future, and though he's kept his mouth shut as instructed after failing his previous mission as an insider at Goldstone, he's fallen too far into a black hole to be worth anything to me. Now, instead of a resource, he's a loose end.

I slip leather gloves on, smooth and soft as butter, as I get out and close the SUV door quietly. Two knocks at the door have shuffled movement sounding from inside the house.

"Patricia?" he slurs out in the false, desperate hope of a truly broken man. The door opens a heartbeat later, and the light in his eyes goes out when he sees me on his doorstep.

He knows why I'm here. I know why I'm here. But still, he tries to dance away.

"Mr. Blackwell, nice to see you." He lies horribly, the only truth the cheap whiskey on his breath.

I don't wait for an invitation, stepping inside and closing the door behind me. The house is a mess, a bachelor pad of the worst kind, and I suspect, based on the rank smell in the air, that the garbage hasn't been taken out in days.

"Is there anything you'd like to tell me?" I ask the open-ended question, interested in what he'll spill as his last words. Mere gibberish, or something useful, perhaps?

He shakes his head, his eyes losing focus at the fierce movement, but it must rattle a memory loose because he changes, nodding just as hard. "Yeah, yeah. There was a guy, a guy at work."

He stumbles, his steps deeper into the house, and I follow, maintaining my distance. Tonight's work will not be up close and personal. "A guy at work?"

Since his trial, a showcase that resulted in some pre-trial detention as a warning and a quick plea deal that resulted in a supremely generous probation, he's been working a blue-collar job, laying tar on roofs. I did it as an exercise to him, not only of the breadth of my reach but as a way to keep an eye on him when I thought he could be useful. Even his job was useful. He's tarred a few of my roofs recently.

A significant downgrade from his previous office life, but since he failed so spectacularly at that, the menial labor seems an appropriate prolonging of his punishment.

"At work, a temp guy chatted me up. Nothing too weird, just asking how I ended up pulling roof duty. Which wouldn't have been a big deal, but he knew my name. Most guys who know who I am, they stay far away, telling me rats get bats." He falls to the couch, unable to stand any longer with the alcohol in his blood, but he manages to mimic swinging a bat, as if to take off someone's head.

My lips quirk at the saying I haven't heard before, finding it amusing in its promise of violence. But the man seems lost in self-pity, as if his lack of friends at work is a sadness I could possibly empathize with.

"This man, what did he look like?" I say, feigning interest in his story. There is only one tidbit of information I truly want, whether he spilled anything incriminating.

He blinks, like he's trying to remember through the boozy haze of his wasted mind. "Big guy, dark hair, young . . . maybe thirty?"

"And you told him what, precisely?" My patience is wearing thin. It's time to get to the crux of the situation.

His eyes widen as he hears the warning in my voice. "Nothing, I swear it, Mr. Blackwell. Just told him that life takes you on bad trips sometimes, that I'd lost my job, my wife, my daughter in one fell swoop when I went on trial, but I was working my way back. That's it, that's all I said."

I give him a slight nod, like he's a good dog. "I believe you," I say, and he sags in relief, a feeling that doesn't last. "It's too bad you won't succeed."

Tension shoots through his body, the smell of fear scenting the air as he looks around the room, searching for a way out. But there is none, only one last choice to make.

I sit on the coffee table in front of him, pulling a gun from my waistband with my right hand and a rope from my back pocket with my left. I hold them out, like a magician who just did an amazing trick and expects applause. Ta-da.

The man offers no applause, only a slight widening of his eyes in horror as he sees the items.

"You have a choice to make. Option one, I will shoot you in the heart. You will die, but be certain that no investigation as to your murder will take place." I pause, letting him remember that I have significant sway over the police and everyone in this town.

He gulps, looking to the rope.

"Option two, you can hang yourself. Choose option two, and I'll make sure your wife gets a nice payday. It's doubtful your family will mourn you either way."

My every word is ice-cold, no sway either way. This is a game to me, one with a deadly result no matter his choice, but I find entertainment in the mental gymnastics he goes through, first looking for a way out and finding none, deciding which fate is the lesser of two evils.

I can feel my own heartbeat racing with excitement, anticipation of seeing the light leave his eyes. I'm not an innocent by any means, but I do not have the amount of blood on my hands as say, Gabriel Jackson. Witnessing the moment where life truly ends is like a fine wine, something to be cherished as the gift it is. I look forward to savoring it tonight.

His hands twitch, and I turn my right hand, pointing the gun at him. "Ah, so you have chosen."

Tears stream down his face as he nods. "If I choose the rope, can I write a note? I just . . . I want to say goodbye to them."

It's almost moving, his single final desire. I don't need to ask who 'them' is, his estranged wife and daughter. Not that I'm moved.

And the experiment continues as I agree, interested beyond measure at what his last words to his family will be. He's brought this upon himself, upon them, when he betrayed Goldstone in favor of me. He knew the devil he bargained with. I never hid it from him.

He reaches for the pen and pile of papers on the coffee table. They are, ironically, legal papers. It seems that Patricia, instead of wanting to come back to him in an attempt to rekindle their failed marriage, has served him with papers. Divorce.

How appropriate, then, that his final message to his family is written on them. His hand shakes, the writing nearly illegible except for its simplicity.

*I'm sorry. I love you.*

He pauses, like there's more to say or as if he wants to postpone the inevitable, but finally, his head falls, his elbows resting on his knees, and the cheap Bic falls to the dirty carpet.

Sobs rack his body, but he stands, his eyes meeting mine. Sad resignation shines from their depths, but also relief. He's thought of this himself, a way out from the catastrophe he created. Oh, I helped, guiding him and feeding his hatred, but the first step was his. The last will be his as well.

He takes the rope, already tied, and slips it over his neck, ironically similar to the silk ties he used to wear so often.

Stepping to a chair, he loops the rope through the unique little cutouts in the walk-through arch between his living room and the kitchen. Looking at me one last time, he pleads.

"Take care of my family as you promised. Please."

I nod, wondering if he'll have the guts to actually do it the way it needs to be done for this. "I am a man of my word. The payment will be made as soon as the coroner deems your death a suicide."

I lick my lips, ready for the show and to move on with my plans.

His lips move, as if he's praying, and time stretches. He goes to step off the chair, but as the rope tightens, he chickens out, standing up again. He looks back over his shoulder, tears trickling again. "I can't. Help me."

I sigh, disappointed. Maybe he was strong . . . once. But not anymore, so I kick his feet out from underneath him. His weight jerks down, tightening the noose savagely.

He flails, jerking, and his hands go up to his neck reflexively, and I watch, fascinated. All he needs to do is pull his feet underneath him and step back to the chair. It's right there. But alcohol, panic, and the quickly diminishing oxygen in his brain have robbed him of any rational thoughts.

It's riveting. I can't look away, not that I would. I feel God-like and want to remember every moment as his life drains out, filling me with exaltation and renewed vigor.

When it's over, I shudder, euphoric at my dominance and ability to make a man perform such a feat. He was useful for a while, but in his death, his true disposability is what is most remarkable.

I do a thorough scan to insure there is no trace of my presence left behind. Though I was careful the entire time, it wouldn't do to leave accidental evidence. Not when I've gone through so much to set the scene.

Back in the car, I can't stop the smile that sweeps over my face. It feels foreign, an odd stretching of my lips and cheeks as I enjoy the pleasure of a mission accomplished. I will send his wife a payment, true to my word, through a shell company, of course.

But this was merely a cleaning up of one loose end.

I have so many agents in motion, so many plans in play, that Goldstone will never see what's coming next. Rough laughter rings through the SUV, my belly shaking with diabolical mirth at how I will bring the Golden Boy to his knees, fell his empire, and shake the very foundation of Roseboro. They will all remember me, the man who built this city, who will always rule even long after I've turned to ashes.

Roseboro is *my* legacy.

# CHAPTER 15

## Charlotte

I T'S AMAZING HOW THINGS CAN RETURN TO SOME SURREAL SENSE OF normalcy after such an earth-shaking event.

The morning after we fell into bed, Lance and I went downstairs together to start the morning baking and found Trixie already hard at work in the kitchen. Well, she'd been taking selfies in the kitchen, but she'd had the ovens pre-heated, at least, with a mixer of cupcake base mixing on the stand.

I couldn't even give her any shit for a photo break either when she'd been so shocked at seeing Lance and me obviously post-hookup that her screech had brought the security guards running.

But after some teasing questions that I dodged as much as possible, we got to work in the kitchen, the guards went back outside with apology muffins, and Lance sat down at his table in the front.

And that's been our normal for three days. Bakery work for me and Trixie, laptop work for Lance, cleanup, and then back upstairs for some cupcake fun that has zero to do with flour and sugar.

But our phones have been blowing up, both our families texting us and calling like mad.

Lance got pretty lucky. His parents were aghast at his lack of manners but basically agreed to disagree on what would make him happy. It seems their desire to have him home and coming into the fold at Jacobs Bio-Tech is the main priority. His mom had just thought that a good woman would be another way to keep him here. But as long as he's giving daily reports on his assessments of that day's spreadsheets and making headway on analyzing current and proposed projects, they're mostly copacetic, or so he says.

I know Lance is worried about his brother. Not that Cody gives a shit about us or whatever we're doing here, but Lance shared that he thinks Cody isn't getting the recognition he deserves at work and that it's driving a huge-ass wedge in the whole family.

My family, on the other hand? Basically, I started World War III, with me on one side, Priscilla and Sabrina on the other, and Dad staying as neutral as Switzerland.

According to Priscilla, I've always been selfish but now my need to be the center of attention is physically harming Sabrina, who has taken to her bed in a state of depression over my betrayal of our sisterhood. It was hard keeping my eyes from rolling with that one. Sabrina and I are about as far from sisterly as we can be.

Sabrina's texts started out angry, blaming me for everything from her lost Barbie when she was ten to resigning her to a life of spinsterhood, but they've gotten more desperate, basically pleading with me to let her have Lance. I want to explain to her that her whole issue is treating Lance like some sort of toy when he's a man. He's not like her Barbie . . . which I will secretly admit I stole.

But I can't really hide Lance in the flowerbed like a Princess Diana Barbie, although the thought of getting a little dirty with him sounds like fun. I bet he'd look great with a few streaks of mud on his washboard abs to highlight just how deep those ridges are.

"Ooh, do tell what naughty thoughts are running through your head," Trixie teases, breaking me out of my thoughts. She would catch me the second they turn dirty, not in the previous thirty minutes I've been on auto-pilot thinking about how to make things up with Dad. I could care less about Priscilla and Sabrina, but I want him to understand.

"My family drama and trauma," I reply, and she winces like she sucked on a lemon. I did tell her that dinner was awful, and she's seen some of the texts coming in, calling me a bitch and worse. She's put two and two together.

"Ugh, leave their drama to your stepmama. I know the dreamy look and red cheeks didn't have a thing to do with that. I want to hear the sexy thoughts about Lance, or the dirty details from last night, if you're feeling generous." She clasps her hands beneath her chin, eyelashes blinking heavily.

"I told you that what happens between Lance and me stays between us," I remind her for the billionth time. She's been hounding me like crazy for anything I'll spill, which isn't much. It feels too personal and private, and honestly, as close as Trixie and I are, this feels beyond big, and the only people I'll share that type of thing with are Mia and Izzy.

"Come on, Char," she pleads with an exaggeratedly fake pout. "It's not like I can't tell that you're walking like you rode in the Kentucky Derby last night. How many times did you ride that stallion . . . two? Three? Did you even get any sleep at all? I'm living vicariously through you. Help me out or I'll be forced to imagine him licking icing off every inch of your skin, you sucking that Twinkie dry, and sweat glazing every bit of his skin." She looks over at Lance, who's typing away as per usual, and my eyes follow hers, hungry to look at him every chance I get. "He's hung like an eggplant, right? And a six-pack better than Miller Light too?"

I shake my head, even though she's right. "Is everything about food to you?"

"Food porn is a thing," she deadpans. "Have you seen that video where they make chicken cordon bleu? They butterfly the chicken breast so that it totally looks like a spread-open vajeen, stuff it full of ham, then pour white, creamy béchamel sauce over it. I damn near had an orgasm just from the chef slicing into all that creamy, meaty goodness. I couldn't decide if I was hungry or horny."

She pauses like she's thinking, but we finish her sentence together. "Both."

We giggle loud enough that Steven and Lance both look our way. Lance gives me an *I know what you're laughing about* wink and his cocky smirk promises to fulfill whatever dirty ideas Trixie and I are discussing.

I turn back to Trixie, calming down a little. "Everything's great there. But I'm just worried about my Dad. I just know that whatever Priscilla and Sabrina can't unleash on me, they're probably doing to him. He doesn't deserve being stuck like that."

Trixie places her hand on my shoulder. "He's not stuck, honey. He's choosing to be there. I know that hurts and sucks eggs, but it's the truth. Has he called or texted?"

I nod, biting my lip. "He did." I pull my phone out of my apron pocket, pulling up the text Dad sent the afternoon after Lance and I stomped out of dinner, and show it to Trixie.

*It seems your focus was not as you'd led me to believe. I do hope that you can be successful, both with the bakery and Lance.*

It almost sounds like a dismissal or a goodbye, which slices into my heart deeply. My apologetic response has gone unanswered so I'm not sure whether he's angry and giving us both some time to cool off or if he's written me off completely.

Trixie coughs. "Damn, that's . . . hard. Sorry, babe."

"I know. Can you, uhm . . . I need a minute," I blurt, making a dive for the kitchen and praying Trixie can handle things up front for a second.

God, everything is such a mess. Not with my pristine baking space, but with my life outside these walls. Here, I'm safe and I know what I'm doing, the recipe for success so easy to follow. Add ingredients, mix, bake, and voila . . . happiness in every delicious bite. But out there, in the rest of the world, I'm falling flat.

I've got a business I'm only just beginning that requires all the time a newborn baby does. A family who's angry at me. Friends who are in danger from a madman. Hell, it's possible that I could be in danger, a real enough risk to warrant guards.

The oven dings, and I pull out a tray of cupcakes, ironically dubbed 'Sinful Secrets' because of their decadently dark chocolate cake that surrounds a rich pocket of chocolate-flavored liqueur. The frosting is an ooey-gooey ganache.

Sinful Secrets.

As of late, it seems like I have more than my fair share. I've been hiding Lance from my family, hiding the reasons I need security from everyone, and hiding the fabulous details of Lance's lovemaking from my friends. That one can probably stay hidden, but the rest, I need to come clean about. As much as I can.

I take the tray of cupcakes out to the front, their presence mocking me every step of the way. "Hey, Trixie. Do you think you can handle closing duties tonight? I need to"—I look over at Lance, who is staring at me intently—"deal with some things."

Trixie doesn't tease like I expect her to, reading that I'm not taking Lance upstairs for more fun and games. "Go ahead, I've got this. Steven will hang out with me, right?" she flirts over at the quiet man by the door.

He lifts his chin in agreement, and Lance is already at my side, his laptop stowed away in his bag.

"What's wrong?" he asks, his eyes worried.

I shake my head, taking him by the arm. "Nothing, not really. I just need to check out for a bit. Can you stay?"

His smile warms the cold pit in my stomach and his voice is quietly reassuring. "Char, I'm not going anywhere."

Upstairs, I move into the kitchen to make spaghetti for dinner. It's one of the first things Grandma Winnie taught me to make as a little girl. It was fun because she would let me literally throw the cooked pasta against the wall to check for doneness, though I'm not sure that really works. But it was fun and I love the memory of us both flinging pasta and giggling when it would fall to the floor.

Lance sits at the counter, watching me move around the small space. "What's up?"

"The fallout's just gotten to me a bit. Trixie asked about my dad." His brows lift in question because he already knows what my dad's text said. "He hasn't responded."

"I'm sorry. I know you're close to him or want to be close to him. But I still wouldn't change what happened at dinner. They were talking about us like chess pieces to be used, but I'm not a player in anyone's game but my own. And you are so much better than anything that was being said about you that night. I just couldn't stand by any longer."

It's basically a repeat of the same conversation we'd had the morning after and several times since then. We've shared a lot about our families in the aftermath of that night, from his desire to make his own way in the world to my feeling like I didn't have a place in my own family. In a twisted way, both of us have made life choices for the same reason, in an attempt to make our fathers proud of us but also not to live under their thumbs.

"I know. I wouldn't change it either," I say softly.

Lance swears under his breath and starts pacing around the living room and fluffing the pillows on the overstuffed couch. He's a neat freak from his time in the military and can't help but set things right when he sees them out of place, even if they're barely mussed.

It's cute and lets me know that he's anxious too.

He strides to the window, peeking through the blinds. "What about them?" he says. I don't have to look myself to know what he's talking about. The bakery closes in thirty minutes so the overnight guard is likely getting into place and getting an update from Steven. "I thought you had guards because of your family. It's not unusual in a certain tax bracket, but your dad doesn't quite seem the type to pay for round-the-clock skilled coverage for you. No offense."

I stir the pasta, coating the strands with the sauce I jarred myself. He doesn't know it, but what he's asking is a test, a barometer of how deep I'm in with him.

The cynical side of me, the one that wants to focus on the bakery and not on another relationship that will likely burst into flames like every one before it, says to dodge and redirect.

The tiniest seed of hope in my center, the one that still hopes Dad will come around, wants to confide in Lance, wants him to know and accept the craziness my life truly is.

He's taken my resolution to focus on the bakery in stride, backing off when I needed to work but being right there, ready to catch me when I couldn't help but fall for him.

He's handled the outrageous behavior of my family, and his own, in a way I'd only dreamed of doing, my knight in camo armor who threw down the gauntlet when I was ready to retreat. Lance won't let me hide behind that reflex. He wants me to shine like a diamond.

But can I tell him this? It's not only my secret. That's the biggest risk of all. Not that I'm putting my life into his hands, but my friends' as well.

I take a steadying breath, praying to the gods of pasta as I sprinkle parmesan on top of the spaghetti that this is the right thing to do. "Thomas pays for them, the security."

Lance lets go of the blinds, looking back at me. "Your best friend's soon-to-be husband pays for you to have that type of security? Why?"

He's already standing taller, recognizing that if this isn't some familial show of wealth through guards, there must be an actual threat being monitored.

I set the plates on the table. "Sit down and I'll explain."

He does, his eyes steady as he looks into my soul. "Tell me what's going on, Charlotte. I'm here, and I'm not going anywhere."

As we eat, I tell him everything. About Mia finding a saboteur implanted in Thomas's company and how they sent him to prison. About Izzy helping catch the spy, which resulted in a hitman contract on her head. But Izzy being Izzy, she made the hitman fall in love with her instead.

"You know Gabe? Who sits with Steven sometimes?" I say, trying to help him place everyone in the huge web of a story I'm weaving.

"The scary dark-haired guy?" Lance says, thinking.

"Well, he is scary, really scary, in fact, but usually people think he's more boy-next-door charming," I say with a shrug.

Lance leans close. "I'm a soldier, Char. I can see the wolf in sheep's clothing. That guy might have a panty-melting grin, but he's stone-cold."

I wipe at my mouth. "Never melted my panties, that's for sure."

"Good. So does Thomas think you're the next target?" Lance asks, his mind making the important jump.

He looks ready to go to battle for me, and I can't explain, even to myself, how secure that makes me feel. I've never been one to depend on a guy, but something tells me Lance is someone I can count on.

"It's precautionary," I explain. "We just don't know what Blackwell is going to do, but now that we know he's got some big grudge against Thomas and went as far as going after Izzy, Thomas wanted me to be safe. And the bakery, too, since he's a silent investor. Mia's got guards, Thomas has guards, Izzy has Gabe, Gabe has himself, and five days a week, I've got Steven and Larry and Curly."

Lance laughs at my list, lifting an eyebrow. "Larry and Curly?"

For the first time in a long hour, I laugh too. "That's what Trixie calls them. She used to call Steven 'Moe' but that ended about the time she started thinking he was hotter than a fresh-baked apple pie."

"I feel sorry for him," Lance says after a moment. "I don't think he'd know what to do with her in full-on Trixie mode."

"I don't know . . . he might be good for her. The calm waters to her craziness."

Lance nods, and I can see the thoughts swirling in his head. Have I given him too much?

# CHAPTER 16

## Lance

I feel like Charlotte just dumped a lot on my plate, and I'm not talking about the spaghetti we've barely picked at. It's delicious—everything she makes is—but the information is too heavy to leave room for anything else.

Charlotte lifts her glass, taking a long sip of the iced tea she poured for us before she began her tale. "What do you think?" she asks, like she's already sure I'm about to bolt for the door.

I say nothing at first, just processing the twists and turns her explanation took. It's definitely far beyond what I'd expected when I asked about the security guards.

My fists clench in anger that someone would want to hurt her or her friends.

No, her family. More than the people who share her name, these people are her family.

"Sometimes, the people we choose are more important than the ones chosen for us," I say, and her brows knit together in confusion. I'm not sure where I'm going with this, but I try to tease out the words from the knot in my stomach. "Your family, your Dad, let you down by not being there for you. So you went out and made your own family with Mia and Izzy."

I look around the room, pointing at the framed pictures Charlotte has, all of them containing her with her two friends. "The family you chose is growing with Thomas and Gabe. And you're a fierce believer in family, Charlotte, with expectations of what that word truly means. Your own family might not have lived up to that, but you damn sure will yourself. I think you're doing exactly what a family does, circling the wagons, watching each other's backs, and preparing for war."

Tears glisten in her eyes, and she sniffles. "Thank you. I never tried to explain it before, but that's perfect. I just don't know why you'd want to get involved with me when I'm literally in the middle of this mess."

"Because I chose a family once too, and now I'm choosing another." I reach over, taking her hand, and her soft smile eggs me on. "When I left, I was young and thought I knew everything. I mostly needed to get away, not because my family was awful but because they thought they knew me when I didn't even know myself. I had to pass through the crucible of the Navy to find out what is really important, though."

Flashes flick through my mind like an old-school movie projector. Men and women I got to know almost as well as myself, each of us searching for something. A purpose, a meaning, a mission.

Charlotte touches my hand. "I've seen videos. Tough isn't a strong enough word to describe it."

I shrug. Even those who make it through have their moment in the dark. Mine just happened to actually be at night.

*The sound of the bell rings out in the middle of the night. It's the third day of Hell Week and it's too dark to see who's next to you, so I don't know who just gave up. All I know is . . . it's not me.*

*I want to, though. Whether it's the surf breaking, or the swims, or everything else they've thrown at me, I've taken it.*

*But this . . . this is so much. I huddle with my boat crew, our wet bodies pressed together in a futile attempt to stay warm and fight off the hypothermia, but all I can think is . . . whose bell was that?*

*"Focus," my closest buddy named Wisenbury says to our boat crew. "Stay steady, one evolution at a time. Right now, our only goal is staying alive till sunrise. Anything after that, we'll worry about then. Don't quit, don't ring the bell."*

*He's right, and I find the strength to shiver a little more.*

*Don't quit.*

"You're right," I admit, coming back to the present. "It was harder than tough, but there isn't really a word for it. I learned about who I am, and that was enough. I was happy. At first."

"At first?" Charlotte asks, and I nod. "What happened?"

"Reality happened," I explain simply. "During training, it's all artificial to some degree. I mean, they're never going to intentionally let someone die. Their goal is to push your boundaries further than you think you can go to show you what you're capable of. And that's dangerous, but there's always this sort of safety net that you knew was there. No one on that beach with you actually wanted to kill you."

Charlotte's eyes meet mine, horrible realization dawning. "But on missions, they really did want to kill you."

"The first time I truly felt how real it was, I busted through a door," I reply softly.

"The door went, and a bullet cracked off the frame six inches from my head. I turned to see the gunman, and I . . . shot. Just like I'd been trained to do. In my head, I was glad I was alive, but at the same time, I realized that the gunman who tried to kill me couldn't have been a day over sixteen. Not even a man himself."

The pause stretches out as I get lost in the memories, but Charlotte lets me be, not pressuring me to continue unless I want to. When I look up, she's chewing a bit of spaghetti slowly.

"I shot a kid. Yeah, he had an AK, and all that *him or me* justification can run through my head on a loop, but . . . it stayed with me a long time. I've seen and done some awful things in the name of my country. It's left . . . scars." I swallow thickly, forcing down the memories that threaten to overwhelm me.

"We all have them," Charlotte says. "You've seen every inch of me and know that my greatest damage isn't visible to the naked eye. It's here," she says, touching her heart, "and here." She touches her temple.

I know exactly what she means. I do have some physical scars, lines where cuts didn't heal cleanly, nicks from the occasional piece of barbed wire, and even a gnarly one on the back of my left hamstring from an IED.

Luckily, I wasn't any closer than I was, and even luckier, it hasn't impeded me in any way. But the deepest, angriest red scars are internal, the ones that pull and pucker, turning me into the man I am now, no longer the ready-to-tackle-the-world dumbass I'd been but something sharper, more careful, more intention-filled.

"I don't think I can go back," I whisper, looking down at my hands. I'm used to seeing them chipped, a line of black under the nails, ragged tears along the cuticles, but now they're clean, trimmed, and soft. The confession pains me. It's something I hadn't fully given form to in my mind, but now that I'm home, it's not only my parents' desire for me to stay that's keeping me here. It's not only the sexy, sweet redhead in front of me either.

It's me. When I was in the thick of things, training day in and day out, with missions sweeping me around the globe at the drop of a dime, I could stay in character. But now, it's like those sharp edges have washed away. I'm still hard, but I've lost the drive. I don't have anything to prove to anyone by trying to be a wetsuit cowboy out to save the world. Maybe I can stay right here and save Charlotte's world, and that can be enough.

"Then don't. Stay here," Charlotte says just as softly. Neither of us says that I could stay for us, but we're both thinking it. I know I'm choosing to focus on her, the curve of her smile from across the table, the flipped-up red hair at the end of her braid, and the way she makes me feel like I'm enough just the way I am.

"I want to stay here with you. See where this goes. I'm not going anywhere, Char." It's a declaration, not of love, not yet, but of intention, that she's not scaring me off with her busy life, her crazy family, or her baggage. I hope she feels the same way about me.

She reverts to humor, awkwardly telling me, "Well, you're not moving in, if that's what you're after. I'm not really the married, two-point-five kids kinda gal."

I let it fall flat, not letting her escape the deeper truths we've been exposing. "Do you really believe you'll never find that?" I ask with a cocked eyebrow, probing the wound, not to inflict pain but so I can heal it appropriately.

Her shrug is answer enough, her doubt and cynicism revealed in its power. "Guys say they want the whole fairy tale and get you to believe you want the same things, but when push comes to shove, it's all a pretty lie. A carrot on a string to tease you along."

I get up, pulling her to the couch to sit beside me. I leave the dishes on the table for later, though it pains my habitual tendencies, but this is more important. I wrap an arm around her shoulders, and she lays her cheek on my chest as she curls her legs beneath her. "Tell me who hurt you, Char. Tell me everything."

She doesn't speak for a long time, but the words come.

"Daniel. He was my college sweetheart. We met soon after I started college and were joined at the hip almost from day one. We had all the wedding plans for after graduation, but he wanted to save up for a ring. We had an apartment together, and we both got jobs at Blackwell. It was perfect."

A tear lands wet and hot on my shirt, her pain hurting me more than a knife would. "Until he started spending late nights with his boss—his older, beautiful female boss. They were doing more than working, obviously."

"Bastard," I whisper, and Charlotte nods, probably thinking quite a few other names for him.

"After that, I tried online dating, mostly. Met a few frogs, but I was doing okay. Until I met Ryan. He was a little older than me and divorced. He said he wanted the whole fairy tale, and I bought it hook, line, and sinker. Right up until his wife walked in on us in bed, their baby girl on her hip. They weren't divorced after all. I'd been the other woman and hadn't even known it."

She closes her eyes, like she's waiting for my judgement, my sneered blame that she wrecked that guy's happy home. But that's not true at all. She was an innocent victim of both those guys, of her Dad's crappy choices, of Blackwell's plotting. Like a precious stone, she's been sliced away, shaped and filed into the woman she is now, with jagged edges and flaws deep inside.

But beautiful, not despite that but because of it.

She won't take her fairy tale for granted when she gets it. She'll grab it with both hands and never let go, thanking the heavens every day for it. But not until she believes she deserves it, until she trusts her prince won't go anywhere.

I tilt her chin up with the soft touch of my fingers and look into her eyes. "I don't like carrots, Charlotte. Dangling or otherwise. And I don't believe in pretty lies, but I do believe in happily ever afters."

I lean in and kiss her, letting her taste the truth, hoping she can feel the honesty in my soul.

Forgetting the plates still on the table, I scoop her up and carry her in my arms. In her bedroom, I set her down before slowly, methodically un-dressing her and then myself. Carefully, I unplait her hair, letting it fall wild and free around her shoulders.

Charlotte looks up at me through her lashes, more vulnerable than she's ever been. Not because she's nude, but because we're both naked, having re-vealed more of ourselves tonight than I think we have in a long time. Maybe ever.

Pulling the blankets back, I tell her, "Climb in." She does as I say, lying on her back like she's ready for me to cover her with my body. I want that too, but not the way she thinks.

As much as I love being inside her physically, right now, we're so emotionally inside each other that I need to just hold her. I lie down beside her, rearranging her so that she's curled up, the little spoon to my big spoon. I pet her hair, twirling the ends around my finger. "Get some sleep. I'll be right here."

I think she's going to argue, her sass coming out when I least expect it, but tonight, she gives in, sighing as she settles. Within moments, she's fast asleep, worn out not only from her baker's hours but from the energy it took to give so much to me at once.

It's a long time before I fall asleep too, cocooning Charlotte in my arms, keeping her safe from any threats, inside or out.

# CHAPTER 17

## Charlotte

I DON'T REMEMBER FALLING ASLEEP. WE WERE SNUGGLED UP AND MY mind was racing, fears and worries washing over me, drowning me. But Lance was holding me close, giving me time, giving me space, giving me oxygen to be okay.

But I must have fallen asleep because I'm waking up, still surrounded by his arms, his warmth permeating me where our skin touches.

He touches me everywhere, not just where my back is pressed to his chest or where my ass cradles his cock, and not only where even our feet are tangle together. He touches me inside my soul.

It's terrifying, it's exhilarating, it's everything I've always wanted but been too afraid to wish for. The little seed of hope is the scariest thing I've ever felt, because I've felt it before and had it ripped away, ugly strands of my innocence left in its wake.

I need to stop this or slow this down. Put us back where we were somehow, before I slice myself open and give him my heart. Because he's going to leave. It's what men do. They lure me in, make me think I can have it all, be it all, do it all, and then they leave. I'm left to pick up the pieces of my shattered soul, again and again, ever since I was a little girl.

I can't do it again. I can already feel that if Lance leaves, the shattering will be epic, a disaster I don't know if I can recover from.

*Reset. I need a reset.*

I must move, or somehow twitch, because Lance pulls me in closer, his arms caging me against him. As he rearranges, his hips press forward, drawing my mind and focus to where we are only inches apart.

That's what I need to pull us back to before, thrashing and pounding and exuberant in the physicality of fucking. No drama, no baggage, no gamble that he might destroy me.

I wiggle again, this time purposefully, grinding my ass back to tease him. Slowly, Lance wakes up, a moan already on his lips. "Good morning to you too," he says, gravel in his tone.

"I need you. I need to feel . . . everything . . . nothing," I say, likely revealing too much.

Lance's hand grips my hip, stilling me, but he thrusts against me, his cock sliding through my ass cheeks. "I've got you."

He slips an arm underneath me, holding my chest in place. He kicks the blanket off, his other hand pulling my thigh up and back over his, opening me to the cool air of the room. It feels cleansing, purifying, vulnerable to be held in place, though the physical exposure is so much less than the emotional.

His cock nudges at my entrance like he's testing my wetness, but I'm drenched for him, needing this. "Please . . ." I beg, my head falling back to his shoulder. "Hard."

He nuzzles my neck, inhaling me, and I grip his hair, holding him to me too. With a fierce thrust, he enters me to the hilt, impaling me on his cock. I jerk at the intrusion, the feeling a perfect blend of pleasure and pain, much like Lance's presence in my life, but when he starts to stroke into me, pleasure takes over.

He's rough in the dark, both of us only going by feel, the sound of slapping skin filling the room. I can't hold back the moans, the symphony pouring from my mouth as he plays my body like an instrument he already knows too well.

His hand moves from my thigh to my clit, teasing it in slow circles, soft in comparison with the hard way he's fucking me. "I know what you're doing, Charlotte. But don't be scared. I can handle your demons. Can you handle mine?"

I don't answer, afraid the answer is no . . . more afraid the answer is yes. He smacks at my pussy, a sharp sting that puts me on the edge, crying out as I teeter, ready to fall into my orgasm. Ready to fall into him.

He pops me once more, punishing my lack of faith, my unwillingness to jump, and I spasm. I can't hold back the tidal wave washing over and through me any longer. "Yes. Yes . . . yes!" I cry. We both know I'm not simply calling out my pleasure but answering his question.

I tried to fight, tried to deny, tried to protect myself. But it didn't work. In one orgasm, he's decimated my defenses and we both know it. I may never get a happily ever after, if such a thing truly exists. But I'm fully on this ride with Lance until it goes off the tracks, which I know it inevitably will.

But I'll take as much of him as I can get. Soak it up to get me through the days after he's gone because even if he doesn't go back to the SEALs, he'll leave me eventually. They always do.

For now, though, I feel him bucking deep into me, bottoming out like he can imprint himself on my most private of places and make me believe. As he comes, his hot cum splashing inside me, I almost do.

Afterward, Lance stays inside me, his long fingers tracing along my skin like he's leap-frogging from one freckle to the next in the dark. It feels right, like we could stay here like this forever, no ghosts of the past, no shimmery future, this moment enough to live in.

But sleep overtakes us, and once again, I relax into him and let the dreams wash me under.

My alarm is an annoying chirp that's loud enough to wake the dead. It has to be to rouse me from the peace of the early morning hours to begin baking, but this morning, it's even worse. I feel like I've been running all night, mind churning from dream to nightmare and back again.

Lance reaches over, swatting at the alarm, and blessed silence returns. But he doesn't let me fall back asleep. He kicks the covers off us, the shocking cold making me cry out. My eyes only open to slits, but I look back and see him smiling. He's one of those chipper morning people, which usually I don't mind since he makes coffee first thing, but this morning, I could really use a few more minutes of shut eye.

I relax back into the soft mattress, mumbling, "Five minutes." Or at least I think I say that.

Lance is having none of that. He spanks my bare ass, the pop loud but not as loud as my cry of surprise. "What the hell?" Yeah, as much of a morning person as he may be, I'm most definitely not.

"Rise and shine, porcupine. We've got work to do, muffins to muff, cupcakes to cup, and pies to . . . pie? I don't know. I was on a roll, so work with me," he says, laughing.

It doesn't feel weird or heavy. In fact, it's like he's doing his best to make things between us seem just the way they were before, but I can see the darkness in his blue eyes, the way he's watching me carefully, even though I've only got one eye fully opened now.

"Coffeeeee," I say, sounding like a zombie hunting for brains.

"On it," he snaps, salute and all, before disappearing out of the bedroom. I can hear him in the kitchen, the beep as the coffee maker starts, then the water turning on as he cleans up the plates from last night.

He's nervous too. That's his tell. Or maybe he's just being a neat freak. Hard to know for sure, but I should get out there and help him.

I roll over, stretching long and lean on the bed, and stand, reaching for the ceiling once again to get all the kinks out of my muscles. I don't bother making my bed—not my tendency, unlike some people—instead, grabbing Lance's T-shirt from the floor and pulling it over my head.

When I pop through, he's standing in front of me, blessedly bitter nectar of the gods in hand. "Thank you," I say, taking it. It's so dark I can feel my body getting energized just from the smell.

"Hop in the shower. I'll make you breakfast," he offers, taking my half-empty cup from me. "Promise, it'll help."

I smile. "I'm headed downstairs to make breakfast for half of Roseboro. I can grab a muffin hot out of the oven."

His single lifted brow dares me to argue with him. "You need protein for the long day, and I saw eggs and bacon in your fridge. Now, get." He swats at my ass again, and I squeal, running for the bathroom like he's chasing me.

*I want him to chase me*, I think.

God, I'm wishy-washy as fuck. From my middle of the night freakout to wanting him by the light of day.

I suds up my hair and body, noting that I'm deliciously sore from the rough, pounding way Lance took me in the middle of the night. After a quick rinse, I dry off, braiding my hair out of the way and foregoing makeup. It doesn't do me any good in the hot kitchen, mostly melting right off.

I yank on jeans and a *Cake Culture* shirt, the smell of bacon teasing at me enough to make me hurry. In the kitchen, I see Lance standing at my stove, naked save for the apron he's tossed on. His bare ass looks downright edible peeking out the back.

I slide up behind him, standing on my tiptoes to peek over his shoulder. "Something looks delicious," I purr.

"SEALs can cook, you know. You don't have to sound so surprised."

I grin, smacking his ass the way he did mine before getting in a pinch. "Wasn't talking about the bacon."

He kisses me, quick and casual, before telling me to sit down. I sit at the now clean table, and he sets down two plates of eggs and perfectly crisped bacon.

As he sits, he says, "Wanted to talk to you about something."

*Shit. That didn't take long for the shoe to drop. Some fucking Cinderella I am, shattering glass slippers everywhere I go.*

The bacon that was delicious a second ago now tastes like ash as I swallow, forcing it down. "Okay," I say, resigned.

"Thomas's challenge, the Hope Initiative. Are you doing anything yet? I thought we could do something together if not."

*Errrk!* My brain gets whiplash as his words sink in. "Wait. What?"

He picks up his own fork. "The Hope Initiative. Wanna do it together?"

I can feel my eyes widen, my heart grow, and my stomach flip-flop. "You want to do a project together?"

When he nods, I almost don't believe it. Is he for real? Like for-real, for-real? I keep feeling like I'm getting punked, but maybe that's my own cynical self-sabotage? That starts a whole hamster-wheel of thoughts running through my mind, so I stop them with a single word. "Yes."

With one question, my fears are pushed away and we end up discussing ideas to make a difference in Roseboro at four thirty in the morning, over breakfast in my apartment. It feels . . . amazing. As long as I keep the door shut on the little demon in my head that whispers *it won't last.*

"So, Trixie suggested we do a subsidized preschool at a nursing home, bridge the generations-type thing. Or scholarships for those who need them for a brighter future." I can't help the grin that crosses my face at her *Scholarships for Strippers* idea.

"You think she'll be okay working with me too?" Lance asks, and I can tell he doesn't want to step on anyone's toes by jumping in on this.

"Might cost you a couple of stories about sweaty soldiers playing volleyball in the sand, complete with descriptions of the guys' bodies, but you can handle that, right?"

"Oh, yeah," he says, a devilish smile on his face, and I wonder how he's going to torture Trixie with the tales. "But seriously, the bridging the gap type deal is a good idea. We could call it 'Generations of Hope' or something like that. There was something similar for our K-9 dogs when they'd retire or get injured. Usually, they'd go to their handlers, but for the dogs who needed to be adopted, they'd pair them up with a vet, usually someone with PTSD. The K-9 acts as a type of emotional support for them because they've both been through the same things. It's a perfect match for them both. The generations thing sounds like that, helping them get through similar things or address universal issues."

"Wow, I didn't know anything like that even existed," I say, sad at the need for something like that but thankful it exists.

Lance shakes his head, shrugging. "It doesn't in Roseboro. But we don't have to do that specifically. We should all get together—you, me, and Trixie—and figure something out."

Plan made, he takes my empty plate to the sink, rinsing it before putting it into the dishwasher. "Have I told you how sexy you are when you clean things?" I say, a sultry tease woven in the question.

He flexes his arm and winks at me. "Yep, I figured that's why you were letting me wash your cookie sheets every night. Wait, no . . . suds your pan." He smirks like his pun is creatively hilarious.

I can't help but laugh. He's trying so hard sometimes. "Stick with the food puns. They're tastier."

"You've got me there." He looks down, noting that he's still naked except for my apron. He pulls the white fabric over his head, hanging it on the hook and damn-near strutting back to the bedroom, dick swinging like a fucking god. Or a Fucking God. Honestly, he's both.

Which both scares me to death and thrills me beyond measure.

*It's okay, Char. You've got this.*

# CHAPTER 18

## Lance

I N CHARLOTTE'S BEDROOM, I GET DRESSED, GRINNING THAT MY T-SHIRT is back on the floor where she dropped it. I leave it there, grabbing a fresh one out of my duffel that's sitting in the chair in the corner. I'm far from moving in, but after the crazy dinner, it'd seemed prudent to mostly stay out of my house and be backup for Charlotte. I travel ultra-light so it didn't seem like a big step.

But after last night, it does. I want to put my socks and underwear in her drawers. Literally, that's not even a pun. I want to wake her grumpy ass up with coffee every morning and cuddle her to sleep each night. I want to fuck her until she realizes she's mine. I want to prove to her that a man stays.

That I'll stay.

We head downstairs, and just as I reach for the doorknob, it opens to reveal Trixie. "Well, good morning, you two. Hope you had a *good, long, hard* night." She drawls out every syllable, making it sound as dirty as possible.

I don't have to look behind me to know that Charlotte is blushing hard. "It was great. Uh, thanks again for taking over closing duties so I could . . . uh . . ." Charlotte trails off, and I grin, knowing she just unintentionally lobbed that softball in the air for Trixie.

Trixie's glee is obvious. "So you could open? Your legs!" She laughs like it's the height of humor, and I can't help but laugh too.

It takes Charlotte a beat to give in, but she laughs too.

I press a kiss to her cheek and toss her a rescue line. "You made a delicious dinner, thank you. But now I need to go run five or twenty miles or so to burn it off, so I'll see you later. After that, I'm going to reach out to Thomas and see if I can help at all with security."

She shakes her head, her braid bouncing from shoulder to shoulder. "No, he's got it covered. You don't have to—"

I give her a firm look, inviting no argument. On this I won't budge, not on her safety. Everything else, I can take at her pace, even when it's two steps forward and one back.

But this is life or death, possibly, and I won't take no as an answer. "You said Izzy has Gabe because of who he is?" I ask, and she nods, eyes flicking to Trixie. I guess Trixie doesn't know that part of the story. "Well, you have me, and I've got some skills of my own. I just want to help, be in the loop. I think I know the guy Thomas has coordinating things. I'll just have a friendly conversation with him."

She bites her lip, still not sure, but nods.

Trixie is done being patient, though, and shoves at me, pushing me toward the back door. "Yeah, yeah . . . smoochey, smoochey. I'll see you later and all that jizz. Get it? Jizz, not jazz because well, you know. That's why you need to go. We've got girl talk to do, dicks to dissect, orgasms to evaluate, and such. So buh-bye."

I laugh, grabbing at the door frame and hollering back, "Hey, are you really going to tell her about my meat? The bacon, I mean." I toss her a big wink, which she swats out of the air with a laugh.

I don't care in the least if she's in there spilling the dirty details of every last bit of what we do. Especially to Trixie, who I'm pretty sure is on my side and will tell Charlotte to hang on tight to me with everything she's got. Good thing that only makes it easier for me to hold on to her too.

Getting in my car, I pull a card out of my wallet.

"Hello," the voice answers flatly. "Who's this?"

"Hey, Jon, it's Lance Jacobs. Could I take you to lunch today?"

After Charlotte's story, it seems ironically appropriate that we meet at the Gravy Train, the diner that seems to be the lynchpin of not only the three girls' friendship but the scene of so much of the skull fuckery that's led to all this.

The coffee's good, the company not so much so. Gabe Jackson, the wolf in sheep's clothing, stares at me openly from across the room. He probably thinks his look is neutral, but I can read the hostility and distrust plain as day. I've handled guys like this before, though, and I know that what most people would see as friendliness he sees as weakness.

But I can't 'swell up' on him either, as he'd see that as a threat. So instead, I give him a nod. He's part of Charlotte's chosen family. I must pass his muster, as he slides his eyes back to Izzy, who's running her ass off.

I've only met her once when she came into the bakery, but she feels familiar because of the way Charlotte talks about her and the numerous pictures in Charlotte's apartment.

I finish my first cup just as Jonathan Goldstone walks in, looking for all the world like a Secret Service agent in his black suit, white shirt, and shined black shoes. I can even see the slight print of his piece under his jacket, and the sight reassures me.

"Lance, good to see you again," Jonathan says, shaking my hand as he slides into a booth. Izzy comes over, already carrying a cup of coffee, which she sets it down in front of him. "Thanks . . . tell Henry no usual today. Maybe tomorrow?"

Izzy nods and leaves, and I'd bet my left nut she's already texting Charlotte and Mia to make sure they know about this meeting. I give Jonathan a raised eyebrow. "You've become a regular here? You have my interest piqued."

"Good food, conveniently located . . . and the coffee's not too bad," Jonathan says, but I can read something behind his eyes. He's always been one to play things close to the chest, and I realize that he chose this location for our meet because Gabe would serve as his backup. Smart guy, one I can respect. "What can I do for you?"

"I'm sure you're well aware that I'm seeing Charlotte?"

Jon's smile is placating, neither confirming nor denying.

"She told me everything," I continue, moving this conversation ahead a few hops and skips. "I assume you're the coordinator on all of this."

His posture changes, from his relaxed meeting-a-friend laidback style to something more serious. He leans forward, hands stacked on top of one another on the table, letting me see that he's not making a move. Yet.

"Depends. Define *everything*."

"She told me about the saboteur. And Gabe." My eyes flick to the side, seeing that Gabe is taking a keen interest in our conversation.

"Stop. Don't say another word. Let's go outside," Jon says, already getting up. He tosses a five on the table and heads for the door. Gabe starts to get up too, but Jon gives him the smallest headshake, confirming what I already knew.

Jon's here at Thomas's behest, coordinating the security and likely doing more. I know he's a skilled man, perhaps better-equipped mentally than I am for this job. Para Rescue is about saving lives, not taking them, even if he's skilled tactically as well. He's got cojones that would help him stand strong against the likes of someone like Blackwell, especially for family.

Outside, he doesn't head to a car, instead motioning for me to follow him. We walk side by side down the sidewalk, and he talks without looking at me. "Bad history with mics. But directional mics on a moving target with ambient traffic noise involved are pure shit eighty percent of the time, so we walk. And fill me in on what you think *everything* means."

I sigh, giving him the basic rundown of what Charlotte told me last night, finishing with, "You're on this, right? You're going after Blackwell? I'm in."

Jon shakes his head, seeming almost amused at my go-getter attitude, but I can sense the anger underneath. "Figured you would, but it's not that easy. We've already looked at it from every angle. This isn't a door kicker op. A ghost couldn't get into Blackwell Tower right now, not even an angel, fallen or otherwise." He looks back at the diner, but I don't get the joke he seems to be in on.

"So we sit on our hands?"

Jon shrugs. "Thomas is taking a different tack, more strategic long-game. He's cutting away Blackwell's supports, one by one, until he's ready to fall. In the meantime, we secure the perimeter."

He doesn't sound happy about that. We're men of action. But if the higher-ups say hold, then we hold, and I guess in this instance, Thomas Goldstone is the highest-ranking officer on this op.

"Okay, then loop me in the security detail. Gabe is watching Izzy. I can help watch Charlotte." It's not what I'd hoped for, but it's something, at least. As much as I don't want to go back to war, for Charlotte, I'll go to battle right here on my home ground.

Jon wavers for a solid minute, eyeing me up and down like he can measure my intention, value, and more if he only looks hard enough. I must pass his inspection because he finally says, "Unofficially. In uniform, you outranked me, but this is my team. Still, another pair of eyes and set of hands couldn't hurt. I'll introduce you around, keep you informed, but that's it. You're backup, not the primary. You armed?"

I shake my head. "Recommend a local store?"

"I'll cover you," he says. We've made a lap around the block, returning to the Gravy Train parking lot. He heads to his SUV and opens the back door, flipping the seat to reveal a hidden compartment below. He reaches in and hands me a beauty of a Sig, just like the ones I'm used to. "Too big for my carry rig, but it's a good gun. Don't fuck it up."

I nod, sliding it in my waistband and pulling my shirt over it. It's too big to really hide this way, but I only need to get to my car across the lot.

"Let's go meet the team," Jon says, and I nod, glad to be able to help.

# CHAPTER 19

## Charlotte

THE END OF THE WEEK COMES, INCLUDING ANOTHER SUCCESSFUL custom cake creation, this one for a birthday party. It's perfect, nothing big and fancy like the wedding cake but a small, double-layer round with a rainbow of flowers laid out to look like a mane, flowing from a golden unicorn horn. I'd even played with edible glitter and candy sequins to make it more 'extra'.

Throughout the busy week, Lance is still here. He's spent every day working on his laptop, leaving to make appearances at the office, or to get what he calls PT in, but coming back to help me in the kitchen or feed me takeout for dinner.

It's nice to have someone to lean on, and I'm trusting more and more that he's got my back.

He's a genuine American hero who wants to make me his number one. I might be his toughest mission to date, but I'm trying to have a little faith.

"I know that look," Trixie says, jostling me from my reverie as she takes the tray of Ooey-Gooey Buttery Goodness Bars from my hand. "The *'I'm in love but don't want to admit it because I'm a scaredy-cat that's scared'* look." She fakes a cat hiss, grinning. "All you're missing is a damn yellow daisy to pluck at as you chant, 'He loves me, he loves me not.'"

"Oh, stop it," I protest, trying to sound stern but failing miserably. "I was thinking about the Generations of Hope event."

Trixie smirks, one brow lifting in a twist and the other lowering over her eye. She looks like a girly version of The Rock with his famous expression. She's not remotely convinced but offers me a lifeline. "Fine, if you're thinking about the event, then tell me all about it. Give me the latest update."

Trixie had been thrilled to go in with Lance and me on the Generations of Hope idea. Over several days, we spent every spare moment trying to figure out how to make the biggest impact and finally landed on a big festival-type event for the kickoff with smaller get-togethers on a regular basis after that. We're hoping to win Thomas's funding to keep them going.

But first, we have to make the kickoff a huge hit to showcase the idea. So Lance has been steering the ship, making every wish we come up with actually come true.

"Well," I tell Trixie, going through my mental checklist, "he's scouted several locations, and I think he's actually going to get Main Street to let us use the park in front of the community center. We'll be able to use the basketball courts for a charity game, set up tents with the various activities, and he got a burger place to sponsor the food. It's actually happening, Trix! We're going to bring everyone together, from the youngest to the oldest, and Roseboro will be better for it."

She nods but frowns. "Hey, I thought we were doing the food?"

I shake my head, transferring mini-tartlets to the bakery case. "We're doing mini-cupcake samples and sponsoring the Bake-a-Thon tent, where grandmas like my Grandma Winnie can teach the next generation how to bake. But we'll also have a grill for burgers that the grandpas are going to man."

She smiles. "We are doing it, aren't we? I talked to Terry Maxwell, the computer fixer guy, about having a booth too. He said he'd facilitate a social media workshop for the older set, get the tech-savvy kids to help out. He said he'll have everybody, young and old, safely on Instagram before the end of the event."

"And I talked to Mrs. Petrie, Izzy's neighbor, about doing an arm-knitting demonstration," I conclude. "She makes these monstrous blankets out of fluffy yarn. I think the kids will love them. Hell, I love them so much I'm hoping I have time to get to her booth to learn myself."

We stand back, looking at the case filled with the first round of today's goodies. "Ready for the before-church crowd?" Trixie asks, and I see the first car pull up outside.

I nod, and Steven flips the lock and turns on the buzzing neon sign.

Trixie is helping the first customer when I feel my phone buzz in my pocket. I look down, seeing it's Mia. "Hey, Trix, I'll be a second," I say, waving my phone at her.

I can't be gone long. The rush is going to start any minute, but I always take time to answer Mia if I can. Besides being my bestie, she'd be the one to notify me if there was something to worry about with the whole Blackwell situation.

"Hey, girl," I answer as I swoosh through the double doors to the kitchen.

"What's shaking, bacon?" she says, my food puns rubbing off on everyone.

"Busy, busy, just starting the Sunday rush. You awake already or still awake?" Either option is equally likely. Mia is a total video game nerd and will start a game at ten p.m. to play for 'just a minute', and boom, here comes the sun. She's tricked me into that more than once, but not since I opened the bakery and had to start getting up around the time she goes to bed after a gaming session.

"Still awake, actually, though not from gaming. A little birdie told me to do a full background check on your boy, which of course means I need to know what the fuck's up with you and GI Joe!"

My jaw drops, even though somehow, I'm not surprised. "You did not do a background check on my boyfriend."

The word rolls off my tongue before I can stop it, but it feels good. It feels true, and I like that. A lot.

I can hear her eye roll. "Of course I did. I checked Gabe out too, though his file is unsurprisingly thin. Your man's, though? Thick, like thiiiick. I know it all, family, military, et-cetera, et-cetera. But what I don't know is, how're you doing and what're you doing with him?"

I fidget, drawing invisible shapes on the clean stainless-steel prep table. "I'm good, I'm . . . uh, I'm *seeing* him?"

Mia isn't one for pussyfooting around, and she slips into her Russian accent, which makes everything sound like a threat. "In Mother Russia, man is seen or not seen. No questions. So which?"

"Seeing," I admit. "I'm still not sure what he's doing with me when he could have someone easier, more beautiful, less *me*, but he's still here so I'm trying to believe him when he says he's not going anywhere."

"Wow," Mia says breathlessly. "It's about fucking time. You are the shit, girl, and we've been telling you for years that you deserve the very best and to stop settling for assholes. It's not that all guys are shit—helloooo, Tommy?"

I can't decide if she's merely talking about how awesome her guy is or if he just walked through the room, but the result's the same either way. He's one of the good ones. A moment later, she continues. "You've had your pick of the assholes, or let them pick you. I don't know which is worse. Sounds like you got a good one this time, though."

"He is, isn't he?" I know I sound like a lovesick teenager, but honestly, I feel a little spun out like I did the first time the boy I was crushing on looked my way. And that was in third grade. Her words start to sink in and I can't help myself. "What do you know about him?"

He's already told me so much, but I want more. I want it all. Like maybe if I truly understand everything about him, I can somehow figure out how to make him stay. I know it's a weakness, but my experiences weigh on me, making me feel like not enough no matter how many times my friends tell me I am.

"Well, Jonathan knows him well enough to vouch for him. Jon's the guy who controls your security and is helping me snoopity-doo-dah into Blackwell. I hear the guys on the ground respect Lance, but *you'd* know that better than *me*," she accuses.

"We went out to meet the SUV guys. I'd only ever met Steven, but Lance introduced me to Brian-slash-Larry and Paul-slash-Curly too," I say, confirming her accusation and reminding myself to use their real names, not the *Three Stooges* ones Trixie prefers. "Jon got Lance a gun, which made me nervous at first, but he showed me how he takes it apart, cleans it, and stores it safely. I don't want to ever touch it, but it helped me feel comfortable that he was confident with it. Silly, I know, considering he's a SEAL."

"Look," Mia says quietly, "he's clean as a whistle on paper. The timing just makes me nervous. Are you sure he's not some Blackwell sleeper agent? I mean, Blackwell's got more tentacles than a giant squid, ones we never even considered." For all my trust issues, Mia has some of her own. I know she feels guilty she didn't catch on to the saboteur's deception at Goldstone sooner.

"I trust him, Mia, and that speaks volumes," I reassure her. "Not just in my brain, but in my gut too. I know my picker's been a bit broken in the past, but I really think I'm doing the right thing this time."

Funny how trying to convince Mia helps me convince myself. Not that I need convincing, exactly. I do trust Lance, can feel it in my bones that he's good for me, but my pesky demons keep trying to steal my happiness. But I won't let them. I refuse to lose something this good because of my cynicism and lack of faith.

"Okay, if you're with him, I'm in. I'll let Tommy know the family grew by two feet. What size shoe does he wear, anyway?" Mia says casually. Too casually.

"Big enough for me to feel it the morning after," I reply to the question she's really asking. I don't know where the stereotype came from that only guys engage in locker room talk because Mia, Izzy, and I share way too much. I know everything from how dominant Thomas can be to how sweet Gabe often is, which seems counter-intuitive if you knew the men, but I guess you never know what goes on behind closed doors. Unless you spill *all* like we do.

"Gotta go, honey. Trixie is going to kill me if I leave her out there alone for the rush much longer," I tell her honestly. She says something about our usual lunch date, the ones I've been missing out on in favor of doing custom orders, and I agree noncommittally.

As soon as I hang up, Trixie pokes her head through the doors, her eyes wide. I get a good look at her eyes and see the horror there. Something's wrong.

"Oh, my God, Char, you have to come!"

# CHAPTER 20

## Charlotte

OUT FRONT, STEVEN IS ON HIS FEET, HIS PHONE PRESSED TO HIS EAR.
"What's wrong?" I ask, customers looking around in confusion.
From behind me, I hear Lance barreling down the stairs, so he must
be who Steven is calling in as backup. But from what?

I make my way toward the counter and see a small man in a brown
three-piece suit who somehow reminds me of wheat bread. He adjusts his
glasses down his nose, somehow managing to look down at me though we're
basically the same height.

"Are you Charlotte Dunn, proprietor of this establishment?" he sneers,
running a finger along the glass case, leaving a smudgy fingerprint.

"Yes, can I help you?" I reply, even if I'm pissed about that fingerprint.

His eyes are sharp, his smirk arrogant as he speaks slowly and clearly
so that everyone in the room can hear him. "I'm Barrett Williams, Roseboro
Health Department. I'm here to investigate some rather troubling complaints."
He glances at the clipboard in his hand. "Red hair in several cupcakes, unclean
surfaces in the kitchen, and most disturbing of all, a nasty roach infestation."

He leans in as he says the last part, like he intends to keep it between
us, but everyone in the room has gone silent and hears every bit, judging by
the gasps of disgust that resonate through the crowd.

My head is already shaking, refuting his words. "That's patently untrue.
We're exceptionally clean here and follow every rule regarding health and food

safety. You're welcome to do an inspection now, if you'd like," I say, pushing the double doors to the kitchen open.

There's nothing to see but a standard working kitchen. Food storage containers on a baking rack by the wall, several prep tables in the middle with treats in various stages of preparation, a sink full of this morning's dishes waiting to be scrubbed and run through the washer, which is steaming with its current load.

But Mr. Williams doesn't frame it like that. He looks disgusted. "Are those pies uncovered? A fly or a roach could crawl right up onto them. And is that butter at room temperature? That can lead to foodborne illness if not refrigerated properly."

I can see my customers shuffling uncomfortably, several with their phones out, either typing away or discretely filming.

"The pies are cooling as per protocol. And butter has to reach room temperature to make frosting. There must be some misunderstanding. We're compliant with all the guidelines." He's hearing none of my explanations, though, and I hear the jingle of the bell as people make an escape for the door empty-handed.

My mouth opens and closes, no sound coming out. This is ridiculous, unfounded complaints and accusations that aren't even in the food handling safety guidebook.

"I'm afraid we'll have to close for the day for the inspection. I certainly wouldn't want to eat anything from here until this *misunderstanding* has been cleared up." He sneers, like my label is obviously untrue.

Trixie and Lance help escort customers out, promising them that everything is fine and that we'll be cleared of any concerns and reopen with an A-plus rating as soon as possible. Murmurs of 'Well, I still won't be back' and 'Roaches? Ew!' sound as loud as a death knell for my fledgling bakery.

I turn back to Mr. Williams, wanting to wipe the congenial smile off his face with my fist. But I force myself to stand tall, escorting him into the kitchen for a thorough inspection.

An hour later, he's been through my dish machine with a cotton swab to look for mold, he's knelt down in my freezer to look beneath the storage racks for any evidence of infestation, and he's bagged several different foods as 'samples' for lab inspection. From what I can tell, he's found nothing. My kitchen is virtually brand-new and we take great care of it.

Lance has been typing away on his phone, but I've been too busy worrying to give it much thought until there's a knock at the back door. "Finally," he sighs. "This isn't my kind of fight."

He opens the door, and Thomas steps through with a severe-looking woman in a black suit and sensible heels.

I can feel Mr. Williams shrink next to me, the snarky bite he's had dulled just by this woman's presence. Her words neuter him even more. "Anita Culpepper, Ms. Dunn. I'm the Health Commissioner for Roseboro. I oversee all public health inspectors, including Mr. Williams here. Mr. Goldstone asked that I be present for the investigation. May I see the complaint?"

Mr. Williams flips to a page at the back of his clipboard, handing it over to his boss, who reads it aloud. "First complaint, two weeks ago . . . *several red hairs found in red velvet cupcakes.* Second complaint, one week ago . . . *door to kitchen opened and 'it looked grody back there.'* Third complaint, yesterday . . . *disgusting place, roaches everywhere, even upstairs where the owner lives.* That one has a vomiting emoji added." She flips the paper over and scans it again before looking around the kitchen.

"Have you found any evidence of health code violations?" she asks Mr. Williams.

"I sliced into a few cupcakes but didn't see any hairs," he starts, but I interrupt, anger boiling over.

"Four dozen cupcakes! He destroyed forty-eight cupcakes to crumbs looking for something that's not there."

He has the decency to look chagrined, at least. "Freezer and dish machine are clean. I was just about to look behind the equipment for evidence of roaches and mice."

Ms. Culpepper's jaw is set in stone as she grits her teeth. "By all means, do so." We all watch closely as he goes over to the stovetop, turning on his penlight and looking at the burners. He kneels down and looks underneath, then behind. "Anything?"

He gets up, shaking his head.

"So what you're telling me is that you bust in here, loudly proclaiming to all of my customers that I have a filthy business, making sure to enunciate for every camera as you made claims that you can't remotely substantiate. Is that what you're telling me, Mr. Williams?" I stare him down, thankful for my business classes. The lessons are still in the filing cabinet of my brain, and I pull them out, ready to rage now. "That sounds like defamation, malicious intent to destroy my business, and a gross disregard for standard protocol."

Ms. Culpepper takes over before Williams can dig his own grave with his own mouth. "Miss Dunn, you have the apologies of the Health Department. It does appear that everything is in proper order here. Your A-plus rating of a month ago stands unchanged, and I will be sure to review investigative protocol with Mr. Williams."

She turns to go but pauses, looking back. "In my experience, when a new business opens up, people are harsh, sometimes needlessly so, going so far as to file unwarranted complaints. Perhaps there's another baker who is jealous of your new and successful venture? I hate to suggest that, but it wouldn't be the first time I've seen something like that. Just be certain to uphold your own high standards, and everything will come out okay in the wash."

Her hand on the doorknob, Lance calls out. "Wait, Ms. Culpepper. Would you possibly help alleviate some citizen concerns about the food of *Cake Culture*?"

Her eyes narrow, the ironclad persona once again coming out. "I do not accept bribes, if that's what you're suggesting. Nor make recommendations. I merely verify that rules are followed."

"No, nothing like that," he quickly reassures her. "It's just that, given how clean the kitchen is and the fact that there are zero concerns with any violations, would you consider eating a cupcake of your choosing on the way to your car? It'd go a long way in making it seem like everything is okay here if you're willing to eat one out of the very kitchen you're inspecting, know what I mean?"

She tilts her head, almost as if she's reading bylaws in her mind. "That is acceptable under the guidelines." A grin breaks out across her face, making her look ten years younger. "Can I have a Sinful Secrets? I've been dying to try one."

I start to box up a Sinful Secrets, but she holds up a hand. "No sense in boxing it. The point is to eat it." She takes a dainty bite, moaning in delight. "Oh my gawd, it's as good as I thought it'd be. I'll be back. You just gained a customer."

And with that, she and Mr. Williams walk out. Her, cupcake in hand and a smile on her face. Him, sad and droopy, and likely a bit scared at facing her wrath at the office.

I look around the room at my people. Trixie looks worried, nibbling on her lip like its candy. Lance looks pissed but under control, while Thomas looks resigned.

"I'm sorry, Charlotte," Thomas says. "I've dealt with this before. False complaints are one of Blackwell's tools." His brows knit together, and he looks around. "Though I'm not sure I see the play here."

"I don't think it's him this time," I respond. "Did you hear Ms. Culpepper? Jealous rivals?"

"But there's not really another bakery that we're competing against. It's just grocery stores, for the most part, that make cakes around here," Trixie protests. "Though I guess their bakers might be out of work if you go huge?"

"Not a bakery rival, a family one," I explain. "I think Sabrina did this because I took Lance away from her in the twisted fairytale in her mind. She's trying to get back at me by taking away something important to me."

It makes sense. I haven't heard from Priscilla or Sabrina since the third run of bitchy texts they sent me. And this is just nasty enough, juvenile enough, that it fits Sabrina's style perfectly. She's not the type to come at me directly. Having someone else do her dirty work is right up her alley.

"Oh, shit," Trixie whispers, covering her mouth with her hands.

Lance seems unsure but says, "It's worth a conversation. Do you want me to go with you?"

I shake my head, wishing he could but knowing differently. "Thank you, but no, I need to do this alone."

# CHAPTER 21

## Charlotte

THE HOUSE LOOKS LIKE IT DID LAST TIME I VISITED, BUT IT FEELS different. The anger and disgust I've been getting from Priscilla and Sabrina feel tacky, like their oily aggression is reaching out to me, pulling me into their games.

It took me so long to escape, right up until I graduated high school, then I ran like hellhounds were on my heels. Ever since, I've visited infrequently, and usually by force.

Today, I come freely, no longer the scared little girl they can keep under their thumbs. Today, I'm ready to war. Don't mess with my baby, my bakery, or I'll go full Mama Bear on your ass.

I knock on the front door, my heart already racing in anticipation. But it's not Sabrina's smug face when the door opens. It's Dad. Probably a good thing, because there's a fair-to-good chance I would've punched Sabrina on sight. I guess that's still to be found out.

Dad looks exhausted, his face drawn and his shoulders slumped and withered. It's like he's aged ten years in only a few weeks. "Dad? You okay?"

His huff of laughter is humorless as he waves me in. "Of course, but it's been a rather taxing time."

He walks off, not waiting for me to apologize or explain, though I don't truly feel the need to do either. I follow him into the kitchen, closing the door behind me. Dad grabs a glass from the cabinet and then his own personal disgusting poison, V8 juice, from the fridge. He pours carefully, talking to the glass. "I've been chastised rather fully over that dinner, and after. I hope it was worth it?"

I nod, biting my lip and feeling like a little girl who's disappointed her daddy once again. "I am sorry it all went down like that, but I'm not sorry I didn't let Priscilla and Sabrina steamroll over me again like they always do. I'm not sorry that Lance stood up for himself and for me."

He sighs, turning to lean against the counter and give me a hard look. "Am I to take it that you and Mr. Jacobs are still seeing each other? That this is something more serious, and you weren't stealing your sister's man just because you could?" I can hear the tagline Priscilla and Sabrina have been selling in his words.

"Is that what you think?" He doesn't answer but tilts his head questioningly. "I met Lance at the gala. After that, he started coming by the bakery every day. He'd do his work, and he'd help me. We spent quite a bit of time together, then the dinner came. Priscilla and Sabrina obviously had all these plans, but by then, Lance and I were . . . something." I don't know how to describe us now. I certainly don't have a label for what we were then.

"So he stood up for you when he felt you were being insulted," Dad summarizes. "And now?"

I move closer to him, standing right in front of him so he hears me loud and clear. "I'm following my heart, which is hard and scary, but he's being patient with me."

Dad looks at me carefully, and I feel like he's weighing our future. If he can't see that I've done nothing wrong here, I don't know that I'll ever forgive him. It's not about Lance, or not just about him, but about how my Dad perceives me. Growing up with Sabrina was hard on me, and he didn't get that, but this is far beyond any petty insults and stunts we pulled as kids.

This is my heart. This is my life.

I freeze, realizing that I'm thinking about both Lance and the bakery.

Finally, after an eternity, Dad nods. "My little girl is seeing an American hero, one who will stand up for her, protect her, and care for her. I guess I can't be angry at that, now can I?"

He smiles, and I can't help but hug him. He hugs me back, patting me softly. It's on the tip of my tongue to tell him about what Sabrina's done, but I don't want to ruin the moment, the progress we just made. So I keep my mouth shut to him, but I won't to Sabrina, who deserves my full wrath.

"Is Sabrina here? I'd like to talk to her," I say carefully.

Dad seems to think I'm here for amends with my stepsister as well because his smile grows. "She's upstairs. Go on up."

Upstairs, I pause outside her door, taking a steadying breath. "I'm an adult, not a kid she can walk all over. I can be mature about this," I remind myself as I knock.

"Come in," I hear through the door. I open it slowly, seeing her Princess Barbie room, white and pink with frou-frou ruffles. It feels like a Southern Belle child's room, circa 1950.

Sabrina is lying on the bed on her stomach, scrolling on a tablet. If I had to guess, I'd say she's online shopping.

"What the hell are you doing here?" she bites out, flipping over to glare at me.

I grit my teeth, forcing my voice to not quaver. Not with fear, but with fury. "I had a rather surprising visit at the bakery today. I thought you'd be interested in it," I say, baiting her to see if she'll reveal anything.

"Why would I give a fuck about anything at your little sweatshop?" she says with an eye roll.

"Because it seems someone made some rather specific complaints to the Health Department, completely unfounded ones designed to hurt my business. Would you know anything about that?"

Her smile is pure malevolence, her glee palpable. "You think I made complaints to get back at you for Lance?" Her laughter is sharp, bitter, but she shakes her head. "Hell, I wish I'd thought of that. Pretty fucking genius, if you ask me."

I can't hold my anger back anymore. "Is this a joke to you? This is my livelihood. I've got every cent tied up in that bakery, not to mention my blood, sweat, and tears. It's off limits from whatever family shitshow we have going. Be mad at me about Lance, bitch and whine to your mom about it like you always do, but leave my bakery alone."

"Or what?" she says, smirking. "Did you think I'd just sit back and be happy you got some grade-A dick? Lance is a fucking catch, *my* catch, and you stole him. As far as I'm concerned, this is Karma coming back to bite you in the ass like you deserve."

"He was never going to be interested in you. Ironic that you talk about Karma, but this is what happens when you're a shallow, vindictive, entitled brat."

I take a breath. God, that feels good to say. Ugly words, but a long time coming. The vitriol continues to pour out from my soul, repressed so many times that the dam has given way. "Good guys see that coming a mile away, and the number-one bro rule is 'Don't stick your dick in crazy.' Making false complaints just shows how far gone you are. And a little FYI, those complaints aren't anonymous, not really. Thomas Goldstone is on the paperwork as an investor in *Cake Culture*. You think he won't get that info?"

It's a huge bluff, an idea that just occurred to me, but she doesn't know that. "Fine," she finally admits, intimidated. "I didn't do it. But I'd shake the hand of whoever did, that's for damn sure."

"Whatever." I'm losing steam, not because I'm reverting to my teen self but because I'm never going to trust her, to be honest. I've been burned too many times by her. She could tell me the sky is blue, and I'd go check for myself before believing her.

"Really. I didn't do it. I wish I had," she says, and that at least sounds like the truth.

But if not her, then who?

She sees the track my mind is already racing down. "And Mom didn't either. She can barely even text, says it's bougie, so filling out an online form is beyond her. I have to do her online shopping or she has the maid do it." She points her thumb at the tablet she set aside when I came in. "Trust me, if I had done it or if she had, I'd be dancing around, yelling for you to *suck it, bitch*. But *we didn't*."

She makes a point. She would be gloating over her victory if she'd done this. And she's not.

"Fuck. I'm sorry, I guess. I just figured . . ." The apology is bitter on my tongue.

She rolls her eyes. "You figured that if something bad was happening to you, it had to be the evil stepsister's fault?" Sabrina shoots back bitterly. I glare at her, not disagreeing with her assessment. "Newsflash, you're not exactly the sister I wished for either," she says snidely. "Man-stealing bitch."

"I think we're just going to have to agree to disagree there. He was never yours. But he most definitely is mine." I turn, opening the door to escape, then closing it behind me.

I hear a loud thump, a pillow hitting the door, probably, and then a strangled cry. "Ugh!"

Yeah, you're not my idea of a dream sister either, girl.

## CHAPTER 22

### Lance

CHARLOTTE'S VISIT HOME MAKES ME CONSIDER A BIT OF A TRIP DOWN memory lane. While her relationship with her sister has always been shitty, my relationship with Cody was once so much better.

I've got to figure out what the hell is going on with him, so I head home too, figuring I can refresh the gear in my duffel bag, grab a workout, and see if Cody's around for a chat, brother to brother. Hell, maybe I can get Dad involved too, and we can really lay all this shit out and get ourselves straightened out.

I don't even have a chance to knock on the front door before Hamilton's opening it, looking professional, as always. "Mister Lance."

"Hamilton, good to see you. Anybody home?" I ask, coming into the foyer.

He dips his chin, his eyes neutral. "Indeed. Mister Jacobs is in his study. Mister Cody is in his room. Can I get them for you? Or perhaps you're trying to avoid them?"

He has a glint in his eye, and I'd bet he doesn't miss a thing that happens around here. I grin before telling him, "Nah, I got this." I lick my lips, putting my thumb and index finger in my mouth and letting out a piercing whistle that echoes through the house. "I doubt you use that one?"

"Indeed, sir." Still, Hamilton looks slightly amused as doors suddenly slam and heads pop out. Dad, Cody, and Mariella stick their heads into the foyer, but Mariella quickly disappears again.

"What the hell's going on?" Dad asks.

"Wanted to talk to you two, if you can spare a minute," I say, already walking toward the great room.

I can hear Cody grumble, "Oh, of course we can . . . for you." But he follows.

We sit down, and Hamilton offers everyone a drink, but I decline for us all, giving Cody a look that dares him to disagree. He sighs and waves his hand at Hamilton, telling him it's fine.

Once Hamilton excuses himself, I look from my Dad to my brother. "I've been going over files, reports, projections, spreadsheets, and more until I'm damn near blind. I wanted to tell you what I've found."

Dad leans back, listening. Cody's eyes glaze over, already done with the conversation.

"Admittedly, I'm coming in at a disadvantage. I'm a SEAL, and my MBA isn't from a fancy school like Yale. But I didn't need that to get a fair assessment of the current standings. What I've found is that the company is doing well, exceedingly well." Dad's brows shoot up, and even Cody looks slightly more interested.

"Compared to?" Dad asks.

"Compared to the rest of the bio-tech industry."

Using visual aides from my computer, I explain the points where the company is doing well, above expectations in most areas. "The only area I see that needs true improvement is employee retention, which in my experience is based on morale. The company can use some more *esprit de corps*."

Dad remains unconvinced. "What about the prototype project for spinal cages with brain-computer interfaces? It was an utter failure, to the tune of *millions*."

Cody tenses, jaw so tight I'm surprised his teeth aren't breaking from the sheer force. Dad looks at him accusingly, and I start to get a clearer picture of what's going on here. Dad is a brilliant man but can't see the forest for the trees because he's stuck, running the same loop in his mind about who and what we are—Cody, me, even the company.

"Dad, one of your biggest failures is the coffee on the first floor," I shoot back, a side flank attack to wake him up. "I've had better on a hospital ship in the North Atlantic, and it's the first impression you make. You never could make a decent cup of coffee, so why are you even trying? Make tea or smoothies or something else because you're a shitty coffee maker."

It's a nonsense approach, but I need something to shock him out of his rutted path. Dad's face immediately pinches, and I know I've made an impression. "What the hell are you talking about? Coffee? Who cares about that? I don't even make the coffee! If it's shitty, talk to whoever makes it."

He looks at me like I've lost every marble out of my skull, and I deliver my point. "Exactly. You don't make it, just like Cody didn't make the spinal cages. But yet, you're blaming him for the whole project just because he managed it. You know what I saw when I took a close look at that venture?"

Dad huffs. "Is this the part where you gang up on the old man?"

"You asked me to do this," I growl. "Do you want to hear it or not?" I take his silence as answer enough. "I saw a project that was earmarked as a long-shot from the get-go, but one with the potential for a huge payoff. And *you* were the one who signed off on it. No one else. So, project underway, budget is within parameters, initial reports promising but very early. Then, the expo comes up and it was decided that the cages should be paraded out as the wave of the future, one that Jacobs Bio-Tech is designing themselves. Who decided to show the cages at the expo?"

Cody looks at Dad, who begrudgingly admits, "Me. They were promising at the time."

"I know, but your hurry to showcase led to overtime hours, rush orders on materials, and other costly expenditures," I point out. "None of which would have been a problem except the tech didn't work. It's still in R&D but looking less promising than some other projects, so their budget's been slashed."

Dad growls, looking at Cody. "That's right. It didn't work."

I growl right back, frustrated that he's not seeing the big picture here. "Cody, what settings do you use for the microscopic lens to see as you work?"

Cody smirks, already seeing where I'm going. "Not a fucking clue, since *I don't use them.* I'm a paper pusher." Then he looks Dad dead in the eye, years of resentment in his words. "Not a barista."

Every bit of Dad's air escapes as he plops back in the chair, his hands going to his salt and pepper hair to pull at the strands as his volume gets louder and louder. "But this isn't coffee, it was a multimillion-dollar project! And all that money was lost on your watch."

"You'll never get it, will you? I'm not a fuck-up!" Cody says, standing up. "I'm the one who's done everything you've ever wanted—stay here and work the family business. Hell, if you'd asked me to marry the damn blonde and start popping out grandbabies, I would've hopped to it. But I'll never be *him*. And that means no matter what I do, it'll never be good enough."

He stomps out of the room, and from far away, I hear a door slam and music start blaring.

Dad shakes his head, exhaustion and frustration washing through him. "Do you see what I'm dealing with? He's immature, always folds under pressure. This is why I need you here, Lance. It's too much for me. I'm not old, still got some years in this ticker," he says, patting his chest. "But I thought I'd be able to slow down by now. I promised your mother I'd take her to Europe for her birthday, but I can't even see leaving for a week, much less the month-long trip she wants to take."

I lean forward in my chair, looking Dad in the eye. What I'm about to say is one of the hardest things I've ever had to say, and I've informed wives that their husbands are never coming home.

I steel myself, thankful for my years of training to face the hard shit head-on.

"Dad, Cody's not the problem. *You* are."

That gets his attention.

"I don't know what happened between you two after I was gone, but he's a good worker. His projects are managed well, on time and under budget, and his staff loves him. You, on the other hand, are this tornado that blows through the office, blowing his projects up and then blaming him. I don't know if it's stress or just something you've got personally with Cody, but it's clear. *You're* the problem, not him."

I wait, expecting the explosion of justifications, explanations, and arguments. But he sags, broken, his eyes unseeing as he stares at the floor. I wish he was yelling instead of *this*. He's always been larger than life to me, a role model I hoped to live up to, but now he looks small, uncertain, and it kills me.

Still looking down, he says quietly, "Did I ever tell you how I took the company from pharmaceuticals to bio-tech?"

I shake my head, not seeing the connection.

"I'd been working at Jacobs Pharma for decades under your grandpa, and it was getting to be a tough market to capitalize on. Fewer and fewer projects were panning out, and the amount of work to get that one-percent edge over the competition was ridiculous. So I proposed that we expand at least, diversify a bit so we had a more stable revenue stream." He huffs, his eyes glassy as he remembers. "We argued so loudly and so often the walls of the old headquarters would shake and people would scatter if we were in the same room together. Dad wouldn't hear of it. He was convinced I was throwing away two generations of hard work to chase some crazy dream. He just wanted to make another cholesterol med, a sure thing."

"Build a better mousetrap?" I say, and he nods.

"And so we held steady until he retired and I took over the reins. I made the transition slowly at first, but when the name changed, he was furious. Accused me of ruining his legacy, of being a young upstart who didn't know my ass from my elbow, and vowing that I'd see the day he was right and I was out on the streets." He's quiet for a moment, and I try to think back to the grandpa who died when I was just a boy. I have impressions of peppermint and pipe smoke, but not much else.

"He died before he saw the success I'd made of what he started. Never saw the dream come true. He died thinking I was a fuckup, and he knew best," he says sadly.

"But you did know what you were doing and have done a damn fine job of turning Jacobs into the primary bio-tech company on the West Coast, and it's positioned well to be a global force against the big dogs of the industry. You did that."

He looks up at me, pride shining in his eyes, but I have to finish the thought. "But you didn't do it alone. Let go, Dad. You're holding on too tightly, to the company, to Cody, to me. And it's killing you and killing everyone around you. You've earned some time to relax. Take that trip with Mom, and trust that the people you trained will take care of Jacobs Bio-Tech."

"I don't want to become obsolete," he confesses. "Hell, maybe now I know how your grandpa felt. I thought your coming home would help. Though I'm not sure if I thought it'd give me more time because you'd have to be trained or less time because you've always been your own man. Maybe a bit of both?"

"You don't need me, Dad. You never have, and I'm not sure I'll ever come onboard at Jacobs. Cody's your guy. He knows that company inside and out. He's young, and you're stressing him out to his limits, but he's a believer in bio-tech and that'll make all the difference. I'm not saying you just toss him the ropes, but you need to step back, let him shine on his own. You might be surprised what he'll show you if you let him engage and show you his skills. He's got plenty."

He looks down the hallway where Cody disappeared, pensive and thoughtful. "I really fucked up with him, huh?"

I nod, agreeing with him. "You really did. But he wants to please you, so I think you can make it up to him. Admitting you're wrong will go a long way, and better behavior going forward will go even further."

Dad turns back to me, smiling for the first time in over an hour. "I raised two strong-willed, intelligent, good men. You two are my greatest accomplishment."

I lift a brow, grinning wide. "Pretty sure you had help there too, Old Man. Mom was the one who patched us up when we did stupid shit. You were the one who yelled at us for doing it."

"Both equally important parts of parenting," he jokes before narrowing his eyes. "You know, I think your mother is having a bit of a crisis herself. My guess is that's what the matchmaking was all about. I'm having growing pains about stepping back from the company, and she's having the same thoughts, that her family doesn't need her anymore. A grandbaby seemed like the perfect solution to her, I think. Don't be too mad at her, okay?"

"I'm not. She's backed off after the dinner," I admit. "Or I guess juked and is now throwing her eggs in Charlotte's basket for a grandkid. Wait, that sounds . . . wrong."

Dad laughs. "I know what you mean. Just promise me that you won't let Mom influence you in this. You've always gone your own way, and I've always been proud of you for doing it. I am proud of you, Lance."

My eyes burn. The words feel good down to my soul. I think every child has a desire to make their parents proud, and though I've never acted with that goal in mind, it feels good to know that I've done something good.

"Thanks, Dad."

He gets up, and I swear his eyes are a bit teary too. "If you'll excuse me, I think I have another difficult conversation I need to have, some crow to eat, if you will."

I smile, glad that he's going to make amends. "If you'd like, I happen to know a great baker who could probably put those blackbirds into a rather delicious pie. Might make it easier to get down?"

He shakes his head, laughing lightly as he heads down the hall, shoulders wide and proud.

# CHAPTER 23

## Lance

"**A**LL SET?" I ASK BRIAN, STANDING BEHIND THE RIBBON. He holds up a finger, using his other hand to press a button on his headset. Moments later, he gives me a thumbs-up to let me know security has done their full sweep and we're clear to proceed.

I take Charlotte's hand on my left, Trixie's on my right as we step onto the small stage just off Main Street. Charlotte steps forward, happiness shooting off her like fireworks as the assembled crowd claps.

"Thank you so much for coming. Today, we begin a new chapter in the story of Roseboro. Once upon a time, families spent hours together. I remember my Grandma Winnie teaching me so much. How to bake, how to garden, how to sew—though that lesson didn't go so well." She pauses as everyone laughs.

"But over the years, our culture has succumbed to the dreaded 'busy' bug, and the divide between generations grew. There aren't Sunday dinners where everyone gathers around the table together, or daily phone calls to catch up. In my Grandma Winnie's honor, I'd like to see this change."

She looks back at me and Trixie, smiling. "*We'd* like to see this change. So welcome to the first ever Generations of Hope event. We've been fortunate to partner with people of every age, businesses of every industry, and hopefully, your hearts today. Meet, talk, share, impart knowledge, and let us bridge the gap and create a new generation of hope."

Trixie and I step forward, giant scissors in our hands, and Charlotte holds the ribbon as we cut, the three of us kicking it off together, making the idea we sprouted over work in the bakery come to life before our very eyes.

The crowd cheers as the ribbon drops, the mob surging forward. It's a good mix of seniors and kids, and everything in between, which I'm glad to see. That's the vital key to making this a success.

"We did it," I say proudly. "Mission accomplished."

Trixie rolls her eyes, punching me in the shoulder lightly. "Military talk, really?" She moves her hand, mimicking a talking mouth. "Roger wilco, hooah, hooah, sir!"

Charlotte, though, has stars in her eyes. Admittedly, they probably have more to do with the smiling faces all around us, but I'll take some credit for her smile when she curls into my side, wrapping an arm around my waist. "Hush, I like it when he talks all military."

*Oh? I could think of some orders I'd like to give her.*

But now's not the time, even though Trixie says, "And that's my cue to leave you two alone. Don't do anything to scar the little kiddies or cause one of the old farts to have a heart attack." She winks as she walks off, laughing.

Charlotte and I walk around, checking in with the various booths and getting to see our handiwork firsthand.

In the first tent, Jeanine Matherson, a retired fine arts teacher from Upstate who retired to Roseboro, is leading a beginner class on pencil drawing. She's got a group of mixed students, some young and some old, but all concentrating on the line technique she's demonstrating. The next tent has a tiny, grey-haired woman with thick ropes of yarn looped over her arms as she coaches her students through some tricky method of over-under.

"I'll be back for your second lesson, Mrs. Petrie," Charlotte calls out, and the woman smiles and nods. Turning, she giggles. "And there's the competition."

I look over to see a white-haired woman with a gleaming smile handing out cookies, waving when Charlotte waves. "Who's she?"

"Joan Harris, the police chief's wife. I don't think there's been a single school bake sale, charity event, or church bazaar in town that she isn't there with her cookies."

"Oh?" I ask, amused. "How are they?"

She sighs, but not unkindly. "They're delicious, and gorgeously decorated by hand. Each and every one of them piped to perfection. Diabetics are warned to stay ten feet away from her at all times. That's why I stick to every other treat and let her have the corner on the decorated cookie market."

We watch the storytelling area for a while, where kids are sitting enraptured as older citizens read them stories. A few of them seem to be telling stories of their own, sharing their wisdom with the next generation.

The picture of the day has to be a little girl, probably only three or four years old, fast asleep in the arms of a grey-haired man in a wheelchair. She'd asked if she could sit in his lap, declared him her new grandpa, skin color differences notwithstanding, then promptly passed out from all the excitement.

It's enough to make a hardened soldier like me get a bit choked up.

We walk on, and I find Cody at a booth showcasing the Jacobs Bio-Tech arm prosthesis. It's a current offering from our product catalog, though it's always being updated as new technologies become realities. But the kids and adults gathered around him don't seem to think it's outdated. Based on his current discussion of whether the 'robot arm' or Iron-Man would win an arm-wrestling competition, he seems to be doing quite well, actually. My favorite is the young man who's explaining to a grandma who Iron-Man is, using the image on his shirt as a show-and-tell.

I offer a wave, which he answers with a bro chin lift and a smile. Then his eyes turn to Charlotte, and he calls out, "Thanks again for inviting Jacobs Bio-Tech, Charlotte. Your Generations of Hope event seems to be a raging success!" The crowd around him turns to look at Charlotte, who's blushing at the attention as they all thank her, saying how much fun they're having and asking when the next one will be.

Eventually, we make our way down the rest of the row. "Your brother is pretty slick with the name dropping," Charlotte says, "and the gaggle of people mobbing him."

Pride bubbles up, not that I had anything to do with Cody's prowess as a representative of the company or the family, but just that he's my brother and is doing so well.

"You want to head to the grills and grab a bite to eat before your cake decorating demo this afternoon?" I ask Charlotte, who's looking around with a beaming smile on her face.

She agrees, but before we take a step to follow the delicious aroma wafting through the area, a deep voice sounds from behind us. "Charlotte."

She whirls as I automatically reach for my Sig, which is stored in a fanny pack, much to my displeasure. Unfortunately, it'd been the best family-friendly way to carry. Instead of a threat, though, I find Thomas and Mia approaching.

Charlotte lets out an ear-splitting 'eeeee' and grabs Mia in a big hug, the two of them going total girl-giddy.

Thomas eyes me up and down. "Things look wonderful, Charlotte. And you're enjoying yourself, Lance?"

"Always. It's better to build than destroy," I reply honestly. We didn't get too much of a chance to talk during the whole Health Inspector drama, but that's okay. I've gotten my measure of the man, and he's good.

"You know, Lance, you're quite the subject of conversation," Thomas says with a chuckle, glancing at Mia. "These two seem to be unable to stop gossiping about you."

"Hopefully, good things," I hedge, and Thomas grins, not really divulging any more.

Mia shoves at my shoulder, grinning. "All good, trust me. You were the topic of a whole dinner a couple of weeks ago. Jonathan vouched for you. That's the only reason we didn't sic Gabe on you. Well, that and Charlotte says you're quite—"

"Sweet!" Charlotte interjects, splotches darkening her cheeks as she gives Mia a look that communicates 'shut up' loud and clear.

I laugh at the obvious compliments she's been divulging, throwing my arm around Charlotte's shoulder and kissing her on the temple. "As long as it's good, I guess I'm okay with that."

Mia smirks, nudging Charlotte with her elbow. "Humble, too? Looks like you've got a keeper, girl. Lucky bitch."

I look to Charlotte, half expecting her to have questions, doubts, and nerves rising in the depths of her eyes. But what I find takes my breath away.

I can see the trust she's placing in me, the hope that I won't betray her the way others have. It feels like the most important responsibility I've ever taken on, one I won't fail to live up to. Especially not when I know what it's costing her to have faith in a future with me.

"I think I'm the lucky one as she's adding me into her busy schedule," I say, letting Charlotte off the hook. "We were heading over to grab a burger. Want one too?"

Mia links her arm through Charlotte's, pulling her away from me. "Absolutely! You think you're getting away from me that easily?"

Thomas and I meet gazes, both of us happy to trail along after our women as they chatter away.

Once we all have burgers in hand and Charlotte has thanked the guy manning the grill for his sponsorship of the event, we find a tall table to perch at. Mia steps away for a moment to grab us all cold bottles of water, returning quickly, and we dig in.

Conversation is light, and Charlotte relaxes without teasing digs for gossip from Mia.

Our burgers disappear bite by bite, and the girls start rambling about a video game I've never heard of before, something called TERA.

"They do this often?"

Thomas grins, shrugging like this is a normal occurrence. "Give Mia two months, and she'll have you playing too."

I look around and see a surprising sight heading this way.

"Dad! Mom!" I call, giving them a welcoming hug. "Good to see you here."

Mom is smiling at Charlotte like she hung the moon and stars, or like she might be the key to keeping her baby boy here in Roseboro. Dad, however, is focused on Thomas.

"Great to see you again, Thomas."

"You too, Bishop. Couldn't miss an event like this."

"All for a great cause. Lance and Charlotte did a wonderful job with this," Dad says, beaming, "launching from idea to reality so quickly. It'd be an amazing asset to continue the get-togethers throughout the year, help the connections grow for all the citizens of Roseboro for generations to come."

"No need for the hard sell, Dad," I warn with a chuckle. "Whoever Thomas chooses as the winner for his Hope Initiative will be deserving. And the real winners are the people of Roseboro, no matter what."

Thomas inclines his head. "Didn't I see your other son here too?"

"Yes, Cody has really gotten on fire with this. He's demo'ing our prosthetic arm. He's quite the showman, but he knows that product inside and out, manages that project team in fact," Dad brags.

It's been a little over a week since our sit-down chat. I don't know what Dad said to Cody or what Cody said to Dad, but their relationship has been improving. It's still not perfect, but I think Dad finally sees that his fear of the future was the real problem all along, not Cody's work, which Dad admits is significantly better than he'd let on.

The best side effect of Dad's epiphany is that Cody and I are no longer getting pressured to perform, at work or with the whole wife-kids-picket fence combo platter.

Thomas and Dad begin discussing how a Jacobs prosthesis project might help with patients at Goldstone Health, and Charlotte leans over to me.

"I need to head over to the community center kitchen for the decorating demo. You coming with me?"

I nod, whispering so I don't interrupt Dad and Thomas. "Of course. You're my number-one priority. I'm on your six all day."

Heat fills her eyes, and I know she reads my double meaning. "Excuse us. We've got to be in the kitchen in fifteen. Thanks so much for coming, though."

Dad and Thomas nod, going back to talking immediately. Meanwhile, Mia is watching us with a knowing look.

Before we're three steps away, Charlotte pulls on my hand to stop me. She lifts up to her toes and presses her lips to mine. She tastes salty and sweet, my favorite combination.

When she pulls away, I lick my lips, getting one last taste of her. "What was that for?"

Pulling me down, she whispers into my ear, her breath hot and her tone suddenly sultry. "One, for helping me pull this off. Two, for that military talk. You know what that does to me."

My lips quirk as I fight the smile that wants to stretch my face so desperately. "Oh, you like that? Well, I'll be on your six all night, making sure every bit of intel is drawn from your body. Three, four, five times, if I have to. I won't stop until my mission is complete."

It's the weirdest dirty talk I think I've ever said, but if she knew radio code, I'd fill her ear with word salad. Whatever this woman needs from me is what I'm damn well going to give her.

She laughs, pushing back a little. "On second thought, I think my baking puns are better."

I growl, pulling her in tight. "You think your dirty talk is better than mine?" I feel her head nod against my shoulder. "Red, all damn day, I've been walking around being polite and well-mannered for your event. But what I really want is to take you home, yank those jeans off your ass, leave on that Generations of Hope T-shirt that fits you so damn well, then fuck you until your screams bounce off the walls. I want you coming on my hand, my tongue, and then, if you're real nice, I'll stretch that pussy with my thick cock until you come on me again. Then I'll flip you over, wrap that braid around my fist to force you to arch for me, and I'll fuck that bubble ass of yours until I fill you up with so much cum you can't even hold it. But I'll help you slip your panties back on, pat that pussy, and hold you all night while you sleep in the mess we made."

She shudders in my arms, and I wonder if she just had an orgasm from my filthy words. And when she pulls back, I can see that she's damn close, ripe for the picking.

Her eyes are blue flames, fire I want to burn me, mark me as hers. Her chest rises and falls as she pants, her puffy lips open and waiting for mine.

My cock surges between us, thick and hard and wanting to mark her too. Inside and out, cover her with cum so she always knows that she's mine and I'm not going anywhere.

The lust is palpable, electricity sparking on our skin, but there's a deeper layer to it, a foundation we've built brick by brick, sometimes slowly and other times, faster. All at whatever pace Charlotte needs.

But I can see it now. She's with me, no longer dancing around the fire but engulfed in it with me.

She bites her lip, taking a jagged breath. "You fight dirty. Because all I want to do is run straight for home, or hell, the nearest deserted corner, and do just that. Fuck yes, to all of that. But I can't. I have to—"

"Not fighting. *Promising.* That's my mission tonight," I say with a soft vow in my voice. "But right now, you need to go decorate some cupcakes, so let's go." I run a finger down the bridge of her upturned nose, an oddly intimate gesture, then *boop* her at the tip. "Let's go, Sweet Scarlet. There are cupcakes that need frosting."

I pull her hand, directing her to the community center kitchen, but I hear her growl behind me, "Yeah, there is. *My cupcake.*"

# CHAPTER 24

## Blackwell

I PEER THROUGH THE TELESCOPE, WATCHING THE STREET BELOW FROM my living room window, sneering as the happy rabble leave the community center. Of course, the ginger honeypot will be there for hours, breaking down equipment and finishing up the event.

I'm sure she feels it was a success, and from a standpoint of charitable goodwill, it probably was. Too bad charity is a misplaced effort, a pathetic attempt to level the playing field when, by life's very nature, there are leaders, followers, those who achieve, and those who are sacrificed.

The greater good for the many? No.

The greatest good for *me*. Earned through strategy and manipulation. And it will be mine.

I'm growing impatient, ready to move past the small annoyances to the large-scale plays that will truly get me to the top of the mountain. King of the hill? I'll be King of the entire Pacific Seaboard, no matter what it takes or who I have to step on to get there.

Speaking of destroying the weak and useless, I decide to reach out to a resource, one well-placed and with the potential to be exceedingly useful. For a time. They are all only useful for a time, then they are parceled out the same fate as so many others before them.

The fate I will receive too, for none of us escape the Reaper forever. But

I will go out on my own terms, cheating him with a golden crown proclaiming that I created this town, and it will forever be mine.

"Hello?" the voice answers.

"Are you alone?" I ask, wanting to be sure I maintain the utmost secrecy for the next phase of my master plan.

There's some muted conversation in the background, then my pawn speaks again. "My apologies, sir. I'm alone now."

"Any suspicions?"

My pawn laughs lightly. "No. Not at all. Can I help with something?"

Though they are obviously eager to get off the phone, I'm more than eager to move pawns where I wish them. "Today's charity event disturbs me. Everyone mingling with smiles on their faces and Goldstone's 'hope' in their hearts. Useless drivel."

Though I can't see my operative, I can hear the shrug. "It doesn't make a difference if people have hope. You'll do what you want and they'll be left in your wake, but you'll still be in control." Such resignation is in contrast to my pawn's previous commitment to my goal, but as long as orders are carried out, I can tolerate some flagging spirits.

"I see," I muse. "You'd do well to remember that as well. When the dust settles, I will be in control. Of Roseboro, and of you."

The threat need not be more explicit, though I let my mind wander for a moment at the joyous beauty an extra death would bring. Shock and surprise for some, and glorious victory for me.

"Of course, sir."

The speedy acquiescence pleases me. Most of my minions think themselves strong. And perhaps to the average person, they are. Most of them are self-starters, overachievers who have reached and tried to grasp the proverbial brass ring. But like a Shakespearean hero, they all have that tragic, fatal flaw. Hubris, insecurity, lust for power, it doesn't matter. I take it, I mold it, and when they think they are free, I show them the full extent of their self-made prison. Only then are they ready to be the weapon I desire, to strike down my enemies like an arrow loosed from a bow.

Even if Golden Boy knows I am coming, it is the unseen dart that strikes deepest.

"I will have use for you soon. Be aware, be cooperative, and you will reap what you sow." I toss out the promise that has always yielded results, with of course, the irony unnoticed. The wishes aren't outlandish, merely a life that they've been denied. But I can easily repair that discrepancy. That is assured. "And maintain secrecy. No one need know of your motivations. Yet."

"Yes, sir. I understand."

I hang up and sit back, considering the fortitude I require of my operative. Each one has been a wealth of information, insights I wouldn't have received otherwise, and have successfully completed backhanded actions at my command. But this pawn is dangerous, moldable by me, yes, but also able to be influenced by those around them. I will have to remind them that my orders are paramount, even more than friends, family, or conscience.

I might need to advance my timeline, not dilly-dally and allow questions to take root. I am ready to proceed and will do so as soon as possible.

One other area of my schedule to address. I make another call.

"Yes, sir," he answers, all business.

"The preparations, are they complete?" I say, not letting my urgency color my words but instead feigning mere interest in his progress.

"Nearly, sir. We were delayed ever so slightly because we do have to actually do the upgrades Mr. Goldstone requested to his systems or our presence would be noticed. But I'll do my final assessment to sign off on the completed work and will make the special adjustments you requested."

"Excellent. And when it's completed—"

"You will be in total control." I do not appreciate that he interrupted me in the least, but his promise of control is an exhilarating one. Another step in the direction I will take Roseboro.

I smirk at his choice of words. "Aren't I always?"

He chuckles, agreeing, and hangs up with a promise to notify me when the job is complete.

My mood lifts from the dark pall today's events brought over me. Because it's true. I am always in control, and this time, there's nothing Golden Boy can do to stop me.

I will take it all. His money, his friends . . . but most importantly, his life.

And Roseboro will once again be mine alone.

I take a piece of stationary from my top drawer, heavyweight linen beneath my black ink pen. It is an old tradition of sorts. A declaration of war, an opportunity for surrender. But there will be no mercy given by my hand.

Not now. Not ever.

My hand flows surely across the page.

*Thomas,*

*I will admit to you a failing. A breach of the confidence I bore for so many years, heedless of the future and certain of my standing as the rightful creator of this fine town of Roseboro. For it is my town, my creation.*

*But much like the intrusion of the Black Plague in 1348, you came to Roseboro. I am a bit of a history buff, you see, and much like the Italians attempted to forestall the spread of the destruction, I did the same.*

*Small movements to slow your progress, underhanded deals to stop you at every opportunity. For your attempts to become the King of the Rose-Covered Throne were unwelcome, most of all by me.*

*But the time for sacrificial pawns has passed. Checkmate.*

My pen starts to flow faster and faster, and before I know it, I'm smiling with mirthless glee at a future he doesn't even see coming for him, faster than a speeding bullet and more dangerous than he could imagine.

This rough draft might not be perfect, but it will be. Just in time for his ultimate destruction.

# CHAPTER 25

## Lance

"WE DID IT!" CHARLOTTE EXCLAIMS.

Coming up to the roof of the *Cake Culture* building was a stroke of inspiration, and now I'm glad I agreed to her idea to grab the fire escape ladder and head up here.

Laid back on a blanket on the roof above her apartment, the night sky glittering above us, she's stunning. Her red hair is fanned out over my arm, her head cradled on my chest as she curls up next to me.

"You did it," I correct her, grinning to myself in the dark. Trixie and I certainly helped, but Charlotte was the driving force behind the whole event. She's already got ideas for the next one. It'll be smaller, for sure, not a kick-off event like today's, but still just as impactful for the generations of people who have already committed to coming.

She snuggles in closer, sighing happily. "Thank you, for today and for . . . everything."

I press a kiss to her forehead, inhaling her scent. "Anything for you."

I mean it. She's set my world off its axis. She is why fate brought me here. I'm sure of it. I was put in this place for her. And she, for me.

She says she doesn't believe in happily ever afters, but I do. I believe enough for the both of us. And something tells me she's starting to believe too.

"Did you see that?" she whispers, tension shooting through her body.

"What?" I say, moving to get up and defend her if necessary. We're safe here on the roof. The fire escape ladder is one of those hyper-secure ones that you can't reach from the ground level. But her alarm puts me on alert.

She pulls me back to her, laughing softly. "Down, boy, I meant the shooting star. No need to go Battle-Bot on me."

I relax back into the blanket beneath us, rolling her to her back and looming over her, keeping her caged in the frame of my arms. "A shooting star, you say? Did you make a wish?"

She bites her lip, driving me mad before confessing, "Well, I remembered some rather filthy things you said to me earlier. What if I wished for those to come true?"

"Then I'd be happy to make that wish come true."

I press my lips to hers, not sweetly, not this time, but rough and forceful, all the need we built up from our little touches and looks over the course of today driving me hard. I take her mouth, owning her as we share breaths, promising more. More pleasure, more time, more us.

She writhes beneath me, moaning as she returns the passion in my kiss in equal measure. Moving lower, I kiss along her neck, tasting her salty sweetness, savoring the air of vanilla that permeates her. She turns her head, giving me access and begging for more.

I nip and suck at the satiny skin, whispering in her ear. "Tell me what you want."

"Everything," she repeats, her earlier word having a new meaning in the heat of the moment. "Fuck me."

"As you wish," I tell her, committed to making her every dream come true.

I trace my hand along her side, following the curve and brushing along the side of her breast. Her back arches, and I shove her shirt up, revealing her lacy bra. "Shit, you've had this on all day? These candy-pink nipples barely covered by lace? If I'd known that, I would've pushed you into the first deserted alleyway I could find and fucked you right there."

She grins, like she thinks I'm exaggerating. I'm not.

I nuzzle her cleavage, feeling her softness against the scruff of my cheeks, and reach behind her to unhook her bra. She reaches for the hem of her shirt to pull it off, but I stop her. "Nuh-uh, I told you I was going to fuck you in this T-shirt and I'm going to." I pull the loosened bra down as she watches, letting her tits rest on the shelf it creates before I trace her pinkness, biting her playfully, just the way she likes.

I unbutton her jeans, and she lifts her hips to help me, kicking her shoes off with a toe. Grabbing her waistband, I pull at her jeans as I lift up, turning them inside-out as they come off, leaving her bottom half-bare, save for her panties. I rip them off too, revealing her slick and needy pussy.

"Fuck, Char." My voice is a deep rumble against her hip as I tease a finger along her wetness, tracing her lips. "On my hand first," I tell her, slipping a finger inside her.

She whimpers as I curl my finger, petting the front wall of her pussy. The wet sounds of my pumping finger send electric tingles through my spine as I speed up, holding her down with my free hand until she's on the edge.

With a final stroke, she spasms, her scream rising in her throat. I swallow her cry in a kiss, and her hips rise, bridging up to my hand. I plunge into her as deeply as I can, stroking her inside as she falls apart for me.

"I've got you. Let it go, Charlotte."

Her honey coats my fingers, thick and sticky. Needing a taste, I kiss my way down even as my finger keeps stroking her. She's still coming when I flick my tongue over her clit. She bucks, her hands going to my hair.

"I can't, too much," she protests, though her hands are pulling me to her, not pushing me away.

"On my hand, on my tongue, and on my cock," I remind her. "You can go again, I know you can."

I hold still, letting her have control for a moment. She lifts and lowers her hips, running her clit over my flattened tongue. My tongue dips inside her every chance she gives me, lapping up her sweetness and swallowing her down.

"That's it . . . use me, fuck my mouth." She tries to keep going but she's getting so close already, the edge rising up to meet her. Her movements stutter, losing their rhythm, and I take over.

I suck her clit into my mouth, fluttering my tongue across the hardened nub. Her back bows and then reverses, curving her hips and shoulders together as a guttural grunt, primal in its depths, erupts from her. It's music to my ears, a buffet for my tongue as she comes again.

I've waited for her my entire life, the one I never even knew I was looking for as I escaped to save the world. But she's here now, with me in this moment, and I need her.

I rip my shirt over my head and unbutton my jeans, shoving them and my boxers down my hips but not able to wait long enough to take them off entirely. Charlotte looks down my body, drinking me in with her eyes. I rub my hand across my chest, over the ridges of my abs, and down to take my throbbing cock in hand. I stroke for her, enjoying the way her eyes widen and her lips open like she wants to suck me.

"You want it?" She bites her lip, nodding. "Where?"

I had a plan, a promise I'd made to her, but the way her tongue peeks out to wet her lips taunts me, teasing me to diverge from the path. She drives me mad with the desire to claim every sweet inch of her, inside and out.

"My mouth," she whispers, breathless but sure.

She sits up, flipping her knees beneath her and sitting back on her heels. She leans forward, licking my crown, making a slow circle to taste the precum that's leaking freely for her. My knees spread, dipping into her mouth deeper, and she takes me inch by inch into her mouth and throat.

I weave my fingers into her hair, cupping her head to guide her as I begin to fuck her mouth. She moans, the vibration zinging all the way to my balls, which are already tightening up, ready to come for her. The *gluck* sound as my cock leaves her throat is sexy and thrilling, and she swallows reflexively. I give her a moment to breathe before sliding back into the wet heaven of her mouth. Her cheeks hollow, her tongue curling to tease my shaft, and suddenly, I'm right on the edge.

I pull back, leaving her mouth gaping open, a line of spit from her lips to my cock. "Not yet, not in your mouth this time."

She nods and lies back on the blanket, knowing what I want. Her eyes sparkle in the moonlight, full of lust, full of *more*, speaking to my heart.

But I don't say the words, not yet. Though I feel them, deeply and acutely, I don't want to scare her. Not now, when we've come so far.

She surprises me when she flips over, giving me her back. At first, I think she's overwhelmed with the emotion of the moment and hiding once again. But she looks over her shoulder, braid swishing along her freckled skin, and she arches, presenting herself to me.

"You did promise me something naughty." Her hips sway seductively, reminding me of what I vowed earlier today. I'd been teasing in a way, testing her limits, but now . . .

My God. She's committing to me fully, trusting me to stay with her, to give her exactly what I promised. And I'm a man of my word.

I fall over her, catching myself on one hand and wrapping her messy braid around my fist to keep her eyes on me, not letting her escape this moment. The moment she is mine, I've already been hers.

Dipping my fingers into her wet honey again, I coat them before reaching up to massage her asshole, watching her eyes. She moans thickly as I press in, pushing back as my finger penetrates her.

I take my time opening her up, preparing her for me. When she's ready, I line my cock up with her ass, watching the spit-covered head nudge against her. "Ready?"

"Please," she begs. "I'm so ready."

I thrust into her slowly, relishing her body stretching around my thick cock. I can feel the quivers of her body, the tight ring of her ass squeezing me and not letting me go, as if there's anywhere else I'd rather be than inside her. Body, mind, and soul.

When she pushes back again, I pound into her just like I promised, feeling her orgasm rising quickly. "Come for me, Red. I need to feel you come on my cock."

She's riding the edge, a hairsbreadth away from falling but clinging on. "What do you need?" I ask, and she whimpers.

And I know. She's ready. Fuck knows, I'm ready.

I pull her hair harder, turning her head to look at me, not letting her doubts color the moment. I need her to hear me, see me, trust my truth.

"I love you, Charlotte. With all my heart. I love you."

She cries out to the dark night, the words releasing not only her orgasm but the restraints she's placed on her own heart too. And as she shudders beneath me, I hear the words fall from her mouth too.

"I love you too."

It releases me, and I claim her final secret . . . her heart. Finally mine.

It's hours later, or maybe minutes, when I slip out of her. I turn her to her back, lying beside her and tracing the curve of her collarbone. Everything has changed tonight, here on this roof.

"Did you mean it?" she asks, but the teasing tone says she already knows the answer.

I tickle her, making her squirm and laugh. "I think I made good on my word," I say, touching my thumb to my fingers as I tick off, "on my hand, on my tongue, and on my cock."

She rolls her eyes, and I give her what she wants. "Yes, I meant it. I've felt it for a while, but didn't want to scare you. Are you scared?"

She dips her chin, closing her eyes for a second, but she's smiling so I don't get too nervous until the moment stretches. My heart stops beating until she opens her eyes once again, her blues meeting mine.

"Surprisingly, I'm not. I feel bubbly, warm inside. Like bread dough is rising inside me and I'm so full of carb-y happiness I want to explode like the Pillsbury Dough Boy."

I can't help but laugh. She's funny and sexy and perfect just as she is. "I don't think I've ever heard of love being compared to bread, but somehow, it seems fitting for you."

Eventually, I do pick her up and carry her back downstairs to bed. I don't put her messy panties on her, though, instead curling up behind her, both of us naked, to fall asleep.

I'm awakened by the sound of a buzzing cell phone, and I look over to see it's Jonathan. It's the middle of the night, hours before Charlotte's alarm will go off to start her morning baking.

I extract myself from Charlotte's side and quietly head to the living room so I don't wake her. "Hello?"

"Am I interrupting?" he asks, a chuckle in his voice. "Heard there were some fireworks over the bakery tonight."

"Shut up, asshole," I joke back. "I'm sure you're not calling in the middle of the night to give me shit. What's wrong?"

"Just an update, like you asked. We've got some reliable intel that Blackwell's got local law enforcement in his pocket, all the way to the top. You got a problem, call me or state police. Got it?"

"I understand. Keep me informed."

I hang up, sensing Charlotte behind me. "Who was that?"

"Jonathan. He just wanted to give me an update. Nothing actionable, but he knows I'm here to help keep you safe," I promise.

Charlotte wraps her arms around me, burying her head in my chest. "Thank you. You're one of about a half-dozen people I trust right now, so thank you for watching my back."

I kiss her forehead, picking her up in my arms and carrying her back to bed. "I've got you, Charlotte. I'll keep you safe, body and heart."

She relaxes into my arms, falling asleep quickly with the reassurances. But as I lie awake for hours, I find my mind analyzing every angle Blackwell could be coming at her and at Thomas from. I'd been worried about the event today, enough to work with Jonathan on adding extra security, but it'd gone off without a hitch.

So if not something big like that, what's he planning? Because a man like Blackwell is always planning something. And we need to figure out what it is before anyone else gets hurt.

# CHAPTER 26

## Charlotte

THE BAKERY IS HOPPING BUSY, A LINE OUT THE DOOR ONCE AGAIN. The Health Department issue fizzled quickly, and the Generations of Hope event had an added benefit of making my bakery *the* place to go for all your baked good needs. Old and young, and every age in between, have been clamoring for *Cake Culture* for the last week.

Trixie and I have been baking our asses off, and Lance has been helping even more than usual. With his dad and Cody patching things up, he hasn't been as needed at the office, nor at his secondary office at the table in the corner. I'm glad because I wouldn't have been able to get through these last few days without his support. He's my number-one dishwasher.

Right now, he's in the back, though, doing his other specialty, making buttercream. It's the tenth batch of the day, a creamy lemon sorbet frosting for the 'Sock It To Yo Mama Sucker Punch' cupcakes that are cooling on a rack.

As I serve up box after box, I smile and thank each customer from the bottom of my heart. They're the ones letting me do exactly what I've always dreamed of doing, and I appreciate their business.

A blonde woman in a fitted dress that highlights all of her assets steps up to the case next. She looks like she's ready to go on a date, hair and makeup perfect and high heels shaping her calf muscles. If I weren't so damn busy, I'd feel like a frumpy-frump next to her, but luckily, I'm way too busy to care about my barely-there face or pulled-up hair. *Function over frivolity* has become my motto.

"How may I help you?" I ask, already grabbing a box.

She looks at the case but seems to be uncertain, her eyes darting to the tables throughout the space. Twirling a lock of stick-straight hair around her finger, she says quietly, "Uhm, there's usually a guy here. He helps sometimes, but mostly, he sits over there." She tilts her head like she doesn't want to get busted pointing. "I think he's like the owner or manager or something. Is he here?"

Trixie hip-checks me, a beaming smile on her face. "Oh, you mean Commander Cookie? He is here, but unfortunately, he's elbows-deep in frosting at the moment. I'm sure Sweet Scarlet here can get you a delicious treat, though, and if you sit down, maybe he'll come out to deliver some hot, fresh cookies right out of the oven."

It's on the tip of my tongue to tell the woman that his name is Lance and he's mine, mine, mine, but Trixie's wink makes me back off. Staking my territory is a bit of a new instinct to me, but I don't know if I've ever been this far gone over someone, so maybe it's normal?

The woman nods in thanks to Trixie and asks me for a 'Shangri-Vanil-La' cupcake. Once she's served, she makes her way to an open table, barely pecking at the cupcake and obviously wasting time as she waits for Lance to make an appearance.

"What the hell?" I ask Trixie, about ready to resort to the 'licked it, he's mine' defense. Or is that an offensive move? Sports have never been my strong suit, so I don't know the first thing about offensive or defensive. Hell, I'll go for both, just to be sure.

Trixie rolls her eyes but smiles. "In case you didn't know, while the cakes and cookies and pies are popular, we're also famous for serving up a fair bit of eye candy to go with it. And despite our obvious assets, it's not us."

She pouts, but it's fake as can be, and I can sense her desire to flip her hair around, but the messy bun at the back of her head doesn't lend itself too much drama. She looks towards the double doors that hide Lance from the front of the shop.

"Ain't nothing sexier than a hot man who can cook, bonus points that he can string more than three words together."

She gestures to the line of women who are focused on the case and menus on the wall until . . .

Lance comes out from the back. "Got the next batch of zucchini bread in the oven. What's next, Boss?"

His eyes are on me, but I can see every head in the place swivel in his direction. Jealousy squirts into my bloodstream, hot and sour, and heat rises in my cheeks.

Trixie whispers from right next to my ear, chuckling. "He's only got eyes for you, Char. Don't worry your pretty little head about that boy. Hook, line, and sinker, he's done for."

It's not her words that soothe the beast in my belly but Lance's smile as he comes over. "How's it going? Need anything?"

My body, semi-functional brain included, wants to say that I need to take him upstairs and claim him. Ride him like I did before, blow him like I did before, remind him that he's mine and everyone else can step the fuck off. But he doesn't need the reminder. His eyes tell me that he knows exactly what's going through my head.

He stands next to me, possessively throwing his arm over my shoulder and rubbing lightly at the skin below the short sleeve of my T-shirt. Leaning down, he whispers in my ear, "Whatever you're thinking, I fucking *love* that idea. Let's serve all these people as fast as we can, then you can slowly and with lots of adjectives tell me exactly what you have in mind."

His cocky smirk is full of heat, but I don't mind because it's warranted. He's mine, I'm his, and every woman in here is wishing he was whispering sweet nothings and dirty somethings in their ears. But he belongs to one person. Me.

"All right, Commander Cookie," I say, lifting my brows. "Let's get these people fed. Everyone's starving today."

There's a murmur through the crowd, and I think I hear someone murmur, 'hungry for him,' but Lance ignores it and gets to work. He's friendly and charming but professional, and slowly but surely, the line shrinks.

There's only a few more people waiting when the one person I don't want to see comes strolling in the door. Actually, scratch that, one of the two people I don't want to see.

"Charlotte, can we talk, please?" Sabrina says haughtily.

Gesturing to the line, I tell her, "Kinda busy here. Can it wait?"

*Or just never happen*, I think, wishing she'd just leave.

I'm still not 100% sure she didn't send in those anonymous complaints, even though she denied it. I'm also not 100% sure she did it. Which leaves me in a state of limbo. I don't like her, that's a ship that sailed long ago, but there's a difference to who we were as kids and who we are now, as adults. Or at least, there should be. Lance taught me that with Cody, their relationship evolving and improving now that they're talking more.

"You think I'd be here if it wasn't important?" Sabrina hisses, her eyes narrowing. I don't answer for a moment, trying to see what her play is here. Because there's always a play with her.

"Fine, let's step to the back so we don't air our family laundry in front of everyone. Can you guys watch the front?" I ask Trixie and Lance. When they nod, I lead Sabrina to the kitchen.

"Okay, what's up?" I ask, not wanting any small talk. Whatever she's here for, she can speak and get the fuck out. Especially since I'm betting it's more whining about Lance.

I cross my arms, leaning back against the table, but she paces a bit, looking at the kitchen. "This looks great," she says, and it's all I can do to bite back the remark about her saying the opposite on her complaint form to the Health Department.

When I don't thank her, she sighs and says, "I'm worried about Dad."

"What's wrong with him?" I say, instantly scared to death that Priscilla has finally done something that will drive him into an early grave.

Sabrina shakes her head, holding up a hand. "Not like that. He's not dying or anything. Or at least, no more than the rest of us, but he's just . . . stressed. More than usual, and it's wearing on him. I can tell by the worry on his face, and he's not eating enough. I think *we* wear on him. Not that I think we're ever gonna be besties, but a little less 'at each other's throat' would probably help."

It's a ridiculous request, one I have serious doubts I could honor even if I wanted to. But he's my dad, and he's forgiven me for so much over the years, only asking for one thing . . . that I be kind to his family.

They're not mine, but as much as I chose Mia and Izzy and the whole gang and would defend and support them no matter what, Dad's chosen Priscilla and Sabrina to be a part of his family. And I can respect that, or at least I should.

The door creaks open, and Trixie's head pops in, blonde permed hair springing from her bun. "Sorry to interrupt, but we need you for a minute."

I nod to Trixie before turning back to Sabrina. "Can you wait one second? Let me deal with this and I'll be right back." I run out front, dealing with a customer who wants to order a custom cake.

It takes a little longer than I'd expected, and after a few minutes, Sabrina comes out of the kitchen. She waves as she walks by, calling out, "Check in on Dad. He'd like to hear from you."

It irks me that she's telling me what to do once again, but she's only suggesting that I get closer to him, like maybe she knows he needs me. That's oddly *kind* of her, which is not a descriptor I'd typically ever use for Sabrina.

When Sabrina's gone, I go back to helping the lady who's ordering a tiered quinceañera cake with various edible pearls, sequins, and icing designs. It's going to be another major showcase for my decorating skills, and I'm excited about it, ready to tackle more large-scale orders.

While the line is manageable, Trixie sneaks off to the back to take the zucchini bread out of the oven, toss a batch of muffins in, and grab a tray of cookies. It feels like we successfully made it through another rush.

"What'd Sabrina want?" Trixie asks cautiously. "World War III beginning today?"

I shake my head, still not completely believing Sabrina. "Surprisingly, no. She was telling me that she's worried about Dad and thought I should give him a call. She even said maybe we could lighten up on each other for his sake."

Even as I repeat her missive, I can't believe she would be so mature, not after our last near-knockdown-drag-out fight over the health inspector.

"Hmm, that is surprising—" Trixie says.

But she's interrupted by a loud BOOM.

My eyes meet Trixie's, whose are wide with alarm. Lance jumps into action, moving straight for the double doors to the kitchen.

But when he opens them, the wafting air from the back fills the front room, smoky and hot.

"Oh, shit, the kitchen's on fire," Trixie blurts out.

They say there are two types of people in crisis situations, fighters and flighters. I'm here to say that there's a third type, freezers. Because I'm frozen in place, disbelieving my eyes.

Through the open doors, a haze of white billows near the ceiling, and flames jump from the oven. Lance grabs the fire extinguisher, quickly pulling the pin and aiming at the base of the fire as he sweeps the white foam through the chaos.

Finally, the alarm goes off, a shrill beeping tone that repeats annoyingly, then the sprinklers rain down cold water on everything. It's the signal for people to go from 'Oh, my God' to 'get me out of here', and there's a mad dash for the front door.

Steven pulls on my arm with a firm grip. "Miss Dunn!"

"Everyone out," I call out, finally coming out of my shock. It feels like an eternity has gone by, but it's only been an instant. Just an instant, but my dream is going up in smoke, in flames that are reaching the ceiling now despite Lance's efforts. "Come on, Lance. We have to go."

He tries to shake me off, his eyes gritted against the heat and smoke. "I can save it. I can—"

"Save you, save us. That's all I need. Let's get out of here," I say, pleading with him. He lowers the near-empty extinguisher, realizing I'm right.

The three of us are the last ones out, me, Lance, and Steven busting out the door as the fire trucks are pulling up. Firefighters pull hoses, aiming for the bakery, and with a whoosh of water, they begin fighting the fire.

It's terrifying and heartbreaking, but at the same time, I feel an overwhelming sense of relief that we're all okay.

"What happened?" I ask, not expecting an explanation but needing to give voice to the question running on repeat in my head.

Lance shakes his head, looking at the flames. "I don't know. The oven was completely engulfed."

Trixie's mouth drops open in horror. "Oh, my God, I was right there by it. I took out the bread and put muffins in. If it'd exploded a minute sooner, I would've been standing right there." She's shaking, and I gather her into my arms, patting her hair that's gone wet and frizzy from the sprinkler water. "How did this happen?"

Ice chills my veins. This isn't an accident. I haven't even fully absorbed what's happened, but I know this isn't an accident. This is Blackwell. It has to be.

"Blackwell."

The word galvanizes Lance and Steven, the latter grabbing his phone from his pocket, pressing one button. He starts talking to whoever he quick-dialed.

Lance puts a hand on my shoulder, careful to not disturb Trixie, who's crying silently, tears running down her cheeks to puddle on my shirt. "We don't know it's him. It might've just been an accident."

"We just had a clean inspection and everything was in tip-top order," I hiss incredulously. "This wasn't an accident."

My vehemence catches the attention of a police officer standing nearby. He must've responded to the 9-1-1 call for the fire.

"You said this wasn't an accident, ma'am?" he asks. "I'm Officer Vaughn. And who are you?"

I stand straighter but still keep Trixie and Lance at my sides for support. "I'm Charlotte Dunn. This is my bakery. *Was* my bakery."

He nods sympathetically, flipping open a notebook and taking out a pen. But my announcement has also caught the attention of several customers too. Most of them lean in, as hungry for gossip as they had been for cake. One guy, in particular, comes stomping over.

"This is your bakery? We could've all been killed! What the hell kind of business are you running here?" He's yelling, angry, and aggressively gesturing with his arms, but for the life of me, I can't remember ever seeing him before.

"Sir, I'm sorry for any inconvenience, of course. Right now, we're just glad that everyone's okay." I try to be reasonable, digging deep and finding a degree of customer service, even though what I really want to do is curse the sky for this disaster.

But the man is having none of it. He gets right up in my space, his long finger pointing in my face threateningly. "You're lucky, bitch, you know that? I should sue you for almost killing us all."

Lance tries to intervene, wanting to calm the situation. "Sir, we're all upset, but this is not the appropriate way to treat someone who just lost their business."

The man turns his beady eyes to Lance, and you can almost see his excitement at a new target. He moves his hand from my face, using both to push at Lance's shoulders as he sneers. "You gonna defend your bitch here now?"

Lance is static, not stepping back at all. "Chill out, man!"

The angry customer rears back, telegraphing a punch so big that even I can see it coming. One tight fist heading straight for Lance's jaw. Trixie and I yell out, but Lance steps in, letting the haymaker go over his head and back before lifting the man into the air. When he's up, Lance twists, his hand planted in the man's chest as he does a WWF-like suplex and slams him to the concrete hard and so fast that I don't even have time to call out. He points to the man, his eyes burning in anger.

"Stay down. Last warning."

The guy looks to Officer Vaughn, who's been standing there, uselessly watching the whole showdown. "You saw that! I want to press charges!"

"Go ahead," Lance growls. "You press charges, and so will I. You laid hands on me first. And my lawyers are a lot better than yours."

Another officer helps the guy to his feet, escorting him off to the side, probably to ask the guy questions about what happened. I look around, watching in horror as I realize people are filming, typing on their phones. Great, just what I need . . . more bad press.

But bad press won't matter, though, because the bakery is demolished.

Officer Vaughn clears his throat, getting my attention. "Ma'am? Can you tell me who has access to your ovens?"

I answer reflexively, picturing my pristine kitchen. "We all do. Me, Trixie, she's my assistant manager, Lance, he's my boyfriend who helps out, and Steven, who's . . . a friend." I don't say that Steven is our guard because I know that'll only lead to questions I think are best answered by Thomas, or at least if I have to answer them, I want to make sure I'm saying what Thomas wants me to since that part of the party is all his.

He scribbles something down. "Anyone else? Maintenance workers, customers, family, friends?"

"Sabrina, my stepsister," I whisper, my stomach dropping. "She came to see me out of the blue today, we talked in the kitchen, and I left her alone to deal with a customer. But I don't think she would know how to tamper with anything." I'm arguing with myself even as the suggestion that she could be responsible gets written down too.

"I think we're going to need you four to come down to the station to answer some more questions," the officer says.

But Lance balks. "Take Charlotte and Trixie, and Steven too. I have some things I need to attend to, but I'll be along as quick as I can to answer any questions." It seems reasonable, but something in his eyes tells me he's not spilling his guts, not fully. I wonder if he's going to go after Sabrina or to talk to Thomas about the possibility of this being a Blackwell act.

Vaughn's demeanor flips like somebody pulled his switch. "Mr. Jacobs, I said you're all going down to the station for questioning. You, especially," he says, lifting his chin toward the assaulting guy who's loudly proclaiming that Lance started it. "Let's not have an incident."

He grabs at Lance, who steps back, calm and controlled. "On what grounds are you detaining me?" His voice is loud, drawing attention as questioning eyes look our way.

Vaughn comes at him again and they tussle, arms flailing. I can tell Lance is trying to not hurt the cop and is just defending himself.

Still, Trixie gets into the mix, throwing catfight-worthy scrabbling arms and flailing hands as she yells like a banshee, "Leave him alone! We have rights!"

Somehow, I end up trying to separate all three of them. "Stop it, all of you. Stop!"

I see a phone fall from Lance's pocket. I drop down to pick it up, thinking I'll hold it for him until after this weird attack by the police. But it's not his usual phone, the one that sits on my nightstand every evening as we drift off to sleep in each other's arms.

*Why would he have two phones?*

My gut drops like I'm on a roller coaster as one answer bubbles up. *It's a hoe phone.* Been there, done that, burned that bridge to the ground with kerosene and matches.

Wait, that's not funny, given the current situation.

But my heart cracks at the thought.

The screen lights up as I turn it over and the last message displays.

*Blackwell—Mission is a Go. Execute.*

Bile rises in my stomach at the jargon and the name attached to the message. I look up to Lance, my heart painfully shattering in my chest. It's not another woman. It's another man. The worst man in all of Roseboro, telling Lance to do what?

Did Lance blow up my bakery?

Hot tears flow as he calls out my name, but I shake my head. The officer grimaces and hauls Lance away, shoving him into a waiting police car.

I fall to my knees, right there on the street in front of my dream. Both of them . . . the bakery and Lance.

I thought I was finally going to get everything, that maybe happily ever afters could be true and happen to me. But I know better. It'll always be the happily *never* after for me.

# CHAPTER 27

## Charlotte

TRIXIE HELPS ME UP, SHOOING ME OFF TO THE SIDEWALK TO SIT ON a bench. "Oh, my God, I can't . . . I thought Sabrina . . . I never thought Lance would . . . Blackwell—"

I can't string a coherent sentence together, but Trixie gets the gist. She saw the same thing I did.

Lance had a phone with a message from Blackwell. All signs point to his being a sleeper agent, just like Mia said.

But how? He couldn't have been faking everything all along, could he?

The charming smiles. The panty-melting kisses. The dick me downs. My heart cries out. Not just the sex, but the emotions are what I really can't believe he faked. He made me believe again, made me hope. And I thought he was right there with me.

He said he loved me. I said I loved him.

I meant it, I really did. But for him, was it all just a ploy? A way to get close to me, a way to hurt Thomas?

I don't want to believe it. But the phone holds the proof. I look at it again, though tears cloud my vision, and Trixie looks over my shoulder.

There's no passcode, so it's easy enough to look through the data. There are pictures of the kitchen, of Steven, of me. It's almost like he was building a file on the bakery for Blackwell.

But it's the messages that hurt the most.

*Concerns about your cover?*

*No sir.*

Then weeks later . . .

*Expect a visit.*

That had been the day before Barrett Williams had shown up for his health inspection with the phony complaints. Apparently, that was Blackwell too. Sabrina really is in the clear. It seems I'm a worse judge of character than I thought. I suspected her both times, but it was the one person I never considered who was betraying me the worst.

And today's message . . .

*Mission is a Go. Execute.*

The betrayal burns me to the core, and the tears that have been pouring slowly refresh their hot trails down my cheeks. Trixie holds me, taking the phone and putting it in her apron pocket.

"Honey, I get that Lance has done something really awful, but I don't get *why*. Why is Steven pacing around on the phone like someone tried to kill the president? What the hell does Blackwell have to do with the bakery? This is all just . . . *what?*"

She looks to me, fear lining her face as her brows pinch together.

"It's a long story," I say, drained after all this.

She shrugs, looking across the street where the firefighters are doing all they can do. "Hell, the bakery just burned down. We've got time. Tell me what the fuck's going on."

But I can't. It's not my story to tell, and the last time I told someone, he ended up being Blackwell's agent.

The phone buzzes, and both of us jolt.

Trixie pulls it out, holding it so we can both see the screen.

*Blackwell—Move to final phase.*

Our eyes meet, horror dawning. Burning the bakery wasn't the end of whatever plan Blackwell has.

"Should we give this to the police?" she asks, looking at the cops and then the phone. She's acting like the phone is a snake, about to bite her.

I shake my head, knowing the truth. "No, I need to give it to Thomas."

She tenses as an SUV peels into the lot across the street, drawing everyone's attention and putting us all on alert. But it's just Jonathan, who looks at me with haunted eyes. "I'm sorry, Charlotte. Are you all right?"

"It was Lance all along," I say sadly.

"Start at the beginning," he says crisply, all business.

I give him the basics that we've put together and hand over the phone. He listens carefully, asking questions about what I saw today, but shakes his head when I say it had to be Lance and that the police took him in for questioning. "It doesn't make any sense. I know Lance Jacobs and this isn't his style. Did the police see the phone?"

"No, it fell out of his pocket when he was scuffling with the police officer who was trying to arrest him," I reply, shaking my head. "I thought it was just his phone, so I held onto it, for safekeeping, you know? Then I realized I'd never seen it before and read the messages on it."

"So they took him in with no evidence? But left you here?" he clarifies, looking at the phone in his hand, and I nod.

"The last message said, *final phase*. What do you think that means?" My voice is shaking, but I can't help it. Today has just been too much.

He looks grim, slipping the phone in his pocket. "I don't know yet. Stay here, stay with Steven, and Brian is on his way to be backup. Don't talk to anyone." He runs back to his SUV, catching Steven's eye and pointing at us, assigning responsibility.

Trixie leans in to me, whispering, "Who the hell are you? A secret princess or something?"

My mouth opens and closes, wanting to tell her everything, but no sound comes out.

She sighs, looking worried. "Fine, I get it. But whatever the fuck is going on, I don't think that guy is right."

I look to her and she explains. "You said you needed to get the phone to Thomas. It doesn't take a genius to know that this has something to do with your friends. Whatever is going on, you need to get to safety. And it sure ain't sitting on a sidewalk bench in the open, across the street from the bakery that just got burned down. You need to get together, circle the wagons, and have each other's back to stay safe." Trixie points at Steven, who's still talking in his earpiece. "Don't keep him here, Char. Go be safe."

I can hear the fear in her voice, the concern that something else is coming and we're out here like sitting ducks. I look around, seeing the crowds gawking and pointing, the building, and finally, the stress on Steven's face.

She's right. I need to go, get to Thomas and Mia's so we can all be together and be as safe as possible. Blackwell can't take us all out, not with full security.

"You're right, Trix. Safety in numbers, that's what they say. Come with me," I suggest.

She shakes her head, sadness in her eyes. "Honey, you can't even tell me what's going on because I'm outside the circle. I get it."

I take her hands, desperate. "You're important to me, Trixie. I don't want anything to happen to you."

She smiles, but I can tell it's forced, given the situation. "I know. You're important to me too, and that's why I don't want anything to happen to you, so go. But I don't want anything to happen to me either, and you've got some shit coming, I think. I'm just going to head home and chill. But I'm still on the clock." The tease is bitter. I know she's hurting and is scared for me.

I hug her tight, her arms wrapping around me too.

"Love you," I tell her honestly.

"Love you too. Now go give Blackwell hell, rip his nuts off, though still not for a 'Nutz for Nutz' cupcake. Ew," she says, her nose crinkling. "Still the grossest thing you've ever thought of."

"Thank you, though you're a crazy bitch, you know that?"

She grins, and it seems the slightest bit more real this time, until she looks across the street and the smile fades. "This is our bakery, damn it," she spits out. "Nobody gets to take it."

# CHAPTER 28

## Lance

T HE INTERROGATION ROOM IS FREEZING COLD, LIKELY TO MAKE suspects talk. Same reasoning behind the uncomfortable chair, the plain table in front of me, and the cuffs locking me in place.

My internal clock says I've been here for less than an hour, but staring at my own reflection and wondering who's on the other side of the one-way mirror is making time stand still.

*What the hell happened at the bakery?*

One second, we were all thankful to have gotten out, blessedly breathing fresh air and watching as the bakery burned. I'd been so glad no one was hurt because it'd been a full house in there. The next minute, some guy is throwing punches and a cop's going Full Metal Jacket, trying to bring me in without reason.

Resisting arrest probably wasn't my best move, but something felt off and I was worried about leaving Charlotte.

Charlotte. Her face when she saw the phone.

She was arguing for me, standing up for her man like the badass I know she can be, but something on that screen broke her. Her face had gone pale, well, paler than her usual, and her eyes were shocked and angry.

I don't know what she could've seen. Or where that phone came from. Was it hers? If so, I'd never seen it before, but maybe she has a backup from Thomas?

My mind is swirling, questions layering on top of one another as I try to dissect and consider each one carefully and methodically. I'm still trying to figure it out when the door opens.

An older man, grey-haired with a paunch belly, comes in, shutting the door behind him. He sits down across from me, a gentle smile on his face that makes the thick mustache over his top lip wiggle at the ends. "I'm Frank Harris. Wanted to ask you a few questions."

"Lance Jacobs. I have a few questions of my own too," I reply, keeping myself steady. If he thinks his little act so far has me intimidated, he's got another thing coming.

Jonathan warned me about the police, and I'm not going to play this like some greenback. I've handled interrogations myself, and this Harris guy won't be resorting to waterboarding to get his answers, which bodes well for me. I'm leaving this room with more information than I give, that's for damn sure.

"Hmmm . . . your information says Navy. Do we need to call the Pentagon?"

He shrugs like it doesn't matter, but he's just trying to get under my skin and we both know it.

"Currently on terminal leave, but I can give you my old CO's name, sir. Should I call you 'sir'? I'm afraid I didn't catch your role here at the Roseboro Police Department." I look around the interrogation room like I'm evaluating it for a Yelp review.

His mustache twitches, then he inclines his head. "Chief Harris, at your service."

What the fuck is the Chief of Police doing interrogating me? First off, there's no reason for them to hold me, but his presence hints at something much larger. Chiefs don't get involved for a swing at a cop, even in Mayberry.

Needing more information, I hedge my bets. "Nice to meet you, Chief Harris. Though I do wish it were under better circumstances."

He shrugs, opening a file on the table between us and pretending to read it. I can tell he's faking. His eyes aren't focused. So, this is a show, but for what? Or maybe more importantly, who?

"Says here you were behaving suspiciously at the fire over at Cake Culture today. That true?" he says casually.

"No." It's the only answer I need to give because it's the truth.

He grunts. "Why don't you tell me about today." It's an order, not a question.

"It was a busy day at the bakery, so we were all out front, serving customers, when there was a loud boom in the kitchen. We went to the back, I tried to put it out with the fire extinguisher, but it got too big, too fast. We had to get out. Outside, a guy got physical and I defended myself. An officer was asking the same questions you are now. Then he said we needed to come in to the station—"

"And that was Officer Vaughn?" he interrupts to clarify.

I nod. "Yeah, Officer Vaughn wanted us to come in. I told him to bring everyone else down and I'd be here shortly. He didn't like that, became aggressive, and next thing I know, I'm here and everyone else was dismissed without further question. Are they okay?" There's something going on here, but I need to at least know if everyone else is fine after the fire.

"As far as I know," he says, a gleam in his eye. "Though I haven't seen Miss Dunn yet."

He's trying to make me worry about Charlotte, but why? Is it a tactic to get me to talk, hoping to get back to her? Not going to happen. I don't trust this guy. He may be the boss around here, but he reads slimy to me.

"So, you didn't want to come with Vaughn. Where were you planning to go?" Harris asks slyly.

Thank God for my training. There's a time to be emotionless, and a time to lose it . . . coolly. This is one of those times, and I spit out, "To my parent's, to a friend's, to take a shit . . . it doesn't matter. He had no right to detain me, and you have no right to hold me."

Harris's good-old-boy act disappears. "I may not be able to charge you with burning that bakery down just yet, boy. But I've got a guy out there talking about pressing charges for you doing some body slam move, a serious accusation with your being a trained killer and all. And an officer with a helluva shiner, so yes, assaulting a police officer is the charge right now. See what your CO thinks about that."

If it was just the bakery misunderstanding, I'd get up and waltz out of here. But the officer assault is a serious accusation, one I'm not sure isn't true. I don't remember hitting Vaughn when we tussled, but I wouldn't swear to that in a court of law.

"In that case . . . lawyer."

Chief Harris turns a mottled shade of red and knocks on the mirror two times. An answering single knock must communicate something to him, or at least he acts like it does. "Your family has been notified and my guess is they'll have your lawyer running up here to save your entitled ass any minute now."

I dip my chin, not speaking.

"Got a little story to tell you. Now, you don't talk." He points a thick finger at me in warning. "Just wait on that lawyer, but you can listen, right?"

He waits for me to answer, but I just glare at him.

After a moment, he continues.

"Once upon a time, there was a guy called Prince Charming, and you'd think he'd be the hero of the story, but no. Instead, he went into the kitchen of the local bake shop and waited until he was alone. Now, everyone thought he was just baking some cupcakes or something, but he wasn't. No, our not-hero was tinkering with the ovens, opening the gas intake too much until BOOM!"

I grit my teeth, needing to refute these accusations, but I know he's baiting me. So as hard as it is, I just keep my mouth shut.

He smirks, like he knows exactly what he's doing to me. "This Prince tries to make his getaway. But he gets caught and his web of deceit is discovered by everyone. He's arrested, goes to trial, and ends up spending the next twenty years of his life in prison."

He eyes me, gauging my reaction to his story and the threatening ending. But I give him nothing.

He tries a few more times, saying variations of the same accusations to see if I'll flinch, but I'm stone-cold against his onslaught.

In my mind, I'm still trying to piece things together. I don't believe for a minute that the oven blowing up was an accident, and the obvious person to do something like that is Blackwell.

But what does he stand to gain from destroying a bakery? From hurting Charlotte?

From what Jonathan has told me, Blackwell is escalating, getting grander and more complex in his elaborate plans. And this seems small, comparatively, even though it's everything to Charlotte. And she's everything to me.

Unless . . .

It's not about the bakery or Charlotte. It's a power move, a play that directs the next few steps. But how is he funneling this to get at Thomas, because he's most definitely the end game?

Harris is getting frustrated with his lack of progress and my lack of attention. "Are you listening to me?" he barks.

I refocus my eyes on him, cold and collected to his mad fury. "Law-yer."

He growls, pushing the table toward me as he lumbers up. He grabs my upper arm, strongly *encouraging* me to stand. "You want to be that way, fine. But we need the room. Guess you'll have to wait down in holding for your fancy lawyer to get here."

It sounds like a threat if ever I've heard one. He uncuffs me from the table but makes sure to sneakily press each bracelet a notch tighter around my wrist. The delight in his eyes at the small shock of pain is more worrisome than the discomfort.

Downstairs, he leads me through a checkpoint, where the officer on duty acts like the president is coming through. I'm betting the chief doesn't come down here too often, especially not hauling a prisoner. It's another odd puzzle piece in this picture.

Why in the world is someone like Harris the one investigating me and the fire, and not a run-of-the-mill detective? It must be because he wants this case for some reason.

The bars slide open in front of me and Harris shoves me. He's obviously hoping I'll lose my footing and go sprawling across the filthy concrete floor, but I do a good job of maintaining my balance. It's a small win given today's catastrophes, but hopefully the start of a good roll.

The door slides closed, and Harris sneers from the relative safety on the other side. "I'll be sure to let you know when that lawyer gets here." His tone tells me that he'll have me waiting long after the family attorney arrives.

Once he's gone, I turn around, looking at the handful of other guys in the holding cell with me. There's a drunk and disheveled guy curled up in the corner, snoring lightly. A tall, bald guy with tattoos on both forearms who looks menacing, but I'm betting it's his version of resting bitch face. And lastly, a middle-aged guy in khakis and a polo, with gold-rimmed glasses. He looks like someone who'd love to discuss the merits of quantum physics.

I lift my chin, greeting each of them silently, then move toward an empty section of bench to claim it for myself. My mind is still working, churning over everything we know and trying to piece together the rest of the puzzle.

I've got my head hanging down, my elbows resting on my spread knees when I hear a quick shuffle of feet. I look up to see the physics guy making a run at me, murder in his eyes.

I stand up fast, chin tight and ready for his assault. Not going to happen, but I'm surprised he's more than I thought. "Sit down," I growl.

Physics guy freezes a foot from me and veers off to sit down on the bench next to me like that was his goal all along. Creepy and strange.

Baldie lifts his eyebrows at the scene, then nods his head at the bench next to him. I take the invitation, moving to sit down. "I'm Dave, in for drunk and disorderly," he says with a shrug. "I'm a happy drunk, what can I say?"

"And him?" I ask, looking to Physics Guy.

Baldie twists his lips, scowling. "Don't know, but I can sense that little fucker's wrong in the head."

I concur, but thankfully, the buzz of the gate down the hall opening stops further conversation.

A familiar face soon appears in the bars. "Holy shit, I'm glad to see you, man!"

Jonathan smiles, but it's grim. "Let's just get you out of here. We've got a lot to talk about."

Paperwork to get released takes twice as long as it did coming in when they were ripping my watch off and damn near drooling to get their hands on my wallet. I don't know how much cash I had in it, but I'm betting it's a little lighter now.

Finally, we get to Jonathan's SUV and he pulls out of the lot, looking in the rearview mirror more times than safe driving requires. But he must see there's no one tailing us, and my sideview mirror tells me the same.

"Thanks, man. I feel like there's so much we need to talk about," I say as he pulls out of downtown.

His jaw is set, teeth clenched. "Not yet."

After a long stretch of silent minutes, he pulls into a treed driveway on a rural country road outside Roseboro. He reaches into his pocket and pulls out his jammer. He flips it on and sets it on the dashboard.

Then he pulls his gun on me.

# CHAPTER 29

## Charlotte

S TEVEN HANDS ME ANOTHER TISSUE FROM THE CONSOLE, WHICH I
take thankfully. "Sorry I'm such a mess," I say between sobs.
    I'd cried through telling Trixie what I could, but sitting still in
this quiet car is too much, and the sobs have been racking my body for the
last fifteen minutes as we get closer to the Goldstone building. Poor Steven
seems at a loss and just keeps handing me tissues. Guess they didn't teach
him about this in badass school, whichever one he went to.

We pull into the garage, and I swear his shoulders lower a solid two
inches from his ears. But he clears his throat and says professionally, "Miss
Dunn, let me help you upstairs."

I let him open the door after scanning the parking lot, then lead me to
Thomas's private elevator. After a whoosh that makes my belly climb into my
throat, the doors open to reveal Mia.

Her eyes are red and puffy too as she launches herself at me. "Oh, my
God, Char," she says, gathering me in her arms. I let her hug me, soothe me,
and eventually, my arms come up to circle her too. She's mumbling into my
shoulder, "Could've lost . . . what the fuck . . . so glad you're . . ."

I nod, hugging her back. "I know, but I'm okay. Well, physically, anyway. My heart hurts."

I rub at my chest, and Mia's eyes shoot to Steven. "Why didn't you take
her to the hospital if she's injured?" she demands.

He shakes his head almost imperceptibly as I place a staying hand on Mia's arm because she looks like she's about to launch herself at Steven too, and not in such a caring way. "Not from the fire. Lance."

"Lance?" she asks, confusion pulling her eyebrows so tightly together they look like caterpillars about to battle above her nose. "What about him?"

She looks between me and Steven, who's staring into space like he wishes he could be anywhere but here in this moment. Mia's fire is growing by the millisecond, her face already a deeper shade of pink than her current hair. "What? Somebody better start speaking or I'm gonna track him down and introduce him to Thunder and Lightning." She holds up one fist, then the other. "And then a friend I like to Hail, because it'll drop you to your knees." She kicks her leg up in a hi-yah motion.

Even through the tears, she breaks me into a laugh. A snotty, ugly one, but a laugh, nevertheless. "Can we sit down?"

"Oh, yeah, of course." Mia leads me to the couch, and Steven stays at his post by the elevator, pulling his phone back out to text. I wonder if he's texting Jonathan and if he knows anything about what's happening to Lance down at the police station.

We sit down, and I curl my feet up underneath me, needing to be small and less of a target because it feels like the universe is taking pot shots at my life today. Mia waits exactly two heartbeats before saying, "Speak, *Tovarich*. Tell me what the fuck is going on."

I don't know where to start. It feels like I've lived a lifetime in just a few hours. "You know about the fire?"

"Yeah, something about an oven, but everyone got out, right?"

"Yeah, so we got out ,and I'm watching my baby burn when this cop comes over and starts asking questions. He's all 'who has access' and I tell him just me, Trixie, and Lance, but then I remember that Sabrina came by today and I left her back there for a second while I stepped to the front." My eyes are unseeing, cloudy behind unshed tears as I remember, but I blink them back.

I've cried enough. I need to be strong. I've been through bad shit and come out the other side, stronger for it. This is worse than anything else, for sure, but I'll be invincible, savage and cold as ice after this. *And alone again*, a small voice whispers.

"Sabrina?" Mia growls. "That bitch!"

I shake my head before she can get too far. "I thought the same thing, and thought it might be Blackwell too. Just grasping for straws, you know?

But then the cop wanted us to go to the station to make statements and Lance lost it. At first, he said he'd meet us there, but then when the cop tried to force him to go, Lance fought him. That's when the phone fell out of his pocket."

I swallow thickly, wringing my hands. The hands that held the proof of his betrayal.

"What phone?" Mia asks quietly. I think she can tell this is the crux of the issue, the reason for the tears. Even more so than the bakery. I can rebuild that, but my heart? It's shattered beyond repair this time.

I meet her eyes, wishing she could erase the memory, that I could go back a couple of hours and never have seen that screen. "Lance had a second phone, and his last text message came up on the screen when I grabbed it. It was from . . . Blackwell." The tears won't be held back, but I don't give into them fully. I let them trail hotly down my puffy cheeks but keep my head held high, refusing to break.

Mia jumps from the couch, pissed. "Blackwell? Lance is . . . he's working for . . ." She turns down the hallway, bellowing, "Tommy!!"

He comes running, phone held to his ear. His eyes search the room wildly, looking for a threat, but when he sees only Mia and me, he tells who-ever's on the phone, "Hold up."

He looks at Mia, and he says, "What's wrong?"

"Did you know about Lance? That he's working for Blackwell?" she de-mands, a hand on her hip. If you didn't know her, it wouldn't seem all that scary. I mean, she's a small, nerdy woman with streaked hair who's currently wearing ripped jeans and a K-pop T-shirt.

But you'd be wrong. Mia's the second-scariest person I know. Second only to Gabe, but he's a different kind of scary.

Thomas cringes, nodding. "Yes, we're working on it."

Mia sputters, and I think she was hoping Thomas would tell her it was all a big misunderstanding. "But he . . ." She turns back to me, sadness in her eyes. "I thought he was going to crack that cynical heart of yours and be your happily ever after."

"Me too, honey. Me too," I agree hollowly.

I shake it off, remembering why I came here in the first place. "He's got a head start. None of us saw this coming, least of all me. So we need to circle the wagons," I tell Thomas, using Trixie's phrasing that rings true. "You've got to get Izzy and Gabe here. Whatever Blackwell's planning, he can't get us all at once, not if we're here, surrounded by security."

He nods, taking his phone back out. He presses a couple of numbers and has a quick conversation with Gabe. When he hangs up, he tells us, "They're already on their way. Steven reported to the crew that you were coming here, and Gabe said he couldn't hold Izzy back from getting to your side. They'll be here any minute."

The tiniest smile tries to break free at the idea that Gabe couldn't hold Izzy back. She's strong, but he's . . . Gabe. Which is actually why he couldn't stop her, because as scary of a guy as he is, and as deadly of a hitman as he used to be, Izzy's got him wrapped around her little finger.

The elevator whirs, and Steven lifts his gun, pressing the button on the headset at his ear.

There's a tense moment where I irrationally fear Blackwell himself is going to walk off the elevator. But when the door opens, Gabe and Izzy walk into the apartment.

Izzy rushes me, much like Mia did, wrapping me up for a hug. "Motherfucker, I'm going to slice his balls off and serve them as the Blue Plate Special." Izzy's language has taken a turn for the worse, or at least the more creative, since she started seeing Gabe. It's oddly funny because I rarely hear him curse, but Izzy says he curses like a sailor.

A sailor . . . *my* sailor.

Lance.

Fuck, is everything going to bring me back to thoughts of him? I sigh, telling Izzy, "Thanks, honey, but don't blow the Gravy Train's health inspection over me. Those people are hardasses."

It's the barest hint of humor but the first sign that I'm going to be okay. Eventually. After I kill Lance, slowly and painfully. I chance a glance at Gabe, wondering how much it'd cost me to hire him, but he winks like he already knows what I'm thinking and I'm betting his family discount is pretty steep.

Gabe breaks into my murderous thoughts. "What do we know? What's the plan?"

I appreciate the move to action, because I can't stay stagnant in my pity party of heartbreak or I'll drown. I need to do something about this attack on my bakery and my heart. Action, that's what I need. Retaliation.

I sit back down on the couch, Mia on one side and Izzy on the other, while Thomas and Gabe face each other. I feel like I've got my people around me, but my stupid broken heart still feels like there's someone missing.

"Jonathan and Mia have been digging, and we've made some moves.

Business moves to hurt Blackwell, but obviously, they're not enough," Thomas says.

"And we've found sketchy stuff, loads of it, actually," Mia adds. "But no smoking gun, and we don't know where enough of the bodies are buried, literally or figuratively."

"We need more time," Thomas growls. "We need solid proof or making an accusation like this could backfire majorly. He's got major clout in Roseboro, damn near built the city. We can't let anyone he's got in his pocket sweep this under the rug. We need undeniable evidence that he's doing all of this."

Thomas looks to Gabe, but Izzy gets up and stands in front of him. "No, we've talked about this. I get that the most damning evidence we have of Blackwell's wrongdoing is that he hired Gabe to kill me, but if we go to the police with that, they'll arrest Gabe, especially if they do any looking into his past. So no, there's got to be another way. He's a maniacal mastermind. He's got to have left a trail. We just have to find it." She looks off into space like she's searching too, but she's coming up empty-handed, like we all are.

"There is another option to get information," Gabe says carefully. He looks at me, apology in his eyes. "We have another of Blackwell's pawns. We could ask him questions."

I flinch, electricity shooting through me. "Bring Lance here? Why? He's already in jail."

Thomas clears his throat. "Jonathan bailed him out fifteen minutes ago."

I look at Thomas incredulously, bile in my gut threatening to come up. "What? Why would he do that?"

Thomas looks at Gabe, who says gently, "Because it's our best option. I'll take care of it."

I know he's not just talking about walking Lance back down to the police station to turn him back in. And as much as Lance has hurt me, I don't want the ending Gabe would give him. He might deserve it, but I'm not the sort of person who could do that to someone, nor let Gabe do it in my stead. As much as my superficial knee-jerk reaction is *kill the bastard*, my true nature isn't so sadistic. I won't become that for Lance's betrayal, not for anything.

I don't begrudge Gabe for what he's done, but I won't bear the same weighty responsibility he does for that drastic of an action. I don't want him to kill Lance. So why bother asking the questions he won't answer when the threat isn't real?

"It's not like he's going to spill his guts and tell us everything. He's obviously a great liar, had me completely fooled and believing in fairy tales," I say, and everyone in this room knows how unlikely that is, and by extension, what a good liar that means Lance must be. "We need to just go after Blackwell head-on."

Thomas and Gabe meet eyes over my head, and I've never felt so inconsequential. I'm just a cog in the wheel, but Thomas owns the wheel and Gabe is the one turning it. I pull my legs up to my chest, placing my head on my knees and sighing as I close my eyes.

I'd thought my life now was different. I'd finally stepped out of my stepmother's control, Dad's passive awareness, and all the heartbreaking drama there. I was in control, free to make my own way, my own choices. But it was an illusion.

My bakery, the one I'd poured every bit of my blood, sweat, and tears into? Partially Thomas's. My friends have men of their own now. My life, the one I thought I was master of my own destiny for? It's just a linchpin in someone else's game.

I'm just a pawn, always have been. And apparently, always will be.

"Fine, whatever you want to do," I say, the words echoing in the cavern between my chest and my thighs.

I just don't want to hurt anymore.

# CHAPTER 30

## Lance

H IS GUN'S A GLOCK 29, SMALL ENOUGH TO FIT COMFORTABLY between us in the small space of the SUV's cab. The doors are locked, and I'm betting Jonathan has the child safety engaged so that I can't open the door next to me without his unlocking it from his side.

"Explain," he says evenly. He's stone-cold in this minute, not the friend I shared a battlefield with but the cold-eyed warrior I remember. He may or may not like what he has to do right now, but he'll do it either way.

I hold my hands out, though he knows I'm unarmed since he watched them check the returned inventory they handed me at the jail. Wallet, set of keys, and a small pocket knife. No gun.

"There was a fire, everyone got out, asshole cop power-tripped about us going down for questions and arrested me. Got the full-court parade of interrogations, complete with the damn Chief of Police, then you showed up." I narrow my eyes, looking at him carefully. "But you already know that. What's going on?"

I'm hoping he'll tell me what's brought this on because I'm clueless.

Something Charlotte said echoes in my mind. Blackwell has people all over the city, and she doesn't trust anyone. *Oh, fuck.*

"Are you working for Blackwell? Are you spying on Thomas for him?" I growl.

It'd make perfect sense, Infiltration 101, get close to your target.

Jonathan's insinuating himself as the head of Thomas's security team would be perfect, getting him into all sorts of top-secret places and able to direct every move Thomas makes, for good and bad.

I'm already looking for an opening to take Jonathan out, grab the gun, and remove the threat to Charlotte and her friends, when he scoffs.

"Me? Nice try, but you're the operative for Blackwell. What does he know? What's he planning?" Jonathan says quietly, ice in his voice.

I read his face, looking for any sign of dishonesty but finding none. "Wait, you're not on Blackwell's payroll?" He shakes his head slightly, but his eyes and the gun stay locked on me. "I'm not either. Charlotte said Blackwell was a sick fucker, with resources all over the city. But I'm not one. I swear it. On Stockton's grave."

James Stockton. He wasn't the first death letter I'd had to write, nor was he the last, but it was the hardest. And Jonathan knows that because he was there for the worst of it.

*We're most of the way through the dusty field, just after 2200 local. Ahead, less than a hundred meters now, is our target when the AK opens up and we grab dirt.*

*"Move, move, move," I yell to my men. We're a small group tonight, just one platoon of sixteen, but we're good. My guys do as trained, alternatingly laying down covering fire and hauling ass for the single shack on the property.*

*Inside, the family of caretakers, employees of the area warlord, shrink back in fear, but they each hold weapons. A father, a mother, and a ten-year-old boy. Thankfully, they're more scared of us than their warlord.*

*Stockton, our interpreter, tells them we aren't there for them and even gets them to lower their guns, which we promptly secure. We stay still and quiet for two hours as a patrol sweeps the fields outside.*

*We're ready to kill every one of those patrolling men, which in the civilian world sounds horrifying, but there in the quiet of the night, I'm ready to do whatever I have to for my men.*

*Eventually, the guards retreat, and I silently celebrate that our cover held. I call for pickup, and we prep to leave as the tut-tut-tut of the chopper blades gets closer in the distance.*

*Stockton speaks to the father, something I can't understand but sounds kind, like he's thanking the man for our safety. Stockton even smiles, a flash of white teeth in the dark shack.*

*Suddenly, the man lashes out with a knife. I return fire automatically, killing the father instantly as the mother and child cry out, yelling in a language I don't understand.*

*He'd been sitting on it the whole time, and he gets Stockton across the calf, taking him down. We'd all been so close to surviving this unexpected meeting, but the father forces my hand.*

*We leave the shack, one dead, two grieving, but all of my men alive. They're my responsibility, and I'm not going to fail them.*

*We haul ass for the Blackhawk that's just setting down. I help Stockton, who's limping badly and not able to put much pressure on his left leg. We make it aboard, and one of the guys who's already loaded helps me pull Stockton inside.*

*He's half in-half out when the ratta-tat-tat of automatic gunfire loudly sounds out, even though we're right under the helicopter's rotating blades.*

*I shove Stockton in, climbing in behind him. We both take hits, I can tell by the way his body jerks in my arms and the fire that shoots through my leg. But the chopper takes off, getting us out of there.*

*"Are you hit?" someone asks, and I nod because my mouth is so dry, I can't speak. But I'm okay. It's not serious, even though it hurts like a motherfucker. "Stockton?"*

*No answer.*

*I roll over, where the medic's working, but I can tell already that it's not good. Five seconds. If we'd been five seconds faster . . .*

I'd had to tell his wife, as she held the tiny baby Stockton had kissed goodbye less than a week before, that he hadn't made it. I'd been the man right next to her husband as he kept us all safe in that shack and paid for his kindness with his life. She hadn't said it, but I know she'd wished it'd been me.

An inch or two to the right and it would've been.

I tell Jonathan, back in the cab of his SUV at gunpoint, "You were on pickup that night, Jon. Your boys were our backup, so you know. I swear on Stockton's grave, it's not me."

Jonathan lowers the gun, sighing. "Fuck. I had to be sure. It'd be so much easier if it was. One and done."

I know just how close Jonathan was to shooting me, can hear the desperation in his voice. "We need to back up. Our intel is wrong. It's not you, and it's not me."

He nods, putting the Glock away. "Then who?"

I look out the window, replaying the day. "Charlotte was sure it was Sabrina, and she was in the kitchen alone for a few minutes this afternoon.

She came by unexpectedly, which could track that it's her. I could even see her being so mad at Charlotte that she could be turned to Blackwell's side, not because she cares about Thomas but just to get back at Charlotte."

Jonathan shakes his head, drumming his fingers on the steering wheel. "But what about the phone?"

"What phone?" I ask. "Charlotte picked up a phone when the police were hauling me away, but I'd never seen it before."

Jonathan opens his center console, pulling out a phone. "This phone. Check the text messages."

I do as he says, and fury rushes through my body, my blood catching fire in my veins. "What the fuck?"

"I know. Charlotte thinks it's yours," he says hollowly.

"No, she knows I wouldn't do something like this, wouldn't betray her. I love her," I protest. But I can see her, the color draining out of her face and the look of hurt in her eyes.

I hadn't understood then, but I do now.

She *would* believe I'd do something like this. Not because she doesn't trust me, but because she doesn't trust anyone and is always waiting for the other shoe to drop. And this? This is like a size-thirteen combat boot dropping on her life. *She'd believe*, I think sadly.

Her scars run too deep. I've been healing them, but not fast enough, not enough for her to know without a doubt that this is a lie.

"I'll make her understand," I vow to Jonathan. "I'll prove to her that it's not me. I love her, and she does this dance. Two steps forward, one step back. This is a giant one back, but I got her to trust me once. I'll get her to do it again."

"That's sweet and all, but not really the issue at hand. Whose phone is this?" Jonathan says. "We were sure it was yours."

I play back that moment.

Vaughn could've dropped the phone in the scuffle. His vehemence that he take me in could be a play from Blackwell to separate us. Even Chief Harris's involvement could track with that. Dirty cops on Blackwell's payroll makes sense, and Jonathan knows the cops are in Blackwell's pocket.

But Vaughn didn't have access to the ovens in the kitchen. He might be dirty, but he's not the guy for this.

I flip to the camera folder on the phone, scrolling.

Steven? Maybe it's not Jonathan who's the plant in Thomas's crew but the guard closest to Charlotte. He'd been there today and has been in the kitchen dozens of times.

But a picture on the phone stops me. It's a picture of Steven. If he's the plant, he couldn't take a picture of himself. He's too far away. I study the picture, horror dawning as I realize who.

Only one person has gotten Steven to smile and flash a peace sign.

"Oh, fuck. I know who it is," I say, still not believing my eyes even though the proof is right in front of me.

"Who?" Jonathan says.

"It's Trixie. She was always taking pictures of Steven. I thought she had a crush on him. And she's got full access. To everything. She was there, fighting Vaughn when he tried to take me in. Maybe the phone fell out of her pocket or she dropped it into mine?"

Jonathan's eyes narrow, and I can see his mind flipping through files in his mental filing cabinet. "Trixie Reynolds, Oklahoma. Business degree, assistant manager at *Cake Culture*. . ." He goes on, repeating things I already know about Trixie, but he's missing the vital piece and so am I.

How in the fuck does she know Blackwell, and more importantly, why would she betray Charlotte?

# CHAPTER 31

## Charlotte

I'M STILL TRYING TO BREATHE, THOMAS AND GABE AND MIA DISCUSSING angles and options like I'm not even here. At least Izzy is rubbing my back in soothing circles and cooing in my ear that everything's going to be okay.

I want to tell her that it'll never be okay again, but that would be rude. She's been through *way* worse things than I ever have, and she came out the other side, strong and fierce. She also got her man by walking through the fires of hell with him.

So, while I'm devastated, I try to believe her, have a little faith that I'm going to recover from this, rebuild my bakery. After that, I'll probably become a spinster because I'm sure as fuck never letting a man inside my heart again.

Steven steps into the room, addressing Thomas. "Excuse me, they've arrived."

I look at Thomas, shaken anew. "They? Is Lance here? Now?" At his grim nod, I shake my head. "I can't do this. I'm going to just go to the guest room."

Izzy's hand is tight on my shoulder, and she sits me back down. "The hell you are. You're going to sit right here, glare holes in him, and show him that he didn't fucking break you. You're better than this, stronger than him. He knows it hurts, and that's why you're going to stand up to the pain, rise from it like a goddamn phoenix, and tell him to go fuck himself and his back-alley betrayal."

Mia cups my face in her hands, her eyes gleaming. "We've got you, *Tovarich*. Let's give him hell."

The contrast in their support helps me in ways I wouldn't have expected. I look at Steven and nod.

Just in time, because the elevator dings.

Jonathan and Lance walk off the elevator, purpose in their stride and looking like the warriors they both are.

Lance beelines for me, but I flinch back into the couch. "No," I say, but my voice is weak. I swallow, wanting to be as strong as Mia and Izzy think I am. "No."

Lance stops, his eyes hurt but searching mine. "Charlotte, I didn't do what you think I did. The phone isn't mine."

My chin stays high, but the tears silently streak down my cheeks. "I get it, really, I do. What better way to get an in with the last mark in Thomas's circle than to play on my loneliness, give me all the things I thought I'd never get, that I never deserved? I made it easy, didn't I? Fell right into your trap and believed you, even though I knew better."

I stuff the hurt down, knowing I'll have to deal with it later, and letting the softness he's brought out in me come through for only a moment. "I loved you. When you look back on what you've done here, remember what you threw away. It might have been an act to you, but it wasn't to me. I truly, honestly loved you."

I get up, having said what I need to say and shown that my backbone, while bent, is not broken by his deception. But he follows me toward the hallway. He grabs my arm, turning me and pressing me up against the wall, caging me in with his arms.

Mia and Izzy cry out, but in my peripheral vision, I see Jonathan hold up a staying hand and shake his head at Gabe, who's pulled his gun.

"Look at me, Charlotte," Lance commands.

I can't help it, I do. That stupid seed of hope that he planted wants to have faith, even as my brain knows the real truth of what he's done. The disconnect is a painful wrenching of my soul from my body.

His blue eyes are fierce, his jaw clenched. I get a glimpse of what he must look like as a SEAL ready for battle. But this is one he can't win, one I've already lost.

"Love," he says gruffly. Confusion mars my face, and he continues. "Not past tense, not *loved*. Love. You love me. And I love you. It wouldn't hurt so damn much if you didn't."

I shake my head, not wanting the words to water that fucking seed, not wanting to feel like I'm home inside the circle of his arms.

"You said what you wanted to say, and now it's my turn," he challenges. "I'm not working for Blackwell. That phone wasn't mine. Yes, I'm here for you, because you are the most gorgeous woman I've ever met, inside and out. I see your damage, just like we talked about." He slowly, torturously moves his hand to brush my hair from my face, pressing the softest of kisses to my temple and tracing a finger down my neck to rest his hand over my heart. "You're dancing away from me again. This time, it'd be warranted, but I didn't do this."

Jonathan starts to speak. "We've analyzed the phone—"

"No, she needs to believe me," Lance growls over his shoulder. "Not a report, not someone else. Me." He cups my face in his hands, fingers woven into my hair and holding me in place with his eyes. "You know me, know that I love you. Trust that, Charlotte. Trust me. I. Love. You."

I want to believe so badly, but it feels like another trap. I'm going to fall back into his arms, only for him to drop me later. I always end up on the floor, broken and forgotten.

But as I search his eyes, beseeching me to believe, I reconsider.

What if he's telling the truth, that the phone isn't his? Blackwell could've done something sneaky to make me think it was Lance all along. That'd definitely be in his wheelhouse. Do I really believe Lance would betray me this way?

I want to say yes. I always believe people will disappoint me, and all signs point to that being the case once again. But in my gut, I know the answer's no. He wouldn't. I have to believe that he wouldn't.

That seed of hope again blooms into a dandelion in my soul. Because I do believe him. For the first time since I was a little girl, I do trust—him, his denial of wrongdoing, and . . . his love.

I sob one time, collapsing onto his chest. "Oh, my God. I'm so sorry, Lance. I thought—"

He shushes me, pulling me into him, holding me until I lift my head and brushing my lips with a feather-soft kiss. "There you are, Red. I love you."

I answer him, but the 'I love you too' is mumbled against his lips as he kisses me again. It feels like a fresh seal on what we are, what we have. What I almost threw away because my cynicism misled me.

I vow to not let that happen again and to have a little faith in myself, the people around me, and the world at large. Yes, there are douchebags, but there are also Prince Charmings. And maybe even a happily ever after or two. *Or three*, I think as I smile against Lance's lips.

A throat clearing interrupts us, and Lance pulls back, but his eyes stay on mine. They shine with joy and happiness that I put there, and I know mine shine back just as brightly. The storm may be raging outside our little circle, but at least I know Lance is by my side through it all. Not sheltering me—I don't need that—but supporting me and letting me support him in return.

He slips an arm around my shoulder, holding me tightly against his body, and we turn back to the room. Mia and Izzy are the ones with tears now, though mine are all dried up. Thomas, Gabe, and Jonathan look a bit touched too but are covering it with an armor of 'time to work' stoicism.

"Now can I say what we've found out about the phone?" Jonathan asks, grimacing slightly.

Lance waves permissively, and everyone looks at Jonathan, who's pulling the phone out of his back pocket.

"I haven't had enough time to have the data fully analyzed, sorry. But Lance could tell. He knows . . ." Jonathan lets the sentence trail off, looking to Lance to see if he wants to be the one to spill.

"Out with it already! Who burned down my bakery?" I shout, pissed. Okay, so whatever Blackwell is doing to Thomas is probably more important in the big scheme of things, but *Cake Culture* is my dream. And someone destroyed it.

Lance places his hands on my shoulders, forcing me to look at him. "I'm so sorry, Charlotte, but it's . . . Trixie."

I laugh, an unladylike bark of disbelief. "No, it's not. Trixie's almost as committed to the bakery as I am."

But if it's not Lance, who? Sabrina was there, so she'd been a consideration, but she wasn't the one with the phone. That scuffle involved the police officer, Lance, me, and . . . Trixie.

I don't want to jump to conclusions, not again, but it has to be.

"It was the pictures, not the text messages."

Jonathan shows me the phone, and the photo folder has all those shots, and I recognize the one that damns her. Steven, with a peace sign.

"I was there. I remember that one," I say, my shoulders shrugging in confusion. "But why?"

"There's no telling what Blackwell's angle with her is. But we'll figure it out," Thomas promises. "We were ready to ask Lance some hard questions, but it sounds like those need to be directed elsewhere."

A phone rings, and Thomas holds up a finger, moving to answer it while Gabe, Lance, and Jonathan discuss ways to ask Trixie some questions.

Thomas nods and sets the phone down. "Steven, my assistant and a courier are on their way up." Steven nods and a moment later, the elevator opens.

Steven does a quick frisk of the assistant and the blue-uniformed courier, who seems surprised by the security. "Just need a signature, man. Order says it has to be Thomas Goldstone himself."

Steven nods his approval of the guests, and Thomas walks over to sign the digital clipboard. The courier reaches into his bag and pulls out a black envelope, handing it over. "Thanks, here ya go."

"Kerry, go home," Thomas says afterward. "It's late."

"Everyone else is already gone home for the day, hours ago," she replies with a smile. "That's why this is the best time to get everything done without interruptions, especially by my boss." Her smirk tells me they have a teasing, comfortable relationship. "But I'm on my way out now too."

She pats her oversized purse and waves 'bye to Mia.

"Careful, this feels like retribution by Blackwell," Gabe says after she leaves. "I might've sent him a little present once that required his signature. It was . . . unpleasant, to say the least."

Thomas nods and opens the envelope carefully, holding it far from his face like there might be poisonous powder in it. He slides the enclosed paper out, unfolding it and reading it, his eyes scanning left and right.

"What's it say?" Jonathan asks.

Thomas's face pales all at once, and he looks up. His eyes are bright with fear, his mouth hanging open in disbelief.

Hoarsely, he barks, "Everyone, OUT! Now!"

He makes a dash for the elevator, shoving Mia as he goes, and everyone follows his lead. Lance grabs my hand and drags me toward the elevator while Izzy and Gabe haul ass. Jonathan and Steven take up the rear, visually sweeping the room to make sure we're clear.

"What's going on? Tommy?" Mia demands fearfully.

Thomas ignores her, pressing a complicated order of buttons on the elevator panel. "Crouch down and hold onto the rails. We're going down fast."

We do as he says, understanding that we need to follow orders more than ask questions right now. Thomas finishes his button pushing by slamming a fist on the fire alarm, and the whole building erupts in a loud siren.

The elevator doesn't so much as lower as it falls all at once, and my stomach threatens to come up at the sudden drop. Only a second later, it seems, the elevator doors open to a concrete corridor.

"Run . . . Run . . . RUN!" Thomas yells.

I don't know what's happening, but I run as if my life depends on it.

# CHAPTER 32

## Blackwell

THE SUIT IS PERFECT, FAR BETTER THAN THE ONE I WORE TO THE office today. An occasion such as this requires the best finery I can afford, and I can afford the best. The custom-tailored handmade suit is a favorite of mine, though only for auspicious events.

A hefty glass of my finest tequila completes the accoutrements, and I sit in my favorite leather chair by the floor-to-ceiling wall of windows, overlooking the city. The first sip is rich with agave notes and the alcohol, a favorable combination along my taste buds, but the intensity builds, becoming darker, deeper as the oak shows its smokiness. The second sip amplifies the flavors even more.

It is a worthy drink, as worthy as my suit to be a hallmark of this moment in my mind when I remember the importance of this day.

I look over the city, watching the ants scatter this way and that. Leaving work and heading home, to what? A second job that pays nothing, cooking for unappreciative partners, or cleaning a worthless shack? Such futile endeavors.

I look through the telescope toward the Goldstone Building, which glints obnoxiously. Run, little ants. You leave every day thinking tomorrow will be another day in the wheel, never reaching new heights because the running is all for naught.

But not this time.

Tomorrow will be a new day, a gift for each and every one of the peons below me in the city.

I don't show them mercy because they are important but merely because a god's power comes from his worshippers. And they will all be mine.

I will not become irrelevant like some pagan deity who's had his day and is no longer remembered, his legacy dying out when his most devout believers pass on.

No, the people of Roseboro will understand that I built this city. They will appreciate that I continue to bring abundance to our borders, making each and every one of them thrive, and they will revere the hallowed ground that I tread.

They will be my congregation, recognizing the true greatness I deign to share with them. This city will be my legacy, and my flock will see that my immortalization knows no bounds.

As soon as I defeat those who dare to oppose me.

Him.

The Golden Boy.

The only one to ever stand up to me, both in action and in achievements. But my greatest success will be in taking him down.

*Quite literally*, I think with mirth.

I listen in to the bug I had placed in his penthouse apartment, amused. Thomas is a fan of bugs. Used one to catch my saboteur, in fact. The irony seems poetic.

He thinks his security is top-notch, and I'll admit that his investigative cousin did a thorough job of vetting each and every member of his team before allowing them to upgrade their system. But not thorough enough to thwart me.

I listen to him opening the envelope, another instance of poetic justice that I hope Gabriel Jackson will note. Ah, he does.

Glee burgeons forth in my soul, righteous joy that I've not known in years.

Finally, Thomas Goldstone will know my wrath.

I hear Thomas's exclamation, instructing everyone to get out. But it's far too late for that. He should've never come to Roseboro in the first place. The day he stepped foot into my city is the day his fate was written.

I have controlled his destiny all along, letting him grow in my fertile soil for this moment where I smash him beneath my shoe like the weed he has become.

A text comes through my phone . . .

*10 . . .*

I continue the countdown myself, eyes locked on the monstrosity across the city.

*5 . . .*

I stand, leaning forward toward the glass, wanting to be as close as possible to the hell I bring to Goldstone's existence.

*3 . . . 2 . . . 1.*

There's a rumble, audible even from here. A growing, deep guttural boom that demands everyone's attention. Down at the street level, ants freeze, cars slow as confusion percolates their dulled minds. But they'll know soon enough.

A deep boom rends the air, then another.

I watch, childlike glee filling me as the Goldstone building implodes in a dramatic chain-reaction series of explosions, just like Thomas Goldstone's empire. Glass shatters upward, floor by floor as each level collapses, and his monument falls from the sky, rushing toward the ground, a cloud of dust billowing out from ground zero.

Chaos reigns.

It's a symphony composed by my own hand. A beautiful destruction, a swarth of dark now visible where gold once stood. Not a new beginning, for I've never stopped my direction of Roseboro, but perhaps a fresh claiming.

A consecration of the land, that this city is mine. Always and forever.

My lips quirk, my teeth reflecting in the glass before me. I've done it, reduced the competing king's castle to crumbs while mine stands tall, resolute, eternal. A laugh erupts, fogging the glass, and my hands move of their own volition, applauding the show I orchestrated.

My phone buzzes on the floor where I dropped it in my excitement. I bend to pick it up and see one last text.

*Mission complete.*

Indeed.

*Bravo.*

# CHAPTER 33

## Charlotte

T HICK DUST FILLS THE AIR AS WE FOLLOW THOMAS, THOUGH WE'RE
at least a few blocks away from where the Goldstone building stood.
*Holy fuck! The building is demolished.*

We were *this close* to being inside when it gave way but sprinted down
the hidden corridor Thomas led us through, and moments later, the world
shook around us. It was like an earthquake, but so much worse. Seconds later,
the rush of dust and smoke billowed up behind us, and we were all running
as hard as we could. Only when our lungs could do no more did we slow
down, but still, we walk.

It's unimaginable, unfathomable. An entire building in ruins.

There's no doubt that it's Blackwell's doing. The pure, absolute madness
leaves no question.

But at least we're all alive.

We emerge into the night, sweet air filling my lungs for the first time
in what feels like forever. Jonathan pulls keys from his pocket, and a huge
Suburban beeps. We automatically aim for it and pile in. Steven takes the
wheel, pulling out carefully. It feels like he should be peeling out of the lot,
getting us clear of the danger zone, but he can't. There are too many onlook-
ers, and debris clogs the street.

Steven carefully makes his way clear and gets us on the move away from
downtown.

"Escape Plan Omega," Jonathan says when we're clear of downtown. Steven nods once and accelerates slightly.

The vehicle is silent as we drive. I think no one knows what to say. I certainly don't. I knew that Blackwell was sick, devious, and cruel, but this is on a completely different level.

This is more than murder. This was wholescale, indiscriminate slaughter.

Lance leans over, putting a hand on my thigh. "Are you okay?" he murmurs in my ear. "Any injuries, anything?"

I shake my head, biting my lip as I meet his eyes questioningly. "I'm clear too. Everyone clear?" he asks the rest of the car.

A hum of 'Okay' and 'Just shocked' sounds out, and while it's hard to believe considering the devastation, we're all uninjured, just dirty and dusty.

The Suburban returns to silence, and Lance takes my hand, like I'm precious and he almost lost me. The truth is, I almost lost him because of my own insecurities and lack of trust. But this second chance is all I need to do better and have a little faith. In him, in myself, in us. And it was almost taken away by Blackwell's devastating action.

Lance presses his lips to the top of my head, rubbing his lips across my filthy red curls, and I sigh, closing my eyes. "I love you, Lance."

"Thank you," he whispers, shuddering as his body starts to purge itself of the emotions inside. "I know how much it cost you to say that. I won't betray that, I promise. I love you too."

Well outside the city, in the woods surrounding Roseboro, Steven pulls into a hole in the trees lining the roadside. I would've driven past and never even seen the opening. He stops, tapping a quick code on a camouflaged keypad, and a near-invisible, green-painted gate slides open in front of us.

Steven continues driving down what's basically a grass path until he pulls up in front of a cabin. Well, it's built with logs, so I guess that makes it a cabin, but it's huge, like a mountain version of a mansion.

Izzy asks the question we're all thinking. "Where are we?"

"A cabin I bought through a line of shell companies," Thomas explains. "It can't be traced to me. It's stocked, secured, and prepped."

"It's basically our *shit hits the fan* property," Mia says. "Just in case."

I think it's safe to say the shit hit so hard, the fan was reduced to bits and baubles. *Just like Thomas's building*, I think sadly.

But we're together. We're safe. We'll survive.

Inside, the cabin is breathtaking, hand-carved creatures shaped into the wood beams and warm, cozy looking furniture dominating the large space. I'd love to come back some time when I can truly appreciate it, but right now, it doesn't seem appropriate to ask about Thomas's decorator.

Not that I have anything to decorate since the bakery is gone. But I'll rebuild, a better 2.0 version of *Cake Culture,* I vow. I only hope Thomas can do the same.

"Okay, here's the game plan," Jonathan says, his voice making me jump in the quiet. He's been on the phone most of the way here, texting away and even having a couple of quick, hushed conversations before we'd plunge back to silence. But he knows things, has been working his network, apparently, because he says, "The assumption is that we are all dead."

My jaw drops open, and Izzy cries out, "What?"

"Emergency personnel are onsite. Looks like the building was already mostly empty, and the fire alarm made everyone else evacuate. But being on the top floor, no one thinks the elevator would've been working, much less get us downstairs in time. Your assistant told the police who was in your apartment when she came up, so the assumption is that everyone is dead. The only good thing is that she didn't see me."

He pauses, pulling up early media reports on the collapse. After a moment, the video shifts, and there we all are . . .

*Thomas Goldstone, CEO. Mia Karakova, fiancée. Gabriel Jackson. Isabella Turner. Charlotte Dunn. Lt. Comm. Lance Jacobs. Steven Wilson.*

"Good," Thomas says, handing the phone back to Jonathan.

"Why is that a *good* thing?" Mia asks, confused. "And no offense, but I'm more than just your fiancée, for damn sure."

"I know. We'll make sure they fix it for the real obituary." Then he looks to Jonathan. "So, what's your read, Jon?"

Jonathan looks around our assembled group, stroking his chin. "I don't know yet, but at least we've got something held to our chest."

Thomas and Jonathan talk through options and scenarios. Honestly, it mostly goes over my head, and since it's beyond my involvement, I just try to stay supportive. Especially of Mia, who looks to be near losing it as Thomas talks about next steps.

"Wait, the first step is making sure we tell our *families* that we're not dead!" she protests. "Papa's going to be heartbroken!"

"We can't," Jonathan says, and in the corner of my eye, I see Gabe and Lance nod. "Your safety really depends on Blackwell thinking you're dead.

And Vladimir Karakov acting like anything other than his daughter being dead would cause suspicion."

"I think Vladimir can be told," Thomas says quietly. "But the folks at the Gravy Train, our colleagues, others . . . they have to be kept in the dark. Charlotte, your family—"

"Priscilla and Sabrina aren't losing any sleep," I assure him. "And Dad . . . it's better if they don't know."

"Lance?"

He frowns. "My family's assumed I've been dead before. They'll understand why . . . later."

Eventually, it's decided that Jonathan will go back and speak as a representative for the company and for the Goldstone family.

"Next, we need to find Trixie," Jonathan says, setting off a new discussion.

I try to dissuade them from that, but in the end, I get outvoted. She's our closest link to whatever Blackwell is planning.

"We have to think strategically," Gabe says, his voice low and rumbling. "Blackwell thinks he has us in checkmate. But he doesn't. We have the advantage. Once Thomas comes back to life, though, that advantage disappears. We need to make our plays before that happens."

"And Trixie could be the key to that," I reply sadly. I look around, seeing the faces of my family.

Plan agreed upon, or mostly, at least, we break. Jonathan heads back to Roseboro to start his end and get a handle on the press while Steven sets up watch on the bank of security camera feeds.

Slowly, we all drift into separate bedrooms in the cabin-slash-mansion.

The guest room Lance and I walk into is stunning, or it would be any other day. There's a dark wooden king-sized bed, covered with white cotton linens, and a bank of windows that look out to the treetops. Through an attached door, I find a well-equipped bathroom decked out in white and grey marble and bright lights that blind me.

I blink, and Lance comes up behind me, adjusting the lights with the dimmer switch I hadn't noticed. "Let's take a shower, wash this grime off." I turn to look at him and realize he's still filthy, remnants of the fire, of jail for him, and the building collapse. I must be too, and all I want is to wash it away, start fresh and clean, hopeful and loving.

"That sounds good."

The shower is hot and steamy, but there's no romance to getting undressed. We both just want to be out of these clothes.

Naked, he opens the shower door, letting me step in first. He follows and watches as I let the hot water sluice over my skin, wetting my hair to run in fiery waves down my back. We switch places, and I watch as he does the same, running his rough hands over his chest and abs.

"Lance," I say, but when he opens his eyes and pins me in place with his gaze, I don't know what to say. "I'm sorry," falls off my tongue, but it doesn't seem like enough, not remotely so.

"I know. It's okay," he says gently, cupping my face. "I get it that it was a shock, and everything pointed to me, and it was all too easy for you to think I was just like everyone else who'd let you down. But I'll keep proving to you that I'm not them. I'm here and not going anywhere."

I lean into him, and he wraps his arms around me. "You're amazing, you know that? You could have anyone. Why me, when I'm so difficult?"

I feel his smile against my hair, and his hands pull me tighter. "I've told you, I like you just as you are. Sassy, fiery spitfire and scared, untrusting heart. It makes you real, makes you mine, and I'll keep proving that to you, show you that you're safe with me."

I snuggle in, warm in the water and his embrace. "I am safe with you—heart, body, and soul. I just . . . *forgot* for a minute?" I say, letting a bit of levity into my tone.

"I won't let you forget again," he rumbles, his voice full of lush, dark promise. "I'll make sure you know, without a doubt, inside and out, that you're mine. Always."

His hands rub up and down my back, and instead of the comfort he offered earlier, this is an offer to make me forget.

Forget the war raging at our door. Forget the way I almost destroyed us as surely as Blackwell destroyed Thomas's building.

"I need you," I whisper. "I need to apologize . . ." I don't finish the sentence but slip from his arms, sliding down his body and lowering to my knees before him.

"Char, you don't have anything to apologize for, and you damn sure don't have to do it on your knees, ever," he says gruffly, but his cock is thickening before my very eyes, bobbing toward me greedily.

"I know. I want this." He's right, and I'm not blowing him as some sort of twisted apology but because I need to feel him, love him, worship him.

The way he does me. I want his light to suffuse me, fill in every dark corner of pain I hide, and show him that I am worthy of his love. Because finally, I believe that I am. He's taught me that, and I will forever be appreciative of his patience with my 'fraidy-cat heart.

I lick a long line from just above his balls to his crown and press a soft kiss to the velvety skin there. After a swirl of my tongue around the ridge, I take him into my mouth fully, getting deeper, inch by inch, as I bob up and down on him. He looms over me, blocking the water with his broad back as he watches his cock disappear into my mouth.

His thumb swipes along my brow, catching the few water droplets that threaten to run into my eyes, then his hands weave into my wet tresses. He guides me, feeding me his cock and dipping into my throat as he groans and grunts. "Fuck, Red. Take me."

And I do. I take him gladly, letting him have control. Of my mouth, of my heart, of my everything. It's all his.

He holds me still, thrusting into my mouth so fast I can barely keep my lips closed around him, slurpy, wet sucking sounds echoing against the tile surrounding us. I spread my knees, letting my hands dip down to cup my pussy.

As he fucks my mouth, I slip my slick fingers over my clit, matching his pace. I moan at the dual pleasures, and he freezes deep in my throat. "Do that again," he snarls.

I moan, vibrating my throat along his head, and I can taste the precum that's leaking from his tip, the first tease of the treat I want. He picks up the pace again, long thrusts but occasionally holding me to him, my nose buried in the short scruff of hair at the base of his cock, not letting me breathe.

My fingers speed up too, keeping tempo with him, and we're both getting close.

Without the walls of civility, he fucks my mouth raw and rough. This is punishment for not trusting, absolution and forgiveness wrapped up in one. This is fear that we almost died but celebration that we'll live to see another day. This is a promise for the future, that whatever comes, we'll handle it together.

I cry out around him, ready to fall but wanting to take him with me. He yanks himself free of my mouth, his voice rasping in control. "No, not yet."

I whine, need fiery in my veins and the edge so tantalizingly close, promising release and relief. He grabs under my arms, pulling me up, and takes my honey-coated fingers into his mouth, savoring my flavor.

"Bed. I want you in the bed."

# CHAPTER 34

## Lance

I T'S TOO MUCH, OR I THOUGHT IT WOULD BE TOO MUCH FOR HER, BUT Charlotte virtually runs for the bed. She's tougher than she knows, maybe stronger than I give her credit for, and I think she's pretty fucking badass. There's a core of steel surrounding the fluffy softness of her soul.

But as roughly as I fucked her mouth, she took it. Gladly, gratefully, and so fucking sexy she almost sent me over before I was ready. It's my turn to show her what she does to me.

Charlotte lies down on the white comforter, opening her arms and legs to me, offering to cradle me. But I grab her ankle, pulling her to the edge. "Turn over," I order.

She does as I command, and I shove her knees up underneath her. She's quite literally face down, ass up, presenting herself to me. It's a vulnerable position but one of the lesser ways she's finally opened up to me, though her slick pussy is wide open, her asshole right there, begging me.

I bend down, licking from her clit to her ass, and she writhes wantonly against me. Her sweet taste makes me hungry for more, makes me want to bury my mouth against her until I can't breathe, and I can hold my breath for a long fucking time.

But we both need more right now. I stand back up, gripping her hips so hard my fingertips leave dimples in her skin and she'll probably have bruises tomorrow, but I don't care.

Actually, that's not true. I do care, but I *want* the marks on her skin, need them in a way I never have before. I want to leave indelible, permanent marks on both of our bodies, declarations to the world that she is mine, and I'm hers, and neither of us is going anywhere without the other.

Neither of us needing or wanting gentleness, I slam into her balls-deep in one powerful thrust. I bottom out hard, and she cries out but bucks back into me, ready for more. "Touch yourself," I tell her, my breath harsh as I force the words out.

She wiggles, her right shoulder dropping beneath her, and I feel her fingers brush over the base of my cock where I disappear inside her. I feel her pussy lips kissing my cock, moving as she roughly rubs herself. Not tame circles, not this time. She's thrashing her fingers across her clit, chasing her orgasm, and I oblige, slamming into her over and over.

I want to be deeper in her than anyone has ever been before, in her tight pussy, in her even tighter heart.

I need her eyes, to see her fall over the edge with me. I pull out, manhandling her to flip her over. I watch her eyes trace down my chest, my abs, and her tongue peeks out like she wants to eat me up like one of her cupcakes.

I feel the same way about her.

I pull her legs up over my shoulders, not just her ankles, but to the bend of her knees, and her toes link behind my head. Her hips are up off the bed, totally in my control. When I push back into her, my head falls to the side, resting on her calf.

The hypnotic bounce of her tits drives on my every thrust, and Charlotte's hands flail, like she needs something to hold on to or I'll bounce her away. But I've got her, hips cradled in my hands as I push into her, so rough I fear I might split her in two, but her moans of ecstasy tell me she's loving every brutal bit of our lovemaking.

Because that's what this is. I am fucking her like a damn beast, but there's too much emotion underneath the lust for it to be anything but love.

Her hands finally find a home, one on her tits, teasing and pinching her nipple, and the other at her clit, where she resumes her rough swipes.

Her eyes meet mine, blue to blue, both of us gone for the other. A chance meeting, an unexpected connection, and both of our lives will never be the same. No matter who tries to tear us apart, she will always be . . .

"Mine," I growl at her through gritted teeth. I don't know if I'm telling her or asking her. Not that I'd let her say no, but I need to remind her about who we are and who we are to each other.

But she agrees, mewling out, "Yours. And you're mine." She says it with certainty, finally.

The relief of knowing she trusts in me fully, all doubts obliterated, is freeing, and I fall. My cock spasms before I can hold back, and I grunt, "Come . . . Charlotte." It's half command and half a cry of her name as the wave overtakes me, jets of my hot cum filling her.

I feel her walls clench, milking me as her legs quiver, her thighs shaking against my chest. I hold her tight, staying deep but giving her short strokes as she cries out her orgasm. A combination of her honey and my cum gushes around me, her pussy too full of cock to hold any more.

I hold her there, impaled on me as our breathing returns to normal. I nibble at her calf, then soothe the soft bite with a kiss. Charlotte stretches out, her legs going straight and tight on my shoulders. "Mmm, fuck, that was . . . " She searches for a word.

"Life-affirming," I offer, knowing that after a life and death situation, people will often need something to ground themselves to the reality of still being alive.

She blinks slowly, then nods, eyes on mine. "Life, and love. I love you, Lance."

I lean forward, testing her flexibility, bending her damn near in half to lower my lips to just an inch above hers. "I love you too, Charlotte."

The world may fall to ruins, but as long as I've got her in my arms, I won't give a shit. It's the first time I don't feel the need to rush out and save the world, do my part and make a difference. Instead, I'm locked in place with her, literally and figuratively. As long as I can save her, it's all I need.

As much as she has trust issues, I finally feel like I'm enough just as I am. Charlotte doesn't care what my last name is, where I live, or what I can provide for her financially. She only cares about my heart. And I've already given it to her fully.

The black Cadillac cuts through the late night, heading back to Roseboro. I'm driving, and Gabe sits in the passenger seat, both of us in head-to-toe black.

I don't know the man well, more innuendo and underhanded remarks from Charlotte, but I know he's shutting down. Whatever façade of congenial warmth he wears to blend in with the masses is gone, and he's gone cold, matter-of-fact, and methodical.

I do the same, a mission mentality taking over my mind, but it's harder than it used to be. Before, I was easily able to set aside the part of me that my team called 'Stateside', the kinder halves of our natures that rejected the horror of battle. I could easily divide myself and become who I needed to be. Not this time.

This time, I have something to actually go home to . . . and that worries me.

The SEALs taught me control, care, and caution, and that busting down the front door isn't always the best course of engagement. Missions are not made-for-television action scenes where the good guys always win and plot armor is stronger than Kevlar.

Real men, good men, have died in front of me, and bad guys have won. But with Charlotte counting on me, I find the shields, lock down my defenses, and prepare myself for what we're about to do.

The little house is on the far side of town, the street silent, and in a stroke of luck, the single lamppost light is burned out. Under the cover of darkness, I coast the quiet car to the curb.

"Set?" I ask Gabe, pulling out my Sig.

He repeats, taking out his own piece. "Set."

Silently, we exit the car and make our way to the back of the house. The back door is an easier entry point, with less visibility in case any nosy neighbors decide to check out the sliver of moon in the sky tonight.

Three seconds, through the door and carefully into the house. We're not expecting a fight, but recent evidence points to the fact that maybe our expectations are not exactly accurate.

I point to the hallway, and Gabe nods, moving the other way. I head to the single bedroom to search. A quick check of the bed, closet, and bathroom yields no results.

I hear a quiet lip pop, Gabe's signal, and head back to the front of the house.

He's waiting for me in the living room. "Couch, passed out drunk, I think," he whispers softly.

He goes around one end and I mirror him on the other. Gabe makes a quick move, pulling the target's wrists together and above her head, holding them tightly as he wraps a zip tie around them.

"Wha—what's going on?" she slurs, her voice like sandpaper on her unused and alcohol-dehydrated throat. Before she can react, I have another zip tie around her ankles, not as secure, but enough for our purposes.

Slowly, her eyes creak open, unfocused and twitchy behind half-closed lids. But when I step to Gabe's side and she sees me, her eyes go wide, adrenaline shooting through her blood, waking her up and sobering her a little.

The fear on her face mixed with shame is the confirmation I need. I'd known the truth, trusted my gut, but her reaction at seeing me alive? She might as well spill her guts to us right here and now.

But that's not enough. We have questions, lots of them. And she's going to answer each and every one.

"I thought you were dead," she says, still confused at my presence.

"Death by building collapse instead of death by chocolate this time?" I say, though the slight food pun is dry, bitter with disdain.

"I didn't know, I swear I didn't know." Her head shakes back and forth wildly, begging us to believe her. "Why do you think I'm drowning myself in so much wine I'm damn near pickled from the inside out? I didn't know!"

Gabe is done with her excuses. He pulls a black bandana out from his back pocket and forces it over her mouth. She fights him, thrashing and grabbing at his arms with her bound hands. But in seconds, she sags, the ether knocking her out.

"Let's go," Gabe says. He picks her up, tossing the limp body over his shoulder, and I lead the way out.

At the car, he slides her into the backseat and climbs in next to her. I try to tell him that I'll get back there and he can drive. Even though she's done awful things, I feel nervous leaving her at Gabe's mercy.

"She got you too," Gabe says, looking at me with empty eyes. "Not just Charlotte. She betrayed you, right under your damn nose."

"And you think I'll want revenge."

"No," Gabe explains. "But I'm not risking it when so much is riding on this. Get in the driver's seat."

He's right. He may be a stone-cold scary fucker, and as dangerous as that is, I'm the real danger. Not because I'm bigger or badder than him but because I'm personally invested, and we can't afford any mistakes.

Gabe's a damn pro, for sure, and my respect for the man goes up a few notches. He's still a wolf, but not a lone one, it seems. He's found his pack, and at least he tries . . . not to hide, but to fit in.

And he's right. This isn't a team. This isn't a squad or a platoon. Nobody's here because they're getting a paycheck. This is more. This is a family. Not one by birth, but by choice, just like I told Charlotte. I'm part of them too, now. It feels like home.

Back at the cabin, we quickly get our prisoner down to the basement wine cellar. It was deemed the most secure space, no windows, below-ground, with a single entry/exit point.

Thomas stands off to the side, needing answers but not suited for the type of work that will be carried out here tonight. I could do it, have done multiple interrogations in my time, but Gabe's right. I'm too close because this is personal.

So I stand back, letting Gabe take the lead.

He looks from Thomas to me, his voice hard but also somehow vulnerable. "Whatever happens here tonight stays in this room. I don't want Izzy to see me this way . . . not anymore."

Thomas steps forward, putting a hand on Gabe's shoulder and telling him fiercely, "Izzy knows exactly *who* and *what* you are, better than anyone. She's not upstairs because she can't watch you. She's upstairs because she understands that you don't want her here. So, thank you. For letting us see the side of you she already knows and accepts."

Gabe nods and looks at me. I nod in agreement, letting him know that I'm no threat, in this room or out of it.

He takes a deep breath, and I can see the light dim in his eyes. The humanity fades, and the disconnect between what he's about to do and who he is snaps into place.

I understand. He's a warrior, maybe not the same kind I was, but a warrior, nevertheless.

He shakes the woman in front of him, hard enough to jostle but not hurting her . . . yet. "Wake up, Trixie."

The interrogation begins.

# CHAPTER 35

## Charlotte

I CAN'T SIT HERE BY THE FIREPLACE. NOT WHEN I HAVE A GOOD IDEA of what Gabe, Lance, and Thomas are doing to Trixie downstairs.

I'd seen her when they brought her in, limp and haggard-looking. At first, I thought that'd been Lance and Gabe's doing, but as they passed me, I could smell the liquor on her and realized she was in rough shape before they ever got there.

Lance had offered me a single nod, a sign that everything was going to be okay, then they'd disappeared, leaving us to sit around the fireplace.

I pace, wishing I could go outside and get some fresh air but knowing Steven won't allow us out of the triple-locked doors.

"Sit down, woman," Mia chastises. "You're making me antsy with all your pacing."

I shake my hands out. "Sorry. I just can't believe Trixie did this. I mean, she was close. Not like you two, but . . . like a sister in some ways. She's been there since before I even opened. I just don't know what to think."

"They'll find out everything she knows," Izzy says, trying to be reassuring and failing.

"You mean Gabe will." It's judgmental, ugly, and mean. He's doing what he's doing for us, but I don't know how anyone could be comfortable with Gabe's methods.

Izzy shrugs, accepting. "Yeah, he will. He'll do whatever it takes, and I don't think less of him for it. He takes that stain on his soul because he knows he can bear the weight on his shoulders better than you can. And it's heavy, have no doubt."

I don't know what Izzy has been through. She kept a lot of what happened to her close to her vest, but I know hurt when I see it. And I don't want to be the one who does that to my friend.

"I'm sorry, Iz. This is all just so far beyond my outer limits, you know? I don't think less of Gabe, or you. It's just . . . I never thought it'd go this far."

She gets up, coming over to hug me. "I know. Not exactly the story I wrote for myself, either, but it's mine. He's mine, and I'll do anything for him. And he'll do literally anything for me."

Mia interrupts our moment of friendship to say, "Speaking of our guys, that was some upper-tier Jedi shit that Lance pulled on you back at the apartment before things went to hell."

She gets up, miming waving a lightsaber around in a figure-eight pattern. "Trust yourself, trust me," she says in a high Yoda voice, "and you went all 'Yes, Master' for him."

She starts humming like Yoda, and I laugh at her antics. "I did not go 'Yes, Master' for him. I just . . . realized he was right."

I blush, the splotches hot on my cheeks as I remember that I basically did submit to him last night. But I chose it, and that's between Lance and me, not the girls. Not that I won't overshare with them again in the future, but last night was . . . special, and ours.

But they know me too well, can read the freckles on my face like tea leaves. "Ooh, she might not have been submissive to him then, but she sure has been since," Mia says sagely. "No shame, girl. I like a bossy man."

Lord, does she ever. Again, we overshare on the regular. Fifty shades of Goldstone is pretty much *de rigeur*.

"Seems like you might get that happily ever after you thought was never coming after all?" Izzy says, nudging me. "Gonna make a new cupcake for that?"

I bite my lip, ducking my chin because I was thinking the same thing this morning. Finally. And it feels good and right, warm and beautiful. Like as crazy as it may be, Lance was made just for me, a perfect fit.

An intense energy fills the room, and we all turn to see Lance standing in the doorway. He looks hard, the line of his jaw sharper somehow, the faint lines around his eyes from too much time squinting in the sun deeper than usual. "Char, she's asking to talk to you," he says neutrally. "Your call."

I stand up, not sure I want to do this but my feet already deciding. "I need to know why. I'll talk to her for that, at least. Did Gabe get what you need?"

Lance looks at Izzy, sharing in what I swear looks like respect to her. "He did. He's a good man, and Trixie sang like a bird with very little encouragement. But he'll need you tonight. I think this was *different* for him."

Izzy nods, thanking Lance for the warning.

Lance takes my hand as we walk down the short flight of steps to the wine cellar. I gasp when I see Trixie tied to a chair, her hair a blonde mess of curls, and makeup running down her face in rivers. There's no blood, at least, and she looks unhurt.

"Charlotte, Oh, my God . . . Charlotte. I'm so sorry. I didn't know about the building, I swear it. I'm so glad you're okay. I'm . . . sorry." The words spill out of her mouth, each one chasing the previous in a long run-on torrent of emotion.

"Why?" I whisper, forcing my back to remain straight, my eyes dry. She was my friend, and those emotions don't die overnight. "That's all I need to know . . . why?"

Trixie swallows, looking down. "I'm so sorry. When this whole mess started, I didn't know you. On paper, you were just some rich bitch with a life of ease. From the outside, it looked like you grew up in a wealthy family, a dad and mom, and even a sister. It seemed like you were just doing the crazy dream thing with the bakery, like you didn't have any real worries, just got everything handed to you on a silver platter. I was jealous because I'm . . . me." She says it like it's a death sentence, sadness pouring from her.

"And you kept going even after knowing the truth?" I ask, pissed. She knows all about my life. I shared so much with her during those long hours before we even opened. And even more later, as we got closer. There's only one real question left, then. "Was any of it real?"

Fresh tears shine in the corners of her eyes, and she nods. "Remember what I told you about my life back home? It was all true. And I told myself when I left that hellhole that I was never going back. No matter what. I had nothing after the internship, so when Blackwell made me the offer, I had to take it. I didn't know you, and I was desperate."

I take a deep breath, understanding, in a way.

"And then I met you," she says. "You were nothing like what I thought you'd be. Your life wasn't any better than mine. Just different. You still had worries, and shitty parents, and had to work hard. It was just different than my life. But it was too late. I was stuck."

"Stuck how?"

"If I told you the truth, you would've fired me on the spot. And without a job, I would've had to . . . I don't know, probably dance like the girls back home. I would've ended up just like what I'd run from. And it would've been worse than before. Poor and hungry isn't so bad when it's all you know, but once you've had a taste of a good life, with friends and something to care about, I couldn't—" She shakes her head vehemently, and in a way, I can almost see her point, although it hurts to think that.

I want to frame her as a villainous mastermind in my head, paint her with one stroke of personality, or maybe a personality disorder, that she could do something so conniving behind my back while simultaneously acting as my friend. But people aren't that way, not me, and not her.

"I couldn't go back, no matter what. So I thought if I kept my mouth shut, I could mitigate the damage as much as possible. It was the best I could do in a really shitty situation. So I made false claims to the Health Department, knowing that if they showed up, they wouldn't find anything. And I let a guy in the back door to tweak the ovens. I thought he was making them run hot to just burn the cookies, not the whole store!"

"That was the guy who ended up attacking you," she tells Lance. "I think they just wanted an excuse for the cops to arrest you."

Turning back to me, she says, "I didn't mean for you to find the phone. I'm sorry for making you doubt him. And I swear, I didn't know about the bomb or whatever it was Blackwell did."

"But you were complicit in all of it," Lance growls. "You followed his orders, sent him intel, let Charlotte think I had betrayed her, and guided her to Thomas's."

Trixie sags. I really just want to ask why again, but I think it's one of those questions that'll never have a clear answer. "It didn't have to be like this, Trixie."

Gabe stands up, his eyes dark. "I think you should go upstairs, Charlotte."

I look at Trixie once more. "I loved you like a sister," I tell her honestly. "Truly, in my heart."

She cries out again, "I'm sorry, Charlotte."

But then her eyes flick to Gabe, fresh fear bubbling up as she struggles against her restraints. I go back up the stairs, her apology echoing in my ears until I close the wine cellar door.

I force my feet back to the living room, where Mia and Izzy are waiting for me, each on one end of the couch. I sit between them, and they wrap their arms around me. The Three Musketeers, always. No matter what.

# CHAPTER 36

## Blackwell

*C*HAOS STILL REIGNS AT THE SITE WHERE THE GOLDSTONE BUILDING *stood. The golden building, which served as a landmark for Roseboro, unexpectedly collapsed last night shortly after the majority of the workforce thankfully left for the day. Investigations are still ongoing, but early reports are that there were at least seven deaths, including entrepreneur Thomas Goldstone.*

The screen on my television switches from the microphone-holding newscaster over to a panoramic shot of the destruction. The voiceover continues the update.

*I'm here with Chief of Police, Frank Harris, who is coordinating the investigation. Chief Harris, do you have any evidence of what caused the building's collapse?*

Frank fills the screen, looking right at home in the media spotlight. He's an excellent upstart, one who has served me well over the years.

*Nothing concrete yet,* he says with an aw-shucks shrug. *Right now, we just count it a miracle that the building was mostly empty. Most of the employees had already left for the day. We'll conduct a full investigation, dig through the rubble, look for any workmanship flaws, and determine whether there were structural issues with the tower.*

He's planting the idea that this was a symptom of Goldstone's lack of attention to detail, that he would let his very namesake building be built poorly. The implication that his empire is also built on quicksand is an easy jump.

*Could there be something more sinister at work here? Is there evidence that this could be a terrorist act?*

The newscaster is a persistent pipsqueak, I'll give him that. If he were on my payroll, that'd be a boon, but he's not. I find it annoying and troublesome. The last thing I need is the word 'terrorism' being linked to this.

Frank laughs congenially, looking at the newscaster like he's a young kid who's a bit big for his britches.

*Son, there's no evidence of that, so don't go scaring the good people of Roseboro with your inciteful speech. We live in a good, safe city. We'll find out what happened to this building and you'll be the first to know. Good day.*

Frank walks away, pointing and talking to small groups of officers who are pretty fruitlessly poking through the twisted mess. It gives the effect that he's the boss, the leader in charge, and knows what he's talking about.

Well done, Frank.

My phone buzzes at my side, a message from the chief himself.

*Did what I could.*

The newscaster presses the button at his ear then speaks into the microphone once again. *I'm getting word that Jonathan Goldstone, a relative and friend of the late Thomas Goldstone, will be holding a press conference very soon. We'll send you over to that, live at the courthouse. This is Trevor Olliphant, Channel 5 News.*

Interesting. Jonathan Goldstone.

Former military-cum-private investigator, and cousin of the Golden Boy. I wonder what he's going to do and watch as he takes the steps of the Roseboro courthouse, looking like a rough man who's tried to slick himself up.

He's playing the part of businessman, but his worldliness is readily apparent. Oh, you can hide it from the sheep, Jonathan Goldstone, but I can see you. I can see it in your eyes.

I sense a potential enemy. Not on my level. You are swimming in unfamiliar waters. But you are more than one of the sheep.

He takes the microphone.

*Roseboro mourns the loss of a great man, a man who only wanted to make this city the best it could be. Not only through his business and charity ventures, but by encouraging each and every citizen to be kind, compassionate, and to care for his fellow man.*

*We are all responsible for continuing that legacy.*

*I will be serving as the Interim President of Goldstone Inc, and I vow to continue on as Thomas would. Because Goldstone did not end yesterday with the collapse of a building. It lives on inside each of us.*

*As for last night's tragedy, I have seen that investigations are being specifically targeted in a singular direction.* He pauses, and Frank's vehemence that had seemed so perfect a moment ago now seems like a smoking gun of his erroneous ways.

*There are those who will try to misdirect you. But this was an act of terrorism, a violent and aggressive move by a coward who is more willing to destroy Roseboro than to share the city we all call home.*

This man has stones, bordering dangerously close to calling me out by name. Looking directly into the camera, his eyes narrow and his jaw clenches.

*The truth will come out. Justice will be served. Goldstone will go on, as will Roseboro. In Thomas Goldstone's honor—be good, do good, and leave a legacy of hope for a brighter tomorrow.*

Jonathan Goldstone walks away from the makeshift podium, lights flashing and reporters calling out to him.

My response? I laugh. I laugh at his foolish wish for justice and truth, as if this is some comic book from my youth. Yes, I read them as a guilty pleasure, snuck from the library and enjoyed as banal, nutrition-devoid entertainment. But I would quickly and rightfully return to my studies, my music, my work.

Because that is where the true value lies.

Jonathan Goldstone forgets this, or perhaps never learned it, likely a young, silver-spooned boy, much like Thomas. The latest version, I think, but so much weaker than the original, who at least had innovation and charisma on his side.

The good times roll as the news continues on with their morning reports. It seems that Goldstone stock has plummeted to nearly worthless this morning, as there's simply not much of a business remaining. Regional managers and entities are frozen, chickens with their head cut off.

I have done it, I sank his golden warship, and the city is none the wiser of the monster in their midst.

The only one who knew was Thomas himself, and he took that knowledge to the grave. I do wish I'd been able to hear his fatalistic thoughts as he realized exactly what I had done right under his nose.

I wish I knew what his last thoughts were as he ran for his life.

My phone buzzes again. This time, an incoming call.

"Hello."

"What the fuck, man? I didn't know you were going to do something like that! I *liked* Charlotte. She was good to me. You never said this was going to happen!"

Trixie Reynolds. Her twang comes out when she's angry, like pencils being jammed into my eardrums, highlighting her lack of education in proper enunciation. And people do not speak to me this way. Ever.

"Watch your tongue, Miss. Reynolds. I take it you were unhappy with yesterday's events?"

I'm baiting her, more curious than anything. She's been useful along the way as a low-level resource, stirring up trouble without causing dissention in the ranks of Goldstone's friendly fools.

"Unhappy? Yeah, you could say that," she snarls. "I want to meet, finish our business, and get the hell outta dodge."

I grin, pursing my lips. She is a ballsy one. Though stupid courage has next to nothing to do with intelligence. Because if she were smart, she'd already be on her way out of the city, running like a scared country mouse. That she delays to get payment she feels entitled to is laughable. Survival of the fittest, I'd say, and she's showing her lack of longevity. "I thought your desire was to take over the bakery yourself?"

It is something she mentioned in passing after having been placed in position, and it'd seemed a rather easy payout at the time, less liquid funds and more endorsement of her wares as she began a new business. And potentially another ally in reserve, should her usefulness be needed.

"Nope," she says, popping the *P*. "Those days are past. I want out. Cash money and I'm gone. You and Roseboro will just be a cloud of dust in my rearview mirror."

"Very well," I say, sounding amenable. "I will send a car to pick you up. Be ready in ten minutes."

Ordering a car for her is a simple matter of texting my driver. I don't bother going to my safe to pull out money to pay her off. She won't be leaving with cash in hand. Nor her life. She has run her course of usefulness and dares to have such a demanding demeanor with me, so a loose end is all she's become. How efficient of her to expedite her own demise.

I consider whether I should offer a choice, a game of sorts, as I did with my previous resource when he became a liability. But where that one had held some element of amusement for me, a man who truly believed himself at rock-bottom being forced to dig even deeper for his own grave, Trixie Reynolds doesn't intrigue me the same. She's merely . . . forgettable.

So her death need not be orchestrated and engineered. A quick shot should suffice.

Minutes later, my private elevator dings, announcing the arrival of my guest.

"Come in, dear," I say, guiding her to a chair in front of my desk. She is hesitant, perhaps sensing that this meeting is not as wise as she thought, but she does sit. Her back is straight, both feet on the floor like she could run at any moment. But we know she's not going anywhere.

She thinks she's waiting for the money.

I know she's waiting for a bullet.

I move to the bar, pouring a healthy dose of tequila into a tumbler as her eyes follow me closely. I take a sip, not offering her one. It matters not. The move was merely calculated to place me between her and the door, which she foolishly allowed.

"Well?" she asks, her fear making her bark like a scared puppy.

"Miss Reynolds, have you said anything to the investigating teams looking into the bakery or the Goldstone building?" It is a test of sorts. Frank would've told me if she'd spoken out of turn, but she doesn't know that.

She shakes her head, unruly waves brushing her shoulders. "No, the police asked some questions at the bakery and took Lance away for it. I comforted Charlotte and laid the breadcrumb trail for her to gather her troops. I didn't know what you were planning in getting them all together."

The accusation is meant to be biting, but it's merely a nip on my rough armor. I sip my tequila, saying sagely, "You know what you are meant to know."

"No one said anything to me about the building," she sneers. "Though that Jonathan guy from the news called me to give me condolences on losing Charlotte. Well, he asked if I thought the two incidents were connected, but I told him I'm just a cake maker. I didn't know anything about Charlotte's friends. He seemed to believe that."

Ah, now that is interesting. Perhaps young Goldstone is adept enough to put pieces together, although the two incidents on the same day would be obvious to even the stupidest of people. And Frank says that Jonathan Goldstone isn't dumb, just unaware of how this city works.

"It seems you've done well enough at covering your tracks," I falsely compliment her. "And now you want to simply skip town and start fresh somewhere else?"

She stands, jumpy as the conversation lengthens more than she wanted. "Look, just pay me what you owe me and you'll never see me again."

She holds her hands out, palms facing me as if I need to calm down.

But I am calm, for this is nothing other than business. And I am utterly in control of my destiny where my business is concerned.

I pick up the gun from beneath the bar towel, pointing it at her. "Indeed, I will never see you again, Miss Reynolds. But I'm afraid it won't be because you've left town. At least, not the way you expected."

Her eyes widen, looking comically large with the massive amounts of eyeliner and mascara she has on. Young women these days don't seem to understand that men prefer to see them, not some cartoonishly fake version created with layers of spackle and paint. Her pink lips round into an O, which would be prettier if it weren't covered in sticky gloss. I will need to be careful that her body doesn't leave any trace evidence.

"Blackwell . . . wait . . . let's talk about this, please," she begs, her twang coming on stronger as she pleads for her life.

But the decision has been made.

*My* will, be done.

# CHAPTER 37

## Lance

JONATHAN DRIVES, FOLLOWING THE SUV THAT PICKED UP TRIXIE, staying far enough back to not be busted as a tail. I'm in the passenger seat, having worked with him before, while Gabe and Thomas are in the back.

We correctly assumed Blackwell would bring Trixie to him, but we'd hoped it'd be somewhere more public and less secure. The Blackwell Tower isn't an ideal location, but it'll have to work.

Thankfully, Gabe did quite a bit of legwork on the strengths and weaknesses of Blackwell's fortress when he fought his way out from underneath the man. And while it'd been a fool's mission then, with only one man, our current team is much more experienced and better armed.

Two Special Operations vets, a freshly-retired hitman, and a billionaire.

It'll have to be enough.

Dressed in head-to-toe black, we stick to the shadows, smoothly closing on the tower.

The guys follow my lead, not because this is my show but because I have the most experience leading a team, and though this ragtag assembly isn't composed of the operators I'm used to, what they lack in finesse, they have in heart.

We approach a side door, guarded by a single man. If this were a military op, we'd take him out. A silenced *pffft* in the night air, and that'd be it.

But we'd prefer to not leave a trail of bodies behind. It'd be too messy and lead to too many questions. Plus, while the men we'll encounter tonight are employed by Blackwell, that doesn't necessarily make them evil themselves. We won't punish them for the actions of the man who signs their paychecks.

I hold up a fist and everyone freezes behind me. I scan, looking for cameras, and when I see the dark orb above the doorway, I watch with bated breath. After what seems like an eternity but is probably only seconds, Jonathan places a hand on my shoulder signaling that we're good. His guy did his job, hacking into Blackwell's computerized security system. We should be clear of alarms and all cameras should be disabled for the next ten minutes.

Ten minutes. Watch a clock and the time will drag, infinitely slow and seeming like plenty of time to do just about anything. The reality is, ten minutes is a tight timeline for what we need to accomplish tonight. But the system hack couldn't be any longer, so that's the time we get.

I close the distance with a sprint, using the darkness and the guard's attention to take him low, my shoulder hitting him in the stomach just as I wrap my arms around his legs and lift him. A quick twist, and I dump him to the pavement, his head bouncing off the ground harder than probably necessary, but he's a big motherfucker and he'll be okay other than a bad headache when he wakes up.

Inside, we progress to the stairwell. The elevator would be faster, but it's a blind point we can't risk. Not when everything is on the line. But each floor is a new threat, that we might be seen, that we might be confronted, that we might have to fight our way to the top floor.

The possibility becomes all too real when a door opens just as we start past the fifteenth floor. A tall, broad guard calls out, "Hey!"

Jonathan reacts quickly, his right leg lashing back in a powerful thrust-kick to the man's stomach. The guard is thrown to the wall behind him, the back of his bald head bouncing off the drywall before he sags to the ground.

We're all surprised, but Jonathan puffs up, sarcastically bragging, "I've got some moves too. Not just a supervisor sitting on his laurels."

The smallest of grins quirks my lips behind my mask, and judging by the crinkles around Thomas and Gabe's eyes, they're doing the same small, hopeful smile. It feels righteous, like we have fate's guiding hand endorsing our mission. Two guards, two down.

We don't see another guard the rest of the way up the stairs, but we pause outside the top floor, knowing it's Blackwell's domain and will therefore be guarded by his best man. Gabe has been here before, met with Blackwell himself in his office, so he takes the lead.

He confided on the way here that his natural instinct is to snap the neck of the guard that'll be stationed outside Blackwell's office. Force of habit, he'd said darkly. But he promised to try and restrain himself, to go along with our *less is more* approach, and I hope he can.

He opens the door, shoving his way inside as quickly and quietly as a ghostly breath. I'm glad I've never been on Gabe's bad side. His choke hold is silent but very effective, and he drags the guard into the stairwell. We close and lock the door behind us as we enter Blackwell's private office area, ensuring the guard won't interrupt, even if he does regain consciousness while we're working.

But I can see the adrenaline burning through Gabe, the fire in his eyes. Time for being nice is over. He's out for blood now.

Thankfully, so are we.

We don't go in slowly this time, not wanting to give Blackwell time to arm himself or run. Instead, we burst through the door in a crashing singular movement, guns out, Jonathan and me sweeping the front while Thomas and Gabe cover us.

"What the—"

Blackwell's cursing exclamation of surprise is short-lived. He's standing at a wet bar near the door, blocking Trixie in. But as we enter, he snatches her, grabbing her forearm and twisting her around to act as a shield.

She doesn't cover his entire width, but it's enough. He already has a gun pointed at Trixie's head. He must have already had it pulled and I wonder if we just saved her life from this crazy monster.

"Let her go, Blackwell," I command, lifting the MP5 Jonathan lent each of us. Hopefully, the threat of facing four men with guns will convince him to give up.

He licks his lips like he's eager to put us in our place. "I don't think so. You boys have made a grave mistake tonight."

Thomas pulls his balaclava off his head, raw anger in his eyes as he glares at Blackwell. "You're the one who fucked up."

Blackwell's jaw drops in surprise, his hands going slack on Trixie for a split second. But when she tries to move, his grip retightens as his mouth clicks closed.

Through gritted teeth, he protests the truth before him. "NO! You're dead! The building collapsed with you inside," Blackwell rasps. "There's no way you could've gotten out."

"Ever heard of an escape plan?" Thomas taunts. He pats his chest. "Feels pretty alive to me. Want to check for yourself?"

Ironically, Blackwell does actually take a step forward, keeping Trixie in front of him, and we all prep for battle. But it's not to test whether Thomas is a ghost. It's to threaten him. "How dare you? You should've stayed dead. Never should've trusted someone else to do what I should have done myself."

"Just can't get good help these days, can you?" Thomas needles. He's using his weapon, not the gun but his mouth, pushing Blackwell's buttons. It's smart. It might make Blackwell sloppy and give us an opening to make a move.

"You think you're so brilliant, coming into *my* city, with your insufferable talk of hope and community," Blackwell sneers, while out of the corner of my eye, I see Gabe sliding to the side for a shot. "You make ridiculous business decisions, have the gall to buy my own companies, and go against me on contracts. You're an entitled brat whose only value is in your death. The absence of you from my city will be nothing but a small footnote in Roseboro's history."

"Your city? This city belongs to the people, the ones who get up at the crack of dawn to work their asses off for it," Thomas argues. "The ones who work late into the night to keep us all safe, the ones who work hard, day in and day out. Roseboro is everyone's city."

Blackwell scoffs. "Their city? It's MINE. I own it, from the riverfront to downtown and beyond. It's all mine—the land, the people, the government, all of it. I am Roseboro."

"All I see is a pathetic old man with delusions of grandeur," I growl, pulling Blackwell's eyes to me as Gabe takes another side step.

His eyes go wild, spittle gathering at the corners of his mouth. "They will all bow down to me. *You* will all bow down to me. I have earned it! I have worked tirelessly to reach this point, and I will not have you destroying my grand vision for this city."

"You blew up my building," Thomas charges, tiring of the madman's grandiose rants. Gabe takes another step but doesn't raise his gun . . . not yet.

Blackwell's answering grin is full of malevolence, no sign of remorse for his actions. "I did. Right under your nose, stupid boy. Demolished your building and your entire empire. It will all be mine for pennies on the dollar, every last bit. I will wipe away any legacy you thought to leave, remake it in my own image, and you'll have nothing, even in your death."

His speech is odd, like he's forgotten that Thomas is standing right in front of him, alive and well. He's stuck in a rut of his own making, looping his own maniacal plans for the future.

But his plan becomes clear as he turns his gun on Thomas, Trixie still a shield held in front of him. "Now, you'll stay dead."

Trixie has been silent, frozen in fear in the middle of a circle of men out for blood tonight. But she shows her guts, taking the opening when Blackwell points the gun at Thomas.

She twists, shoving Blackwell away, but before Gabe can take the shot, Thomas rushes into the grappling pair. Trixie's caught, her shirt snared in Blackwell's left hand, and the three of them go dancing across the office, fighting for the gun.

"Thomas, get down!" Jonathan yells as he and I lift our guns, but before he can, Blackwell's gun goes off, freezing everyone.

The split second stretches out, ending when Trixie's mouth opens in a round O of surprise. Her hands go to her belly, a red bloom of blood growing quickly against her pink shirt.

"No!" I call as her legs give out and she collapses to the floor, but no one can catch her or even watch because Thomas is still wrestling with Blackwell for control of the gun. With a hard yank, he steps back, gun in hand, pointing it at Blackwell.

Impotent fury washes over Blackwell's face for a moment before he laughs, a bark of amusement contradictory to being held at gunpoint.

He holds his hands wide, challenging, "Go ahead, *boy*. I dare you."

Thomas holds the gun steady, his eyes narrowed. Jonathan drops to his knees, doing what he can to help Trixie. Gabe moves to Thomas' left shoulder and I take a step closer but keep half-focused on the door.

"Let me," Gabe says, lifting his MP5. "This isn't your—"

"No." Thomas shakes his head, his eyes haunted by what he's seen. "I have to. This has to be me." His voice is hollow, but resolute.

"You won't do it. You don't have the balls," Blackwell taunts. "And even if you did, this city will still be *mine*. Built by my designing hand, my legacy in every corner. You'll never be half the man I am. Even now, you hesitate, letting your friend here die. *So weak.*"

Blackwell looks down to Trixie, who's in Jonathan's arms, but we're not carrying first-aid kits, so there's not much he can do besides hold pressure on her wound. "So pathetic, but a reasonable resource loss so that my plan can succeed."

Trixie looks up with a bloody smile. "Pathetic? Who do you think told them where you'd be tonight?"

Blackwell lunges for her, angry that she might've gotten one over on him, furious that she might've been our pawn instead of his tonight.

A second shot rings out, and Blackwell's head jerks. His eyes look shocked as he crumples to the floor, and Thomas lowers the gun. "My job. My burden."

Shock is setting in quickly, his first kill, especially at close quarters, already hitting him hard. We understand, having all been there once ourselves. Gabe comes up, taking the gun from Thomas's hands.

"It's okay, man. I've got this."

Gabe examines Blackwell's still body, making minor adjustments to his placement then setting the fired gun down. "It'll look like he did it himself."

"You sure? We can't risk being wrong here."

"I'm sure," he tells me. "No fingerprints since we have on gloves, Blackwell has residue on his hands from shooting Trixie, and the placement will look like he fell after a self-inflicted shot. I'm sure." The look in his eyes tells me this isn't his first rodeo at staging either, and I have to trust his skills. We're in this together.

Trixie makes a gurgling noise, Jonathan squeezing her hand desperately. "Trix—"

Her brows are pulled down, her eyes half-closed in pain. I don't know what to say. I can't reassure her that she's going to be okay, because she's clearly not. But she sacrificed herself to try and help us, by coming here at our behest tonight and in fighting for the gun, even if she was unsuccessful.

She tries to smile, her lips trembling at the corners. "Tell Char I'm sorry. Tell her to believe. Take care of her, Commander Coo—"

She doesn't finish the silly nickname she bestowed upon me, a last breath pushing past her lips without sound. She relaxes in Jonathan's arms, no longer in pain, no longer trying to escape her meager beginnings and become something else. She dies as a friend, a member of our family.

Her eyes stare blankly, and though we know we shouldn't touch her, Jon closes them for her.

I look up, realizing Gabe is at Blackwell's desk, his laptop open. "I kept the note simple, just *I'm sorry*, even though I don't think that asshole was sorry for a single thing he did in his life."

"Sounds right for the scene we're setting, at least," Jonathan says, getting up. He's going to take it hard later. He's a born lifesaver, and while he's lost them before . . . it's always hard. I know he remembers each and every one of the souls he's escorted to the Reaper's door.

We gather at the door, the four of us partners in this, and look around one last time. "We clear?"

"Yeah," Gabe says. Thomas finally nods, and I remind myself to check in with him later too. He'll need to purge himself.

I lead us back out the door, down the stairs, and finally, into the dark night.

Mission accomplished. Another hollow victory.

# CHAPTER 38

## Charlotte

THE CABIN IS SILENT, ALL OF US TOO CHOKED TO SPEAK BUT SITTING side by side on the couch, hands wrapped around each other. Three mugs of coffee sit on the table in front of us, long ago gone cold.

"They've got to be okay," Mia says. It's a variant on the one thing we can find to say, begging, pleading, hopeful affirmations that tonight will go as planned. That our men will come back to us.

That we'll all have our happily ever afters. Even me.

Doubt tries to creep in, that anything good will surely be ripped from me, but I squash it down and choose to have faith this time. Lance is surrounded by good men, and they are all uniquely gifted for this work, as ugly as it may be.

Steven calls out from his station in front of the monitors, "They're back."

I'm surprised he can see at all. He's been on duty for hours straight, only catching a catnap when Jonathan traded watch with him. We don't trust anyone else with the situation so tenuous, so Steven has been the only guard.

Thomas had this cabin set up as a safe space, so there's basically an armory, a full security system, and it's completely enclosed with razor-wire fencing.

None of that matters now, because they're back.

We all hop up and run for the door to the garage but stop short when Steven reminds us, "Stay inside."

"Are they okay?"

He shrugs, not helping any. But a moment later, the garage door opens, and they're back. All four of them.

"What happened? Are you okay?" we ask simultaneously.

I'm not sure if they guide us or we pull them, but we all end up in the living room. Thomas pulls Mia into his lap in a chair, Gabe sits on the floor at Izzy's feet, and Lance wraps his arm around me on the couch, pressing us together from knee to shoulder. Jonathan stands, arms at his side and eyes scanning our group.

"Are you sure about this?" he asks Thomas.

Thomas looks slightly shaken, honestly, like still waters on top of churning rapids, and my gut clenches as I wonder what happened.

"I am. We're in this together, and I'm not going to keep tonight from Mia, so I wouldn't expect Gabe or Lance to keep it either. Besides, we all need to have our stories straight."

His words send a chill through me. What would they need to keep secret? What story?

Slowly, they begin to tell us about what their night entailed. The tension builds as they tell us about getting to the top floor of Blackwell tower, but my mouth drops open when Lance gently tells me about Trixie.

"I'm sorry, Char. She was trying to get free, trying to help us. I know you're hurt at her betrayal, but in the end, she sacrificed herself for us. She said to tell you she was sorry and to believe in yourself." The words choke in his throat, matching the tears that catch in mine.

Lance rubs soothing circles on my back as I bury my face in his chest. "She . . . she's gone? I didn't get a chance to tell her . . ."

"She knew."

I hiccup, remembering all the good times. She did awful things, ones I don't know if I could've ever forgiven her for. But I would've liked to have had the chance. At least for us to try. We'll never have that chance. Now I'll . . .

Never hear another outrageous baking pun as she waits for me to laugh at her silliness.

Never pull an all-nighter, high on sugar and karaoke-style singing of old Britney Spears tunes.

Never work by her side, a common dream of success and friendship fueling us.

She's dead.

She gave up her dream of something greater, giving everything she had, even her life. For me, for us.

No matter what she'd done before, in the end, she was my friend. Trixie was in my life for a short period of time, but she burrowed into my soul.

I will always remember her that way. Not confessing her coerced sins, but bubbly and vivacious, singing and dancing, and so full of life that she brightened my world with her very presence.

Mia quietly asks, "Then what happened?"

I can't hear, can't really focus on the rest of their report, too lost in my own emotional tidal wave.

But Thomas keeps talking. "I struggled with Blackwell for the gun and got it. He taunted me, but when he went for Trixie, I had to." His eyes lock on Mia, hard as marbles. "I killed him."

His words jolt all of us. I pick my head up from Lance's chest, but he squeezes my shoulder. I need to control myself.

I see Gabe doing the same to Izzy's calf, where he's got himself wrapped around her leg.

But Thomas, the one who made the confession, is waiting for Mia's judgement.

Her eyes are wide, full of fear, her mouth hanging open. "You killed him?" she asks, looking for confirmation. When Thomas nods, she gathers him into her arms, not condemning him but comforting him. "Are you okay? Oh, my God, are you okay?"

He mumbles something I can't hear, and Mia turns to Jonathan. "You fixed this, right? No one is taking Thomas from me. *No one*, you understand me?"

Her voice is icy, stone-cold threatening. Though Thomas is the one confessing to murder, Mia is the one to fear and we all know it. She loves big and hard and would do anything for any of us. Most of all, Thomas.

"It'll look like a murder-suicide," Gabe interjects. "Not sure how they're going to spin that with the unconscious guards, but there's nothing to point at any of us. We do need to figure out our re-entry to Roseboro, back from the dead. And what you want to share about Blackwell."

The last part is directed to Thomas, but he's had enough for now. "Let's talk in the morning. It's late," Mia says, reading Thomas' mind.

She looks out the window, where the night sky is already lightening from purple to blue. "Or early, I guess. Let's all crash for a few hours and re-convene to discuss what's next."

We make our way to our bedroom, the same as before, but everything is different now.

Before, we'd been scared, running for our lives and unsure if we were going to make it after the building collapsed behind us and we'd escaped by a narrow margin. Now, the threat has been eliminated, and the responsibility of that is heavy on each of us.

Especially Thomas.

But there is also hope, that damned seed burgeoning forth to bask in the sunshine of our safety. No sword dangling over our heads, a sense of free-dom replacing it.

"Is he going to be okay?" I ask Lance, and though I don't name him, he knows I'm talking about Thomas.

Lance pulls my sweatshirt over my head, then moves to undo my braid. Though I hadn't been baking today, it'd seemed familiar and comfortable, giving my hands something to do.

"I think so," he says as he spreads my curls around my shoulders. "He did the right thing. But your first is difficult."

He blinks, then corrects himself. "They're all difficult, but he's not trained. Blackwell forced his hand, made Thomas pull that trigger, sure as if he'd done it himself. He knew Thomas wouldn't let him make a move to-ward Trixie."

I'm quiet, letting that sink in as I pull Lance's shirt over his head. "Thomas is a good man. He did what he had to for all of us."

Lance gives me a small smile, but it's sad. "I know. We all know. He's go-ing to feel that stain is on his soul for the rest of his days."

"Mia will love him, no matter what."

"Which is why I know he'll be okay," he says, smiling gently.

I return the smile, reassured. "If he gives himself too much of a hard time, Mia will rip him a new one and probably order him to 'let it go'. She'd proba-bly even sing it Elsa-style." The joke falls flat, but it's the truth. Mia won't let Thomas beat himself up over this. She'll help him however he needs.

"I need to hold you," Lance says, changing the subject but somehow just as on point. He needs me the way Thomas will need Mia tonight. Likely the way Gabe will need Izzy too.

In the back of my head, I hope Jonathan has someone too, but I've never seen him with anyone, so I don't know.

I let that thought go, focusing on Lance and being what he needs tonight.

I push my jeans off, taking my panties with them as Lance shoves his black cargo pants and boots off. When we're both nude, I pull the covers back.

"Lie down," I say, not allowing any argument.

Lance reclines, his back stiff and straight, and holds out one arm, inviting me to him. Instead of curling up at his side, letting him be my protecting cocoon, I lie on top of him, my knees at either side of his hips, my arms wrapped around his torso, and my cheek laid against his chest. Tonight, I will ground him, keep him here and now, with me, and be his guardian, his shelter from the world.

Incrementally, he relaxes into me, accepting my comfort.

"I love you," I tell him, wanting him to know that no matter what happened tonight, that will never change. He could've gone into Blackwell's tower with guns blazing, shooting his way to the top floor, and killing Blackwell himself in cold blood, and I would still love him. Because I know that he's a good man, *my* good man, and if he did something like that, it would be for honorable reasons.

Because he's an honorable man. One who was patient with me when I ran scared. One who stays. One who loves me.

"I love you too, Charlotte," he says, and I believe him.

Minutes pass, and slowly, heat builds between us as the stress of the night fades into the rising sun's rays. I lift my hips, and he easily slips inside me. We stay like that for a while before I arch my back, beginning to move. I fuck him this time, and he lets me. I choose him, knowing who he is and what he's done.

And when he comes with my name on his lips, I fall apart for him too, his name on my lips, because we know who we are to each other. Everything.

# CHAPTER 39

## Lance

THE MASS OF REPORTERS SWIRLS AND MOBS ON THE COURTHOUSE
steps, surrounding Jonathan like sharks around bait. I, for one, am
glad to remain in the shadows for this one.

Thomas and Mia stand next to me, ready to make their dramatic return
to the living, while Gabe is likely hiding in plain sight somewhere. Izzy and
Charlotte are at Izzy's house with Steven.

Gabe has a top-notch security system in place, more befitting Fort Knox
than a private residence, so it'd seem like a safe place for them to stay while
we break the news to the world that we're all alive.

Jonathan holds up a hand, stopping the barrage of questions being
shouted at him. "Yes, we do have a statement about the news of Custis
Blackwell's death this morning. If you'll please indulge me a moment."

The reporters closest to him stop barking questions and lean in closer,
trying to get their microphones as in his face as possible even though he's
speaking into one at the podium.

He looks back, and that's Thomas's cue. He takes Mia's hand, and together, they step out from behind the column and begin to walk down the
steps toward the podium.

It takes all of two seconds for someone to shout out, "Thomas Goldstone!
Mia Goldstone!"

Thomas smiles congenially, but I know he's still feeling the effects of last night. It's not just playing down to fit into the 'sad news' of Blackwell's death. At least, that's the way the media has been reporting it today.

"Hello, everyone. Yes, I am Thomas Goldstone, and I am very much alive. As is my fiancée, Mia Karakova." He emphasizes her last name, politely correcting the reporter who prematurely gave her his last name. "As are my friends, Gabe Jackson, Isabella Turner, Charlotte Dunn, Lance Jacobs, and Steven Wilson."

There are murmurs all across the crowd, and Thomas waits a moment for them to die down before continuing. "The strikes against Roseboro over the last few days have done more than sadden me. There are no words to describe the pain and horror inflicted on our city. But as is so often the case, there is a lot going on behind the scenes. In the interest of transparency, I would like to pull back the curtain, if you will, for the only way forward is with the truth. It's not comfortable, not pretty and poetic, but it is the truth."

I worry about just how much truth Thomas is going to spill but hold my tongue, knowing that Jonathan and he practiced this speech multiple times today in preparation for this press conference.

"When I came to Roseboro, I found an established and thriving city. At the time, that was under the leadership of one man, Custis Blackwell. He turned a small town into a booming metropolis, but he was not alone. The citizens of Roseboro worked along with him. Unfortunately, Blackwell didn't do this for the good of us all, but for one purpose only. Absolute power."

Speaking ill of the dead apparently is like catnip for the reporters because they're hanging on Thomas's every word.

"I was unaware of his ambitions and set out to make Roseboro my home as well. And I built an empire of my own, with the blood, sweat, and tears of those in the Goldstone family. By that, I don't mean those who bear my last name but every single Goldstone employee. We created that building, that community, together. And I aimed to spread positivity and kindness within its walls and out to Roseboro at large. And we've succeeded. We succeeded so well that Custis Blackwell felt threatened by our community, our caring for one another, as if by my very presence, his importance was diminished."

It's a serious accusation, but just the tip of the iceberg Thomas is about to reveal.

"In the last few months, I discovered a saboteur inside my company. I recently discovered that man was working on Mr. Blackwell's orders. More recently, one of my smaller investments, *Cake Culture*, which is run by a close personal friend, Charlotte Dunn, was targeted by arson. Her employee, Miss Trixie Reynolds, confessed to us that she was also working for Mr. Blackwell." He pauses, swallowing thickly. "And then, our headquarters . . . my home . . ."

The crowd is deadly silent, not a whisper of a question, not a pen scratching on paper. But they are hungry, ravenous for the dirty gossip.

"I was indeed in my apartment with my friends, as my assistant told police. She came up to have me sign for a letter from Custis Blackwell himself. The words will stay with me always. He felt I was usurping a role that was rightly his. In his god-complex-addled mind, there simply was not a place for the two of us in Roseboro. So he was taking out the competition by any means he felt necessary. The destruction of Goldstone Tower was for two purposes—to kill me and everyone I care about and to erase my name from Roseboro forever. It was by the narrowest of margins that we escaped the collapse."

Thomas looks over at Mia, knowing that this is where things get sketchy. "We went into hiding for our safety while we investigated what happened."

I hope Thomas is up to the task because his every word is going to be reported, replayed on every channel at six, ten, and again in the morning. Probably for days to come. The truth must be very carefully shaded.

But I shouldn't doubt him. He may not be a SEAL, but he didn't build his empire easily, and he's commanding with his version of the truth, no matter how directed it may be.

"My security has been working day and night, quite literally, to ensure our safety. And only after Mr. Blackwell's reported suicide and the tragic and unfortunate murder of Miss Reynolds did we feel a return to Roseboro was prudent. As for the future, I feel certain that Mr. Blackwell's involvement in the terroristic destruction of Goldstone Tower will be revealed by the authorities."

Thomas looks over at Chief Harris, who looks red-faced and uncomfortable, but he stops fidgeting with his mustache long enough to nod in agreement.

"These events have shown me that Mr. Blackwell had *friends* in many places inside Roseboro." He pauses, scanning the audience pointedly. "I would like to believe that without his malevolent influence, these *friends*, whomever they may be, will feel the freedom of a fresh start in this changing time. May we all pull together, reconnect with one another, and rebuild Roseboro. Not in the image of a self-appointed, self-aggrandizing king, but because of every one of us. We are Roseboro!"

There's a half-beat of silence, then the audience applauds. Even the re-porters are touched by Thomas's rallying cry. He's a hell of a slick speaker, taking them on a journey through shock, awe, horror, disbelief, and finally, leaving them with a hopeful call to action. I just hope it works.

Thomas steps back from the podium, not taking questions. But a boom-ing voice follows us inside the courthouse. Thomas stops, and we turn to see Chief Harris barreling over.

"Mr. Goldstone, those were some serious allegations you just made. I hope you can back them up," he says, blustering.

I step in front of Thomas, holding out a hand. "Chief Harris. Good to see you again. I was meaning to contact you after our previous discussion. Before she died, Trixie told us that she'd let a man in to tinker with the ovens under Blackwell's order. It was the same man who assaulted me. I'm confi-dent he was employed by Blackwell. I'm sure there's a way to find the con-nection. *There always is.*"

It's a pointed dig, a strong suspicion I already had when such a high-ranking official showed interest in such a low-level charge as a lame as-sault. But he takes my meaning just as intended.

"Are you trying to pussyfoot around saying something, boy?" Harris's face is getting redder, his chest puffing up.

Thomas steps forward. "I think what Lance is saying is that Blackwell had lots of friends in this town. I'm sure they'll all be found with our own investigation and the federal investigation into his business practices. But like I said out there, what I'd like to hope is that those who were caught in Blackwell's web, whether through their own choice or by manipulation and force, can feel free now that he's dead. And we can all work together, doing what's right and doing what's right for Roseboro."

Harris narrows his eyes, searching Thomas's face for something, or maybe searching his shriveled heart for an ounce of integrity. But he offers a hand, and as he and Thomas shake, Harris says, "This is a good city, and I'll do *whatever it takes* to keep it that way. Always have, always will, so you just let me know if there's anything that needs addressing." He dips his chin and saunters away.

He's obviously been on Blackwell's payroll for who knows how long, but maybe he has some twisted sense of trying to do the right thing too. It's obvious that Blackwell preyed on people's weaknesses. It seems Harris's weakness is that while he's a big shot with the police, he wants to play with the big dogs of the city. He's willing to do their bidding, for Blackwell, and now, for Thomas.

"I'd be careful with that one. Fresh start or no, I think he plays to the highest bidder," I warn Thomas, and he nods.

Once we're alone, I call home. Not telling my family that I'm alive has been hell on me, and I know it's been even worse for them.

"Lance? Is it really you?" It's Dad, and I can hear the hesitant hope in his voice, the tears making his voice rough.

"Yeah, Dad. It's me. I'm alive. I'm okay." It's a relief to tell him, and his yell thanking God is a boon to my spirit.

"Miranda! Cody! He's alive!" There's a rustle, then the sound changes as Dad puts me on speakerphone.

"Lance?!?" Mom cries.

"Hi, Mom. Hey, Cody. It's so good to hear your voices. So much has happened."

For now, I don't tell them any more than what Thomas said in the press conference, but I think they're glad to hear it from me. Within minutes, we all feel better, reconnected.

"Okay, I've gotta go, but I'll be home as soon as I can. Probably"—I look to Jonathan, who mouths the answer I'm looking for—"tomorrow."

"Okay, tomorrow then. And bring Charlotte," Mom gushes. "I'll make dinner, I'll make . . . a roast."

She says it like a slab of beef is the cure to all the world's problems. "Mom, you don't cook. Maybe just have Chef make something so we don't die of food poisoning?"

Cody snorts at my dark humor. "Good one, Bro."

But Mom harrumphs. "Lance Jacobs, if I want to make a gosh-darned roast to celebrate my son being alive, then I will certainly do so."

I let her indignant and humorous anger wash over me. It feels good. It feels like home. "All right, Mom. Cook away. We'll see you tomorrow night. And guys?"

"Yes?" Dad says.

"I love you all," I say, realizing how much they need to hear that from me and how much I need to tell them.

# CHAPTER 40

## Charlotte

INNER WITH THE JACOBSES WAS THE ONLY THING THAT MADE ME
able to make this call. That, and Lance by my side in our hotel suite.
I sit cross-legged on the bed, nestled between his thighs.

Lance's parents had exuberantly offered to let me stay at their house, either in a bedroom of my own or with Lance, since my apartment was pretty obliterated by the fire too, but that felt too awkward.

Not staying with him—that's a given and not weird at all. But I think my ideas about parents are pretty fucked up from my own experiences, so staying with the Jacobses seemed wrong in an after-school special sort of way.

Maybe I can learn to accept their style of love the same way I did Lance's, though? It'll just take some time.

Time I don't have as the phone rings.

"Hello?" my dad says. He sounds fragile, older than he is. I remember Sabrina's visit to the bakery before everything went to shit. If she wasn't there to sabotage me, maybe she really was concerned about Dad.

I'm sure the stress of the last few days hasn't helped any issues he's been having.

"Hi, Daddy," I say, the endearment slipping out.

"Charlotte?" he says. "Honey, is that you?" The tears in his voice hit me viscerally, the little girl in my center whispering, *He really loves me*, and sealing over a gaping wound I didn't know was still there.

"Yeah, Dad. It's me. I'm okay. Are you okay?"

He laughs, the sound taking me back to the days when he was happier, less encumbered by the drama the women in his life stir up. Me included.

"Yes. In fact, I'm better than okay. I'm great now that I know you're okay."

We talk for a little while, but before we hang up, I ask Dad to tell Priscilla and Sabrina hello from me. It's a small gesture, but we've got to start somewhere.

Lance runs his finger over my arm, tracing freckles from my shoulder down to my hand. "Well?"

"I think that went really well, actually," I reply, letting loose a pent-up breath. "Shockingly so. Maybe there's hope for us yet."

"And us?" he asks, a cocky grin charging the air between us.

I play along, asking coyly, "What about us?"

He tackles me, laying me back on the bed and tickling me. I thrash beneath him, laughing loudly and feeling so very alive. He pins me with his hands and his blue fire gaze. "Is there hope for us?"

I shake my head, grinning. "None whatsoever." I draw the moment out, but the light in his eyes doesn't waver in the least. "I've completely and utterly fallen for you, and I don't think I'll ever recover. You're stuck with me, Commander Cookie, because believe it or not, I love you."

"Ha-ha, funny girl. Guess what, my Charlotte, my Sweet Scarlet?" His voice drops down, darker and lower. "My Red, I do believe you. I believe enough for the both of us because I love you too."

He presses his lips to mine, soft but sure, like he's sealing our words so I can never take them back. Not that I ever would. He's made a believer out of me. He's my happily ever after.

He pulls back, smiling. "So, there is one thing I need to tell you."

Before, my heart would've jumped into my throat, my mind racing with awful possibilities as fear shot through my veins. But none of that happens. Not now, not with Lance. I just look at him questioningly, trusting that if it's good news, we'll celebrate together. And if it's bad, we'll face it together.

"I've decided to find a new job."

"I've decided to officially retire. I'm not going back to the Teams."

His voice is steady, but I swallow, not because I'm scared for me, but because that's a major life change for Lance. "Are you sure? You don't have to give up something you love, not for your family, and not for me. I will be here for you, a home base for you to return to. And I'll send you sexy pictures of cupcakes, the baked kind, not my . . . you know. I love you, and that won't change, even if you're half a world away doing the thing you love."

He smiles, "I am doing the thing I love." It's half-dirty, but I can tell he means it to be sweet when he continues, "Staying right here with you." He smacks another kiss to my lips, squashing any further discussion of his military career.

"So you're going to work for Jacobs Bio-Tech?"

He shakes his head. "No . . . that's Cody's baby. I was going to tell you. Jonathan sat down with all of us guys. Now that Thomas doesn't need a private investigator, Jonathan is ready to move on. It was always a short-term contract for him. So Thomas needs a Head of Security. I told him I'd only take it if he promised me I never had to protect him from Mia."

I laugh because that's warranted. She might be little and look like your average anime convention attendee, but she would cut a bitch first and ask questions later.

"So you're going to work for Thomas? What about the bakery?" I give him a wink "We made a good team."

"That we did. What's your plan?"

"I've already proven once that I can do it. I'll do it again. Your new boss and I are going to renovate the previous location because it's perfect, other than the fire and water damage. Should be a fast turn-around. The construction crew said I could be opening the doors again in three-ish months."

I pause, biting my lip. "Do you think it'd be weird if I made a flavor in honor of Trixie? It seems weird to do this without her, even after everything."

Lance brushes the hair from my face and says, "I think Trixie would've liked that. What are you going to call it?"

He looks hesitant, like the only flavor worthy of a wild personality like Trixie's would be something outrageous. 'Better Than Sex Cream Pie', or 'Pop That Virgin Cherry Pie', or something Britney Spears-themed, like 'I Know That You're Toxic', a chocolate cupcake with green icing and a gummy snake on it. She'd actually suggested that one once.

"I want to call it Trix—Not for Kids. Like Rice Krispies treats, but made with Trix cereal. And it has to have a white drizzle of glaze on top, of course."

He laughs, getting the reference. "Obviously. I think she would be honored to still be welcome as a part of your bakery."

There are still so many questions. Investigations. A huge building that blew up. Thomas's new headquarters . . . but we'll get there.

Thomas will get his business situation straightened out, with Mia at his side to crunch the numbers. They'll get married soon.

Lance is staying here and has a job. I'm going to reopen the bakery and get my happily ever after.

Izzy is done with school now, ready to tackle the world as a freelance graphic designer. And Gabe . . .

"Hey, with us all being safe from Blackwell now, what's Gabe going to do? Do you think he could work with you as security at Goldstone?" Gabe doesn't need me to solve his career situation, but I can't help but want to fix that final piece of the puzzle.

Lance shakes his head. "Nah, he knows that his background wouldn't hold up to corporate scrutiny. So he's going to do contract work with Jonathan."

My face must show my shock because Lance quickly explains. "Not *that* kind of contracts. Jonathan has lots of different types of gigs—security, investigations—but one of his most lucrative contracts is gap discovery."

"What's that? Tell me faster that Gabe is not going back to being a hitman," I beg.

"He'll be a hitman for a *good* cause, without the death and dismemberment at the end. High-profile people hire Jonathan to find gaps in their security—online, residential, their protective detail. So when it's needed, Gabe will make an 'attempt' on someone's life to see where he can get in, where the breeches in coverage are so they can be corrected. The best part is, a lot of it is in the research, so he can do it from home. And when he has to go out on assignment, it'll be a short trip, usually. With Izzy being freelance, she can probably even go with him sometimes."

I let that sink in, confused but relieved. "So basically, a hitman stopper? If that's even a word."

Lance shrugs. "I'm sure there's a fancy name for it like Security Loss Specialist, but basically, yeah."

"Okay," I say as the last puzzle piece clicks into place in my mind. "So we're all good, then."

Lance nibbles on my neck, and I instinctively tilt away, giving him greater access.

He whispers into my ear, "I've heard I'm not just good, but *great*. Might even make you walk funny tomorrow from having that pussy pounded."

God, I don't know why his cocky arrogance gets me. Well, his silly jokes get me too. So does his sweet and gentle, and his rough and hard.

I can feel his cock already growing between us, hard against my belly. But the thing I feel the most is his heart, beating in time to mine.

Still, I can't let him off the hook that easily or he'll get too big-headed. *Ha!* I laugh but keep the pun to myself as I challenge, "I hear you talking, but I'm not feeling you backing those words up yet. Just a whole lotta chatter without much substance, like a sugar-free cupcake. *Wah-wah,*" I say, mimicking a game show losing sound.

"Sugar-free? That's blasphemy! Oh, you're gonna feel it, Red. Challenge accepted," Lance says, and he sounds like he means it to be a warning, but all I hear is a promise.

A promise for forever.

A promise for happily ever after.

# CHAPTER 41

## Lance

I TAKE THAT CHALLENGE AND DIVE IN WITH EVERY INTENTION OF owning Charlotte, body, mind, and soul, wearing her out as I fuck her all night, and I'll eventually put a ring on her finger.

After dinner with my parents, Mom slipped me her original wedding set, the one my Dad bought her when they were young and poor. It's not fancy or flashy, but it's sentimental. A sign that I believe we can have just as many happy years as my parents have had together.

We're not ready yet, but soon. Last night, I dreamed of a little redhaired girl who looks just like her beautiful momma and holds my heart just as tightly.

But for now, that dream disappears on a wisp of hope for the future, and I take in the beauty laid out before me in the present. "You feel that?" I growl, grinding my hips against her and using her belly to rub my cock.

She gasps and nods but says nothing, a sure sign she wants me to say more. For all her sass and fire, she loves it when I talk dirty, tell her what I'm going to do, then follow through on every filthy promise. She likes the build-up the anticipation gives her.

I've taken it as a personal mission to make her come with my words alone, and one day, I'll complete that mission.

"I'm going to strip you down bare, spread that pretty pink pussy wide open, and fuck you with my tongue so I can taste your sweetness right from the source," I whisper in the meantime.

"I'm going to suck your clit and slide my fingers inside because I want to feel you clamp down on them when you come for the first time. But they'll be a poor substitute for my cock because I'm going to slam into you balls-fucking-deep and fuck you hard . . . deep . . . and rough. You wanna walk funny tomorrow? I'm going to have you bowlegged, with my marks all over your fair skin. Everyone will know that you got fucked all night, will know that you're mine."

"*Fuck*," she moans, loving it. "God, Lance . . . please."

And I know she's mine, totally gone for me. Just like I'm hers.

I make good on my promise, pulling her shirt over her head and using the moment she arches to flick her bra undone. Before she settles back topless, I'm pulling her jeans and panties down in one yank.

Fully nude, I sit her up on the edge of the bed, kneeling between her bent knees, memorizing the feast laid out before me.

I don't delay, plunging right in to lick her with the flat of my tongue, and she shudders beneath me, her hips chasing my tongue. I wrap my arms around her thighs, using my thumbs to spread her slick pussy lips. "Mmm, look at that pussy, already pulsing like it's greedy for my cock. Is that what you want? My cock or my tongue?"

She's too incoherent with lust to do more than moan, so I follow my original plan and lick, suck, and tease along her folds. I dip my tongue inside her, loving the way she tenses even against that small invasion. So hungry, both of us.

I replace my tongue with two fingers, curling them up to caress the front wall of her pussy as I circle her clit lazily. Her cries get louder, begging for more, and I can feel the spasms starting deep inside her, still irregular but growing stronger.

I place a hand above her bare mound, holding her in place, and fuck her as hard and fast as I can, my fingers slamming into her. It looks violent, her cries tortured until . . .

"Oh, my God, Lance!" she cries out, flying into an abyss, my hand the only thing tethering her to this place, still thrusting in and out, forcing more pleasure upon her.

My fingers drip with the evidence of how hard she came, her sweet girl cum coating my fingers. I give her a moment's reprieve, sampling her honey from my own skin and groaning at the sweet taste.

Unable to hold back, I reach behind my head and rip my shirt over my head, tossing it without regard for where it'll land. I unbutton my jeans, shoving them and my underwear down and off.

"You ready, Red?" I ask, notching my cock at her entrance.

"So ready," she replies.

It's heaven. Zero barriers between us, both finally naked, nothing hidden between us. Physically, mentally, or emotionally.

Though Charlotte is stunning, her red hair wild from her head thrashing, the blue of her eyes almost gone from the wide darkness of her pupils, her true beauty is inside her.

Her bravery.

That even when she'd been hurt, disappointed, and betrayed time after time, she courageously got back up and tried again.

I will never let her down. I will earn the faith she has in me every day for the rest of my life.

I shove into her, stretching her pussy around my thick cock even after that hard orgasm. But her cry is one of pleasure, tinged in the pain that only makes it feel better, that teetering edge she loves so much.

I don't give her time to adjust. She doesn't want it, not really. I just start fucking her, bottoming out with each stroke and battering her thighs with my hips. I grip her legs, pulling her to me as I thrust into her, making her take more, take all of me.

Her tits bounce, garnering my attention, and I lean forward to take one into my mouth. I bite and suck, pulling hard enough to raise a bruising mark on her fair skin. The pink connects the brown freckles, making them seem to encircle my mark.

"Do it again," Charlotte orders, her hand cupping her other breast for a matching mark. I oblige, tracing along her fair skin, drawing lines with my tongue to memorize each tiny spot. Until I find one that makes her squirm.

There. I kiss the freckle first, swirling my tongue in a porn-inspired pirate's version of 'X marks the spot' and when she arches, I latch on, nibbling at the skin before sucking hard.

I draw deeply as I mark her, plunging into her pussy as I roughly guide her hips. I can feel her velvet walls grasping me, and I pull off her breast long enough to tell her, "Come, Charlotte."

Her hands grasp for me, one at my shoulder and one on my head, pulling me back to her chest for more. She explodes, her whole body shaking as she cries out my name. She squeezes me so tight, milking the cum from my balls, that I go with her, losing suction on her skin as I grunt out my pleasure through gritted teeth.

We've had sex, we've made love, and we've fucked. This is all of those mixed up together. A foundation of love and trust, with sparkly layers of fun and a future. We're writing our own future, our own fairy tale.

Forever after.

# EPILOGUE

## Charlotte

I POINT A BLUE-TIPPED FINGER, ANNOYED. "TOUCH YOUR FACE AGAIN and I will tie your hands at your side."

I intend for it to sound threatening, but Mia smirks. "You'd probably need to get Tommy for that. He's the only one who can tie me up where I can't get out."

Izzy squeals, shaking her head. "T-M-I, girl. I do not need to know your kinky shit. Save it for the honeymoon." But I can see her thinking. Something tells me that Izzy is going to be asking Gabe to try a little rope play tonight too, in their own way.

"Focus," I say, placing a hand on each of Mia's shoulders. "Hair, check. Makeup, check, if you'd only leave it alone. Dress, check. Potty break?"

She shakes her head, grinning. "No, I'm good. I'm ready. Are you? Got a little extra weight on that bouquet-carrying hand now. Wouldn't want it to be too much for your weak little arms."

Her tease breaks the nerves we're all feeling. Not about the wedding. Mia is more than certain about marrying Thomas. But none of us are particularly 'spotlight' people, and there are going to be lots of spotlights on us today.

Mia and Thomas elected for a small, private wedding. Just family and about fifty of their closest friends and business associates. It's safer than inviting the whole town of Roseboro. But the pictures are going to be the first story on the ten o'clock news and the front-page spread in the paper in the morning.

It's taken a few months, but the timing couldn't be better. The investigations are complete, and all of Blackwell's dirty laundry is out in public.

Well, most of it. Thomas is holding a few secrets close to his vest to call in markers if he has to. He's used a few already, filing suit against Blackwell's estate and getting liens against the Corporation. The Blackwell Building has been renamed the Roseboro Tower, and houses Goldstone Incorporated. Thomas even brought several of Blackwell's companies and subsidiaries under the Goldstone umbrella. He's slowly but surely taking over the Blackwell mantle and reshaping it into something brighter and better. A new start for the city.

What better time for a wedding?

I strike a pose, making sure my new diamond engagement ring is prominently displayed. "How's this?"

Lance proposed six months to the day after our initial meeting at the gala. Crazy fast, supposedly, but he jokes that he knew right away but waited *forever* for me to decide that he'd do for a husband.

I appreciate that he makes it seem like I'm the reasonable one when the truth is, he was healing me, wound by wound, scar by scar.

Mia and Izzy clap, chiming in unison, "Perfect!"

"All right, today's my day. Charlotte, you're up any time now. Izzy, what's it gonna take to make this a done deal with Gabe?" Mia asks, sounding more like a car salesman than a computer genius.

Izzy blushes. "It's not like that, guys. Gabe can't have paperwork floating around with his name on it, especially not with my name too. It's like the number-one way to wave a flag and highlight your weakness. We won't risk it."

"Well, that man is weak for you. Weak in the knees!" I tease.

Mia raises her brows. "He'd damn well better be on his knees for you, girl." We all laugh, already knowing that Gabe going down on Izzy is a regular thing. Again, we overshare. "But what about something unofficial, just private with the two of you or our little group? That way, there's no paperwork. That'd be okay, right?"

Izzy bites her tongue like she's forcing down words. But she loses the battle, her hands covering her face—ugh, her makeup!—as she looks down at her lap. She mumbles something I can't decipher.

Mia looks at me, eyes questioning whether I got that, but when I shake my head, she says, "Louder for the people in the back, Iz."

Izzy looks up, apology in her eyes. "We already did. A month ago, when we went to Mexico for that assignment."

"WHAT?" we both yell.

There's a knock at the door, and Steven calls out, "Ladies?"

"We're fine," Mia calls back. Then to Izzy, "Explain."

"I'm so sorry. I wanted to tell you, but this is your day, Mia," Izzy begs. "I didn't want to take all the attention by getting married first. I mean, you started this . . . us."

Mia scoffs. "Girl, I don't care. I just want you to be happy. Congratulations!"

I repeat the sentiment and Izzy smiles a little wider. "I love you two."

"We love you too."

Mia grabs her hand, lifting an eyebrow. "Uhm, I think he forgot a step though. Where's the bling-bling?"

Izzy flinches and Mia rushes to backpedal. "It's okay if he's saving up or something. The vow is in your heart, not a shiny stone."

Izzy shakes her head. "It's not that. I told him to wait until after, so I know what size my fingers are going to be."

"After what?" I ask hesitantly.

"The baby," Izzy says, her hands going to her still-flat belly.

"WHAT?!" we yell again, and this time, Steven knocks, always the worried security expert. We ignore him to focus on Izzy.

"I'm only two months along, but that was why we wanted to rush the wedding a bit. Not that it'll matter since there's no paperwork, but I want the whole picturesque family. Mom, Dad, baby, picket fence."

It's bittersweet. Izzy's struggled her whole life to feel at home, like she belongs, and I'm so happy for her to finally have the family she's always wanted. With Gabe, her Prince Charming.

"Honey," I say, gathering her in a hug. Mia piles on top, and we're all hugging each other, tears running down our faces as we snottily proclaim to be the best aunties this baby has ever known.

Even though we're not being loud, there's another knock. "Thought you might need a ten-minute warning. Last chance for makeup fixes, bathroom breaks, or to make a run for it, Miss Karakova."

Steven's funny, in a dry humor sort of way. But I also think he'd take Mia right out of here if she asked him to. He might be employed by Thomas, but all the guys on the security team have a soft spot for the crazy, geeky video gamer who captured their boss's heart.

Thomas used to be a bit of a beast, but Mia domesticated that right out of him. Or gave him a better outlet for his monstrous urges. I laugh at my own dirty joke, thinking Mia would approve.

We touch up our makeup and hug one more time. "Ready?" I ask Mia.

She smiles, nodding. "I'm getting married, guys. Let's go!"

And with that, she hitches up her dress and heads for the door, ready to tackle the world. Or forever.

Mia pauses outside the closed doors, taking her dad's arm. Vladdy's in tears, whispering in her ear, probably threatening to kill Thomas if he ever mistreats his princess. Mia definitely gets her scariness from her dad, who's a total teddy bear.

Unless you piss him off, or so I've heard. I wouldn't know, because he's always a sweetheart to me.

The doors open, and Izzy walks in first, slow and steady. She looks beautiful, glowy, and happy. Gabe stands at Thomas's side, looking ready to run down the aisle, snatch Izzy up, and steal away with her.

Then it's my turn. As I walk, I glance over at Lance, who's next to Gabe, thinking that the next time I do this, it will be to become his wife. Where once, that would've terrified me, it now sounds exciting.

I can't wait.

Looking in his eyes, I know he feels the same way. Maybe we could sneak off with the officiant during the reception and do it quickie-style like Izzy did?

We won't, of course. Lance wants to give me the whole princess fairy-tale wedding, his romantic streak unending. I can dig that. It doesn't have to be big and fancy, but something our friends and family can come to.

I want them to see me choosing love, choosing Lance, choosing faith.

The music changes, and Mia begins her trek down the aisle. She's gorgeous. Her hair is blonde and pink, curled up in an elaborate updo with a funky bow, and her dress is pink, of course. But it's the softest, palest shade of blush that just looks warm and ethereal against her skin.

The ceremony is beautiful, with vows of love and promises of all-night game play on video game release days. Gotta love Mia. She thinks ahead and gets that stuff in writing. No take-backsies.

Before I know it, the ceremony is over and Lance is escorting me out behind the bride and groom.

In the hallway outside, we look at each other. The six of us, all from different backgrounds, shaped by different experiences, with different hopes and dreams. But all here together.

Our family, not by birth but by choice.

And forever begins for Mia and Thomas.

It's already begun for Izzy and Gabe and their new addition.

And soon, it' ll be my turn with Lance.

Our version of happily ever after.